THE STATE
OF THE UNION

JESSIE O. ROLAND

Published by Revival Waves of Glory Books & Publishing

PO Box 596 l Litchfield, Illinois 62056 USA

www.revivalwavesofgloryministries.com

Revival Waves of Glory Books & Publishing is committed to excellence in the publishing industry.

Book design Copyright © 2016 by Revival Waves of Glory Books & Publishing. All rights reserved.

Published in the United States of America

Paperback: 978-1-68411-048-3

Hardcover: 978-1-68411-049-0

Table of Contents

This book is dedicated to my family and friends,
especially Big Al; you know who you are, and to my friend
of forty five years, Angie Tripp who encouraged me every day.

UNION

(NOUN)

A marriage becomes a union of a man and a woman.

When states or countries join together to form a union or larger unit.

"Jefferson Lives"

The last words of John Adams, July 4, 1826.

Both Jefferson and Adams died on the fiftieth anniversary
of the signing of the Declaration of Independence.

PROLOGUE

INDEPENDENCE MISSOURI

I'll never forget what I was doing when it happened. I was crying myself to sleep just like I do every night. I didn't actually see it in person, few people did. Millions saw it on live TV. They just didn't know at the time what they saw. I found out about an hour later when my sister called and told me to turn on the TV. I remember asking her which channel. She said it didn't matter, just turn on the TV. I imagine most people in America found out about the same time I did.

I remember September 11, 2001 like it was yesterday. I found out about the Twin Towers about an hour later. It was the second saddest day of my life. The saddest day of my life was when my husband of twenty years just dropped dead. Now those two events dropped down one notch to second and third.

All the TV. stations were showing replays of when it happened. They just kept showing it over and over again.

I sat there mesmerized by it. The camera was on the President. You could see a brilliant white light fill the House of Representatives chamber and then nothing.

The news anchors said that the nuclear weapon was a hundred times hotter than the surface of the sun. I couldn't even comprehend that. The wind generated from it was four to five hundred miles an hour. The so called experts were saying all sorts of things that didn't make any sense to me. Ballistic missile, stealth bomber, suitcase bomb and the one that got me the most, something from a satellite in orbit. After about twenty theories, I was more confused than ever. I didn't know what to believe. Does it really matter how?

The reason I wasn't watching the State of the Union address, I've never paid any attention to politics. A lot of folks watch things like that. They say they want to be informed and know what's going on in the world. Yet, they can't tell you what's going on any more than the guy who barbeques every Saturday afternoon. I know that sounds harsh, but it's true. Our young people don't vote. They think someone is going to take care of them. But WHO?

Everyone says the United States has lost its moral compass. Democrats and Republicans are both saying this. I don't know if either of them are right. All I know is that right now we are crippled. God help us.

We have a President no one has ever heard of. They say he is trying to establish a new government. Good luck with that! The new seat of the United States government is now here in Independence, Missouri. I don't know why they chose here. 'The new President' arrived two weeks ago, one week after I lost my job.

Today was the worst day ever. I had never been so depressed in my whole life. I never thought something like this would happen to me. Here I am though, sitting in a room with about seventy five people. I had been given a number. I walked in here as Myrtice B. Thompson. Now I was number 117. Everyone around me was either reading a magazine or a paperback book. Some were even sleeping. I don't know if they have a number or just came in out of the cold. Things like this happened to other people. I had been here since eight o'clock. I had to go to the restroom; the only problem was they are not calling the numbers in any kind of order. People were still coming in. How many would eventually come in was anyone's guess.

I couldn't take it any longer so I went to one of the windows and asked, what I guess you would call a clerk, if I had time to go to the restroom. I told her I was number 117. She told me if they called my number and I didn't answer that I would be moved to the back of the line. She acted as if she didn't care one way of the other. I went back to where I was sitting and someone had taken it. I found another seat when someone was called. Thirty minutes later, I asked the man next to me if they called my number would he tell them I had gone to the restroom. I told him my number was 117. He didn't answer so I ran as fast as I could to the ladies room. There were two people in front of me. Ten minutes later, I went back to my seat and he was gone. I don't know if they have called my number or not.

I was the only one in the entire room dressed the way a person should be when they leave the house, much less looking for a job. Everyone else was wearing old blue jeans, some with holes in them, and their shirt tails were hanging out. The least they could do was comb their hair. Some of the younger ones don't even have their shoes tied. Their pants are below their you-know-what. I just don't understand some people.

Two years ago, I made a mistake. I was a high school teacher in Kansas City, Missouri. I transferred to the Independence, Missouri school system as the English Literature teacher. Then the cutbacks came and the policy of the last in first out caught up with me. Now I am in the employment office. I don't know why they don't call it the unemployment office. The people around me don't look like they are looking for a job. Most of them will go down the street to get welfare and food stamps. I don't want that. I want a job! The truth is I love working and always have.

At twelve o'clock, someone announced over the loud speaker that they are closing for lunch and would be back at one o'clock. I rummaged through my purse and found a dollar and eighty seven cents. I went to the vending machine and found out a Coke and a candy bar would cost me a dollar and seventy five cents. I shook my head in disgust and went back to my seat. I needed that money for bus fare because my car would not start this morning.

At 2:00 p.m., they called number 117. I went through the door right into another waiting room. This room was much smaller than the first. There were about twenty people waiting in this room. There were three doors in front of me and I could see people behind two of the doors. Every once in a while they called someone. The third one looked as though no one came in and the lights were off.

About an hour later, a man came in from behind me and walked to the empty room. He pulled out some keys, looked through them and unlocked the door. He turned on the lights, booted up the computer and started working. Every once in a while, he leaned back in his chair and studied the screen. Why can't he get up and call someone? I swear, I don't know what has happened to this country. I wanted to break down in tears.

The only thing I knew was right now I was out of a job and I had no money. I had a sixteen year old daughter I had to raise and I had all I could handle! I was desperate with no hope in sight. I already had three strikes against me. I was over fifty-five, I was a woman and I was black.

The man in the office came up to me. He had three one dollar bills in his hand. He was about thirty-five, kind of on the skinny side with thinning hair on top. He nodded his head at me and held out the money and do you know what he asked me to do? He said he had missed lunch and wanted to know if I would run to the deli next door and buy him a ham and cheese sandwich. I said under any other circumstances I would be more than happy to go next door and buy him a ham and cheese sandwich, but if I was not there when they called my number I may miss a job opportunity and that I desperately needed a job. He said he would get a drink and candy bar from the vending machine. I tried to apologize but he just waved me away. With that he left and was back in five minutes. He sat down to eat his candy bar and drink his Coke. When he was finished he came out and called my number. Now I had four strikes against me. He was behind his desk when I came in and I put out my hand to introduce myself. I tried my best to be civil and present myself the best way possible. He either didn't see my hand or ignored it. I don't know which. I sat down across from him while he looked through my paperwork I had filled out over six hours ago. He picked up some reading glasses and stuck one of the legs in his mouth. He wanted to know if I had a resume. I told him I had included one in the paperwork I filled out this morning. I had no idea what could have happened to it. He flipped through the paperwork again and said he couldn't find it. My heart sank. I had spent a lot of time preparing it because I knew how important it was to have a well written resume. He looked around his computer and then his desk drawers. Finally, he pulled it out of a drawer. He was waving it around like he had found an original copy of the Declaration of Independence. I think he was more excited than I was. I was just relieved.

Then he told me to go back into the waiting room and you guessed it, wait. At five o'clock, the other two offices closed for the day. I was the only one still waiting. The man was still there. He would glance at me while talking on the phone, and then he would use the computer for a minute or two. No one had been in his office other than me. He finally stood up, put on his suit coat and closed the office door. He walked up to me and handed me a card. He told me to be at the address on the card at nine o'clock for an interview and testing. I said, "Thank you," and he started to leave then he asked me if I wish I had gotten my degree in Business Administration instead of English Literature. I told him I loved writing. I even told him what my professor had said to us, "String words together and make sentences and sentences together into paragraphs and paragraphs into chapters and chapters into books." I told him I loved writing anything it didn't matter what. Then he asked me if I ever thought of writing a book. I told him I had written two children books when I first started teaching. He wanted to know if it was anything he may have heard of. I mentioned they were in my resume. Then it dawned on me he had only read part of it. I told him the titles and he told me he read those to his younger brother. Well how do you do.

It was seven o'clock before I got home. Now the afternoon battle began. My sixteen year old daughter, Makika, was perfectly healthy; however she was the laziest child on the planet. She refused to help around the house. She would not, for instance, make a peanut butter sandwich for herself. I had to do everything for her. What hurts the most was I had an afternoon job after school when I was her age. I had worked since I was sixteen. I enjoyed every job I ever had. Then my husband died of a heart attack while cutting the grass when she was twelve. I still haven't gotten over his passing. Our world fell apart that day.

I haven't even taken off my coat before she started in on me. She was lying on the couch reading some teen magazine. My feet were killing me, my ankles were swollen and she's asking what's for dinner. I told her I didn't know. I went to the bedroom and slipped my shoes off and tried to get some circulation going. From the living room, I heard her yelling, wanting to know when I am going to cook.

I started crying, asking myself where I went wrong. I did this every day when I came home. If she would just help a little bit it would mean so much to me. I dried my eyes and finished undressing. I put on my housecoat and went to the kitchen. I found some spaghetti noodles and some sauce. I boiled the water for the noodles. We had no meat in the freezer. I walked into the living room and as I neared I could tell the only muscle she has used was when she breathed. I shook my head not able to comprehend what I saw.

She asked me what's for supper and I told her spaghetti. She complained that we have spaghetti all the time. I told her that I was sorry but that was all we had. I answered as civil as I could. Then she started in on me about why I didn't sign up for welfare and food stamps. I countered with we have had this discussion before, like yesterday. She told me that one of her friend's mother was on welfare and made more than I did. I told her I wanted to work, not to be on welfare. Then she got really mad and told me if I did find a job it would be mopping floors and cleaning restrooms I'm not allowed to use. I don't know where young people hear this stuff. I told her I had a job interview tomorrow and maybe I would get lucky.

During supper neither of us spoke. We seldom did anymore. After dinner, I put the dishes in the dish washer. There was no point in asking her. I had to go in the living room and collect the glasses she had used during the time I was gone. Every time she got something to drink she got another glass.

I don't know how many times I had come home from work and she had friends over. I didn't know who they were and every glass and cup was on the coffee table with some amount of soft drink in it. I had to wash dishes before I could even get myself something to drink. After I went to bed she had other friends over and they did the same thing. I had to wash a load of dishes to have a clean coffee cup. I didn't know why she did this to me. I went to bed and cried myself to sleep. Lord, please help me.

I left the house at 7:30. Luckily my old clunker started right up; of course I had to say a prayer or two. There was no need to wake Makika. I gave myself plenty of time. I spent twenty minutes finding a parking space three blocks away. It turned out my interview was next door to the new government building. I had to show my driver's license and appointment card to get in. Then I had to put my purse on a conveyor belt to be x-rayed and I had to go through a body scanner. I wondered what in the world was going on. I made it to the office with two minutes to spare. The receptionist asked if she could help me. I showed her my appointment card and she asked me to follow her. We went into an adjacent office and she pointed at a chair at the folding table and told me to have a seat. I was told that she would be with me shortly. I had never had an interview where the other person wasn't already in the room. I waited and waited some more. Finally this lady came in holding a cardboard box. She introduced herself as Beverly and asked me if I was Myrtice. I told her I was. She brushed the hair out of her eyes. I noticed she was petite, with blond hair and hazel eyes. She was about five feet six inches tall. She was a lot smaller than I am. She looked to be about thirty five or forty. She was wholesome looking and very pretty. She was wearing a sleeveless pullover sweater with jeans and tennis shoes. She didn't dress nice enough for casual Friday. I noticed two pins on her sweater. One looked like a parachute with a wing on each side. The other pin was undoubtedly the cheapest pin I have ever seen in my life. It was heart shaped and looked to be ten or fifteen years old. I hoped that I didn't make her feel out of place because I had on my nicest dress. She went to the other side of the room and brought four smaller cardboard boxes and set them on the table.

Then she gave me some instructions. She said to make sure I put the right letter back in the original envelope. Then she pointed out the boxes and told me to put the letters that needed to be answered in one box and the letters not to be answered in another box and letters from lobbyists in a third box. The last box was for threatening letters. She gave me a dull butter knife as a letter opener and pulled out a double handful of letters. She started opening letters with her knife. She told me it was easy to tell which letters went into each box. I thought this was the strangest test I've ever taken. Maybe she was timing me, I didn't know but she was right, you could tell which box to put it in.

I wondered what would be next. Most questions she asked were simple. Really chit chat like two women cutting coupons out of the Sunday paper. She asked about my daughter. She said she was sorry when I spoke about my husband's passing like he did. Every once in a while she would lean back in her chair and reread a letter before putting it in the box marked answer. I noticed all the letters were addressed to the First Lady of the United States. She must be someone who screened letters for the First Lady. Every once in a while she looked so sad and she would wipe away a tear. Then she said that some of the letters will steal your heart away and stir your soul.

I told her I was reading one like that now. This one was so sad it brought tears to my eyes. She held her hand out for the letter. She read it and shook her head slowly from side to side. Then she put the letter back in the envelope and told me she would be back in a minute. I went back to opening envelopes and reading letters. She was back in a couple of minutes. She laid the letter off to the side. I wondered if she was personally going to give the First Lady the letter because she didn't put it in the answer box. A few minutes later she read it again. She handed it back to me and asked me to read it again. I told her how sad it was, a twelve year old's mother had died and her dad was so depressed that he had nothing to do with her anymore. Her father had not told her he loved her in over a year and then when he came home he sat in his chair and stared at the floor. She was asking the First Lady to pray for her and her father. I couldn't help the tears that ran down my face. Beverly asked me to hold hands with her and pray for this little girl that I had never met and would never meet. I admit I haven't prayed much since my husband's passing, but I felt I had no choice so I nodded my head and two of us prayed for that little girl. I also prayed for me and my daughter.

Then she told me she was hungry. She said there was a kitchenette here and said she would make us a sandwich if I wanted to go ahead and wash up. She said I could use the powder room and pointed the way through another door. After finishing my trip to the restroom, I could hear her humming in the kitchen. I stretched and tried to get the kinks out of my back and the circulation back in my feet. I turned and leaned back against the chair trying to stretch my back. I noticed a photo on the wall. I hadn't noticed it when I came in the room. It was a family photo. I recognized the President right away. I had seen his photo thousands of times on the news. He had his hand on the shoulder of a handsome young man who had a very nice smile. The young man was wearing a robe and mortar board. A high school graduation night. Next to him was a very young girl with black curly hair. She was also wearing a robe and mortar board. Standing next to her was the mother. The two pins on her dress was a dead giveaway. It took my breath away. I almost collapsed. I looked again. I looked toward the kitchen. I broke out in a sweat. I had to sit down. The First Lady of the United States of America was making me a sandwich. I kept asking myself, "Think Myrtice, think, have you said anything stupid?"

She came back with two glasses of tea and then went back into the kitchen. I tried to calm down. I grabbed a tissue and wiped the sweat away. She came back holding two plates, each with a sandwich and potato chips. She told me she had made turkey sandwiches and then she sat down. She looked at me and asked if I was alright. I was able to nod my head and say I was okay.

She asked me if I minded if she said the blessing. She reached out her hands and took mine in hers. She lowered her head and asked the Lord to bless the food. She then took a bite of her sandwich. I couldn't help it; it came out before I could stop it. I remember saying, "Ma'am, are you the First Lady?" She nodded her head, swallowed her food and said she was. She asked me to call her Beverly. I couldn't think of anything to say so I kept my mouth shut. After lunch I offered to clean up the kitchen, but she said she would and that I could go back to sorting letters. She told me I was better at it than she was. I thought for the first time in four years someone else was doing the dishes and for some reason that felt really good.

Later, I asked her if she answered all these letters. She said as many as she could, especially to children and to those that told her they were praying for her and her husband. So many of the letters were sad and she was right; each letter took a little out of you and stirred your soul.

At three o'clock, there was a tap on the door. Someone passed a note to the First Lady. She put it with the letter she had put aside. She told me it was the phone number. I asked her if she was going to call. She nodded her head and said, "Yes." Then she surprised me by saying she wanted to talk to the little girl's father. Well, my curiosity was aroused and I asked her what she was going to say. She shrugged her shoulders and told me she didn't know. She said that her father had always said, "When you know you should do something but don't know what, just wing it." Then she asked me if I had any ideas and I told her I'd wing it myself. What else could I say?

The afternoon passed by a lot quicker than the morning. Before I knew it, it was six o'clock. She looked at her watch. I could tell it was a man's watch. It had a wide leather band. I hadn't seen one in years. People who rode motorcycles wore them all the time. She saw that I had noticed the watch and she told me it belonged to her father. She said he was killed in the line of duty. I told her how sorry I was and she said, "Thank you."

There was a small table in the corner with a phone. She picked up the letter and phone number and dialed. I could tell that it was the little girl that answered the phone. It took her a minute to convince the girl that she was the First Lady. She asked the girl how she was doing in school and said she had prayed for her and her father. Then she told her about losing her father and how much it hurt. I had to wipe my eyes again. Then she asked to speak to her father. It took a while for him to answer the phone. She assured him it was not a prank, that his daughter had written her a letter. She told him he should be very proud of his daughter. Then she got down to business. His daughter had lost someone just as important to her as he had. He needed to start spending time with her and telling her how much he loved her. He also needed to start doing some father and daughter things or he was going to lose her. She told him that she admired him because he had spent his life savings trying to save his wife. She pointed out to him that there were many things him and his daughter could do together that didn't cost money. She said you could take walks, go to the park or just sit and play a game or maybe read a book together. She told him she would be praying for the two of them. After saying goodbye, she left the room and came back with another box of tissues. Both of us had used quite a few today.

What she said next made me think of my relationship with my daughter. She told me it was never too late to give love another chance. You just have to try. It made me realize that my daughter was that age when her father passed. I was depressed for years, still am. I didn't stare at the floor, I stared at the walls.

A few minutes later, there was a knock on the door. She got up and opened it. The President of the United States; all fifty of them, came in. He hugged her and kissed her on the cheek. He told her he had to work a few more hours. She replied that she still had more letters to answer.

Then she introduced me to him. She didn't refer to him as the president, she said my husband. I was honored, but I was also afraid I would lose my voice. The First Lady asked me if I had a smart phone. I told her I did. She wanted to take a picture of my first day on the job. My first day on the job! You can't imagine how it felt to hear those words. A huge burden had been lifted off my shoulders. A lady came in and took several photos of the First Lady, the President and myself.

The lady who took the photos said that someone needed to see me before I left. His name was Alex Jacobs and his office was across from the receptionist's office. I knocked on the door and when he answered it I almost fainted. It was the man from the employment office. He was smiling from ear to ear. He shook my hand and welcomed me aboard. He asked me if I realized the test was yesterday. What could I say? I just nodded my head like an idiot.

He told me I would need to fill out some forms and have an I.D. card made the next day. He gave me a reserved parking card. When he told me that my daughter and I would have full health insurance coverage I almost cried.

What came next was the biggest surprise of the day and believe me a lot had already happened. He handed me a laptop computer and told me that he would like for me to write a book about the First Lady. I just looked at him in disbelief. I couldn't believe someone would want me to write a book about the First Lady. After what seemed like an hour, I came to my senses and asked if she knew about this. He answered that she did and that I could talk to her if I had any questions. He told me that she had requested me when she found out that I was unemployed. (God works miracles, doesn't he?) He cautioned me about telling anyone because I might not get truthful answers. She did not want it sugar coated, just truthful. She wanted a book that would get our young people more involved in our country. If I could get it published, I would receive all the royalties.

On my way home, I convinced myself that I could do this and speaking of young people reminded me of my daughter. I needed to straighten out my own house; put it in order so to speak. I had to rebuild something else. She was lying on the couch when I returned home. It was best to start with a clean slate I thought. I was going to try to rescue my daughter and myself.

Before I even had a chance to close the door she wanted to know where I had been. She stated that an interview and some test shouldn't take all day. She said she was about to starve. I didn't say anything; I just went to my bedroom and changed into something more comfortable. Back in the living room, I sat in my chair and looked at my daughter. She wanted to know why I was looking at her. I told her that I had had a long exhausting day and that we would just have cereal for supper. She made it sound like it was the end of the world. I went into the kitchen and fixed her a bowl and put a table spoon instead of a teaspoon in it. When I handed it to her she looked at the spoon and wanted to know if I couldn't find a spoon that would fit in her mouth. I went back in the kitchen and got the biggest spoon we had and gave it to her. She just looked at it, like what the heck is this. I told her that it was the biggest spoon we had and that it should fit her mouth perfectly. She just sat there looking at the spoon.

I took a deep breath and said a prayer. I asked God to help me out here. The first step was always the hardest. I realized this was going to make or break it. I told her that I lost her when her father died. I told her it was my fault not hers. We didn't have the money to do things we had done before. We had no savings and just my teacher's salary. I didn't know there was a world out there with things to do that didn't cost money. I said that I hadn't really thought about the fact that she had lost someone just as important to her as I had. She had lost her father. I was an adult but she was a child and didn't know how to cope. I told her that she needed me, but that I wasn't there for her as I should have been. She had needed love and reassurance that everything was going to be okay. I told her how sorry I was and asked if she could forgive me.

She was still looking at the spoon. She told me that I had not lost her, but she was the one who had wandered away. And, with a smile, said that the spoon was way too small to fit her mouth. Just then I noticed that tears had started rolling down her cheeks. She told me that I was always there working, cooking and cleaning the house. She said that she had a wonderful role model right in front of her all the time, but never saw it.

We both got up and hugged each other for a long time. It was the best hug I had ever received. We composed ourselves and sat back down.

I couldn't wait any longer and told her I had gotten a job. She wanted me to tell her all the details. I showed her the photos on my phone including the person who I would be working for. She looked for a long time, and then her jaw dropped. She asked if I would be working for the President and I told her that I would be working only for the First Lady. I told her how the First Lady had made me a sandwich for lunch. She thought that was really awesome. Then I told her about the First Lady calling that little girl and how it made me realize how I had done the same thing. Then I told her I wish someone had called me and told me I needed to hug you and tell you how much I love you.

Afterwards, we went for a walk around the neighborhood. I couldn't believe all the things I hadn't noticed in four years. We had new neighbors, lots of people had painted their house, trees were beginning to put on leaves, and spring was just around the corner. I realized how glad I was that we were doing this. I had so much to be thankful for and for four years I never saw it.

I thought of the book I was to write. But that would remain my little secret. Where should I begin, perhaps at the beginning and work my way to the end of the book? But, where was the beginning?

PART ONE

CHAPTER ONE

KERNEY, WYOMING

1994

Last night's thunder storm didn't bring any rain. It moved through Kerney like an empty freight train, lots of noise and nothing else. One of the horses had opened the corral gate and one of the colts was missing. Beverly had her suspicion on which horse was the culprit.

She was holding the reins of the suspect right now. She turned up the collar of her sheepskin coat to ward off the chill. Her horse, Apache, nudged her shoulder. Beverly reached up and scratched behind the horse's ear. The ear twitched and the horse let out a snort.

Beverly grabbed the saddle horn and swung into the saddle. She didn't need the stirrup. The two were on Lookout Point, her favorite place in the whole world. She rose up in the stirrups and looked around. Dawn was approaching and she anxiously waited on the first rays of sun to crest the top of mountains to the east. Gradually the sun rose and a few rays struck the clouds overhead turning them orange. Beverly like to call them pumpkin orange. She smiled; she knew it was going to happen. She had seen it thousands of times and she loved every minute of it. The sun continued its methodical journey. Then it seemed to just pop up and happen. Everything seemed to turn golden. These few minutes were the most precious to Beverly. She said, "This is the day that the Lord hath made. We will rejoice and be glad in it." Psalm 118 verse 24 was one of her favorites. She thanked God for the heavenly sight she was able to witness. It was why she loved this place, this very special place.

Beverly looked around more until she saw the colt in the back corner of the ranch. She waited a few more minutes then headed towards the colt. The colt didn't try to run away. It was lost and just waiting for someone to come and rescue him. She lassoed the colt and headed back to the corral.

Then she went inside the barn and removed the saddle. She swung it onto the tack rack with the other saddles. She removed the saddle blanket, then shook it and placed it next to her saddle where it could air out. She removed the bridle and hung it on a peg on the wall. After checking the saddle, she decided she would saddle soap it tomorrow after school. She checked the feed and water trough. She led Apache out to the corral and closed the barn door. Then she walked to the house and took a shower and dressed for church.

There was a good size crowd at church this Sunday morning and Beverly was starving. She had missed breakfast because the colt had gotten out of the corral. Things like that didn't bother her, that's life on a ranch. Then the sermon had gone a tad longer than she would have liked. Today was the fifth Sunday of the month and a pot luck dinner was held in the fellowship hall. Then the preacher asked Bother Jasper to say the blessing. Brother Jasper always took forever to say the blessing; it was almost a sermon itself. She was looking forward to trying a new dish her mother had made. Fifth Sunday dinners always brought out a crowd. It is always four times a year and when you live in the middle of nowhere, anything is nice. Since Kerney was so sparsely populated and your nearest neighbor may be five or ten miles away, the dinner was the only chance you got to see and socialize with them. Brother Jasper finally finished saying the blessing. In their church everyone was called brother or sister and Beverly liked it that way.

Since Beverly sang in the choir everyone else beat her in line. Beverly had just turned to speak to a high school classmate when the man in front of her realized he had not gotten his spoon and fork.

He turned and stepped on her foot. She was wearing open toed shoes and it hurt like the dickens. She said, "Watch it cowboy," as she was trying to get her foot back in her shoe. It was out of kilter when she jerked her foot back. The man turned to look at who he had stepped on. He had to look down on Beverly to see her.

The man said, "Sorry, I didn't see you." Beverly had to look up to see the man. He was real tall, a lot taller than her dad, who was six foot, and Beverly was short at five foot four inches.

"Are you saying I'm short?" she asked. Beverly was sensitive of her size. In Wyoming it was called puny. She had turned sixteen last month. Her mother had told her she would fill out later. She sure hoped so.

The man said, "Perhaps I was blinded by your beauty," and turned back around. Beverly thought of all the gall, here in church of all places, using a pick-up line. She couldn't believe it. Her mom had warned her about people like him. Her mom had said, "You can't let your guard down for one minute, no sir, not for one minute can you let your guard down." She had never seen him before and around here everyone knows everybody. She turned to the girl behind her and whispered, "Who is that creep?" Sixteen year olds call everyone 'creep'. The girl looked, shook her head and said, "Never seen him before. Why, what did he do?"

"I'll tell you later." Beverly was afraid the man may hear her. When she turned back around the man had gotten the last of her mother's chicken casserole. Doesn't that beat all? Beverly started to say something, and then stopped. No need to start a scene here in church. Her mom and dad had saved her a seat at their table, but Beverly wanted to sit with her friends and pointed that way. Her mother nodded her head to say okay.

Beverly had just gotten up to get a dessert when Jo Beth Gordon grabbed her by the wrist. Jo Beth had moved here last year and had become friends with Beverly, even though she was two years older.

Jo Beth said, "There's someone I want you to meet," and pulled her toward the other side of the room.

"Who?"

"You'll see," and kept pulling her toward the table where the creep was sitting. The man was sitting on a corner chair and was listening to Gus Radcliff. Everyone in the county knew Gus was wounded on D-Day. He had to be close to ninety. The man was leaning over close to Gus so he could hear over the noise. The table seated eight people and there was an empty chair on the other end. Beverly tried to slow down but Jo Beth was bigger, everyone was bigger. She pulled Beverly past the man who was nodding his head at something Gus was saying.

The man didn't even notice Beverly. Beverly thought, thank God for small favors. Then Beverly glanced down at the man's plate. He had hardly eaten any of her mother's casserole. Beverly tried to stop. She made up her mind; she was going to say something. Jo Beth pulled harder.

"Beverly, I'd like you to meet my brother." They were at the other end of the table now. Her brother stood up and nodded to Beverly and said, "Pleased to meet you." Beverly didn't know Jo Beth had a brother and said so.

"He stayed in Denver when we moved. He's in the army now." Beverly sat down in the empty chair as Jo Beth said, "His name is Jack and he's on his way from Fort Gordon which is in Georgia and he's going to Fort Lewis, Washington".

Beverly nodded her head mostly to be polite. Jack was sort of cute and had a nice smile. Beverly sensed he was a shy person, because Jo Beth was doing all the talking.

"They're driving cross country. He was able to stop for the weekend."

"How long will it take?" she asked. Beverly was curious, that had to be close to four thousand miles. "Why didn't you fly?" she asked.

Jack said, "We bought a Volkswagen bus for six hundred dollars and when we get to Fort Lewis we can sell it and get our money back so we travelled for free. We can sleep in the van in bad weather and camp out when it's nice."

"You said we. Who else is driving with you?" Beverly asked.

"A friend of mine. We were in training together." Beverly and Jack had a nice conversation. She found out he was nineteen and wanted to make the army his career.

Jo Beth said, "You two should write to each other. Jack doesn't know anyone at Fort Lewis; pen pals you might say, you have to admit the pickings are pretty slim around here." Beverly gave him her address which was a route number and box number. Beverly asked him, "Did you bring your friend to church with you?"

Jack nodded and looked around and said, "I don't see him."

Beverly looked around also. She saw Mr. Gus going out the door with his walker. The creepy guy was with him. Beverly thought he must be a distant kin to Mr. Gus. Beverly didn't really get a good look at the guy when he stepped on her foot. When he went out the door he pulled it closed behind him. Beverly thought he was an average looking man, close cut black hair and on the thin side with a tan like he was outdoors a lot. She guessed you could call him a "cowboy" because there were more cows and sheep in Wyoming than people. Almost everyone was a cowboy in a way. She put him out of her mind and turned back to Jack and Jo Beth.

The man helped Mr. Gus to his car, folded the walker and put it on the passenger side. It was tough being ninety and having to use a walker. Gus thanked him and asked, "Are you here with anyone?"

The man answered, "My friend Jack Gordon and I are going to Fort Lewis." Gus asked, "What is your name son?"

The man said, "Lewis MacDonald. I enjoyed talking with you and thank you for your service."

After Gus left the parking lot, Lewis decided he would walk around a few minutes. He knew Jack wouldn't leave because Lewis had the keys to the van. He went behind the church. He knew it would be here if they had one. There it was. It wasn't all that big. Lewis didn't necessarily like walking around in a cemetery. It wasn't a hobby or anything like that. He believed you could judge a community by their cemeteries. If the community took care of the dead, they would take care of the living. He was also curios about how long the cemetery had been in existence. He usually determined this by finding the oldest grave. The older graves were usually clustered together in one section and then expanded from there. The oldest grave he found was 1885.

In Virginia where he was born and only been back to a few times for three or four months at a time, it was easy to find graves from 1700. It seemed to him that the farther west you went the graves got younger. In Texas there were a lot in the 1700's.

This cemetery was well taken care of. The grass was cut and trimmed beside the graves. There weren't many elaborate tomb stones here, mostly plain and modest. Lewis liked that. He walked around some more; he wasn't interested in going back inside. He only knew one person in there and that was Jack Gordon. They had met on their first day in the army. They had gone through boot camp and then advance individual training together. Now they were on their way to Fort Lewis, Washington. Lewis had spent four months in Washington State near Seattle. He tried to remember how old he was, maybe twelve. He didn't know anyone in Washington. It was just another place he had lived for a short period of time. He found three graves for someone named Gordon. He wondered if they were related to Jack. They had died in the sixties. He thought about asking Jack later.

He walked through the cemetery looking at the dates and names, no telling who you might find in an old west cemetery. He didn't see any outlaws or anyone famous. Oh well, you never know. He had actually seen a few in other places, especially Texas.

For some reason he thought about the girl whose foot he had stepped on. It was an accident, but still embarrassing. She acted like she got mad about it and he tried to make up for it by paying her a compliment. It just didn't come out right. Well, no problem, I will never see her again anyway.

There was a tree line near the cemetery and he saw a bald eagle take off. Lewis watched as the eagle passed overhead. Then he made a complete circle taking in the beautiful landscape. He could see the flag fluttering in the breeze in front of the small white clapboard church. The sun making it appear to be even whiter than it actually was. The sky seemed a darker blue than he was accustomed to seeing in other places he had lived.

This is America, this place I am in right now; this is what America is really all about, thought Lewis. He remembered something his Mom would say when it was such a beautiful day. He said it to himself as a way of remembering her. "This is the day which the Lord hath made; we will rejoice and be glad in it."

Lewis thought about the eagle. It was the first one Lewis had ever seen in his life. It sent a chill down his spine. It made him proud to be an American. Every time he saw the flag blowing in the wind he felt a sense of pride that most people in the world would never know. Only a few people in the world were truly free. Some flags represented oppression and fear. You could die or be sent to a slave labor camp if you didn't say the right thing all the time. Lewis knew he could never live like that.

As he walked the short distance back to the church, he noticed dark clouds on the horizon. He could see lightning flashes, but they were too far away to hear the thunder. There was a storm brewing on the horizon.

CHAPTER TWO

BOSNIA 1996

MATTHEW 5-9

Jack Gordon was putting on his equipment. Lewis MacDonald was already standing in the door. Jack said, "Four more days, then back to the good ole U.S. of A." Lewis just nodded. He was more of a listener than a talker. They stepped outside to another cloudy day. They were manning a checkpoint. Refugees were moving in both directions to escape the violence. They were part of the International Force. Their mission was to separate the warring factions, trying to keep the peace. They were in a small stone building, the roof leaked and the two windows had broken glass panes but it kept you dry when it rained and it rained a lot here.

Jack and Lewis were part of numerous checkpoints. Six enlisted men and a second lieutenant. Right now there was no traffic which struck Lewis as odd and he mentioned it to Jack. "Maybe we're doing good or just plain lucky."

Jack said, "Let's hope for both."

Two men on for four hours while the others slept. It was almost impossible to sleep with the traffic six feet away. He was thankful for the nightly curfew. No traffic was allowed at night. A little over three hours and maybe he could get some sleep. Each team stayed on duty for seventy two hours and then rotated back to the base camp fifteen miles away. At night two men stood outside with nothing to do except make sure no one came near the building.

"Lewis, why are we here in this God forsaken place?"

"I really don't know, Jack."

Jack said, "Vehicle," and pointed north. Lewis stepped out into the road and held up his hand. Jack unslung his M-16. Lewis put his right hand on his pistol. He didn't have his rifle, it was inside. If there was shooting at a distance of two feet, a pistol was better. Jack was covering him ten feet away. Lewis could tell there were four men in the car and relayed this information to Jack.

The car came to a stop and Lewis asked for ID's. Lewis was six feet four inches tall. He leaned over to look at the ID's. He had a clip board with a list of names, people who were suspected of war crimes. He checked the names carefully. All of the names over here were unusual, no Smiths or Jones someone had joked. Lewis couldn't have pronounced a single one of them. As he was handing the ID's back, a white van followed by a car was pulling up.

"We're getting busy," said Jack.

"Open the trunk," said Lewis. The driver didn't move. Lewis showed the back of the clip board to the man and tapped it. The driver looked at the clip board. Different languages spoken here was plainly visible. The driver sat still and looked to the front. Lewis glanced at Jack and could sense that Jack knew something wasn't right. Jack raised the muzzle of his rifle a few inches. Lewis put his hand on his pistol and stepped back a foot. The car door started opening.

Lewis heard a snap. It didn't register to Lewis that a bullet had missed his head by inches. He had never been shot at before. A fraction of a second later he heard a slap and a groan. Jack was falling face first. Lewis dove to the ground as all three vehicles sped away. Then he heard the shots. Must be two shooters, though Lewis wasn't sure.

The Lieutenant rushed outside followed by a soldier from West Virginia. Lewis couldn't think of his name. The Lieutenant yelled, "Help me get him inside."

Lewis was scrambling to his feet and heard another shot, followed by another. Lewis was scared stiff. The three of them pulled

Jack inside. The Lieutenant yelled, "Get a Medavac," to no one in particular. "Get away from the windows. One man on each side. Don't show yourselves. Bring Gordon over by the back wall. Crenshaw cover the door from back here, if anyone tries to come in, shoot them."

"Are you sure?" asked Crenshaw.

"You're right," said the Lieutenant, "shoot them twice."

The Lieutenant started giving first aid. He turned Jack over, "It didn't go through." The Lieutenant applied a pressure bandage to the wound in an effort to stop the bleeding. The wound was high on the chest. The Lieutenant kept pressure on the wound. He looked up and said, "Don't look at me! Don't let anyone sneak up on us."

One of the men said, "We can't see the back of the building, Lieutenant Jenkins."

"I know," was the answer, and he kept applying pressure.

Thirty minutes later. "Where is the Medavac?"

Crenshaw had pulled the radio over to him and said, "Don't know, I've called three times."

"Call them again. I can't stop the bleeding. I'm on my third bandage."

"Sir, I see someone about two hundred yards away and he has a weapon. He's not near the road and he's trying to get behind us."

"Shoot him," came the reply from the Lieutenant.

"Yes, Sir!" Three seconds later he fired.

Lewis was on the other side of the building and he asked, "Did you get him?"

The other soldier, Watson said, "I'm pretty sure I did. He went down."

Lewis said, "I'm pretty sure there were two shooters. The shots were almost at the same time."

"Could have been an automatic weapon," someone said.

"Too accurate. The second shot, the one that got Jack, would have missed."

"Lieutenant, it will be dark soon."

"I know, where is that Medavac? It has been over an hour."

Lewis felt like a caged animal. The building was only one room and it seemed to be closing in on him. With all seven of them in here at one time, there wasn't much room.

"Lieutenant, what are we going to do?" someone asked.

"We wait, if it's not here by dark, we're leaving."

Lewis asked, "We're not leaving Jack are we, Lieutenant?"

"No, we will have to carry him."

This was such a relief to Lewis. He'd met his family in Wyoming and had come to be his best friend. "No Medavac, Lieutenant." The word was somber and had a profound effect on Lewis.

The Lieutenant stood up and looked down on Specialist 4th class Jack Gordon from Kerney, Wyoming by way of Denver, Colorado. Twenty years old, a good kid.

"I lost him. Would someone like to say a prayer for him?" It was deathly quiet in the little stone building in a country none of the men had even heard of a year ago. That is the life of a soldier. Every man was thinking the same thing; that could have been me.

Lewis crawled over and took Jack Gordon's hand in his. Then he bowed his head and said a prayer. "Lord, we commend the soul of Jack into your ever loving arms. He was a good man, a friend and comrade. Lord you said, 'blessed are the peace makers for they are the children of God.' He tried to be a peace maker and I'm sure you will be eternally grateful for him sacrificing his life for such a noble cause. We ask you to protect us from evil and harm. In Jesus's name we pray, Amen."

The other soldiers said, "Amen", when Lewis finished.

The lieutenant said, "Thank you, MacDonald."

JACK IN THE BOX

ECCLESIASTES 2:14

The sniper was furious. He was very good at his trade. Having come to Bosnia to get experience in a combat situation. He and the other sniper had been in their concealed position for over six hours, not moving a muscle. He was actually training the other sniper, and the teacher had missed. The student had hit his target. The two had observed how the Americans operated at this check point. He knew they were on duty for four hours. The two previous teams had done it the same way each time. Check ID's; use a mirror to check under the car and then the trunk. He would use that knowledge to his advantage.

The three vehicles his men were trying to get past the check point had arrived on time. The American checked the ID's. The sniper couldn't allow him to look in the trunk. He would kill the soldier on the driver's side and his student would kill the other. It didn't go as planned. The soldier evidently was going to use the mirror after checking the trunk. When the door started opening the sniper squeezed the trigger. At the same instant the American stepped back a foot to let the car door open. He had missed. He had never missed before.

He had spent five years in training; not as a sniper, he had only trained as a sniper for six weeks. The school he had graduated from taught everything. How to make bombs from household items, firearms, secret communications, hand to hand combat and the list went on and on.

He remembered the first day he arrived at the training facility. It looked like an abandoned factory which it actually was at the edge of the city. Ten handpicked young men and four women were attending the course.

'The course' was what it was called by everyone, student and instructor alike. He knew before he ever entered the building he and his parents may never see each other again. The building was surrounded by a rusty chain link fence eight feet high. No one left once they came here.

The training was intense, very intense and brutal. In training he had been required to kill four 'Enemy of the State.' There wasn't a shortage of enemies of the state. The prisons were full of enemies of the state. The students helped reduce the prison population.

The students were told what would happen if they failed the course. He didn't know if it was the truth or rumors, but there was enough truth to the rumor to strike fear inside the students. Fear is a powerful motivator. When your instructor happens to mention that you would disappear if you failed, that was a powerful motivation.

After he missed his shot he instructed the other sniper to move behind the stone building. The trainee was a little careless and moved too quickly. A shot from inside the building hit and dropped the trainee. It was time to leave; the occupants would be taken care of after dark. The sniper had to be in Paris, France in a week. No one would ever know he had missed.

The sniper wondered if fate had a hand in him missing the soldier. He was a man who believed in fate. He didn't believe in luck. Fate had kept the soldier alive, but what was the reason fate had picked that insignificant soldier and allowed him to live a few more hours. Because if the attack went as planned tonight all of the men in the stone building would be dead unless fate intervened again. Not likely.

After Lewis finished praying for Jack Gordon, he noticed the Lieutenant had tears streaming down his cheeks. "You did all you could, Sir," and he placed his hand on the officer's shoulder.

The Lieutenant nodded his head and said, "Thank you."

Lewis had come to admire the Lieutenant. He knew nothing about him other than he was a Lieutenant in the U.S. Army and was African American. He also knew he had Jump wings and a ranger tab on his shoulder.

The Lieutenant said, "We need something to make a stretcher. Look around, we can use our ponchos, but we need some poles."

Crenshaw said, "There is some pipe behind the building."

Lewis remembered that Crenshaw was from West Virginia. It had taken two hours to remember that. Lewis thought I might die with him and it took me two hours to remember his name. Fear will do that.

The Lieutenant said, "Check both sides of the building real close then I'll go out and get the pipes."

Lewis thought we can't let him do that. We need him; he's the only one of us that knows what he is doing. I certainly don't. Lewis didn't remember going out the window, he remembered crawling around back and grabbing two pipes. The pipes looked like water pipes of galvanized steel. They were the same length. He crawled back to the window and passed them through. He was still terrified. He went back through the window head first. As he lay on the floor catching his breath, he saw the Lieutenant looking down at him.

"I thought I said I would go out and get them."

Lewis lay on the floor still trying to catch his breath and finally said, "Why should you have all the fun?"

The Lieutenant shook his head and stuck his hand out and helped him to his feet. "In case you haven't noticed I outrank you and I get all the perks, but thanks anyway."

The Lieutenant checked the pipes and said, "These will do fine." The men took a poncho and laid it on the floor and placed the pipes on top, folded it over and snapped it into place. Then they repeated it with another poncho. They placed Jack's body on top and secured him with a rope someone had brought along.

The Lieutenant took a camo stick out of his rucksack and blackened his already dark face and passed it around. "No bare skin, act like your life depends on it."

The team had only one rifle with a starlight night vision scope on it. Lieutenant Jenkins checked both sides of the building and when he was satisfied, he handed the rifle to Lewis. "Since you like playing outside you get to go first. Check behind the building. Two will go out and then the rest of us will pass the body out and then go out."

The Lieutenant put the radio in his rucksack and swung it onto his shoulders. "Let's move out. When we get to the woods I want to stay about fifty yards parallel of the road."

It took ten minutes to move everyone outside. "MacDonald, get in the back with the starlight scope. Make sure no one is following us."

They had only been gone five minutes when they heard a 'whoosh' and a streak of light. Then the explosion. Lewis saw the roof lift a few feet before collapsing back down, the inside glowing bright.

"Rocket propelled grenade. Their reinforcements have arrived. They will know we are gone in about twenty seconds." Lewis didn't recognize who said it. Then they heard automatic gunfire. Lewis could see the flashes from the assault rifles.

"Move deeper into the woods," whispered the Lieutenant. "Stay close to each other. MacDonald move up front. Make sure you check everything especially near the road. I'm hoping they will think we will take the road."

Lewis whispered, "Yes, Sir," and moved up front. When we walked past the stretcher bearers one asked, "Why don't they send a convoy?"

"I don't know." Lewis couldn't tell who had asked.

"Why don't they send a truck?" someone else whispered.

"I don't know." Lewis couldn't tell who had asked about the truck either. In the dark everyone looked alike especially with camo on their faces.

After another hundred yards the Lieutenant stopped everyone and said, "We're being followed. Put the body down and get behind something alongside the trail that we have made. We'll form an L shaped ambush, four men alongside the trail, two at the end of the trail where the body is. MacDonald gives me the starlight." Lewis did as he was told and took the officers weapon.

The Lieutenant went back up the trail a few yards and saw at least ten men coming. He could tell they had no military training. They weren't spread out; they were more in a cluster. He then went to each of his men and whispered, "I'm going to open fire first. Make sure you have a target. There's enough moon out that you can see them and if you are behind something they can't see you. I am going to fire a full magazine and when I stop firing you are going to have to assault them. Shoot each of them twice. Don't waste time checking. Shoot one and go to another one, you understand?"

Each man nodded his head and the Lieutenant moved to the next man. He finally got to Lewis, "When I open fire you fire one magazine fully automatic, then the other guys will assault, you got that?"

"Yes, Sir," was all Lewis could say.

"Get behind that tree and don't fire to the right of it. I don't want to hit our own men. Take the rifle off safe and get ready." Lewis lay down but could barely see the trail. He heard them first. Then he saw them. They were moving fairly fast. Lewis knew what a kill zone was. He had learned that in basic at Fort Gordon. Lieutenant Jenkins waited and waited. Lewis was wondering when he was going to fire.

A successful ambush is over about the time it starts. Lewis knew an ambush is defined as an attack from a concealed position on an unsuspecting enemy when the enemy is in the kill zone. If you are in the kill zone it can be described as hell in a very small place.

The Lieutenant pulled the trigger. Lewis was about a tenth of a second behind him. It takes almost two seconds to fire twenty rounds. The noise was horrendous. In the deep woods it sounded like it was coming from everywhere at the same time. The noise didn't block out the screams, nothing could. Then the men were charging and yelling at the same time, firing two shots at each person in the kill zone. Then it was deathly quiet.

Lieutenant Jenkins went forward, almost at a dead run, quickly counted the bodies. "Nine, everyone get down and face out. I think one may have gotten away."

Jenkins turned in a full circle and pointed back up the trail. "I hear him. I'm going after him."

He headed back up the trail, rifle on his shoulder looking through the scope. The men heard two shots. Crenshaw looked at Lewis and said, "I wouldn't want that dude chasing me."

"You got that right," answered Lewis.

The Lieutenant came back down the trail and asked, "Is everyone alright?" "We're okay. All of us are okay," answered Crenshaw.

"Men you did just as you were trained. I'm proud of you. Search the bodies and put wallets and pistols in your rucksack. We'll find a place to get rid of the rifles. Disassemble them first and throw the small parts away."

"What about these bodies, Lieutenant?" asked Lewis. "Anyone want to say a prayer for them? I didn't think so."

The Lieutenant moved to the front, checked the starlight then handed it to Lewis. "I don't know if the shooting is going to bring anyone else, so be careful." "How do we tell the good guys from the bad guys?" "Tonight we are the only good guys. Now let's get going."

Thirty minutes later Lewis halted everyone. The Lieutenant came up front. Lewis handed him the rifle and whispered, "To the right of the bridge."

The Lieutenant looked and held up two fingers. Lewis nodded. The Lieutenant went back to tell everyone to stay where they were.

When Jenkins was back with Lewis he whispered, "Cover me." Lewis asked what he was going to do. "Just cover me. If they turn around, shoot them," he replied and then he was gone.

Lewis could hear a small stream nearby. Maybe it will mask the Lieutenant's noise. Lewis heard nothing but the stream. He kept his attention on the two men lying on the ground near the road. Every once in a while he looked for the Lieutenant but didn't see him. He sure was taking his time, they weren't very far away. Suddenly the Lieutenant was standing between the two men.

"How in the world did he do that?" Lewis whispered to himself. He saw the Lieutenant bend over the man on the right and place the pistol on his back and heard a pop. It wasn't loud at all; the man's heavy jacket had absorbed the sound. The man on the left started to turn over and Jenkins shot him in the chest, another contact wound. Surely both were dead. Jenkins hit them in the head with his pistol.

He motioned for Lewis to come to him. Lewis moved up, he felt his heart hammering away in his chest. He wondered how long you stay scared.

"Move everyone across the stream and bring someone with you. We need to search these guys." Ten minutes later, Lewis returned with Lofton, one of the stretcher bearers. The Lieutenant was still checking the road. "Do you think anyone heard those shots?"

"No, Sir. I barely heard them."

"Search them."

They found ID's, two pistols, two automatic rifles, and two grenades. "These are American grenades," said Lewis. "Good we may need them. We weren't issued any. I'll disassemble the rifles. Take the bodies and hide them. Then we will dispose of the rifles."

Hiding the bodies was easy. They dragged them a few yards into the woods and covered them with branches. Moving back to where they had laid Jack's body, they huddled up and discussed the situation as quietly as possible. Everyone needed a break. Jenkins decided not to use the road. He took the starlight and said he would walk the point, Lewis was grateful for that.

Two hours later, they halted. Jenkins turned to Lewis and whispered, "I see a small building dead ahead. It looks like there is a light on inside. I think the windows are covered with a blanket or something but there is a hole letting the light out." He handed Lewis the starlight. "See what I mean."

"Yes, sir, I see it." The hole couldn't have been larger than a dime but was clearly visible with the night vision scope.

"See the three vehicles behind the building. Are those the ones at the checkpoint?"

Lewis studied the vehicles. "I'm pretty sure about the van. I can't tell about the cars Lieutenant. They might be, but I'm not sure."

The Lieutenant thought for a minute and asked, "What exactly happened?"

Lewis said, "One vehicle pulled up with four men in it. I stopped it and checked their ID's and then a van pulled up. I only saw one man inside the van, but there may have been more. Then another car pulled up. I couldn't see the people in that car because of the van. I told the driver to open the trunk. He started to open the door and then Jack got shot. All three vehicles sped off. I don't know if they were just trying to get away from the gun fire or were trying to run the road block. I just don't know. I really don't know."

"Did you check under the car with the mirror?"

"No, Sir, I didn't get that far before Jack got shot."

The Lieutenant thought on this for a minute or two then said, "You know what I think; those men knew there was a sniper and they used that to get through. They might be a hunter killer team and we don't know for certain how many there are. The two men back at the bridge may or may not have been with them. They may have been there in case we stopped all of them and was covering for their escape. Now, there is a village not far from the base camp on the road to the east. If it's a hunter killer team then that village is in danger so we need to find out who is in there. I'll take the starlight and check the other side and try to look inside and see what's what."

"Good luck, Lieutenant."

Lewis knelt down on one knee. He was afraid if he got in a prone position he would fall asleep. Lewis couldn't see anything and then the Lieutenant was back. "There are six men in there. They all have weapons and are looking at a map. Get Crenshaw up here."

Then the Lieutenant laid out his plan. Lewis would take the starlight up the lane to the road. Crenshaw was to cut the smallest sapling six feet long that he could find. The Lieutenant taped the grenade to the end of the pole. He put the other grenade on Crenshaw's belt. The Lieutenant believed when Crenshaw struck the grenade through the window the man nearest the door would unbolt the door and try to get out. The Lieutenant would then go in after shooting the man opening the door. "Make sure you don't use the second grenade if I make it inside, okay? If they don't unlock the door run up and throw the second grenade. After you push the first one in, run; they might throw it back out. You got all that?"

"Yes, Sir."

Lewis moved into position and checked the road and the woods beside the lane leading to the house. He looked back toward the house just in time to see Crenshaw shove the grenade on the stick through the window and run. He heard chairs turning over as the men jumped to their feet. He saw the door swing open as one man tried to make it out. The grenade went off with a whump sound. The building absorbed most of the sound. He saw the Lieutenant fire off two shots and dash inside. Lewis heard shots in pairs, pop pop, pop pop, then three more series of double shots. Lewis ran to the building and saw five bodies inside plus the one outside. The Lieutenant told Lewis to bring the body up.

Lewis ran to the edge of the woods and said, "Bring the body." Then he realized that he didn't say bring Jack. Jack had become the body; Lewis felt bad about that.

"Put the body in the van. I want all the weapons, ID's, papers, maps, everything. Grab it quick, put it on the table cloth and put it in the van. Find the car keys. There should be three sets here."

One of the men came inside and said, "Lieutenant there are all kinds of weapons and explosives in the van."

The Lieutenant said, "Put all of this in there also. Did you get Gordon inside?"

"Yes, Sir, we had to lay him on top of all that stuff."

Crenshaw came up and said, "Lieutenant, we only found two sets of keys. We looked everywhere. Maybe one set is in the car. I'll go look." Five minutes later, he came back and shook his head. "No luck, Lieutenant."

The Lieutenant asked which vehicle was without a key.

"The van."

The Lieutenant went to the van crawled inside, reached behind the dash and pulled the wires loose. He started touching the wires together. The engine fired up. He reached on his belt and pulled a Leatherman tool out. It had wire cutters and strippers on it. He stripped the insulation off the wires he needed and twisted them together. "All right, two men to a vehicle. Driver up front, second man in the back with the windows down where you can shoot out both sides. MacDonald and I will be in the van. Drive forty five. Don't slow down. Lead vehicle, I want you to stop one hundred yards before you reach the base camp. I'll get out and walk the rest of the way with my arms up and no weapon. Not many black people around here so maybe they won't shoot. Lead vehicle make sure your lights are on me. I want the guards to see me clearly. I want the van in the middle. Let's get on the road."

On the road, Lewis was thinking what it was like in that cabin. He had seen the Lieutenant shoot the man coming out of the door and how he had dashed through the door and started shooting. When Lewis got there, there were five bodies strewn around the room. Each of them was lying in an awkward position, the living doesn't assume. He wondered how many had been killed by the blast and how many the Lieutenant had killed. He wondered how Crenshaw felt about it. Lewis knew it was possible that the Lieutenant had shot and killed eight men in less than two hours. It didn't seem to be bothering him. Lewis was thankful the Lieutenant was with them. They had cheated death by five minutes back at the check point; actually Lewis had cheated death twice, counting the sniper.

"Why did you go through the window to get the pipe?"

Lewis thought for a few seconds before answering. "I knew the men needed you more than they needed me. It seemed like the right thing to do at the time."

They rode on in silence for a few miles. Lewis said, "Crenshaw did real good, didn't he?"

"You all did."

"I didn't do anything except what you told me to do."

"That's why you did real well."

"But I was impressed by Crenshaw sticking the grenade through the window."

"You know why I put that grenade on that pole?"

"No, Sir."

"Two reasons. Number one that made it harder to throw it back out and number two the first time you throw a grenade in a real situation your arm might turn to rubber, if you know what I mean. He might have missed and hit the wall. It could have gone anywhere, even at me. Don't get me wrong, I trusted him. What if I had went inside and he threw the second one in. I wouldn't have known."

They drove on in silence. They turned off the main road and onto the road leading to the Base Camp. The lead vehicle stopped. Lewis pulled up a few feet. The Lieutenant left his weapons in the van and walked forward. He raised his arms and continued walking. Lewis could see him clearly by looking over the lead car. He saw the four guards pointing their weapons at him. He continued to walk. Lewis said a silent prayer. The Lieutenant stopped ten feet away and turned around. One of the guards came and patted him down. He saw the Lieutenant turn and wave them forward. They stopped the first vehicle and the two men got out of the car and showed their ID's. The guard pointed the men toward a place to park and motioned Lewis forward. The Lieutenant said, "This is the van I told you about."

The guard nodded and looked inside. He saw the body and all the weapons. "We'll, get someone to take the body to the hospital. They will take care of it."

Ten minutes later, an ambulance pulled up. Lewis and the Lieutenant helped the two men unload the body. As they put him on the gurney, Lewis put his hand on Jack's chest and said, "Lord rest his soul." Then added, "Please."

The guard said, "You need to take the van to the intelligence officer," then he waved Lewis through. The third vehicle was also searched and told to park. Lewis and the Lieutenant stopped in front of a large tent. "It's four o'clock. Go take a nap. Reveille is in two hours and after breakfast you can sleep all day. Tell the men for me; I am going to be here for a while." Then he walked inside.

Lewis walked to his tent. He had never been this tired in his life, but he had something to do first. He opened Jack's footlocker. Jack had given him the combination. Lewis knew he could get into trouble, but he was going to take the risk. He knew an officer would be here soon to inventory and take custody of the contents so it could be mailed home to his parents. Lewis found what he was looking for, the letters Jack's girlfriend had written him. He also got the photo of his sister and the girl. It was a shot of them at some kind of gathering, Lewis couldn't determine where or what the function was. He would somehow return them to the girl. He would not read them even though Jack had read parts of them to him. He left everything else including the letters from his family. Lewis placed them in his locker. He would mail them when he got back to Fort Lewis. Then he collapsed on his cot and fell asleep.

None of the men changed uniforms or shaved, they just walked out like zombies for reveille. Jenkins was standing there; Lewis couldn't believe it. He had shaved, showered, put on a starched uniform and polished his boots. He looked like he did for every formation. Lewis wondered how he did it.

He dismissed the platoon for breakfast. Lewis went to him and saluted. Jenkins returned the salute. "Can I speak to you in private after breakfast, Sir?"

"After you shave, shower, change your uniform and polish your boots you can."

"Yes, Sir," said Lewis and gave him his best salute.

Two hours later, Lewis went to the Lieutenant's tent. At the tent flap Lewis called out, "Sir."

"Come in, MacDonald."

Lewis entered. He really didn't know what he was going to say or even how to say it. The Lieutenant was sitting on his bunk. He was cleaning his equipment which he set aside. "Pull out the footlocker and sit down."

Lewis did as he was told and looked the Lieutenant in the eye and asked, "How do you do the things you do?"

"I'm not sure I understand."

"Well, yesterday and all last night, weren't you scared. I know I was."

"Macdonald, I was just as scared as you, but if I showed it would you have done what I told you to do, when I told you to do it?"

"Probably not. I would have been even more afraid."

"It's called leading by example. Of course I was afraid, but I don't ask anyone to do something that I won't do myself."

"Did you learn that in Ranger School?"

"There and in other places."

"Did they teach you how to hot wire a car?"

The Lieutenant smiled. "No, I learned that when I was fourteen. You see, and I am embarrassed to say this, but when I was fourteen I stole a car. I ran out of gas two miles away and was sent to reform school for two years. I learned two valuable lessons. I didn't ever want to go to jail again."

"What was the other lesson, Sir?"

"Always check the gas gauge before you steal a car." Lewis had to laugh. "After reform school they sent me back to what I was trying to get away from."

"What was that, Lieutenant?"

"An alcoholic mother and live in boyfriend who took pleasure in beating the daylights out of me every chance he got. When I got home, I went in the front door and out the back. I never looked back. I was sixteen then and I knew no one would look for me. So, I lived on the street. Now, that was scary."

"I would imagine so."

"There was this Jewish family who owned a little mom and pop grocery store across town and he caught me looking in the garbage cans behind the store. Caught me dead to rights. He asked me if I was hungry and I told him yes. He took me inside, fed me and told me if I wanted a job and a place to stay that he had both. I told him, 'Yes, Sir.' There was a room upstairs with a bath but there was one condition. I had to go to school every night. I would sit with the two of them and they helped me with my homework. I could barely read and write. He paid me minimum wage and didn't charge me room and board. They were always encouraging me to do the best I could. It didn't matter what it was. No job is too small or too big. I owe my whole life to them. They even helped me through college. Everything I am I owe to someone who went out of their way and bent over backwards to help me for no reason at all."

"Not many people like that in the world."

"I wish there were more like that. The world would be a better place."

Lewis thought for a minute and said, "Sir, can I go to Ranger School?"

The Lieutenant crossed his arms, leaned back and looked at Lewis carefully. "I think I can arrange that, but first you have to go to jump school and you have to be a sergeant. Now I happen to know you're being promoted along with Crenshaw tomorrow." Lewis was taken by surprise.

The Lieutenant said, "I was impressed by both of you the last two days and I spoke to the battalion commander and he agreed."

"Thank you, Sir."

"Anything else, MacDonald?"

"Yes, Sir, I wonder if it might be possible to escort Jack's body home. You see we went through basic training and advanced individual training together. As a matter of fact, we bought an old Volkswagen bus in Georgia and drove to Fort Lewis together. We stopped in Wyoming and spent the weekend with his family. We are going back to the states in two days anyway."

"Well, I am glad you are volunteering because I was told to find someone to go. Not many people want to be a Ghost Rider."

"Ghost Rider, what's that?"

"You'll find out."

Lewis looked at Lieutenant Jenkins and said, "I hope it's nothing bad."

"I wouldn't know I've never had the opportunity." As Lewis turned to leave the Lieutenant said, "You did a fine job on the ambush."

Lewis stopped without turning around and said, "I forgot about that." Lewis thought, how can you forget something like that? Some kind of mental block I guess. He jumped when he felt someone's hand on his shoulder. "It happens, sometimes you remember the good things and block out the bad."

"I wish I could do that," The Lieutenant said.

Lewis nodded and started to leave when Lieutenant Jenkins asked, "You married, MacDonald?"

"No, Sir."

"I am. I have a beautiful wife and two kids and I will do whatever it takes to get back to them in one piece. It's why I do some of the things I do. Yeah, I was scared out there, real scared. I don't even know why we are here. I can't tell who is who or what is what. I have seen some of the atrocities that have happened over here. Entire families murdered, bodies mutilated and burned. I have seen vacant stares in children's eyes. They have lost everything. Moving through check points terrified. A child should never be scared. There is a lot of evil in this world and an awful lot of it is right here in this place. In a year or two the same evil will pop up somewhere else. You know what I mean?"

Lewis turned and asked, "What do we do?"

Lieutenant Jenkins said, "We help the children and we teach them not to hate. That's the only way."

Lewis nodded. He would have to think about that. Not that he would ever be in any position to do anything about it. He was just a soldier. He was going back and taking a friend who tried to help and died in the process.

Lieutenant Jenkins said, "You know what the old man said to me when he took me in, gave me a job and studied with me?"

Lewis knew he was talking about the Jewish couple who had changed his life. "No, Sir, what did he say?"

"He said 'a man never stood as tall as when he stoops to help a child.' That's why I say we have to help the children."

Lewis left.

Lieutenant Jenkins went back to cleaning his equipment. After a few minutes, he stopped and started thinking. He was trying to get it straight in his mind for the after action report that he would have to give later. When we sprung the ambush somehow we missed the first man. While I was trying to reload the man rushed us. Specialist MacDonald leaped up and wrestled the weapon away and clubbed the man to death.

Lieutenant Jenkins sat there for another minute thinking. He didn't know if it was fear or just some sort of survival mode. He thought some more. Maybe it was both, fear and survival mode, who knows. Then he thought maybe it was retribution for killing his friend. Lieutenant Jenkins went back to cleaning his equipment.

CHAPTER THREE

GHOST RIDER

At 1400 hours (2:00 p.m.) Lieutenant Jenkins, Lewis and Crenshaw were standing in front of the flagpole. The battalion Commander called the unit to attention. The promotion orders were read by the personnel officer. He presented the Sergeant stripes to Lieutenant Jenkins who pinned them on their collar points, then shook each man's hand. The three then saluted the Commander.

Lieutenant Jenkins told Lewis to accompany him to the admin office. When they arrived the Lieutenant shook Lewis's hand. Lewis saluted the Lieutenant and said, "Sir, it has been an honor and a privilege to serve with you. I hope you never regret doing this."

Jenkins looked at him and said, "MacDonald I think you will go far in the army. Perhaps we will serve together some time in the future. Now, go in and get your briefing on escort duty. Your orders for airborne school and ranger school should be ready, also."

Lewis went inside and approached the clerk typist. "I'm here for the escort briefing."

"See Captain Andrews. He'll give it to you."

Captain Andrews was seated at his desk. Lewis guessed he was about thirty years old and ten pounds overweight. Lewis saluted and took a seat when the officer motioned him to sit.

"I'm going to go over this with you. Sergeant, this is serious business. Everything has to be done in an established protocol. First and foremost, you may never leave the body unattended. At all times either you or an authorized officer must stay with the body from the time you accept custody of his remains. Now, what does that mean? The Air Force will transport the body or bodies on a military aircraft.

The body may be moved from one aircraft to another on its journey to its final destination. On these stops you may request an officer to watch the body while you use the latrine or get a bite to eat. You will have him check the personal information on the coffin and he will sign for it. Then when you get back on the plane you will again check the personal information on the casket and you will sign for it. This is called chain of custody. The Air Force is very good at this and they do not mind helping. They know you can't go three or four days without food. While you are in the air you may sleep. Once you get to the final destination, in other words, the funeral home, you must be awake when anyone is in the presence of the body. Most funeral home directors have done this before and at night; they usually will let you sleep on a couch in the room with the body. During the daytime they are authorized to guard the body while you are in the restroom. Most ceremonies include a viewing for the family then a viewing for everyone else, then the actual funeral and sometimes a graveside ceremony. This is usually a two day event. You must be in a class A uniform. Inside no headgear, outside you must wear you headgear. You will be flown to the nearest Air Force base then the funeral home will pick up the body for the transport. You may sit up front in the hearse. If two people show up you may have to ride in the back. After the service you must make arrangements to get to your next duty station. Any questions?"

Lewis had several questions but he only made one comment. "My Lieutenant said something about Ghost Riders."

The Captain leaned back in his chair, weaved his fingers together and laid his hands on his stomach. "I don't really know how or where the term Ghost Riders came from. You have a dead soldier in a coffin and you're on an airplane by yourself with him, but I don't believe in stuff like that. Look, I will be honest with you, this is not easy duty. You will get bored, tired, sleepy, hungry and other things I can't imagine. Just remember you are honoring a fallen comrade and you are representing the U.S. Army and the United States. Here is a card, put it in your pocket and memorize it. Let me say this. It may take you a week to get there, you may change planes a couple of times. You make take a long ride in a hearse. You will be in a funeral home, in a room with only the coffin at night. You may be the only living person there. The coffin is draped with an American flag. The funeral director and an assistant will fold the flag and hand it to you. Now everything you have done up until this point has been easy. You will walk that flag to a grieving family and you will solemnly present it, probably to the mother, and you will say what is on that card. That is why you need to memorize it."

Lewis looked at the small card. He couldn't believe that something this profound could be on such a small card. He read it twice then he read it out loud. "On behalf of the President of the United States and a grateful nation, I present you this flag."

Lewis looked at the Captain and the Captain nodded his head and said, "See what I mean?"

"Yes, Sir."

The Captain looked at Lewis. "I understand you volunteered for this duty. I don't envy you Sergeant. I don't believe you will ever do it again."

Lewis looked at the Captain and said, "I hope I never have the opportunity."

Two hours later Lewis dressed in his Class A uniform along with his duffel bag was dropped off at the morgue. He had to wait another hour while the body of Jack A. Gordon, Specialist 4th Class, United States Army of Kerney, Wyoming, by way of Denver Colorado was being processed.

Lewis was beyond tired; he was afraid if he closed his eyes he would fall asleep and never wake up. Finally, an aluminum casket draped in an American flag was brought out. A Captain was walking in front of it. The casket was on a gurney pushed by a P.F.C. The Captain had a clipboard in his hand. He pulled a pen out of his pocket, looked at Lewis, "You the escort?"

"Yes, Sir."

The Captain lifted the flag a few inches and pointed at a small plague and said, "Verify the information on it to the information on this card and then sign the card and date it." Lewis did so. "He will drive you to the airport." The Captain saluted the coffin then walked away.

The P.F.C. pushed the gurney to a Red Cross wagon and asked Lewis to help load it. "You can ride up front if you like." After loading the casket, Lewis got in front along with his bag.

The soldier asked, "Where is this one going?"

"Wyoming."

The van went to a point in the road and stopped. "Why are we stopping?"

The P.F.C. looked at him and said, "Waiting on a convoy; too dangerous to travel by yourself. Here it comes now." There was a Humvee with a machine gun mounted on a pedestal followed by five vehicles with another Humvee and a machine gun. The last Humvee slowed up and let the van pull in behind the other vehicles, and then it pulled up behind the van.

"How far to the airport?"

"Thirty five minutes barring any trouble."

At the airport the van went to a different part of the airport and pulled up near a C-5 A Cargo plane. The driver said, "You need to get out and wait here."

Lewis said, "Thank you."

The P.F.C. said, "Good luck Ghost Rider."

Seven men walked toward the van. They were in Class A uniforms. The lead man was an officer. Lewis saluted. Lewis noticed that the six were from the Air Force, Army, Navy and Marines. The officer was from the Army. They opened the back of the van and pulled the coffin out leaving the gurney. The Army officer saluted the flag draped coffin, did an about face, and led the men into the plane.

After securing the coffin he told Lewis there were other bodies coming and it would be at least an hour. "If you need to go to the john, I'll be here to watch the body." Lewis pulled out the paperwork. The officer signed for custody and pointed to the building Lewis was to use. After splashing water on his face he came back. Lewis checked the I.D. tag and signed.

The officer said, "The Air Force will provide you with a box lunch. You have a long journey ahead of you. With any luck there won't be any stops until Dover Air Force Base."

After they loaded four other bodies and strapping in the other coffins, the load master passed out earplugs and told the other escorts, "You may want to catch some sleep. There is no telling when you will get another chance."

Lewis put the earplugs in and lay down adjacent to Jack's coffin. He noticed the others did the same. Lewis sat up and took his coat off and laid it over him. He knew it was going to be chilly once they got to altitude. He had trouble sleeping. The plane's engines were loud back there and he was thankful for the earplugs. He finally drifted off but didn't sleep very well.

When they landed he was still exhausted and sore all over. He could hardly stay awake. An officer came aboard and asked if any of them needed to use the restroom. All of the escorts needed to go. After signing for the remains he said, "Fifteen minutes is all you got."

Again, a quick trip to the toilet and some water splashed on his face was all he had time for. Walking back to the plane Lewis wondered how long it would take to get to Wyoming. After signing again, Lewis waited and waited as a body was removed. Finally they got to him and the body was placed on a C-130 transport. Lewis asked, "Where is the next stop?"

The load master said, "Near Little Rock, Arkansas."

"Okay to sleep awhile?"

The load master said, "If you can over the noise more power to you."

Lewis was out like a light.

The load master shook him awake. "You okay buddy, I didn't think I was going to wake you up."

Lewis rubbed the sleep out of his eyes, yawned, stretched his muscles, stood and looked around as an officer and six men came aboard. All Air Force this time dressed in nomex flight suits. They carefully unstrapped the body and moved it to another C-130. The load master lifted the ramp and said, "Next stop Denver, Colorado." This made Lewis feel good. He was getting closer. Lewis was able to sleep more than two hours. He felt like he was catching up. In Denver, he was told that he would stay on this plane until Laramie, Wyoming and was also told a hearse would be waiting. The flight to Laramie didn't take that long and Lewis slept sitting up for a few minutes. After he woke up he kept looking at the flag draped coffin. He was alone with his friend and for some reason started to talk to the coffin. He felt like he was talking to Jack himself. He felt like Jack was there with him.

After landing and taxiing the ramp came down. Another seven men lifted the coffin and walked to a waiting hearse. They placed the body inside and closed the door. The officer walked up and Lewis saluted the officer; the officer returned the salute. "You are now in civilian hands. I talked to the funeral director. He knows what needs to be done. Good luck Ghost Rider."

Lewis thanked him and got in front with the funeral director. The director introduced himself as Thomas Frank. He looked to be in his sixties with thinning hair.

After clearing the airport Lewis asked, "Do you know the family?"

"Not really. They've only been here a couple of years. I met the sister three days ago when she came in to make arrangements. The body will be cremated. You won't be required to be here for that. Did you know him?"

"Yes, Sir, I did. He was my best friend."

"Were you with him when he died?"

"Yes, Sir."

"No need to tell the family. Trust me on that."

"Yes, Sir."

"It's about an hour to Kerney if you want to catch a nap."

"Thank you. I haven't slept much in the last six days."

"I can tell. Once we get him into a wooden casket and put him in a room you can sleep on the couch."

"You can't imagine how good that sounds. When is visitation?"

"Tomorrow night. The family visitation is at 6:00 p.m. in the room you will be in. I'll let you know at five o'clock. You will have time to get cleaned up and dressed. Then we will move him into the chapel we have here. The church the family goes to is too small to hold a lot of people. It will take about two hours to get him prepared, but you won't be allowed to observe that, but you will have to be outside the room. Then you can get ten hours sleep if you need it, and I'm pretty sure you do from the looks of you."

"That is the best news I have had in a week. Right now I am exhausted. I just felt like I needed to do this. Maybe a time will come when someone will return the favor."

Mr. Frank said, "I understand."

"Thank you, Sir. You have been most kind."

Lewis was glad when Mr. Frank put the coffin in the family visitation room. Lewis was asleep in minutes. He didn't wake up until he heard a knock on the door. He looked at his watch. He realized he was still on local time in Bosnia. He set his watch for five o'clock.

The sleep he had gotten actually made him feel like he wasn't a member of the walking dead. He removed the letters from his duffel bag and looked at the name, Beverly Farmer. He didn't know if she would be at the visitation or the funeral. If she wasn't, he would put them in an envelope and mail them to her. He studied the photo. He was sure the sister would be here tonight. The funeral director said she had made the arrangements. He remembered her from the weekend visit he and Jack had made a year and a half ago.

The funeral director tapped on the door. Lewis slipped his jacket on, buttoned the buttons, slipped the letters in his pocket and opened the door. The director nodded and stepped aside. The sister led the way, followed by Mr. and Mrs. Gordon. They were followed by, apparently, an aunt and uncle. Lewis did not introduce himself. If they remembered him that was fine.

Lewis stood at attention five feet from the head of the casket and slightly to the rear. The mother had to be helped by Jack's father. All were wearing black. The mother was wearing a black veil. She had been crying and kept dabbing her eyes with her handkerchief. Jo Beth, the sister, saw Lewis and walked over. "You are his friend, Lewis, aren't you?"

Lewis simply nodded.

"Jack mentioned you in his letters. Were you with him when he died?"

Lewis remembered what the funeral director had said about telling the family that he was with him when he died. Lewis thought, 'I can't lie to her.' "Yes, Ma'am, I was."

She looked him in the eye and said, "Can you tell me why we're in Bosnia?"

"No, Ma'am, I can't. I don't know the answer to that. I can tell you he didn't suffer. I can also tell you he loved his country very much; I could tell that in everything he did. When he saluted the flag you could see the pride he had in the way he did it. I am proud to call him my friend."

She studied him closely for at least a minute and asked, "I understand you escorted his body back home, is that true? That must have been very hard."

Lewis looked at her and said, "It was an honor and privilege, Ma'am."

She stepped to her mother and said, "Mom, you remember Lewis? Jack and Lewis stopped on the way to Fort Lewis. Lewis brought Jack home Momma."

Jack's mother said, "Yes, I remember, thank you very much."

Jack's father stuck his hand out and said, "Thank you, Son."

Lewis nodded his head in acknowledgment.

"We were very proud of Jack," Jo Beth said. "Mr. Frank said you would need transportation to the airport. We will find someone to take care of you."

"Thank you, Ma'am. I don't think there is very much public transportation around here is there?"

"Not if you can't ride a horse."

"No, Ma'am. I have never ridden a horse in my life."

At 6:40 Mr. Frank walked in and said, "We need to move into the Chapel."

Lewis noted he didn't say body in the presence of the family. The family stepped into the lobby as Mr. Frank and his son moved the casket into the Chapel adjacent to the family viewing room. He took up his position and stood at attention as the family came in and stood next to the coffin to accept the visitors. For a small town Lewis was surprised. The local American Legion and the Veterans of Foreign Wars came in with the Colors of the Armed Forces and stood at attention at the back of the Chapel between the two doors.

Lewis was visibly touched by this patriotic gesture. He knew in all likelihood these elderly men from World War II to the Gulf War had never met Jack. Lewis knew Jack had never lived here and his family had only been here for a couple of years. He imagined scenes like this taking place all over America when the Nation buried one of its fallen.

Then the visitors filed in and hugged the mother and sister and shook hands with the father and uncle and his wife. Lewis guessed the uncle and his wife had lived here for a long time because the people had more to say to them than the father.

After about twenty people had come through Lewis noticed a police officer with a petite blond and obviously her mother approaching the family. The young lady hugged Jo Beth for a long time. Lewis was pretty sure she was Beverly Farmer, but wasn't positive. He wasn't sure what to do; it could be embarrassing if he tried to give the letters to the wrong girl. Then the policeman turned and he saw his name tag. K.A. Farmer. As the girl moved past, Lewis stepped forward and asked, "Are you Beverly Farmer?"

She looked at him and wiped her eyes with her handkerchief. She said, "Yes, I am Beverly Farmer."

Lewis removed the letters from his pocket. "You will probably want these."

"What is it?"

"Letters you wrote to Jack and there is one he hadn't finished writing."

She looked at Lewis and asked how he got them. Lewis explained he escorted the body home. She nodded her head and said, "Thank you," and put them in her purse. One mission accomplished, tomorrow is the hard one. After everyone left he was back in the family viewing room with just Jack and his thoughts.

After a while he said, "Jack I talked with your family today. I know they will miss you. I returned your letters to your girlfriend; she seemed very nice. There was an honor guard that did real well. There was a large crowd and I bet there will be even a larger crowd tomorrow. You were a good friend Jack and I sure am going to miss you. Goodbye Jack, rest in peace and may God rest your soul."

CHAPTER FOUR

THE FUNERAL

The funeral was held at 1:00 p.m. The Honor Guards from the American Legion and Veterans of Foreign Wars were the first to arrive. Lewis guessed the youngest to be forty and a few had to be at least eighty. One man looked to be in his late eighties, but he stood as tall and as proud as someone in their sixties. No wonder they were called the greatest generation. Lewis looked to see if he could see Gus, the old man who told him about D-Day and being wounded on Omaha Beach. Lewis didn't see him and wondered if he was still alive. He hoped so. Then the crowd was let in and it was a crowd. Lewis didn't expect this many. He knew Wyoming was sparsely populated and people sort of lived in clusters, smaller than villages in other parts of the country. Then the family was escorted in, they would be seated in the first two rows, there weren't many. Mother, father, sister, aunt and uncle. A short, heavy set man came in and stood behind the pulpit. He opened his Bible and read the 23rd Psalm and sat in a chair near the organ. Lewis was wondering if the Farmer family was in attendance. He looked into the crowd and picked out the policeman. He was wearing what appeared to be a dress uniform. One uniform paying respect to another in uniform. Lewis noticed there were four other officers seated together. Lewis didn't notice them when they came in. A man got up from where the family was seated. He went to the pulpit and began to speak. He said Jack was his nephew; Lewis was right about him being an uncle. He told stories about Jack as a small child, how funny he was, how he had coached Jack's little league team and going with him when he got his driver's license. He also talked about how sad Jack was when his uncle moved to Wyoming and how proud he was of Jack and how much he would miss him.

Lewis felt like he knew Jack even more after his uncle spoke. He had met Jack only two years ago and he felt sadness about him and a life cut short. As his uncle moved back to his seat Lewis glanced into the crowd. The girl Jack was writing to wasn't there. Lewis had a moment of sadness. Perhaps she had to work or was too sad to attend. Death affected everyone differently.

Then Lewis heard organ music on the other side of the Chapel and the beginning of a song, <u>Amazing Grace How Sweet the Sound</u>. Lewis imagined that's what an angel sounds like. Tears started streaming down his cheeks, and through his vision, which was blurred from the tears; he saw the girl Jack wrote to standing by the organ. Lewis could tell tears were streaming down her face, but she sang on. His eyes locked on hers. Her eyes locked on Lewis. When she finished she sat down. Lewis stood there thinking, 'I never heard a voice like that in my life.' Lewis had to remain standing. There was no place for him to sit. It wasn't proper, anyway.

Then a preacher came forward and introduced himself. He was from Denver and had drove here to pay respects to someone he had respected for a long time. Jack had attended his church for years. His family had been devout church members even before he had arrived as their Minister. He was a fairly young man and he could certainly preach. He spoke for fifteen minutes. He prayed God would comfort the family and sat down.

The organ music started playing again. Beverly Farmer stood and sang <u>Rock of Ages</u>. When she was finished she stood there looking at Lewis. The funeral director and his son came and folded the flag.

Someone from the group of Veterans in the back started playing Taps on a bugle. To someone who never served it doesn't have the same meaning as it does to someone who has had a friend to die. It sent chills down Lewis spine. It is the saddest sound that can be played on one instrument.

The director took the triangular shaped flag and nodded to Lewis. As Lewis approached him, he handed him the flag. Lewis faced the family. Now the hard part. He walked slowly to the family, perhaps fifteen feet, which seemed like a mile, he leaned in at the waist. With one hand on the bottom and one hand on the top he said, "On behalf of the President of the United States and a grateful nation, I present you this flag."

Beverly Farmer watched from across the room. She had never been to a military type funeral before.

The sounds that came from Jack's mother were heart wrenching. She kept rocking back and forth, back and forth, clutching the folded flag and saying, "Oh my baby, oh my baby." Her husband on one side and her daughter on the other were trying to comfort her.

Beverly couldn't bear to watch but she couldn't look away, either. She couldn't believe that there could be a dry eye in the room. Then she saw the most compassionate thing she had ever seen in her life. The soldier who presented the flag to Jack's mother knelt on one knee and put his arms around her neck and rocked back and forth with her. When she had cried herself out the soldier leaned over and kissed her on top of the head. Beverly lost it then. She was wiping tears as fast as she could but they kept coming. At that moment, Beverly Farmer, seventeen and half years old, one week from graduation, fell in love for the first and only time in her life.

CHAPTER FIVE

MEET THE FARMERS

LUKE 10:5

Jo Beth and Beverly approached Lewis who was waiting outside the funeral home. Jo Beth told Lewis that she was too depressed to take him to the airport. "Mom and Dad need me to stay with them."

Lewis said he understood. Jo Beth thanked him for escorting Jack's body home and hugged him.

Beverly told Lewis her family would make sure he got to the airport. Lewis already had his duffel bag and they walked to an old pick-up truck. Lewis guessed it was early sixties and seen its better days, lots of them.

He put his bag in back and opened up Beverly's door, and then he walked around to the passenger side and got in. She fired up the old truck, shifted into first gear, let off the clutch and pulled onto the road. "Mom and Dad should be putting dinner out about now. We are eating a late lunch. Hope you are hungry."

"Yes, I am. I haven't had a decent meal in about a week."

They drove on the highway for about ten miles before turning on a dirt road. As they drove along Lewis noticed the road was terrible. The old pickup was bouncing on every rut and pot hole. They came to another road and turned. This one was even worse than the last one. Lewis was afraid his head would hit the roof if it got any worse. Then she hit a large pot hole and the engine sounded louder. Lewis looked behind the truck and saw the muffler rolling in the road behind them. "Lost the muffler."

With a wave of her hand she said, "Don't worry about it. Daddy will pick it up tomorrow. Stuff's always falling off; tailgate, mirrors, bumper."

Lewis had to laugh. "Would it be cheaper to fix the road or the truck?"

She smiled at that. "Don't know."

"How far from the church do you live?"

"Twenty two miles."

Lewis figured they had drove fifteen miles so far. Lewis studied her face. She was very pretty, blond with hazel eyes. He figured she hadn't gotten any taller since he saw her at the church dinner. She was petite. "Jack enjoyed getting your letters."

She asked, "Did you read them?"

"No." Then he thought I might as well tell her. "He would sometimes read me parts of them; never anything personal."

Beverly said, "I thought it was the least I could do. He was serving our country, and I've always enjoyed writing letters."

Lewis pondered this for a while then said, "I've never been much of a letter writer myself."

She looked at him and smiled.

Lewis went on to say, "I've never had anyone to write to, other than my sister and she is worse than I am." As they drove on and Lewis asked, "How old are you?"

She answered pretty quickly and said, "I will be nineteen," then she thought I'd better not lie to him and added, "In a year and a half. How about you? How old are you?"

Lewis replied, "I'll be twenty five…in a year and a half."

They both had a good laugh. It felt good to laugh.

Beverly asked, "Are you married?" She noticed he wasn't wearing a wedding band, but who knows.

"No, I'm not married. How about you?"

Beverly looked at him like he was crazy. "Of course not. I'm just seventeen." Lewis smiled while she was looking. She looked at him and thought he wasn't what you would call handsome, but he was good looking with a nice smile. "Are you divorced?"

"No, how about you?"

She hit the brakes and skidded to a stop. The dust rose and swirled around the truck. "You're funning with me aren't you?"

"No, Ma'am, I'm not. And what did you call it; funning with you."

"All right, I just don't like to be picked on or made fun of, about anything, especially my size."

Lewis smiled and said, "What about your size? Most women I know would love to be your size; by the way that's a compliment."

"Thank you." She put the truck in gear, raced the engine, popped the clutch and took off again in a cloud of dust. Lewis figured she was doing about forty five, he couldn't tell. The speedometer didn't work; it just sort of bounced between 0 and 10 MPH.

He looked at her again and noticed she had no jewelry on except a class ring. He thought, she is actually very beautiful. "You are a very good singer."

She glanced at him and said, "Thank you. I love to sing and those were two of my favorite songs."

Lewis nodded and changed the subject before she asked him if he could sing.

"There was an old man named Gus. Was he at the funeral? I don't remember his last name."

"Mr. Gus passed away last year. You know he was wounded on D-Day."

Lewis said, "Yes, he told me. I'm sorry to hear that he passed away. He was a very nice man."

"How do you know Mr. Gus?"

"I met him when Jack and I came through here on the way to Fort Lewis. Remember I stepped on your foot."

"Was that you?"

"Yeah, that was me. Sorry, it was clumsy of me."

"Don't worry about it. It doesn't hurt anymore."

"I hope not. That was a year and half ago." Lewis laughed.

Beverly smiled and inside she couldn't believe she had thought he was a creep. "How tall are you?"

"Does it matter?"

"No, not really; just curious I guess."

"I am six foot four inches and a lot of times wish I was shorter."

"Why would you wish you were shorter?"

"So I don't hit my head every time you hit a bump in the road."

"Well, don't worry about it, we're here."

Lewis noticed the house about a mile away. "Nice place. Have you lived here your whole life?"

"Not yet," she answered and then laughed.

Lewis loved her laugh. "I should have seen that coming. Are you funning me?"

"Me? Why, yes I am," she replied as she patted him on the arm.

Lewis got out, walked around and opened her door. "Thank you."

"My pleasure."

They walked up the steps onto the front porch which looked to Lewis like a nice place to sit and enjoy the view. "This is nice."

She opened the door and said, "Come in." Lewis followed her into the living room. She stuck her head into the kitchen and dining room combination, "Mom, Dad, I brought someone to lunch."

The lady of the house wiped her hands on a dish towel. Lewis noticed her father stand from his chair in the dining room. Her mother walked over to them and said, "Aren't you going to introduce us to your friend."

Beverly's eyes got big and her cheeks blushed.

Lewis thought, 'She doesn't know my name.' He stuck his hand out. "Lewis, Lewis MacDonald, but my friends call me Cowboy." He shook hands with the two of them.

"Please, sit down. Alice will you get Lewis a plate and something to drink."

Mr. Farmer noticed that Lewis pulled Beverly's chair out and pushed it in when she sat. He liked to see a gentleman in this day and age.

"Why do they call you Cowboy?" Alice wanted to know.

Lewis leaned back in his chair. "Have you ever noticed when someone is real tall, his friends may call him Shorty?"

Mrs. Farmer nodded. "So, you're not a cowboy."

"Oh, no Ma'am, I have never ridden a horse in my life."

Mrs. Farmer said the blessing and then said, "Please, help yourself."

Mr. Farmer asked, "Where are you from?"

Lewis answered, "Here and there."

Mr. Farmer glanced toward Beverly. Beverly thought what kind of answer was that.

"Ms. Alice, this pot roast is delicious."

"Thank you."

"What kind of work did you do before you went into the Army?" asked Mr. Farmer.

"This and that," he replied and then he looked at Ms. Farmer and said, "The potato salad reminds me of the way my Mom made it. Do you also put mustard in it? I believe that is what makes it taste so good. It gives it that spicy taste."

"Why, yes I do, that way it is not so bland," said Alice.

Mr. Farmer glanced at Beverly again. Beverly thought, he can change the subject faster than a pony express rider could change horses.

Mrs. Farmer asked, "Have you ever worked on a ranch before?"

"Now and then. This potato salad is really good."

Beverly thought, you missed your stirrup there when you changed horses this time Buddy. "Can we talk about something besides the potato salad? Can we forget the potato salad?" asked Beverly.

Lewis looked at Beverly and smiled then he looked at Mrs. Alice and smiled. Mr. Farmer was sitting across from Lewis. He saw Lewis wink at Mrs. Alice. Mr. Farmer realized that Lewis was funning with her. Alice also realized he was funning with Beverly. She almost laughed; she loved it.

Beverly said, "A few minutes ago you said you had never rode a horse before. How did you work on a ranch and never ride a horse?" She had heard her dad talk about people who lived in Idaho.

'Survivor Nuts' he called them. He said they wouldn't give any personal information when stopped by the police. "You're not from Idaho, are you? Not that there's anything wrong with that," continued Beverly. Mr. Farmer glanced at Beverly and almost laughed.

"No, I am not from Idaho," said Lewis, smiling as he said it. Then he turned toward Mrs. Alice and said, "Dill relish, right."

Alice nodded her head and had to cover her mouth to keep from laughing.

"We'll give you the recipe when you leave," quipped Beverly.

Finally, Lewis said, "Maybe I'd better explain."

"You got a lot of explaining to do, buster." It came out before she realized she had said it and she covered her mouth and said, "Sorry."

Lewis was laughing. He had a nice laugh thought Mrs. Farmer. She could tell Lewis was enjoying this. "When my mom divorced my father she was an executive with an insurance company. Every three of four months she would go somewhere and open a regional office or a district office and then move to another area. I have lived in about thirty states, three or four months at a time. That is why I was home schooled. When I turned sixteen I would get summer jobs, you know, grocery stores, bowling alleys, movie theaters, that sort of after school stuff, nothing important. I worked on a ranch in Texas; repairing fences, filling water troughs, putting out hay. We used pickup trucks for all that."

"What was the name of the ranch? I may have heard of it," said Mr. Farmer. "The Three R Ranch; it stood for the Red River Ranch. It was in Texas and Oklahoma."

"I sold them a bull about ten years ago."

"Then you met Bo Weaver. He was the ranch foreman. Little guy, always chewing tobacco," said Lewis.

"That sounds like him. I wonder if he is still alive."

"I imagine so. He was too mean to die," laughed Lewis. Mr. Farmer joined in.

"I noticed you call your mother, Mom, and instead of dad you say Father. Any reason?"

"I haven't seen my father since I was two years old."

"That's awful. Does he know where you are?" asked Mrs. Farmer.

"Sometimes. My sister keeps in touch with him. She understands him more than I do. She's five years older so she remembers him. I don't"

Mr. Farmer forked a piece of meat in his mouth and Beverly was taking a drink of her tea.

Mrs. Farmer asked, "Do you know where your father is?"

"Yes, Ma'am. He's the Governor of Ohio."

Mr. Farmer started coughing.

Beverly spewed tea everywhere. She was sure the tea had shot out of her nose. She jumped up and ran to the bathroom. She thought to herself, 'I am never coming out. I am such a fool. I know, I will climb out the window and go hide in the barn. No, that's the first place daddy always looks.' She took a face cloth and wiped her dress. 'I'm so embarrassed. Why can't he just say I'm from, pick a state, any state, and I was an assistant at a burger joint and please...I worked on a ranch and rode a horse. The kicker is that his father is the Governor of Ohio and he and Jack Gordon buy a forty year old van and drive cross country. The sons of governors don't do that. What's he going to say next?' She put her ear to the door and heard her daddy laughing. "Good for you, Daddy; about time someone laughed at the idiot."

Five minutes later, there was a soft knock on the door. "Beverly are you alright?"

"Yes, Momma. I'm fine."

Again, a knock at the door and someone trying to get in. "Beverly, open this door right now." She could barely hear her Mom. "Beverly, open the door." Her Mom came in. "What's wrong with you? Now you come back into the dining room right this minute. We are not rude to guests in this house."

"Momma, look at the way he answered the questions; here and there, this and that, now and then and my father is Governor of Ohio. Momma, I'm too embarrassed to go back out there."

Her mother folded her arms and looked at Beverly and said, "What would you say if from the time you were two you lived in so many states it would take you ten minutes to name all of them. What would you say if you worked at a different place every three to four months? Would you try to name them? Now, I think he is a very nice man and I've never said this before, but I am disappointed in you." With that she walked out and closed the door. Beverly wanted to scream.

She opened the door and walked into the dining room. When she came in, Lewis stood and helped her into her chair. "Thank you."

Lewis nodded his head.

Mr. Farmer said, "I like this guy even though I nearly choked to death when he said his father was the Governor of Ohio. As soon as you said it, I saw the resemblance. "MacDonald, Charles is his first?"

"Yes, Sir."

"I understand he's running for the Senate. Do you think he'll get elected?"

Lewis cocked his head to the side. "I believe he will. He's very popular."

Beverly quizzed, "Why is he so popular?"

Lewis pointed his finger at Beverly. "Because he will tell you what you want to hear," then he pointed to Mr. Farmer, "And he will tell you what you want to hear," then he pointed to Mrs. Farmer ,"And he will tell you what you want to hear and he hopes the three of you never talk to one another. That's why Mom left him. She couldn't put up with his mess any more. Mom wanted a family life. One that included him. He couldn't or wouldn't change. She didn't want to be a trophy wife. She wanted to be a housewife with a career. He wanted to go to a social function every night. My father's problem is money. The answer to every problem is to throw money at it. If he pulled up to a stop sign and saw a lot of trash beside the road, he'd think if we throw a lot of money out people would stop and pick up the money and the trash, then when he went back the money would, of course, be gone and the trash would still be there. His answer would be we didn't throw enough money out."

Mr. Farmer said, "He's always on the Sunday talk shows."

"Yes, sir, if he hears someone is setting up a camera, he'll run over people to get in front of it."

Beverly said, "So, your father really is the Governor of Ohio."

Lewis smiled at her and said, "If I was going to lie about something like that I would have picked another state like maybe Idaho. Beverly, I won't lie to you and I won't make a promise I can't keep."

She looked at him for at least thirty seconds before answering. "Fair enough."

Mr. and Mrs. Farmer looked at each other and shrugged their shoulders like what's going on.

After lunch, Lewis helped clear the table and put the dishes in the dishwasher. "Mrs. Farmer, that was a wonderful meal. It reminded me of the meals my mom cooked."

"You don't get the chance to visit your mother?" asked Beverly.

"My mother passed away when I was nineteen. She had ovarian cancer."

"I'm sorry. I didn't know."

"That's okay. I guess that's why I went in the Army. I drifted about for a few years and decided to sort of settle down."

"But you move about, I mean, in the Army. You move about, don't you?"

"Yes, every few years, but I figure it would wean me from moving every four months. I was six or seven before I figured out every body didn't move like that. I guess I thought since we did then everyone else did to."

Then Beverly said, "Mom, Dad I am going to change clothes and show Lewis around."

While Beverly was changing, Lewis asked Mrs. Farmer if there was anything he could do to help in the kitchen. She said she was fine and for him just to enjoy his visit.

Beverly came in wearing jeans, a sweater and boots. She picked up a blanket from a chair and asked, "Are you ready?"

"Sure. What's the blanket for?"

Beverly answered, "Lookout Point."

"Lookout Point?"

Beverly said, "It's my favorite place in the whole world. I think you will like it."

"How far is it?" asked Lewis.

"Not far; not far at all."

And it wasn't; not even seventy five yards. A small hilltop. Lewis guessed it was only thirty five feet higher than the surrounding landscape. They had to use the gate in the fence because of the livestock. When they got to the top Beverly said. "From up here you can see most of the ranch. The fence down by the road and back here, she had turned to face in the other direction, the backside. The only place you can't see is what's beyond the barn and there is a little dip way back there near the fence in the back corner. If one of my horses should get out of the corral I can come up here and pretty much get an idea of where he is."

Lewis looked around. It seemed as though you could see forever. He looked at the sky. It was the darkest blue Lewis had ever seen. "It's beautiful up here."

"Thank you. I love it."

Lewis asked, "How many horses do you have?"

Beverly answered, "Usually between fifty and sixty."

"That's a lot of horses!" exclaimed Lewis, rubbing his chin. "What kind of horses?"

"Wild mustangs," she said. "I adopt them, and if I can, I train them and sell them to people who can't afford a quarter horse or some expensive horse. Mostly to teenagers who would never be able to buy a horse. It's sort of a mission to me."

Lewis looked around to her and said, "You must be a very good rider."

She smiled at him and boasted, "You can't believe how well I can ride. Some people say I was born on a horse. I can't ever remember not being on a horse. Mom's got pictures of me when I was three riding on a horse, wearing a cowboy hat, boots and everything."

Lewis said, "I can imagine. This is a beautiful place. You don't ever want to leave a place like this. I have lived and traveled all over and you'll never find a better place to live."

Beverly said, "I don't intend to. This is all I want or need." She spread out the blanket. "Have a seat. Don't worry about Mom and Dad, they can see us here." She turned and waved at the house. "We come up here to watch the sun rise. As soon as the sun comes up in the fall or winter, when the grass is brown, everything turns golden for a few minutes and when the sun sets it seems to be orange. At night I love to look at all the stars. When I was a little girl I use to believe the stars were angels shining a light down on me. I know that sounds silly."

Lewis said, "Not really, maybe there are angels up there shining a light down on you. It's a good thought anyway."

Beverly continued, "When there is snow on the ground and there is a full moon with all the stars out, it is really unbelievable."

"This is a very special place to you isn't it?" asked Lewis.

"Look around you, Lewis. We are in the middle of nowhere. This is the center of my universe."

They were facing the road in front of the house. Lewis was looking across the road. He asked, "Who does that land over there belong to; it seems like it is deserted, there are no cows or horses."

Beverly answered, "That is the Triple D Ranch. The man that owned it passed away five years ago. His wife is in a nursing home in town, I think. She is about ninety three or four. I have heard they are planning on selling it for back taxes or something."

Lewis asked, "How big is it?"

"Five thousand acres with a small house and a barn. You can only see the very top of the house if you stand up," Beverly answered.

Lewis stood up and looked. He could barely make it out in the distance. "You know that could be a beautiful place. It really has potential. It has lots of grass, trees and I can see a couple of small lakes."

Beverly said, "They were good neighbors. I would visit them a lot when I was out riding. I really miss them. We value our neighbors out here because they are so few and far between. We depend on each other."

Lewis said, "You won't find that in most places. I wonder what they are asking for it."

Beverly laughed. "More than I have."

Lewis asked, "If you owned that, what would you do with it?"

Beverly said, "You mean if I owned that and all of this." She waved her arm around to include their land.

Lewis said, "Yes, what would you do with both of them?"

Beverly looked around like she had never entertained the thought. "Well, I would put cattle over there and use this one for horses but I don't pipe dream. I accept what the good Lord has given me."

Lewis nodded his head in understanding and looked at Beverly as she looked across the Triple D Ranch. He thought, she gets more beautiful every time I look at her. Neither one said anything for a few minutes as they both gazed across the road.

Lewis asked again, "I wonder how much it would cost."

She didn't answer.

"Beverly?"

Again she didn't answer.

"Beverly, are you alright?"

"I was just thinking."

"A penny for your thoughts."

"It will cost you a lot more than that." She smiled.

Lewis smiled back. "Must be personal, so we won't go there."

"It's not that. I was just thinking, that's all. Nothing wrong with that is there." They both heard a bell ringing and looked toward the house. Mrs. Farmer was out front ringing a bell that was attached to a post near the sidewalk. Beverly said, "I hope you like homemade strawberry ice cream."

"I don't know that I have ever had any."

"Well, you are missing a treat if you don't try it," she said.

They folded the blanket and Lewis carried it back to the house. Mrs. Farmer said, "Wash up and I will fix you a bowl."

Mr. Farmer said, "We will eat on the front porch. It's too nice a day to be inside."

Half way through the bowl, his chest hurt and he had a bad headache. He stopped eating because everyone else had also stopped. Beverly said, "It will give you a headache, wait a minute and it'll go away."

As his headache eased off Lewis said, "It was well worth it," and started eating again.

Mr. Farmer said, "Where are you being assigned to next Lewis?"

"Fort Benning, Georgia, Sir, for airborne school."

Mr. Farmer nodded his head.

Beverly asked, "What is airborne school?"

Lewis replied, "That's where they teach you how to parachute out of a plane. It lasts three weeks."

Beverly said, "You mean if there is engine trouble or something like that."

"No," said Lewis, "It's a way to put troops on the ground real fast. Usually behind enemy lines."

Beverly thought she needed to get out more often or watch more television. "Why do you want to learn how to do that?"

"I have to so I can go to Ranger school."

Beverly said, "You won't have any trouble being a ranger. Benny Fairchild is a Ranger and all he does is ride around in that ugly brown suburban, wearing that ugly uniform and Smokey Bear hat. Telling everyone 'I saw two elk or a bear this morning'; mostly at the diner trying to pick up girls." She noticed her Dad looking at her and Lewis was too, but he was smiling. She added, "At least that's what I heard."

Mr. Farmer said, "We have a guy on the force who was an Army Ranger. He said it was the hardest school he had ever been to. Living in swamps and mountain climbing. He said he had to rappel out of helicopters and they had to go days without food, water or sleep."

Beverly was listening intently to all this. I really need to get out more, she thought; I will go to the library tomorrow and read up on all this. She put her hand on Lewis's hand and said, "You will be careful, won't you."

He said, "I will try to do just that."

"You promise."

"No."

"Why not?"

"Because, I don't make promises I may not be able to keep. I don't want to get hurt any more than the next guy. Sometimes you have to take chances because, if you are too careful, someone else who is counting on you may get hurt. Do you understand what I'm saying?"

She nodded her head. "Sort of like the three Musketeers; one for all and all for one, sort of."

Mrs. Farmer said, "I am sure you will do just fine."

"Ma'am that was the best ice cream I have ever had. I don't know how you do it."

Mr. Farmer asked, "When do you have to report to Fort Benning for Airborne school?"

"Next week."

"And you have to fly out tonight?"

"Well, I always like reporting in early and I have been thinking of just hitch hiking. America is a beautiful country and I haven't seen it all. After looking around here I realize there is a lot I haven't seen. This is beautiful country here. I'd like to see more of it and the weather is nice. I look at it like an adventure."

"Could be dangerous," cautioned Mr. Farmer.

"So is flying," responded Lewis.

"Can't argue with you there."

"Mom, Dad, I am going to show Lewis around; maybe take a walk."

"Let me help you with the bowls, Mrs. Farmer."

"I can manage just fine but thank you for offering."

"We're going to go look at the lakes. You'll be able to see us, Dad."

Mr. Farmer just nodded his head and went inside with Mrs. Farmer.

As they strolled through the pasture Lewis asked, "How long has your family lived in Wyoming?"

Beverly thought for a minute. "Since 1870 as near as we can figure. My great, great, great, great grandfather came here. I might have put one too many greats in there. I get confused on all that."

Lewis asked, "Was he a prospector, trapper, buffalo hunter something like that?

Beverly laughed and said, "Nothing like that. He was a horse thief."

Lewis looked at her and said, "You're serious, aren't you?"

"Yes, I am. Wyoming wasn't even a state back then and wouldn't be for at least twenty years. After the war ended was when the real western expansion started. People east of the Mississippi had lost everything, and I do mean everything. The only place to go was on this side of the Mississippi. They came here following a dream, I guess, and stayed. Did you know the Oregon Trail came through Wyoming?"

Lewis said, "So you're grandfather, five or six times removed, chased the American dream on a stolen horse and ended up here." He laughed a good hearty laugh and said, "I don't know if I would tell anyone that."

Beverly laughed and said, "Why, that's the most interesting part."

Lewis laughed again and said, "You're right. That would be hard to top. What happened after he got here? Obviously he got away with it."

Beverly said, "What happened is that he got to this part of the state and winter set in and his pursuers had to turn back. He met up with some Indians and lived with them that year. Now the horse he stole was really nice stock so he traded it for another horse and the Chief's daughter. He got the better end of the deal. He married her and had six children. He was later appointed sheriff. You see, he was handy with a gun and most people were not back then. He was paid seven dollars a month, room and board and a percentage of each fine. There weren't many laws back then so he charged people under the notion that there ought to be a law against it or there's probably a law against it or there is going to be a law against it. He got two dollars and fifty cents if the fine was ten dollars. Then he started noticing all these wild horses, mustangs and started roping them and bringing them to his ranch. He tamed them and sold them to the army. He put the horses in a corral, fed and watered them. The horses finally understood they couldn't eat or drink without him.

Horses are smart animals. He hired bronco busters to saddle break them. He actually made a lot of money and you could claim land back then. He bought other ranches out during hard times."

"Sounds interesting. Is the county named after General Phil Kearney, the Civil War General?"

"No, even though there is a Fort named after him. It's spelled different. It was named after Douglas Kerney. He built a trading post. It's long gone now. The courthouse sits where it was. From what I understand even though he went by Doug everyone called him, 'Dug.' They say he dug up half the county looking for gold."

"Did he ever find any gold?"

"I'm sure he did but that's just a guess. Wyoming is rich in history. Yellowstone was the first National Park. We gave the women the right to vote fifty years before the equal suffrage amendment. We even elected a woman governor. Her name was Nettie Taylor Ross."

"I didn't know that," said Lewis.

"I'm proud of her. She's my hero."

"You must study history a lot."

"Not really. I read a lot; every chance I get. There's not much else to do out here. I try to go to the library every chance I get."

They came to a fence and put their arms on the top rail. Beverly said, "Some of these horses may or may not have descended from the horse he stole. I'd like to think they did." They were looking at a small herd of maybe forty. Lewis could tell they were mustangs because the horses he saw in Texas and Oklahoma seemed to be stouter and larger than these. They didn't seem to be under nourished but seemed to be smaller than other horses.

"You only raise mustangs?"

"Actually, I don't raise them or breed them. I get them from the BLM. The Bureau of Land Management. They were nearly starved when I got them and I put them in here to get them in shape."

Lewis asked, "Which one do you pick to saddle break?"

"I don't, they pick me. Some will get use to me and let me get close to them and we sort of become friends. It helps when I ride my horse among them. I think the horse thinks, that don't look so bad but some will never be broke. They are free spirited."

Lewis looked at her as she was looking at the horses. He could tell that she was at peace, happy and content with her station in life. Lewis said, "Beverly, you should keep doing this. This is your mission in life, isn't it?"

She nodded her head and said, "I am glad you understand." She looked at him and studied him before asking, "Do you have a mission in life, Lewis?"

He answered, "I'm sure I do. I just don't know what it is."

She said, "Don't worry, you'll find it. You'll recognize it for what it is, and then never let it go."

They walked some more, walking past two small lakes. "Any fish in there?" asked Lewis.

"Yes, there is. Anytime we want fish we come here and catch a mess. The ranch is kind of self-sufficient. We hardly ever have to buy anything."

"That's nice. Most of the people I know spend most of their time running here and there to buy things they need. You walk out the door and it is right outside. What do you grow in the greenhouse?"

"Mostly vegetables that we can't get because of the growing seasons. Tomatoes, squash and onions; things we like year round. The strawberries in the ice cream came from here."

They walked to Lookout Point and Beverly asked, "Lewis, would you like for me to write to you?"

"I'd like that."

"I will write to you every day. Will you write to me every day?"

"I'll try."

"You promise."

"No," said Lewis. He saw the disappointment in her eyes. "I don't make promises unless I know I can keep them. For the next four or five months I know I won't be able to write every day. In Ranger school you are in the field so much. There's no post office in the middle of a swamp. I'll be lucky to see a building, so I can't make that promise."

Beverly looked at him, nodded in understanding then said, "Lewis, maybe you have found your mission in life and just haven't recognized it."

Lewis asked, "What is that?"

"Not making a promise you can't keep."

When they arrived back at the house Mr. Farmer met them at the door. "Lewis, you still thinking about hitch hiking to Georgia?"

"Yes, Sir."

"I have a friend, a long haul truck driver; he makes a run to St. Louis, you interested?"

"I sure am; that's about one-third of the way. Thank you, Sir."

"Let me give him a call and see if he can do it."

Beverly said, "I will be worried about you doing this."

Lewis said, "I spent two days on a plane getting here. I'm sort of flown out, but I'll be alright. I've done this before."

Mr. Farmer came back after contacting his friend and said, "We'll meet him at the diner outside of town at eight o'clock. I'll give you a ride. You would never get there on time hitching a ride around here. Now, let's eat dinner. Hope you don't mind leftovers."

When they sat down for dinner, Mr. Farmer asked Beverly to say the blessing. "We hold hands when we say the blessing. I hope you don't mind."

"No, I don't mind at all." Lewis held Beverly and Mrs. Farmers hand and he felt like he sort of belonged to this group of nice people. He had never really had many friends. He considered Jack Gordon a friend but he couldn't think of any others. He told himself 'you need to hold on to this family.'

At 7:30, he was ready to go. Mr. Farmer was waiting in the pick-up truck.

Mrs. Farmer hugged him and said, "Thank you for bringing Jo Beth's brother home. Now, you be careful."

"I'll try Ma'am, and thank you so much for welcoming me into your home."

He turned to Beverly. "I'll send my address as soon as I know it." She reached up and hugged him and gave him a kiss, "I know you will."

After dropping Lewis off and settling down in his recliner, Mr. Farmer said, "You know he really seems like a nice guy. I think he likes Beverly and I believe she likes him, too."

"I think you are right because she kissed him right smack dab on the mouth," said Mrs. Farmer.

CHAPTER SIX

MAIL

PROVERBS 25:25

Beverly wrote Lewis a letter every day and twice on Sunday. She didn't have an address yet but she knew in her heart of hearts he would send it to her. She walked to the mail box every day. It was a lot longer on the way back. After he had been gone a week she got the first letter. More important she had an address. The next day she mailed eight letters. There was no incoming mail. The walk seemed that much longer. Each day she mailed a letter to him. Five days later she got a letter. She noticed the walk was shorter. In her room she read it over and over. He explained to her why he had not been able to write and told her how much her letters had lifted his spirits. Three days later he wrote her about having to jump out of a tower that was thirty four feet high and slide down a two hundred foot cable. He had already done it about ten times. Tomorrow they had to be pulled up a two hundred and fifty foot tower and then be dropped with the parachute already opened. Beverly tried to picture this in her mind but couldn't. Five days later she received another letter saying he had already made two jumps out of an airplane and had three more to go. Beverly thought they were just teaching how to jump out of a plane, not that they actually did it. She started to worry. She said prayers for him every day that God would keep him safe.

It would be another week before she would hear from him again. She could only hope that everything was alright and he wasn't hurt. She was outside when a UPS truck came up the long driveway. She wondered what on earth a UPS truck would be doing out here. He was probably lost. The driver stopped and Beverly went to the truck and asked, "Can I help you?"

The driver said, "I need for you to sign for this."

"What is it?"

"I don't know."

Beverly had heard of companies sending stuff and if you signed for it you got billed for whatever was inside. "I'm not signing for anything unless I know who it is from."

The driver looked at the return address and said, "Lewis MacDonald."

"Give me that clip board." She signed for it and the driver gave her a strange look as he left. The package was only about two inches thick and about twelve by fourteen inches. She walked up on the porch and tried to open it. She had to use her pocket knife. She pulled out a book, a letter and a small box. She read the letter first. As she was reading the letter her mother walked out on the porch. Beverly sat with her feet on the steps. Her mother sat down beside her. "From Lewis?"

"Yes, Momma." In the letter Lewis said the book was about airborne school and that his picture was on page forty three, bottom row, third from the left. She found the page and looked at the picture. "Momma, what have they done to my Lewis? He is nothing but skin and bones." She wanted to cry. She went back to reading the letter. Lewis said he was sending his jump wings and he would be honored if she would wear them. She opened the small box. The wings were on each side of the parachute. "They are beautiful, Momma. Pin them on me right now. I'm going to wear them all the time."

Her mother pinned the wings on her shirt and said, "You called him, my Lewis, what has come over you?"

"Momma, I can't explain it. I don't know if you would understand. I think about him all the time. When I am by myself I start talking to him. I know he's not there. Sometimes when I do something I tell myself I'm doing it for Lewis. I know you think I'm crazy but Momma, I love him. I've loved him since the funeral when I saw how he tried to comfort Mrs. Gordon."

Her mother patted her on the knee and said, "Oh, I understand. I had the same feelings with your father. Now aren't you glad I made you come out of the bathroom."

Beverly laughed and said, "I have tried to forget about that."

"Don't worry. I will remind you from time to time. Now, let's get a bite to eat. We can talk while we eat."

"Momma, look at some of the things they have to do. This is the tower that Lewis had to jump from and this is the two hundred and fifty foot tower he wrote about. I can't believe he has done all of this." She had turned the book where her mother could see.

"Lewis is a man, Beverly. Men do things like this. I remember when your Dad went through the police academy he had to do a lot of really hard things. He once told me you train for the really hard stuff, and then when you have to do something it feels easy. I think it's the same thing."

Beverly pondered this a few minutes then said, "After all this, I bet Ranger school will be really easy. I mean, how hard can it be?" Beverly really was in for a reality check. It was only after Lewis didn't write for two weeks that she went to the library and looked up everything she could find on Army Rangers. It scared her to death. Her first thought was these people are crazy. Even the motto of the Rangers scared her; "Ranger Lead the Way." She read about how on D-Day they had to climb a hundred foot cliff while being shot at.

She went home and talked to her mother about all she had learned. She couldn't help from crying. Her mother kept telling her everything would be alright. Beverly cried herself to sleep that night.

Finally, she got a letter from Lewis. He told her some of the things he had to do. This only increased her anxiety, especially when he told her that part of the training would be sliding down a cable and dropping twenty feet into a lake. It was called "slide for life."

Beverly didn't like it, she didn't like it one little bit. She wondered could you die if you didn't do it right.

That night she wrote an anonymous letter to CBS's Sixty Minutes telling them they needed to send a crew to Fort Benning, Georgia and investigate Ranger School.

In his next letter, he said that he would not be able to write for the next three weeks. He was going to the North Georgia Mountains for mountain training. She wanted to go to Fort Benning and tell someone that they had obviously lost their mind. Her mother talked her out of this insanity.

In his next letter, Lewis told her that he had to make a night parachute jump. Isn't it dangerous enough in the day time? Why can't they just do it in the day time and everyone close their eyes and pretend it's night time? The last letter she got topped them all. He had to go through something called, escape and evasion, and they would show them how to eat snakes and other stuff not fit for human consumption, at least in America. If those fools in Fort Benning didn't drop them behind enemy lines they wouldn't have to know all this stuff. They are obviously trying to kill My Lewis. She was fraught with frustration. She was afraid she may lose her hair. She had heard about stress making women lose their hair on an afternoon talk show.

Then it was over. She couldn't believe twelve weeks had already passed. She got a letter on a Monday and then Tuesday. They started coming every day and on Wednesday she always received three. He was writing her twice on Sundays. She was so happy he was able to write every day and that she did not lose her hair. She had also gained five pounds because she had been eating for her and Lewis while he was out eating snakes and other things not fit for consumption, at least not in America.

She found that she had read so much material on Army Rangers she was becoming quite the expert. She faithfully wore his airborne wings and when someone commented on them she would say, "They are jump wings. My boyfriend is an Army Ranger. Rangers lead the way you know."

Beverly was so happy and so proud of Lewis, until the next letter arrived. He had been assigned to a Ranger Battalion. Her studying has told her that there were about seven hundred and fifty men in a battalion. She said to her mother, "Momma, Lewis is going to be with seven hundred and fifty crazy people. Jumping out of planes at night into swamps and mountains, eating snakes and other things not fit for human consumption, at least not in America."

That night, her mother was talking to her father out on the front porch. "Keith, I'm worried about Beverly."

"Why are you worried?"

"Well, she is in love. I guess you have noticed that. I know nothing will probably come out of it, but she is so naïve."

"Alice, if she was someone else's daughter you know what you would be saying."

"What?"

"That girl is dumber than dirt."

"Keith Arnold Farmer, you should be ashamed of yourself."

"Look, you know long distance romances don't last. He will see a pretty girl and the letters will slow down and then stop."

"You think so?"

"He'll probably fall in love with a Georgia Peach and it'll be over."

"Why would he fall in love with a peach?"

"Alice, a Georgia peach doesn't grow on trees."

"Sure they do. All peaches grow on trees," said Alice.

"A Georgia Peach is a pretty girl from the state of Georgia."

"How do you know that?"

"I get around."

"No, you don't."

"Do too."

"Keith Arnold Farmer you've never been out of Wyoming."

"I've been to Casper and Laramie."

"I have to but I don't call that, getting around."

"I've been to Cheyenne," said Keith.

"Keith, that was a school trip in the eighth grade."

"Yeah, but I saw a lot!"

Beverly was crying herself to sleep every night. She was sure the stress would take a toll and she would lose her hair this time. Next time she went to the library she was going to have to look up stress and hair loss.

Beverly and her family went to church every Sunday. On this particular Sunday the new preacher, Brother Lawson, preached a sermon about trusting in the Lord. He even said it was a sin to worry. "If you worry, you are not trusting in the Lord. Even when you can't figure out God's will, I assure you He knows what He's doing." Calm came over Beverly and she asked for forgiveness for her sins. She would still pray for Lewis in all her prayers.

When she was leaving, instead of shaking the preacher's hand she gave him a hug and said, "Thank you, so much."

Brother Lawson saw the airborne wings and said, "I haven't seen any of those in a long time. I know you probably don't know this but I was an Army Ranger."

Beverly smiled and looked the preacher in his eyes and said, "Rangers lead the way. Thank you so much for leading the way."

The next letter said they were flying to some place she had never heard of in California and the whole battalion would be jumping for field exercises. Beverly told her mother, "There are so many crazy people in California; another seven hundred and fifty won't matter." Beverly didn't give it another thought.

Two weeks later, Beverly was reading the letter she had just received from Lewis. She had gotten into the habit of reading his letters while walking back to the house. Suddenly she stopped in her tracks. He asked her what she thought about him buying the ranch across the road from theirs. The Triple D Ranch, five thousand acres, with a house and barn. She turned around and looked across the road. She sat down in the driveway. Her mother saw her and walked out to the driveway. "Beverly, what's wrong?"

Beverly handed the letter to her. She read it and sat down beside her. "What are you going to tell him?"

"Momma, I don't know. I guess I will tell him that's a decision he is going to have to make."

Her father pulled into the driveway and when he saw them he stopped. He got out and walked up to them. "What's wrong?"

Mrs. Farmer handed him the letter. He read it twice and looked across the road then he sat down beside his wife. "He obviously doesn't know how much land cost and how much is there."

"He knows Daddy. I told him five thousand acres."

Mr. Farmer said, "He can't possibly afford it. No bank is going to loan him any money. It would be different if he already had the livestock to go on it. I mean, he's a sergeant in the Army. He might make a couple of thousand a month at the most. What's for dinner?"

The letters kept coming and Lewis was now able to call her at least once a week and talk for a few minutes. He said there was always a long line to talk on the phone. She had told him it was his decision to buy the ranch so it wasn't discussed anymore.

Lewis told her that every morning they had to go for a long run in their combat fatigues and boots. They would sing a song called, 'I want to be an Airborne Ranger.' The next time she was in Casper she went to an Army Surplus store and bought some Army fatigues and combat boots. Every morning she would put them on and go running. She didn't know the words to the song Lewis was talking about so as she ran she sang, "I want to be an Airborne Ranger, I want to be an Airborne Ranger," she sang it over and over. When she ran and sang she felt like she was close to him. After a few weeks she told Lewis what she was doing.

He said, "That's my girl." Those words made her day.

She kept running and singing then one day when she got home, her mother was on the phone and she heard her say, "She's not moving to Idaho," and then she hung up. "That was Freeda Boyd. She wanted to know if you have joined some right wing militia group and moving to Idaho."

"What makes her think that?"

"She has seen you out running in that getup and just assumed that. She wants to know if she can go with you."

Beverly started laughing.

Her mother rolled her eyes and laughed, too.

"Is it that bad?"

"I'm afraid so. You just keep doing what you're doing and don't worry about Freeda Boyd."

Beverly was walking back from the mail box. She read the letter then read it again. She sat down in the driveway. Her mother came out to her and she read the letter and sat down beside Beverly.

Mr. Farmer pulled up and saw the two of them. He muttered to himself, "Now what," as he got out of his vehicle. As he walked over to them, his wife handed him the letter. It said, "Howdy neighbor." He sat down beside the other two. All of them looking across the road like three monkeys. Hear no evil, speak no evil and see no evil.

The next time Lewis was able to call, they spoke for a long time.

A month later, while Beverly was preoccupied in the house, Mr. Farmer told his wife he wanted to talk to her. So the two of them went out on the porch and sat in side by side rocking chairs. "What do you want to talk about?"

He said, "I want to talk about Lewis."

"What about Lewis?"

"Well, I don't want Beverly to know what I've done, I wish I hadn't done it, but I did and I need to tell you what I found out."

"What did you do Keith?"

"I want you to understand I did this for Beverly, alright. I was concerned for her is all."

"I understand you want to protect our daughter, but what did you do that you don't want her to find out about?"

"I had some friends run a background investigation on him, strictly off the books you understand. I couldn't figure out how a sergeant could borrow that kind of money to buy a ranch. I went to the court house to find out what bank held the lien on the property. You know what I found out?"

"No, what did you find out."

"He didn't borrow any money. He paid three and half million dollars for it."

"So, you thought it had to come from drug money, right."

"Yep, that's what I thought."

"Keith, please don't tell me Lewis is involved in something like that. That would kill Beverly."

"No, it wasn't drug money. You remember he said his mother was an executive in an insurance company."

"Yes, I remember that. That's why she moved so much."

"Well, I found out his mother is from one of the richest families in Virginia. They are worth millions. Banks, real estate, you name it and they are in it. I also found out she was the executive vice president and she made millions. She got bonuses every year and put that in a trust fund for the two kids. All the child support from his father went into another trust fund. That trust fund alone is worth over five hundred thousand dollars. When she died, Lewis inherited over ten million dollars. Alice, can you imagine that? Ten million dollars!"

"Good Lord, Keith, you can't be serious."

"I am serious and I don't know if Beverly knows. I know she loves him. I think the world of him myself. I don't know if I can look him in the eye after doing what I've done. That's why I don't want Beverly to know I did this."

"You're right. I wonder why he doesn't buy a car."

"The will was probated two months ago. His father contested the will. He was running for the Senate and needed money for his campaign. Someone leaked it to the press. The voters of Ohio found out about that and turned against him. He lost the election; the low life jerk. We don't need people like that running the country. I'm glad he lost."

"I remember him losing," said Alice. "So you agree we don't tell Beverly?"

"Yes, we won't tell Beverly."

"Won't tell Beverly what?" They both looked behind them and saw her standing there.

"Nothing dear," said the mother.

Beverly walked in front of her parents and stood looking at them with her hands on her hips. "What is it, Momma?" She didn't get an answer so she looked at her Dad. "What is it, Daddy? What is so all fired important that you don't want to tell me? Is this about Lewis?"

Her Daddy looked away. He couldn't look her in the eye.

"Daddy what is it that you don't want me to know about Lewis? Now you tell me this instant. If it concerns Lewis, I have a right to know."

So he told her all he had learned about Lewis.

Beverly stood there looking at both of them. They couldn't tell if she mad or not. "Is that all?"

"Yes, that's all. I am sorry I did this but I was just trying to protect you. I'm sorry, will you forgive me?"

"Yes, I will forgive you but I already knew all that." She went back inside. Mr. and Mrs. Farmer just sat there looking at each other.

In the next letter, Lewis said he was transferring to a Base in southern California. He was part of a training unit and other Army units would go there to train against them. They would be the aggressor unit against other Army units. He said it sounded like a lot of fun. He would be in the field for a week and then off a week. Every other week a new Army unit would show up. A lot of them would be National Guard units. Lewis and three other guys had bought a station wagon to drive cross country. It would take them four or five days, maybe six if they had car trouble. He told her he had one year to go and was getting out. He was leaving on Tuesday morning and would call when he got to California. Today was Tuesday; he would be on the road already.

CHAPTER SEVEN

DUTY

JOHN 15:13

Sergeant Keith Arnold Farmer left for work at 5:30 that morning. He had eaten breakfast and drank his usual two cups of coffee, with cream and two sugars. He pecked Alice on the cheek and said, "Love ya."

She had answered, "Same here."

Sergeant Farmer was a Sheriff's Deputy for the Kerney County Sheriff's office. Twenty five years on the force; forty five years old. Could retire today if he wanted. He had seriously considered doing just that. He wanted to wait until his daughter, Beverly, finished college. He had no idea when that would be. She was content riding horses and working on the ranch, but that had changed lately. She was head over heels in love with Lewis. Sergeant Farmer thought that was okay. He thought, she could go to college and then be head over heels for someone else. He liked Lewis and respected him a lot. He still poked fun at Beverly about the first time she brought him home from church. Beverly had never told him exactly when she fell in love with Lewis. Then Lewis had done up and bought the ranch, five thousand acres, adjacent to theirs. There was an old house, torn down fences, and not one single cow or horse on the place. What in the world had made him do that? They had only spent six or seven hours together. Lewis had only written Beverly a few times a week even though she had written to him every day and twice on Sunday. He had to admit his daughter was happy. A three thousand mile romance. What sealed the deal were the airborne wings he had sent her. No matter what she was wearing she had them displayed. Sergeant Farmer admired her for that, but what if either of them met someone else? He didn't want to think about that. He knew it wasn't the money. She loved him before she knew about him getting the ten million.

At the office, he handled a few routine reports, said 'howdy' to everyone and went on patrol. At twelve o'clock, he stopped at the diner and had the blue plate special. Today's special was meatloaf, green beans, mashed potatoes and gravy. It was Valentine's Day, so he ran by the florist and ordered a floral arrangement. He would take his wife out to dinner tonight.

Even though the Kerney Police Department was responsible for calls within the city limits, the Sheriff's Department and Police Department helped each other out during emergency calls. The dispatcher, which served both city and county, came over the radio. "Alarm, possible 110 at location number three. All units respond."

Deputy Farmer said, "Responding to possible 110 at number three." 110 was robbery in progress. Location number three was the Kerney Citizen's Bank. They used location codes so people with police scanners wouldn't go to the location and get in the way.

A Kerney police officer said, "300 Bravo on the way to possible 110 at number three."

Deputy Farmer accelerated his Chevy SUV the three blocks to the bank. There was a front parking lot, a back parking lot and a drive through. He pulled to a stop twenty five feet from the front door. He saw the Kerney police cruiser go around to the back. In the event it was a false alarm there was a protocol the bank employees followed. The manager was to walk out, walk over to the police car and put his hands on the hood. This was a sign that everything was okay. If it was a hostage situation and the robber let someone go they were not to approach the police car. Deputy Farmer glanced at the cars in the parking lot to see if anyone was sitting in one with the engine running. A getaway driver was also a danger. He saw no one. He removed his Remington shotgun from its safety rack next to the driver's seat and got out of the Sheriff's car. He placed the shotgun on the hood and removed his Smith and Wesson model 57, .41

caliber magnum from its holster and waited. The manager didn't come out; instead a man came out walking behind a bank employee with a pistol to her head. Famer recognized her. Carmen Barber, a very pregnant Carmen Barber. She was screaming, "Please, don't hurt my baby."

Farmer was standing on the other side of his police SUV leaning over the hood. "Police! Drop your weapon. Drop the weapon now!" Farmer didn't know if there was anyone else inside. He knew the Kerney Police would stay where he was in case anyone went out that way. The man pointed his weapon at Farmer and fired. His bullet hit Farmer's windshield. Carmen Barber twisted free at the sound of the gunshot. The robber fired at her. She went down with a scream. Farmer fired his Smith and Wesson revolver as soon as Carmen Barber went down. The .41 magnum round struck him in the chest and he went down. Farmer rushed around the vehicle. The robber fired another round from the ground. The bullet clipped the front bumper and deformed into a jagged point and ricocheted into his right leg. The deformed bullet tore a jagged hole in Deputy Farmer's leg making a large entry wound. Farmer fired again and hit the robber in the head.

Farmer hobbled over to Carmen Barber. Blood was spewing out of her wound with every heartbeat. The policeman in back was screaming into his handset, "Shots fired, shots fired, Kerney Citizen's Bank, send ambulances." His job was to stay where he was. He didn't know what the situation was inside or out front. He could only hope Farmer was alright.

Farmer wasn't all right. Every step blood gushed down his leg. He made it to Carmen. He knew he had to stop the bleeding and stop it fast. He jerked his tie loose and tied it around her leg. He took his Maglite flashlight and pushed it under the tie, then twisting the flashlight to make it tight. His tourniquet was working. The blood stopped spewing out. As darkness engulfed him he knew he had done his duty.

Twenty minutes later at the emergency room, Todd Archer, the ambulance driver, was waiting at the emergency room door. He saw Carmen Barber's husband come into the parking lot and run up the ramp. He met him at the door. All three had gone to high school together. Todd stopped him as soon as he stepped inside. "Carmen is in surgery right now, Gabe."

"Is she going to be alright?" Gabe asked.

"I think so, but you never know. She has lost a lot of blood. They are doing everything they can. Come with me. She may be in there for hours."

"Well, what about the baby? Is the baby alright?"

"Gabe, I don't know. They have to save Carmen first." Todd walked down the hall with Gabe beside him.

"Where are we going?" Gabe asked.

"There is something I want to show you." Todd led him into a room. There were two bodies inside. A sheet was covering each of them. Todd pointed to one of them. "That's the guy that shot Carmen." He walked around to the other body and pulled the sheet down to his waist. Gabe walked over beside Todd. "You recognize Deputy Farmer?"

"Yeah, I recognize him. Why did you bring me in here? We aren't supposed to be in here."

"Notice anything unusual about him?"

"Todd, what are you talking about? I want to go find out about Carmen and the baby."

"We have plenty of time. They won't tell you anything right now, anyway. Do you notice he's not wearing a tie, Gabe?"

"I don't understand Todd. What are you trying to say? What has this got to do with anything?"

"Both were shot in the leg. Deputy Farmer used his tie to put a tourniquet on Carmen's leg."

"Why didn't he use it on his own leg? That's what you are trying to tell me. He could have saved his own life but he saved Carmen's instead."

"That's what I am saying, Gabe. His family will be here soon. I think you need to speak to them. I would want to if I were you." Todd walked out of the room leaving Gabe looking at Deputy Farmer.

Beverly was in the barn feeding the horses and brushing them, one of her favorite things to do on the ranch. She heard a car pull up. She didn't pay that much attention to it. Her mother was outside pruning the flowers. She saw her mother walk toward the car. Her mother put her arms around her like she was cold. Then she saw her mother cover her mouth and bend over. When Beverly saw the sheriff and Preacher Lawson get out and go to her mother she knew in an instant, "Daddy! Something has happened to Daddy!" She ran from the barn as the two men helped her mother to a chair on the porch. As she got to the porch she heard the sheriff say, "There was nothing they could do."

Beverly stopped in her tracks and started sobbing. This can't be happening; it can't be happening. Brother Lawson walked over to Beverly and put his arms around her. "I'm so very sorry." He helped her over to her mother and said, "She needs you Beverly." All she could do was nod her head in understanding.

The longest ride Beverly had ever taken was to the hospital that day. It was forty miles but seemed like a thousand. She and her mother held each other. Beverly rocked her mother and kissed her on the head the way Lewis had done with Mrs. Gordon. She whispered, "Lewis, I need you so bad and I don't even know where you are."

All the way to the hospital Alice kept saying, "What are we going to do?" The only answer that Beverly could give her was, "We have to go on, Momma. We have to go on."

That evening when they arrived back home there were two Valentine arrangements on the porch. One from Lewis and one from Keith Arnold Farmer.

The funeral was on Friday. Beverly and her mom sat on the front pew. There were hundreds of police there to honor a fallen Brother. They came from adjoining states. They had a police escort for the body and officers stood along the route and saluted as the hearse went by. They held the salutes till all the cars passed. All the flags in the city were lowered to half-mast in honor of Deputy Farmer. Gabe Barber asked if he could sit with them. They said yes, they were bound together by an unbreakable bond.

Saturday evening, Lewis called. "Hey, pretty girl."

"Lewis, Daddy is dead."

Silence.

"Lewis can you hear me?"

"I'm here, Beverly. What did you say?"

"Daddy is dead."

"I'm in shock!" said Lewis. "What happened?"

She told him everything that had happened, especially about her father saving someone else's life and not sparing his own. Everyone knew about his heroic deed. It had spread like wildfire.

Lewis said, "He was a good man, Beverly. I thought a lot of him."

"He thought a lot of you, Lewis. The Mayor presented Mom with the Flag and the Sheriff presented me with his badge. I will cherish it forever."

"I'm sure you will, you have every reason to. He laid down his life to save someone else's."

"I miss you, Lewis. I really needed you and I didn't know where you were."

"Well, that won't happen again."

People had come to the house to pay respect and condolences since it happened. On Sunday, Jo Beth Gordon and some other ladies were joined on the front porch. Mrs. Farmer was inside with the older ladies. "Did you ever hear from Lewis?"

"He called yesterday. I really miss him, Jo Beth. I know he would have been here had he known."

A sheriff's car pulled up. They had been coming for days. Everything was a blur to Beverly. She couldn't remember who had dropped by. There was a book for people to sign and it was already filled. They were writing their names on notebook paper now. Jo Beth saw the sheriff get out and someone in uniform. "Look who's here."

Beverly didn't even hear her. The ladies stepped aside and Lewis walked between them. He hugged and kissed Beverly on top of the head. Beverly looked up. "Lewis, how did you get here?"

"The sheriff brought me."

Beverly stood and wrapped her arms around him and laid her head on his shoulder and started crying. Lewis patted her on the back, "Cry all you want, baby."

When she was all cried out she said, "Momma, come out here! Lewis is here!

Mrs. Farmer came out and hugged him. "Somehow I knew you would come. I just knew it."

A week later, Carmen Barber delivered a healthy seven pound, four ounce baby boy by C-section. Gabe had to go to the administration office to have the birth certificate completed. When he got to Carmen's room, she said, "Come, say hello to Gabe Jr., honey."

"He's not a junior."

"I thought we agreed to name him after you?"

"I changed my mind. His name is Keith Arnold Barber. I named him after the police officer who saved your life. We'll call the next one Junior. I want him to know how fortunate he is to be alive and have a mother. I thought it was the least we could do."

CHAPTER EIGHT

LOOK BEFORE YOU LEAP

PROVERBS 8:5

Lewis was out of the Army. He bought a ten year old Jeep. It was the first vehicle he had ever owned. The shocks were shot, but the brakes and engine were fine. It had large oversized mud grip tires and a winch on the front bumper. It was perfect for off road use.

He had a lot of work to do. The house and barn were sound but needed a lot of work. He spent a lot of time repairing the fencing on the property. He would wait on livestock until he finished the house. It was hard work but he enjoyed it. More than anything else he got to see Beverly every day. She would ride over on one of her horses and Lewis would make a peanut butter and banana sandwich for the two of them. He would show her what he was doing; no major remodeling just repairs from years of neglect.

There was no furniture or appliances in the house. He slept on an air mattress with a sleeping bag. Lewis didn't mind as long as he got to see Beverly every day. She thought it was cool. Roughing it builds character.

Most importantly on Friday nights, Lewis, Beverly and her mother would go out to the diner in Kerney. Lewis enjoyed being around Alice; she was so much like Beverly. Lewis was always telling corny jokes that Alice laughed at first, then Beverly would catch on a minute later. When she laughed then Alice and Lewis would laugh at her.

"The two of you missed all the excitement in town today."

"What happened?" asked Alice.

"I was coming out of the hardware store when a UPS truck came down Main Street. He must have been doing thirty and right behind him was a Fed Ex truck. The UPS truck turned left at the end of the square and the Fed Ex truck turned right."

"Then what happened?" asked Beverly.

"That was pretty much it, but it was pretty exciting."

Alice laughed.

Beverly said, "I don't get it."

Alice said, "It's so boring in Kerney that it's exciting when two delivery trucks come through at the same time."

Beverly laughed, and then the three of them laughed together.

Beverly asked, "Do you regret moving here, honestly?"

Lewis didn't hesitate. "No, this place is as close to perfect as it can get."

On Saturday nights, Lewis and Beverly would take in dinner and a movie in Laramie or Casper. It was a long drive, but it gave them a chance to be alone. They had many long conversations there and back. Sundays was church day. Lewis and Brother Lawson hit it off right away. Both being an Army Ranger sealed the deal. Lewis would eat lunch with them at their home. Sunday was also visitation day.

Beverly's maternal grandparents were living about ten miles away. Lewis didn't even know they were still alive until he moved to Kerney. Both were in their eighties. Every time they left, Beverly would say, "Thank you for coming with us. I know Mom appreciates it."

"I always enjoy seeing them," Lewis said.

Then one day out of the blue, Beverly said she wanted to join the Sheriff's department. Naturally Lewis wanted to know why.

"Well, why did you want to join the Army?"

"I wanted to serve my country."

Beverly said, "I want to serve my community. Dad always thought that people should serve their community in some way."

"Beverly, you know the danger that is involved. You know what happened to your dad. I don't want something like that to happen to you."

"I understand that, Lewis. I've talked to the sheriff and he said I could do follow-up on reports and interviews. Mostly to free up the other deputies. I wouldn't be out on patrol or anything like that. I don't meet the size requirements for the police academy."

"Will you be able to arrest someone?"

"No, you have to complete the academy in order to do that. It's like I will be an outdoor secretary."

"Okay, but you still have to be careful."

When Lewis asked Beverly to marry him the furniture was just being moved in. She had helped him pick it out. Nothing fancy, but sturdy, something that would last. They did splurge on the appliances. Lewis loved to cook and he had not had a stove or refrigerator since he moved in. Beverly said yes to his proposal. They both had known that they would be married one day. They set the date for the second Monday in September. She would have preferred to be married on a Saturday or Sunday but the rodeo was in town that month and in Wyoming a wedding can't compete with a rodeo. She also had her sights on winning her third consecutive barrel racing championship. No one had ever won it three times in a row and with a little bit of luck she would be able to do the hat trick. It always brought the crowd to its feet.

Lewis said, "Any day is fine with me as long as we get married."

The Tuesday before the wedding, Lewis dropped by. Beverly was home alone. Her mother was in the reading club and today was book discussion day. There was snow on the ground with predictions of up to six inches that night. Beverly loved it when it snowed early. Beverly met him at the door with a hug and a kiss. She noticed he was holding a blue folder in his hand. They went into the kitchen for a cup of coffee. "What's in the folder?"

"It's something we need to sign." Lewis put it in front of her. "It's a prenuptial agreement. I'd like for you to sign it." The folder stayed on the table. Beverly never expected something like this. "Aren't you going to read it?"

Beverly took a deep breath then said, "No, Lewis, I am not going to read it and I will never sign it. I can't believe you would want me to do this."

"Please, read it, Beverly. I'm sure once you read it you'll be happy to sign it. Please, just look at it."

"No, Lewis. I will not read it!"

"Then let me read it to you." He reached out for the folder. She put her hand on it.

"Lewis, I would like for you to leave."

"Please, read it Beverly or let me tell you what it says."

"No, Lewis! I don't want to know what it says. I am very upset right now and I just need to think. Please, just leave." She could see the hurt in his eyes. She didn't even look at him as he left. She picked up the folder and threw it in the trash where it belonged. She started crying, then went to her room and put on her pajamas. She lay across the bed and cried her heart out. How could he ask her to sign something like that? Did they not have any trust between them?

She heard her mother come home. She didn't get up. She couldn't face her mom right now. She couldn't face anyone.

Two hours later, her mother knocked on the door. "Beverly, are you alright?"

"Yes, Momma, I'm alright." What was she going to tell her mother? Her mom thought the world of Lewis. She was going to be so heartbroken to think it all came down to possessions. Wedding plans had already been made. Invitations had been mailed a month ago. The Bridal shower was last week. She would have to return all those gifts. That would be so embarrassing. How was she going to tell all those people that there would be no wedding? There was a knock on her door.

"Dinner is ready, Beverly. Come eat, you will feel better after you eat something. Come on, let's eat."

Beverly wanted to stay in bed the rest of her life. She didn't want to tell her mom what had happened. She didn't want to tell anyone. She walked in the dining room and stopped. Her mother had found the folder and was reading it. "Momma, please, don't read that. You knew it was in the trash. I wish you would just put it back where you found it."

Her mother shook her head. "I can't believe he would want you to sign this. I don't blame you I wouldn't sign it either."

"I know, Momma. It hurt so much when he asked me to."

"It's not but one page. It's not worth the paper it's written on. It's got the entire whereas and party of the first part and party of the second part."

"Momma, I don't want to hear it! Please, just throw it back in the trash where you found it."

"Just listen to this nonsense. I promise to laugh when you laugh and cry when you cry. I can't believe he would want you to sign this. I hope you told him to never come back. If you did, good for you."

Something wasn't right here. "What did it say?"

Her mother was headed toward the trash can. "About what?"

"About laughing and crying."

"Oh, you don't want to hear it."

"Momma, what does it say?"

"It says 'I promise to laugh when you laugh and cry when you cry.' That's all it says. There is only one page and places for two signatures."

Beverly was across the room in two steps. "Let me see, Momma."

"No, you have seen his true side. I think that it's best just to throw it away."

Beverly snatched it out of her hand and read the document. Her heart sank. "Momma, what have I done?"

"I don't know. What did you do?"

"I told him to leave, Momma. I've got to go apologize."

"You can't go now, Beverly. It's dark and the snow is really coming down. They say it's a blizzard."

"I'll take daddy's truck. It's a four wheel drive." She grabbed the keys and ran out the door.

"Beverly, at least put some warm clothes on. You are going to freeze!"

Beverly was already gone. She felt like she was froze before she even reached the truck. She had on flannel pajamas and a ratty old housecoat that her mother had threatened to throw away. Her bedroom slippers were wet from the snow. Her daddy's old work boots were still in the floor board. She left her slippers on and pushed her feet into the boots. There was a yellow rain slicker hanging from the gun rack. She struggled into it. There was enough room for two of her. She found his hunting cap on the dash. It was orange and black checkered and had ear flaps. Beverly always called it his Elmer Fudd hat. She found some work gloves in the glove compartment. The fingers were mostly gone from stringing fence.

She could hardly see the road. The windshield wipers weren't much help. The driver's side window was halfway down, having quit working years ago. The heater only put out cold air. She drove on. The snow was really coming down now. She was only able to drive what she guessed was ten miles per hour. At this speed it would take at least twenty minutes. She ran off the road twice. Thank the Lord for four wheel drive. She drove on. No way could she stop; she was past the halfway point. She turned on the road going to Lewis's. The snow was coming down harder now. She had never seen it snow like this before. She had to slow down and said a prayer that she had enough gas to get there. "That's his driveway." She almost went passed it. Then, she went off the road taking out about thirty feet of fence before she got straight on the driveway. As soon as she got even with the house she ran out of gas. She switched off the lights and ran to the porch. She knew he never locked his door. She knocked once then went in and shut the door behind her. When she turned around she was face to face with a very beautiful woman. Beverly thought, boy he don't waste time; eight hours at the most. The woman was wearing a dress that looked like it cost more than all of Beverly's clothes put together. She was wearing a string of pearls that must have cost a fortune. "I'm sorry. I have made a big mistake." She turned and reached for the door.

"You're not going out in this weather." The woman put her hand on the door.

"Please, let me go. I have made a terrible mistake."

She heard Lewis yell from the bedroom, "Who is it?"

"What is it is a better question."

She heard Lewis coming down the hallway. He was pulling a heavy sweatshirt over his head. He stopped, looked, and started laughing. He bent over holding his side laughing. He had to sit down and his face was red. Beverly thought, first the woman and now he's laughing when he got caught.

"Please, just let me go." She had had enough and she started to cry.

The woman was sipping on a glass of wine and Lewis had told her he never drank.

"Beverly, I would like for you to meet my sister, Cynthia. She has been dying to meet you."

"I could have waited," said Cynthia. She walked to her chair and removed something from her purse. "If you are her about the prenuptial agreement we're not budging an inch"

"You know about the prenup?"

"Yes, my law office prepared it."

Lewis walked over and put his arms around Beverly and gave her a big, long hug.

There was a flash, then another and then a third. Beverly looked at Cynthia who took a fourth picture. Beverly screamed, "Noooo!" Then reached out with both hands. Then a fifth picture was taken. Lewis was smiling.

Cynthia yelled, "Watch it! She's making a break for the door!"

Lewis grabbed her by the wrist. "You're not going anywhere tonight! I've already talked to your mother. Cynthia, will you watch her while I call her mother and tell her she's safe. Better move her to the fireplace where it's warm."

Lewis was back in a minute. "Lewis, I'm sorry about the way I acted. I should have known better." Beverly was looking at the fire with her hands outstretched feeling the warmth of the fire. "I can only ask for your forgiveness."

"You're forgiven and we will never speak of this again."

"Wait till you see the pictures," said Cynthia, grinning.

"Oh Lord, I forgot about those. You are not going to develop those are you?"

"Honey, I'm a lawyer. What do you think?"

"Cynthia would you take her to my room and get some warm clothes on her."

When they reached the hallway Beverly turned around and said, "Lewis you do forgive me don't you, and I will sign that agreement."

"Yes, I forgive you."

"Do you forgive me for running over thirty feet of your fence?"

"I'll have to think about that." He smiled at her and said, "I love you, Beverly."

"I love you too, Lewis."

Beverly slept in the guest room. Cynthia slept in Lewis's room and Lewis slept on the couch. At one o'clock Beverly knelt down beside the couch and said, "Lewis, are you asleep?"

"Not anymore."

"Lewis the agreement is only twelve words long. I wanted to tell you they were the most beautiful words I've ever read." Beverly leaned over and kissed him on the cheek. "Goodnight, Lewis."

"Goodnight, Beverly."

*****

Beverly wore a simple white wedding gown. She was the most beautiful woman Lewis had ever laid eyes on. Lewis wore a tuxedo. Jo Beth Gordon was her Maid of Honor. Gabe Barber stood in for her father and gave her away. Lewis asked Brother Lawson to be his Best Man. The Associate Pastor performed the ceremony.

The honeymoon would be in Yellowstone National Park. They had reserved a cottage and would leave early the next morning. In Casper they stopped for gas to make the long journey. Lewis went in to pay and after waiting in the car for what seemed like fifteen minutes Beverly became concerned and went in. Several people were staring at the TV behind the counter. She worked her way through to Lewis and looked at the screen. The second plane hit the World Trade Center. She said, "Oh my God! What happened?"

Lewis put his arm around her shoulder and pulled her close. While still trying to take in that this was terrorism and not an accident, she questioned, "How could someone do this?"

"I don't know," answered Lewis. He pulled her closer and kissed her on top of her head.

It was a quiet drive to Yellowstone as their thoughts were consumed of the events they had witnessed on the TV. How can the happiest time of your life also be one of the saddest? The honeymoon was a somber one in all respects. "What will we do, Lewis? Are we at war?"

"I'm afraid we are. I don't know with whom, but yes, we are."

"Will you have to go?"

"I don't think so, but you never know." In spite of all that was going on in the world Lewis and Beverly were deeply in love. On the morning they were to leave Yellowstone, they were standing on the balcony of the cottage. Lewis put his arm around Beverly and pulled her close. "Beverly, you don't know how good this makes me feel."

"What's that, Lewis?"

"You standing beside me."

"I will always stand by My Lewis."

When they returned to Kerney they stopped by to pick up Beverly's belongings from the house she had lived in her whole life. They sat in the living room and had a cup of coffee with her mom. She had lots of questions about their honeymoon trip. Then Alice surprised them both by saying, "Lewis, Beverly, what do you think about trading houses." Lewis had never thought about something like this.

"Mom, this house is worth more than ours. This is a three bedroom and ours is only two."

"I only need two; one for me to sleep in and one for sewing. It just makes sense to me. Beverly has her horses and their barn, corrals and watering troughs. You would have to build all of that or come over here every day to feed and water them. When would you have a chance to ride them?"

Lewis said, "If we do trade, I insist on paying you the difference."

"Fair enough. I will get my things. I'm already packed."

"You've been planning this awhile, haven't you," said Beverly.

"When you have children, you will be glad we traded." Beverly and Lewis had not thought about children.

JACK IN THE BOX

Just as Lewis and Beverly had witnessed the attack on our country so had millions of others. It was the news around the world. The phone systems were over loaded by people calling friends and relatives telling them to turn on the television. I didn't matter what channel as long as they had news. America had been dealt a severe blow.

In the Arab world, there was celebrations in some places, fear in others. No one knew what America's reaction would be. One man in particular had grave misgivings. The loss of life didn't concern him at all. What may happen next was something to be concerned about.

He hadn't been in America very long; two years, but it seemed a lifetime. It had taken five years to get here. He considered himself a patient man, but this, this event had changed everything. He had spent two years in France. Paris was indeed nice in the springtime. He enjoyed the sidewalk cafes. Then he moved to Spain. Madrid was crowded and loud but he wasn't outside much there. He was in a class to learn Spanish. He could speak and write Spanish fluently but that wasn't good enough. It had to be perfect. Then a year in Mexico City. The smog and the altitude along with the crowd were overwhelming to him. When he arrived in Mexico City he applied for a work visa to go to America. He had the necessary documentation and the money to bribe any official to make it happen. A year later he was in America. He had a job waiting on him in Fargo, North Dakota. He would be working with the phone company. Anyone who met him had the impression he was Spanish. No one would have dreamed he was Iranian. He went to night clubs, strip joints, and had friends over for parties. Muslims are forbidden to drink alcohol and lust after women. He had been given permission to do all these things. He had to fit in. People had to believe. He even told Arab jokes and called them camel jockeys. The Arab jokes didn't bother him, he was Persian.

He had to find out about the attack on the World Trade Center. He had six sleeper agents in America. Iranians just like him waiting to act against America. He needed to find out if everyone was in danger. He was in charge of the six men.

He drove to Minneapolis. Once he arrived he made a call from a restaurant that lasted thirty seconds. He got an answering machine. He knew he would. He said, "Ishmael, are you there? I'm already at the restaurant." Then he hung up. The man he was calling was not named Ishmael. It could be explained as a wrong number. The Iranian didn't know the person he was calling. He had a business card with a phone number. The phone number on the card wasn't the number he called. He had to add a one to the last digit. Even though he didn't know the man, the man knew what he looked like and that was all he knew about the Iranian. Neither man could implicate the other. The two men had a way to confirm each other. If one of the two didn't know the correct confirmation signals he was to walk away.

Two hours later, he was sipping on a drink in a strip club. He was sitting at a corner table in the back. There was an empty table next to him. Ten minutes after his arrival, a man came into the strip club and stood by the door for a minute to let his eyes adjust to the dim interior. He went to the nearby table and sat down. He looked at the agent and asked, "Excuse me, isn't your name Ishmael?" The first confirmation.

"No, Sir, you must be mistaken." The Iranian pulled a pack of cigarettes out of his shirt pocket, shook one out and put it in his mouth. Then he patted his pants pocket for his lighter. "Excuse me, Sir; I seemed to have left my lighter at the restaurant." The second confirmation. One more to go. "Do you happen to have a light?"

"Here take these," and he handed him a book of matches. The Iranian opened the book of matches. One had been used but still in place. The third confirmation.

Anyone paying attention to the two men would never have noticed anything unusual or out of place. The two men sat in their chairs for ten minutes. Then the Iranian said, "Did we have anything to do with the hijacked planes?"

"No, I don't know who did that," answered the man.

"Does this change anything?"

"Just be more careful. Be very careful. I'm leaving next week but everyone knows that. Make sure your people are very careful."

Then the man left. The Iranian agent watched him leave. No one came in or out while he was there. He would spend the night here in Minneapolis, Minnesota before going back to Fargo, North Dakota. He made his first mistake when he had too much to drink. When he left the strip club he saw three women, obviously prostitutes standing on a street corner. He walked over and struck up a conversation and offered one of the women money for sex. The women were vice cops. When they tried to arrest him he became what is termed disorderly. He had at least taken the precaution of having false identification. Then he made the second mistake. He told him he worked for the phone company, which was true. He realized he should have lied as soon as he said it.

He was taken to the police station and fingerprinted, then the mug shot. He had enough for his own bail. He knew he had been instructed to leave the country if he was arrested or fingerprinted for any reason by law enforcement. He knew if he left the country for solicitation of a prostitute he would be put to death. There was too much at stake. He couldn't leave. If he left on his own he would be tracked down and killed. There would be no safe place on the face of the earth if he left without permission.

Halfway to Fargo, he realized he had made a third mistake. He had used a Muslim name. He should have picked another Spanish name. He had lots of fake identifications hidden away. He had chosen a Muslim name when he left Fargo because of the large number of Muslims living in Minneapolis. Nothing he could do about it now. When he arrived in Fargo, North Dakota he destroyed that identity. No way could they track him unless he was fingerprinted again.

The other man had been right when he said, 'Be careful.' He wouldn't take any chances. They would never take him alive. If they were successful he would return to Iran one day as a hero. All six sleeper agents had been here since the Iranian revolution. They had come across the Mexican border one at a time. Each agent went to different parts of the country. The Iranian didn't even know their names or locations. He would be told that information when the time was right; now was not that time. If one was caught he couldn't inform the others. They didn't even know there were others. He was the only one that knew there were six.

CHAPTER NINE

THE PROMISE

2 PETER 3:13

Beverly had been with the Sheriff's Department for a month. She really enjoyed her job. She was going all over the county doing a wide assortment of duties from funeral escort to filling out accident reports. She had many where motorists hit deer. These were simple reports that had to be filled out for insurance claims. She also had to take photos of the damaged vehicle.

One day as she arrived home Lewis told her that a package had come for her.

"Who sent me a package?"

"It's from Cynthia."

"Your sister?"

"Yeah, it's on the sofa."

"Why would Cynthia send me a package?"

"Maybe it's a wedding present. I don't know. It's on the sofa."

Beverly opened the package. It was a tri fold picture frame 11x14 inches. She unfolded it. In the left frame was a picture of Beverly and Lewis. Lewis had his arm around her waist. Beverly was trying to reach for the camera. Elmer Fudd hat, earflaps, yellow rain slicker, ratty old housecoat hanging down to her knees, flannel pajamas and muddy, untied work boots. The middle frame held the prenuptial agreement. The frame on the right held the wedding photo. Beverly walked to the fireplace and placed it on the mantle. She stepped back and smiled. She loved it.

Beverly loved her job. She knew she wasn't doing real police work but it freed up the deputies so they could do the real police work. Several deputies told her that it really meant so much to them. She typed statements for them when she had time. She felt like she was serving a community she truly loved.

One day, Lewis called her at the sheriff's office. "Honey, I have some bad news. Apparently your grandfather has had a stroke. I'm taking your mother and grandmother to the hospital now. I'll see you there."

"Is he going to be alright?"

"Honey, I don't know. He wasn't conscience when the ambulance picked him up. You know Sunday when we were there he seemed just fine. When you get to the hospital meet us out front with a wheelchair for your grandmother."

"I'll be there in five minutes."

"It will take us a lot longer than that. Maybe thirty minutes or more. Love you, gotta go."

Beverly first went to the emergency room. Her grandfather had already been taken to the intensive care unit. Her first indication of the seriousness of his condition was they wouldn't let her see him. Beverly had never felt so helpless. She rounded up a wheelchair and waited outside for her family. Twenty minutes of pacing back and forth was all she could do. When they finally arrived the first thought Beverly had was her grandmother looked ten years older than she did last Sunday. She hugged her grandmother and then her mom. Lewis parked the car and joined them inside. Beverly pulled Lewis to the side. "Lewis, I'm so afraid."

"I know, me too. We can only hope and pray for him."

Two hours later, the doctor came out and walked over to them. "Let's step into here." It was a small waiting room. Beverly figured this is where they give the bad news to the family. "He has had a massive stroke. I'm afraid there is nothing anyone can do. It is simply a matter of time. We are moving him to a room where you all can be with him, but please only one at a time. We will be continually giving him medication and monitoring him. We don't need people in the way. I hope you understand and I am terribly sorry."

"If we could have gotten him here sooner would it have mattered?" Lewis was thinking about Jack Gordon in Bosnia and the Medevac not showing up.

The doctor didn't hesitate. "He could have been laying in ICU and I don't think it would have changed anything, sorry."

Lewis nodded in understanding.

Beverly said, "I will go in first."

She went in. She couldn't believe how frail he looked. Grandpa was always vibrant looking. He never looked old until about five years ago. She loved him so much. She remembered him teaching her how to lasso, starting with a fence post. Then she moved on to harder and harder things. When she started lassoing cows and horses he told her one day she'd be able to lasso a jack rabbit. Beverly smiled when she actually tried it one time and almost pulled it off. She sat in the chair beside his bed, took his hand in hers and squeezed it gently. "Grandpa, this is Beverly. I am so sorry this has happened to you. I will be praying for you Grandpa. Grandma and Momma are here. We are all praying for you. I know God will be waiting for you in Heaven. I can't think of anyone who deserves to go to Heaven more than you. The way you lived your life has been an inspiration to me. Grandpa, do you remember how you taught me to shoot and Daddy didn't know you were doing it. Then when Daddy started teaching me how he couldn't believe how well I could shoot a pistol and a rifle. Daddy said I was a natural and might be another Annie Oakly. I never told him different. You taught me how to ride a horse and most important you taught me to love horses. You taught me everything I needed to know and everything I wanted to know. I hope there is a little bit of a horse thief running through me. I can never tell you how much I love you. There are not enough good words to say it all. I remember when I was in the third or fourth grade I told everyone my grandpa was the world's greatest cowboy. You were the greatest cowboy in the world to me. When I do the hat trick everyone ask me how did you do that? I tell them my grandpa taught me, but I never tell them how to do it. I tell them, get your grandpa to show you how. I love you, Grandpa, and when you see Daddy up there tell him I love him and miss him so much."

She stood up and kissed him on the forehead and left the room. Alice went in next and stayed only a few minutes. When she came out Lewis pushed Beverly's grandmother's wheelchair into the room. Lewis came out and sat down beside Beverly and put his arm around her. He pulled her close and held her.

Alice said, "It hurts so much to see Daddy like that."

Beverly nodded her head. "I don't believe he will last through the night."

Lewis went in and brought Grandma out and walked back in the room.

After a few minutes, Beverly went to the door and as quietly as she could went in. Lewis had his back to her. He didn't know she was standing behind him. She saw Lewis was holding his hand. She heard him say, "Grandpa, there is something I want to tell you. An angel of the Lord is coming to get you. I promise I will take care of Grandma all the days of her life, so you can lay that burden down and I will take it for you."

Beverly eased out of the room and stood in the hallway and said to herself, "A promise has been made and I know he will keep it."

Beverly's grandfather didn't make it through the night. The next morning Beverly went to her grandmother's house and picked up her clothes and other things she would need. Lewis went to the funeral home and made arrangements for the burial. Now there were three in the MacDonald household. Two weeks later, Lewis asked

Beverly if she knew of someone that could come sit with her grandma and keep her company while they were at work. The ranch kept Lewis busy from early morning till late evening. Lewis knew she had to be lonely there by herself. Beverly said that she knew the perfect person. She had known her for her whole life.

"Who is it?"

"Miss May," Beverly answered.

"You'll love her."

CHAPTER TEN

MISS MAY

1 TIMOTHY 5:10

Beverly left early the next morning and returned before lunch with Miss May in tow. When Lewis opened the door he was looking at an elderly Native American lady that may have stood five feet tall when she was younger. She now stood only about four and half feet. She was grey haired and had wrinkled and leathery looking skin. She looked like an old catcher's mitt that had been left outside for a long time; a very long time. She wore thick glasses and leaned on a cane. It wasn't actually a cane but a stout stick. She was wearing an honest to God granny dress with an apron tied around her waist. An old fashioned bonnet was on her head. At first glance Lewis thought his eyes were deceiving him because she was wearing old fashioned army combat boots that were untied; there weren't even any laces to tie.

Lewis moved out of the way as she tromped into the living room. She looked up at Lewis and blinked behind the coke bottle glasses. "How tall are you, Sonny?"

Lewis didn't answer.

Miss May looked at Beverly, "Must be hard of hearing." She patted Lewis on the stomach and said to Beverly, "He's skinny as a rail, now don't you worry. I'll have him fatted up in no time."

Lewis started to say something but didn't.

"Well, show me the kitchen and then get out of my way. We'll eat in thirty minutes." Then she pointed a gnarled bony finger at Lewis. "Now don't you be late, Sonny."

"I won't Miss May." Lewis stopped Beverly and asked, "How old is she?"

"Nobody knows."

"Does she know?"

"Nobody knows."

Miss May went into the living room first to grandma and took her hand in hers and gently patted it. "I'm sorry for your loss, Mrs. Thomas. It seems the good die young, doesn't it. Don't you worry. I'm here to take care of you. You need anything let me know."

As she walked past Lewis she nodded. "I'll have you fatted up right quick like."

Lewis could hear pots and pans rattling around in the kitchen. The old lady was humming as she worked.

"Beverly, we need to talk."

"About what?"

"I think it's pretty obvious about what."

"Don't worry. You'll love her."

Lewis shook his head. "I hope you're right."

"Why don't you ask Grandma?"

Grandma came over to Lewis. "Thank you, Lewis and Beverly. I know I don't have much time left on this earth. I can't think of anyone I'd rather spend my last days with than with Miss May."

Lewis looked at Beverly and asked, "How long have you known her?"

Beverly said, "Why Lewis, she delivered me."

Lewis said, "I don't want to be fatted up. You don't think I'm too skinny do you?"

"No Lewis, I don't think you're skinny but she is a good cook and you may put on a pound or two. Don't worry about it. Grandma needs to enjoy her last days, don't you think?"

That night at the dinner table, after making sure he wasn't late, he didn't know if he had ever laughed this much. Everything Miss May said and the way she said it was funny. When Lewis said something Miss May would look at him through the coke bottle glasses, blink a few times and go off on another subject just as funny. Grandma Thomas was crazy about her. Beverly would smile at Lewis and say, "I told you so."

Lewis started calling dinner time at the table "Happy Hour." The four of them loved talking and laughing together. Miss May would bustle around as she worked; cooking and cleaning. If she wasn't humming she was saying something that made them laugh. She loved watching the westerns. One night a movie came on and the cavalry was making its charge; bugles blowing, sabers outstretched and gleaming in the sun, horse hooves flying in a cloud of dust.

Miss May looked at Lewis and said, "General Custer wore the first arrow shirt." Lewis had to think a minute and then he laughed so hard his side hurt.

Another night they were watching a rerun of the Andy Griffith show. Miss May said, "It didn't seem like Andy had aged a bit in forty years. I wonder how he does it."

Lewis answered, "Miss May you see these shows are…" He noticed Miss May was looking at him and blinking at him behind the thick glasses. "I wonder the same thing, Miss May."

Beverly just smiled and patted him on the knee.

Every morning Lewis woke up to the smell of brewing coffee and breakfast being cooked. When he came in the kitchen Miss May would ask, "Did you wash up, Sonny?" She always called him Sonny.

"Yes, Miss May."

"It says in the good book that cleanliness is next to godliness. That's in the book of Deuteronomy."

When Lewis and Beverly were in the bed one night Lewis asked how long Miss May had known Grandma Thomas. "I don't know if grandma ever remembers life before Miss May. When Momma was born Miss May was there to deliver her. When I was born Miss May was there to deliver me. She was probably the first person I ever saw. I know she was the first person to ever hold me. She's very special to us Lewis."

Saturday nights were something Lewis would never forget. Every Saturday night after happy hour at the dinner table everyone would go into the living room. Miss May would say it was about time for "rasslin." The show would begin; The Miss May Show. Lewis had never seen anything like it. Miss May was so excited and would grunt and groan and scream with delight. She would punch the air with her bony fist, jump out of her chair and go halfway across the room leaning on her walking stick to get a better look at the TV through her coke bottle glasses.

"The Masked Predator, now that's a "rassler" if there ever was one", said Miss May.

Lewis asked, "Which one is the Masked Predator, Miss May?"

"He's the one with the mask on, Sonny."

"But, they both have a mask on, Miss May," Lewis said.

"Respect your elders, Sonny. That's in the good book, in the book of Ecclesiastes."

"Miss May, I heard someone say wrestling was fake. Have you ever heard that?"

"Of course not. Anyone can see that it's real. You let them tell that to the Mask Predator and they'll change their mind right quick like. No sir, "rasslins" not fake."

Lewis loved teasing Miss May. He couldn't help it. It was just so much fun. "Miss May, I saw in the paper the other day that some people say the moon landing was fake. Have you heard that?"

"Don't need to hear it. Anybody with half a brain knows that. I bet they filmed it in that Hollywood town where they filmed the

Roy Rogers show. That's probably why Roy Rogers don't come on anymore. The government won't let him use it. You can fool some of the people all the time. That's in the good book, in the book of Lamentations."

"I thought Teddy Roosevelt said something like that."

Miss May nodded her head and said, "Teddy Roosevelt, he quoted the good book a lot from what I hear."

Lewis really fell in love with Miss May. If and when Lewis said something funny, which was seldom, Miss May would cackle a laugh and say, "It does a body good to be happy. That's in the good book, in the book of Leviticus."

Lewis would read the Bible at night trying to find what she was referring to. He never would find it. He mentioned it to Beverly and she just smiled and said, "She got you to read the Bible though, didn't she?"

"Well yeah, so you're saying she says things like that so I will read the Bible looking for it."

"Don't worry, Lewis, it won't hurt you and to ease your mind she did the same thing to Momma and the same thing to me."

Grandma Thomas passed away in her sleep seven months after Grandpa Thomas. Lewis could tell she had a smile on her face. They, actually Miss May, had made her last days enjoyable. Grandma had left the house to Beverly, her only grandchild. Lewis asked Beverly what she was going to do with it. They didn't need the house and they didn't need the money if she sold it. Beverly said, "Lewis my grandpa built that house. Momma was born there. I was born there. I can't just sell it. I have so many memories of that place. When I was a child I would go there and play. Grandma and Grandpa would tell me stories. We played games at the kitchen table. I just can't bring myself to sell it. Let's just wait awhile before we make any decisions."

After the funeral, Beverly asked Lewis to drive Miss May home. She would stay with her mother while he was gone. Lewis drove Miss May to her house. Lewis had never been there before. When they pulled in the driveway, Lewis couldn't believe his eyes. The front porch was about to fall in and the house looked like it had never been painted. It actually looked dangerous. It was the saddest place Lewis had ever seen. "Miss May, is this where you live?"

"Yes, this is it, Sonny."

"Not anymore." He backed out and went straight to Grandpa Thomas's house. He pulled in and said, "You live here now, Miss May." Lewis could tell she was shocked and didn't exactly know what to say but for the first time he thought he saw a tear rolling down her cheek. He helped her in with her bags. As he drove home he wondered what Beverly was going to say when he told her what he had done. He hoped she would understand.

When he went in the kitchen, Beverly asked, "Did you get her moved into her new house?"

Lewis looked at her and said, "You knew I was going to do that, didn't you? That's why you had me take her home, right."

"Yes, and I know my grandparents would want it that way. Miss May has always done for others. It's time someone did for her. She is a proud person Lewis. She's not going to take a hand out."

"She wants to pay rent," Lewis said. "We decided on a dollar a month and we have to go by every month and collect it or she will walk here to pay it."

Beverly smiled, "I told you that you would love Miss May."

On the first of each month, Lewis would go by to collect the rent. He also brought two rocking chairs for the front porch where the two of them could sit outside and talk. Lewis looked forward to his visit with Miss May every month.

On one visit, Beverly collected the rent and brought along a dress. "Why that dress is way to pretty to wear. It's pretty enough to be buried in."

"Don't talk like that, Miss May."

Beverly noticed that Miss May never wore the dress. She was saving it for a special occasion. After Lewis and Beverly had been married over a year, he and Miss May were sitting outside enjoying the weather and talking. Miss May asked Lewis, "When you two going to have some children?"

"Well, Miss May, we haven't really talked about children. I figure when the good Lord wants us to have children we will."

"Do you want children, Sonny?"

"Well, I wouldn't mind having a couple. Maybe a boy and a girl."

"How's about Miss Beverly?"

"I imagine she wouldn't mind having a couple. You know she's an only child. I think her being by herself as a child; she would have liked having a brother or a sister. Someone to play with, you know what I mean?"

"Well, I will pray ya'll have a boy and a girl. Twins would be nice don't you think?"

"Yes, Ma'am, that would be nice. I'll tell Beverly you are going to pray for us to have twins."

"You know prayer works, don't you, Sonny?"

"Yes, Ma'am, I sure do," answered Lewis.

PART TWO

CHAPTER ELEVEN

A MAN NEVER STOOD

SO TALL

Beverly glanced at her watch. She wore her dad's watch with the wide leather band since he was killed. She also wore his badge and Lewis's jump wings. No one ever said anything to her about it. They knew she was paying honor to the two most important men in her life. It was six o'clock and time to head home. She was near where she would turn on the dirt road when the dispatcher said, "Domestic dispute, 310 Casper Highway, any unit respond." Beverly was one hundred yards away. She knew she wasn't supposed to answer callouts but she was here. How would it look to a caller to see a deputy sheriff's car drive by?

Domestic disputes were one of the most dangerous calls. A lot of officers were injured and even killed coming between two people fighting. Maybe the police presence would diffuse the situation. Beverly hoped so. She stopped the vehicle in front of the address. A large man, on top of a woman, had his left hand on her throat and was punching her in the face as hard as he could. Beverly jumped out of the car. She grabbed her Daddy's Maglite flashlight, ran up behind him and hit him as hard as she could on the right side of his head. He fell off the woman and sprawled out face first on the ground. Beverly had handcuffs in her vehicle in case other deputies needed extras. Beverly cuffed him.

The woman had turned blue in the face and was bleeding profusely from where she had been beaten. Beverly didn't want to take a chance and cuffed her, too. She walked back to her car and called dispatch. When dispatch answered Beverly said, "I need two ambulances at 310 Casper Highway."

"Beverly, is that you?"

"Yes, Mary, it's me."

"What are you doing there, Beverly? You're not hurt are you?"

"No, I'm fine."

"You didn't hurt anyone did you?"

"Let's hope I did. I also need an arresting officer, quick."

"One's on the way and I'll get those ambulances out to you. Two of them, huh. Wait until the sheriff hears about this. You didn't shoot anyone, did you?"

"No, Mary, I didn't shoot anyone." She heard the siren before she saw the car. "Got to go, Mary. I'm on my way home."

The Deputy got out of his car and walked over to Beverly and the two people on the ground. "You okay, Beverly?"

"I'm fine. I think both of them need to go to the hospital." He nodded his head in agreement. "Fill me in where I can fill out the paperwork."

Beverly told him what had happened.

"Have you searched them?"

"Haven't had time."

The Deputy searched the man and found a packet of white powder in a small plastic bag in his jeans pocket. "Do you know if they have a vehicle?"

"I don't know. There's not one in the driveway."

"I'll call an investigator on the drugs."

"What will happen to them?" asked Beverly.

"Domestic violence for him; assault and battery, and drug possession charges if this turns out to be anything. Probably drug charges for both if they are cohabitating or married. You did a good job, Deputy MacDonald."

"Thank you." Beverly smiled. Everyone called her Beverly. No one had ever called her Deputy MacDonald.

The ambulances pulled up, loaded up the two and drove away.

"I need to go to the hospital with these two to get some details." He patted her on the shoulder and got in his car.

As Beverly was getting in to her car, an elderly lady ran up to her vehicle and tapped on the side glass. Beverly got out of the car.

"You can't leave those children here by themselves."

"Children?" asked Beverly.

"Yes, there are two children in there. This is the third time I called about something like this."

"What happened the other two times?"

"I guess they talked to them and gave them a warning."

"Were they fighting the other times?"

"Not that I know of. Just shouting and throwing things at each other."

"Who owns the duplex?"

"I do. My husband bought it before he died. Someone needs to do something. The lights have been turned off for two weeks." She explained that the children were orphans and the girl had been raising them. "I don't know if that's true. She looks mighty young to be a foster parent for two children."

Beverly checked her flashlight to see if it was still working. She stepped through the door and stopped. Trash was everywhere and beer cans were strewn about. Beverly thought, this is evidence of child neglect and she went back to her car and got the camcorder. She checked to make sure a fresh tape was inside. She filmed as she went, living room first, then the kitchen. The kitchen was full of dirty dishes. The only food in the cabinets was oatmeal and macaroni and cheese. She saw a partial loaf of bread on top of the refrigerator. She opened the refrigerator door and saw a jar of mayonnaise and some baloney. She turned on the gas stove and then the water, both worked. She checked the bedroom on the right. The bed was covered with filthy sheets and clothes were tossed in the corner. She went into the other bedroom, no sheets on the bed, just a blanket. A Raggedy Ann doll and a toy fire truck were on the floor. This looks like the kids room but where are the kids? She looked in the closet but there were no clothes hanging. She went into the bathroom and looked in the tub. She didn't see the children anywhere. Beverly was about to go ask the lady if she was sure about the children. Then she heard them. One was crying softly. She followed the sound to a coat closet that was obscured by the front door being open. She closed the front door. There was a combination lock on the door.

Beverly put her ear to the door. She could barely hear them. She heard a little girl say, "Joshua, you have to be quiet. You are going to get us both in trouble."

"Please don't let him beat me, I can't take it anymore."

Tears came to Beverly's eyes. She went outside and got the tire tool out of the trunk. She hoped she could use it as a crow bar. As she went back inside she thought of what she needed to say to the children. She put the tire tool behind the lock and pulled as hard as she could. The hasp popped off. Beverly had the camcorder pointed along with the flashlight at the closet door. She opened the door and knelt down.

The little girl was standing in front of the boy. She had her arm out in front as trying to protect him. Their faces were filthy, clothes were nasty. Paper plates were thrown in the corner. Beverly kept the camcorder pointed at the children. "My name is Beverly. I am here to take you to a safe place."

The little boy ran past the girl and threw his arms around Beverly's neck and started sobbing. Beverly hugged him to her and gently patted him on the back. The boy leaned his head back and looked at Beverly. Tears were running down his cheeks. "Are you an angel?"

Beverly didn't answer. She didn't know how to answer. Then the little girl came out of the closet. "Where are you taking us?"

"To a safe place," answered Beverly. Then she said, "Let's get all your clothes." She put everything she could find in a blanket including the doll and the fire truck. She carried everything to the car. She put the children in the back seat and fastened their seatbelt. Once they were secured she called dispatch. She requested Mary to call Family and Children Services.

Mary called back a few minutes later. "I'm not getting an answer. It's almost seven. They are gone for the weekend."

"What should I do, Mary?"

"Let me call the sheriff at home." Ten minutes went by before Mary called back. "Beverly, the sheriff wants to know if you can keep them this weekend."

Beverly didn't hesitate. "I can do that."

"You need to take them to the hospital to be checked for child abuse."

"Mary, that's thirty miles in the opposite direction. Doc Fletcher is only five miles. He's on the hospital staff and his office is at his house."

"Wait one minute."

Beverly waited five.

"You can do that. Make sure he knows about the child abuse, okay. He may have to testify in court. I'll call him for you."

"Thanks, Mary."

Ten minutes later, she and the children pulled up in front of Doc Fletcher's office. The doctor lived in the upstairs section. Beverly brought the camcorder and the kids inside. He was waiting for them in the small lobby of his office. Doc Fletcher was in his sixties and on the small size. He wasn't wearing his doctor's jacket. He looked more like a trusting uncle than a doctor. He said hello to the three and motioned them into an exam room.

He unbuttoned the boys clothing and turned him around. Beverly had the camcorder going. She gasped when she saw the bruises on the boys back, buttocks and legs. He had bruises everywhere on his backside. She could tell some were older and had turned yellow, some were almost gone, but there were a lot of recent ones. Beverly's heart sank. How could anyone do this to a child? She asked the doctor why most of them were on his back.

The doctor said, "That's where they usually are when you are running away while being hit." Then the doctor asked, "How old are they?"

The girl answered. "We're five."

"Both of you?"

"We are twins," answered the girl.

The doctor looked at Beverly and said, "About twenty four bruises as best I can tell."

"What's your name, son?" The boy was shaking and looking at the floor. "Son, can you tell me your name?" The boy looked over his shoulder at his sister and then looked back to the floor.

The girl answered, "His name is Joshua."

Beverly could tell he was scared to death. She just wanted to wrap him in a blanket and hold him. The doctor weighed him, checked his heartbeat and looked for signs of other damage. "His size is the size of a four year old. He is undernourished and I think he has a lot of stress related issues. I don't detect any internal problems.

I think he needs to be cleaned up and put on a proper diet and he will be okay."

He then checked the little girl. "And what is your name?"

"Deborah."

She had eighteen bruises and was about two inches taller than the boy. Doc Fletcher looked at both the children's hands. He turned toward Beverly and in a low voice he whispered, "Her fingernails are broken."

Beverly asked, "What does that mean?"

"She tried to fight them off; the boy didn't."

Beverly couldn't imagine the hell the two children had lived in. Beverly had so many emotions. She was angry, sad, and she wished she had hit the man more than she did. After the kids were dressed, Beverly asked, "If they are twins, why is her hair black and his is blond?"

"Happens," was the only answer he gave.

Before they left she asked what she needed to feed them to get their weight to normal. "Just a normal diet. They need stability and love more than anything."

On the way home, the children didn't say a word and Beverly wondered how Lewis would take this. Beverly got the children out of the car and ushered them in the house. A thought occurred to her and she called a friend that had children and asked if she had any extra kid's clothes and shoes. Beverly went to her closet, took out a couple of long t-shirts. She got the kids undressed and put the t-shirts on them. Then she put the children's clothes that they had gathered at the house in the washer but she didn't even think the clothes would fit the kids anymore.

"Are you hungry?"

Both the kids nodded their heads. She had a chicken casserole her mother dropped off the day before. She warmed two plates in the microwave and put the plates on the table along with a glass of milk.

She heard Lewis pull into the garage. He stamped his feet to get any dirt off his work boots before coming inside. He saw the two children and froze.

Beverly stood up and said, "Lewis, I'd like you to meet Joshua and Deborah. They will be staying with us this weekend."

Lewis said, "Hello," but neither child answered. "Will you excuse us for a minute?"

He pointed to the living room and Beverly followed him. At the doorway, he looked at the children. They reminded him of the children he had seen in Bosnia. The same vacant stare. He could see the fear in their eyes. He sat on the sofa. Beverly sat down beside him and started telling him everything that had happened. She had tears streaming down her face when she told him about them being locked in the closet and the bruises. "What do you need me to do?"

"I need you to bathe the boy while I bathe the girl."

"I can do that."

"Be careful when you bathe him. His body has to be sore. Wash his hair and tell him to close his eyes while you rinse his hair out. I have their clothes in the dryer and they should be ready by the time we are finished. I have called Mrs. Parker and she is bringing some extra clothes and shoes."

Lewis went in the hall bathroom and ran some water in the tub making sure it wasn't too hot. He took Joshua in the bathroom. He left the door open and undressed the boy. "Joshua, we are going to get you cleaned up." Joshua just stood there staring at Lewis as he helped him in the tub. Lewis's anger raged inside him when he saw all the bruises. He bathed him as gently as he could. He washed and rinsed his hair. He got a towel and dried him off. Lewis knelt down to put Joshua's socks on. The boy had his hands on Lewis's shoulders and continued to stare at him. Lewis thought back to what Lieutenant Jenkin's said, 'A man never stood so tall as when he stoops to help a child.'

Lewis tried to put the boy's shoes on but they were way too small. "Do they hurt your feet?"

He nodded yes.

"We'll leave them off then." Lewis asked, "Feel better?"

The boy just nodded his head. Lewis had not heard the boy speak at all.

After dressing and combing the boys hair Lewis took him in the living room and turned on the TV. He tried to find something the boy would be interested in but it was already primetime. The boy just kept his eyes on Lewis.

Beverly and the girl came in the living room just as there was a knock at the door. Beverly answered the door and asked Mrs. Parker and her two kids to come in.

Mrs. Parker said, "I brought what I could find in a hurry. I'll look some more tomorrow. Tommy, give Mrs. Beverly the shoes."

Beverly said, "These will do just fine." She knelt down and hugged the boy. "Joshua, come over and thank Tommy for the shoes." Joshua came over and hugged the boy just as Beverly had done.

"That's so sweet," said Mrs. Parker.

Joshua went to the sofa with the pair of shoes. Lewis knelt down to help him put them on. Again the stare.

"I also have a pair of pajamas, two shirts and two pair of jeans. They are like new. Tommy is growing so fast. There is a dress, a nightgown, a sweater, shirt and a pair of jeans, some sandals and a pair of tennis shoes she should be able to wear. Paula outgrew them a few years ago but they are still good."

"Deborah, thank Paula for the clothes," said Beverly.

"Thank you. How old are you?"

"I'm seven," answered Paula.

"I'm five," said Deborah. She went back to her chair checking out the clothes and shoes.

"Mrs. Parker, thank you so much. If there is ever anything I can do, please let me know."

After the Parker's left, Beverly said, "I know everyone has had a long day, so I say let's go to bed." She put the two children in the guestroom, leaving the door open.

Lewis said, "I need to get an early start tomorrow. I'll try not to wake you when I leave."

Lewis left at daybreak. Beverly woke the children up two hours later. She made them a bowl of cereal for breakfast. She made her plans for the day and then at 10:30 she started dinner. She had some homemade cookies and put a few on a saucer with two glasses of milk. "Here are some homemade chocolate chip cookies and some milk. I think you will like them."

The two children went into the dining room. A few minutes later Beverly went in and sat down. The boy reached for his milk and it slipped out of his hands. Beverly jumped up to grab a towel and the boy let out a scream and ran past her. The girl jumped up out of her chair and stood between her brother and Beverly. "Please, don't beat him! He didn't mean to spill it."

Beverly froze in place. "What did you say?"

"Please, don't beat him. He didn't mean to spill his milk."

Beverly knelt down and took the girl in her arms. "Deborah, I would never beat you or Joshua. I was just getting a towel to clean it up."

The girl just looked at her. Beverly picked up a towel off the kitchen counter and cleaned up the milk. "Deborah, everyone has accidents and we don't cry over spilt milk, you understand?"

The girl nodded.

"Can you do me a favor? Take these cookies and milk to Joshua." Beverly put a half glass of milk in the girl's hand. She put three cookies in a plastic freezer bag. "When he's finished, the two of you come back in here, okay."

Ten minutes later, Deborah was back with the glass and an empty freezer bag. "Where is Joshua?"

"He won't come in here. He had an accident."

"He's not hurt is he? Did he fall down?"

"No, Ma'am. He wet his clothes."

"Oh, that kind of an accident. Where is he?"

"He's already in the closet."

"Why is he in the closet?" Then she understood why.

Beverly went into the room and opened the closet door. Joshua was sitting in the corner. Beverly went into the closet and sat on the floor across from him. She looked around and said, "I need to clean this closet out." Joshua looked around, also. "Joshua, you know what I think. I think you spilt your milk because you are trying so hard not to spill it and you get nervous. Everyone makes mistakes when they are nervous. I wish I had a nickel for every time I've dropped something. And don't get me started on Lewis, why that man is as clumsy as an ox. Now let's get you bathed off and changed into some dry clothes. Don't you worry about that milk, okay?"

Joshua nodded his head.

Beverly looked out and saw Deborah watching her. She knew Deborah was trying to protect her brother. There was no telling how long she had tried to spare him from beatings. All they had was each other.

Beverly put what she needed in the trunk of the car then brought the children out. She put them in the back seat and fastened their seatbelts. "Where are we going?" asked Deborah.

"You'll see in a minute." It wasn't far, less than a mile. "Wait here," she told them. She got out of the car and walked toward Lewis who stopped working when he saw her. They started talking.

Deborah was standing up in the back floorboard. She could see between the headrests.

"What are they doing?" asked Joshua.

"She's waving her arms all around and pointing back at us."

Joshua stood up too, trying to see what was happening. "I can't see."

"He looks mad and she's crying. Hide, he's looking this way. She told him about the milk and you wetting your pants."

"I can't see! Is he mad?"

"Yes, he's walking back and forth. He's saying something and looking at us. Get down, they're coming this way."

"Don't let them beat me, Deborah. I can't take it anymore."

"If they do, we will run away."

"Where will we go? We don't even know where we are."

"We'll go somewhere; anywhere they don't beat kids."

They watched as Lewis and Beverly went to the trunk and removed a cardboard box and a blanket. They went back to where they were and spread the blanket out.

"What are they doing?" Joshua asked.

"They put a blanket on the ground."

"Why."

"I don't know, Joshua."

They came back to the car. Beverly on Deborah's side, Lewis on Joshua's side. They opened the doors and Joshua looked up at Lewis. "Okay come on, we have a surprise for you."

"I want to stay in the car," Joshua said.

"No, you need to come with me."

"Please, let me stay in the car. Please."

Lewis said, "We can't eat in the car."

"We're going to eat here?" asked Deborah.

"Yes, we are. Now come on." Lewis held Joshua's hand as they walked toward the blanket. Deborah and Joshua sat down next to each other. Lewis noticed the boy was shaking and asked, "Joshua, are you cold?"

"No, Sir," as he looked down at the blanket.

"Why are you shivering?"

Beverly said, "He's not shivering, Lewis, he's trembling. He's scared to death." Lewis looked at Beverly. She was trying to hold back the tears, but it wasn't working.

Lewis took two steps and he was standing in front of Joshua. The boy was looking straight up with tears in his eyes. Lewis knew as tall as he was he must be scaring the boy even more. Lewis knelt on one knee and put his hand under the boys arm pits. When Lewis started lifting him up, the boy reached out to his sister. Deborah started to get up but Beverly put her hand on her shoulder to keep her in place. When Lewis had fully stood up the boy had both hands our reaching for his sister. He was crying now. "Joshua, look at me." Lewis was holding the boy as if he were a two year old. He took his hand and turned the boy's face to him. "Joshua, listen to me. I promise I will never beat you or Deborah. I promise you Beverly will never beat you or Deborah. Do you understand? No one will ever beat you or your sister again. I promise."

The boy nodded his head. Tears were streaming down his cheeks, and his nose was running. Lewis took out his handkerchief and wiped the boy's face. "Now, why don't you give me a hug, I need one." The boy threw his arms around Lewis's neck and started sobbing. Lewis knew these weren't tears of joy, fear or pain. These were tears of relief. Lewis walked around a few minutes, rubbing the boys back and telling him, "Everything is alright; everything is going to be alright."

Beverly watched Lewis and thought every time I think I can't love him anymore than I already do, he does something to make me love him more. Lewis put Joshua down between him and Beverly. "I want to sit beside Deborah."

"She's right there across from you. Now let's all hold hands and say the blessing."

After Beverly asked the Lord to bless the food and the four of them, Lewis asked, "What's for lunch?"

"Fried chicken, potato salad and baked beans."

Lewis said, "We are having a family picnic. Have you ever been on a picnic before?"

"We've never had a family before," answered Joshua.

Lewis looked at Beverly and then turned his head. He had to wipe his eyes. The boys answer stuck in Lewis's mind. Was the boy thinking we are a family now? Lewis didn't know the mind of a five year old. One day in someone's life doesn't make a family; a family was a lifetime, or it should be.

Lewis thought of Miss May saying she would pray that he and Beverly would have a boy and a girl. Twins. He dismissed that thought as soon as it entered his mind. Beverly put some of each item on the plates.

Five minutes later, Beverly felt a tap on her knee. She looked at Joshua. "Can I have a little more chicken?" he asked.

Deborah mouthed under her breath to him, "You're going to get us in trouble."

"Of course you can! I have plenty." She put more chicken and potato salad on his plate.

She reached out to Deborah. "Would you like more?"

Deborah answered, "Yes, Ma'am, please."

When everyone was finished eating, Lewis said, "Let's put the food away and go for a walk." He picked up the blanket and folded it. As the four walked Lewis held Joshua's hand, Joshua was holding Deborah's hand and Deborah was holding Beverly's hand.

"Where are we going?" Deborah wanted to know.

Beverly replied, "To our favorite place in the whole world. We call it Lookout Point."

Later, Lewis and Beverly watched as the kids played nearby. Joshua would pick up a blade of grass or clover and study it like he had never seen one before. Deborah would chase Joshua, who was laughing like crazy. He ran by and stopped. "I can run real fast in these shoes." He stretched out the word fast, and then took off. Deborah right behind him.

"I wonder if they have ever played outside before?" asked Beverly.

"It doesn't seem like they have."

Joshua ran by with his arms outstretched like a plane. "Look, I can fly."

Deborah came over and flopped down on the blanket and tried to catch her breath. "I can't catch him since he got those magic shoes."

Joshua ran by again and Deborah took off after him.

"Lewis, I would like to keep them. I can't stand the thought of them ending up somewhere like the place they were in. It would break my heart."

"Beverly, I don't know. I would love for them to be able to stay here, but we've only been married a little over a year and you just turned twenty one. I don't even know if they would let us keep them. I guess it wouldn't hurt to try. I wouldn't even know where to start."

"I know a Judge," said Beverly.

CHAPTER TWELVE

NOTHING VENTURED

NOTHING GAINED

They cleaned up the children and loaded them in the car. As they were pulling away, Beverly said, "Stop the car. There is something I need to take with us." She ran to the Deputy vehicle and retrieved the video tape of the duplex and the children.

On the way, Lewis asked, "What Judge do you know?"

"Jack Gordon. He's Jack Gordon's uncle. You probably met him at the funeral."

"I shook hands with him but that was all."

"I know. I've run into him several times and he asked about you. He said he has never had the chance to thank you."

"He doesn't have to thank me."

It was a long drive and they arrived at 3:45 p.m. While Lewis parked the car on the street, he saw Beverly with a child in each hand in tow. Lewis thought, she is on a mission.

Beverly had already rang the doorbell when Lewis caught up to them. A lady answered the door. Lewis assumed it was the Judge's wife.

Mrs. Gordon said, "Yes, can I help you? Oh, Beverly, I didn't recognize you."

"That's okay, Ma'am. We need to see the Judge."

"He said he didn't want to be disturbed. Could this wait until Monday?"

"No, Mrs. Gordon this can't wait until Monday. Please tell him we are here." She left them standing on the front porch. She came back five minutes later.

"He prefers you wait until Monday."

Beverly stepped inside. "Tell the Judge this will only take seven and a half minutes."

Mrs. Gordon went back to see the Judge again. A few minutes later, Judge Gordon stepped into the living room.

"Your Honor, I want you to watch this. It only lasts seven and half minutes."

"Beverly, its Saturday. The football game comes on in five minutes."

"Your Honor, these two children are more important than your football game." She pulled the two children in front of her. She didn't know if the Judge had seen them or not.

"But its Texas and Oklahoma. The Red River Classic."

"Yes, Sir, I know you went to Oklahoma and your brother went to Texas and the two of you have a five dollar bet every year."

"How do you know all that?"

"Everybody knows that, Your Honor."

"You are not going to give me any peace and quiet unless I watch this, are you?"

"No, your Honor. I'm not."

"Out of respect for your father, I am going to give you seven and a half minutes. But that is all. You understand?"

"Yes, Sir."

"Have a seat."

Lewis glanced at his watch as the Judge left the room. It was exactly 4:00. The children were sitting between the two of them.

Deborah said, "Who is that man?"

Beverly answered, "Right now he is the most important man in the world."

Lewis kept looking at his watch. He showed it to Beverly. The watch showed that it was now 4:30.

"That's good."

"Why is that good?"

"You haven't seen the tape. Trust me, that's good."

At 4:35, the Judge came back. He stuck his head in the adjacent room. "Honey, can you watch the children for a few minutes?"

Mrs. Gordon came out. "Sure."

As the children were walking into the other room with Mrs. Gordon, Joshua looked over his shoulder and waved. Then he said, "Bye."

Beverly smiled and said, "We're not leaving you."

A timid, "okay," came from Deborah.

The Judge said, "Come with me. Let's talk in my office."

In his office, he directed them to two chairs. "I watched it four times."

"Yes, Sir, your Honor, I don't want these two children to ever be put in a situation like that again. They have suffered enough."

"I agree they have, but there are procedures that have to be followed."

Beverly said, "Your Honor, we would like to adopt them." She had decided to shoot for the moon and settle for foster parenting.

Judge Gordon knitted his fingers together, leaned back in his chair, and rested his hands on his stomach. "Beverly, how old are you?"

"I just turned twenty one."

"Lewis?"

"I'm twenty six, almost twenty seven."

"How long have the two of you been married?"

"A little over a year, your Honor."

"You see where I am going with this, don't you?"

"Sir, I don't think age can always be a sign of maturity and responsibility," said Beverly.

"I agree," said the Judge. "But the State likes, number one, that the parents be married longer than a year and number two, be older than twenty one."

"There must be something we can do. It breaks my heart to even think about them being moved from foster home to foster home. Who knows what situation they may be in next?"

"Lewis, you are not having much to say about this."

"Your Honor, I couldn't say it any better than my wife. Those two children are precious. They are certainly precious to us. I made them a promise and I intend on keeping that promise. I don't make a promise I can't keep."

"What did you promise them?"

"I promised them that no one would ever beat them again."

"I see."

"Your Honor, if you will speak to them, I'm sure you will find they are very special children. We want what is right for them and we feel we are the right ones to raise them," said Beverly.

"All right, I have missed most of the game already, send one of them in." "They are twins, your Honor. It may be best if you speak to them together."

"I can do that."

The children came into the office. Lewis and Beverly went back into the living room and sat down. The Judge looked at the two children and asked, "Do you know who I am?"

Deborah said, "Yes, Sir, you are the most important man in the world."

The Judge chuckled and said, "Sometimes I think that myself." The kids just looked at him. "Why do you like living with Beverly and Lewis?"

Joshua spoke up for the first time. "Because they don't beat you when you spill your milk."

Deborah said, "We hold hands with them when we walk to Lookout Point."

"Lookout Point?"

"It's our favorite place in the whole world," she added. The Judge couldn't think of any place around here like that.

"I'm not sure I know where that is?"

"Come visit us and we'll show you," said Joshua.

"What would you do if you had to live somewhere else?"

"Run away and come back to them."

The Judge said, "Let me see what I can do. Can you tell them I will be with them in a few minutes?"

"Yes, Sir," said Deborah.

"The four of you can wait in the den and watch the football game. At least someone will get to watch it."

He picked up the phone and called the Sheriff's office. "Kerney County Sheriff's office, Mary speaking, can I help you?"

"Mary, this is Judge Gordon."

"How may I help you, Judge?"

"I need to know the names of the two people arrested yesterday evening. This is about the two minor children." Mary gave him the names and the Judge wrote them down. "Can you tell me if they are still in jail?"

"Both are still in the hospital, your Honor."

"The hospital? I didn't know that."

"Yes, Sir, the man had beaten the woman up pretty bad. She's lucky to be alive."

"And the man? How did he end up in the hospital?"

"One of our deputies had to use force to prevent him from killing the woman."

The Judge nodded his head in understanding. The sheriff's deputies were big fellows. They could handle about anyone.

"Who was the deputy?"

"Deputy MacDonald, your Honor."

"Deputy MacDonald! You mean Beverly MacDonald?"

"Yes, Sir. She knocked him out and handcuffed him. We're real proud of her."

"What did she hit him with, a tire iron?" He remembered seeing a tire iron used to pry the lock apart.

"No, Sir. She used an official police equipment item."

"What did she use, Mary?"

"Her daddy's Maglite."

"The one he used to make a tourniquet?"

"One and the same."

"So, it saved two people's lives."

"Looks that way," answered Mary.

"That flashlight needs to be put on display in a museum."

"She would never part with it, your Honor."

"I should buy stock in the company."

"You want the number?"

"I'll get it Monday. Thanks Mary, you have a good day."

His next call was to his brother in Texas. When his brother answered, Judge Gordon said, "I've got a big problem."

"You bet you do. We're winning 21 to 3."

"No, this is more important than the football game."

"More important than Texas and Oklahoma? Now that's a big problem. Talk fast its halftime."

Fifteen minutes later, he called Lewis and Beverly back into his office. "I talked to my brother. He is a law professor in Texas. He knows about things like this, much better than I do. I handle criminal cases not family and children services."

Beverly had a sinking feeling in her stomach. "Please, God, don't let them take them away."

"He said I could grant you temporary custody until it goes through the system. He sees no problem with it being made permanent. In four or five years, you can then apply for adoption."

"Thank you, Lord," said the two in unison.

As they were leaving Beverly hugged the Judge. The Judge could see the tears in her eyes. He shook Lewis's hand.

"Lewis, I never got to properly thank you for bringing Jack's body home. I want you to know it meant a lot to the whole family. I wished I would have thanked you sooner."

"Your Honor, it was an honor and a privilege to be able to escort Jack home. Jack was the best friend I ever had."

The Judge said, "Thank you."

As Joshua was leaving the den, he looked over his shoulder at the game. "What are they playing?"

"Football," answered Lewis.

"When I get big, I want to play that."

CHAPTER THIRTEEN

HAPPY HOUR

That night at the dinner table, Lewis and Beverly reinstituted 'Happy Hour.' They would spend one hour laughing, talking and playing games with the children. They had no actual children's games in the house. They would make do with what they had.

Lewis went over the rules three times with both of them until they understood what they were supposed to do. Lewis said, "Since Beverly is the lady of the house she will go first."

Beverly looked at Joshua, then Deborah and finally at Lewis. She let the suspense build.

"Joshua, do you have any sixes?"

"Go fish."

Lewis knew nothing about child psychology but he noticed Joshua seemed to be more trusting of people than Deborah. He held his cards where anyone could see them. Deborah held hers close to her chest and didn't spread them very wide. She would peek at her cards. She would make a Mississippi riverboat gambler proud. Lewis figured she's very competitive. If only he knew.

Beverly tucked the children into bed and taught them a simple prayer. She told them a good night story. For the time being they would sleep together. She didn't want any sudden changes the children wouldn't understand.

In the middle of the night, she heard a scream. She and Lewis sat up immediately. Beverly said, "I think that was Joshua," and got up. She quietly moved across the hall. She heard Deborah saying, "Joshua, you have to stop crying. You are going to wake them up. You are going to get both of us in trouble."

"I had a bad dream and it scared me."

Beverly walked into the room and turned on a small lamp on the dresser. Joshua tried to hide under the cover. Deborah was still raised up on her elbow.

"He's okay now. He got scared is all. He's quiet now."

Beverly went to Joshua's side of the bed and sat down on the edge. She pulled the covers back a little where she could see him. He was wiping his eyes.

"Joshua, did you have a bad dream?"

"Yes, Ma'am."

"Do you remember what the dream was about?"

"No, Ma'am. But it scared me."

"I have bad dreams every once in a while," said Beverly.

"You do?"

"But you know what. When I wake up and see where I am and I know I am in my safe bed in my safe home, I go right back to sleep. Everyone has bad dreams now and then."

"Deborah doesn't," said Joshua.

"Maybe Deborah has bad dreams and doesn't tell you."

"Deborah's not afraid of anything."

"Well, that's good. You know what? I have good dreams, too."

"You do?"

"Sure, let me tell you some." She pulled the covers back and climbed into bed between the two children. "Not long ago I would dream that I would marry the most wonderful man." She looked toward the door and saw Lewis standing in the shadows. "He would love me all the time and take care of me. Every day he would do something that was so kind for me. He was really handsome and you know what? He would sometimes get up early and cook breakfast for me."

She saw Lewis give her the thumbs up on breakfast and go into their bedroom. "He would be the best husband in the whole, wide world."

"Why did you end up with Lewis?" asked Deborah.

"I heard that," said Lewis laughing, which caused Beverly to laugh. The children giggled, too.

"Let's snuggle up and go back to sleep," said Beverly with a smile.

CHAPTER FOURTEEN

RAISE YOUR HAND

2 TIMOTHY 3:15

The next morning, Beverly dressed the children for Sunday school and church. She went into the children's Sunday school class with them. Every once in a while Joshua would look at her and smile. It was an adorable smile, not too big. Not a posed smile just a natural smile.

After Sunday school, she met Lewis and they entered the church. Brother Lawson was in the vestibule greeting everyone. Beverly said, "Brother Lawson, I'd like to introduce you to Joshua and Deborah."

Brother Lawson shook Joshua's hand and said, "Joshua is one of my favorite people in the Bible." Then he shook hands with Deborah. "What a pretty name for a pretty girl. There is a Deborah in the Bible, too. Did you know that?"

"No, Sir," answered Deborah as she looked up at Beverly.

"Oh yes, both are very famous as a matter of fact." Then he said to Beverly "Are they here for the weekend?"

"I hope a lot longer than that. We will talk about it later," answered Beverly.

"Lewis, how are you?"

"Very well, thank you."

When everyone was seated, the congregation sang a few songs then went over the prayer list. Collecting tithes and offerings came next. Beverly gave each child a dollar to put in the collection plate. The children sat between Lewis and Beverly. Joshua was next to Lewis.

Brother Lawson stepped to the pulpit and welcomed everyone then led them in prayer. Brother Lawson was ending his third year at this church. He had discussed with his wife about leaving and moving to a larger church. He would speak with the deacons after the service. He felt like he was in a rut here. The congregation wasn't responding like he had hoped.

He had a folder with his sermon. He opened it and asked the congregation to turn to the Gospel of John, chapter eight. He read the first six verses. Jesus had been asked by the scribes and Pharisees about stoning a woman caught in the act of adultery.

"Now I want you to notice Jesus stooped down and with his finger wrote something in the dirt. No one knows what he wrote. That is lost to history. Wouldn't it be nice to know what he wrote? We can only speculate. Then Jesus said something and I would like to read to you what he said, 'He that is without sin among you let him cast the first stone.'" Brother Lawson paused for a few seconds. "Now I ask you," looking out at the congregation, "If there is anyone here who is without sin, I want you to raise your hand."

Two small hands were raised.

This had never happened to Brother Lawson before. It rattled him so much that his folder with the sermon fell to the floor. Compounding the problem, he had run out of staples that morning. His sermon fluttered around his feet. Then he was hit with a mental block. Every preacher's worse nightmare. His brain just seemed to shift into neutral. He looked at Joshua and Deborah. Joshua and Deborah, that's it. I will preach on Joshua and Deborah.

Lewis had lowered Joshua's arm and Beverly finally managed to lower Deborah's. Then Brother Lawson did something he had never done before. He moved from behind the pulpit and stood in front of the congregation and started to preach. "Faith and responsibility. I want to talk about faith and responsibility. God picked two to lead Israel. Why those two? They had faith and they were responsible people. Faith and responsibility. I will be using those two words a lot today. It seems as though lately this nation has drifted away from faith and responsibility. We see it on the news all the time. We see people doing all sorts of evil things. Not just here but everywhere; everywhere we look we see evil lurking out there ready to harm someone.

"The Bible tells us a lot of people had the Faith. Abraham, Moses and most important our Savior Jesus Christ. Somehow, God wants me to talk about two people of great faith. a man and a woman. The man I am sure you have heard about, the woman you may not have. Sadly, a lot of times the woman doesn't get the credit she deserves." He paused and several women nodded their heads. Several poked their husbands in the side with their elbows. The preacher smiled and continued.

"The two people are Joshua and Deborah. We are privileged to have two children here today named Joshua and Deborah. I would ask them to raise their hands, but they beat me to it." Then he smiled at the MacDonald's.

Lewis smiled. Beverly blushed.

"God put the Nation of Israel into the hands of Joshua and Deborah. Then God guided them in their paths."

Brother Lawson heard an "Amen" from the back of the church, and then he got wound up. He heard several "Hallelujahs and a "Preach it Brother." He had a revival going on. Pacing back and forth Brother Lawson said, "I wonder if there is anyone in this congregation that God would point out and say, 'I choose you.'" He pointed his finger directly at Lewis. "I wonder if there is anyone else in this congregation." He pointed to someone else. "How about you?" The man shook his head. "It doesn't have to be a man, it could be a woman. Is there a woman here that God would pick to lead this nation? I would like to think every man and woman in this church has the faith and is responsible enough to lead this great nation of ours. You see if God chooses you, He will guide you. How can you fail if you are being led by him?"

Several "Amens" were shouted.

When Joshua heard his name he was straining to see but someone was sitting in front of him. "I can't see." Lewis picked him up and put him in his lap. Beverly smiled and put Deborah in her lap.

Brother Lawson continued to preach. Neither he nor the church had been this excited in the three years he had been here. Then he wound down and asked those to come forward for the alter call. Almost half the congregation came forward. There was not a dry eye in the house. Brother Lawson was exhausted and invigorated, if you can be both.

As the congregation was leaving more people than ever told him it was the best sermon they had heard him preach. When Joshua and Deborah came through he thanked them for coming and told them to be sure and come back. Beverly said, "I apologize, Brother Lawson."

"Why?" asked the preacher.

"About them raising their hands."

"How old are they?"

"Five."

"Perhaps they are without sin. Beverly, when we say everyone has sinned, and they have, I don't think they are talking about someone that hasn't reached the age of accountability. I'm glad they pointed that out to me."

After everyone left, his wife said, "That was the best sermon you have ever delivered. What made you change your topic?"

"Divine intervention," he replied and laughed. Then he added, "We're staying."

On the way home Lewis said, "Oh, I meant to tell you this Friday but we got sort of tied up with other things. I was talking to Miss May and she asked about us having children. I told her I wouldn't mind having a couple, maybe a boy and a girl. Guess what she said?"

"I don't have a clue what Miss May might say," she replied as she laughed.

"She said that she was going to pray that we would have a boy and a girl...That we would have twins."

"Lewis, you don't think for one minute that us getting custody of the children was because of Miss May saying she was going to pray we would have twins, a boy and a girl. I believe in prayer just as much as anyone else, but that's a little fast, isn't it?"

"Well, when I walked in Friday and saw them, it was downright spooky."

CHAPTER FIFTEEN

SHED A TEAR

After the children were in bed they made some plans. The children were the center of the plans.

"I hope it works," said Beverly.

"I hope it does, too. I don't know if they have ever been separated. Especially for an hour."

They left the house before breakfast. By prior arrangement, Lewis and Joshua were up front. With, as Lewis said, "Ladies in the back."

He pulled up in front of the strip mall at the edge of town. Beverly and Deborah got out. Lewis drove off.

Joshua started screaming. "You're leaving Deborah!"

"We'll see them in a few minutes." In the rearview mirror Lewis saw Deborah point and start running after the car. Beverly caught her and picked her up. Deborah was still pointing at the car when they went inside.

Joshua screamed even more and started crying. Lewis was feeling bad about making him cry. He was expecting him to be upset but not like this. Joshua was panicking. Lewis tried to quieten him but it just wasn't working. He pulled the car into the diner and parked. Joshua was a little quieter now. He wasn't screaming anymore but tears were streaming down his face.

Lewis carried him inside and sat on one side of the booth and Joshua stood at the end of the table. He didn't want to sit down. "I want Deborah. Please, Deborah is all I got."

Lewis didn't say anything. He just sat there feeling like the biggest jerk in the world.

"Where's Deborah? I want Deborah!"

Lewis ordered hot cakes and sausage for the two of them.

"I want to go find Deborah. Deborah is all I got." The biggest tears Lewis had ever seen were rolling down Joshua's face.

Lewis bowed his head and said his blessing. He added, "Lord, help me out here, please."

"Joshua, you need to sit down and eat your food."

"I'm not hungry! I want Deborah!"

Lewis kept eating. By now he was almost finished. He couldn't take it anymore.

"Eat your food and I will take you to Deborah." Lewis thought, 'Well, this didn't work. Don't know when we will try something like this again.' Joshua picked up his spoon. Lewis figured he would either, take a bite and say he wasn't hungry anymore or he would try to gobble it down as fast as he could. Joshua put a bite in his mouth and chewed real fast and swallowed. Suddenly a look came over his face. He licked his lips and took another bite. He climbed into the seat opposite of Lewis and sat on his knees. He took another bite and chewed real slow this time. He seemed to be savoring every morsel. He saw Lewis was finished eating and he put his arm around his plate and pulled it closer to him. He was watching Lewis. Lewis smiled. Joshua was thinking I got my eye on you. Between the first bite and the second he seemed to forget he needed Deborah.

When Joshua was finished Lewis wiped his hands and mouth. He picked him up and they went outside. They walked to a small kid's playground next to the diner. Joshua looked at all the things to play on. He had never seen anything like this before.

"Joshua, you can play. I will be right here with you."

The boy ran to a plastic horse mounted on a coil spring. He got on and rocked back and forth for about ten seconds. He got off and ran to a seesaw and bounced up and down. Then the monkey bars and then the slide; never staying longer than a few seconds on each one. After trying them all he looked around to see if he had missed anything.

Lewis asked, "Which one of them do you like the best?"

"I like the horsie the best."

"Well, let's go back and ride it some more."

"Okay."

Thirty minutes later Lewis said, "There's Deborah."

Joshua ran up to her and said, "Where did you go?"

"Shopping."

"How? We don't have any money."

"She does! She bought all kinds of stuff."

"Did you get something for me?"

"Of course! I wouldn't buy something for me and not get something for you."

"What did you get me?"

"Well, how about a real live cowboy hat and some cowboy boots, a big winter coat, some clothes and some toys and some games."

"Wow."

"You can see everything when we get home," Beverly said. "How did it go with you?"

"He wasn't a bit of trouble." Beverly looked at Lewis for a long time. "Okay, he pitched a fit for twenty minutes. I thought it wasn't going to work."

"What won him over? He looked like he was having a blast when we got here."

"Hotcakes and sausage. You wouldn't believe what happened Beverly. He was really scaring me and after one bite he was fine. I've never seen anything like it."

The four of them went to a store specializing in household items. Beverly had a shopping cart. Lewis had one, too. They went down the aisle that had bedspreads, curtains and lamps. Lewis stopped and picked up a bedspread. He called to Beverly, "I've never seen anything like this, have you?"

"What is it dear?" This also got Joshua and Deborah's attention.

"It's a bedspread with a race car on it." At the mention of a race car, Joshua had to see.

"Wow, a real live race car," said Joshua.

"Look, here are some curtains with airplanes on them," remarked Beverly.

Joshua piped up, "Can I see them?"

"Sure! Do you like them?"

Joshua had a big smile on his face. "I sure do. I love airplanes."

"Hey, over here is a lamp made from a football helmet. I wonder where they come up with these ideas." Lewis said this like he was amazed. "Look here, this is a painting of a cowboy riding a horse. This is really good. Don't you think this looks real, Joshua?"

"It sure does. I like horses."

All these items went into the shopping cart. They had agreed that when Joshua decided to sleep alone he could. They were not going to push the issue.

After getting home they unpacked everything. They showed Joshua the things that Beverly had picked out for him. Deborah then showed Lewis and Joshua what she had gotten. They put the spread on the bed. Hung the curtains and plugged in the lamp. Beverly was holding the painting. "I don't know where to hang this, Lewis?"

"I don't know either, dear."

Joshua said, "I'd put it right there." He pointed to a place on the wall opposite the head of the bed. They hung the painting.

"Why did you want it there?"

Joshua answered "So you can see it when you're in bed."

No one slept in the room that night. Joshua did go in a few times to look around. He liked everything in it.

The next morning, Lewis was up early. Joshua came into the dining room where Lewis was drinking his coffee and sat down. "Good morning, Joshua."

"Good morning," said Joshua as he was rubbing the sleep out of his eyes. "What are we going to do today?"

"I don't know," Lewis answered.

"I know what we can do today. We can go back to the diner and get hot cakes and sausage. Then we can go to the playground and the toy store."

"Well, what about Deborah?"

"She'll be alright with Miss Beverly."

"I'll go tell them," said Lewis.

They took the old Jeep. When you were going thirty miles an hour it seemed like you were going ninety. Joshua laughed at every bump in the road.

"Lewis drives real fast," said Joshua.

"I'm not going real fast."

"Uh huh, Lewis drives real fast."

Lewis thought with my luck, I will get stopped by the police and he will say, "Sir, do you know how fast you were driving?" and Joshua will say, "Lewis drives real fast." Lewis slowed down.

After the diner and the playground, they went to the toy store and bought a toy airplane for Joshua.

"How about Deborah? Shouldn't we buy her something?" asked Lewis. They made another round through the store. Then Lewis ran by the hardware store and then home.

When they were home the kids played in the family room. Beverly and Lewis were sitting at the dining room table. "Well, how did it go?" asked Beverly.

Lewis laughed and said, "Let me tell you about it. It was so funny, you had to be there."

"Why? What happened?"

"Well, after breakfast and the playground we went to the toy store. There is a storm drain in the middle of the parking lot, just a metal grate. I was carrying him because cars come through there pretty fast and they may not see him. When we walked past the storm drain Joshua said, 'Water goes down that hole.' I stopped and acted like I didn't know what he was talking about, so I asked him what he said. 'Water goes down that hole.' I asked him, 'What water?' He said, 'Rain falls out of the sky, hits the concrete, runs downhill and goes into that hole.' He was pointing at the sky and then the concrete, then he pointed at the drain. So I said, 'I don't understand.' He took in a deep breath and then let it out. He shook his head like I can't believe he doesn't know this. Then he said, 'Look, rain falls out of the sky, hits the concrete, runs downhill and goes into that hole.'" Well, I put my hands on my knees and he did the same. It was bone dry in the bottom so I said, 'Then where does the water go?' He looked at me and I could tell he hadn't thought that far ahead. He shrugged his shoulders and said, 'I don't know.' I could see another pipe in the bottom and said, 'I bet rain falls out of the sky, hits the concrete, runs down the hill, then goes down that hole and I bet it goes in that other hole. I wonder where it goes then.' I picked him up and we walked around looking for where it goes from there. Beverly I wish you could have seen him. It was so funny. We had fun. He is really a smart kid. Then we went into the hardware store and I thought I was going to die laughing in there."

"What did he do there?"

"Well, it wasn't just him. You know Chester Farris; he was sitting on a stool by the counter and I was paying for my items. He stuck his finger out at Joshua and asked him to pull it. Well, Joshua pulled it and when he did Chester broke wind."

"Oh, no!" exclaimed Beverly.

"Oh, yeah! Joshua ran to the other side of the room and was looking at Chester like, I got my eye on you."

"That's awful," said Beverly.

"Oh, it doesn't end there. Jimmy Parker and Tommy came in. Chester stuck his finger out at Tommy and said, 'Pull my finger.' Well, Joshua was watching and said, 'Nooo, don't pull that finger,' and he ran across the room and said, 'Whatever you do, don't pull his finger.' Tommy said, 'What happens if you pull his finger?' Joshua walked off and said 'You don't want to know. You really don't want to know.' Well, Tommy being curious like anyone that age laughingly pulled his finger. Then both boys took off to the other side of the room laughing. Joshua said 'I told you not to pull his finger but you had to do it anyway.'

When we left Joshua asked me who 'was that man.' I said, 'He's Chester Farris.' Joshua said, 'him a nut.'"

Beverly shook her head and said, "You need to keep him away from Chester Farris."

"I will. But you don't have to worry; Joshua won't get within twenty feet of him."

"Have you noticed that Joshua is always watching you?"

"Well, I noticed the first day he was always staring at me but I haven't noticed it since then. Why? Why do you think he's watching me?"

"You know how sometimes you put your hands on your hips when we're talking."

"Yeah, what about it?"

"Well, he tries to copy you. Every few seconds he'll look at how you are standing or if you crossing your legs or you cross your arms, he will do the same thing."

"So, you are saying I am the posture role model?" he asked and then laughed.

After happy hour at the dinner table they grabbed a blanket and headed up to Lookout Point. Lewis walked about twenty feet away and was looking at the Triple D Ranch across the road. Joshua walked over and stood beside him. Lewis put his hands on his hips. Joshua did the same. Lewis folded his arms across his chest and Joshua glanced over at Lewis and did the same. Lewis put his hands in his back pockets. Joshua did the same. Lewis was changing positions about every twenty seconds.

Beverly was laughing.

Deborah asked, "What are they doing?"

"It looks like they are playing 'Simon says.'"

Lewis reached down and picked Joshua up and hugged him. Lewis said, "I love you."

Joshua answered, "I love you, too."

Beverly hadn't felt this way in a long time. Until the children came here, she hadn't realized something was missing in her life. She put her arm around Deborah and hugged her closer. "I love you," she said and squeezed her.

"I know. I love you, too."

Eight hundred miles away a Veteran sat in a wheelchair and hoped and prayed.

THINKING ALIKE

The next day, Lewis was working at the Triple D Ranch. Beverly had bought some crayons and coloring paper to keep the children occupied. She showed them the paper and said, "Draw and color whatever you like; just make sure you only do it on the paper."

"But I don't know how," Joshua said.

"Well, that's the fun of color crayons. You don't have to know how. Just draw anything, a bird, a horse. You've seen the horses on the ranch. Draw one of them. Whatever makes you happy. Just draw and color."

She put Deborah at the dining room table.

"Joshua why don't you use the coffee table. Remember; just draw on the paper, okay."

After an hour, she asked Deborah if she was finished. Her drawing was a small hilltop. A man was holding hands with a small boy. The boy was holding hands with a small girl who was holding hands with a woman. The four were looking towards the sun which was colored yellow.

"This is very good, Deborah. Is this Lookout Point and the four of us are watching the sun come up?"

"Yes, Ma'am."

"Does that make you happy?"

"Yes, Ma'am."

She went into the living room. "Are you finished Joshua?"

"I think so." Beverly looked at his drawings. She didn't know what to think. Joshua had drawn the same scene except his sun was colored orange.

"Is this Lookout point at sunset?"

"Yes, Ma'am."

"And does this make you happy?"

"Yes, Ma'am."

She couldn't wait to show it to Lewis. She knew the two had not looked at each other's drawing. She didn't know what to make of this. To think alike in different rooms was amazing to her.

When Lewis got home, she showed him the two drawings. He rubbed his eyes and his chin and ran his hands through his hair.

"What exactly did you tell them?"

"Well, I told them they could draw whatever they wanted, a bird, a horse, whatever made them happy."

"Maybe when you said, 'what makes you happy' suggested to them to draw what makes them happy. I don't know? Maybe they can communicate with each other, being twins, in a way that we don't understand. I don't think we should be carrying out experiments with them. We will just watch them and see how it goes."

"It may be like ESP."

"No, Miss May is the one that does stuff like that."

After breakfast, Beverly would sit with the children and teach them to count, identify colors and the letters of the alphabet. She taught them how to spell simple words. They were so proud to know how to spell and write their names. The children enjoyed learning. Beverly was afraid they would be behind the other children in class.

After they had been there for two weeks, Beverly realized she hadn't worked in the greenhouse since they had gotten there. She thought the two of them would enjoy seeing things growing; things they had planted themselves.

After lunch, she took them to the greenhouse. Beverly enjoyed working there. She planted food and flowers year round.

"What do you do in here?" Deborah wanted to know.

"We grow food," answered Beverly.

"We have to grow our own food?" asked Joshua.

"Well, someone has to, right. It doesn't just do it by itself," answered Beverly.

The two children were looking at each other. Beverly didn't notice. She started gathering what was ready. "Okay, let's plant some squash and I believe okra would be nice."

At the dinner table, Lewis noticed they didn't eat very much. "Aren't you guys' hungry?"

Deborah said, "No, Sir."

"We didn't mean to eat all of your food," Joshua said and looked down at his plate. Lewis looked at Beverly and held his palms up like 'what's going on?'

Beverly said, "I think there has been a misunderstanding." She looked at the two children then went to the freezer and opened the door. "Come over here and let me show you something."

The two walked over and peered into the freezer.

"See, there is plenty of food in here." They just stared into the freezer. They had never seen so much food before. "I grow things in the greenhouse because I like to work with dirt and plants. It's fun growing your own food. There are some vegetables you can't get at the grocery store year round. And, they just taste better when you grow them yourself. In a week or two those seeds that we planted today will start to sprout and it's fun watching them grow. Now, let's go sit down and eat your food. I didn't mean to make you feel bad. I will have to show you how we get it ready for the freezer."

The next day, Beverly loaded the children into the car and put some food in a bag. "Where are we going?" asked Joshua.

"We are going to see a very special friend. You will like her."

After they arrived, Beverly and the kids got out of the car. She knocked on the door. "Miss May, it's me, Beverly."

"Hold your horses. It takes me a while to git my giddy up agoing," came from in the house. Miss May opened the door and blinked a few times. "Come in, come in."

"Miss May, we brought you some fresh vegetables. There are some tomatoes, okra, squash and some really nice strawberries. We picked them yesterday."

"Just put them on the counter, Miss Beverly."

When Beverly came into the living room, Miss May was leaning on her stick, stooped over at the waist. She was looking at Deborah and Joshua.

"These are the twins I was praying that you and Lewis would get; a boy and a girl. What are their names?" asked Miss May.

"Joshua and Deborah," answered Beverly.

"Those are great names. Straight out of the good book." Beverly was thinking, how does she know they are twins and how does she know they are living with us.

"Joshua and Deborah, say hello to Miss May."

"Hello," they said at the same time.

Miss May blinked a few times. "They sure are pretty smart, too. I can tell."

"Miss May, is there anything I can do for you while I'm here?"

"Naw, I's fine. Jest a little slow moving is about all."

"Well, we're going to be going then."

"Well, let me pay you for all that." She dug her handkerchief out and untied the corner and handed Beverly two dimes.

"That's way too much, Miss May. Let me give you some change." Beverly handed her a nickel.

In the car, Joshua asked, "How old is she?"

"Nobody knows."

Joshua thought about it for a while. "I bet she's a hundred."

Beverly laughed and said, "You might not be far off."

CHAPTER SIXTEEN

BIRTHDAY WISH

When Beverly pulled into the driveway, she saw Lewis talking with the sheriff in the driveway. Beverly said, "How about going inside and eat some cookies and drink a glass of milk."

After watching the children go inside, she walked over to the sheriff. Beverly had resigned from the department when she got custody of the children.

"How are you doing, Sir? What brings you out this way?"

"Hey, Beverly. I thought I would drop by and fill you in on your case."

"My case?" asked Beverly.

"The child abuse case, when you rescued the kids. Well, the strangest thing happened. The woman pleads guilty at her arraignment. She got six years. When we moved her back to jail, I was curious because we didn't have much on her. I asked her why. She said it was the only way she could get away from him; meaning her husband, and be protected. I think it was one of those cases where she was beaten into submission, if you know what I mean."

Lewis nodded his head, "I've heard of that. Hard to believe stuff like that goes on in a civilized country."

"Did she say anything about the children? I'd really like to know what."

"As a matter of fact she did. She said, 'Please, make sure they are placed in a loving home.' She gave me their names and their birthday. I gave those to Lewis already. Then the public defender told her not to talk to me anymore. The low life jerk! He probably wants to soak the taxpayer for money on an appeal. The husband's trial isn't coming up for another month. I think she's afraid he won't get sent to prison and if both were out, she's afraid he'd kill her and she might be right. He's pretty big and strong. You took a chance Beverly. Don't get me wrong; I am glad you did what you did. If not, she would be dead. It could have gone the other way you know. One trip out here for a notification is enough for me.

"By the way, the kids look happy and healthy and with a birthday coming up day after tomorrow, I'm sure they'll be even happier."

"Birthday! You mean their birthday is Friday?" asked Beverly.

"I believe that's the date. You may want to double check it."

Beverly looked at the paper Lewis had been holding "Yep, its Friday. We have a lot of work to do."

"Birthday party?"

"Birthday party. I need to call Momma and see if she can bake a cake and buy some presents. She also needs to call and invite the neighbors and their kids. I won't be able to do that and keep it a secret."

Lewis said, "Thank you for dropping by, Sheriff."

Beverly called her mother and asked her to take care of things. There was also something she wanted her mother to buy for her. Alice was excited about the party.

"I'll try to remember what I bought for you. I bet I have a photo in the scrapbook."

"Don't forget Joshua."

"What do you buy a six year old boy? Don't worry. I will think of something."

Beverly decided that six o'clock was the best time for the party. Now, how to get the kids out of the house for an hour. Lewis came up with an idea he thought would work.

At 4:50, he loaded the children in the Jeep and drove to the far corner of the Triple D Ranch. He parked thirty yards from the tree line. "Okay, we need to be very quiet. I saw a deer a few weeks ago and we want to see if he comes back."

"What do we do if he comes back?" asked Deborah.

"Well, we will watch it and see what it does. It's a lot of fun."

Joshua pointed to the front and said, "Deer."

Lewis looked and didn't see anything.

Deborah said, "I don't see it."

"Maybe it was something else," said Lewis.

Joshua shook his head and said, "Deer."

Lewis looked again and didn't see it. "Are you sure, Joshua?"

Joshua nodded his head and pointed and said, "Deer." The deer stepped out. It just seemed to materialize there.

Lewis said, "Be very quiet, okay. We don't want to spook it."

The kids were fascinated. The deer grazed twenty yards away. Joshua pointed again and tapped Lewis on the shoulder as another one stepped out and then another. Finally, a nice buck joined them. The deer were so close even Lewis was amazed. He had only seen one deer a few weeks ago.

He smiled and thought he really didn't even expect to see one. He was just trying to get the kids out of the house for an hour.

After the deer moved on, Lewis started up the Jeep and drove to a small lake. "Let's get out. Don't get too close to the water." He went near the water's edge. He had a slice of bread in his shirt pocket. He pinched off a small piece and rolled it into a small ball the size of a pea. He threw it in the water. A fish took it as soon as it hit the water. He pinched off another piece, rolled it into a ball and handed it to Deborah. "Go ahead and throw it in." He was pinching off another piece for Joshua. He kept doing this till the bread was gone.

"Sometimes when I am back here I will see an eagle. I think there is a nest nearby." The kids looked around, up in the air and the trees but didn't see one. "Maybe next time we'll see one. That was a good job spotting those deer, Joshua."

Joshua beamed and flashed a smile. When they pulled into the driveway, the children saw all the cars.

"Why are all these cars here?" asked Deborah.

"Well, let's find out. We must have company."

"SURPRISE!" Then everyone started singing Happy Birthday. Joshua and Deborah didn't know what to do so they did nothing.

Beverly walked over and hugged Joshua. "Happy Birthday, Joshua," she said. Then she hugged Deborah. "Happy Birthday, Deborah."

Lewis rubbed the top of their heads. "Happy Birthday, guys."

"Are you ready to open your presents?"

"We're getting presents?" asked Deborah.

"Sure, on your birthday you get presents."

"And you get a birthday cake made especially for you," said Alice.

As the guests crowded around, they handed them their gifts. Deborah opened hers first and she got a doll. Her eyes got huge and she hugged the doll to her.

Joshua opened his first one and it was a book. He was disappointed because he didn't know how to read. He opened it and let out a shriek. "It's got planes in it." He flipped through the pages. He was so excited he ran around the room showing everyone. "There must be a hundred planes in here. I love planes. When I get big, I want to fly a real plane." He couldn't take his eyes off the book.

Lewis leaned down and said, "Be careful, you don't want to tear it. You have some other gifts to open."

"This is the best present in the whole wide world."

"Let me put it somewhere until you finish opening your other presents and eat your cake, okay?"

Joshua slowly handed him the book and said, "Be careful and don't tear it."

"Don't worry, I won't," said Lewis as he smiled and rubbed Joshua on the head.

"When I get big, I want to fly a plane," said Joshua.

Each of the children brought a small gift. The adults brought gifts that were a little more practical. Each gift they opened was like opening a treasure chest.

Lewis was standing beside Beverly. "They sure are excited, aren't they?"

Beverly smiled and said, "They probably have never had presents before, much less a birthday party. I'd be excited, too."

Alice walked into the room and said, "Everybody ready for some cake."

Everyone went into the dining room. There were two cakes; a chocolate cake and a vanilla icing cake. Each had the kid's names on it and six candles. Joshua's was the chocolate cake. There was a chair in front of each cake.

"Sit down now." Alice had already lit the candles.

Beverly said, "When you blow out the candles, close your eyes and make a wish and don't tell anyone or it might not come true. Now, close your eyes and blow out all the candles, okay."

After the candles were blown out, each one got the first slice out of their cake. After enjoying their cake Joshua and Deborah played with their toys with the other kids. Lewis and Beverly were glad to see how well they did with the other children.

Joshua came over to Beverly and said, "Can we tell each other what our wish was?"

"Yes, you can, but don't tell anyone else."

After everyone was gone, Lewis said to Joshua, "Let's put your toys in the room with the race car. That way you can find them real easy." He helped Joshua take everything.

"Where is my book? I want to look at my book." There was a small desk and chair in the room.

"It's on the desk. You can sit in the chair and look through it. It's almost bedtime so don't stay up late."

He left Joshua looking at the book. In the living room, Beverly was reading the directions for the thing she had asked her mother to buy for her.

"What's that?" asked Lewis.

"Baby monitor."

"You're going to spy on them?"

"Of course not. I'm just going to listen to them and see what they talk about."

"I believe that's called spying."

"Lewis, both of them have wants and needs that we don't know about. I think if we understand them more we can help prepare them better. We have no idea the extent of what they have gone through and how much damage they have suffered."

"Well, considering everything I think they are doing real well. I have to admit, you may be right."

Beverly put the monitor near her ear; she didn't want it too loud. Lewis leaned over. Beverly smiled, "Why Lewis, are you spying on the children?"

"In for a penny, in for a pound," was his answer.

They heard Joshua go into his room. They listened as the two said their prayers. She could hear the two get into bed. She could even hear when they turned off their bedside lamp.

"What did you wish for?" asked Joshua

"I wished we could stay here with Beverly and Lewis. What did you wish for?"

"I wished we could stay here, too, and I wished for a horse for us."

"Joshua, you were only supposed to make one wish, not two."

"Well, nobody told me."

"She said make a wish, not make a bunch of wishes. If we don't get our wish, it's your fault."

"I'm sorry, I didn't know. Maybe nobody heard me about the horses."

"Did you say horses?"

"Yeah, one for me and one for you."

"So, you made three wishes?"

"Well, really just two."

In the living room, Lewis said, "We have a problem."

"About Deborah being a little bossy."

"No, not that, even though she is a little bossy. I haven't told you but a week ago I bought two colts for them. They are delivering them tomorrow and building another corral."

"That's fantastic, Lewis. I was riding a lot younger than they are."

"Well, the problem is they are going to think they can get things just by wishing for them."

"Yes, I see where you're coming from. What are we going to do?"

"You're the spy. I'm going to let you figure it out. Any cake left?"

That night Joshua didn't have a bad dream. He had a good one; he was flying a plane.

Beverly and the children spent the next day with her mother. Beverly gave them classes on colors and numbers. "You'll have them doing long division in a week if you keep this up," said Alice.

"Momma, I don't know what they need to know going into the first grade. I don't remember what we did."

"I remember you were pretty dense back then," said Alice laughing.

"Momma."

"Well, you were. You came home complaining about they didn't teach a single thing about horses or shootouts during bank robberies," then she stopped and thought about Keith dying during a bank robbery. "I shouldn't have said that. I'm sorry."

"It still hurts, doesn't it, Momma."

"More than I can say. I still talk to him every day when I'm alone."

At five o'clock, Beverly pulled into the garage. After getting out of the car, they went to check on things in the greenhouse. The children saw Lewis standing near the barn with his hands on his hips. They ran over to say hi.

"What are you looking at?" asked Beverly.

"These two colts. I came out here and there are two colts and a new corral. I don't know where they came from. I better call the sheriff. There might be some horse thieves around and they are hiding them here. The sheriff will know what to do."

"That's our horses," said Joshua.

"How did you get horses?" asked Beverly.

"Joshua wished for them," said Deborah.

"We're not supposed to tell Deborah. Remember, we are not supposed to tell what we wish for."

"Oh….does it count if you accidently tell?"

"Yes, it does," said Lewis.

"Well, I guess we can keep them, but I'm afraid now you won't get any more wishes on your birthday. Some kind of state law," said Beverly.

"Which one is mine? asked Joshua.

"The black one looks like it might be yours, Joshua," said Lewis.

"And mine is the white one. I am going to name him Cloud."

"I'm going to name mine Midnight," said Joshua.

"When can we ride them?"

"Let's wait a few days. They need to get use to their new home and get use to us. Let's go in and pet them." Lewis and Beverly held the kids hands and they walked into the corral. The horses stood still while they petted them. "Owning a horse has responsibilities. You have to feed and water them. I also don't want you out here without us. We'll show you what to do I'll brush them and stuff like that until you get older. Now let's go in and eat some dinner and try out some of those new games you got at your party."

Saturday night wrestling came on. Joshua asked Lewis, "Do you want to rassel?"

"Yeah, we can rassel. We need to move the coffee table and this chair."

Lewis was on his knees and Joshua was on the other side of the room. Lewis was the announcer. Beverly and Deborah were the spectators.

"In this corner, weighing in at fifty four pounds, from the great state of Wyoming, Big josh." Joshua had his hands clasped together moving them back and forth over his head. The crowd went wild.

"In this corner, weighing in at one hundred and eighty five pounds, from parts unknown, Big Mac." The crowd booed.

Joshua was stretching on the other side of the room.

Suddenly Joshua flung himself at Lewis. He grabbed Lewis by the hair and had both feet on Lewis's chest. He almost knocked him over. "Oh, that hurts."

The crowd went wild.

Lewis was able to get Joshua on the floor. "Oh no, he's got him in the tickle hold." Joshua was screaming and laughing at the same time when Lewis tickled him. Lewis let him go. Joshua was giggling as he tried to crawl away. Lewis grabbed him by the ankle and pulled him back.

"He's got him in the kissing hold now." He was kissing him on the cheek. Joshua was screaming and giggling at the same time.

The crowd was booing.

"Wait a minute, wait a minute," said Joshua. "Nobody said ding, ding."

Lewis let him go.

On the other side of the room, Joshua said, "This time no tickle holds and no kissing holds," as he was wiping his cheeks on the arm of his pajamas. Then they started over.

At bedtime, Joshua asked if he could look at his book with the planes.

"Only for a few minutes," said Lewis. A little while later, Lewis went back to check on him. "Time for bed Joshua."

As Joshua was leaving the room, he looked around and asked, "Can I sleep in here every once in a while?"

"Sure, anytime you want. It is kind of like a boy's room and the other room in kind of like a girl's room, if you know what I mean."

"I know what you mean. I was thinking the same thing; it's pink and has a lot of lace."

"You think Deborah would get scared by herself?"

"Deborah's not scared of anything."

"I guess that's good. Do you like your airplane book?"

"Yes, Sir. I love airplanes."

"When I was in the army, I parachuted out of airplanes, did you know that?"

"Really, were you scared?"

"Yes, I was, but you do it anyway."

"I don't like doing things that scare me," said Joshua.

"That's good. You're not old enough to do things that scare you. Don't you worry about it, okay?"

The next night, Joshua announced at the dinner table that he was going to sleep in the other room. "If Deborah gets scared she can just come get me and I will go in the room with her."

"That's fine Joshua. You can sleep in there anytime you want. You can sleep in there every night if you want," said Beverly.

That night, Lewis tucked him in and said, "I'll have a lamp on so if you wake up you'll know where you are, okay."

"Can you stay with me a few minutes and maybe tell me a story?" asked Joshua.

"What kind of story do you want me to tell you?"

"Tell me a story about Bubble Bear and Pumpkin Man."

"I'm not familiar with them. What kind of story is it?"

"You know like Bubble Bear and Pumpkin Man goes to the toy store and they buy some balloons and Bubble Bear blows one real big and starts floating away. Pumpkin man, who is a pumpkin, grabs him by the leg and they both float away and they went real high and this bird flies by and lands on the balloon and pecks a hole in it and they fall and land in a swimming pool and have to run home and dry off so they won't get into trouble. Tell me a story like that."

So Lewis made up a story about someone named Bubble Bear and Pumpkin Man. Beverly asked him what took so long. "I had to make up a story about someone named Bubble Bear and Pumpkin man. He's fascinated by them."

"I think he just likes spending time with you. I think he is fascinated by you Lewis and that's a good thing."

"You know what I think. He's my little buddy."

CHAPTER SEVENTEEN

THE BIG NICKEL

A week later Beverly and the children were walking in the parking lot of the grocery store. She always held their hands. Joshua broke away, ran ten feet and picked something up. "Look Mommie, I found a big nickel." He showed her the nickel. That's the first time one of them had called her Mommy. It wasn't a nickel either, it was a half dollar.

"Oh Joshua, this is a very special coin. We want to make sure we keep this."

"I can't spend it," said Joshua. He had a sad look on his face.

"Tell you what, I'm going to give you a dollar for it and I will keep this for you."

"What about Deborah? She was with me."

"I'll give Deborah a dollar, also." This excited both of them. Next to the grocery store was a store that sold almost everything. Beverly still called it the dime store. When she was little it was the five and dime store. They went in and Beverly found a small 3x5 inch frame. The children went looking for something to spend their dollar on.

In the car Deborah said, "We bought you a present." She handed it to Beverly. It was a heart shaped pin.

"It's beautiful." She pinned it on her blouse. "I will wear it every day. Thank you."

When she got home she took a piece of cardboard and cut a circle in it and put a piece of felt over it and glued the felt down. She put the coin in. She pulled out the old manual typewriter and typed in the date and "Joshua found this special coin on this date." She put it on his dresser. She pointed it out to Joshua. "Here's your special coin." She didn't tell him it was all about him calling her Mommie. She would do that when he was older. "Now you can look at it anytime you want."

Sometimes the smallest things are more important than the big things. This was one of the small things that meant everything to Beverly.

AT THE OTHER PLACE

After dinner one evening while Lewis and Joshua were working on a model airplane, Beverly and Deborah were baking cookies. Beverly said, "Joshua sure is interested in airplanes isn't he?"

"Yes, Ma'am," answered Deborah.

"I wonder why?"

Deborah was mixing the cookie dough in a large bowl and said, "When we were locked in the closet at the other place he would tell me, 'If I had a plane, we could fly away.'" She said it so matter of factly. She didn't even look at Beverly when she said it.

Lewis and Beverly had agreed they would never discuss the situation of where they had lived before coming to live with them. Both hoped the children would simply forget over time. This was the first time it had been brought up.

That night, Beverly did something she hadn't done since her Daddy was killed. She cried herself to sleep. She kept repeating in her mind over and over what Deborah had said. 'When we were locked in the closet at the other place Joshua would tell me, if I had a plane we could fly away.' She couldn't get it out of her mind. Especially the 'When we were locked in the closet at the other place.'

Beverly promised God that the children would never regret one single day of coming to live with them. Her last thought before falling asleep was 'When we were locked in the closet at the other place.' 'When we were locked in the closet at the other place.'

CHAPTER EIGHTEEN

MACDONALD VS.

WYOMING

The children had been at the ranch eight months. They had started riding the horses in the corral. Beverly used the camcorder and would play the videos for them when nothing was suitable for the kids to watch on TV. Every time Joshua would ride by, he would flash that smile of his.

School would be starting in a few weeks. Beverly had prepared them as best she knew how. Every day they learned something new.

At happy hour Joshua had developed a dry sense of humor and was always joking with Lewis. The four felt like they had the perfect lives. The ranch was doing really well. Winter had come and gone. Everything was just fine until the day the registered letter arrived. The letter was from the state of Wyoming Family and Children Services. In essence the state wanted the children turned over immediately. 'To be placed in a more permanent environment.' The MacDonald custody was only temporary.

When Lewis came home Beverly was on the couch. Lewis could tell she had been crying. They went into the dining room to talk.

"What's the problem?"

She couldn't answer. She handed him the letter. He read it twice. He leaned back in his chair. "Do the children know?"

"No, I sent them out to the greenhouse. You don't know how hard it was not to let them see me crying. I don't want them to see how upset I am. Lewis what can we do?"

"I don't know, but I do know where to start."

He picked up the phone and before he started dialing he said, "Try to compose yourself in case they come in."

Beverly nodded. She felt better with Lewis here and knew if anything could be done he would do it.

A minute later he said, "Cynthia MacDonald, please. This is her brother calling. Tell her it's urgent, very urgent."

Cynthia answered the phone. "Lewis, what's wrong?"

"Cynthia, the State wants us to turn the children over to them. Let me read you the letter." After reading the letter there was a long pause. Long enough to make Beverly nervous. "It says immediately. I don't know if that means today, tomorrow or next week. Cynthia, this can't happen. We don't know what to do."

A pause. "I don't know." Another pause. "Every three months? Are you sure?" A long pause. "No they haven't, I'm sure of it, but let me ask Beverly. Hold on a sec." He covered the mouthpiece of the phone. "Has the State sent a caseworker out to inspect the living conditions?"

"No, no one has come out." answered Beverly.

"Have we received any correspondence from the State?"

"No, we've never received anything."

"No, we've received nothing; no mail and no one has visited," said Lewis into the phone. There was a short pause. "We've had the children eight months." There was another short pause. "Judge Jack Gordon," answered Lewis. Another pause. "I assume he still has an Attorney's license, but I don't know for sure." Another pause. "You can, I'll pick you up at the airport. Thanks Cynthia."

He looked at Beverly. "She will be here tomorrow. We need to see Judge Gordon tonight."

"I'll get the children. We'll eat when we get back."

When they showed the letter to Judge Gordon it would be an understatement to say he hit the roof; he went through the roof, then went ballistic. "Why this pompous bureaucrat. He has had those documents for eight months. He sat behind his desk yawning for eight months and out of the blue he does this. I'm a duly elected Superior Court Judge. He is some flunky at the State level. He probably spent six months getting one of his underlings to find Kerney on the map.

"I won't stand for this, no siree. I will write a restraining order right this minute. I am a Judge and my decision will be respected and adhered to. I will not stand for this. We will fight them tooth and nail."

When Lewis and Beverly finally had a chance to speak the Judge calmed down a bit.

"My sister is flying in tomorrow to help out. She wants to know if you still have a license to practice law."

"You bet your colt 45 I do. Why is your sister flying in?"

"She is a lawyer in California and a few other states, your Honor."

"What does she plan on doing?"

"She mentioned she would lay waste to the State of Wyoming," said Lewis.

"A real firebrand is she," said the Judge, "I like that."

"Yes, Sir, she is. However she doesn't want to appear as an interloper in this case. She wants to know if you would also represent us in this matter."

"You can bet your boots I will. I wouldn't pass this up for anything."

Lewis said, "She intends on using a secret weapon, your Honor."

"Secret weapon. What secret weapon?"

"The children Sir and publicity. She wants Beverly to write letters to every newspaper, radio station and all the TV stations in the state. She wants Beverly to personally challenge the Governor to come inspect the living conditions and to talk with the children himself."

"I like the plan. We can get every church and school to hold a vigil in the front yard. I know a reporter in Cheyenne that will do a human interest story on the kids. We go proactive right this minute. About my fee. I'm so ticked off; I will do it for free. No pompous bureaucrat is going to do this to the Honorable Jack Gordon."

Judge Gordon was pacing back and forth, hand raised over his head, index finger extended. He hadn't felt this alive in years. "I've sat on the bench and held my emotions in check and admonished lawyers for expressing their emotions." Judge Gordon felt twenty years younger. He wasn't going to take any prisoners. This was a fight to the finish, last man standing.

After they left, the Judge went in his office. He found what volumes he wanted and settled down to read. He said to himself, out loud, "I wonder what kind of lawyer his sister is. What will she bring to the table?" If he only knew.

The drive to the Laramie airport lasted the better part of an hour. As they neared the airport, Joshua went crazy with excitement. When he saw the first plane in the distance he started jumping up and down. He almost trampled Deborah going back and forth from one side of the car to the other. Lewis loved seeing how excited he was. In the terminal, his face was glued to the window as large jets were arrayed outside. Joshua couldn't believe the size of the planes.

When Cynthia came down the jet way and greeted Lewis and Beverly with a hug, she said, "You still mad about the photo."

Laughing Beverly said, "No, it's my favorite. It's on the fireplace mantel. Cynthia, this is Joshua and Deborah."

Joshua grabbed her by the hand and pulled her to the window. "Which plane did you fly on?"

Cynthia pointed to the nearest one. "That one right there."

"Wow, when I get big I want to fly a plane. Is it a lot of fun? Were you scared? How do things look up there?"

"It is a lot of fun. You go real high and real fast." She glanced at Deborah and saw she was appraising her. "And Miss Deborah, what do you want to do when you grow up?"

Deborah pointed at Beverly. "I want to be just like her."

Beverly's eyes watered up and she said, "You are already like me."

Cynthia crossed her arms and was looking at Deborah. She said, "I believe you have got about the prettiest hair I have ever seen."

Deborah smiled and said, "Really." Then she ran her fingers through her curly hair.

Cynthia nodded her head. "I wish mine looked that good but I am stuck with this." Cynthia knew she had won her over. Tell a girl she has pretty hair and she's in your corner.

Lewis dropped Cynthia off at Judge Gordon's the next morning. Judge Gordon opened the door and Cynthia stuck out her hand. "Judge Gordon, Cynthia MacDonald, are you ready to get started?"

"Well uh, yes, sure please come in."

Cynthia was dressed in a business suit. It was conservative cut attire. Judge Gordon had a woman lawyer in his courtroom from time to time. The first thought Judge Gordon had was power lawyer. He would not mistake her for just any lawyer.

In his office he said, "I've been reviewing the law on cases such as this. I see no reason why we can't win this case on its own merit."

Cynthia nodded her head and said, "I would still like to use statistics that would be beneficial to us."

"What statistics are you referring to?"

"Most children over six years of age never get adopted and become wards of the State until the age of eighteen. Most children live in a succession of foster homes where they are sometimes mistreated. Some are exploited sexually. Some foster parents are in it only for the money. Some children are used for nothing more than domestic servants. All states have statistical information on the categories I've mentioned. While Wyoming is ranked very well in comparison to other states; if one child falls through the crack lives are destroyed.

"We also will point out the higher percentage of youth violence and incarceration in penal institutes. All this information should be brought to light, don't you think."

"Yes, yes of course," intoned the Judge. She had brought up a lot of things he hadn't thought of. Never underestimate a woman, especially when it comes to children.

"You seemed to be very informed on this subject. Would you be willing to argue your points in the preliminary hearing?"

"I'd be most happy to prepare a brief, submit to the presiding Judge and argue that position. However I don't think there will be anything other than the first day. It is my intention that at the end of day when we walk out, this will be forever a thing of the past. Have you seen the tape Beverly made of their prior living conditions?"

"Yes, I watched it here. That was the reason I gave them custody."

Cynthia said, "The State doesn't know we have it and that, Sir, is where I blow… sorry, you blow them out of the water. They will have no alternative but to allow them to keep the kids and I would like for you to recommend the family be allowed to adopt the children right away."

"I couldn't agree more. Those children are precious and it's obvious how much they love Lewis and Beverly and there is no finer couple in the country."

On the second day, letters went out to every media outlet in the State. Pastors in their pulpit asked for character references for the MacDonald's. They came in by the hundreds. The people of Wyoming were standing by one of their own. Protests were held by concerned citizens in front of state buildings. Statistics were quoted mostly from nationwide. Horror stories begin to emerge about orphans and foster care. Everyone agreed, most people who had anything to do with foster care were good people. People with compassion and love in their hearts but everyone knows there are always those bad apples.

The vigil at the MacDonald ranch was not all that large but they were faithful. They came every day and brought their children. Joshua and Deborah did not fully understand the extent of the situation.

When the TV reporter from Cheyenne arrived, the cameraman started filming while the reporter did her lead in. The crowd, mostly the children, started chanting, "LET THEM STAY, LET THEM STAY."

They knocked on the door and Beverly opened the door and invited them in. After introductions, the reporter asked if it would be possible to film the living conditions.

"Yes, of course. Joshua, Deborah, please show the lady and this gentleman around."

From Joshua's room they heard her say, "That is a real live race car."

Lewis had to smile at that. Joshua came back leading the way with that smile on his face.

"Do you mind if I interview the children by themselves, without the crowd."

"No, Ma'am, please do. We have nothing to hide," said Lewis.

"We can go to Lookout Point," said Deborah.

"Where is Lookout Point?" asked the reporter. The cameraman was still filming.

"It's not far. It's our favorite place in the whole wide world," said Joshua as he raced to get the blanket.

Five minutes later, the children were seated on the blanket with the reporter. "Why do you like living here?"

Joshua answered, "Because they don't beat you if you spill your milk. They tell us bedtime stories and they are always telling us they love us. At happy hour we play games and laugh and talk."

"What is happy hour?"

"At the dinner table after dinner we take an hour to do things families are supposed to do. It's a lot of fun."

"We never had a family before," said Deborah.

"And we get to ride horses."

"You have a horse?"

"Yes, Ma'am, we both do. I thought everybody had a horse," said Joshua.

"Well, I don't. I live in a big city. Not many people own horses in the city."

"You can come here and ride one of ours," said Deborah.

The cameraman waved to the reporter and pointed to the driveway. A black sedan and a limo that was followed by another car eased up the driveway. The three car convoy stopped in front of the house. Someone opened the rear door of the limo and Governor James T. Carson emerged.

The camera man said, "It's Governor Carson."

"Kids let's go back inside, okay?"

The Governor had already entered the house when the reporter and the children went in. The cameraman continued to film.

"Governor Carson, we truly appreciate you coming. This is Joshua and Deborah, whom I believe you have heard about," said Beverly.

Lewis said, "Will the two of you show the Governor around please?"

"Yes, Sir," said Joshua.

They heard the governor say, "That's a real live race car you have there, Son." Lewis had to smile and shook his head. That bedspread was worth its weight in gold.

When everyone entered the living room Beverly said, "Would you like some coffee, Governor?"

"Yes, please, this is a very nice place you have here."

Joshua ran into the kitchen and returned with a plate of cookies. He set them in front of the Governor and sat beside him. Joshua picked up a cookie and started eating. He was the most relaxed person in the room. "Would you like a cookie? Mom made them."

The Governor made note that he said Mom. How do you take a child from someone they call Mom? That is just wrong. The Governor picked one up and said, "Thank you."

Joshua said, "You're welcome."

"Do you get to hunt and fish around here Lewis?"

"Yes, Sir," answered Lewis.

"I haven't been able to do that lately. It's something I miss a lot," said the Governor.

"Well, Governor, you are welcome here anytime," said Beverly.

"Thank you, Ma'am," and a friendship was born.

They chatted for a while and finally the Governor rose from his seat and patted Joshua on the knee. "Well, I'd better get back to the Capital."

Joshua ran into the kitchen and came back with a plastic bag full of cookies and handed them to the Governor. The Governor looked at him and then at Deborah and said, "I wish you the best of luck. I don't know what I can do except say that I personally inspected the living conditions and found them outstanding. These two children deserve the best and I believe this is the best. I'm going to take you up on that fishing and hunting, Lewis."

"Yes, Sir, I would be honored if you would do that." Cynthia and the Judge were hard at work on the upcoming hearing. They heard about the Governor's visit from Mrs. Gordon. "Wonder how it went," asked the Judge.

"If he talked with the kids it went fine."

JUDGEMENT DAY

The hearing started on time. Lewis, Beverly and the two children were in an adjacent room and would be called one at a time. This was not a trial hearing. Cynthia had taken care of everything in a manner that impressed the daylights out of Judge Gordon. She had picked out the clothes the children would wear. She had Beverly dressed in a conservative cut business suit. Lewis had on a nice suit. Most important was the statistics and the all-important tape which she had added footage to at the end. When they sprung the secret weapon it was indeed impressive.

Joshua came into the room and flashed that smile to Cynthia. He was dressed like a little man with one exception. He was wearing khaki slacks, navy blue blazer and light blue dress shirt with a red tie. The red tie matched his red tennis shoes. Cynthia wanted to kidnap him, he was so cute.

Judge Gordon approached him and asked, "And you are Joshua, is that correct?"

"Yes, Sir, but sometimes when people are in a hurry they call me Josh."

"Well, Joshua, are you doing okay today?"

"Yes, Sir."

"Joshua, do you like living with Lewis and Beverly MacDonald?"

"You mean my Mom and Dad, yes, Sir. I love living with them."

"Counsel objects your Honor," said the Family and Children lawyer.

"On what grounds Counselor," asked the sitting Judge.

"On using the term Mom and Dad. That has not been determined yet and it may sway your decision, your Honor."

"Objection noted and overruled. As a member of the bench, it is my job to be swayed, as you say, and you will get ample opportunity to try to sway me when it is your turn."

"Your Honor, we know nothing about this child and yet we are asking him if he likes living there."

"Sit down and wait your turn. I'm sure we will find out a little about the child in due time" said the Judge. Judge Gordon looked at

Joshua and said, "Well, Joshua tell us a little about yourself for the Counselor," he motioned towards the other attorney.

"Well, I'm six years old. My favorite color is red. My favorite T.V. show is Sesame Street, but I know Big Bird isn't really a bird. My favorite day of the week is Thursday because Mom makes homemade pizza and she puts lots of pepperoni on it because I like pepperoni. Do you like pepperoni? I like to go fishing and ride my horse. His name is Midnight, and my sister, her name is Deborah, we're twins. Her horse's name is Cloud because she's white and Midnight is black.

"Why do you like living with, pardon the phrase, your Mom and Dad?"

"Because they don't beat you if you spill your milk. Dad tells me bedtime stories and they tell me they love me. They tell me that all the time. I love them, too."

"Have you started school yet?"

"Not yet, but I've learned a lot. Mom studies with us every day. I've learned all kinds of stuff."

"What else do you do as a family?"

"Well, we go to Lookout Point. That's my favorite place in whole wide world."

"And what do you do at this place called Lookout Point?"

"Oh, different things. Sometimes we watch the sun come up or go down. Sometimes we look at the stars if there are no clouds. If it's windy, we fly a kite and what I like the most is when we have a family picnic. See, we've never had a family before."

The silence was deafening and hung in the air. Finally Judge Gordon said, "Thank you, Joshua that will be all."

"Counselor, do you have any questions for Joshua," asked the presiding Judge.

He got up and walked toward Joshua. He couldn't think of anything to counter with. The boy had said everything. He looked at Joshua, "Did anyone tell you what to say in this meeting?" He was grasping at straws.

"Yes, Sir," answered Joshua.

"What did they tell you to say?"

"Mom told me to tell the truth." Well, I walked into that one thought the lawyer.

"No more questions, your Honor."

Joshua got up and smiled at everyone.

Next Deborah came in. After she was seated, the opposing counsel asked the Judge if he could question her first. "Judge Gordon, do you have any objections to that?"

"No, your Honor, certainly not. Counsel may go first," replied Judge Gordon.

Counsel approached Deborah and asked, "How are you doing today?"

"You are wasting your time."

"I'm sorry, what did you say?"

"I said you are wasting your time. If you take us away we will just run away and come back home. No matter where you send us we will find a way to come home."

The attorney looked at the Judge. "Your Honor, the witness is badgering the counsel."

The Judge leaned forward in his chair and looked at the attorney. "In thirty five years on the bench I have heard thousands of times that counsel is badgering the witness. This is the first time I've heard that the witness is badgering the counsel. For crying out loud, she is six years old and you are a grown man. Suck it up. Have you got any more questions for this little lady?"

Deborah had her arms folded and was glaring at the attorney.

"No, your Honor." That's one mean little girl he thought as he returned to his seat. Judge Gordon got up, smiled at Deborah and said, "That's a very pretty dress you have on."

"Thank you, sir, my Mom made it for me. It's my favorite color and she knows I like lace on my dresses. She let me help her make it."

The opposing counsel thought well, I just lost the case. She went from a pit bull to a sweet little girl in two seconds flat. The State attorney looked at Cynthia. Cynthia smiled at him, but the look said more than that. Then it dawned on him. She looked like a nice young woman, but she can turn into a pit bull in two seconds flat.

Judge Gordon questioned Deborah for a few minutes before excusing her. Then the Judge said, "Your Honor, may we go into the chamber and discuss a few things. These are very important items; I'm sure counsel would appreciate if we do this. It will embarrass the State if we discuss this in open court."

The States counsel said, "Discuss what?" I don't know what they could be talking about, your Honor."

Cynthia spoke up for the first time. "Trust me; you don't want it out in open court."

"Let me be the Judge of that," said the presiding Judge.

"It's a video tape, Your Honor," said Cynthia.

"I know nothing about a video tape. I object, Your Honor."

"On what grounds, Counselor?"

"I demand to see the contents of the tape before we decide if it is to be shown."

"I think that is the point she is making, Counselor. I don't know what you are thinking. This is not a criminal trial. There are no discovery rules here. If the tape is to be played, where it's to be played is the question? We are trying to decide that issue right now. The tape will be played. I have made my decision. Now, where is the question?"

"I say here in open court," said states counsel.

"I warned you," said Cynthia.

It took five minutes to set the system up. She put the tape in and pushed the play button. She was now the 'Pit Bull.' Cynthia didn't narrate the tape. No one needed to. It lasted seven and half minutes. The Judge asked her to rewind it and play it again. She gladly did so.

"There is more footage I would like to have the court view. Not of child abuse but of the happiness of two children in a loving environment." She didn't wait for approval, she pressed play again. The tape showed the children riding their horses. She smiled every time Joshua rode by and flashed that smile of his. Then scenes from the birthday party and Joshua running around showing everyone his airplane book. She had never seen a child that excited, that happy.

"This is Lookout point, Your Honor, that Joshua told you about." Deborah was chasing Joshua who happened to be wearing the same red tennis shoes. Both children were squealing with delight. There was video of Joshua fishing and he and Lewis wrestling. Footage of Deborah helping Beverly bake cookies. She had flour on her nose and her cheeks. And there was footage of the four of them at the dining room table during happy hour playing games. Then, Cynthia stopped the tape. "There is more, Your Honor, but I realize the time constraints. We also have other material we would like to present. One thing I would like to point out is the State wants to take these two wonderful children and place them somewhere else. Where, is anyone's guess?"

"What else do you have?" asked the Judge.

"A compilation of statistics, Your Honor, and over three hundred sworn depositions of character of reference. It will probably take fifteen minutes of your time, Your Honor. There is also a financial statement on the MacDonald family."

"Let's take a thirty minute break and I will look at these in my chamber."

Thirty minutes later they were back in court. The Judge called the three lawyers up to the bench. "Is this financial statement up to date and correct?" asked the Judge.

"As of yesterday at close of business, Your Honor," said Cynthia. The Judge handed the statement to the States counsel. He flipped through all the pages and looked at the last line. He looked at Cynthia, then the Judge and finally Judge Gordon.

"This amount here, is this the total of all the statements accounts?"

"Yes, it is, and the amount is verified by an independent auditor not affiliated in any way with the MacDonald family."

"And these letters, these sworn affidavits, are these people prepared to affirm the content and signature?"

"If need be, Your Honor," said Cynthia and seconded by a nod from Judge Gordon.

"You may return to your seats. Would the bailiff bring in the family? All four of them."

"Yes, Sir."

Beverly, Deborah, Joshua and Lewis came in and stood before the Judge.

"Would counsel please come forward?" When everyone was in the proper place the Judge said, "It is an embarrassment to me and to the State of Wyoming that this hearing ever took place. I am giving full and permanent custody of Joshua and Deborah Williams to Lewis and Beverly MacDonald. I realize that you are both young and haven't been married for a great length of time but I can't remember seeing a happier family. If you would like to start adoption proceedings, I will sign them."

Cynthia stepped forward and said, "Your Honor, I believe you will find the necessary paperwork here."

The Judger leaned forward and said, "You work fast, Counselor."

"When it's something I believe in, yes I do. Thank you, Your Honor."

Looking at the State Counselor the Judge asked, "Do you have any objections, Counselor?"

"No, Sir."

The Judge picked up his pen and signed all the necessary paperwork. "This court is out of session." He rapped his gavel once and left the room.

The four MacDonald's were hugging and crying tears of joy.

Deborah ran over to the States attorney and kicked him in the shin. She pointed her finger at him and said, "That's for making my Momma cry."

Cynthia walked over, gathered up her material and looked at him as he rubbed his shin. "I warned you but you didn't listen."

As Judge Gordon walked by him he said, "Never underestimate a woman." The States attorney simply nodded his head as he hopped around on one foot.

SCHOOL

On the first day of school Beverly loaded the children up. "You guys ready?" "Yes, Ma'am," they both said at the same time.

"I'll be there with you. I've volunteered as an assistant. I may not be in the room with you but I'll be in the building, okay."

"Yes, Ma'am."

"Are you looking forward to school? You'll meet a lot of other children."

"I guess," said Joshua.

"How many other kids will be there?" asked Deborah.

"I'm not sure but it doesn't matter."

Beverly held their hands and took them to the first grade class. "Mrs. Winslow, this is Joshua and Deborah."

"Hello, Joshua and Deborah. Why don't the two of you sit here?" She pointed to two desks on the front row.

"Do you want me to stay in here with you, Mrs. Winslow," asked Beverly.

"That will be fine Beverly. Let's see how they do. After talking to you that may be a good idea for the first few days."

"Let me know what you need me to do to help out. I know this is unusual but given the circumstances I sure do appreciate you letting me stay."

"I think they will do just fine," said Mrs. Winslow.

Mostly, Beverly stayed in the back of the room. If a child needed to go to the restroom she took them. She sharpened pencils, passed out papers and helped anyway she could. Her main purpose was to see how Joshua and Deborah handled this new experience. At lunch she was able to sit with them while they ate. The other children didn't notice Beverly at all.

"Are you enjoying school?"

They both nodded their heads.

In the class when the teacher asked a question the first two hands to go up were always Joshua and Deborah's. Beverly was so proud of them. She was so afraid that they were going to be behind in their learning compared to the other kids. Mrs. Winslow didn't always call on them which pleased Beverly. She didn't want them to be singled out; she wanted them to fit in.

On the second day, Joshua told her, "We'll be alright if you need to do something else."

"Does it bother you that I'm in your class with you?"

"No, Ma'am, but we'll be okay."

Beverly talked to Mrs. Winslow and she agreed with the children. "You can always come back if there is a problem but I really don't see where there will be one. They behave very well."

After three weeks, during recess, Beverly went out to the playground with the second grade class. She looked around but didn't see Joshua. She walked over to Mrs. Winslow, "Do you know where Joshua is?"

"Beverly, let's take a walk."

"He's not in trouble is he?"

"No, come on let's walk around and I'll tell you about it."

"Yes, Ma'am."

"I understand you've been teaching the kids at home, whereas, you put it they wouldn't be behind everyone else."

"Yes, Ma'am, I was afraid that since they've never been around other children and no one has helped them learn there would be a lot of things they wouldn't know. I've done the best I could and if they are behind in anything I will help them catch up."

Mrs. Winslow smiled and said, "Let me tell you a story. Last week someone gave me a Canadian dime. I'm sure it was by mistake. I put it in my change purse. I wanted to show it to the class compared to what ours looks like. You know to get their curiosity up. Children who are curious learn more. You understand what I'm saying?"

"Yes, Ma'am, I do," said Beverly.

"Well, I called Joshua up front to write his name on the blackboard."

"Now I know Joshua can write his name, Mrs. Winslow. I can't imagine why he couldn't in class."

"Let me finish Beverly, yes Joshua can write his name but that's not what the story is about. I couldn't find the dime so I dumped all the change out. Joshua had finished writing his name. I had spread all the coins out. They weren't separated or anything. Joshua said, 'Wow, Mrs. Winslow, you have a dollar and forty three cents.' I counted the money and guess how much I had?"

"Don't tell me you had a dollar and forty three cents," said Beverly.

"That's exactly what I had. It gets more interesting. I picked up a dime, nickel and three pennies. I asked how much was still on the desk. He looked and said a dollar and twenty five cents. Then I asked him if I had a dollar and forty three cents before and now there's a dollar and twenty five cents, how much is in my hand? Well, he scrunched up his face and closed his eyes and said, 'Eighteen cents' and then smiled that smile of his. Have you noticed when he draws there is always an airplane in the picture. In art class that's all he draws."

"That doesn't surprise me. He is fascinated by planes. He saves his money to buy books and models of planes. Lewis gives them his change. Joshua is always counting his money so he knows when he can buy something else. That's probably why he was able to tell you how much you had," said Beverly.

"Beverly, I don't know why Joshua is more advanced than anyone else in class. I don't think it's because you've been studying at home. I doubt you have taught him anything a normal first grade boy shouldn't know. Now let's talk about where he is right now. He's in the principal's office with the science teacher from the middle school. They are not testing him or anything like that. They are just a couple of guys talking. I know I should have asked you about it but then his answers wouldn't be the same, you understand?"

"Yes, Ma'am. He's so small I don't know how he will act around grown-ups he doesn't know."

"Well, let's go find out," said Mrs. Winslow. They stood at the principal's door. They could see Joshua pointing out things on a model airplane. Beverly could see the science teacher nodding his head and smiling. Beverly could tell Joshua was enjoying himself. She motioned to Mrs. Winslow that everything looked fine and they could leave.

"What should I do?" asked Beverly

"You may want to move him up a grade next year. He is clearly very intelligent for his age, especially in math."

"You mean separate him from Deborah? I would never want to do that. I'll talk to my husband, but I'm sure he would agree with me on this."

"Well, don't limit his horizons. He is a very smart child. Also, keep working with him at home because if you stop he may think he's learned enough."

"Yes, Ma'am, I understand," said Beverly.

When they arrived home Beverly went into the living room. She wanted to see the crayon drawing of Lookout Point Joshua had colored. Sure enough there was a small plane on the horizon. Beverly had never noticed it before.

After the children were in bed Beverly told Lewis about the day's events. Lewis didn't act surprised by any of it.

"You know I've noticed the way he talks. The answer he gives is like a boy older than he is. I agree with you we shouldn't move him to a higher grade. Deborah is also smart but in a different way."

CHAPTER NINETEEN

PLAY BALL

The next year the Kerney County Parks and Recreation department decided there were enough children in the county to form a baseball/softball league. A field was established complete with fence, dugouts, and backstop. When Deborah heard about what was happening she said she wanted to play baseball.

"Hadn't you rather play softball with the other girls," asked Beverly.

"Softball is for sissies," said Deborah.

"Well, I don't know about that. Besides, I don't know if girls can play on the boy's teams. Joshua would you care if there were girls on the team?" asked Lewis.

"Let me think about that. I'm only seven and I need some time to figure that out." Deborah looked at Joshua a few seconds.

"I don't think it would bother me. You might want to ask someone else."

Beverly called the parks and recreation director and asked about the rules.

"There is nothing in the rules that says a girl is not allowed to play on any of the baseball teams."

It became apparent right away that Deborah was one of the better players on the team. Joshua, on the other hand, seemed as though he didn't mind if he didn't even play. When Deborah was playing she swung the bat just as hard as she could. She was very aggressive running bases. She was constantly stretching a double into a triple. She was always sliding into bases. In the field she was diving at every ball near her. After every game her uniform was always the dirtiest.

Joshua would usually say, "Mom, you don't have to wash my uniform." He never hit the ball out of the infield. If it made it out of the infield it was because a player missed it. There was one thing Joshua was good at. He could run like a deer. He was almost impossible to throw out. He was so fast that Lewis had to put a chin strap on his batting helmet. Joshua would outrun his helmet. Several times Lewis swore he would leave a dust trail when he was running. Every time Joshua got on base he would look at Lewis and Beverly and flash that smile. It was a natural smile and only lasted a few seconds.

In one game, a parent from the other team was sitting behind Lewis and Beverly. Joshua hit an easy roller to the second baseman. Joshua flew down the base path and beat the throw. The man sitting behind them said, "That little buggar can fly."

Beverly stood up, turned around and said, "That little buggar is mine and his name is Joshua but you can call him Josh."

"I'm sorry, Ma'am. I didn't mean to be disrespectful to your son."

"Apology accepted," said Beverly.

Later in the game Joshua was distracted when he saw a plane flying in the distance and had his back to the plate. The batter hit a ground ball down the first base line and it rolled into right field. Everyone was screaming, "Joshua, get the ball." Joshua turned around; saw the ball and the runner headed to second base. Joshua ran and picked up the ball. He didn't throw the ball into the infield; he gave chase, in a round-about way. He ran to first then headed to second. Halfway to third, the coach sent the runner home. Joshua rounded third and turned on the speed.

Lewis was on his feet, "This is going to be close."

Joshua tagged the runner out before reaching home. From the dugout Joshua's coach yelled, "Joshua what kind of baseball was that?"

Joshua took the ball out of his glove and looked at it. "It's just a regular old baseball."

"No, I mean what kind of baseball was that?"

"Oh!" Joshua looked at the ball and turned it around in his hand. He looked at the coach. "It's a Wilson."

"Never mind Joshua," the coach said, shaking his head.

Beverly turned around to the guy sitting behind her and said, "You're right, that little buggar can fly."

Later Deborah was at bat and a pitch hit her in the side. Beverly stood up "Oh no!" She started toward the field.

Lewis stopped her. "Let her be."

Deborah got up and trotted to first base. Halfway there she yelled at the pitcher, "Is that as hard as you can throw? You throw like a girl." She reached third on a base hit by the next player. On the next pitch the catcher missed the ball. Deborah was off and running. The catcher caught up with the ball and threw to the pitcher who was covering home. He turned to apply the tag thinking the runner would be sliding. Deborah wasn't thinking of sliding. The impact was tremendous. Deborah's helmet came off. The pitcher's hat went flying up in the air. Both Deborah and the pitcher were on the ground.

The umpire looked in the glove and saw the ball. "You're out."

It's a long ride home when you lose. Deborah sat in the back seat with her arms folded. She was fuming. "If Clark had caught that fly ball we would have won. How do you miss a fly ball?"

Joshua was sitting beside her and said, "It's easy to miss a fly ball. It's real easy."

With the season almost over the coach was going over the scorebooks. He was figuring out batting averages for the players. He thought they would like to know. Just like the major leagues. He totaled up hits, base on balls, strikeouts, runs batted in and runs scored. When he was finished, he sat back and shook his head. Joshua's batting average was the lowest, but he walked a lot. His strike zone was smaller because he was smaller than the other players. None of this surprised the coach. What did surprise him was that Joshua led the team in scoring. The little rascal scored almost every time he got on base. The coach checked the figures again. They were right. How can I keep him from getting distracted in the field? It's like he's in a trance every time a plane flies overhead. Once he ran over to centerfield just to point an airplane out to him. Maybe I can speak to his parents about this. He was sure they had noticed his obsession with planes, too. I think I will pay them a visit. He took the statistics with him.

Deborah answered the door. "Hello, Coach, would you like to come in?"

"Is your Mom and Dad home?"

"Yes, Sir, I'll go get them."

"Is Joshua home?"

"Yes, Sir, he's studying his airplane books."

That explains a lot. Maybe he just has an interest in airplanes. I'm sure it's just a phase and it will pass as he gets older.

"Afternoon, Coach. What brings you here?" asked Lewis.

"Coach would you like something to drink?" asked Beverly

"No, thank you, Ma'am. Is there somewhere we can talk, you know, without the kids?"

"Well, it's a nice day. How about on the porch?" suggested Lewis.

On the porch the coach said, "I went over the records of all the players. I'm happy to say Deborah has a very high batting average."

"What's a batting average?" asked Beverly.

"It's a percentage of how often a player gets a base hit verses how many times they bat, if the player walks it doesn't count on their average."

"I think I understand," said Beverly.

"Well, Deborah has the second highest batting average on the team."

"Well, that's great!" said Lewis.

"Yes, it is. She's a remarkable little girl. A great player. Boy, she hustles and tries harder than anyone on the team. I had my doubts about a girl playing but she's removed any doubts I had. I wish the other players tried as hard as she does. And, that brings me to Joshua. Deborah is so competitive and Joshua is not at all. I have noticed he gets distracted so easily. If a plane goes overhead he can't take his eyes off of it."

"We both have noticed that. Beverly and I have talked about this. We have both decided not to put any pressure on them to participate or not participate. If they show an interest we will support them."

"Well, I know that's great. I know some kids play baseball or softball just because their parents insist they play. I wish other parents had your attitude. It's just a game. I want to see kids have a good time and enjoy the sport without all the pressure. I've seen parents scream at their child if they missed a ball. It's sad when you think about how it must make that child feel.

"The real reason I dropped by was to tell you how well Deborah was doing. You have every right to be proud of her. She is like a little pioneer out there. Next year I bet we will have more girls interested in stepping up to the plate."

"You haven't mentioned Joshua's, uh, what did you call it?"

"Batting average."

"Yes, that's it, batting average," said Beverly.

The Coach cleared his throat and said, "His average is the lowest on the team."

"I see," said Beverly.

"I don't think you really do, Ma'am."

"Why is that?"

"Well, Joshua leads the team in scoring is why. He is so fast if he gets on base he steals second then third and usually scores. Scoring is more important than getting a base hit."

"I see, so Joshua is doing fine except he gets distracted when a plane comes within a hundred miles. Is that what you are saying?"

"Yes. Ma'am, but it's just a game. I believe he's happier than Deborah on the way home, am I right?"

"Yes, you are, and in a perfect world Deborah would be a little less competitive and Joshua would be a little more competitive. We don't live in a perfect world and I wouldn't change either of them one bit."

"Oh, you can't believe how much he loves planes. He saves his allowance so he can buy more plane books. He has models all over his room and pictures everywhere," said Lewis.

"Well, he will probably outgrow that. Something else will interest him later. Cars, girls, it happens."

"I sort of doubt it. I've never seen any child that obsessed with planes," said Beverly.

As the Coach was leaving Lewis shook his hand and said, "Coach, you don't know how much it means to see people like you volunteer their time. You're showing these kids that someone other than their parents love them. You are teaching them about sportsmanship and that's important."

"Thank you, Lewis."

"I once knew a man who told me that a man never stood so tall as when he stooped over to help a child, and I believe that."

"Maybe that should be our league motto," said the coach.

"That would be nice," said Lewis.

"And who knows, Joshua may be a pilot one day," said the coach.

"Only if he wants to be one," said Lewis. "We are not going to encourage or discourage one way or the other. Like you said, he may find another interest later. He has been on the planes for at least two years. He got a book for his sixth birthday and he just about went crazy. I've had to learn about planes myself, just to answer his questions."

PLANES

The next year Joshua was still studying airplanes. Lewis and Joshua were assembling models of every type of airplane he could get. Joshua also got more involved in math. He had asked Lewis what two words were in one of his plane books.

"That's aeronautical engineer," said Lewis.

"What do they do with airplanes?"

"Well, from what I understand they design airplanes."

"That is so cool; you mean they decide what a plane is going to look like?"

"I think so," said Lewis. "I bet they know all about flying a plane."

"You can do both?" asked Joshua.

"I think so."

"Wow, when I get big I would love to do that."

Lewis always smiled when Joshua used the term 'when I get big.' He knew Joshua was small for his age and probably would never get big as big is considered. That wasn't all that important now. Lewis knew he ate like a horse. He also knew Deborah seemed to be catching up with children her age.

"Of course you have to be real smart in math."

"I'm real smart in math, my teacher said so."

"Yes, but I bet you have to be even smarter than you are now, but of course you will learn even more the older you get.

"I'm going to learn even more, you'll see," said Joshua.

"In a few years you will have to learn algebra. You know what I always called algebra?"

"No, sir."

"I always called algebra, 'Big Al.'"

Joshua canted his head to one side and squinted his eyes.

Lewis noticed and asked, "Something wrong?"

"No, Sir, I was just trying to remember something."

That night Joshua didn't go to sleep right away. He was trying to remember who or what was 'Big Al.' He had heard it before but when or where had he heard it.

"Dad, why am I smaller than everybody in my class?" Lewis was tucking him in at bedtime. Lewis knew that one day he would probably be asked this question. It was only natural to wonder why.

"I don't know, son. I don't know why you are the smallest and I don't know why you are the smartest in your class, either.

"I think I know why," said Joshua.

"Why?" asked Lewis.

"Because that's the way God made me."

"You know what, I think you are right, Son. Actually I know you are right and guess what."

"What?" asked Joshua.

"God has a plan for you just like he has a plan for everyone. That's why you should always do your best with the gifts he has given you. That way whatever plan he has for you, you will be ready to carry it out."

Joshua thought a while and said, "You know what Miss May told me yesterday."

Lewis thought there is no telling what Miss May told him. "What did Miss May tell you, Son?"

"She said that one day I was going to do something amazing. I don't know what she was talking about."

"You do something amazing every day, son. The way you love the three of us is pretty amazing to me."

"Deborah loves the three of us just like I do," said Joshua.

"That's pretty amazing isn't it," said Lewis.

"Yes, I guess it is."

"Don't forget to say your prayers," said Lewis.

At the age of eight, the kids were very good riders. After going to the rodeo and seeing girls participate was all the incentive Deborah needed. Joshua was amazed at the clowns. Deborah loved riding horses and always rode faster than Joshua. Joshua was a good rider but he was no match for Deborah. Beverly was proud of the way they took care of the horses, not just theirs but all of them. One day Joshua asked Beverly, "Why doesn't Dad like to ride horses?"

Beverly laughed and said, "Well, he has his jeep and it's less likely to throw him than a horse. Your Dad is not a horse person."

"Can he ride at all?" asked Deborah.

"Well, I'm pretty sure if there was an emergency involving life or death he could."

"You mean if the jeep won't start," laughed Joshua.

"Right, if the jeep won't start."

Beverly and Lewis believed in being active members of the community. Beverly was a den mother for the girl scouts. Lewis was a scout master for the boy scouts. He enjoyed taking the seven boys camping. He would show the boys some of his survival skills he had learned in Ranger school. He would tell them, "Always be prepared and don't lose your cool. You can find a way. It may save your life one day or someone else's life."

Joshua and Deborah both participated in the junior rodeo and sang in the children's choir at church. It was unique to see her barrel racing on Saturday and singing solo on Sunday. Her favorite song was 'There Will be Peace in the Valley.' Joshua would also sing a solo from time to time. He would always sing 'I'll Fly Away.'

Both children made the honor roll every year. When the school held the annual spelling bee everyone would speculate on which MacDonald child would walk away with top honor. The same went for the geography bee. At the close of each contest there were only two children still on stage. It was anyone's guess who would be the last one standing. Every night Beverly helped the two children study. She actually learned a lot herself. They made learning a game and Beverly developed a method for remembering things she would learn. She thought it was a lot of fun and she would study the material herself so she could ask the children questions about any given subject. Beverly was becoming more intelligent every day, so were the children.

Eight hundred miles away a veteran sat in his wheelchair and hoped and prayed.

CHAPTER TWENTY

THE NERD

The kids were now thirteen and the school year was coming to an end. They would be in high school next year. Where has the time gone? Beverly knew the eighth grade would be different than middle school. Beverly knew that there would be more stress on the children. There was not much stress back when she was that age but it was different now and things had certainly changed. She was thankful for happy hour. It was a great stress reliever. It was a stress reliever for all of them. Playing games and not worrying about the state the world was in. Happy hour was also a way to kind of stretch the truth. It was always in jest and Joshua could outdo anyone else.

"I am the self-proclaimed nerd of Kerney Middle School," he began one night.

"How so?" asked Lewis.

"What do you mean, self-proclaimed?" inquired Beverly.

"No one else wants the title," Deborah chimed in.

"I have everything going for me, size, weight, the goofy looks and brain power. That is with a capital B and P. Brain Power. Others use brawn, I use brain power. Everyone knows nerds are small. Now look at this physique." He stood up and made an attempt to flex his muscles. "I have devised a method for storing pertinent information, really for instant recall."

Lewis looked at him and grinned, "Will you share this discovery with the rest of us?"

"Certainly, the brain has lots of nooks and crannies. I store the mundane information in there."

"In those nooks and crannies," said Beverly with a not so sure grin.

"That is correct. This allows me to store important information in a centralized location. I have moved it closer to the front for easy access."

"I think I understand the concept," said Lewis nodding his head in understanding.

"As you can see this allows for easy access. I have placed everything in alphabetical order by height and color. I can systematically recall information. This allows me to help my fellow man. If they need to know something, say they fall asleep in class, they can come to me and for a modest fee I share this knowledge with them. I am the go to guy for knowledge," said Joshua.

"Did I hear you say for a modest fee? How much is a modest fee?" asked Beverly.

"He charges a nickel," replied Deborah.

"A nickel?" quipped Lewis.

"That is correct, a nickel," said Joshua.

"He made thirty five cents today," said Deborah, "including a nickel from me."

"Joshua! Surely you didn't charge your own sister." Beverly was aghast.

"She asked a two part question, so she actually got a discount."

"Oh, I see, I think," said Beverly.

"Business is business," said Joshua and smiled.

THE FIGHT

On the last day of school, Beverly was helping the third grade class at their end of the year party. The middle school was between the elementary and the high school. She drove to the school expecting to see them standing outside. They weren't there. Where could they be? The other students were gone. "Oh Lord, I hope nothing is wrong," said Beverly to herself.

She went into the office and asked, "Have you seen Joshua and Deborah?"

The secretary glanced at the principal's office and said, "They are in there with Mr. Queen. You can go in. They are waiting for you."

Beverly knocked and opened the door. Mr. Queen was behind his desk. Joshua and Deborah were seated across from him.

"Come in, Mrs. MacDonald." Joshua and Deborah looked in Beverly's direction. Beverly saw the black eye on Joshua immediately.

She went over to him. "Joshua, are you alright?"

"Yes, Ma'am, I've been hurt before. This doesn't hurt."

She looked at Mr. Queen. "What happened?"

"They were fighting."

"I can't believe Joshua and Deborah were fighting."

"Not with each other."

"Well, where is the other student?"

Mr. Queen cleared his throat. "He's at the High School. I sent him over there. He is not even supposed to be over here. I assume his parents have taken him home."

"Joshua, you know you are not supposed to be fighting. Haven't we always taught you to just walk away?"

"Yes, Ma'am, I tried to just walk away and he hit me anyway."

Mr. Queen said, "Joshua wasn't the one who was fighting, Ma'am." He looked at Deborah. "Deborah was the one fighting."

"Deborah how could you?" snapped Beverly.

Mr. Queen said, "I saw the whole thing. The kid punched Joshua and Deborah saw him do it. I tried to get there but the other students were already gathered around and in the way. Deborah screamed at him, 'You leave my brother alone,' then he shoved her down. She got up and said, 'Did you hear what I said; leave my brother alone.' Then he shoved her again. When Deborah got back up she landed the first eight or ten punches. She had him on the sidewalk and she was trying to pull his ears off. She was saying, 'If you won't listen, you don't need these.'"

"Deborah, what do you have to say for yourself?" asked Beverly.

"I broke a nail!" She held it out for Beverly to see.

Beverly was shocked by the answer and said, "Young lady when we get home you have some explaining to do."

Mr. Queen said, "Have you ever seen a wild cat go after a dog?"

"No, Sir, I have not."

"Well, that's what it was like. It took three of us to pull her off."

"Mr. Queen, I am terribly sorry about this. What happens now?" Beverly knew the school policy on fighting and she was dreading the answer.

"Well, I am supposed to expel her for two weeks."

"But school is out," said Beverly.

"Yes, and that makes it impossible to expel her for two weeks. I'm supposed to fill out a report and file it, but I don't know where the form is. All the office help is gone and I'm retiring next week. So if you just go on home, we will forget this incident ever happened."

"Yes, Sir, thank you so much Sir," said Beverly.

"And I wouldn't worry about the boy. After she beat him up all the other kids were making fun of him for getting beat up by a girl. I don't think he will be showing his face any time soon."

In the car Beverly looked at Joshua. "I'm taking you by the doctor."

"Mom, I'm fine, this doesn't hurt."

"Let's not forget about my nail," said Deborah.

"What am I going to tell your father?"

"We could tell him I ran into a door knob," said Joshua.

"We are not going to lie to him."

"Maybe he won't notice. I could put on a hat and wear sunglasses. That wouldn't work he'd want to know why I was wearing a hat."

Beverly had to laugh at that. Even with a black eye he still had a sense of humor.

They were at the dinner table when Lewis came home. He washed his hands and sat down. He looked at Joshua. "Door knob?"

"Sorta," said Joshua.

"That's a beaut," said Lewis.

"Yes, Sir."

"You know the problem with black eyes don't you?"

"No, Sir."

"They only last a week or ten days. You really can't show it off for longer than ten days."

"Lewis, please don't make jokes about this, they were fighting."

"I know that."

"You do? How did you find out?"

"At the hardware store. Anytime something happens around here someone calls the hardware store first then the newspaper and then the radio station. You can get the news a lot faster through the hardware store. So I already know all about it."

"Well, aren't you going to do something? I don't want them fighting."

"I don't either. Now Joshua, did you try to walk away?"

"Yes, Sir, I did, but he hit me anyway."

Lewis looked over at Deborah, "Deborah, did you try to avoid a fight with the boy?"

"Yes, Sir, he pushed me down twice then he said something that made me mad so I hit him."

"What did he say?" asked Lewis.

"I'd rather not say," answered Deborah.

"Joshua, do you know what the boy said?"

"Yes, Sir" Joshua was looking down.

"What did he say?" asked Beverly.

"I kind of promised Deborah I wouldn't tell."

"Kind of," asked Lewis looking at Beverly.

"Well, I sorta promised I wouldn't tell."

"Joshua did you promise Deborah you wouldn't tell what the boy said?"

"Yes, Sir."

"Well, then you don't have to tell," said Lewis

"Lewis, they were fighting. Now I know he promised her but this is different."

"How is this different? Both of us have taught them to keep their promise so he should keep his promise."

"You should have seen her, Dad," said an excited Joshua. "Pow, pow, pow, she hit him in the snotlocker then between the running lights and then in the breadbasket."

"Joshua MacDonald! We do not use words like that," Beverly said.

"Yes, Ma'am, I mean his protruding oxygen intake apparatus."

"His what?" asked Lewis.

"His nose," answered Joshua.

"And the other thing? I know what a breadbasket is but what's running lights?" asked Lewis.

"Running lights? I thought everyone knew running lights were the eyes."

"I see," said Lewis.

"See, that means you're running lights are operating satisfactory" Joshua said with that smile.

Lewis shook his head. He's a regular comedian thought Lewis.

"She was on him like a wildcat on a possum or a raccoon; I forgot what Mr. Queen said."

"He said a dog," said Deborah.

Lewis looked at Joshua and asked, "How old is this boy?"

"I heard he's old enough to vote." Then he flashed a smile.

"Deborah, if you decide to tell me what he said then you can tell me, okay. Were you hurt?"

"I broke a nail." She got up and showed Lewis.

"Lewis, I can't believe you are making light of all this, don't you understand they could have been expelled."

"Beverly, I understand. Each one tried to avoid the fight. I am not going to tell them they can't defend themselves. Sometimes people won't take no for an answer.

Now, young lady," Lewis was looking at Deborah. "You will be in high school next year and boys will start looking at you in a different way. You don't want all the boys afraid you will beat them up now, do you?"

"Well, maybe." Deborah looked at him and smiled and said, "No, Sir, I guess not."

"If they're not interested then pow, pow, pow," said Joshua grinning. Then Joshua said, "Dad can we go to town tomorrow?"

"Why do you need to go to town?"

"Well, it would be a good chance to show off my black eye it being Saturday and all."

"We'll see," answered Lewis.

"I wish you would grow up," said Deborah.

And grow he did…That summer Joshua started to grow, really grow. He lost his stature as the school nerd. Nerds were known to be small and Joshua was growing like a weed.

HAPPY HOUR

"Well, what's it feel like to no longer be the school nerd?" asked Lewis during happy hour.

"It's alright; it was only a matter of time. Every drifter and gunslinger that comes through think they have to try their skills against yours. Now I don't have to constantly watch my back."

"Who's the new nerd now?" inquired Beverly.

"A new kid named Pierre from the Dakota's," answered Joshua.

"North or South?" asked Lewis.

"Does it really matter where he is from? He's got the size, the weight, and the goofy looks and did I mention he wears black horn rimmed glasses, how can I compete with that?"

"I don't suppose you can," said Beverly.

Joshua held up his hand with his fingers extended. "See these fingers. They will never grace the keys of a common calculator. My slide rule is gathering dust."

"Oh, this guy is good, he's real good," said Deborah.

"I guess it's hard to charge a nickel for information now; you know now that you are not the top dog anymore," said Lewis.

Joshua nodded. "That's the sad part. Guess what Pierre charges. A dime. I heard he was opening up an off shore bank account to hide his money. The guy is good; he's real good."

Deborah laughed. "Guess you paid him a dime today?"

Everyone looked at Joshua. "I was just checking him out, you know, finding out if he knows his stuff."

Lewis was smiling and asked, "So, what was the question you paid him twice the going rate for?"

"I asked him about the infield fly rule in baseball."

"I've never heard of it before, what is it?" asked Lewis.

'It's too complicated to explain."

"You haven't mentioned his term paper," said Deborah.

Lewis asked, "What was his term paper about?"

Joshua sighed. "He concluded Einstein was overrated. He's good, really good. Guess what his favorite phrase is, you're going to love this. 'Are you joshing me?' You say something to him and he will say, 'Are you joshing me?' So now everyone is calling me Josh. You all can still call me Joshua if you like."

"I kind of like Josh, don't you, Honey?" said Beverly. "Sounds more grown up."

"It sounds cool to me," said Lewis.

"He will always be little brother to me," said Deborah.

Eight hundred miles away a veteran sat in his wheelchair and hoped and prayed and waited. He had waited a long time. He would never stop hoping and praying. He would wait as long as he had to. Hope, pray and wait. That was all he could do and he would never stop.

JACK IN THE BOX

The Iranian had spent five years at the phone company in Fargo, North Dakota when he was instructed to turn in his notice and move to Washington State. He was to direct an operation that would take place on the Canadian border. He changed identities but was still in Spanish mode.

He had been given a large sum of money to conduct the operation. The money was for bribes and to live a fairly lavish lifestyle. He knew westerners would do anything for money. He approached the customs officers and made them an offer they would have been a fool to refuse.

He was posing as a drug smuggler. "You let my trucks go through and you can retire early." His company owned six trucks. The trucks were clearly marked as trucks belonging to a furniture company operating in Canada who shipped to America. The custom officials would also receive a percentage of the drugs worth. The Iranian made sure there were never any drugs on the trucks, only furniture.

The customs men were told to let the Wednesday truck pass through with only a curious glance inside the cargo section. The Iranian had been running this operation for a year and the other trucks were rigorously inspected. The Wednesday truck would not be.

The Iranian did not know what the end result was supposed to be. He lived in a nice condo in Seattle and drove a nice Lexus automobile. He wouldn't mind doing this for twenty years.

THE GOOD DIE YOUNG

After cutting Miss May's grass they were sitting in the rocking chairs on the front porch. She had already paid him a nickel. Josh tried to decline but he took it after she insisted. They went through this ritual every time he cut her grass.

"Joshua, did you know that Joshua took Moses' place in the good book."

"Yes, Ma'am." Josh knew Miss May was the only person who still called him Joshua. He also knew she never said the Bible; she always called it the good book.

"Maybe one day you are going to take someone's place."

Two days later the mail man was making his deliveries. He always went to the door and knocked so she wouldn't have to walk to the mailbox. But today, she was in her rocker on the front porch. The first thing he noticed was she didn't wave and her rocker was perfectly still. He checked her pulse or tried to. She had obviously passed away. He went inside and called the sheriff's office. He went back outside and waited. He knew there was no chance of foul play. She had to be a hundred or maybe even more.

A large print Bible was in her lap. She was obviously reading it when she passed away. A purple silk bookmark was clutched in one hand. The mailman slipped it out and read it to himself. "This is the day which the Lord hath made. We will rejoice and be glad in it." He noticed her index finger was resting on a Bible verse. The verse had been highlighted with a yellow highlighter to make it easier to read or perhaps find. He took the Bible out of her hand and read the verse "And be kind one to another, tenderhearted, forgiving one another, even as God for Christ's sake hath forgiven you." The mailman nodded his head in acknowledgement. "You did all that and more

Miss May." He closed the Bible and read the first page. "Merry Christmas from Lewis, Beverly, Joshua and Deborah." He carried the Bible inside by her chair. He was sure the MacDonald family would like to have it returned. Then he went back outside and sat in the rocker and waited.

MATTHEW 5:8

Lewis made the arrangements for her burial. Beverly went into her closet and picked up the dress she had given her years ago. Miss May had said, 'It was way too pretty to wear. It was pretty enough to be buried in.' Beverly couldn't help but think that was what Miss May was saving it for.

At the funeral there was an overflow crowd. She knew everyone and had done something for almost every family in the county. Several people spoke about her and what she had done for them. Some of the stories were funny, some were sad. When it came time for Lewis to speak he went to the pulpit. Lewis was a man of few words. Most people in Wyoming are. They say what they mean and mean what they say. Lewis had never spoken to a crowd, big or small.

Lewis said, "We don't know what day she was born, only the day that she died. We don't know where she came from but we are glad she stopped and we're glad she stayed. That's in the good book in the book of Judges."

When Beverly spoke she had to wipe away a few tears. "I would like to quote a Bible verse that is fitting for Miss May. It is the Gospel of John, chapter eleven, verse thirty five. 'Jesus wept.'"

CHAPTER TWENTY ONE

BULL IN A CHINA SHOP

Josh continued to grow. Beverly became concerned enough to call Doc Fletcher.

"He's growing like a weed," said Beverly.

"It's about time!" replied Doc Fletcher.

"Do you think something could be wrong with him?"

"I doubt it. Sometimes kids just suddenly get a growth spurt and can grow a foot taller in a year."

"I think he has already done that."

"I'm sure he's alright. Don't let him walk around in the corral without his boots on," Doc teased her, chuckling as he hung up.

Lewis asked Beverly, "You remember how Josh was always saying 'when I get big?'"

"He hasn't said that in a while has he," said Beverly.

"At least a year, maybe two."

Josh continued to grow. He loaded and unloaded bales of hay, jerking them around like they were nothing. In his senior year he was the biggest boy in school. Wide shoulders, barrel chested, huge long arms, small waist and big long legs. He stood six foot, five inches tall and weighed two hundred and sixty five pounds of pure muscle.

Josh's friend, Tommy Parker's dad, had died after a long bout with cancer. Tommy lived a few miles from the MacDonald's ranch. Josh and Deborah would stop by each morning and give him a ride to school. Tommy was the best player on the Kerney County High

Rustlers football team. Everyone thought Tommy would win a football scholarship to a major college. After his father died, Mrs. Parker had to start working at the diner in town. Tommy would go to school and then go to football practice. After practice he would go to where his mother worked and hang around until closing time at eleven o'clock.

Josh knew Tommy wouldn't be able to keep doing that and would probably have to stop playing football. Josh said he was planning on trying out for the team and Tommy could ride home with him.

"That's great," said Tommy.

Josh didn't know a thing about football.

The Kerney County football coach was so disappointed in Josh that it made him furious. Josh wouldn't tackle and hardly blocked. All that size gone to waste. He let him stay on the team because he only had thirty five players. He tried putting him at defensive end hoping his size would make the other team run the other way. The coach found out that wouldn't work in the first practice. He put Josh on the bench. That didn't bother Josh at all. Josh rode the bench every game. He never played a single play the whole season. He never told anyone that the only reason he stayed on the team was so Tommy would have a ride home.

Lewis volunteered to help out on the sidelines giving players Gatorade during time outs, wrapping sprains and taping cuts.

The Coach thought about talking with Lewis and see if he could motivate his son. He decided against that when he realized he needed Lewis helping out. He would let sleeping dogs lie.

The first game was a total disaster. They played the Cheyenne High Wranglers. The Wranglers had won the last two State Championships. The score was 44 to 3. Then the team jelled and won the next nine games. The team only averaged seventeen points a game, but the defense led by Tommy Parker held their opponents to fourteen points a game.

In the playoffs, they won three in a row. Tommy had been selected as All State Defensive End. He was all over the field making tackles. In the playoffs alone, he had blocked two punts and a game deciding extra point.

The Kerney County Rustlers were riding Tommy's coat tails and everyone knew it, especially their next opponent. The Cheyenne Wranglers were 13 and 0 going into the State Championship game. They were averaging 38 points a game while giving up 17.

"Welcome to the Wyoming High School Championship football game being played tonight here in Cheyenne, Wyoming. The Cheyenne High Wranglers against the Kerney County Rustlers. I am Ted Malone and I will be joined by my good friend Jim Bowman. Jim, is there anything you would like to point out to our viewers?"

"Thanks, Ted, well one thing that has to be noted is Cheyenne is eyeing its third consecutive championship title. Cheyenne defeated Kerney High in the first game of the season 44 to 3. If you look at the sidelines you see almost seventy players on one side and thirty five on the other. That in itself should tell you something. Cheyenne has averaged 38 points a game.

"The fans are sensing this, too. There are twenty thousand on the Cheyenne side because they are playing at home.

"Kerney County has brought 1200 faithful here on this cold December night. Back to you Ted."

"Thanks, Jim. Any predictions?"

"Cheyenne 38, Kerney 17 that's my prediction. Cheyenne has five players selected to All State; Kerney has one. I don't see Kerney County pulling this off."

"Any key match-ups you see?"

"Yes, Kerney County has an outstanding defensive end in Tommy Parker and across from him is the best tight end I've ever seen. Pat Fleming might just negate the All State Defensive End that Kerney County has."

"The teams are meeting for the coin toss. You will notice the team colors for both teams are red and white. Cheyenne is wearing red jerseys with white numbers, white pants and white helmets. Kerney is wearing all white with red numbers and red helmets.

"Here comes the toss. Cheyenne has won the toss and elected to receive. Kerney County has selected the end zone to our right. I don't think wind is going to be a factor tonight. The only factor is the temperature. It was freezing last night and the field is still frozen."

"Jim, do you think the crowd noise will be a factor?"

"Could be; twenty thousand fans can make a lot of noise."

"They're lining up for the kick-off. We are underway."

The game started with Cheyenne driving the ball for a touchdown. Kerney County didn't have any luck on their first possession and punted to Cheyenne. Kerney was able to stop this drive. On Kerney's next possession, they had to punt the ball away after three plays.

Cheyenne was overwhelming Kerney County at the line of scrimmage and moved the ball down field on their third possession and punched the ball in for a 14-0 lead. Kerney just couldn't mount an offense and punted the ball away. Cheyenne stalled on their next drive and punted. Once again Kerney couldn't move the ball and with six minutes left in the half they punted. Cheyenne marched down field. They smelled blood. Score here and take a 21-0 lead into halftime.

With fifteen seconds left on the clock at Kerney's ten yard line, Cheyenne called 'power right triple option.' This play would put most of the Cheyenne team running to Tommy Parkers side of the field. The quarterback had three options, pass, lateral to the halfback or keep the ball himself.

On the snap, the big tight end straightened Tommy Parker up and the fullback, who was leading the way, hit him low on the leg. Tommy's right leg snapped. The quarterback lateraled the ball to the trailing halfback. Somehow the Kerney linebacker ran the halfback out of bounds at the five with ten seconds left in the half. Tommy Parker wasn't getting up. The Kerney players were frantically waving for the trainers.

Lewis ran on the field. They were on the far side in the corner. Josh had seen the play. His friend was hurt. Josh ran as fast as he could to help. As soon as Lewis saw the leg he knew it was broken. "Josh, don't let him move, okay."

Josh knelt down and took hold of Tommy's hand. "Don't move Tommy" was all he could say.

Lewis ran to the middle of the field and waved for the ambulance. Once the ambulance started moving Lewis returned to Tommy's side. "Don't move, son. I know it hurts, but don't move."

The ambulance crew took over and secured his leg so he couldn't move it and do more damage. Josh was looking at the Cheyenne players. They were high fiving each other and laughing. Something was building inside of Josh. An anger he didn't know he had.

One of the trainers said, "They did that on purpose. You don't play like that, it's just a game."

Then Josh said, "It's not just a game anymore." As they loaded the stretcher on the ambulance Josh picked up Tommy's helmet and ran into the huddle. A linebacker said, "We got twelve in the huddle. Someone's got to leave."

Josh said, "It's not going to be me."

Tommy's mother was sitting with Beverly and her mother. Alice said, "Come on Mavis, I'll drive you to the hospital. We can follow the ambulance."

Beverly asked if she needed to go, too.

"No, you stay," nodded Alice, and they were off to the hospital.

Well, that was the worst thing that could happen right now. That was their best defensive player and if Cheyenne scores here with no time left I'm afraid that's the ballgame. I just don't see Kerney County coming back down 21-0.

The Linebacker looked at Josh and saw something in his eyes. "Alright, safety out," he yelled and pointed at the safety. When the Coach saw the safety run off the field he grabbed him by the arm.

"Why did you come out?"

"We had twelve in the huddle, Coach."

"Who went in? I only sent one player in. Who else is in there?"

"Josh MacDonald, Coach"

"MacDonald, I didn't send MacDonald in. I need someone who can tackle." The Coach ran to the defensive coach. "Did you send MacDonald in?"

The defensive coach looked around and didn't see number 94 who was always seated on the end of the bench with the kicker. "No, Sir, I didn't send anyone in."

"Call time out."

"We can't Coach. We don't have any time outs left."

The Coach was furious. He threw his clipboard down. He wanted to kill someone, namely Josh MacDonald.

"We're going to lose this game right here, right now. Why did he go in? I need someone who can tackle. You know they are going to run right at him."

The Coach couldn't bear to watch; but knew he had to.

"Look at him; he is not even in a stance. He's just standing there. At halftime I am going to rip his jersey right off of him. He is off the team."

Josh was just standing there. He was leaning forward a little at the waist. His feet were planted the width of his shoulders. His right foot was two feet behind the left. His long arms just hanging down.

The big tight end stepped up to the line of scrimmage and looked at Josh. "Hey, we got another country boy here."

Josh said nothing. He was looking at the ball.

"You should have had the ambulance wait on you."

Again, Josh said nothing, just kept looking at the ball.

"I'm going to knock you into the middle of next week."

Josh said nothing. He just looked at the ball.

On the snap, the big tight end fired off the line. It would have been a perfect block if a huge forearm swung at incredible speed hadn't hit him in the chest, lifted him off the ground and threw him on his back.

Josh was across the line of scrimmage. He saw the fullback coming parallel with the line of scrimmage. He dove at Josh's knees. Josh decided if the boy wanted a knee he would give him one. Josh timed it just right and dropped the fullback face first. The quarterback was sprinting to his right with his eye on the trailing halfback. When he saw Josh he froze like a deer in headlights. Without looking, he lateraled the ball to the halfback. Josh stretched his left arm out and tipped the ball. The halfback saw he wasn't going to catch the ball and tried to reverse his course and a foot slipped. He lost a couple of steps but didn't go down. The ball hit on the ten and bounced knee high.

In practice everyone is taught to fall on the ball. Josh had no intention of falling on the ball. He caught it with both hands a foot off the ground. Two strides later, Josh was streaking down the sidelines. Only one Cheyenne player knew the ball was loose and gave chase. He was one of the fastest players on the Cheyenne squad. Josh was eating up huge amounts of yardage with each long stride.

The Cheyenne player wasn't gaining ground he was losing ground. People that big can't run that fast thought the Cheyenne player.

On the Kerney side, no one saw Josh running down the sideline. His white uniform was streaking in front of red jerseys with huge white numbers. However there were three people there that night who were focused on number 94.

His dad went to the far end of the bench and stood on top of it. He was looking at Josh, number 94, eighty yards away. Deborah, the cheerleading captain, called for two cheerleaders to stand beside each other, she stood on their shoulders, and six girls were behind her to catch her when she fell backwards.

Beverly was in the stands. When she saw Josh on the field she framed him in the center of the camcorder. She wanted to capture his first play as a football player.

"The ball is loose! Kerney County has it. Look at him go. He only has to beat one man. He's at the fifty, the thirty, the ten, touchdown! Now a touchdown separates the two teams. Oh, this is a remarkable turnaround."

As Josh ran down the sidelines, the Cheyenne crowd stopped cheering when they saw him with the ball. All Josh could hear was the wind in the earholes of his helmet. He knew the kid wasn't going to catch him. No one had caught him since he was five years old.

When he crossed the goal line he didn't spike the ball or jump up and down. He didn't celebrate at all. He stopped and walked over to the side judge who finally reached the end zone and signaled a touchdown. He handed the ball to the referee. The referee who was forty five years old and winded after running ninety five yards said, "Thanks."

Josh said, "You're welcome," then trotted to the sidelines.

When Lewis saw Josh come out of the cluster of players with the ball he hopped down and started running down the sideline behind the players. Deborah didn't fall backwards she jumped down and was running behind everyone else. When she saw Josh score she started doing cartwheels. Beverly was filming the entire play. On the tape you could hear her saying, "Run, Josh, run. Oh, thank you Lord for blessing this family."

The Kerney coach was trying to get to Lewis. He was going to give him a piece of his mind. He saw Lewis hop down and start running. The coach didn't know his team had scored. When Josh reached the sideline Lewis shook his hand and patted him on the back.

Deborah jumped on him and threw her arms around his neck. "That was awesome little brother, just awesome."

Josh went to the bench and sat down.

The coach saw the players jumping up and down. "What happened?" he asked, to no one in particular.

"We scored coach, we scored a touchdown."

"How?"

"Fumble recovery I guess. I didn't see it but they are signaling touchdown."

"Who scored?"

"Josh MacDonald, Coach," someone said.

Twenty thousand fans on one side of the field were praying for a penalty flag. Twelve hundred on the other side was praying for no flag. God smiled on the twelve hundred.

Lewis went to the bench while Kerney High lined up to kick the extra point. He sat down beside Josh. "Josh I'm proud of you, especially the way you acted after scoring. That took class. The defense needs someone to become their leader with Tommy out. It doesn't matter who it is; they just need a leader."

Josh nodded his head.

Well, Jim we got us a different ballgame now 14-7. Do you think that last touchdown that was scored will be the difference in the game?"

The third quarter was a defensive struggle. Kerney's first possession was three and out. Cheyenne managed a first down before having to punt it away. Neither team crossed the fifty yard line.

A quiet leader emerged on the Kerney defensive unit. He was leading by example. That was the only way he knew how. In the third quarter, Cheyenne had the ball for four series. Josh made six tackles. He also batted a pass down at the line of scrimmage and caused a fumble that was recovered by Kerney. He was all over the field. He dominated the line of scrimmage. The Cheyenne team stopped running or passing on that side of the field.

In the fourth quarter neither team was able to move the ball. On two consecutive plays, Josh sacked the quarterback for a five yard loss. Midway through the fourth quarter Kerney County got its second break of the game. With the ball on the Kerney County forty, a back-up running back went in for an exhausted halfback. His name was Jerome 'Slick' Washington. He was the smallest player on the team; one of the only two African Americans on the team. He took a pitch out and ran right. There was nothing there. He reversed the field and ran all the way to the other sideline. He reversed again and actually ran behind his own thirty yard line. Finally he saw an opening and headed up field. He reversed directions yet again and went across the field. Then he headed for the end zone at an angle. When he crossed the goal line he collapsed. He had to be helped off the field.

"Well, that was the longest touchdown run I believe I have ever seen. He crossed the line of scrimmage four times. I believe he ran two hundred and fifty yards.

"Yes, Jim, he did and I think what happened, the Cheyenne defense wore themselves out chasing him. Did you notice no one touched him? If I didn't know better, I would say he was running for his life."

"Well, that won't be mentioned in the record book. It will go down as a sixty yarder. By the way, that was the longest run by Kerney County all year."

"Jim, the only two scores Kerney County has been able to muster up were by back-up players."

"That's right. How do you factor something like that in your game plan? When Tommy Parker was taken out you just knew this game was over and the very next play they go ninety yards on a deflected lateral for a touchdown. I'd like to add, this MacDonald Kid, number 94, has been impressive. Look at his size and I've never seen someone that big move that fast and I've seen a lot of great players in my twenty five year career."

There was someone else in the stands that started taking notice of Josh. He had come to scout six players. The six All State players in the game. He had a form to fill out on each player. He added a seventh. Number 94, Joshua MacDonald, defensive end, 6'5", 265 pounds, Kerney High School. He had already written down big, fast and strong. Then he added dominates the line of scrimmage. He would mail the forms and video to Norman, Oklahoma tomorrow morning. He often wondered if anyone read them. He was a recruiting scout for the University of Oklahoma.

With five minutes remaining in the game, Cheyenne had to punt from their own forty. Josh literally ran over his blocker and with those long arms outstretched he blocked the punt. Now the question on everyone's mind was can the Kerney County Rustlers move the ball. They desperately needed to score. The team was exhausted and if the game went into overtime could they stop Cheyenne.

Kerney County managed two first downs in a row. Their first consecutive first downs in the game. The Cheyenne defense stiffened and stopped them on the fifteen yard line. A thirty two yard field goal would put Kerney County ahead with a minute and a half left in regulation. The only bright spot on the Kerney County team was their kicking game. They had won six games by a field goal.

On a cold December night, with the field frozen, the kicker lined up and booted it through the uprights. Kerney County was too exhausted to celebrate.

The kickers name was Pierre Longfellow. He was small and had lived in Kerney County for three years. He had moved from North Dakota. He said kicking was a science having to do with temperature, humidity, barometric pressure, trajectory, ball placement, and other stuff no one understood.

Josh was his holder. He held Pierre's glasses when he kicked.

"Jim, Kerney County has just done something no other team has done in three years. The Cheyenne Wranglers have not trailed in a game in three years."

"You're right, Ted, but ninety seconds is a long time down on that field. If Cheyenne can manage the clock and either tie or score a go ahead touchdown that would be a heart breaking loss to Kerney. Or if Cheyenne fails to score and don't win their third consecutive championship that would be a huge loss. It's a shame someone has to lose. Both teams have played their hearts out tonight."

After the field goal, Pierre Longfellow went to the bench and put his glasses on. He wanted to see how much time was left on the clock. Pierre was like a lot of geniuses. He would forget to tie his shoes, comb his hair, or wear the same color socks. He weighed 134 pounds in all his equipment. His I.Q. was 142.

On the ensuing kickoff, the kick returner spotted a seam in the Kerney team. He headed that way. As he was about to break into the open he saw a scrawny kid flying through the air. The runner did a double take; the scrawny kid was wearing black rimmed glasses. Pierre Longfellow had never made a tackle in his life. The other players joked that Pierre couldn't tackle his sister. Pierre bounced off and slid to the ground. The Cheyenne runner tripped over Pierre and fell on the thirty. On the sideline, a Kerney player slapped Pierre on the shoulder. "Good tackle."

"Someone pushed me," answered Pierre, then he went to the bench and looked around. "Has anyone seen my glasses?" He would find them in a few minutes; he was wearing them.

Cheyenne seldom passed the ball. They were a running team that could grind out the yardage and eat up the clock. Now the role was reversed. Cheyenne started throwing quick down and out passes to the sidelines and would get out of bounds to stop the clock. Each play was taking five or six seconds for four or five yards. They reached the fifty but needed to reach the twenty five for a long field goal.

First down at the fifty. Thirty seconds on the clock. On first down the Kerney defense rose to the occasion and tackled the runner in bounds. The clock continued to wind down. Ten seconds, ten precious seconds was lost.

On second down, the Cheyenne receiver caught the ball and headed up field and went past the first down marker. A Kerney defensive back put a bone jarring tackle on the receiver and the ball squirted loose and went behind the first down marker. Both teams scrambled for the ball. Once the pile became somewhat stationary the side judge blew his whistle and signaled to stop the clock. It was deathly quiet in the stands. Who has the ball? That was the question on everyone's mind. At least ten players were in the pile. The refs were pulling players off the pile, those that obviously didn't have the ball. At the bottom of the pile, a Cheyenne player was in a fetal position with his huge arms wrapped around the ball. The referee had his hands on the ball to make sure it wasn't moved forward even an inch. The umpire signaled for a measurement. One referee had a chain link in his hand to make sure the measurement was precise or as precise as possible. The chain is ten yards long, thirty feet. Three hundred and sixty links in the chain. The referees stretched the chain as far as possible. The players were gathered around watching closely. The spectators couldn't see for the players. The ref stood up and held his arms over his head. His palms and fingertips one inch apart. One link, then they signaled third down. The game clock read ten seconds.

Football is said to be a game of inches. It is also a game of passion. The referees huddled once again. The umpire announced, "Reset the game clock to twelve seconds-twelve seconds." A collective groan went up from the Kerney bleachers. Twelve seconds is time enough for three plays, maybe four. Twelve seconds; games have been won or lost in less time. Twelve seconds can go by in a blur or in slow motion.

One player was behind the two teams watching the measurement. He faced the Kerney bleachers and started lifting his arms, palms up. He pumped his arms up and down, again and again. He wanted noise, lots of noise. All is not lost; he seemed to be telling the Kerney crowd. In the stands someone lifted his boots and started stomping the floor of the bleachers. Someone else joined in and then another. Young and old all joined in. Twelve hundred fans were stomping their feet. The noise reverberated throughout the stadium. For the first time that night, Kerney County was wound up to a fevered pitch. The player signaling for noise was number 94. In the huddle he said above the noise, "You hear that? How can we let them down?"

Football is indeed a game of passion. These modern day gladiators were fighting for their school, their community, their families and for themselves.

On third down, third and an inch, Cheyenne tried the safest play in the play book, which was a quarterback sneak. He was met by a wall of men, who seconds ago were mere boys. He bounced backwards and tried to run left. Josh caught him from behind for a three yard loss. Cheyenne called time out. Forth and three, eight seconds on the clock when Cheyenne called their last time out. Both teams went to the sidelines and huddled with the coaches.

"Do you think they will go for the first down or go for the score?" asked the Coach.

The defensive coach said, "If they go for the first down and don't make it out of bounds that's the ballgame. I would go for the score. That's what I would do."

"What do you think they will call? A Hail Mary?"

"That quarterback can't throw into the end zone from there. No way; it would be a fifty yarder."

"What defensive line up are we going to use? You know it's going to be some sort of trick play. It's got to be."

The defensive coach said, "We need five defensive backs in case they throw deep. Three down linemen, three linebackers spread out and five defensive backs."

"We don't have five defensive backs. Our backups are hurt."

"Let's put MacDonald on the five yard line. That's what I would do."

"We need the pass rush," said the coach.

"It will be over before that. Coach, he hasn't missed a tackle all night. They can't throw over him in the end zone."

"I don't know. I just don't know."

"Coach, you're always telling me a turtle never makes progress unless he sticks his neck out."

"You think I should stick my neck out?" asked the Coach.

"Yes, I do."

"You better tell him what he needs to do. Don't let them get by him and to bat the ball down. We don't need to lose this on the last play."

"I'll tell him."

He called Josh over. "Son, I need you on the five yard line. Please don't let them get by you and be careful on pass interference, okay."

Josh nodded and went to the five.

Beverly was wondering why is he all the way back there. He looks so lonesome back there all by himself. Cheyenne lined up. The Kerney Coach saw the alignment. He turned to his defensive coach. "Why is the tight end in the blocking back position?"

"I hope he's planning on blocking."

"They have three wide receivers in Coach," another coach pointed out.

"Why do they have a running back in? There's no way they are going to run?" asked the Coach.

On the snap, the quarterback faked to the huge tight end. It wasn't a very good fake, it wasn't supposed to be. He went through the line unmolested and drilled the middle linebacker. The quarterback pivoted. Seven seconds…The quarterback lateraled the ball to the running back that sprinted to his left. Six seconds…The wide receiver on the left side sprinted to his right. The running back lateraled the ball to the wide receiver. Five seconds…The wide receiver ran to the middle of the field and lofted a lazy spiral to the big tight end racing downfield. Four seconds…

The Kerney coaches were yelling, "Reverse, reverse," then "Pass, pass." The big tight end caught the ball on the twenty five yard line going full speed. Only one player stood between him and another

State Championship. He had a score to settle with number 94. Three seconds…

The big tight end didn't try to run around Josh. He headed straight for him. Josh held his ground. Two seconds…

If there had been a physics professor there that night he would have thought of Sir Isaac Newton's theory. A body in motion tends to stay in motion. A body at rest tends to stay at rest. An irresistible force meeting an immovable object. Each weighed 265 pounds. There was one factor that couldn't be computed. No one knew how strong Josh was. Josh didn't know how strong he was. You don't load and unload twenty thousand bales of hay in a year and not become strong. One second…

The tight end lowered his helmet and aimed at Josh's chest. Josh lowered his helmet. Twenty one thousand people heard the impact. It sounded like a gun shot. Zero…The clock stopped, but not the play. The impact knocked Josh back on his heels. Some spectators said they heard a mighty groan even though they couldn't tell from whom. Josh straightened up with his arms around the big tight end and slammed him to the ground. The tight ends helmet came off and rolled to the end zone.

The ball had popped loose and was bouncing toward the ten, then the fifteen. The wide receiver was racing down the field. Josh was trying to get to his feet. His knees were wobbly from the impact. As he staggered to his feet, Beverly could be heard on the video, "Josh get up! Please get up. You've got to get up Josh!"

The wide receiver scooped the ball up at the fifteen. All he had to do was angle away from Josh. He chose not to. Holding the ball out with one hand he wanted to taunt Josh before scoring. That was a huge mistake. Josh's legs started working and he launched his body from ten feet away at the wide receiver. The kid never had a chance. Josh flattened him.

There would be arguments about which tackle was the most vicious. Josh got up. He was holding the ball. The game was over.

Twenty thousand spectators on one side were hoping, praying for a flag. Twelve hundred were praying there was no flag. God smiled on the twelve hundred for the second time that night.

"Jim, have you ever seen a player make two tackles in one play?"

"Sure lots of times, but not like that. They are both still down and number 94 is waving the trainers over. We've watched this guy for the second half and each time he tackles someone he gave them a hand up. He didn't on this play. Maybe he realizes they won't be able to stand up. What a way to win and what a way to lose."

Josh walked towards the referee and held the ball out to them. "Game ball, Sir."

"You keep it, son. You deserve it."

"Thank you, Sir."

The Kerney County Rustlers who had just pulled off an unbelievable win were walking around in a daze. They were not celebrating. They were too tired. Meeting the Cheyenne players at midfield and shaking hands was even exhausting, but that had to be done no matter how tired you were.

Josh moved through the players and walked up to Jerome 'slick' Washington.

"Game ball, Slick." It was the first time Josh had ever called him 'Slick.'

"You're kidding right?"

"No, you rushed for two hundred and fifty yards in the State Championship game. You deserve it."

"Thanks, man."

"You should get everyone to autograph it and you can show it to your grandkids someday."

"Good idea. You know I was running for my life out there."

"It looked to me like you were running for a touchdown," said Josh with a smile.

The two coaches met at midfield and warmly shook hands. Each man had his other hand on the other man's shoulder. They spoke briefly. What was said is lost to history. No one recorded the brief exchange. The Cheyenne coach turned and trotted to his sideline. The Kerney coach walked slowly back to his sideline. Halfway there he looked to the Heavens and said, "Thank you."

His team had something no one would ever be able to take away. A State Championship and a place in history. Football is indeed a game of passion.

Three men wearing suits and heavy overcoats walked across the field. One held the Championship trophy. Another held a plaque. A Kerney player nudged a teammate to look, "City Slickers."

The Kerney players were exhausted. Several were bent over at the waist, hands on their knees gulping for air like a fish out of water. Many were looking at scrapes and cuts they didn't realize they had till now. Several were kneeling on one knee trying to rest legs that had given out ten minutes ago. They were a motley looking bunch. Yes, football certainly is a game of passion.

It's amazing how fast twenty thousand people can leave a stadium. Twelve hundred weren't going anywhere soon. The State School Superintendent and two other high ranking athletic board members were holding the championship trophy at the fifty yard line on the Kerney sidelines.

"Coach Brown, on behalf of the State of Wyoming, I'm proud to present you with this trophy. Congratulations!" Coach Brown had not prepared a victory speech. No one had expected them to win. His speech was the gracious loser's speech. Coach Brown was a man of few words, most people in Wyoming are.

"Thank you, Sir. I'd like to say it was an honor to play a fine team. Our boys, uh correction, our young men played their hearts out. On behalf of our school, our team and our fans, thank you."

The State Athletic director stepped forward, "On behalf of the State of Wyoming, I would like present this plaque to the most valuable player. Number 94, Joshua MacDonald, where are you Joshua?"

The players had to push Joshua to the front. The athletic director presented him with the plaque. Josh looked to his family twenty feet away. Josh looked at the plaque and spoke into the microphone.

"I don't deserve this award. The player that deserves this award is Tommy Parker. He led this team all year. He is the reason we are here tonight. If it wasn't for Tommy we would all be sitting home tonight watching someone else play." He held the plaque out to the athletic director. "Can we do that, Sir?" No one had ever turned an award down.

"Yes, we can," said the school superintendent.

Josh walked to his family and everyone hugged him. All three were saying, "We are so proud of you and so proud you recognized Tommy with the plaque."

"Coach Brown, do you have any more to say?"

Coach Brown cleared his throat and leaned toward the microphone. "Yes, there is. Twenty thousand people had the privilege to see a boy become a man tonight. I'm proud to have seen it myself. Thank you all and now I am off to the hospital to present this plaque to Tommy Parker." All this time he was watching the MacDonald family.

CHAPTER TWENTY TWO

THE REASON

MATTHEW 6:4

The Kerney County football team had rented rooms to spend the night in Cheyenne instead of having to drive the four hundred miles back to Kerney. Most of the fans had also rented rooms in Cheyenne and the surrounding areas.

After returning to their rooms, Deborah and Josh showered and changed into their street clothes.

"Dad, can we go to the hospital and see how Tommy is? I know Grandma is still there with Mrs. Parker."

"All of us will go. Mrs. Parker needs all the support she can get," replied Lewis.

When they arrived at the hospital they found Coach Brown outside Tommy's room. He had found a chair to sit in. Alice was coming down the hall with a cup of coffee. She handed it to the Coach.

"Thank you, Ma'am. I sure can use it."

Beverly asked, "Is Mavis in the room with Tommy?"

"Yes, Ma'am," answered the Coach.

"How is he, Coach?" asked Josh.

"I'm afraid he will never play football again. From what I understand they are doing surgery in a few days to put pins in his leg."

"I hate to hear that. That's just awful," said Beverly.

"They have him on pain medication. I haven't seen him except for a couple of minutes when they brought him to his room. I gave him the plaque Josh. That was an honorable thing for you to do."

Josh nodded his head in recognition of the compliment. Mavis Parker came out of the room and saw the MacDonald family. "Thank you so much for coming. I expected you to show up. Josh, Tommy is asking for you."

Josh went in and saw Tommy lying there. He was watching T.V. He had it tuned to the Public Television Station. They were replaying the game. "You played a great game Josh." He picked up the plaque from beside him and looked at it.

"All I did was what I thought you would have done," said Josh.

"Well, I would have fallen on the ball because, if I picked it up like you did, they would have caught me before I ran five yards."

"Aw man, you could have out run that guy."

Tommy held up the plaque and looked at it for a long time before he looked at Josh.

"About this…what in the world were you thinking? You deserve this. I never saw anyone play like you played tonight. As a matter of fact, I think the only reason you went out for the team was so I could play. Am I right?"

Josh was looking at the floor. He nodded his head.

"Why?" asked Tommy.

"It was my way of repaying you for something you did for me when I was five years old."

"What are you talking about Josh? I'm the one on medication. What in the world did I do for you when we were five years old?"

Josh looked at Tommy. Tommy could see the tears in his eyes. "You gave me a pair of shoes."

Outside in the hallway Coach Brown said to no one in particular, "I don't understand how in practice I couldn't get Josh to block or tackle and then in the game he played like he did. I just don't understand it. With his ability I don't understand it at all."

No one answered for a long time. Finally Deborah spoke up. "Everyone on the team is a friend of Josh's. He didn't want to hurt someone."

Lewis thought on this for a moment, "How do you know that?"

"Josh told me," answered Deborah.

When a nurse came in Josh joined the others in the hallway. Mrs. Parker went back into the room. She wanted to know if there were any complications.

Coach Brown said, "Well, I guess that means no scholarship. That's sad. There is no way he can afford to go. His grades aren't good enough for an academic scholarship."

Lewis was about to speak up when Deborah said, "We can raise the money."

"How?" asked Beverly.

"Everyone in the county knows Tommy. The cheerleaders can have bake sales. The football players can have car washes. The middle school can cut grass. We can put jars in businesses and collect change. We can do it if we all pull together. I know we can!"

Coach Brown said, "You know Sammy Campbell that owns the rodeo arena. He thinks the world of Tommy and he's a big supporter of the school. I bet if we asked him he would have a benefit rodeo and donate the proceeds to send Tommy to college."

"Well, let's get it done" said Beverly.

Coach Brown looked at the MacDonald's and said, "If I ever have children, I hope they are just like these two," pointing to Josh and Deborah.

"I hope they are too," said Beverly.

And get it done, they did. If a traveler happened to pass through Kerney, Wyoming, population 1700, they would notice all the lawns were well maintained and people drove the cleanest vehicles in the state. On certain weekends the town looked deserted; everyone was at the rodeo.

Tommy Parker would go to college. He went to a small college in Laramie. On his first day of school he decided he wanted to be a teacher when he graduated. He knew he wanted to go back to Kerney High School and teach. He felt like he had a debt he had to repay. He knew he had no legal obligation to repay it but a moral obligation. In Wyoming, a moral obligation was just as important as a legal obligation.

THE WALK-ON

After graduating, Josh entered the University of Oklahoma. Deborah had selected Texas. This would be the first time they had been separated in their young lives.

For some reason, Josh decided to try out for the football team. He was what coaches would refer to as a walk-on. He made the team. He was starting left defensive end. The defensive front four made the cover of College Sports magazine. The caption above it simply said, "THE WALL." Three of the players were scowling, looking tough with their arms folded. Josh has his hands on his hips and he was smiling.

Near the end of the season the director of recruiting was analyzing the results of their recruiting program. He was interested in how well the program was working. He was looking at the evaluations of the recruiting scouts. He was comparing the names to see if any made the Oklahoma team or if they made the team of another college. Since Wyoming is last in the alphabet he got to it last. Of the six names that were reported he found two had been awarded a scholarship to major schools. They weren't starters. Another two had tried out at smaller schools and were getting some playing time on special teams. One had not made the academic grades and was dropped from the program. One didn't play at all. This was Tommy Parker, and then he saw the reason. The injury, oh well it happens.

Then he noticed the recruiting scout had written a report on someone else. He read the report more out of curiosity than anything else. Then the name sunk in, Joshua MacDonald, starting left defensive end as a freshman for the Oklahoma Sooners. He wanted to rush downstairs and tell the head coach. He stopped at the door. "Wait a minute. We hadn't recruited him. Hadn't so much as called him or anything. The kid just showed up." Then he realized that this would make him look bad. He put the folder back with the others. "Don't throw a rock at a hornet's nest."

CHAPTER TWENTY THREE

THE WILD BLUE

YONDER

1 CORINTHIANS 13:11

Josh had joined the Air Force ROTC program. He wanted to be a pilot with a degree in Aeronautical Engineering. The Friday before Thanksgiving in his sophomore year he had an opportunity to take a fight on a real Air Force jet. He went to Mountain Home Air Force Base in Idaho. It was only for one day, a familiarization flight.

On the morning of his flight, Josh was on the flight line waiting for the instructor pilot. Josh couldn't take his eyes off the plane. He didn't see the pilot walk up beside him. The pilot had seen Josh and wondered where in the world they found a flight suit big enough. The kid was huge.

"Well, what do you think?" asked the pilot.

"It's the most beautiful thing I have ever laid eyes on," answered Josh.

"Well, let's take her for a spin. I'm Captain MacArthur. Let's do the pre-flight inspection. Do you know what type of aircraft this is?"

"Yes, Sir, it's an F-4 Phantom configured as a Wild Weasel," answered Josh.

"Pretty good, not many of these old war birds around anymore." The pilot noticed the cadet was interested in everything he said or done. Most students didn't really pay that much attention.

"How much flying time do you have?" He knew a lot of cadets had some flying time on private airplanes. Several had their private licenses. One rich kid owned his own plane.

"I've never been in a plane before, Sir."

"Really?"

"No, Sir, I've always wanted to fly. I had a few hours in a flight simulator in college, Sir."

"Where do you go to college?"

"Oklahoma, Sir."

"If I was as big as you, I would try my hand at football."

"I play football, Sir," said Josh.

"I hope you can fit in the cockpit," he said with a laugh.

"I'll be terribly disappointed if I can't."

"Look kid, I'm not going to show off or anything. I'm not going to try and make you throw up or anything. You know why?"

"No, Sir," answered Josh.

"I don't want to have to clean it up after you. Down here is the ejection mechanism. Do not under any circumstance touch anything in the cockpit. Do you understand?"

"Yes, Sir. Don't touch anything."

"The weather is getting a little thick. We'll only stay up for an hour or so. Maybe we can get back before the weather gets here."

The pilot got into his seat and said over the intercom, "We use this aircraft to pick up enemy radar sites and anti-aircraft sites. We use it a lot in the aggressor role trying to sneak in and bomb surface to air missile sites. A lot of times you have to fight your way out. Modern fighters have the advantage over this old war bird. It's a nice plane to fly. It's actually a lot of fun to fly. When you go into the Air Force you may actually fly one of these. Being a Wild Weasel is an important role in modern warfare. We blind the enemy and that gives our bombers a chance especially if we can blind them and take out their air defense."

"Yes, Sir."

"We are going to take off and go to twenty thousand feet. No steep climbs or dives, okay."

"Yes, Sir."

The pilot taxied to the runway got clearance and accelerated down the runway. When he lifted off Josh had to smile. His dream was coming true.

Forty five minutes later the pilot said, "Down below us is the Rocky Mountains even though you can't see them for the clouds."

"It is beautiful up here, Sir."

"Yeah, all we can see is clouds." Josh looked in every direction. Clouds everywhere. He had never had this much fun in his life.

Then an explosion rocked the plane. Warning lights started flashing and all kinds of beeps and bells were coming from everywhere.

"What happened, Sir?" asked an excited Josh

"Engine failure. Fire on left engine." Captain MacArthur popped the canopy and said, "Mayday, Mayday," then over the intercom excitedly said, "Eject, Eject!"

He could see Josh reach down to pull the ejection seat. "It's not working, Sir."

"Try it again."

"It's still not working, Sir."

The aircraft was shuddering and making a long turn to the left. It was losing altitude fast. "We'll try to get below the clouds. Maybe the mountains are far enough below us."

"Captain, eject."

"No, I'm not leaving you kid."

"Captain eject…Please!"

"I'm sorry kid." He reached down between his legs and pulled. The rockets fired pushing him clear of the aircraft.

Josh was leaning forward when the rockets fired. Josh screamed. It felt like his neck was on fire.

Four hundred miles away Deborah felt a burning sensation on the back of her neck. She went to the bathroom, wet a face cloth and applied it to her neck. She asked Beverly if it looked like something had stung her. Beverly looked and said she didn't see anything. Beverly said, "Put some lotion on it and see if that helps."

Deborah said, "It feels like it's on fire."

PSALMS 34:4

As Captain MacArthur's chute opened he saw the plane go into the clouds trailing smoke. Josh was looking at the altimeter and saw it was going down fast. Then he heard a ripping sound from the port side and behind him.

For the first time in his life he put his hands on the controls and said, "It's just you and me Lord; just you and me."

Then he heard a voice. "You can do this Joshua."

He looked at the horizon indicator and moved the stick to the right and pulled slightly to the rear. He saw he was bringing the plane level and slightly climbing, not a lot, but he was level and was going up. He was afraid the airplane may be damaged and he didn't want to climb too rapidly.

As Captain MacArthur floated in the clouds Josh came out. The captain never saw him. He listened for an explosion but didn't hear one. The captain was thinking he must have crashed on the other side of a mountain. Then he hit the ground and everything went black.

Josh tried to look behind him to see if the plane was trailing smoke. He had to put the plane in a long turn to see the smoke trail in the distance. Josh remembered a World War II movie where a bomber had to dive to put out an engine fire. Diving was out of the question. He pushed the throttle forward and saw the planes airspeed increase. He was hunched down as far as he could. The wind was beating him and he didn't know how long he could take it. I've been hurt before was all he could think of, but never like this. Two minutes later the fire warning light went out. Josh said a prayer. Josh kept it up for another minute. The pain was awful. "I can't take it anymore." He pulled back on the throttle and watched the airspeed indicator slow to 175 knots. The windshield was diverting most of the airflow now but at this altitude, without the canopy, Josh was freezing. He couldn't stop shivering. He had never been this cold in his life.

Everywhere Josh looked there were clouds. He knew most weather systems moved from the south to the northeast. He headed southwest. "Where am I?" He had no idea. He tried to use the radio but didn't really know how. He was afraid to touch anything. He knew if he turned the wrong dial on the radio he'd never be able to use it.

He maintained the southwest course. He wondered how long he could fly at this speed. He didn't know if the instruments were right or not. He just kept flying to the southwest. He could picture in his mind where mountains were but he didn't know where he was. All he could see was clouds. When the captain was flying they flew in a different direction. Josh figured they had flown in a huge circle. He said the Lord's Prayer and then the 23rd Psalm. They were his favorites. Then he thought of his Mom singing 'Amazing Grace.' Josh quietly sang the song. After all, at this point Josh was just along for the ride. The plane was flying level and in a straight line.

Beverly also liked 'Rock of Ages.' When he started singing 'Rock of Ages Cleft for me' He saw a small break in the clouds off to his right. The break only looked to be a mile wide and five miles long, but it was closing fast. He made the turn.

Josh started saying the 23rd Psalm again. When he got to the last sentence, "And I will dwell in the house of the Lord forever," he nosed the plane over.

Most people don't believe in divine intervention, but if something happens to them they may very well believe that God had a hand in it somehow. Josh was one of those that believed in divine intervention, always had since he was five years old. God had surely intervened then.

His left hand was on the throttle in case he needed to give power to the climb. The clouds were thick and closing even faster now. When he came out below them he didn't see mountains. He was over the desert. "I wonder where I am." He had no idea. He tried the radio again but no luck. He looked at his watch. He couldn't believe he had been in the air for three hours. He slowed even more and lowered the flaps and the landing gear. He had heard of pilots forgetting to lower the landing gear on normal flights. He was afraid when he had to make a landing he would be so nervous he would forget.

Josh saw no signs of anything man made. No roads, buildings or even power lines. He also saw no sign of water. Josh flew on.

An hour later, he saw a plateau that looked level. Josh flew over it and made a wide turn to the left and flew over it again. He timed it on his watch. It took four minutes to fly over at one hundred and fifty knots. The plateau was at least nine miles long and appeared to be sandstone. He knew a good pilot could land in less than a mile. Josh wasn't fooling himself. He knew he wasn't a good pilot. He wasn't even a pilot. He made another turn and came in over the plateau again. He estimated he was twenty or thirty feet high. He wanted to make another run at it when the engine stopped. Josh told himself, "Keep the nose up ten degrees. Touchdown on the rear wheels to avoid an end over end flip." Josh wasn't scared; he didn't have time to be scared. "It's just you and me Lord; just you and me." Then he heard the voice again. "You can do this Joshua." Then touchdown. It was rough to say the least. For a second he was glad no one was watching then he wished a lot of people were watching. He used the rudder to steer the plane and let it coast to a stop.

He climbed out of the plane and knelt down to pray. He thanked God for delivering him safely. Then he walked around the plane. The right side looked fine. He walked to the front and could see the left engine intake. He moved closer and could tell one of the turbine blades had broken loose and destroyed the ones behind it. He walked to the rear and saw the fire damage. The compressor blades had come out of the side of the engine and tore a three foot long section off. Josh figured it had peeled off before breaking loose. This would have caused a huge amount of drag on the port side. That was why the plane went in the long left turn and caused the loss of altitude. After it broke away he could control the plane.

"You have work to do Joshua," again said the voice. Hardly anyone called him Joshua now. He couldn't figure out the voice. It didn't sound like anyone he knew, but he vaguely remembered a voice from a long time ago.

It was hot for November but Josh knew the night time temperature was going to drop drastically and it would get cold. His flight suit was wet with sweat. He needed a dry flight suit if he was going to make it through the night.

Josh had only been on the ground for a few minutes. He laid out what he had to survive. The Air Force had given him a survival pack that contained two small containers of water; each six ounces, two protein bars; each 3 ounces, a pen light and a pen flare with three flares. The pen flare was the size of a ball point pen; a signal mirror, three inches by five inches. He would use that a lot. Josh knew someone would be able to see it from miles away, a lot further than he could see a plane.

He hoped and prayed Captain MacArthur was unharmed and had been found. Josh wondered if the Air Force was looking for him and if they even knew where to start looking for him.

A survival radio was included but what was the range? He turned it on and said, "Mayday, Mayday." He got no response. He tried all the channels then put it away. He had a Leatherman tool, with a folding knife, a screwdriver and pliers, Deborah had given him for his fourteenth birthday. He had a small Bible his mother had given him when he went away to college. He also had a pen and a small spiral notebook. He opened the notebook and wrote down the date then he started his journal.

This is the journal of Joshua A. MacDonald, Kerney, Wyoming, I

landed here by the grace of God. If for any reason I don't survive,

please tell my family I love them. Also I would like to point out I

hold no one responsible for what happened to me.   The Captain

did not want to eject. He did everything by the book. He is a very

brave man and I hope no one holds him accountable.

Then Josh closed the notebook and began unpacking the parachute. He cut some of the suspension lines. He took off his flight suit and tied a suspension line to the left wing. He ran the line through one arm and then one leg and tied it to the horizontal stabilizer. It made a nifty clothes line. Then he cut the parachute into sections. He made a large one for a ground cloth. It was large enough to fold over him twice and this would be his blanket. He cut a large section and rolled it into a pillow. He took another section and tied suspension lines to the corners and ran lines to the landing gear and took more line and ran it to the landing gear struts as high as he could and made a small tent under the plane. He knew silk could hold heat in and the wind out. He cut a large piece four feet wide and eight feet long and cut a neck hole in the center for a coat. He cut a long narrow strip for a belt. Then he cut a piece three feet by three feet and tied suspension lines to the four corners and tied these to the right wing and right horizontal stabilizer. He found a rock and placed it in the center. If it rained, the silk would help capture the water and drain to the center where the rock was. He found some small rocks and placed them in a circle and turned his helmet upside down in the circle. The rocks would keep it from overturning. If it rained, the helmet would catch the water. Josh looked at the overcast sky. . Maybe it would rain, but he had his doubts.

BAD NEWS

Lewis had just gotten home and the family was about to sit down for dinner when he heard a car pull up. He looked out the dining room window to see it was a blue sedan. Two Air Force officers got out and came to the door. Lewis figured they were lost. He opened the door before they rang the doorbell.

"Can I help you?" asked Lewis.

"Mr. MacDonald, may we come in?"

"Sure."

Beverly came into the room at this time followed by Deborah.

"Mr. Macdonald, I am Major Holloway and this is Captain Robbins, United States Air Force. I am sorry to have to inform you that your son, Joshua…"

Lewis saw that one of the men was a Chaplain and his knees went weak.

"…was on a flight this morning from Mountain Home Air Force Base. His plane was lost. We assume it crashed and we are still looking for the aircraft. The pilot managed to eject and we found him four hours ago. He said your son's ejection seat failed. I'm sorry, Sir."

Beverly let out a moan and Lewis had to catch her. He moved her over to a chair and helped her sit down. The Chaplain went to Beverly and tried to comfort her. He said, "Let's pray." Beverly nodded. When they finished praying, she overheard the Major saying things like, "Very mountainous terrain, searching with all available aircraft," and the one that hurt the most; "Not much hope."

Deborah snapped, "I refuse to believe my brother is dead; you hear me! You keep looking."

"Yes, Ma'am, we will definitely keep looking, but you have to accept the facts."

"I think my brother is alive. He is my twin, and I would know otherwise."

"Ma'am, we will continue to search. The pilot saw him go into the clouds."

"What would happen if the pilot ejected and Josh didn't? Would Josh be burned in any way?"

"I'm not sure I understand, Ma'am. I guess it's possible exposed skin could be burned when the ejection seat rockets fired if that's what you're asking."

"That's what I'm asking. Mom, you remember this morning, I asked you if something had stung me. Remember I said it felt like it was on fire."

Beverly nodded in remembrance.

"You keep looking for my brother, you understand," insisted Deborah.

The Chaplain's curiosity got the best of him. He had read about this phenomenon of twins that were miles apart feeling the same pain.

"Ma'am, we are doing everything possible to find Joshua. I'm praying that he is alive and I believe you when you say what you just said."

The Major looked at the Chaplain like he must be crazy but Deborah did calm down some.

"We will keep you informed as soon as we find out anything. Again, I'm sorry." He handed Lewis a card with a phone number. "If we can be of any help let us know."

"You keep looking for my brother."

"I promise, Ma'am, we will keep looking."

After they left, Beverly stood up and walked over to the fireplace mantel. The special coin, 'The Big Nickel', was sitting there. When Josh went off to college he put it there along with a note that read 'When you see this, think of me.' She held it to her breast and started sobbing.

"Mom, he's alright. I can feel it.

Lewis said, "God, I hope you are right." Then the three of them embraced and said a prayer for Josh.

"Mom, he's alright. I just know it."

Beverly just nodded. Then she saw the two crayon drawings of the four of them holding hands at Lookout Point hanging on the wall. They do think alike. Could Deborah be right? Beverly had a glimmer of hope. Hope. Hope was all she had to cling to, that and her faith.

CHAPTER TWENTY FOUR

VOICES

PSALMS 91:11

It took an hour for Josh's flight suit to dry. He stayed in the shade of the aircraft as much as possible. Only his hand was exposed to the sunlight as he flashed the mirror constantly hoping someone would see it. As the sun started going down, Josh noticed the sky turned orange with the last rays of the sun. It reminded him of the sunsets back home. Home; he thought a lot of home. Then Josh started talking to God.

After the sun went down he put his flight suit back on and tugged on his homemade coat. He had already spread his bedding down. Then he said his prayers, asking God to protect him and keep him safe. Josh didn't need to get right with God, as a born again Christian he knew he was right with God. For some reason, Josh could feel a presence with him like someone was watching him. He couldn't see anyone; he just felt it. He had felt this presence near him since he was five years old. The only person he had ever confided in was Deborah. She had also confided in him that she felt like someone was watching her especially when she was alone. Twice he sat up and looked around to see if anyone was nearby. He even called out, "Is there anyone there?"

Then he heard the voice again. "Trust in the Lord, Joshua."

He fell asleep, pondering about the voice and trusting in the Lord.

Eight hundred miles away Deborah had tossed and turned for hours thinking of Josh. She felt like she was freezing. She knew the heat was on but she couldn't get warm. She got out of bed and put on a jogging suit hoping that would help. She was also thirsty and needed some water. She wondered if she was coming down with the flu. She slipped on her house shoes and started towards the door and then she heard a voice. She hadn't heard the voice since she was thirteen years old.

"Deborah, trust in the Lord."

She returned to her bed and sat on the edge.

"I do."

She lay back down and went back to sleep, pondering about the voice and trusting in the Lord.

SURVIVING

JOSHUA 1:9

The thunderstorm struck in the middle of the night waking Josh. Before lying down, he had put his helmet out along with his boots in case it rained. It came down hard for two minutes and then quit. Josh got up and checked his helmet; maybe a quarter of an inch. Josh drank it and then checked the boots; not much there. He remembered his dad telling him about an Army Green Beret that would bet five dollars he would drink a beer out of his boot. He took the helmet to the plane and used his hand to wipe off what water was on the wing into the helmet and drank it. Then he placed it under the small piece of parachute and let the water drip down. There wasn't very much but every drop was precious.

At daybreak, Josh woke up and thanked the Lord for seeing him safely through the night and providing the water. When he stood up, he put his hand on the wing and it was damp. Of course, dew. He pulled out his handkerchief and wiped it up and squeezed it into his mouth. He still hadn't eaten anything since he landed.

He wrote in his journal and flashed the mirror at the same time. This time to the east. In the afternoon when the sun was overhead he would flash up into the sky. His plane was painted desert camo and would be hard to spot. Later he would flash to the west. He needed the sun to use the mirror and he could only cover a pie shaped area. Josh had no way of knowing that a candlelight vigil was held the night before in Kerney, Wyoming at the MacDonald Ranch.

Each morning Josh would wake up early and see if there was any dew on the aircraft. He had been able to get a few ounces at the most. The sky had cleared and he knew it would not rain today. He stayed in the shade as much as possible and read his Bible. He found he could flash the mirror and read at the same time. Reading the Bible and talking to God gave him comfort and strength.

He still hadn't used the water from his survival kit. He decided he would drink half of one of the containers that night after he ate one of the protein bars. It was only three ounces. He knew as long as he didn't have to exert himself he could go a few more days without food. He couldn't imagine having to exert himself. He had seen nothing from the air that he would try to walk to. Besides, he knew the plane would be easier to find than him walking alone.

CHAPTER TWENTY FIVE

MY BROTHERS KEEPER

HEBREWS 11:1

Once again, Deborah had chills during the night. She got out of bed and put on a jogging suit. She still couldn't get warm. The next day she felt like she was burning up. She checked her temperature and it was normal. She was thirsty all the time; she just couldn't seem to get enough water. That night the chills came back. The following morning she was burning up again and she felt as if she was starving.

She said to herself, "Josh, where are you?" She sat on the edge of the bed. "Where can you be?" Then she thought about what her dad had told her when he was in the Army and training in the desert in California. He had said 'You burn up in the daytime and you freeze at night, and you're always thirsty.'

She knew her mom and dad had a feeling of helplessness; just like she did. Her dad had called the phone number several times that the Air Force Chaplain had given him but he didn't receive any new information. Deborah didn't like feeling helpless. Her brother needed her. Then a thought entered her mind. She felt like she knew where Josh was. Getting someone to believe her would be the problem.

She called the Air Force Chaplain. When he told her he couldn't give her any information at this time she noticed he sounded guarded in his reply. She said, "Please don't think I'm crazy, but you are looking in the wrong place. He's in the desert."

"Why do you think he is in the desert?" asked the Chaplain.

"Because I'm freezing at night and burning up during the daytime and I'm always thirsty."

"Ma'am, the Air Force isn't going to change the search area because you're hot or cold and you're thirsty."

"Please, I'm begging you. Please just look."

"Ma'am, I'm a Chaplain. I have nothing to do with the search. Even if I wanted to change the search area I couldn't. The Air Force is enlarging the search area every day. We are adding twenty five miles a day."

"What if you're wrong and he's not there?" asked Deborah.

"Let me ask you the same question. What if he's there and we go looking in the desert. He couldn't possibly be in the desert, Ma'am. It's too far."

"How could you know that?"

"Ma'am, I don't know if I should tell you this, but we found a piece of the aircraft."

"When?" asked Deborah. She could hear the Chaplain let out a breath of air.

"About an hour ago. It was only five miles from where we found the pilot. We believe the plane exploded in midair and is probably scattered over a large area. It snowed that night and the snow could cover up the wreckage. I'm sorry, Ma'am, but we have gone from search and rescue to search."

"Then you are saying they believe my brother is dead."

"We have not absolutely ruled on that Ma'am," said the Chaplain.

"Please don't talk that way. I just know he is alive."

"Ma'am, the plane was going down over the mountains when the pilot ejected. Now we will continue to search. We won't give up no matter how long it takes."

"If he were in the mountains I would be cold all the time, not hot in the daytime. Don't you understand that?"

"Ma'am, we will continue to search and I pray for your brother every day."

"So do I," and she hung up.

Deborah went back to her room and sat on the edge of the bed. "Deborah, Joshua needs you," said the voice. She wondered how can I help him when I have no idea where he is.

"Deborah, Joshua needs you," said the voice again. She stood up and went to Josh's room. She stood in the doorway before entering. Josh was a neat pack rat. If it involved planes and flying he kept it. Everything was in a systematic order. Photos, books and models were everywhere. Josh could find anything in a minute. Josh would laugh and say 'it's in alphabetical order by height and color.' She looked at all the books neatly stored in the bookcase. She ran her fingers along the spines of each book.

"Deborah, Joshua needs you."

"Help me please!" pleaded Deborah.

She looked at the models. There were a lot of jets but there were also some small planes. She remembered what Josh would tell her when they were locked in the closet at the other place. They always referred to it as the other place. 'If I had a plane we could fly away.' "But I don't have a plane," said Deborah.

"Deborah, you can do this," reassured the voice.

She looked around the room desperately looking for something, anything that would help her. She noticed Josh's laptop computer on his desk. There was a small die cast metal airplane sitting on top of it. Deborah picked it up. She remembered buying it for Josh when he was seven or eight years old. Then she thought, a lot of people own airplanes, not just the Air Force. If I could get the word out and others could search too, maybe we could find him.

She opened up and turned on Josh's computer. She knew Josh was on Facebook. She thought 'birds of a feather flock together.' People with the same interest would communicate of

Facebook. She went to Josh's last entry. 'Going on my first flight tomorrow.' Someone had replied, 'Congrats, if something happens I'll look for you. Ha Ha.'

Deborah thought that was strange. She looked at the person's profile. He was a pilot and was in an organization called the Civil Air Patrol. "What's that?" She went back to the bookcase and ran her fingers over the spine of the books. She found an old volume titled 'A History of the Civil Air Patrol.' It didn't take long to find out the organization was a group of pilots who volunteered to search for missing aircraft and people who were lost. "Perfect."

She went back to the computer and typed a message under the man's comment. She explained who she was and that she believed that Josh was in the desert. She included the man's own words 'If something happens I'll look for you.' She left off the Ha Ha. She got no response. She thought maybe the man could help find Josh. She could only hope. Hope. Hope was all she had to cling to, that and her faith.

CHAPTER TWENTY SIX

THE VERSE

ROMANS 8:25

On day four, Josh was reading his Bible and flashing the mirror. The wind started picking up. It was blowing hard enough to pick up sand. Josh placed his Bible on the ground and made sure his bedroll and coat was secure. He really needed those two items. He felt like he was freezing every night even with them. When he returned to his Bible he noticed the wind had blown one of the pages over like a bookmark. He picked up the Bible and read that page over and over. He seemed to be fascinated by one verse in particular. He must have read it a hundred times that day.

On day five, there was no moisture on the wing. Josh drank some more water from the survival container. He sat in the shade and flashed his mirror. He was flashing in a random pattern hoping someone would see it. He could only hope. Hope. Hope was all he had to cling to, and his faith.

Josh talked to God a lot that day and pondered about the voice.

There Is A Place Where Hope And Faith Becomes One.

PSALM 39:7

Forty miles to the east of Josh, two men were flying in a Cessna 172. They were returning from a fishing and hunting trip in Colorado. They had agreed on no cell phones, laptops, or anything to interfere with their trip. They were going to live off the land. In five days, they had caught two small fish and killed two squirrels. Both were about to starve and called the whole thing off . There was no way they could have lasted the rest of the week. After breakfast at the airport, they headed home.

"We're never going to do something this stupid again, are we?" questioned the pilot.

"If I ever mention something like this again, I want you to smash my tongue with a rock."

"Gladly, with a big rock." The two men didn't know an Air Force jet was missing and presumed lost in Utah. "I'll be glad to get back to Reno and sleep in my own bed and eat some of the wife's cooking."

"Speaking of wives, you know they are going to make fun of us for coming home early."

"I've been made fun of before. Right now, I am willing to put up with it."

"What in the world were we thinking? Trying to live off the land like the pilgrims did for Thanksgiving.

"I don't know. It seemed like a good idea at the time. I thought you knew what you were doing."

"Me! I thought you knew what you were doing." Both men had a good laugh.

"They won't let us ever live this one down."

"I know and I don't know what our story is going to be," said the pilot.

"You could tell them you needed to work on your sermon for Sunday."

"Actually, I do need to work on it more."

"What are you going to preach on?"

The pilot glanced at his friend and said, "Well, it is Thanksgiving. I am going to preach on how blessed we are. You know sometimes we take that for granted."

"I guess with the fast paced world we live in it's easy to forget that."

"Yep, and from time to time we need to be reminded."

"What's the title of your sermon?"

"<u>Trust in the Lord</u>." I think the reason we are blessed is because we trust in the Lord. I am going to read from the gospel of Matthew chapter five verses three through eleven."

"The Beatitudes?" asked his friend.

"Yes, because each verse begins with the word blessed. I can't think of any other verses beginning with the word blessed, especially nine verses. Then I will close with verse twelve telling us to rejoice and be exceedingly glad for great is your reward in Heaven."

"I've always liked those verses. You know, those verses brought me to Jesus."

"I know, remember I'm the one who read them to you. You were going through a tough time when you lost your son in Kuwait in the Persian Gulf War."

"And you showed up on my doorstep. That's when we met for the first time."

"That's right; you see what I mean when I say a Christian becomes a missionary when he steps out of the church."

The man in the right seat saw something out of the corner of his eye.

"Hey, Pete, I just saw something back there."

"What was it?" asked the pilot.

"I don't know; a reflection or something."

"Probably the sun reflecting off a pool of water. It rained a few days ago."

"Do you think we ought to check it out?"

"There is nothing within a hundred miles of here."

They flew on.

A few minutes later the passenger said, "I'd feel bad if it was someone needing help and we didn't look."

"Where was it?" asked the pilot.

"Well, I'm not exactly sure. It's behind us now."

"It's probably nothing but I'll turn around." A few minutes later he asked, "See anything now?"

"No, I don't see it anymore. I'm not even sure we went back far enough."

"We don't have a lot of fuel to hang around here long. I'm sure it was the sun reflecting off a puddle of water."

Two hours later, the men landed in Reno, Nevada. The first thing they did was wolf down some breakfast for the second time that day. "Let me check my email and then I'll give you a ride home." He had an office at the airport. He booted up his computer. There were several messages. He started scanning them. Then he got to a longer message. He started reading it slower. Then read it again. He let it sink in, and then read it for the third time.

He had been corresponding with a guy who wanted to be a pilot. He had never met the young man. He remembered the guy telling him he was making his first flight the next morning on an Air Force jet. He had answered and said if something happened he would look for him. Of course, he had been joking, but now the boy's sister was asking for help. She believed her twin brother was alive and in the desert. She said she could feel it.

The pilot remembered his twin sister and the connection they had shared. When one of them was sad the other felt the same way even though they lived hundreds of miles apart. And before he lost her to cancer, he could feel her pain.

"The reflection! Could it have been the reflection that he saw?" he asked himself. He looked up a website for the Civil Air Patrol. There was information on the search. He went to the wall where the planning maps were. Taking a grease pencil, he drew a line from Boulder, Colorado to Reno, Nevada. He drew an elongated oval twenty five miles wide and seventy five miles long. He was estimating where his friend thought he saw the reflection. Then he drew a line from the Air Force search area to the oval he had drawn. Then he calculated the distance.

"It's possible," he said to himself. Somewhere those two lines would intersect. He could only hope. Hope. Hope was all he had to cling to, that and his faith. What more did he need.

He went outside. His friend was already asleep in the car. He shook him awake.

"We've got to go back to the hangar."

"What did you forget?"

"I forgot who I am."

"What do you mean?"

"I'm a member of the Civil Air Patrol remember."

"We need to look for a missing plane or someone who's lost."

"The Air Force thinks one of their planes crashed in Utah."

"We're going to Utah?"

"No, we're going to try to find that reflection you saw."

"How?"

"I don't know."

"Why is the reflection so important now? That's nowhere near Utah?"

"I know but it's in the desert."

"The desert? Why in the desert?"

"His twin sister thinks that's where he is."

His friend remembered when the pilot lost his twin sister and how it had affected him. He had said they could feel each other's pain.

After refueling and getting in the air, the pilot said, "We're going to try and retrace our flight path. I want you looking for anything that may remind you of where we were when you saw the reflection."

"Roger, I can do that."

Two hours later the pilot said, "We should be in the area now. I'm going to do some figure eights. Maybe we will see it again."

Fifteen minutes later as they were making a turn, the passenger yelled, "There! Straight ahead, I just saw it."

"Keep your eye on it."

"There it is again. Up on that plateau."

"Get the binoculars from the back seat."

Two minutes later. "You're not going to believe this. There is an Air Force fighter jet just sitting there pretty as you please."

"That's it. The signal is constant now."

Ten minutes later, the pilot could see the plane. He rocked the plane's wings. A flare was fired from the plane.

"How in the world did he land it here? I figured it had crashed."

"I don't know. We have to tell someone." He tried the radio and got no response. He tried his cell phone and got no signal.

"No signal; we're out in the middle of nowhere."

Five minutes later they were circling the plane. The passenger asked, "What's he doing?"

"It looks like he's praying."

"I don't blame him for that. He is a blessed man."

"Is there any coffee in the thermos? Why didn't we think to bring water?"

"Maybe a cup."

"Get that windbreaker from the back seat. Tie the arms through the handle. There is a magic marker in the door panel. Write on the bottle, 'Sit tight, we'll get help.' I'm going to slow down as much as I can and you drop it out. While I'm circling you write down the GPS coordinates. Do you have your smart phone with you?"

"Sure."

"I want you to take some pictures because people aren't going to believe us."

"Where do you think he came from?"

"The Air Force said Mountain Home, Idaho. There's an Air National Guard Base about a hundred miles from here. We're going there."

"Will they let us land there?"

"Probably not but we're going to fake a reason. We've got to tell someone."

Josh ran to the thermos and shook it and said a prayer. He read the message and prayed again.

Even the best laid plans can go wrong. The radio didn't work at the Air National Guard base. They landed anyway. An hour later, the two men were still surrounded by Base Security and their plane was still being searched. The security officer wasn't happy at all. The two men were trying to explain why they had landed without permission. They showed the photos on the phone to the sergeant. He knew with computers you could generate any photo you wanted.

One of the security men, said "Excuse me, Sergeant, can I speak to you for a minute."

"What is it?"

"I saw on the news four or five days ago a plane went missing in Utah. Maybe that's the plane. I don't think we can take a chance. We need to report this."

"Alright secure this aircraft. We'll take them to the Administration building. We'll let them decide."

Fifteen minutes later, the Sergeant was showing the photos to the Administration Officer.

"Tell the two men to have a seat." He knocked on the door of the Commanding Officer.

"Come in," was shouted from inside.

"Colonel, two men landed a few minutes ago in a civilian aircraft. They claim they saw a military jet sitting out in the desert. They have photos, Sir." He showed the photos to the Colonel.

The Colonel was in the process of discussing budget cuts with his staff. One member of his staff was the Public Information Officer (PIO). He looked at the photos.

"Sir, if these are real we need to take advantage of it."

"What do you mean take advantage of it?"

"Colonel, every time the Air Force cuts its budget, the first place they look is on these little outposts of freedom like here. This is an opportunity we shouldn't pass up, Sir."

"You're saying we're worth keeping because of this incident?"

"If we take advantage of it Sir. We can rescue this guy a lot quicker than anyone else. We can have an F-16 there in fifteen minutes and a helicopter in an hour. The F-16 can verify if he's there or not before we tell anyone. We rescue him and then tell the Air Force we got him."

"Well, let's get this show on the road. Brief the pilot. Give him the coordinates. And warm up the helo so they can take off if he's there."

"Are you going, Colonel?"

"I wouldn't miss it for the world. I want someone to film it at the site and back here."

A captain burst into the ready room.

"Who's on deck?"

"I am. What's up?"

"Fly to these coordinates and tell me what's there."

"What's supposed to be there?"

"An Air Force fighter. Now get going. If he's there radio, 'Bingo on package.' You got that. That's all you say."

"Bingo on package."

"Go man, full throttle, you got that." Ninety seconds later, the pilot ran his engine to full military power and released the brakes. He shot down the runway like a drag racer. At one hundred and forty miles per hour he lifted off and climbed almost straight up. He leveled off at five thousand feet, punched in the GPS coordinates and was supersonic in forty seconds.

JAMES 1:3

Josh heard the sonic boom and knew what it was. What else could it be? Josh's plane was painted desert camo and the pilot had missed him on his first pass. He turned around for a second look. Josh saw the plane turn and head back towards him so he fired one of his pen flares. The jet rocked its wings. Josh would have cried if he could have made tears.

The pilot said, "Bingo on package. I say again bingo on package."

Two UH1 helicopters lifted off one hundred miles away.

The F-16 pilot then put on a show for the smallest crowd to ever watch an air show. One person, Josh, just watched in awe. Fifty minutes later, the plane left and Josh heard the unmistakable sound of a helicopter. No, it was two.

"Thank you, Lord, for answering my prayers."

Josh had already secured everything and was ready to go. As his dad would say, 'travel light, freeze at night.' Josh watched as the two choppers landed side by side fifty yards away. Josh saw a cameraman get out, then a Colonel. Josh didn't know what he should do so he decided he would meet him half way. Josh walked toward the Colonel, stopped ten feet away and saluted.

"Cadet MacDonald, Sir, ready for inspection." He didn't know anything else to say. The Colonel returned the salute. A Captain handed him a bottle of water.

"Go easy on that Son," said the Colonel.

"Sir, yes Sir. Thank you Sir."

"You might want to wait in the chopper, son."

"I'm fine, Sir, just real thirsty."

The Colonel walked to the plane. He noticed the cadet was one step to the right and one step to the rear. The Colonel smiled. He stopped twenty yards from the plane. It looked fine from this side.

"Isn't she the most beautiful thing you've ever laid your eyes on, Sir." They walked over to the other side and looked at the fire damage and the ripped panel.

"You did a fine job landing this, son. How many hours flying do you have?"

"This was my first flight, Sir." The Colonel turned and looked at Josh. He had heard of natural pilots even though he had never met one.

"Well, I guess you are ready to go right?"

"Can I get my belongings Sir? It won't take me but a minute." He was back in less than a minute "Sorry about the parachute. I needed it for other things."

"Don't worry about it, son."

On the way back, Josh asked if someone had told his family he was safe and sound. He was told they would be personally notified.

An hour later when they landed news people were waiting. The PIO officer had called every news outlet he could think of. He was going to milk this dry.

PRAYER WORKS

In Kerney, the Air Force sedan pulled up in front of the MacDonald ranch. Well-wishers for the candlelight vigil were already setting up for another night.

Lewis saw the two officers come to the door. He had his arm around Beverly's shoulder. They rang the doorbell. Lewis said, "I don't want to open the door."

Beverly said, "They won't go away, Lewis." He opened the door. The two officers came inside. The three men nodded to each other. Then they heard a shriek and Deborah ran out of her room. "Mom, Dad, turn on the TV. They found Josh! He's alive!"

Beverly broke down crying. "Oh, thank you, Lord. Thank you so much, Lord." Lewis held her.

Deborah turned on the TV. They could see Josh stepping out of the helicopter. He looked exhausted as he walked through the crowd of reporters. Lewis looked at the two Air Force officers. "You came to tell us didn't you?"

"Yes, Sir, since we deliver bad news it's only fair we get to deliver good news, also. Your son is dehydrated but that's understandable. He will spend the night in the hospital where they can give him some fluids, but he's fine. Then they will want to ask him about what happened."

"What about Thanksgiving?" asked Beverly.

"Ma'am, I'm sure you understand. We need to find out what happened. We don't want anyone else having to go through what your son went through."

"We understand," said Lewis "The main thing is he's safe."

Deborah noticed the Air Force officers for the first time. She poked the Chaplain in the side with her elbow. "Told you so. Told you my brother was okay."

"Yes, Ma'am, you did. And you were right; he was in the desert. I think there were two miracles performed by the Almighty. I'm going to give a sermon on this event. I hope you don't mind."

"No, I don't mind," replied Deborah.

The news had already reached the crowd outside for the candlelight vigil. A cheer went up. Lewis didn't know how they found out and it wasn't important right now. Then he remembered fifteen years ago most of these same people had met here when the state tried to take the children. There was no doubt in his mind he was living in the right place. When the two officers left, the MacDonald family went outside and had a party. It seemed fitting.

CHAPTER TWENTY SEVEN

THE INTERVIEW

2 CORINTHIANS 2:14

In Nevada, the Colonel and Public Information Officer visited Josh in the hospital. He was watching reruns of Gunsmoke. Festus and Doc were arguing.

"How are you doing, son?" asked the Colonel.

"I'm fine, Sir. They have loaded me up on fluids and food."

"You feel up to an interview tomorrow before you go back to Idaho?" asked the PIO.

"What kind of interview?"

"Well, just regular questions for the press. People want to know how you are doing. Nothing wrong with that."

"Well, I guess that will be alright."

They concluded their visit and left Josh to get some rest. In the hall, the PIO stopped the Colonel. "You know Sir, it would be a shame for him to miss Thanksgiving."

"What you got up your sleeve?"

"We could make a stop on the way to Idaho. I know it's out of the way but I think of the press."

"Go ahead and do it," answered the Colonel.

The next morning Josh was seated at a table in his flight suit. There was a bank of microphones in front of him. The PIO started thinking maybe I should have prepped him on his answers. Too late now.

The first question was from a reporter from Reno, Nevada. "Sir, what sustained you during your five days in the desert?"

"My faith in God and my family. I knew everyone all across America who heard about me was praying for me. I also knew the Air Force wouldn't give up until they found me."

The PIO wanted to jump up and down. The kid had mentioned God, family, America and the Air Force. He could have hired a Hollywood script writer and it wouldn't have been this good.

"I understand you play football for Oklahoma. Do you dream of playing in the NFL?" This question came from a woman from Las Vegas.

"Ma'am, my dream is to be an Air Force pilot."

The PIO thought he had died and gone to Heaven.

"What about the pilot. He ejected. Do you have anything to say about that?"

"Ma'am, he wanted to stay in the plane. I pleaded with him to eject. I have the utmost admiration for him. He is a very brave man. I also figure he owes me the rest of my ride," then he smiled and laughed. The reporters laughed along with Josh.

In Idaho, the pilot was watching. He had thought his career was over. He sat up and paid more attention.

"How did you survive without water?"

"Well, it rained the first night. I was able to catch some water, not much but some, in my helmet and my boots."

"In your boots?"

"Yes, Sir," said Josh.

"What did that taste like?"

"It tasted like a boot." There was laughter in the room. The PIO could die a happy man. These people were not eating this up as much as he was but they were eating it up.

1 CORINTHIANS 15:51

In Kerney, Wyoming, the MacDonald's were watching also. Lewis said, "When Josh gets home, I don't think we should ask him a lot of questions. If he wants to talk, we let him talk. This has had to have an effect on him. I hope it hasn't but it may have."

"He acts fine to me," said Beverly.

"No, Momma, he has changed."

"How has he changed?" asked Beverly.

"He was my little brother. Now he's my big brother."

At the MacDonald ranch, the Thanksgiving dinner was on the table. Alice was spending the day with them. Alice insisted on putting a plate in Josh's normal place. "He's not physically here but he's here in our heart."

They sat down and each one said a blessing for themselves then held hands and said the blessing.

Lewis picked up the carving knife and fork. He was about to start carving the turkey when he heard something. He canted his head to the side and listened. He put the knife and fork down. The noise was getting louder and he recognized it for what it was. He had heard it hundreds of times in the Army.

"What is it?" asked Beverly.

"A helicopter. I wonder where it's going." It was getting louder and closer. Then it passed directly over the house causing the house to vibrate.

"My, Lord," said Alice.

Lewis walked out on the front porch. Beverly followed close behind him. A few seconds later, Deborah and Alice came out.

"It's landing!" Lewis saw the helicopter flare just before touching down on Lookout Point. The side door slid open and Josh stepped out.

"It's Josh!" They all shouted at the same time.

All four ran to the gate. Each was trying to open it at the same time. There was an inside latch and an outside latch. It was comical to Josh. With all four of them trying they couldn't get it open.

He turned to the PIO officer and said. "You know how many MacDonald's it takes to open a gate? Four; if you give them enough time."

Deborah climbed the fence and was running to Josh. Grandma Alice pushed Lewis and Beverly aside and easily opened the gate. Deborah jumped up and threw her arms around Josh. When the others got to Josh, they hugged him. They couldn't seem to let go. No one noticed the cameraman filming the homecoming.

"I brought some company. I hope you have enough food."

CHAPTER TWENTY EIGHT

THE JOURNEY BACK

IN TIME

ST. MARK 3:33

"Mom, do you know who our real parents were?" asked Deborah. Beverly was not surprised by the question. She had known it would eventually be asked. It had taken fifteen years. The answer was the same today as it would have been five, ten or fifteen years ago.

"No honey, I don't know." Beverly, Deborah and Josh were sitting at the dining room table. Lewis was at an American Legion meeting.

"Why are you asking now?" asked Beverly.

"I'm just curious. Well, both of us are, right Josh."

"Yes, Ma'am, just curious I guess. I mean do we have other brothers and sisters? Are our real parents dead or did they just abandon us? You understand you and Dad will always be our mom and dad."

Beverly thought for a minute and then replied "Your Dad and I have always known that this day would come. It is only natural. If I can help you find out I will be more than glad to help. I have to confess I don't know where to start. Both of you will be going back to school tomorrow. I will see what I can find out here."

"Deborah the University of Texas and Josh, Oklahoma should have something that tells people how to track down things like this."

"That would be great, Mom. I hadn't thought about that" said Deborah.

"But, why are you trying now."

"Well, I have been thinking about it since the eighth grade" said Deborah.

"What happened in the eighth grade?"

"You remember the fight?" asked Deborah.

"Oh yes, I remember the fight. You know you were wrong to fight that boy no matter what he did."

"You remember I told you he said something that made me mad?"

"Yes and you wouldn't tell us what he said."

"He said, 'Your own momma didn't want you,'" said Deborah. "So you see it is not what he did, it's what he said."

"How awful. That is an awful thing to say. Now I am glad you beat him up. Don't worry, I'll tell your Dad what he said."

"He knows Mom. I told him the next day. I couldn't keep it from him. He said if I wanted to tell you I could. He said it was my decision."

Beverly thought about that for a moment. "Josh, Deborah, you don't know where this path you have chosen will lead you. You understand that don't you. I'm not trying to discourage you. I just want you to be prepared for what you may find."

"We understand Mom," said Deborah.

"Do you mind if I talk with your dad about this or have you already discussed it with him?"

"No, Ma'am, we haven't mentioned it to him but we're sure he will give us his blessings."

After Josh and Deborah left for college Beverly talked with Lewis. "I wonder what took them so long," was all he said.

Beverly didn't mention to Lewis that it seemed as though Josh didn't have much to say. Deborah did most of the talking. Since the desert it seemed like Josh was quieter than normal. They had agreed not to bring up what happened in the desert. If Josh wanted to talk, they would talk.

Beverly didn't sleep well that night. She kept asking herself "Where do I start?" She decided she would start at the beginning or the beginning as she knew it to be.

Beverly knew in most organizations the secretary was perhaps the most knowledgeable to find out information from. She went to the Kerney County Sheriff's office. Mary had been the secretary for almost thirty years.

"Hi, Beverly, I haven't seen you in a while."

"Mary I need to look at some old records."

"How far back are you talking about? We're still transferring cases to computer files."

"You remember when I got the kids?"

"Sure do. I remember transferring those about a month ago. You want to look at them?"

"Please, it's the only place I know where to start."

"To start what?"

Beverly told her what she was trying to find out and why. Mary had the file on her computer in less than a minute. Beverly wrote down all the pertinent information.

"Now where do I go from here?"

"District Attorney's office at the Court House. You want me to call? I have a friend over there."

"Oh Mary, that would be great." Ten minutes later, Mary was telling Beverly what she had found out.

"Now the prison?" asked Beverly.

"Let me call the DA's office again. They probably do that sort of stuff all the time," said Mary. When Mary hung up the phone she said, "This may take a while. Let's go get a cup of coffee. If a call comes in they will page me."

Beverly and Mary waited for a call that may never come in. Time dragged by for Beverly. Mary wanted to chat and Beverly was obliged to go along. At one o'clock, "Mary, line one," came over the speaker.

"Come on let's go to my office." Beverly noticed Mary was writing things down. This had to be good right, or did it? Finally Mary said, "Thank you, goodbye."

"Okay, I think that's a start."

"What did you find out?"

"The woman served three of a six year sentence. The man died of a brain tumor after spending less than a year. End of story on him. The woman was put on three years' probation. When the probation ended she lived at this address." Mary wrote it down for Beverly. "You know when her probation ended she was not required to give another address. Most people, when their parole has ended, move as soon as possible."

"I would imagine so. I know I would," said Beverly.

"It's at least a start. There is a little irony here. You want to guess what kind of job she had on probation?"

"I don't have a clue." said Beverly.

"She worked at a shelter for battered women. You know she had some experience on the subject at hand wouldn't you say."

"Yes, I would. She may still be there, got an address?"

Both the home and the work address were in Casper. Beverly decided she would wait another day to track her down. She wanted to put some thought into this and talk to Lewis. What do I say if I locate her? "Hi, remember me? I caused you to go to prison for three years."

She got in her car and started to leave the Sheriff's office. No, I said I would do what I could to help them find out about their parents. That did not mean I would wait.

She headed for Casper. She decided to try the home address first. Maybe someone would remember her and could steer her in the right direction. She didn't want to go to her work address. She didn't know if her employer knew she had a prison record. That could be one of the worst ways to meet. Beverly realized the woman may not even know who or where the children came from. What happens then, a dead end? Beverly found the address. It wasn't a bad neighborhood or didn't appear to be. She parked on the curb and walked to the door. She didn't know what to say if the woman still lived there. "I guess I will wing it." She had her Father's Sheriff's badge in her purse 'only as a last resort.' There was no doorbell, she knocked. A moment later the door opened.

The woman who answered the door was about five foot seven. She was dark headed and Beverly guessed about her age, maybe a year or two older. Beverly thought she was rather attractive but dressed rather plain, but there was something else.

"Ma'am, I hate to bother you but I am trying to locate Carol Duncan who lived here about ten years ago."

"I'm Carol Duncan. Wait a minute, I recognize you." And she stepped out on the small front porch. Beverly would have never recognized her from her mug shot when she was arrested.

"Ma'am, I'm not here for any confrontation." She had her hand on the badge.

"You saved my life. I'm sure I would be dead if you hadn't showed up when you did."

Beverly was speechless.

"Please, come inside."

"Ma'am, I don't know if I should. I have been approached by the children who were in your custody to find their birth parents." Beverly thought this is not a lie. The children had approached her.

"Then come inside and I will tell you everything about Joshua and Deborah and their parents. I have some things I'm sure they would want."

Beverly didn't want to go inside but she threw caution to the wind and followed her in. Four hours later she was driving back home. There was just too much to digest and the children would be home in two weeks for Christmas. She needed that much time to digest all of this. She thought the woman was telling her the truth but you never know. She wanted to verify a few things. Things that had nothing to do with Josh and Deborah. It was already getting late. She would start that tomorrow. She stopped by the cemetery on the way home. She wanted to check a date.

Doc Fletcher had retired five years ago. She started there. She assumed he was still able to read an x-ray. He could and it verified one point the woman had made. Beverly decided she would go on to the next point and not stop till she found a lie. Then and only then would she proceed with caution.

After verifying everything the woman had told her she was ready. She said a prayer and got ready to deliver everything to Josh and Deborah. She had not told Lewis anything, but she knew Lewis would agree she had done the right thing. All she had to do was wait until they came home for Christmas.

All three were out feeding and watering the horses. They would be home shortly. Beverly was as ready as she would ever be. She had gone over it a hundred times in her mind. She had actually rehearsed it by talking to herself earlier. The only question that remained was could she go through it without making a mistake. It was so sad to her. She didn't know if she could even do it without crying. She had put three chairs on one side of the dining room table and one on the other side; this is where she would sit.

When they came in she asked them to sit. She wanted Lewis in the middle.

"When you left after Thanksgiving you asked me to help find out about your real parents. I have done what you asked me to do. Now, I want to say that any decision you make I will support and I'm sure your Dad will agree." Lewis said, "Maybe I should let you do this. I don't see how it would be fair for me to be a part of any discussion. You know I will support any decision they make." He started to get up.

"You are part of this," said Beverly.

"How, I know nothing about this."

"But you do. You just don't know it yet." Lewis sat back down. More out of curiosity than anything else. "Go ahead then."

"The woman who had custody of you was your Aunt."

"Our Aunt! You have got to be kidding me."

"No, Deborah, I'm not kidding. I met and talked with her. She told me everything."

"And you believed her?" asked Deborah.

"Yes, I believed her, but I verified what she told me. She told me the truth. The evidence is irrefutable. That part was actually easy." Beverly was holding a folder in her lap. She pulled out an 8x10 photo and laid it on the table in front of Lewis.

"This is a photo of your father." Josh leaned to his left and Deborah leaned to her right. Then Deborah and Lewis looked at Josh.

"He looks like you Josh," said Deborah. Josh looked at the photo and then held it in his hand. He nodded his head in agreement.

"He's dead isn't he?" he asked and then looked at Beverly.

Beverly nodded her head and said, "Yes, he is. I'm so sorry." She felt her eyes watering up and had to wipe a tear away.

"Do you know how he died?" asked Josh.

"He worked at an oil refinery in Texas. There was an explosion and a fire. I'm sorry, Josh. I have his obituary. You can read it later, okay." Josh kept looking at the photo and just nodded his head. Beverly didn't know if she could go on because it got harder, it got sadder.

"How old were we when he died?" asked Deborah.

"Fourteen months," answered Beverly as she pulled another photo from the folder.

"Your mother." This time Deborah got the looks. Her mother was a few years older than Deborah was now when the photo was taken. The resemblance was uncanny. The same black curly hair. The eyes and nose even the smile was almost the same. There was no doubt in anyone's mind, this was their mother.

"She left us didn't she? I was right all along, she left us. That boy I had the fight with was right. She left us. Our own mother didn't want us. I feel like such a fool."

"Yes, she left you but there is more to it than just leaving you. Please let me finish."

"No, she just left us. How do you leave your own children? There's nothing to say but she left us."

"Deborah, please let me finish. This is hard on all of us and it gets harder, especially for me. Here is a photo of the day she left." She took the next photo out of the folder.

"I don't want to see it. She left us and gave us to her sister. No way, I don't want to see anymore. I thought I could handle this, but I was wrong. No mother leaves her children."

Beverly started crying, "God, why didn't we do this sooner?"

"Mom, don't cry," said Josh. "I want to know."

Deborah started to get up from the table. Josh said, "Deborah, please don't. I need to know."

Deborah sat back down, and then said, "Josh you may want to know, but I don't. I wish I had never even brought it up. Nothing could make me leave my children."

Lewis got up and went around the table. He put his arm around Beverly's shoulders and pulled her close. He reached down and took the photo from her hand. He looked and squinted his eyes, then pulled his reading glasses from his shirt pocket and put them on. He walked slowly back to his chair.

Deborah turned away and closed her eyes and covered her ears with her hands. "I don't want to see or hear about it. She left us! That's all there is to it!."

Lewis sat down.

Josh looked at the photo and said, "She was in the Army?" Then looked at Beverly.

"Yes, she was," answered Beverly.

Lewis looked closer. "Was she a doctor?"

"She was a surgeon," said Beverly.

Even though Deborah had her ears covered she heard everything that was said. Now Deborah looked at the photo.

Lewis said, "She was a Major."

"Yes, she was," said Beverly.

Deborah was now holding the photo. There was no doubt about it. Josh who looked about two years old was smiling and holding the toy fire truck that was now in his room. He was sitting on her left knee. Deborah was on her right knee and holding the same rag doll that was in her room. The one in the picture looked new. The Mother was wearing her dress uniform.

"Ragmuffin," said Deborah.

"She was on her way to Bosnia. Lewis, what day did Jack Gordon get killed?" Beverly knew the answer.

"Well, I came home on May the sixteenth. I was supposed to come back on the eighteenth but I was able to leave two days early. Remember his funeral was on the eighteenth."

"Yes, I remember. What day did he die?"

"Jack was killed on the fourteenth. Why do you want to know that?"

"You said the Medivac didn't show up, right?" asked Beverly.

"That's right, it didn't…I should have seen that coming. That's why you said I was part of this, right?"

"Yes."

"I don't understand what you are talking about. What does that have to do with this," said Deborah.

"The citation that she received said that a Medivac went out to retrieve a wounded soldier. It had engine trouble and had to return. Your mother being a surgeon and realizing time was of the essence volunteered to go on another helicopter. The helicopter was shot down and all aboard was killed. I'm sorry."

Lewis said, "So you believe she died trying to save Jack Gordon?"

"I think so. The date is right."

"But why would the Army make a mother leave her children? That doesn't make any sense to me at all," said Deborah.

"That's the way things are. She had a commitment of her time. She had to designate someone to care for her children. There are a lot of single parents in the Army. You don't get to pick and choose. If they need you, you have to go," said Lewis.

"So you are saying she left us with her sister while she was in Bosnia?"

"She didn't leave you with her," answered Beverly.

"Well, who did she leave us with?" asked Josh.

"Your maternal grandparents," said Beverly.

"Then how did our aunt get us?" asked Deborah.

Beverly pulled out another photo and laid it in front of Lewis. "This is the family photo on the day of their wedding." It was a typical wedding photo. Bride and Groom in the center. Their parents slightly behind them on either side.

"With the exception of your aunt this is your entire family," said Beverly. "On the left are your maternal grandparents. They were killed in a car accident not long after your mother passed. Your mother left the two of you in their custody. Your paternal grandparents are on the right. Your paternal grandmother had Alzheimer's at the time of the wedding. She died when the two of you were four years old. Your paternal grandfather, the man in the wheelchair is still alive. He lost his legs in the Vietnam War. With the condition of his wife and both living in an alternative care facility he couldn't care for two three year olds. I think that is obvious."

"Let's get back to our aunt. Did she say why she would lock two five year olds in the closet for what seemed like forever? When you talked to her did she say why she put us through that?" asked Deborah. Beverly could tell she was upset.

"To protect you," said Beverly.

"To protect us! You can't be serious? She's saying she locked us up to protect us!" exclaimed Deborah.

Beverly pulled out the booking photo of their aunt. It was sickening to even look at. She had been beaten severely. Everyone was quiet as they looked at the photo.

"Yes, to protect you. Her husband, who by the way, died in prison less than a year after you came here, became very violent. He couldn't hold down a job and turned to drugs and took it out on the three of you. They had no money, no car; there was no escape for her. All you ate was oatmeal, bologna sandwiches and macaroni and cheese."

"So that's why we never have oatmeal, bologna sandwiches and cheese and macaroni?" asked Lewis.

"That's right. I'll cook you anything you want as long as it's not one of those," said Beverly.

"Your aunt was able to obtain her husband's medical records from the State when she got out of prison. She asked a neurosurgeon if the brain tumors could have made him violent. She said when she married him he was a kind and sweet man. The doctor said it was likely. I showed the x-ray to Doc Fletcher and he said the same thing. There were over twenty tumors and where they were located would have caused that. He would have had decreased motor skills and probably slurred his speech and keeping his balance. He said it would have been difficult to find any type of work."

"Josh picked up the family wedding photo and looked at Beverly. "You said our Grandfather is still alive."

"He was at nine o'clock this morning."

"You talked to him?" asked Deborah.

"No, I called the alternative care facility."

"You know where he is?" asked Deborah.

"Yes, he's in Beal, Iowa."

"Where's that?" asked Lewis.

"Just across the State line. It's almost in Nebraska."

Deborah got up from the table and went toward her bedroom.

"Josh if you are going with me you better get packed." She turned around and went back and hugged Beverly, "Thank you, Mom, you're the best. You don't know what this means to me."

Josh said, "I guess we are going to Iowa?"

Beverly wiped her eyes and just nodded. That was all she needed to hear. Sometimes joy comes from sadness.

Josh came around the table and hugged her. "You're the only Mom I've ever had and you'll always be my Mom. This changes nothing. I love you." Then he leaned over and kissed her on the head.

"Are we going with them?" asked Lewis.

"Yes, we are."

"Then we better pack."

"Our bags are in the car."

"You never cease to amaze me."

"And you never cease to amaze me, Lewis," said Beverly, wiping her eyes.

They decided to stop and spend the night an hour before reaching Beal, Iowa. A town none of the four MacDonald's had ever heard of. They didn't want to be exhausted when they met the Grandfather.

CHAPTER TWENTY NINE

BEAL IOWA

MATTHEW 5:14

At 8:30 the next morning the four walked into the lobby of the Beal Alternative Care Facility. They approached the receptionist desk. "We would like to visit Mr. Alfred Williams please," said Beverly.

The receptionist looked up, stood and crossed her arms and looked at Josh and Deborah. "Lord have mercy, you're Joshua and Deborah aren't you. I would know you anywhere."

"How do you know who we are?" asked a puzzled Josh, before looking at Beverly.

"Honey, he's got a picture of your mom and dad in his room and you're the spitting image of them. Every time they clean his room he tells them to make sure the photo is where he can see it.

"Every morning he goes out on the sun porch. He has told me at least a thousand times that one day the two of you will come here to see him. I guess todays the day. Now, ya'll go out on the sunporch. I'll bring him out. Good Lord, no way. I wouldn't miss this for the world. Hardly a day goes by he doesn't mention you by name, Joshua and Deborah, and now you are here in the flesh."

They went out on the sunporch and had a seat. They had to wait a few minutes. They saw him when he came through the door. Josh and Deborah both stood. The receptionist was behind him. When he was in the center of the room she turned him ninety degrees where he was facing them.

Other than being twenty five years older he looked almost the same as the wedding photo. His hair was gray and he was thinner in the face. When he saw them he said, "Joshua! Deborah!" For a few seconds his mind forgot he had no legs and tried to stand. Then he collapsed back into his wheelchair. When he was back in his chair he held his arms out and started weeping.

Josh and Deborah went to him and hugged him. They both said, "Hello, Grandpa."

The old man said, "That's the sweetest words I've ever heard. I've waited here for almost fifteen years. This is the best Christmas present I could ever get. I've prayed every day for this day. How did you find me?"

"Mom found you Grandpa," said Josh.

"Grandpa, I'd like you to meet our Mom and Dad, Lewis and Beverly MacDonald," said Deborah.

Lewis and Beverly both came over and shook hands with Mr. Williams. Mr. Williams noticed Beverly was wiping the corners of her eyes with a tissue.

"When did you find out where I was?"

"We found out yesterday afternoon. We left home as soon as we found out," said Deborah.

"Where do you live?"

"Kerney, Wyoming," answered Beverly.

"The two of you look so much like you're mom and dad. It's like they have come back also." Then he started crying.

"It's okay, Grandpa. We're here now and that's what's important" said Josh.

"Come on lets go somewhere. There is something I want to show you. Can you get the door, Ma'am?"

"Is it alright if you leave?" asked Beverly.

"Sure, I leave all the time. I own the place. Besides it's not far." Out on the sidewalk he said, "I'd like for you to visit the cemetery. Would you want to do that?"

"Yes, Sir, we would," said Josh.

The old man headed in that direction. He was right; it wasn't far.

HONOR

EXODUS 20:12

"I come here almost every day if the weather's not bad." The old man had no trouble with his wheelchair. He finally stopped in front of the graves.

"Your maternal grandparents are buried to the right of your mother. Do you notice anything unusual about them?"

"The last name Beal. Is the town named after them?"

"Yes, it is," said the old man.

"Is there anything else?"

Josh spotted it right away. "They were born on the same day and died on the same day."

"They knew each other their whole lives, lived next door to each other. Happens a lot in small towns. Is Kerney, Wyoming a large town?"

"No, as a matter of fact it's a lot like this. Not much different at all. We only have one traffic light. I noticed Beal has two."

The old man laughed and said, "We didn't want to be known as a one red light town so we installed another one."

Lewis had to laugh at that one.

"And this is your Mother and Father. I was so proud of him. He married the prettiest girl in town. A doctor in the Army. When

327

she got transferred he didn't complain. He just packed up and moved with her."

Josh noticed the inscription at the bottom of the granite slab. 'Beloved Father of Joshua and Deborah.' He pointed it out to Deborah. Then they looked at their mother's grave. There were two inscriptions, one above the other. The top one was simple. '2 Timothy 4:7.'

"Mom would you look in your Bible and see what second Timothy, chapter four verse seven says?" asked Deborah.

Beverly started to take out her Bible from her purse when Josh said, "I have fought a good fight. I have finished my course. I have kept the faith."

"That's very good Joshua. That was her favorite Bible verse. She wanted people to be curious and look it up and maybe read the next verse. 'Henceforth there is laid up for me a crown of righteousness which the Lord, the Righteous Judge shall give me at that day and not to me only but unto all them also that love his appearing.' I see you study the Bible."

"Yes, Sir, but I remember the first verse when I was in the desert."

Lewis looked at Beverly. This was the first time Josh had mentioned the desert. Both noticed Deborah kneeling down at the foot of her mother's grave. She was running her fingers over the inscription at the bottom. 'Beloved Mother of Joshua and Deborah.' Her back was to Lewis and Beverly. Her shoulders started moving up and down. She was obviously crying.

Beverly started to go to her and Lewis stopped her. "Let her be. She needs to do this." Then they heard her. "Momma…Momma, I am so proud of you."

Josh put his hand on her shoulder.

"Momma, please forgive me." Then she lay down on the grave and hugged it, her body racked with sobs. "I am so sorry, please forgive me, Momma. I am begging you, please forgive me."

Josh helped her up and both were rocking back and forth, still kneeling at the foot of the grave. Deborah was still crying. Josh was patting her on the back and rocking back and forth. Josh leaned over and kissed her on the top of the head.

Beverly was crying. She couldn't help but remember how and when she fell in love with Lewis. Lewis was holding her and doing the same as Josh.

Lewis turned to Grandpa Williams and said, "We have never seen her cry before. If she got hurt she never cried."

Lewis and Beverly went to the two of them. Deborah threw her arms around both Lewis and Beverly and said, "Thank you, thank you for being who you are and doing all you've done. Thank you so much for this. This is the happiest day of my life. I will love you two forever and a day."

Grandpa Williams said, "Your mother had a life insurance policy. I put it in a trust fund for the two of you."

"Oh Grandpa, we don't need any money. You use it to take care of yourself," said Deborah.

"I don't need any money, honey."

"But you're bill at the alternative care, that must set you back a lot," said Deborah.

"When your Grandmother needed help, I built it for us. I own the place, literally."

Josh spoke up. "Why don't you use it to start a college scholarship fund for kids that wouldn't be able to go to school. It could be a memorial scholarship fund in their name. I'm sure you could find someone to manage it for you."

Grandpa Williams looked at Beverly and Lewis then said, "You did a good job raising them."

"We had good stock to start with. We're very proud of them," said Beverly.

"There is one other place I'd like for you to visit before we go back. It's across the street."

THE GOODBYE

As they were leaving the cemetery both Josh and Deborah stopped and looked back. "Did you hear her?" Josh asked Deborah.

"Yes, I did," answered Deborah.

Lewis, Beverly and Grandpa Williams stopped and turned back when they realized Josh and Deborah had stopped. All five saw a small whirlwind form at the graves for a few seconds. Then it lifted up and dissipated as quickly as it had formed, leaving no trace of its existence.

Of the five witnesses, three paid no attention to the small whirlwind. It happens all the time in Iowa. Tornados they notice. They also happen all the time. To two of the five it meant something. It brought tears to the eyes of Josh and Deborah.

"That was amazing, wasn't it?" said Josh.

"It was beautiful," said Deborah.

"It's gone without a trace of its existence."

"Except in my heart and memories," said Deborah.

"You know, I feel like this is the most important day in our lives," said Josh.

"I truly think you are right. I think our Mother feels she has been forgiven," said Deborah.

"I think she has forgiven us forever doubting," said Josh.

"I believe you are right."

Across the street was the Katrina Beal-Williams memorial Park. "The city named it after her when she was killed," said Grandpa Williams.

"This dedication stone was placed here in her honor." Everyone noticed there was an inscription at the bottom. "An Angel of Mercy."

"After my son was killed and your Mom could come visit, she would bring the two of you here to play. One day I came over here and she was sitting on that bench. She was crying. I found out my son proposed to her on that bench. This was a very special place to her. Do any of you have a special place?"

"Yes, we do. All four of us have a special place," answered Beverly. "Then never let it go."

Lewis knelt down beside Grandpa Williams and placed his hand on the man's forearm to get his attention.

"Mr. Williams," the old man looked Lewis in the eye. "Mr. Williams, I was in Bosnia. I had a friend, his name was Jack…Jack Gordon and he…he got shot and the Lieutenant…the Lieutenant couldn't…he couldn't stop the bleeding…"

Beverly could tell Lewis voice was choking with emotion.

"I think…I'm pretty sure…we're pretty sure…" Lewis looked to Beverly for help.

Beverly took Mr. William's hand in hers and squeezed. Mr. Williams looked to Beverly. "Sir, Lewis was in Bosnia and a friend of his was shot by a sniper. We believe…we're pretty sure that Katrina died trying to save his life."

Mr. Williams looked to Lewis and saw he had taken his handkerchief out to wipe his eyes. Mr. Williams patted Lewis on the arm. He understood. Sometimes we have burdens we can't put behind us. He, himself had burdens he had tried to put behind him and move on. Those burdens were still with him. He couldn't put them aside and continue his journey in life. You simply had to bear

the burden and try. You had to try. Mr. Williams wiped his eyes, "It's
a small world isn't it."

CHAPTER THIRTY

SMALL WORLD

When they were back at the Alternative Care Center Lewis asked how long the two families, The Beals and the Williams, had lived in Iowa. "Since 1871. They were originally from Kentucky. This was about the time horse racing came about. They were the best of friends. They had lost most of their horses to the two armies during the Civil War. A rich German came through and offered them two thousand dollars for their prized horse but they had to deliver it to Kansas City, Missouri. The two of them transported the horse to Kansas City. When they got there the German said he would only pay five hundred for the horse, and they had to let one of his men ride the horse to see if it was any good. Well, they were stuck in Kansas City. They had no money. With only one horse, how were they going to get back to their families? Well, this rider rode the horse and when he got back he saw what the German was doing. After he paid them this rider took off on the horse. The German called the Sheriff. The Sheriff said he wasn't going into Kansas. There was still bad blood between Kansas and Missouri from the Civil War.

"My relatives said they would go with the Germans for a thousand dollars each, plus a horse, a saddle, a pistol and a rifle. Well, they chased this man through Kansas, Colorado, and into Wyoming."

"Oh boy," said Beverly.

"I'm sorry, what did you say, Ma'am?"

"I said, Oh boy. I love a good cowboy story."

"Well, every time they got close this cowboy would take off again. You know how legends get mixed in with facts. They were about two hundred yards behind him when his hat flew off. He jerked the horse around and went racing back for his hat, leaned down, snatched it up off the ground, turned that horse around and skeedaddled off. They never saw him again. That's when they knew he was toying with them. Winter was coming on, they turned back and made it to here and holed up for the winter. Built a cabin right here. Sent for their families and have been here ever since. Just imagine if that hat hadn't blown off, no telling where they would be."

"It's a trick Grandpa," said Deborah smiling.

"What's a trick?"

"Picking your hat up off the ground."

Lewis couldn't resist saying "I understand it's passed down from generation to generation." Beverly kicked him under the table.

"How do you do this trick?" asked Grandpa Williams.

"The Lariat is around the saddle horn. You hold on to the bottom loop of the lariat and you can reach another eighteen inches to the ground. Josh and I can do it. Mom showed us how."

Beverly, red faced said, "Mr. Williams, I have a confession to make."

After her confession the old man said it was the best thing that ever happened to them. Then he looked at Josh and said, "It seems like yesterday you would sit in my lap and ask me to tell you a story. I had to make them up. I even made the characters up. I named them Bubble Bear and Pumpkin Man. I had to tell them over and over. I know you don't remember any of that."

"I remember the characters. I didn't remember who told them to me. I'm sorry. I wish I could remember more." Lewis said, "Mr. Williams, he asked me to tell him those stories. He even told me what they were about so I know he remembers some of it. I just thought it was his imagination."

Josh said, "They were as real to me as anything else."

Mr. Williams continued, "I even had a nickname for you. You're middle name is Alfred and I always called you 'Big Al.' If we went somewhere and people knew you, as soon as we went in everyone would say 'Big Al' at the same time. It always made you smile. I guess you will always be 'Big Al' to me."

Then Mr. Williams looked at Deborah. "Deborah, when you're Grandmother started getting disoriented you would watch her like a hawk. If she went into another room you would bring her back and tell her to sit in her chair. You were always looking out for her. What was amazing is how you cared for her and you were only three years old."

This brought tears to Beverly's eyes. She thought, she is only twenty and she has protected someone else most of her life. First her grandmother and then Josh. She was so proud of the two.

That night in the hotel they talked about the day's events. Beverly started off first. "Did you guys realize this is the first time I have ever been out of Wyoming in my life?"

Josh said that this was a memorable trip for him, and then he added that he wished he could remember more of his grandfather.

Everyone was quiet for a few minutes before Deborah said, "Can you imagine how hard it had to be for a mother to have to leave her children behind and go halfway around the world for who knows how long."

"I can only imagine. It would be harder than anything I have ever had to do in my life," said Beverly.

Deborah and Josh nodded in agreement.

"You don't know how much I respect your mother. I don't think I would have had the strength to do that," said Beverly.

"Thank you, Mom," said Deborah.

"Yes, thank you. It means a lot to hear you say that. It also means a lot to both of us that you did all the leg work to help us connect with our roots," said Josh.

"The two of you should be very proud of your mother," said Lewis.

"We are," answered both Josh and Deborah. "You can't believe how proud we are of her and I am so ashamed of the way I acted when you were trying to tell us. Looking back I know I probably disappointed you, Mom. I wasn't brought up that way, I'm sorry."

Deborah then asked the question that was on everyone's mind but no one had brought up.   "I wonder if our lives would have been different, for the four of us, if we had done this ten years ago." No one answered; there wasn't an answer. Deborah said, "This is the best Christmas present I've ever had. A trip I thought I would never take. I can't believe how easy it was to find our biological parents."

"Things just sort of fell into place. If Mary wasn't with the Sheriff's office things might have been different. She did almost everything. We would be a square one without her," said Beverly.

CHAPTER THIRTY ONE

THE VERSE

2 TIMOTHY 4:7

Lewis looked at Josh. "Can you tell us about the Bible verse?"

"Yes, Sir, I was reading my Bible and the wind picked up. I laid the Bible down to make sure everything was secured and the wind blew the pages and bent that page over. When I picked the Bible back up that verse jumped out at me. I must have read it a hundred times that day. That verse gave me so much comfort and strength. I knew I had fought to stay alive and I would continue to do that. I knew if I didn't survive I would keep my faith."

Beverly noticed his voice begin to break up with emotion as he finished. "Is there anything else you want to tell us about that time?" asked Beverly.

There was a long pause by Josh. "Yes, Ma'am, I talked to God, a lot." There was silence in the room for a few seconds.

"You talked to God?" asked Lewis, who then looked at Beverly.

"Yes, Sir, all you need is a nice quiet place," then he smiled.

"Did God answer you?" asked Lewis.

"He answered my prayers. But no it wasn't a two way conversation. I talked, he just listened. I got the feeling he already knew everything, anyway."

"Is there anything else that happened that you want to tell us about?" asked Beverly again.

Josh looked at Deborah.

Deborah nodded her head. "Tell them about the voice."

"Well, I would hear this voice," said Josh.

"You would hear a voice? I don't understand," said Beverly. She looked at Lewis when she said it.

"Yes, Ma'am, a voice." Josh glanced at Deborah, and then he continued. "I know this sounds crazy but ever since we got to the ranch, we always felt like someone was watching us. Right Deborah? Especially when we were alone."

"That's right," answered Deborah.

"Well, that's different than hearing a voice, right Hon?" Lewis was asking Beverly.

"I heard the voice also," said Deborah.

Lewis looked at Deborah. "You heard a voice, too?" Then he looked to Beverly and raised his eyebrows.

"Yes, Sir, I've heard the voice"

"When did this start hearing this voice?" asked Beverly looking from Josh to Deborah and back to Josh.

"The first time I heard it was when Josh spilt his milk and ran into the closet and you told me you weren't going to beat him."

"What did the voice say?" asked Beverly.

"She said, 'Deborah believes her.'"

"Josh, when did you first hear the voice?" Lewis was looking at Josh.

"On our first family picnic. You picked me up and promised me no one would ever beat me again. I guess the guy in the eighth grade didn't get the memo" then he chuckled.

"What did the voice say to you?" asked Lewis

"'Believe him, Joshua.'"

"That's all. It only said, 'Believe him Joshua?'"

"Yes, Sir" answered Josh.

"I don't understand. There is nothing special about the ranch. You never heard the voice before that?" asked Lewis looking from one to the other and then back to Beverly.

Josh answered, "No, Sir."

"And you haven't heard this voice since then?" asked Beverly.

"Yes, Ma'am. I heard it in the plane and after I landed."

"What did this voice say to you then?" asked Beverly.

"She said, 'You can do this Joshua.' She said that twice. Once while I was flying and when I was landing. After I landed I heard her say, 'You have work to do' and I also heard her say, 'Trust in the Lord Joshua.' I heard her say something at least four times."

"The voice also told me to trust in the Lord," said Deborah.

"When?" asked Beverly.

"When Josh was in the desert and several times she said, 'Deborah, Joshua needs you.' The voice always called him Joshua. She also said, 'Deborah you can do this.' That's why I sent that message. I was hoping it would get others to look in the desert for Josh. That's why I looked in the bookcase and found that book on the Civil Air Patrol."

"I don't have a book on the Civil Air Patrol," said Josh.

"Yes, you do. I looked at it. I know you have a book on the History of the Civil Air Patrol."

"I don't know where I got it. I don't remember it. I don't know where it came from."

"I do." Everyone looked at Lewis.

"I bought it at a yard sale. I paid fifty cents for it. I thought Josh would like it. I put it in the book case."

"When?" asked Beverly.

"I can't really remember; maybe the week before Thanksgiving."

"So you heard it when you first got to the ranch and didn't hear it again until Josh was in the desert?" asked Lewis, changing the subject.

Then Deborah said, "There was one other time. When I got in the fight in the eighth grade. When that boy pushed me down twice. Twice, I would like to remind everyone," she repeated, looking at Beverly and smiling. "And the boy said, 'Your own momma didn't want you' and then the voice said, 'Deborah defend yourself.'"

"Why didn't you ever tell us any of this?" asked Lewis.

"I don't know. I don't know why I never told anyone but Josh."

"Same here," said Josh "Maybe we couldn't believe it ourselves and figured the two of you wouldn't understand."

"So you're saying it was like a guardian angel?" asked Lewis.

"It was more than that," said Josh.

"You keep saying, 'She said', was the voice always a woman's voice?" asked Beverly.

"Yes, Ma'am, it was always a woman and both of us believe it was our mother. We believe she's gone now, right Deborah?"

Deborah answered with, "Yes, she's gone."

"Why do you think that? What makes you believe she is gone now?" asked Beverly before looking at Lewis.

"Today we both heard it again."

"When?" asked Lewis.

"When we were leaving the cemetery," answered Josh.

"What did the voice say?" asked Beverly.

"Goodbye, Joshua. Goodbye, Deborah. We both heard the same thing. Isn't that right Deborah?"

"Yes, we heard the same thing like she was leaving and then we saw the whirlwind."

"What whirlwind?" asked Lewis. He glanced at Beverly. He saw a small smile on her lips and she was slightly nodding her head.

"The whirlwind; I saw it," said Beverly. "I didn't pay it any attention at the time, but I remember seeing it." Then Beverly looked at Josh and Deborah. "Do you think the whirlwind was your mother and that is when she left?" asked Beverly before glancing over at Lewis.

Deborah answered first. "I think so. I want to believe it was her."

"I know it sounds impossible, but I want to believe it was our mother, too," said Josh.

Beverly smiled and said, "I want to believe it was your mother, too. That is so cool."

Deborah and Josh both smiled and shook their heads. They had never heard Beverly use the phrase 'That is so cool.'

Lewis didn't know what to think of this. He thought, 'These three believe in ghost or spirits or who knows what.'

"Let's get back to this voice and forget about the whirlwind," said Lewis.

"It's kind of hard to forget about the whirlwind," said Josh.

"Right and I don't ever want to forget about the whirlwind," said Deborah.

"I didn't mean it like that," said Lewis. "The whirlwind can be explained. It may have been just a whirlwind, but the voice, now that's different. Are you sure it was a voice, or could it have been the wind or something else. You know like a radio in another room or a car passing by. Sometimes if you're going to do something that you know is wrong you may hear a voice inside you saying 'Don't do that' you know, like your conscience telling you not to do that. That's your own voice; you're thinking you're not actually hearing something. Under the circumstances you couldn't tell the difference. I'm sure that's all it was," said Lewis satisfied with his explanation.

"Lewis, they heard a woman's voice, isn't that right?" said Beverly, looking at Josh then Deborah.

"Yes, Ma'am. It was always a woman's voice," answered Deborah.

"And you didn't hear this voice at the other place, right?" asked Beverly.

"No, Ma'am, only when we got to the ranch," said Deborah.

"And both of you, both of you, believe it was your mother, and she's gone now. That she left on a whirlwind. Is that right?"

"Yes, Ma'am, I believe she's gone now. Why would she say goodbye if she was not leaving."

"I believe she's gone now," said Josh.

Lewis asked, "Son, I understand why she would say, 'You can do this' and 'Trust in the Lord,' but I'm curious about when she told you, 'You have work to do.' What did she mean by that?"

Josh took a few seconds before answering. "Dad, I don't know. That has bothered me ever since I heard it. I thought it was doing what I did in the desert to stay alive. You had taught me most of that stuff in the boy scouts. It was common sense really. I would have done the same thing even if she hadn't said that. Now, I think she was talking about something later on, you know, in the future."

"Do you have any idea what it is that you are supposed to do in the future?" asked Lewis.

"Dad, I don't have a clue. Ever since I can remember you have told me God has a plan for everybody. I remember you saying he may reveal it to us or he may not. Maybe that's part of God's plan, not telling me. I'm sure I will know when the time is right."

"Son, that's why I always told you to do the best you can."

"Yes, Sir, and I am going to try to do that," answered Josh.

There was a pause in the conversation. It seemed everyone was pondering the subject.

"I bet you were amazed when you saw the same Bible verse on her grave," said Beverly.

"No, Ma'am, I sort of expected it to be there," answered Josh.

"What! How can that be? Until yesterday you knew nothing of your mother. You didn't even know she was dead. You certainly didn't know that was her favorite Bible verse until Mr. Williams told us today. How could you have possibly expected it to be on her grave?" asked Lewis, surprise clearly showing on his face.

"Dad, I can't really explain it. I had a lot of time to think in the desert. No one has called me Joshua in a long time. I wondered who would call me Joshua. She was the answer I came up with. I know it sounds strange but when I was in the desert I never felt I was alone. I never got lonely. I always felt a presence around me."

"I didn't tell Deborah about me thinking it was our mother. That's the reason I wanted to find out and when Mom told us about our mother I felt like the verse would be there on the grave. I was right, I can't explain it, but I was right."

"But why didn't you hear it at the other place?" asked Lewis.

"I think I know the answer to that," said Beverly "If it was their Mother."

"Well, I certainly like to hear it," said Lewis.

"At the other place she couldn't bear to watch."

CHAPTER THIRTY TWO

LEAVING ON A WHIRLWIND

Later that night after Josh and Deborah had returned to their room, Lewis and Beverly were still talking. "You know what I think is strange or unusual, or at least it is to me," said Lewis.

"What's that?"

"Let's say for instance they both imagined the voice, and let's say that the whirlwind was just a common every day run of the mill whirlwind. The wind blew the pages in his Bible to the same verse that is on the grave. Now we know he quoted that verse. We both heard him. The Bible verse is chiseled in stone so to speak. I just find all that unusual."

"God works in mysterious ways Lewis. You are wasting your time trying to figure it out."

"You don't think that's strange or unusual?" asked Lewis.

"Yes, I do Lewis, but other unusual things have happened."

"Like what?"

"Tell me about the book," said Beverly.

"What book?"

"The book you bought for fifty cents at a yard sale."

"Well, it was before they came home. I went into the auto parts store and you know the vacant lot next to it?"

"Yes, I know where you are talking about."

"Someone had a couple of tables there and I thought I recognized someone. I thought maybe she had come home early. I went over and this woman was looking at a book. Well, when I got close to her I realized it wasn't who I thought it was. She put the book down in front of me instead of putting it back with the other books. Then she walked away. I picked it up and thought Josh would like it, so I bought it."

"Lewis, who did you think it was?

"Now don't go jumping to any conclusions."

"Lewis, who did you think it was?"

"I thought it was Deborah."

"So, this woman who you thought was Deborah was looking at the book and you bought it for Josh."

"Yeah," answered Lewis.

"Do you wonder who the woman was?"

"Well, yeah, I wonder who she was, but I know what you're thinking and I can tell you right now she wasn't a ghost."

"How do you know she wasn't a ghost?" said Beverly smiling.

"Well, you can see through a ghost, right?"

"I don't know, can you?" she teased still smiling.

"All I know is when I saw the picture of their mother I thought she looked familiar. Beverly don't tell me you believe in ghost."

"You didn't see a ghost, Lewis. I know who the woman was. At least I'm pretty sure I know who it was."

"Who."

"Their Aunt Carol, Katrina's sister, they look an awful lot alike. When I first saw her I knew she was related to Deborah."

"What was she doing in Kerney? Did you tell her Josh and Deborah lived in Kerney?"

"Lewis, you saw her the week before Thanksgiving. I saw her the week after Thanksgiving. She couldn't have been here for that and no I didn't tell her where they lived. That is not my decision to make. That is Josh and Deborah's decision."

"Well, I wonder why she was in Kerney," said Lewis.

"She works at the center for the battered women in Casper. Sometimes they help relocate women and children away from an abusive spouse. She was probably doing a follow-up on someone."

"Let me ask you this. If I hadn't thought she was Deborah, I wouldn't have gone over there and I wouldn't have bought the book. Do you think they would have found Josh if I hadn't bought the book?" asked Lewis.

"Only God knows the answer to that, Lewis. I'm just thankful she was there. I'm thankful you thought she was Deborah. I'm thankful that book was about the Civil Air Patrol. I'm thankful Deborah found it. I'm thankful for the two men that answered the message. This had been two days of many blessings to be thankful for. Josh and Deborah have been able to heal a wound we didn't even realize they had. We can only imagine what Josh went through in the desert, but I think he is stronger for it. I think Deborah has a new meaning to life. I can see the pride she has for her Mother. Something was missing in their lives and you and I never saw it. And Grandpa Williams, can you imagine what he went through. For fifteen years knowing you have two grandchildren somewhere out there and you don't know where. To go out on that sunporch every day for fifteen years hoping, just hoping they would show up some day."

"Lewis, you and I have so much to be thankful for and in a span of two days three lives have been changed. We have given an old man hope. We have given Josh and Deborah their real parents. And a big part of that may have been a case of mistaken identity, in you thinking Carol was Deborah. God does work in mysterious ways don't you think."

"Well, I don't know about that, but when I saw the photo of their mother I expected you to tell us she was still alive. I thought I had seen her five or six weeks ago. But now you sound like you believe in ghost. Beverly, tell me you don't believe in ghosts."

Beverly didn't answer.

"Beverly, say something."

"Let me ask you this," said Beverly. "Josh and Deborah told us about the pilot who found him. We heard Deborah say a few minutes ago that this voice that she believes is her Mother said, and I quote 'Deborah, Joshua need you.' She also said the voice said 'Deborah you can do this.' Is that what made Deborah go into his room, find that book and then send that message? I would like to think it did."

"Beverly are you saying you believe in ghost?"

"Before I answer that let me ask you a question. How much longer could Josh have lasted?"

"I don't know the answer to that."

"So she heard this voice 'Deborah Joshua needs you' and then 'Deborah you can do this.' Do what? What could Deborah do? So she goes into his room, his computer is there. She sends a message to the man who found him. Did she send messages to other people, not that I'm aware of? The guy with him had seen a reflection. They flew back there. Now, you and I never thought to do what she did. Something compelled her to do something."

"So you do believe in ghost?"

Beverly smiled and said, "I don't believe in whirlwinds either. Let them believe if they want. What's the harm? All I know is that both of them basically heard the same thing. They were not anywhere close to each other when the voice said 'You can do this' and 'Trust in the Lord.' I do not believe they are making it up. Do you believe they are making this up?"

"Of course not. They wouldn't do that," said Lewis.

"Then, where does that leave us."

"I don't know. I honestly don't know," said Lewis letting out a breath of air and then looking at the ceiling.

"There is one thing I do know Lewis. Josh wouldn't be with us today if Deborah had thought it was her imagination. If she had thought it was her imagination she wouldn't have went into his room and sent that message."

"So, what do we do?" asked Lewis.

"We don't do anything."

"Nothing?"

"Let me ask you a question. You remember the day I brought them home?"

"Sure."

"You remember the bruises?"

"Of course, I couldn't ever forget those," said Lewis.

"Would you have trusted or believed anyone if that had happened to you?"

"I doubt it, but I can't say for sure."

"Yet, the very next day this voice tells them to believe us, and guess what. They believed the voice. Then they believed us, two complete strangers." Beverly paused for a minute before saying, "They were five years old at the time. Maybe somehow they remembered their mother's voice. Babies can recognize their mother's heartbeat even after being in an incubator for weeks. Their mother died two years before. Maybe they recognized the voice and knew she would tell them the truth. I don't know. Anything is possible.

"Lewis, I believe that both Deborah and Josh are perfectly normal twenty year olds. For fifteen years they have wondered about their real parents. In the last two days they have found out a lot, and I mean a lot. They hear something, a voice, if you will and they see a whirlwind. Their mother is a hero, Lewis. Maybe heroes get to leave on a whirlwind. You and I have raised two amazing children. I think they deserve to believe their mother was watching over them and said goodbye and left on a whirlwind. Oh, think of the stories they will be able to tell their children and grandchildren."

"No, Lewis, I don't believe in ghosts, but I do believe in Josh and Deborah. I do believe they think they heard something. Maybe it was their imagination, and it seemed real to them. I don't know but in a strange way I'd like to believe that somehow their mother was watching over them. Maybe a mother's love can transcend time and space and even violate the laws of physics. That's a good way to look at it and it makes me feel good."

"I just don't like our children hearing voices, that's all I'm saying."

"Lewis, they are not our children anymore. They are both grown and like it or not we have to share them. We have to share them with their real parents. I will be honest with you; I don't mind that one bit. We will love them the way we always have. That will never change."

"So you are not concerned about them hearing voices?" asked Lewis.

"They will never hear voices again, Lewis. Remember, she said goodbye. She's gone."

Lewis nodded his head.

"Lewis, sometimes I hear my daddy. I always thought it was my imagination, but after today I'm not so sure."

Lewis wiped his eyes with the back of his hands. It had been a long two days. "Sometimes I hear my momma."

Beverly didn't answer. They sat in silence for a few minutes.

Then Lewis started talking. "Ever since you told me about their mother dying the same day as Jack, it made me think of a couple of things."

"Like what?" asked Beverly.

"When they put Jack's body on the plane we had to wait about an hour for the other four bodies."

"And you think their mother was one of those bodies?"

"Well, it's possible. They died close to each other probably within fifty miles. A medivac would have had a least four people. The pilot, co-pilot, crew chief and the medic."

"I don't suppose we will ever know," said Beverly.

"I always wondered why they didn't send a convoy to get us. They may have been out looking for the wreckage. I was so tired when we got back to the base camp I didn't notice."

Lewis thought for a few minutes before saying, "Did I ever tell you I was a Ghost Rider?"

"No, you didn't. I'd love to hear about it. I love a good ghost story."

So he told her.

CHAPTER THIRTY THREE

FAMILY

Beverly was already dressed and packing their suitcase for the trip home. The Christmas program was tonight at 7:00 p.m. They would have enough time to drive to Kerney, rest a few hours, and then go to church. Beverly and Deborah were both singing in the musical. Christmas was special to her and the children. They were also exchanging gifts tonight in the fellowship hall. The congregation had drawn names.

Lewis was in the shower. A sense of dread came over Beverly. Christmas should be spent with family. She thought of Grandpa Williams spending Christmas without his family. It saddened her. She sat in the chair by the window. Looking out she could see the alternative care home.

Lewis came out of the shower. He was wearing a motel robe and was drying his hair. He saw Beverly by the window.

"Are you already finished packing?"

"No, I was thinking of something."

"What were you thinking?"

"I was thinking of Grandpa Williams spending Christmas by himself."

"You don't think it's right that Josh and Deborah, who have never spent Christmas with him, as far as we know, are headed back home, right?"

"Something like that."

"Well, what are you going to do?"

"Let me think on it a few minutes."

In the room next door, Deborah was looking out the window. She could see the alternative care home.

"You thinking about Grandpa?" asked Josh.

"Yeah, you know we have never spent Christmas with him. It seems a shame. No one should spend Christmas by themselves. It's just not right. He is part of our family."

"Well, we have two choices. Take him with us or stay here. If we are taking him with us we need to come to a decision pretty quick."

"Let's talk to Mom and Dad."

They saw Lewis and Beverly as soon as they stepped out of their room. Beverly said, "Why don't we ask Grandpa Williams to spend Christmas with us?"

"We were going to ask you the same thing. Do you think he will go?"

"It won't hurt to ask," said Lewis.

Two hours later the five of them were on the road. It was a long drive. In good company time flies.

They made it to church with time to spare. The church members thought it was a great Christmas story. Two grandchildren finding their grandfather and spending Christmas with him for the first time in their lives. Beverly loved showing off Grandpa Williams to the congregation.

In the fellowship hall after the musical all of the older women were hovering around him bringing him a slice of cake or pie.

Deborah thought she was going to have to beat them off with a stick. Lewis thought it was funny. Josh wanted to find out his secret. Knowing something like that could come in handy.

FORGIVENESS

LUKE 2:10

Her past was eating away at her like a cancer. She had always heard you don't have to look far to find someone worse off than you are. She didn't know if that was true or not. She had been awake for two hours. She had brewed a pot of coffee. She hadn't touched the cup she had poured. She was sure it was cold by now. She had not even turned on the lights. She sat in the dark with the blinds and curtains closed.

Solitude. Christmas was always a day of solitude. She had no family. She had no friends. Everyone she knew and met at work were sad people. People that had no place to go. People, who just like her, had hit rock bottom.

She hadn't celebrated Christmas in over fifteen years. She felt she had no reason to celebrate. She didn't know how much longer she could go on like this. It was slowly but surely killing her. Everyone said Christmas was a time of joy. There was no joy to be found in her life. She had no Christmas tree, no presents, not even a single Christmas card. Tears formed in her eyes and rolled down her face. She wiped them away, she didn't know why because more tears would follow shortly. It had been this way for what seemed like forever.

She knew she would eat a sandwich for lunch. She never bought anything for a Christmas dinner. Why, because she knew she would be alone. She had no one to invite. No one to turn to. No one to talk to. Everyone she knew was just like her, some, even worse.

There was a knock at the door. She wouldn't answer it. There was no reason to answer the door. The knocking continued. They will go away, they always do. She sat in silence. The knocking continued. She sat and listened. The knocking continued.

She got up and peeked out the window. She couldn't see who it was. The knocking continued. She went to the door. She didn't know why but she opened it.

"Aunt Carol?"

Carol Duncan stepped out on the small porch.

"Deborah?" Then a pause. "Joshua?"

"Yes, Ma'am" said Deborah.

"You look just like Katrina and Joshua you look like Alfred. Would you like to come in?"

"No, Ma'am. We don't have time. We want you to come with us," said Josh.

"Where?" asked Carol

"Well, it's Christmas and we want you to spend Christmas with us," said Deborah.

Josh said, "Grandpa Williams and Grandma Alice are also spending Christmas with us and we would like for you to spend Christmas with us, too."

"Christmas, I haven't celebrated Christmas in over fifteen years."

"It's like riding a bike, once you learn how you never forget." said Josh and smiled.

"Are you sure?" asked Carol.

"Yes, Ma'am, we're sure. I never thought I would say this, but I have learned so much in the last few days and I understand everything now. We, Josh and I, forgive you. We now know you were trying to protect us. We want so much to spend Christmas with you and Grandpa Williams. Our Grandma Alice will be there, too. Please come with us."

"Let me freshen up real quick and get my coat."

She was back in a minute. On the way to the car Carol said, "Did your Grandpa tell you I went to see him after I was paroled?"

Josh answered, "Yes, Ma'am. He told us. He said you asked him for forgiveness and he said he forgave you."

"That was the hardest thing I have ever done in my life. What happened to the two of you is a burden I will carry for the rest of my life."

"Ma'am, we have forgiven you, both of us, so you can put that burden down now," said Deborah.

"Right," said Josh. "Let's enjoy Christmas."

There was snow on the ground that night in Kerney. It was a full moon and all the stars were out. The reflection of the snow made it a perfect Christmas card picture. A tarp and blanket was spread out on Lookout Point. Seven people were sitting in a circle, holding candles. They were singing Christmas carols. They sang 'Silent Night' several times, it seemed to be everyone's favorite. Carol Duncan realized she had received the most precious gift of all, forgiveness.

DÉJÀ VU

Beverly had never been out of Wyoming before going to Beal, Iowa. Six weeks later, she would leave Wyoming again. Lewis's sister, Cynthia, had passed away from ovarian cancer, same as his mother. Cynthia had never informed Lewis she was battling the disease. He found out the day after when he received the phone call from a member of her staff. Lewis was simply told she wanted it that way. It was the saddest day of his life.

She was five years older and they communicated by Christmas and birthday cards and the occasional phone call. Cynthia was a very busy woman. Lewis knew the real reason she didn't tell him of her impending death. She didn't want to bother anyone.

Beverly, Josh and Deborah would drive to Virginia and make the arrangements there. Lewis would fly to California and retrieve the body. He was met at the airport by one of her partners and taken to the church for the funeral.

"Lewis I know this is a bad time for you, but after the funeral we need to read the will."

"It would be best to do it while I'm here," said Lewis.

"Mr. Carlton is the executor of her will. While they transport the body to the airport we can do the will. I understand you will fly on the same aircraft. Is that correct?"

"Yes."

"We have made those arrangements for you."

"Thank you; I wouldn't even know where to start."

After the funeral Lewis was escorted into Mr. Carlton's office. After the introductions were made Mr. Carlton read the will.

"Cynthia left her share of the firm to the firm. The three of us opened it over twenty years ago.

"I have no objections to that," said Lewis.

"Since you live in Wyoming, she knew you would not be interested in her condo. I will place it on the market tomorrow. Any objections to that?"

"None whatsoever. Can you give me a ball park figure on its value?"

"Between seven hundred and eight hundred thousand," answered Mr. Carlton.

"I would like to establish a memorial college scholarship fund in her name with that money. Can you handle that for me?"

"Certainly," answered Mr. Carlton.

"She left twenty percent of her assets to the Cancer Society."

"That sounds like Cynthia. She's going to fight what killed her even after her death."

"She was the most competitive woman I've ever met," said Carlton.

"You should meet my daughter," said Lewis.

"The eighty percent remaining is to be divided four ways. Twenty percent to each party. You, your wife, your son and your daughter. The kid's portion will be placed in a trust fund until the age of thirty. I guess she thought it best to do that."

"I have no problem with that."

"It's a lot of money, Lewis."

"I'd rather have my sister," said Lewis.

The aircraft the law firm had rented was waiting for Lewis. The seats were removed except for one. It was mounted sideways next to the coffin. She would be buried alongside her Mother in Virginia. Cynthia wanted it that way.

Once again Lewis felt like a Ghost Rider. Lewis was able to sit in his seat, which was facing the casket and put his hand on her casket. He talked to her a lot on the flight. He would tell her about the kids, she was instrumental in securing their adoption. Every once in a while he would say, "I wish you had told me, Cynthia. I know you didn't want me to worry, but I wish you had told me."

The graveside funeral was simple, another request by Cynthia. A few distant relatives were in attendance. There were no friends. She had had a church funeral in California. Lewis knew she had no friends in Virginia, having moved away when she was seven.

Lewis stood beside the graves and wept. "I brought her home, Momma," was all he could say.

PART THREE

CHAPTER THIRTY FOUR

THE CALLING

KERNEY, WYOMING

1 CORINTHIANS 7:24

"Lewis, if I win the presidency I want you on my cabinet," said Senator Carson.

"Senator, the election is months away. I know you are the best man for the job, but anything can happen, you know that."

"How long have we known each other Lewis?" asked Senator Carson.

"Since you were Governor and you came here on a challenge from Beverly," answered Lewis. "At least fifteen years."

"And all that time you have been honest and forthright with me. When you didn't agree with me you told me face to face. I need someone I can trust and tell the truth. I shudder when I think about being surrounded by liars and thieves."

"Well, I appreciate that Senator. You know my father would roll over in his grave if he knew I was supporting an Independent candidate."

"The main reason I want you is your love of the land. I've never known anyone who cared for the land like you do. That is why I want you as my Secretary of the Interior. Will you accept it if I win?"

"Senator, you know I have to run that by my family. That is a decision I'm not going to make on my own. Now, let's go fishing while you still have a chance."

"One thing I will miss is this time that I have to go hunting and fishing."

Senator Carson knew the American people were tiring of the Democrat and Republican parties. Both parties were run by extreme factions, the ultra-liberals and the right wing conservatives. He believed there was a middle ground and that was the forgotten fifty percent. Senator Carson wanted those voters and went after them with a passion. One news analyst pointed out the week before the election "If neither candidate gets the two hundred seventy electoral votes necessary to win, the House of Representatives will choose from the top three candidates. Each state only gets one vote. The republican can garner thirty five of the fifty votes.

"The Senate chooses the vice president from the top two candidates. The Senate is evenly split and each senator gets one vote. They would never choose an Independent over a republican or democrat. In theory we could end up with a republican president and a democrat vice president. There is no way an independent can win under those circumstances. If this happens this may cause a loggerhead in American politics like we've never seen before."

Senator Carson's running mate delivered his home state of Ohio. Senator Carson knew how important Ohio had become in recent years to both the democrat and republican parties. You had to win in Ohio to be elected president. He was amazed neither opponent had selected a running mate from Ohio to help win the twenty electoral votes. The real clincher was his running mate had played quarterback for the Indiana Hoosiers thirty years ago and they won there with its eleven electoral votes. What put him over the top were the three electoral votes from his home state of Wyoming. The election was close, but close only counts in horseshoes and hand grenades.

Carson carried all of the south and the states in the middle of the country. He failed to carry the west coast, California, Oregon, and Washington. Carson knew he wouldn't win there and didn't even campaign in those places. He spent his money where he had a chance to win and it paid off. He knew individual votes weren't important. Electoral votes were the only votes that really counted. If you won a state you would get all the electoral votes except for two states that could split the electoral votes.

Carson got two hundred and seventy one electoral votes. Two hundred and seventy being the magic number to be elected president.

The republicans and democrats split the remainder. The republican was hampered by problems from the start. His age became apparent weeks after the Republican Convention when he suffered a mild heart attack and spent four days in the hospital. He never recouped the momentum. He carried his home state of Nebraska and came in a close second in several states.

The democrat candidate didn't fare much better. Allegations kept cropping up on various items. Mostly unproven allegations from the republicans that he constantly had to defend.

Senator Carson stayed out of the fray and hammered away at the forgotten fifty percent. It paid off for him.

None of the news organizations gave an independent candidate any chance of winning. It was seven in the evening on Election Day when one news announcer was saying, "We got us a three way race here folks."

At nine o'clock, one announcer was saying, "This is a nail biter."

Most people went to bed. They were not all that interested anyway. It wasn't decided till the wee hours of the morning. On Wednesday morning, America woke with a new president elect. James Taylor Carson from Wyoming, the first independent president.

People went off to work like nothing had happened at all. There was no dancing in the streets or any rioting. In Wyoming, it snowed that night. Not much had changed.

President Carson nominated his cabinet to be voted on by the Senate. There were the usual occupations. Lawyers, judges, business owners, politicians and one man no one had heard of before. A rancher from Wyoming named Lewis C. MacDonald.

At his confirmation hearing a senator asked him why he should be Secretary of the Interior. Lewis answered him the best way he knew how.

"I can't think of a single reason why you should consent to me holding this position other than I have lived all over this country.

"Senator, I love this land. I love this country and I want it to be as enjoyable to my children and grandchildren as it is to me. I want an environment that is as beautiful as nature made it. Nothing more, nothing less.

"Yes, I enjoy this land that belongs to all of us. I have never taken anything from it that won't grow back on its own. This nation is rich in resources and those resources can be taken from the ground and with proper oversite can be placed back the way it was.

"Am I the best man for the job? Probably not. Will you find someone that loves this land more than I do? You won't find anyone. I hope I have answered your question, Senator."

A news analyst remarked after the hearing, "Simple answers from a simple man."

Lewis C. MacDonald was confirmed. Most presidents get their way as long as no one was controversial. Lewis C. MacDonald was as bland as rice without salt and pepper, butter or gravy.

CHAPTER THIRTY FIVE

JACK IN THE BOX

The Iranian was instructed to eliminate the two customs inspectors he had been bribing at the border customs checkpoint. The last critical shipment was on a Wednesday. He was instructed to move all of his trucks to a warehouse in Seattle, Washington. There the critical items would be distributed among the six trucks and sent on their way to different parts of the country. He would meet all of his agents at that time, not as a group but individually.

The elimination of the customs agents would take place Thursday night. He would continue to operate his trucks for another month and close the operation down. He would then assume a new identity.

On Thursday night, a beaten and rusty twenty year old Oldsmobile pulled up to the customs checkpoint. The driver was instructed to open the trunk. The driver got out and went to the rear of the car. An argument ensued when the driver started complaining. The man finally opened the trunk. While the agents looked in the trunk the passenger slipped out and fired several shots, killing the two agents.

The two men leaped back into the car and sped away. The incident was captured on four different video cameras. The car was found four miles away. The trunk was opened as if something had been removed, probably drugs. It had been burned.

The car was reported stolen at 7:00 a.m. on Friday morning, a few minutes before the FBI showed up on the elderly lady's doorstep. The FBI conducted a thorough investigation. Photos of the two suspects were shown on TV to help identify them. The shootings stayed on the news for five days. It was never solved. A twenty thousand dollar reward was offered. Hundreds of tips came in, none panned out. It was speculated that they were drug dealers and were probably back in Mexico.

The Iranian was told a month later to change identities and move to a small town on the Canadian border. He was going to work in a convenience store and operate a telemarketing company across the border in Canada. He was told both were legitimate businesses and he would receive other instructions.

The Iranian felt like he was being put in seclusion. The import business had gone well, at least he thought so. There was no link that could be traced back to him.

Six weeks later he was told his mission. His six sleeper agents would be activated and would bring America to its knees. "Praise Allah," was all he could say. He had waited twenty years. Patience had paid off. "Praise Allah."

Now he would be playing the part of an everyday American. His name would be Jack Carr.

Jack was a busy man. Playing the part of an American was easy. He had been in America long enough to pick up their habits and the American lingo. He even had a favorite football team, the Seattle Seahawks. He drove an American car, a fifteen year old Ford. He fit into the American landscape as any other American.

The entire plan had been laid out for him. All he had to do was insure that it was carried out. He was lucky because the most important agent lived about a hundred miles from him. He paid him a visit. He pulled to the side of the road two hundred yards past the agent's house and parked. He turned on his emergency flashers and raised the hood. He pretended he was working on the engine for ten minutes. Even though Jack had excellent hearing he was wearing hearing aids. He wanted to know if anyone was lurking nearby and watching the house. The hearing aids would help to detect any sounds coming from the woods nearby.

Jack turned up the hood on his heavy jacket and started walking. To any observer he looked like a stranded motorist. When he reached the agent's house he rang the doorbell. When his agent opened his door on a cold, wet Wednesday night Jack said, "Sir, I'm having car trouble. May I use your phone?"

His agent said, "Sure, come in out of the cold." Jack didn't know if his agent had noticed that he didn't remove his gloves or remove his hood.

"Show me the device," said Jack after the door was closed.

"It's in the basement," said the agent and turned and walked into the hallway, opening the basement door. Jack just looked at the device. He couldn't take his eyes off of it.

"I thought it would be larger."

"So did I," answered the agent.

"Here are the instructions. You will notice the first thing you will do is have the truck you have sanded and painted. Then you will make sure that truck is in perfect working order. Then you will drive the truck as much as possible. We don't want it looking like it has been repainted. You understand?"

"Sure. That's no problem."

"Then when the time comes you will be given more instructions. Do you understand?"

"I understand. You have nothing to worry about."

Jack looked at the other agent for a long time before saying, "I have everything to worry about."

After returning upstairs Jack looked around the house. Trash was everywhere. Jack wondered how the man lived in this garbage dump.

"How long have you been in America?" asked Jack. He was concerned about the man's mental state.

"Almost forty years," came the reply.

"Do you like America?"

The man spit on the floor and said, "I spit on America." Jack didn't figure anyone would ever notice the spit with all the garbage everywhere. One fear Jack had was one of his agents becoming to Americanized.

"I spit on the great Satan," he said and spit again.

Jack nodded his head.

"Would you like me to get my prayer rug? Perhaps you can join me."

Jack glanced at his watch and said, "I have to leave."

During the two hour drive home, Jack had a lot of time to think and even more time to worry. Jack worried a lot. His agent didn't seem to be concerned. Maybe it was confidence on his agent's part, but confidence can be deceiving. It doesn't lead to success each and every time. Jack worried even more.

Jack had one year to implement phase one of the plan and phase two would be eleven months later. Almost two years for the completion of the plan and returning home. Home. He thought a lot about home. Would he even recognize it after being gone for so long? He could only hope. Hope. Hope was all he could cling to, that and his faith.

CHAPTER THIRTY SIX

THE FAMILY

EPHESIANS 6:7

Lewis MacDonald's family was supportive of him in every way. Josh would be going into the Air Force in eighteen months.

He was an asset to the football team on and off the field. He helped tutor players with low academic grades. What Josh enjoyed most about being on the team was the community outreach programs the team sponsored. Visiting hospitals was something Josh took great pride in. Young and old seemed to brighten when a few Oklahoma Sooners showed up to visit. Some of the players were household names and for the first time Josh realized how important football was in Oklahoma. He was able to travel all over the state. One community he was impressed with was Claremore. The home of the Will Rogers Museum. He had always admired the man. He spent hours in the museum dedicated to a true American. Someone whose words still rang true a hundred years later. Josh believed those words would still ring true a hundred years from now. Josh was surprised to learn that Will Rogers had died in a plane crash in Alaska in August of 1935. He was flying with someone named Wiley Post. Josh had never heard of the man. He was amazed to learn that Wiley Post was the first person to fly solo around the world. It had taken almost eight days. It bothered Josh that someone could be the first to accomplish the feat and he had never heard of him. Someone like that should be remembered. Josh also couldn't help but ponder the fact Will Rogers dying in a plane crash. Josh's ambition to become a pilot wasn't dampened by Will Rogers' death.

Josh thought about studying planes for fifteen years. It dawned on him what one of his ROTC instructors said, "The pilot makes the machine complete. Without the pilot it is an expensive piece of a lot of small parts."

Josh decided to study the men and women who made the machine complete, the pilots. He realized you always had to be careful. The sky was like the ocean, it is very unforgiving, and your craft is so small in such a big expanse. Even if you are famous; death can sneak up on you.

Josh decided to pay tribute to Wiley Post by having him as a role model. He knew young people like him had the wrong role models. Sports figures, rock stars or movie stars. Josh already had his parents, both living and dead. He didn't believe you could have too many, especially if they were the right ones. Josh also read a lot about Chuck Yeager, the first man to break the sound barrier. Another role model for Josh. Josh knew he wanted to be a fighter pilot in the Air Force. Perhaps one day he could also break the sound barrier, but for now it would have to remain a dream.

As an art student at the University of Texas, Deborah had landed a plum assignment. She would get college credit for painting a mural in a small southwest Georgia town named Colquitt.

As soon as she parked the car and looked around, she was amazed at how closely it resembled Kerney. On one corner of the square was a remodeled two story Inn called the Tarrer Inn. She would be spending her nights there. There was a large upstairs veranda that overlooked the square. She planned on sitting under one of the ceiling fans and just relaxing. When she went inside to register she was amazed at the attention to detail. She knew right away she would be doing a lot of sketching in this beautiful place. There was a side courtyard that took her breath away. Yep, she would work a lot out here. The sidewalk out front was brick pavers and reminded Deborah of New Orleans. She had spent one night in New Orleans in the French Quarter on her way here. When she finished here she would return to Texas with a lot of ideas for Kerney.

Deborah was able to watch a folk life play called 'Swamp Gravy.' There were about a hundred volunteers that put on an unbelievable performance. She couldn't believe there was that much talent in a small town. This was another idea to take back to Kerney.

About the only difference in Kerney and Colquitt was where the hardware store was located. In Kerney it was on the square. Deborah found out the building near the Tarrer Inn was once the hardware store but now it was a gift shop. Deborah wanted to find a memento of her visit here. This gift shop had everything from gifts to lawnmowers. They even had a used corvette for sale. Deborah thought now that would make a really nice gift for someone. She found a small plaque of her mother's favorite Bible verse 'This is the day the Lord hath made. We will rejoice and be glad in it.' She had to look one more time at the corvette before she left. Yes, she wasn't dreaming, there was a corvette in the store.

Next to the gift shop was a used book store. She went in to browse around. An old man, obviously the owner, was asleep in a corner chair. She picked out two paperbacks and left the money on the counter, never waking him from his nap. You got to love small towns. She took her bought items back to the Tarrer Inn and headed back out to look around. As she went back by the book store she could see the man still sleeping through the window. She thought to herself 'I hope he is just sleeping. What if something is wrong with him?' She walked back in and cleared her throat, still no movement, and then she leaned over and shook his arm. The man jerked awake and looked at Deborah.

"Just checking to see if you are okay," said Deborah.

"Why wouldn't I be?" questioned the man.

"Well, I'm sorry I woke you. I bought a couple of books and left the money on the counter."

"You didn't wake me. I was just resting my eyes." The old man glanced at his watch and said, "Two o'clock, time for me to sit outside. I sit outside and wave at people going by from two to three o'clock."

"You wave at people?"

"Yep, someone has to do it, don't you think. Don't look right to drive around the square and no one wave at you. What kind of town would that be?"

Deborah smiled. Chester Farris sits outside the hardware store in Kerney and waves at everybody and tries to get kids to pull his finger.

Deborah wondered where people got the latest news. The local paper was a weekly. In Kerney you got the latest news at the hardware store. She found out three weeks later when she needed her hair trimmed. She decided she would treat herself to a manicure, too. She went into a beauty salon that was also on the square. The owner was moving around at ninety miles an hour cutting and coloring hair and also doing pedicures. The phone was ringing off the hook. It didn't take her long to figure out this is where you find out the local news.

"Are you always this busy; going ninety miles an hour?" asked Deborah while the young lady was trimming her hair.

"No, Ma'am. I'm usually going a hundred and ten," as she kept clipping Deborah's hair.

"That last call sounded serious. Nothing bad I hope."

"No, Ma'am, that was about Tadpole Brewer. He had an accident a few minutes ago. He had a three o'clock appointment and didn't show up. Now if he had been here at three o'clock like he was supposed to be he wouldn't have had an accident and got snake bit. You know what I mean? But, that's Tadpole for ya."

"Tadpole?" asked Deborah.

"That's just what everybody calls him. They call his big brother Froggy so naturally they nicknamed him Tadpole. His big brother Froggy is always going frog gigging. You know how good frog legs are."

"I can't say I've ever tried them before. What was the accident?" asked Deborah.

"Oh, Tadpole was riding down the road and saw a rattlesnake. He stopped in the road trying to catch the snake. He was between his truck and the snake when a combine rear ended his truck and then the truck rear ended Tadpole knocking him down and he got bit by the snake."

Another lady sitting in the salon said, "Didn't the same thing happen to him about a year ago?"

"Yes, Ma'am. A logging truck headed to the paper mill in Cedar Springs hit him that time. You know what that's called don't you?"

Deborah answered, "Déjà vu."

"No, Ma'am. That's called being dumber than dirt." Deborah didn't really get homesick here. It was so much like Kerney. Things like that happened in Kerney all the time.

Beverly would stay at the ranch and operate it. She had been doing it almost all her life and it was where her heart was. Her Mother helped out as much as she could. The ranch kept them busy. Beverly felt blessed because there was plenty of grass for grazing. The cattle pretty much took care of themselves. She didn't get to ride as much as she liked but sometimes sacrifices had to be made. She worked in the greenhouse along with her Mother. Beverly come to realize her mother was funnier than she had remembered. Or maybe time had taken away some of her grief.

Lewis was in a unique situation as secretary of the Interior. America is a huge country. He spent little time in Washington. He was visiting different places every day. Lewis and his small staff of three traveled in a small SUV. He wanted to see things up close and personal. That was the main reason Beverly stayed at the ranch.

Lewis never looked at himself as a politician. He was a messenger from the White House and to the White House. Lewis wanted more people visiting national parks and traveling to and fro, spending money at mom and pop stores seeing this beautiful country that everyone was blessed to live in.

The Federal Government owns huge tracks of land out west. Lewis believed if people visited those places they may decide to move from large cities and settle in rural America, developing in those areas. The large cities were overcrowded and taking a huge toll on the Federal Government. There were more people than jobs and this cost a huge amount in government welfare benefits. Almost every rural area could absorb a thousand people which would create jobs in those communities. People won't move if there are no opportunities.

Lewis's normal work attire was a blue work shirt, jeans and boots. He always wore a cowboy hat and handkerchief around his neck. None looked new, but worn. He was a hands on person. No one thought of him as a bureaucrat. When people met Lewis they felt they had known him for years.

Lewis believed if there was another large work project it should involve water. He knew there could be floods in one area and drought a few hundred miles away. If you can move oil why couldn't you move water without the environmental impact of an oil spill? If a pipe ruptured simply turn off the water. Crops and livestock out west were dependent on water. This would help America to continue to feed the world. Normal dry stream beds could be used instead of pipe, wild game wouldn't lose their habitat. Lewis believed in protecting wild species. He was also smart enough to realize if you protected one species you may harm another. He knew there was a delicate balance at play. Lewis believed he was helping his country. It was a calling to him. He had managed his ranch the same way.

CHAPTER THIRTY SEVEN

JACK IN THE BOX

2 TIMOTHY 3:17

Jack hadn't slept in two days, and knew he wouldn't sleep for another two. How could he sleep? He had set in motion an event that would change the world. He watched the news constantly. He knew if it was discovered it would surely be on the news. He had already informed his employer he would not be able to work Tuesday, February seventh. He was the best man at his brother's wedding. He had even printed up a wedding invitation and mailed one to himself from Seattle, Washington to show his boss. Jack didn't have a brother. He wanted to watch the State of the Union Address.

Lewis had been Secretary of the Interior for a little over a year. The President had asked Lewis to sit out of the upcoming State of the Union Address the first week of February. This sounded great to Lewis. He wasn't a politician and wasn't interested in politics. The President explained that by law one cabinet member is required to be in another secure location to ensure the rules of succession. The United States cannot, will not go one second without a president.

"Lewis, you know I have tried to bring the Republicans and the Democrats together on the issues," said the President. They were alone in the oval office. It was only the second time Lewis had ever been in the room.

"Mr. President, I know you have reached out to both sides of the aisle," answered Lewis.

"That is why when I selected my cabinet I tried to pick from both parties. To try to please both sides of the aisle."

"Mr. President, I know that. I know you picked me because I don't belong to a political party. I have always voted for the best qualified candidate. Sometimes I had to choose the lesser of two evils."

"Sometimes when you try to please everyone you end up pleasing no one," said President Carson.

Lewis didn't answer.

"You know I honestly believe both parties put their party before country." Lewis nodded in agreement and then said, "I'm afraid that will never change."

PENNSYLVANIA

On Monday night, Lewis along with six Secret Service agents left Washington and went to a secure location in Pennsylvania. A score of people were already there. Communications people, staff for cooking meals and six other Secret Service agents. There was even a doctor, nurse and a Judge. The U.S. Government has hundreds of sites like this all over the country. There is one fairly close to Washington that can house the whole congress.

The State of the Union Address to both Houses of Congress has been done this way since Woodrow Wilson was President. He was the first to address the full Congress. Before this a letter was sent to each Congressman. Thomas Jefferson was the first to do this. The President is required by the constitution to do this every year.

For the last seventy five years, it has become more of a campaign speech or wish list than a State of the Union which would be nothing but numbers and percentages and in theory be as dry as dust. Almost every news outlet in the country covers the address. It is also beamed to almost every country on the face of the earth.

WASHINGTON

At 8:50 p.m. on Tuesday, the networks and cable news outlets started their broadcasts.

'Good evening, we would like to welcome you to the State of the Union Address. President James T. Carson will enter the House Chamber shortly. The State of Union Address is being held in the House of Representative Chamber which is large enough to hold all five hundred and thirty five members of Congress.

'I see the Supreme Court Justices are now entering the Chamber. All nine Justices are present tonight. They are followed by the Chairman of the Joint Chiefs of Staff and the Chiefs of Staff of the Army, Navy, Air Force and Marines. Now the Attorney General is coming in followed by the Presidential Cabinet. One member of the Cabinet is not present tonight. By law one cabinet member must sit out to ensure the line of succession. Tonight he is the Secretary of the Interior, Lewis C. MacDonald; he is also from Wyoming the same as the President.

'I see the Vice President and the Speaker of the House have already taken their places behind the podium. When the President comes in he will give a written copy of the speech to the Vice President and the Speaker of the House.

'I see the First Lady has entered the gallery. As you probably know the Vice President is a Widower.

'The Sergeant of Arms is ready to announce the President's arrival.'

'Ladies and Gentlemen, the President of the United States. And here he comes, President James T. Carson, our nation's first Independent Party President.

'We have been informed he will speak for 55 minutes to an hour. His main topics are the economy, the twenty trillion dollar debt, the high unemployment rate and of course something he has given many speeches on, the trade deficit.

'The President is stepping to the podium. We will now see what the President of the United States view of the Union is.'

The time was precisely nine o'clock. Lewis MacDonald was in a room he assumed was the communications center. There were several televisions mounted on the wall. Each set was tuned to a different channel. The picture was the same; evidently they were using one feed for all the stations.

Lewis could see several men and women sitting at their work stations around the room. Computers and telephones were being used. These people were not watching the speech.

Lewis noticed two men standing by the door, one on each side. Two were standing slightly behind him, one on each side. They were not watching the speech either. They were watching everyone else including Lewis. The four men were obviously Secret Service.

At precisely 9:30 p.m. Eastern Standard Time, all the screens were filled with white light and then nothing.

"What happened?" asked someone seated on Lewis's left.

"Check the signal feed," replied someone.

"Try another station. Let's find out if we've got a problem here."

Someone turned the channel on one of the TVs to another station and got a rerun of a situation comedy, and then a game show.

"Maybe we lost the feed at the Capitol."

"Call someone! We've got other signals, but we've lost the State of the Union Address. There has to be a problem at the Capitol." This came from a man who stood up near the bank of TVs. Lewis assumed the man was in charge of communications at the facility.

One of the Secret Service men looked to the man on his left and said, "Call headquarters and see if you can find out what's going on from the duty officer."

Two minutes later the other agent said, "There's no answer. It doesn't even ring."

"Try another number."

"I already have. Something is wrong boss!" came the reply.

"Call any number you can near the Capitol. Find out what has happened." Then the agent put his hand on Lewis's shoulder and said, "Come with me."

Lewis stood up and asked, "Where are we going?"

"To another room, Sir."

Lewis followed the man. He noticed the other men he assumed were agents fell in behind him. They went down the hall and entered another room. One agent turned on the TV. and picked up a phone and dialed a number. In two minutes, other agents entered the room. Lewis saw four agents, with automatic weapons in their hands, take up positions outside the door. Then one agent closed and locked the door.

"What's going on?" asked Lewis.

"Just following procedure. It's nothing more than a precaution."

One agent was constantly going through the channels on the TV. He would only stop for a second before going on. He finally stopped on a local news broadcast from a Baltimore station that was on a cable network. He turned the volume up. The announcer was interviewing someone. The eyewitness was stating that he saw a blinding flash in the direction of Washington almost thirty miles away. A towering mushroom cloud was still visible and was illuminated by fires from below.

Everyone in the room was transfixed by what they were seeing. They didn't want to believe or accept it. Then the phone rang.

The agent that had directed Lewis to this room answered and listened. Every few seconds he would glance at Lewis so he assumed the conversation was about him. Then the agent hung up the phone.

"Sir, we should be able to verify the extent of the situation in about an hour." Lewis didn't consider himself to be an intelligent man, nor was he stupid.

"I refuse to be sworn in until we know for certain. Do I make myself clear?"

"Yes, Sir, we would not have it any other way," answered the agent.

"How are we going to confirm it? I know how important this is but how can we know?"

"Sir, that is above my pay grade, but rest assured we have people working on that even as we speak."

"For situations like this…Is that why a Judge is here?" asked Lewis.

"Yes, Sir, for situations like this."

"You have to plan for any situation don't you?"

"Yes, Sir. We try to plan for any possible scenario."

"I'm going to ask a stupid question here. Have other bombs gone off and are we retaliating in any way?"

"Sir, I don't know the answer to that."

"So you are saying let's hope for the best and expect the worse. Who can authorize a strike if the President and Vice President are not able?"

"The Speaker of the House but he was in the same room. So, in saying that, I would say it would fall on you."

"But, I haven't been sworn in," said Lewis.

"You become President on those people's death, regardless if you have been sworn in or not."

Lewis tried several times to get in touch with Beverly, but the lines were jammed or either wouldn't work at all. He prayed that his family were all alright.

At 3:50 Eastern Standard Time, Lewis was sitting in a chair in front of the TV. A Secret Service Agent came into the room and said to Lewis, "Mr. President, we need to go back into the communications room to be sworn in."

Lewis looked at the floor and nodded his head. His heart sank for the lives lost and their families. The agent started to leave and looked back to Lewis. The agent saw that Lewis's lips were moving but he was making no sound. He's praying, good he's going to need them. God help us all thought the agent. Lewis stood and walked to the communications room.

"I should wear a suit. Give me ten minutes to change."

As Lewis was leaving the small room he had slept in last night he grabbed his Bible. Beverly had given it to him on their first anniversary. Lewis always carried it with him when he traveled. The Bible had a zippered cover. It measured five by seven inches. Lewis had to wear his reading glasses when he read it. He remembered saying to Beverly he wished the lettering was larger. She had replied, 'The word is the word; it doesn't matter if it's small print or large, it's still the word." Lewis left the room.

Lewis C. MacDonald placed his left hand on the Bible, a King James Version, raised his right hand and took an oath to protect and defend the Constitution of the United States of America.

"Mr. President, the communications gear here can contact any number in the United States. We have no evidence that any other bombs have been used anywhere in the world. We have been informed our nuclear weapons are on standby if we need them. No credible country or group has taken responsibility.

"When you were sworn in that signal was beamed to any station worldwide that wanted to broadcast it. Sir, do you wish to make a speech to the American people?"

"Yes, I do. I think it would be appropriate, but first I want to activate all National Guard units to active duty and turned over to the states governors. They will know best how to utilize them. We can't know where they are needed from here. Do you agree?"

"Mr. President, I am a Secret Service Agent. I do not give advice."

"I'm asking you man to man, face to face."

"In that situation, I think that would be a good idea," said the agent.

"I also think our nuclear force should standby not stand down, but we don't need an accidental launch. Can we do that from here?"

"Yes, Sir. We can do that."

The agent went to a work station and brought a man over to Lewis. Lewis gave him clear and concise instructions. The man went back to his work station and transmitted coded messages to all U.S. forces worldwide.

"Do you need some time to prepare your speech Mr. President?" asked the agent.

"No, I need to do this now."

"Come with me, Mr. President."

He took Lewis to an alcove and pulled a curtain back. There was a desk with an American flag behind it. The seal of the President of the United States was on the front.

"Please, have a seat, Mr. President. It will take a few minutes until we're ready."

Five minutes later, a haggard faced man looked into the cameras. An expert on body language would reach the conclusion the weight of the whole world rested on his shoulders.

Lewis glanced at his watch. It read 4:30; four thirty in the morning. Lewis doubted anyone was sleeping. Someone had mentioned that the explosion had probably disrupted electrical power in as many as ten states. The internet had crashed throughout the

United States and Canada. The message had to get out to the nation and it was about to be delivered.

"My name is Lewis C. MacDonald. Earlier this evening I was Secretary of the Interior. As you may know, those of us who still have electrical power and phone service, a nuclear weapon has been used to destroy the city of Washington. One cabinet member is required to be in a different location in order to meet the constitutional requirement of succession of the presidency. I was selected to be that person. I was sworn in ten minutes ago as your President. I humbly ask for your thoughts and prayers. Our thoughts and prayers also go out to those people and their families who lost their lives or were injured. He paused. "I do not know who did this to us. We will find out and the retribution will be a terrible swift sword. I have activated the National Guard and turned those units over to the individual states governors. They will know best where they are needed." He paused briefly, then he continued. "I am ordering all active duty military to return to their bases if at all possible. If you are on leave, your leave is cancelled. I am ordering the F.A.A. to ground all flights. We don't know how this device was delivered. I am ordering all banks, credit unions, savings and loans institutions closed for the remainder of the week. On Monday you may withdraw ten percent of what you have in your account. I am ordering all trading and brokerage houses closed for the remainder of the week. They can reopen Monday with no block sales of stock and bonds. I am requesting that news stations, both T.V. and radio be given government access to give updates on the situation. I am asking those same outlets to rebroadcast this speech every four hours for the next forty eight hours. The people of this country will be kept informed as we find out more of who is behind this and where we go from here." Another slight pause. "I have been told that rioting and looting are already taking place. The American people have a right to defend and protect themselves, their family and their property. You need to ask yourself if there is anything inside that store or home that is worth dying for. There will be zero tolerance for these crimes and you will be prosecuted. We have been severely wounded as a nation.

We don't need to be hurting each other." He cleared his throat, then continued. "I am ordering the FBI, DEA, ATF, Border Patrol, Secret Service and all Federal Law Enforcement personnel to report to work immediately. I am not and I repeat, I am not declaring Martial Law.

The state governors and legislatures need to reseat a congress following their states existing laws. That is the responsibility of the individual states. I want a congress seated in forty five days. Everyone should stay home and protect their family and friends. Stay indoors, we don't know where the radiation has spread and which areas are the worst. I recommend that everyone boil your drinking water just to be on the safe side. We have everyone working on this and will know more in time. This is still a very fluid situation and when the sun comes up we will have a better picture of the damage and what we are dealing with.   We are a nation at war. I don't know who we are at war with. Am I scared; am I afraid; yes I am. We have been grievously wounded. The American people will decide if we have been fatally wounded. May God bless you and this great nation of ours."

Those in the communication room thought it was a good speech considering there were no notes, rehearsals or prep time. It was brief and to the point.

The new president called all of the staff into the communications room. He wanted to address them. They were now his staff, his advisors.

"I don't believe we can reestablish the government here in this location. I want the government visible to the American people. Does anyone know of a location we can use?"

A Secret Service agent spoke up. "President Carson was scheduled to attend a ribbon cutting ceremony for a new federal courthouse in Independence, Missouri, Mr. President."

"Can we move what we have here to there in a week?" As he said this the President waved his arm around the room to include all the equipment.

Someone spoke up from the back of the room. "No Sir, not this that you see here, but we can take another site like this one and move that equipment there. We need to stay here until that site has been moved."

"Good thinking, son. What is your name?" asked Lewis.

"Alex Jacobs, Mr. President."

"You work for me now. I'm putting you in charge of all that."

"Yes, Sir, Mr. President."

"What about a Vice President?" a Secret Service agent asked.

"I know I need one right now, but I want the right one. I'll be honest with you, I don't know anyone to pick. I'm not going to start putting friends in high places. I'm just going to trust in God that he will keep me safe."

Alex Jacobs spoke up. "You are not required to have one. Several presidents have served without one. Teddy Roosevelt didn't have one after President McKinley was assassinated."

"Okay, we will go with that right now. We need to get this ship righted and moving again. I know it won't be full speed for a long, long time, maybe never. The American people need to see that and know that."

Lewis looked around the room and studied each person.

"I want all of you to know that right now you are most important people in government. We have nothing right now. No Supreme Court, no Joint Chiefs of Staff for the military. We don't even know if the Pentagon is functional. We can assume for the time being that it is. I assume the Central Intelligence Agency is operational because of the distance. Who is the Senior Secret Service agent here?"

"I am, Sir." This was the same agent that had moved Lewis from room to room earlier.

"What is your name, Sir?" asked Lewis.

"Ronald McIntyre, Mr. President."

Lewis nodded. "You're in charge of the presidential detail. I want a name by nine o'clock for a temporary head of the Secret Service or as you say the Treasury Department."

"Yes, Sir, Mr. President."

"Okay from now on we can drop the Mr. President. I don't feel like the president. If I had my choice I would have been in Washington last night and hope someone more qualified than me would be addressing you. Mr. McIntyre, can I speak to you in private for a minute?"

In the hallway, Lewis looked at the agent. The man was about fifty and stood six feet tall. There wasn't an ounce of fat visible on the man. He looked like he could run ten miles and not be winded. His dark brown hair was neatly trimmed.

"About my family," said Lewis.

"Sir, we have a go team on two hour standby for any emergency. Any address and phone numbers would have been in Washington. We need that from you."

"I understand that wasn't foreseeable."

"No, Sir, it wasn't," said the agent.

"My wife is at the ranch. My son is at the University of Oklahoma. My daughter is at the University of Texas. Their name is Josh and Deborah. I need to give you the directions to the ranch. The roads out there may not be on the map."

"Don't worry, Mr. President. We'll take care of it."

"You don't know how much I appreciate it."

"I'm sure they already know about what happened last night."

"I don't know about that. The phone and the power go out at the least amount of bad weather out there and my wife hardly ever turns on the T.V. She works outside and hardly ever around the phone. I have tried to call and haven't been able to get through."

"We'll take care of it, Mr. President."

"Where is the Go Team located?"

"St. Louis, Missouri."

CHAPTER THIRTY EIGHT

JEFFERSON

ST. LOUIS, MISSOURI

Treasury agent Marsha Jefferson loaded her bags in the agency car at 9:45 p.m. She didn't wait on a phone call. The thirty seven year old African American woman had been an agent for ten years. She was in her fourth year as a Go Team member.

After graduating from Auburn University in Alabama she joined the Birmingham Police Department. She spent five years with the police department. Marsha was an ambitious woman and knew she would never reach the heights she wanted to attain working at the police department. On a whim, she applied for a position with the Treasury Department. She had had a lifelong dream of working for the Secret Service. She admired the dedication and the professionalism of the department. She knew she would never be assigned to something as high as the presidential detail. She couldn't believe she was accepted. When she informed her Lieutenant he had said, 'Yeah, right.' She pushed herself relentlessly. In training she was always the first to arrive and the last to leave. She could run as far and as fast as any of the men in training. She wasn't as strong as the men, of course, but she made up for it by cheating. She had started this practice in high school and perfected it in college while playing basketball. She was an intimidating force on the court. She was a couple of inches taller than most women. The opposing team quickly learned if you went up for a rebound against her you might get an elbow or a knee or even a shove. Her favorite was landing on the other girl's foot. This was perfectly acceptable in a dog eat dog environment.

Her policy with the Secret Service was don't shoot them twice, shoot them three times. She had been reprimanded for aggressiveness several times. One superior had even suggested she take anger management counseling. She told him to kiss off. That didn't help her career path. She had calmed down some in the last two years she told herself. Actually it was the last two months.

She pulled into the parking lot, retrieved her bags and glanced at her watch. Twenty minutes, Jefferson smiled. The Go Team was prepared for a two hour call-out.

This position had its advantages and disadvantages, doesn't everything? She never knew where or for how long she would be gone, or when. This was a rung on the ladder to promotion. The disadvantage was no personal life. No pets, no house plants to water, paying bills in advance. She ate it all up. She had shown them that she could play marbles with the big boys and go home with all the marbles.

She walked into the office and the duty officer said, "I was about to call you." Marsha smiled, woman's intuition, she had beaten the call out.

"We have an assignment yet?"

"Not yet, but I'm sure we will get one. I don't know what they would do with the go team. Probably doing other things," said the duty officer.

"Any word on how bad it is?"

"Not yet, we've had lots of calls but nothing definite, news people wanting a situation report. I have been telling them not at this time. We're in the dark here just like everyone else; of course I couldn't tell them that."

"You're doing the right thing."

"Thanks."

"Need help calling the Go Team?"

"Yeah, that would be great. Here's the numbers for Alpha Go. I'll take care of Bravo Go. Some may already be inbound."

The Secret Service is the most professional organization in the U.S. government; most were already inbound to the office. The Secret Service has had its ups and downs but always seemed to bounce back and land on its feet. They take their duty very seriously.

Once all the Go Team was assembled it became hurry up and wait. The Go Team is capable of handling almost any situation. If counterfeit money shows up a lot in any area the Go Team can flood that area with agents. That was what Marsha Jefferson loved about the job, the instant release of energy and power. She had made numerous arrests of counterfeiters. Catching one man while he was paying his bar tab at a strip joint in Omaha, Nebraska.

At five in the morning, the Go Team Commander called a mission briefing. The Go Team would be split into Alpha and Bravo teams. Their mission, secure the presidents family, then stay at the ranch and await further instructions. Cut and dried, a piece of cake from outward appearances. Appearances can be deceiving as Marsha Jefferson was about to find out.

The B Team headed out in four SUVs. They would split again, one to Texas and one to Oklahoma. The A Team would head to Kerney, Wyoming. Marsha headed to the map room and couldn't find Kerney. She had to use the index. "This place is out in the middle of nowhere," she said to one of the other agents. This should have given her a clue. Then she saw that there was a Kerney and a Ft. Phil Kearny. It took ten minutes to clarify it was Kerney. With the internet down she couldn't use the mapping system from the satellite photos.

They headed west. Crossing the Kansas line in three hours. Each SUV had four agents. There were four women in one SUV. First Ladies require women as the closest security and that security would be around the clock.

They would take turns driving, two hour shifts. Two large communications and office vehicles would leave within the hour. They were the size of Greyhound buses. The agents could eat and sleep inside on small bunks. They had enough weapons on board to fight off a small army if need be.

Marsha was riding shotgun in the lead vehicle. She glanced at the speedometer, 85 MPH. When the sun came up they were well into Kansas. Kansas was a breeze. They gassed up in Colorado. The driving got tougher, up and down mountains. They had been on the road for seven hours when they turned north and headed for Wyoming.

Marsha started driving when they hit the state line. They were now on secondary roads, paved but winding up and down. Marsha felt like they were in oblivion. They drove on and on. After an hour, one of the agents in back said, "There's a dinosaur graveyard in Wyoming. Thousands of dinosaurs died in one place. I wonder why so many died there."

Marsha said, "I bet I know what they died from."

"What?"

"They came here and died of boredom. When was the last time we saw a human being or even a house? We haven't seen a trace of civilization in how long?"

"Thirty two minutes," said one of the agents in the back.

"Somebody take that watch away from her," said Marsha.

The others laughed. Marsha didn't.

They skirted Laramie and headed towards Casper. The instructions said to turn about halfway between the two and go northwest toward Kerney. These people live in the middle of nowhere thought Marsha. Marsha had been awake for thirty hours. She had napped a few times when she could.

They needed gas and something to snack on. They finally reached a gas station in between two towns. An old man came out of the station. Marsha thought, now that's what a mountain man looks like.

"You want gas?" asked the man.

"Yes, Sir. Fill up the four cars." She pulled her government credit card out of her purse.

"Don't take plastic; only money and gold."

"Sir, I can assure you the card is good; United States Government."

"Ya'll government people?" asked the man and spit a stream of tobacco juice on the ground.

"Yes, Sir."

"Don't take plastic," he repeated as another stream of tobacco juice hit the ground.

Marsha wanted to scream. She went to the other vehicles and collected what money everyone had.

"Put forty dollars in each vehicle. That should get us back to civilization."

"Where you going?" he asked as another stream of tobacco juice hit the ground.

"Kerney."

"Can't get to Kerney from here," he said as tobacco juice was still streaming to the ground.

Marsha ignored him. You can get to anywhere from any place.

Twenty minutes later they were back. The old man walked out and put his hands on his hips and waited. Marsha was out of the car before it stopped. She walked as fast as she could and stopped within inches of the man.

"Why didn't you tell us the bridge was out?"

"You didn't ask." He spit again.

Marsha reached inside her purse and pulled her identification out and put it in the old man's face.

"You see this?" she snapped, waving it in front of him.

"That's right pretty, Ma'am."

"I could bring the full weight of the United States Government down on you. Do you understand that?"

Another stream of tobacco oozed from his mouth. "They were here a month ago."

"Who?"

"The Government."

Marsha noticed the streams of spit were getting closer to her new shoes. Her two hundred dollar new shoes. Marsha turned in disgust and headed back to the car. They went back towards the main highway. A mile down the road Marsha stopped, got out of the SUV and kicked the front tire. Then she went around to the other three and kicked them. Now she felt better. Getting back in she said, "Thought we had a flat."

They found another gas station forty miles away. A young man came out and said, "Howdy."

"Do you take credit cards, Sir?"

"Yes, Ma'am. Would you like me to pump the gas fer you, seeing how I ain't doing anything else?"

"Yes, thank you. Can you tell us how to get to Kerney?"

"Sure, let me draw you a map."

"The bridge isn't out on this road is it?"

"No, Ma'am. I wouldn't tell you to go that way if the bridge was out."

"Well, the last guy didn't tell us about a bridge being out."

"That must have been ole Jake."

"I don't know his name but it was about forty miles from here."

"That would be ole Jake. He's not all that bad. Why he'd give you the shirt off his back. A friend of mine's wife left him and ole Jake showed up the very next day knowing he'd be all depressed. Ole Jake gave him a whole case of his special whiskey. You know, just to get him through his pain and suffering. The very next day the revenuers raided ole Jake's gas station. They didn't find a drop. Then ole Jake went back to his friend and asked for some of that special whiskey back to get him through his depression. Yep, that ole Jake, he's a real nice man. Now, ya'll have a good trip, Ma'am."

Marsha was running her fingers through her hair. She was actually thinking of pulling it out. On the way back to the SUV the thought of suicide went through her mind and then she thought no, that would be embarrassing for her family. She could ask one of the agents to shoot her and make it look like an accidental discharge. She would be buried with full honors.

CHAPTER THIRTY NINE

THE FIRST LADY

KERNEY, WYOMING

After reaching Kerney, Wyoming the Secret Service agents got directions to the MacDonald ranch. Ten miles from the ranch they saw power company and phone company bucket trucks working on the power and phone lines. A tree had fallen on the lines.

"I hope they have power and phone service at the ranch," said Linda Compton.

"Let's stop and ask," said Jefferson.

The agents were informed the power had gone out the day before but was now back on.

"She may not even know what has happened. I doubt they even have cell phones. I haven't seen a tower in the last fifty miles. Good thing we have satellite phones."

"How do we tell her if she doesn't know? Shouldn't someone higher up have that responsibility?" asked Compton.

"Right now there is no one higher up," said Jefferson.

The agents finally reached the MacDonald ranch without Marsha Jefferson having a total breakdown. She was stressed out. The drive had taken a toll on everyone. Marsha figured they were running two hours late, maybe three.

The agents went to the front door and rang the doorbell repeatedly without an answer. They went around the house.

Everything looked normal. There was a light snow on the ground with no tracks anywhere.

"Well, where do you suppose she could be?"

"I don't know. What do we do now?"

"Let's split up and look in all the out buildings and the barn," said Marsha.

Two agents went to the greenhouse. Another two went to the workshop. Marsha and another agent went to the barn. As they reached the door they heard a voice from inside.

"Stop it before you hurt me." Clearly it was a female's voice.

"Stop it right now, do you hear me? You are going to hurt me."

Marsha drew her weapon and said to the other agent, "I'm going in first. I'll go to the left, you go right."

The agent nodded. Marsha went in with her weapon held by both hands and went to the left. The other agent was a half second behind her and went right. They saw what they assumed to be a teenager dressed in insulated coveralls and insulated cap that covered most of her face. She was trying to get a horse into his stall. The horse was not cooperating.

The agents holstered their weapons and went in closer after she had successfully got the horse in the stall and a rope was fastened to keep him in. Then the girl turned around and saw them.

Startled she said, "Can I help you?"

"Yes, we came to see your mother," said Marsha.

"My mother is not here."

"Do you know when she is expected back?"

"My mother doesn't live here. She lives at the other ranch."

"The other ranch? I thought this was the MacDonald ranch," said Marsha.

"It is but my mother doesn't live here."

Marsha figured she wasn't getting through to the girl.

"We're looking for Mrs. MacDonald."

"I'm Mrs. MacDonald. Who did you say you were?" She then pulled off her cap and they could tell she wasn't a teenager. Marsha guessed thirty five to forty.

"We're with the Secret Service, Ma'am."

"The Secret Service? Why would the Secret Service be looking for me?"

"Ma'am, do you know what happened in Washington last night?"

"No, I don't. Between the power outage and phones lines down I haven't heard anything. What happened?"

"Ma'am, Washington was destroyed by a nuclear weapon last night," said Marsha.

Beverly, fell against the stall. She couldn't believe what she was hearing. So much was running through her mind, she couldn't think. Finally she looked at the agents and said, "Please, don't tell me my husband is dead." Tears were welling up in her eyes and she sat down on an upturned feed barrel.

"No, Ma'am, your husband is fine. We came to tell you your husband is now the President of the United States," said one of the agents.

Beverly just sat there trying to take in everything that was being said. "Oh Lord, Cowboy what have you gotten us into," mumbled Beverly MacDonald, First Lady of the United States.

"I'm sorry, Ma'am, what did you say?"

"Nothing. I am just trying to understand all of this."

Marsha stepped over to the other agent and said, "Go get everyone else. Cover all the vantage points. The communications gear should be here soon."

As the other agent left, Marsha looked at the First Lady and said, "Let's go inside. Other agents are securing your children."

Beverly nodded, stood up and walked towards the house.

Marsha was behind her. "Ma'am, I should go in first and make sure everything is secure." Beverly was too stunned to even acknowledge or object. Marsha went into the unlocked door. She was in the laundry room. She went through the house checking each room and closet. Marsha estimated the house to be two thousand square feet. The three bedroom, two bathroom house was nice but nothing special. Millions of homes like this dotted the American landscape.

Marsha went back to find the First Lady. She was in the laundry room removing her insulated coveralls. She was somewhere between petite and puny estimated Marsha.

The First Lady went into the kitchen and turned on an old fashioned percolator coffee pot.

After Beverly tried to get as much information as she could she realized the agents didn't know much to tell her. Everything had happened so fast. Beverly said, "I'm going to take a shower and change clothes."

"Yes, Ma'am."

"There are coffee cups in the cupboard."

"Thank you, Ma'am," said Marsha.

Twenty minutes later she came back wearing blue jeans, a sweater and tennis shoes. On the sweater were the jump wings and a heart shaped pin. She sat down in the breakfast room. She put her face in her hands and started crying. Marsha didn't know what to do. Crying First Ladies was not in the training manual. Marsha's womanly instincts finally kicked in and she went over to the First Lady. She didn't know what to say, so she said what she would want someone to say to her.

"Ma'am, you have to be strong. Everything is going to be alright."

Beverly nodded but kept crying. Finally she stopped and asked about her husband. "Where is Lewis?"

"He is in a secure location right now."

"And my children? How do I know my children are alright?"

"Your children are fine. The Secret Service has gone to get them now. They will take them to a safe place." Linda Compton, one of the female agents, came in and pulled Marsha to the side away from the First Lady.

"We can't find the children. They are not in their residence at the college. At Texas, no one has seen the girl since ten o'clock last night. No one has seen the son at Oklahoma since about ten, either. Both their vehicles are gone. What do we tell her? There is no reason to believe something has happened to them, but you never know."

"Do they know if they packed any clothes?" asked Marsha.

"They didn't know about that. They just left."

"At about the same time?" asked Marsha.

"As near as we can tell."

"Did they call each other? It's strange they would both leave about the same time don't you think?"

"We don't know any of that. It will take days to find that out. Oh, by the way, the two commo vans, guess where they are?"

"Trying to turn around at that bridge."

"Yep, you guessed it! Ole Jake has struck again."

Marsha looked for the First Lady in the breakfast room. She found her in the family room. She was looking at something on the fireplace mantle. Marsha approached her and said, "Ma'am," to get her attention.

"I heard what the other lady said about Josh and Deborah. They are on their way here."

"You have talked to them? I didn't know that."

"No, I haven't talked to them but I know my children. As soon as they heard they would have left to come here."

"Why would they come here?" asked Marsha.

"To protect me," said Beverly.

"I see," she replied, even though she didn't. Marsha looked around the room. It was indeed a family room, but more like a shrine of sorts to two children. There were framed crayon drawings and photos everywhere. In the center of the fireplace mantle was a trifold picture frame with a legal document in the center of it. Marsha read the document. She was touched by its simplicity. She could tell there was a lot of love displayed in this room. She couldn't help but notice a police badge with black tape across it in a small display case. Beverly noticed her looking at the badge.

"My father's. He was killed in the line of duty."

"I'm sorry."

"Me too, I adored him. Mom has the flag."

There was a framed half dollar and a locket of black curly hair with chewing gum in it along with a date on the two. Marsha wondered, what's that about? Other than the hideous photo and wedding photo there was only two other photos of the First Lady in the room. She could tell it wasn't a posed photo. She had her arms crossed on top of a fence railing. She had a glove on one hand and was holding the other glove in her gloved hand. She was wearing a sweat stained cowboy hat made of straw. There were a couple of feathers in the front. The brim was bent down. She was wearing sunglasses. She had a slight smile on her lips. She looked peacefully content, happy with her station in life. Marsha wondered how many people in the world were ever that peacefully content, happy with their station in life. Not many she guessed. She knew she wasn't.

Jefferson pointed to an older snapshot of two children perhaps five years old.

"Is this your son and daughter?"

"Yes, that was taken right after we got them."

"Oh, so they are adopted?"

"Yes," answered Beverly. "And I love them with all my heart and soul. I thank God every day for the joy they have brought into our lives."

Then the other photo of the First Lady. This was a family photo on graduation night. The children were in the middle. There was a photo of the President. Marsha had to smile, he was holding up a fish about three inches long still on the line. He was wearing an old baseball cap, black with gold letters, with EIEIO across the front. It took Marsh a few seconds to catch on, MacDonald and EIEIO.

Beverly moved to the other side of the room and Marsha followed. There was a wedding photo of a family. Beverly didn't say who it was. Next to it was a photo of an Army officer in her dress uniform. A boy and a girl were sitting in her lap. Marsha could tell the children were the same as the other photos. She could tell this woman was in the wedding photo she had just seen.

"Their mother was killed in Bosnia right after this photo was taken." The next photo was of the boy and girl, now grown, beside an elderly man in a wheelchair.

"Their grandfather."

Beverly moved around the room again, Marsha followed her. She saw a framed cover of a sports magazine of the Oklahoma defensive line. She picked him out right away, the same smile. Next to it was an article about a pilot landing in the desert.

"I remember that. So that was your son?"

"Yes, I was so afraid for him. They didn't know where he was for five days. They assumed he had died in a crash in the mountains. God does indeed work miracles, doesn't he?"

"Yes, Ma'am," answered Marsha.

There was an article about the first girl to play baseball in Kerney. It had a picture of her sliding into home. The girl reminded Marsha of herself when she was that age.

"Your daughter is very competitive isn't she?"

"Yes, she is; maybe too competitive, but I wouldn't change anything about her. I am very proud of both of them."

There was a framed article from a South Georgia newspaper with the girl standing in front of a large mural. The painting was being dedicated.

Marsha guessed the First Lady knew her life had changed a few hours ago and she wanted to remember what life was like before. Marsha didn't blame her; things would be different from now on.

Linda Compton came back in. Marsha introduced her to the First Lady.

"The commo vehicles should be here in an hour. We've got everything secure. There is a good vantage point about a hundred yards from here. You can see everything."

"That's Lookout Point," said Beverly.

"Lookout Point?" asked Compton.

"It's our favorite place in the whole world. Now, if you will excuse me I need to feed Comanche."

"Is Comanche your horse? The one in the barn," asked Marsha.

"That's right. Would you like to see her?"

Both agents agreed and the three went to the barn. To Marsha the horse looked scrawny but somehow full of energy. Small muscles rippled when the horse moved. Marsha had no idea what kind of horse it was. Its color was pale in front and got darker toward its rump with spots in the lighter color. Marsha figured it was a mixed breed and wasn't very pretty.

Beverly said, "She's a mustang. Born in the wild. I've had her about a year. She's a good horse and wants to go for a ride. It'll warm up this afternoon and if the snow melts we'll go riding."

The two agents looked at each other.

"You can go in the Jeep," said Beverly and smiled for the first time since Marsha had met her.

"That would be fun," said Compton. Jefferson looked at her like she was crazy.

Beverly asked, "Have you met my husband?" Both agents noticed she didn't call him the President. Other First Ladies usually addressed the President as the President.

"No, Ma'am," both agents answered at the same time.

"He doesn't ride either. Now the children, that's a different story. Both of them love to ride. I guess they learned to love it from me."

The commo and office vehicles arrived at dusk. All the agents worked as a team until they were finished. Marsha approached Beverly and told her she would be inside the house until six a.m. Linda Compton would take over till two p.m. A third agent, named Sandra Clarke that Beverly hadn't met yet, would take over until ten p.m.

At six a.m., Marsha was relieved by Compton and went to the office Van where her bunk was located. At seven a.m., she heard one of the other agents come inside. He told Marsha to get up. It was the agent in charge, Dean Gilmore.

"What is the First Lady doing?"

"What do you mean? I guess she's in the house with Compton."

"No, she's sitting on a horse on that hilltop," said Gilmore.

"You mean Lookout Point?"

"Whatever," said Gilmore.

"Where is Compton?" asked Marsha.

"She's on a four wheeler we brought with us. She's behind the hill. She's watching her, but I want to know what she's doing."

Marsha got up and put her coat and shoes on. It was dawn but Marsha could see her.

"How long has she been out there?"

"Since six thirty. Did she tell you anything?"

"No, she didn't say anything to me."

They could tell she was dozing off and then her head would snap up. Even the horse looked like it was asleep. The horse's neck was bent down like it was eating but its head was a foot off the ground.

"Someone needs to tell her it's freezing out here and it's starting to sleet," said Gilmore.

Marsha looked at Gilmore and said, "You want to tell the First Lady to go inside, you go ahead and do that. I'm not."

Then the agents heard a call from the commo van which was monitoring video sensors placed at strategic points about a mile from the ranch.

"We have a vehicle approaching and turning on the road out front."

Several agents came out of the van. One yelled to Gilmore. "It's a dark colored pick-up truck."

Marsha and Gilmore looked at the First Lady. At that time the sun crested the mountains to the East. The sunlight made everything look golden. Marsha couldn't believe how everything looked. Not much took her breath away but this was absolutely beautiful.

The First Lady's head came up; the horse lifted his head, too. The First Lady rose up in the saddle and nudged the horse with her boots. The horse started picking its way down the hill. They heard the four wheeler start up and move slowly to the top of the hill.

"That's the scrawniest horse I have ever seen in my life," said Gilmore.

"That's Comanche," said Marsha.

At the bottom of the hill Beverly leaned forward and slapped the horse on its rump. It was like releasing a coiled spring. The horse accelerated to a full gallop.

"She's going to get killed," said Gilmore.

Marsha smiled and said, "She knows what she's doing."

Beverly was leaning all the way forward in the saddle. Her hands were on the reins about eighteen inches from the bridle. Chunks of mud were flying from the horse's hooves. It looked like steam was coming from the horse's nostrils. Its ears were laid back and the mane and tail were almost straight out. Beverly would lean either to the left or the right to go around small cottonwood trees. On the four wheeler Compton was bouncing up and down and losing ground. It was almost comical.

Gilmore said, looking at Beverly, "Good Lord! That woman can ride."

Marsha was smiling too much to answer. Pride was building up inside her.

Suddenly Beverly's hat flew off. She jerked back on the reins. The horse's front legs went straight, her back legs bent; her flanks were almost on the ground. Beverly jerked the left rein and the horse spun around without coming to a complete stop. Then another slap on the rump and the horse took off at a full gallop, back towards the hat. As Beverly approached the hat she leaned down further than it seemed possible and grabbed the hat. She slapped it back on her head. She braked the horse as she had done before and spun it around and took off again at a full gallop.

Gilmore's heart skipped a beat. For a second he thought she was falling off the horse.

"My God, did you see that? How did she do that?"

Marsha was grinning from ear to ear.

The pick-up turned into the driveway at the same time Beverly reached it. The horse skidded to another stop. Beverly dismounted before the horse came to a full stop. Beverly ran to the fence, climbed two rungs, hopped over and ran to the pickup.

The pickup came to a stop. Both doors opened and a woman got out of the passenger side and a huge man got out of the driver's side. All three met and embraced with a hug, a big hug. Compton had stopped the four wheeler at a discrete distance and cut the engine off.

Marsha said, "The children are home safe and sound."

Gilmore was shaking his head. "We violated every protocol in the book Jefferson."

"Who are we going to tell and who would believe us anyway?"

"No, you're right. No one would believe us. I saw it and I don't believe it."

They looked toward the security van. Everyone was outside and giving each other high fives and patting each other on the back. They had enjoyed the show.

CHAPTER FORTY

INDEPENDENCE

MISSOURI

Alex Jacobs grabbed his carryon luggage and climbed out of the taxi, and looked at the possible new location of the United States government. He had flown in on a military aircraft from Pennsylvania. Civilian aircraft were still grounded by the FAA.

He was standing in front of an eight story building that was supposed to house the new Federal Court House. Those plans had come to a halt the morning after the nuclear weapon. He was met by ten other men and women from some of the other secure sites from around the country.

"Is everyone here?" sked Jacobs.

"No, Sir. I expect them to trickle in all day. It's almost impossible to get any type of transportation from anywhere to here. They're doing their best," said a tall man with a Midwest accent. Alex Jacobs assumed he was from someplace nearby.

"Where are you from, Sir?" asked Jacobs.

"Kansas City."

"That's great. We need someone who knows the local area. What is your field if I may ask?"

"Computers," answered the man.

"Even better," said Jacobs. Then he continued, "I need a volunteer."

"What for?" someone asked.

"We're going to go in and look around first. I need someone to stay out here and direct new arrivals in and to put these on." He removed some old cards from his pocket.

"I want you to write your name, first and last and what your specialty is. It will save us time today. I don't need to tell you important this is. The United States government may have to fit in that building. Kick around in your head how we can do that. We have to think out of the box. So, let's get started, who's my volunteer?"

A young man stepped forward. "I'll do it."

"Good, make sure they use a magic marker so we can see it plainly."

"Yes, Sir."

Alex Jacobs was relieved no one questioned his authority. He had a signed document placing him in charge. He was glad he didn't have to use it.

Inside they found eight courtrooms on the first two floors along with a cafeteria on the first floor and a coffee and sandwich shop on the second. The top six floors were offices. There was a huge basement that could be used for something. He noticed new people were arriving and were taking notes and drawing sketches. Four hours later they were back on the sidewalk.

"It doesn't look good does it?"

No one disagreed.

"Mr. Jacobs, what about the building next door?"

"What about it?" said Jacobs.

"Well, it belongs to the Federal Government."

"It does. I didn't know that."

"Yes, Sir, it's slated for demolition to build a parking deck for the courthouse and other buildings around here."

"You sure about that? We need a building more than we need parking. Wouldn't all of you agree?" Everyone nodded their head. He addressed the man from Kansas City.

"Since you're local more so than any of us, your assignment is to first save that building. Now why don't we go and look at the building we just commandeered." Everyone laughed as they were leaving. Jacobs walked up to the man from Kansas City and said, "There is something I want to show you." They had stopped while everyone went on. He unfolded the directive from the President and handed it to the other man who read it.

"I really don't want to use this but I will. If you have any problem securing that building let me know and we'll use this. Legally we can seize it if need be. I don't want to do that."

The man agreed and asked Jacobs the question that was on everyone's mind. "How long have you known the President?"

"I met him shortly after he was sworn in," said Jacobs.

"Sounds good to me," said the man as they started walking to the other building.

"My name is James Reynolds. A lot of office space is in that building. It's not in bad shape, just needs painting and some minor stuff."

"I'm afraid we don't have time for paint, especially for it to dry. Time is of the essence. The new President wants a government the American people can see. Not hidden in a bunker in Pennsylvania."

"Do you think we can pull it off?" asked Reynolds.

"We have to James, we have to."

Toby Burke, investigative reporter for the World News Examiner, told the receptionist for the owner, president and publisher of twenty daily newspapers and magazines, "The old man wants to see me."

The receptionist answered. "I know, be careful, he's in one of his moods." Toby nodded. May I go in now?"

"Remember, be careful."

"I will. Thanks." Toby opened the door.

"You wanted to see me, Sir?"

"Sit down."

Toby sat down in a plush leather arm chair. He didn't lean back or try to get comfortable. Toby was sitting in front of the largest desk he had ever seen. Rumors floated throughout the building the desk had to be brought up on the freight elevator. It was also rumored the office door had to be enlarged to get it in the office. This was before Toby's time and Toby knew often rumors were true.

There was no typewriter or desk top computer in the room, not even a laptop. Toby didn't even see a notepad, pen or pencil just a huge expanse of desk. Other people did the old man's work including himself.

The old man leaned forward and said, "Do you know who the President of the United States is young man?" He called everyone young man or young lady.

"Well, Sir, all I know is his name."

"That's right. His name is all anyone knows. You know he has never held an elected office before, and by some strange twist of fate he's President of the United States of America…that's preposterous."

Toby Burke didn't agree or disagree with the old man. No one ever disagreed.

"Here's what I want to do. First of all I'm writing a full page editorial that will be in every newspaper we own. I will be calling for; no, make that demanding he resign and a special election take place as soon as possible.

"An Independent President, now we can't have that, not in this country."

Toby interrupted and said, "President Carson was an Independent."

The old man glared at Toby. "Young man, don't ever interrupt me when I'm talking."

"Yes, Sir. I'm sorry."

"Now, where was I?"

Toby waited a few seconds before saying, "You were pointing out we can't have an Independent President."

The old man nodded his head then said, "The President has to be accountable to a party where they can keep control of him. This guy, well, there's no telling which way he might go. He may wander all over the place. Now, here is where you come in. You are our best investigative reporter. I want you to dig up everything you can on him, his wife, his kids, even his dog. I want him destroyed, you understand me. I want him crushed.

"This will show how ridiculous this Constitution is. The whole thing needs to be scrapped and start over. I want dirt. I want enough dirt to bury him. You, young man, will."

Toby Burke interrupted and said, "What if there is no dirt?" Toby cringed as he realized he had interrupted him again. The phone rang; the old man grabbed it on the first ring. "Didn't I tell you I didn't want to be interrupted? Who is it? Why didn't you say so, of course put him on."

Three seconds later, "Chuck, how are you? How's the weather out there in California?"

Toby Burke knew that the caller was important. The only person he could think of that was important enough to disregard an order from the old man who was in California and named Chuck was Senator Hunt, or the former Senator. He hadn't run for election, opting instead to run for President.

The old man said, "I know, I'm working on that right now. I know it's ridiculous. I'm doing what I can. Don't worry, I won't let you down. Good day, Chuck and tell the wife I asked about her." Then he hung up.

"Where were we?"

"You wanted dirt. Lots of dirt."

"Right, lots of dirt. If you can't find any dirt, make some up. Things he can't challenge. Things that the American people will believe. They believe anything the media tells them. I want it to be made clear this man will not survive, you understand me young man."

"Yes, Sir."

Burke hated to ask the next question because he already knew the answer, "And who do you think would be his replacement?"

"My good friend from California, Senator Hunt."

"Senator Hunt lost the election to President Carson. Do you think he can be elected?" asked Burke.

"With my backing, yes I do. Now, get to work. I want this done as soon as possible."

"Yes, Sir." Toby started to rise from his chair

"Oh, by the way young man, we conducted a poll last night. Do you know when we asked a thousand people if MacDonald was the best man for the job, do you know how many people said yes?"

"No, Sir, I have no idea."

"Twelve percent! Can you believe twelve percent?"

"Sir, I guess I should start with his college information first and then go from there."

Toby noticed the old man leaning back in his chair and grinning.

"He took a few night classes at a junior college on animal husbandry. See how easy this is going to be?" said the old man.

"Why did President Carson choose him for his cabinet?" Toby was curious.

The old man grinned even more. "He was his fishing buddy." Then he started laughing. The old man had turned red in the face and a blood vessel in his temple looked like it may pop at any time.

"See how easy this is going to be?"

Toby looked at the old man. "Sir, where do you suggest I start?"

"Kerney, Wyoming," answered the old man.

"Never heard of it," replied Toby.

"That's a good one. A man no one has ever heard of from a place no one has ever heard of…make sure you put that in your investigation."

"Yes, Sir, I will mention it every chance I get."

At the door, Toby stopped. "Sir, one last question."

"Spit it out. I have a lot of work to do young man."

"Do you think President Carson picked MacDonald to sit out of the State of the Union because he was the only one on his cabinet he felt qualified to lead the country?"

The old man didn't answer he just glared at Toby.

"Just food for thought," said Toby.

Outside on the sidewalk, Toby turned to look at the sixty story building. The emblem of the World News Examiner was positioned over the main entrance. A globe twelve feet in diameter was affixed to the wall. Above the globe was an eye. Above the eye in large gold letters was 'WORLD NEWS EXAMINER. Below the globe in slightly smaller gold letters was the papers motto 'KEEPING AN EYE ON THE WORLD.'

"Someone needs to keep an eye on us," Toby said to himself before walking away.

PENNSYLVANIA

JEREMIAH 17:7

At seven a.m., Lewis sat down at a desk in the corner and dialed the phone. His first call was to the Governor of Alabama. He bluntly told the Governor this wasn't a social call and he didn't have time to chat. "I've got forty nine more after you, Sir. What I need from you is for you to tell my assistant what we can do to help your situation, let me put him on."

Lewis transferred the call and dialed the next in line. He was calling them in alphabetical order. He was finished by ten o'clock. The states near Washington D.C. took longer, Lewis knew it would. Their needs were greater and Lewis felt compelled to stay on the line longer.

Reports were coming in about damage and fallout. Lewis felt lucky that the weather system had carried a lot of the radiation out to sea off the Eastern Seaboard, but that only gave the European countries a few days to prepare.

He had already given the pentagon instructions. Evacuate as much as you can to safety. The Pentagon was built like a fortress in World War two and had survived. Lewis thanked God for that but the radiation levels were very high in that area. Lewis told them to send the ranking General in each armed force to Pennsylvania and he wanted them by ten a.m. the next morning. These Generals would be his Joint Chiefs of Staff.

The Central Intelligence Director would be here at eleven. The National Security Agency at twelve. The Federal Bureau of Investigation already had four agents here. They were here when it happened. Lewis was amazed at how fast the Federal Government could move in some areas and was disappointed at what they couldn't do in a short period of time in other areas.

He hadn't called Beverly yet; there simply had not been enough time. He knew she would understand. Lewis Hadn't been this tired since Bosnia, way back when, then a thought entered his head. He picked up the phone and made a call. It was to the Pentagon. He wanted to know if a certain officer was still on active duty. They would get back with him.

"Make sure you do."

INDEPENDENCE

Alex Jacobs called the meeting to order. There were thirty men and women in the cafeteria on the first floor.

"Okay, what do we have?" he said.

"An impossible job. I don't see how it can be done," said a man in the back.

"What is the biggest problem you see?"

"Space; where can we put Congress. The House and Senate would need this entire building. Their staff alone would take up half of it." Most people in the room nodded their heads in agreement.

"Mr. Jacobs," a hand was raised in back by a young lady. She was only about twenty five with short black hair. Jacobs couldn't see her name tag.

"Okay, everyone thinks we can't do it because of space for congress and its staff. I'm agreeing with that. What else can we do? I'm open for discussion."

"Mr. Jacobs," the same young woman was speaking. She had stood up to get his attention after he hadn't called on her.

"Yes, you have something you want to add?"

"Yes, Sir, I do. If I remember right, you said we should think out of the box. I've been thinking; now please let me explain what I'm talking about."

"If this is about Congress, we have already decided that issue, Ma'am. Everyone here agrees with that assessment."

"I don't," said the young lady.

"You don't?" asked Jacobs.

"No, Sir, I don't."

"Okay, I will entertain any suggestions you may have."

"The Constitution only requires that they meet one day a year. I looked it up. They take office on January 3rd and have to meet one day a year." She held up a small pamphlet. On the front in bold type it simply said 'THE CONSTITUTION OF THE UNITED STATES.'

"The twentieth amendment sets these guidelines. It was passed in 1933."

"Go on, Ma'am. I'm listening."

"Congress can come here one day a year and then go back to their districts. We can do everything over the internet. Select committees can meet here in one of the court rooms and hold meeting or hearings."

Alex Jacobs sat down on one of the tables and looked at the young lady for a full minute. "What's your name, Ma'am?"

"Riley Mason, Sir. I'm from Atlanta."

"What you are suggesting would mean our Senators and Representatives would have to walk among their constituents and listen to their complaints. If I am correct in your suggestion they wouldn't be detached from the people who they represent. Is that what you are implying?"

"Yes, Sir, they can vote by secure email to prevent someone voting illegally in their place. It is public record how they vote."

Someone yelled out, "All of them have district offices. They can use those. Some have two or three."

"Alright, listen up everyone. You heard the lady. Can we make that work?"

Then it seemed like everyone was talking at once. They were moving again, slowly but surely, but at least they were moving.

"What about the Supreme Court? Where do we put them?" asked someone.

The Congress problem seemed to be behind them. Jacobs felt pretty good.

"They only meet for a month and hear a few cases. They can come here for that and then go back home," someone said.

"Yeah, they all have home offices. They don't need a whole building twelve months out of the year."

"Let's give the Justice Department one floor. They have district offices everywhere. I know there is one in Kansas City. We just have headquarters here. The same goes for the Treasury Department."

At eight o'clock that night, Alex Jacobs said, "I want everyone to think about what we have talked about tonight and we'll try to work any kinks out tomorrow. You know Washington was only twelve square miles and we've reduced it to two city blocks. I like the name Independence."

"Will the President go along?"

CHAPTER FORTY ONE

JENKINS

HEBREWS 11:34

FT. BENNING, GEORGIA

Major Dexter Jenkins, United States Army, was packing his personal items. His unit had just returned from a seven day training exercise. Tomorrow was his retirement date. Jenkins reflected back on his army career. It didn't seem like it had been twenty five years. Most of the years had gone by fast, but the last five had seemed to drag on forever. His first twenty he had led men, real men. Airborne Units, Ranger Units, he relished those years. Once he had made Major all that changed. The Army had changed. Now it was paperwork. The Army had been reduced to a skeleton crew in the important places. It was a paper tiger now. He knew just because you had a battalion or company on paper didn't mean you had a battalion or company in the field. When a government wants to reduce its budget the first cuts were always the military. Then they increase social programs. Someone didn't understand on social programs you pay people who do nothing. At least the men and women in the military were earning their money.

He was looking forward to tomorrow. He cleaned out his desk. Nothing in there he wanted to keep. He threw everything in the trash. He carried two boxes out to his car and returned for the last box. As he walked by the clerk he heard, "Yes, Sir, hold on please. It's for you, Major."

"Who is it?"

"Who's calling please?" The clerk stood up and came to attention. "Yes, General."

Jenkins thought, General. What General would be calling him? He went around the desk and looked at the caller ID. Army units had had so many threats in the last few years that the Pentagon had installed caller ID on every official phone. It did indeed say USA for United States Army and PENT for pentagon.

Jenkins went into his office, picked up the phone and punched line one.

"Major Dexter Jenkins, how may I help you General?"

"Major Jenkins, this is General Upchurch from Army Personnel."

"Yes, General."

"I didn't know you had friends in high places."

"High places, General? I'm afraid I don't follow you."

"Yes, you know the new President."

"I do? I'm sorry, General, I'm afraid I don't know the new President." Jenkins thought someone must be pulling a joke on me.

"You don't know President MacDonald?"

"Not that I'm aware of, General."

"Well, I pulled his records and I pulled yours. The two of you were in Bosnia together."

"We were? General, I'm sorry I don't recall him. That was almost twenty years ago. I'm afraid I don't remember most of them."

"Look Major, my father stormed the beach in Normandy and he remembers everyone that served with him."

"General, I'm sure your father was a remarkable man. But I can't place the name. I was a young Lieutenant in Bosnia with forty men. I remember a few but that's it."

"You've seen his picture, right?"

"No, Sir, I haven't. I just returned from the field a few hours ago. I know the President's name and that's it."

"Is there a photo in your unit? A chain of command is supposed to be displayed in every unit."

"There is one, if you will allow me to step into the hallway."

"Please do," said the General. The photo rang no bells in his memory.

"Sorry, General, I don't remember him."

"Well, why would he request that you be assigned to him?" Major Jenkins sat down.

"He requested me? I don't understand. General, I'm retiring tomorrow."

"Those orders have been rescinded. I'm faxing your new orders now."

"But General, I've already packed and my wife has already left."

"Listen Major, I don't know why he asked for you, but I have been instructed to point out to you a few weapons systems we have in the works that we want approved in the near future. Two of them are drone systems to give battlefield commanders real time intelligence and the other is the new tank defeating missile we have in the works."

"It was my understanding the new missile failed the test trials last summer. I thought it was scrapped."

"It was, but we think with enough money we can fix all that."

"How much money are we talking about, General?"

"I don't have those numbers handy right now," said General Upchurch.

"I understand."

"I'm going to make a recommendation to you."

"Yes, General, and what would that be?"

"Figure out who the new President is. Listen, we're not sending a Major to work for the President. You have been promoted to Lieutenant Colonel."

"Thank you, General."

"And don't forget that missile system."

"I won't forget." He made a mental note to mention it when pigs fly.

The Pentagon wanted missiles even though there were no soldiers to fire them. It was insane, no it wasn't the military. It was a congressman who forced it on the military.

The clerk knocked on the already opened door.

"Congratulations on your promotion, Sir. You are going to be a Special Liaison Officer."

"Thank you, Sergeant." Jenkin's mind was swirling with questions, and then he asked, "Have you ever heard of a Special Liaison Officer?"

"No, Sir, it's not in any file I can find. Oh, by the way you will fly by Air Force aircraft to Independence, Missouri. Civilian clothes required, that seems unusual to me. What's going on, Sir?"

"Don't know, Sergeant. What's in Independence, Missouri?"

"I don't know, Sir."

"Me either. Is there an Army base there?"

"Not that I can find."

"When do I leave? Does it say?"

"Yes, Sir, 1800 hours today."

"That's only three hours away! What do you think is going on, Sergeant?"

"I don't know, Colonel. Do you have any civilian clothes?"

"Yes, I do. They're halfway to Detroit now."

LTC Jenkins aircraft had been in the air for an hour. He was in deep thought. The way he saw it, he had two problems. Number one on his list, try to remember someone from over twenty years ago. Bosnia was nothing in comparison to his three tours in Iraq and two in Afghanistan after 9-11. Jenkins had commanded hundreds on each tour. How am I expected to remember one man out of thousands in twenty five years? Even so he gave it the old college try. It was still evading him. He tried to picture everyone. A few stood out as either good or bad, no Lewis MacDonald. He was holding the President's photo in his hand. He had grabbed it when he left Ft. Benning, Georgia.

He would think on his other problem for now. What in the world do I tell my wife? He couldn't even call her. She was already on the road. She was going to be madder than a wet setting hen when she arrived in Detroit with the kids. There was also a part B to this problem. He had maxed out his credit card when he had to buy civilian clothes. His orders said civilian clothes. Why would he have to wear civilian clothes? Again he stared at the photo, no luck.

He didn't realize when he dozed off. He awoke with a start. He looked around the plane. He was the only one in the cargo bay. This is downright spooky. Then it hit him like a sledgehammer! Spooky! The Ghost Rider! Now I remember. The man killed by the sniper. Moving through the woods. The ambush; MacDonald beating the man to death. The cabin; hotwiring the van. Volunteering to escort the body. Wanting to go to airborne and ranger school. Specialist Jack Gordon. LTC Jenkins remembered every man who had died under his command throughout his career. He would always remember them. He would take those names to his grave.

INDEPENDENCE

When Jenkins landed in Independence, Missouri it was dark. No other planes were landing or taking off. The FAA flight restrictions were still in place. He had heard that power was being restored along the East Coast from South Carolina to New York. The entire electric grid on the coast had gone out. Cell phone and internet service was still unavailable. He didn't know if it was intentional or not by the government. He could see why the government would try to control the information right now. He knew the military had shielded systems, that's why they still worked. He knew a nuclear blast can actually blind a satellite.

A car pulled up beside him and a man got out and opened the door.

"Mister Jenkins?"

"Yes, I'm Jenkins." Jenkins loaded his bags in the back seat and got in front with the driver.

"Where are we going?"

"The new Capital building."

"It's here in Independence?"

"Yes, Sir, it is."

"Is the President here?"

"Not yet. It will be a day or two."

"What do I do until he gets here?"

"Move desks," answered the driver.

ISAIAH 40:31

And they moved desks, lots of desks. For two days the men and women moved desks. The desks came from surplus at military bases all over the country. Gray metal desks, every single one alike. Jenkins didn't know how many he had sat behind in twenty five years. He felt like he had found some old friends. The day shift moved desks; the night shift moved filing cabinets. Computers were being hooked up in offices and tested.

Jenkins was impressed by how organized this team was. No one was wearing suits or dresses. He was thankful he had bought casual clothes. He would have ruined a suit. Then they were finished. The entire team took a tour of both buildings. Alex Jacobs was looking at everything. He couldn't believe they had pulled it off. Then he let out a groan. "We forgot something."

"What?" someone asked.

"Where do we put the President?"

Everyone froze.

"Okay folks, we knew we would have to fine tune some things. We can do this."

This came from the back of the room. Everyone turned around to see who had spoken up. It was the new guy. He had flown in two days ago from some army base in Georgia. He was about fifty years of age and muscular looking. A tall African American. He was the only person who hadn't needed a break since they started. He hadn't even broken a sweat. He never appeared to get tired. He walked toward Alex Jacobs and took the sketch out of his hand and studied it for a minute.

"Put him in this small conference room on the eight floor. We were going to use it for a break room. I don't think anyone will be taking a break for a while, a long while. He'll like it."

"Do you know the President?" someone asked.

"I've known him for twenty years. He was an Army Ranger and he'll make it work. Rangers lead the way."

No one commented.

CHAPTER FORTY TWO

THE COLD HARD FACTS

PENNSYLVANIA

Everyone stood when the President walked into the room. "Is everyone here?"

"Yes, Mr. President," the Air Force General said.

"Okay, this is what I want. I want the cold hard facts in layman terms. I want to know how much damage we've suffered, how big was it, how was it delivered, and most important who is responsible."

An Army General stood and said, "We believe a fifty kiloton weapon from one mile away. That is what our scientist are estimating. That may be off ten percent one way or the other." Then he sat back down.

"The means of delivery was not a missile or aircraft unless someone has stealth technology we don't know about. My estimate is a vehicle or it was in place already. I'm leaning towards the latter Mr. President. Everyone knows the Capital area was blocked off for two miles around the Capital. Our satellites would have picked up something if it was flying." The Air Force General sat back down.

The new director of the CIA stood up. "The list of suspects is not that long and they are the usual groups, Russia, China, North Korea and Iran. I would like to point out Mr. President that this was done by a nation. It was not a terrorist group. None of the nations I just mentioned would be willing to go that far. They would be afraid it would be used against them. The four countries I named don't trust anyone. So I'm leaning against one of them handing over a nuclear weapon to someone else. I can't come up with a scenario for that."

"Could someone else have developed it outside of a nation, you know, in a secret facility?" asked Lewis.

The CIA man continued, "We don't believe so. If it had been smaller I would say it's possible, but one of this magnitude I would say very unlikely." Then he sat down.

"How much damage was done to the Pentagon?" asked Lewis.

"The two nearest sides; the East side suffered damage but it was built like a fort in World War Two. Windows blown out, nothing major," said the Marine General.

"Is it functional?" asked Lewis.

"I'd say eighty percent., Mr. President if the device had been placed between the Capital and the Pentagon we might have lost both. Since it happened where it did it was a blessing. I hate to use that term considering what was done."

Lewis thought on this for a minute and then he spoke. "They had to know what you just said. That leads me to believe what someone said earlier that it was placed there previously. That leads me to the conclusion that that was the only place they could put it. If they had other choices they would have used them. It is possible cameras might have captured it on film from miles away. Maybe we can triangulate it and find out exactly where it was. Then it might lead us to whom."

"We are working on that now but there are so many. There's thousands and thousands of cameras. Everything from banks, liquor stores, pawn shops, grocery stores and the list goes on and on. The FBI is working on that now in Cleveland, Ohio. I don't know if you know this Mr. President but the FBI headquarters was also destroyed. We are working on that twenty four hours a day. I can assure you the

Justice Department won't stop until we know who did this" said the new Attorney General.

"Thank you and I guess it's possible we may never know, but we have to try. We owe it to the American people. Are there any threats on the horizon we should know about? Are any armies on the move or anything like that?"

The acting CIA Director stood back up and said, "Well, the usual. Protecting their own borders and major cities in case we retaliate but there is one point I can't explain. I've talked to everyone here and I think we agree," he paused and looked around the room.

Everyone nodded their head in affirmation.

"Iran has done nothing as near as we can tell. Nothing has moved. In the past if a rat ran across the border they went to full alert. It's just unusual considering it's the Middle East. It just doesn't figure. It may mean nothing or it may mean everything." The CIA man sat back down.

Lewis thought about that for a minute. "Mr. Rosenburg," he said looking at the CIA man. Rosenburg stood back up.

"Yes, Mr. President."

"For the last twenty years or so, hasn't Iran always said if they developed a nuclear weapon they would destroy Israel? I remember someone in the government saying it would only take one, since it's such a small country."

"That is correct, Mr. President."

"Then why wouldn't the Iranians, if it was the Iranians, use it on Israel instead of America."

"I don't have an answer to that Mr. President, but if they used it on Israel, especially the size they used here, some of the most sacred places to the Muslim religion such as the Dome of the Rock would likely be damaged, especially by the radiation. Maybe they want to give it to the Palestinians. If they used it on Israel it wouldn't be worth owning."

"I see," said the President.

Rosenburg continued, "Mr. President there are other ways to destroy a nation without reducing it to rubble."

"How?" asked the President.

"With ground troops," answered the Marine General.

The President just nodded his head. "Let's go to domestic issues now. If we are certain this weapon wasn't delivered by air can we resume air traffic now?" asked Lewis.

"Let's go domestic first and get the system back up and running. I'm not sure about the East Coast. The fall out has moved out over the Atlantic. Mr. President we were extremely lucky there. If the prevailing jet stream had been more to the north, New York, Boston and all the major cities would be in a lot more danger," answered the Air Force General.

"Do we know how many casualties?"

"No, Sir, and we may never know the full count."

"I see, and how about essential government officials, how many did we lose?"

"Mr. President, we may not know for weeks or months what kind of loss we've experienced."

The Marine General stood up. "Mr. President, I would like to say something here and I don't have a solution. I would just like to say let's not make the same mistake again, Sir."

"What mistake are you referring to General?"

"With all due respect, Sir, we should have seen something like this coming. We overlooked something years ago."

"What was that?" asked Lewis.

"We put all our eggs in one basket, Mr. President. I know Washington was designed during horse and buggy days. Everything vital was in walking distance of each other and it cost us dearly."

"I agree General. It was done before nuclear weapons. You cut the head off a snake and it dies. We had everything there as you say in one basket and it came back to haunt us, because someone took advantage of that."

"Yes, Sir, we need to spread everything out where one weapon crippling us in the blink of an eye will never happen again. It was just too much of a lucrative target."

"How about the major cities; has the violence slowed down?"

"Yes, Sir. The National Guard is getting a handle on it, Mr. President."

The Treasury representative asked, "Can we open the banks and get Wall Street back up like we promised. People need access to their money. They have to live and the longer we wait the more panic there will be and the greater risk we will have of a run on the banks."

The President had placed the Agriculture department, which was responsible for the food stamp program, under the Treasury department for ninety days.

"We promised and I intend to keep that promise. We can only hope and pray for the best." answered Lewis.

"I think we can do it, but it will be touch and go," said the Treasury representative.

"Are the networks giving us access to the news? We need to keep the American people informed. I only want them to hear the truth, not a bunch of speculation and opinions," said Lewis.

"Yes, they are but they are giving their opinion many times so it is just a question of who the people believe the news or the government. I'm afraid over the last two decades the American people don't put a lot of trust in either," said someone.

"Do you blame them?" asked someone else.

"Mr. President, Thomas Jefferson said the government has the inherent right to lie in order to protect itself," said the CIA director.

"That was then, this is now. There was no internet or twenty four hour news cycle back then. Let's stick to the truth. That way we don't have to remember what we said," said Lewis.

"Mr. President, do you think we will ever recover from this?"

"That depends on the American people don't you think. Now, let's move on shall we. Another consideration we need to address is social security checks going out on time. The elderly need those to survive. We need to get a handle on that as quickly as possible."

The Treasury department official stood and cleared his throat. "We are working around the clock on social security, welfare and food stamps, Mr. President." He remained standing.

"I'm going to make a decision here that's going to make a lot of folks mad. I want you to concentrate on social security first. That is money we owe. They paid into it. I want that your number one priority."

"Yes, Sir, Mr. President," and then he sat down.

"Thank you, our senior citizens have enough to worry about already."

KERNEY, WYOMING

VULTURES ARE CIRCLING

When the citizens of Kerney woke up on Thursday morning, thirty six hours after Washington was destroyed, they were overwhelmed by the news media. Vans with satellite dishes mounted on extension arms were everywhere.

432

One local man was overheard saying, "They are circling like vultures looking for a scrap" which was true. In a sense they were looking for dirt. They were sticking microphones in people's faces, asking questions. The media didn't seem to be interested in the answers. They were in a race with the clock to be the first reporting the story so the viewers would stay on their network.

The Mayor was quoted as saying, "They were in a media frenzy."

Local folks would ask each other how many times someone had tried to interview them. The answer was pretty much the same. "Four or five." One incident did make the news however. A reporter tried to ask a five year old girl a question. She stuck her tongue out at the reporter. The mother patted her on the head and said, "Good girl."

Toby Burke was racing the clock and was running late. Finding gasoline was a major problem. It seemed like everyone was filling their tank and any gas can they could find because it was rumored there might not be any more deliveries. Credit cards were pretty much useless because phone lines were out almost everywhere on the East Coast.

When Toby finally made it to Wyoming he felt close but still so far away from this town called Kerney. The last seventy miles he had seen thousands of cows and thousands of sheep and almost as many horses, but no people. "Where are the people?" Toby kept asking himself. He finally saw a sign of human habitation. It was actually a sign, a stop sign. It was rusty and had about twenty bullet holes in it. He remembered a friend from Alabama who once told him 'I wouldn't live anywhere you can't shoot a stop sign.' Toby drove on.

The investigative reporter for the World News Examiner pulled into Kerney at lunch time. Kerney was like most small towns he had been to. Four roads in, four roads out like a giant Tic Tac Toe game with the courthouse in the center square where the first player usually places their X or O.

Toby was starving. He hadn't eaten in eight hours and so he pulled into the diner. He had been able to find this morning's edition of the World News Examiner when he went through Cheyenne. He sat in a corner booth and read the paper. The place was packed with other journalist and news people like himself. He ordered the blue plate special when the waitress finally got around to him.

The editorial page from Thursday was indeed a full page. As he read it, it was obvious the old man hadn't written it. The entire staff had to have done this. No one could research and write a full page overnight, but the old man's name was on it and no one else. This disturbed Toby. You don't claim you wrote something when someone else had done all the work. He had never respected the owner, editor and publisher. That was too much power for one person. Newsprint was a powerful weapon and should be used properly.

Toby knew he wasn't sent here to find the truth. He was sent here to destroy someone and this someone just happened to be the President of the United States of America. You can't damage a President without it affecting the nation.

After eating, he thought about his assignment and figured that he would end up at the MacDonald ranch. He overheard a reporter say you couldn't even get close to the ranch. Secret Service had the place locked down. Toby figured if he was to find any dirt he would go to the MacDonald ranch and confront the family. They would have to answer the allegations. But first, he had to find some dirt.

He went to the library to find out where all the government offices were located. This was a small town and from experience knew everyone knew Lewis C. MacDonald. Other reporters were also in town. He recognized the network news people. Their vans were clearly marked with their logos and satellite dishes for instant link-up.

Newspapers were slower; therefore they could get by without the breaking news stories. In the past fifteen years newsprint was always to coin a term 'a day late and a dollar short.'

In the library he noticed an archives section and headed that way. At the door he noticed a man was working in the corner. Burke knocked on the door.

The man turned and said, "Please, come on in."

Burke identified himself and wanted to know if he had any information on the President. He was writing an article for his newspaper.

"That's what I am working on now. I knew everyone would be interested, so I'm putting it all together right now. You want to see what I have?"

"If you don't mind. Has anyone else seen what you have put together?"

"Nope, you are the first."

"That would be great." Toby thought I may get out of here today without being tarred and feathered and run out of town on a rail.

"Do you know the president?"

"I know him and his whole family."

"How would you describe him and the family in as few words as possible?"

"Salt of the earth."

"I see, let me ask you this, what do you personally think of him?"

"Oh, I think the world of him. You know he has never held any kind of office before being named Secretary of the Interior, and now he's President. Who would have ever thought that could happen."

"Do you think he will make a good President?"

"I think he will do what is right if you know what I mean."

"I think I do, but sometimes presidents don't always do right even though their intentions are good."

"You haven't met Lewis, have you?"

"No, Sir, I haven't."

"He'll do right. You can count on that."

"What information do you have?"

The man showed him everything on both Macdonald and his family. When Burke left the library the first thought was, there is no dirt here. He walked across the street to a park. The name of the park was 'Keith Arnold Farmer Park.' The name struck a bell. The First Lady's father. The park was named after him. He inquired people about the naming of the park. He found out it had been named after him because he had saved a woman's life when he could have saved his own. He also discovered there was a memorial college scholarship fund named after him.

Burke realized he had an awesome task in front of him. There was nothing here and if he wrote anything the truth would eventually come out and his name would be attacked to it. He left town at six. He called the office to report in. He was told the old man, the owner, wanted to talk to him and was transferred. The old man picked up on the first ring.

"What have you come up with?"

"There is nothing here, Sir."

"That's impossible; everybody has skeletons in their closet."

"Not him, not here anyway."

"Where are you going now?"

"Don't know," was the only answer he could give.

The cable news networks would stay another four days. They had the resources and the on air talent for their trademark twenty four hour news cycle. They also finally drifted off and Kerney returned to its normal self. Everyone was grateful it was over. The town of Kerney had never experienced anything like this before and hoped and prayed it never happened again.

CHAPTER FORTY THREE

DAMAGE REPORT

PENNSYLVANIA

Ronald McIntyre, Lewis MacDonald's Secret Service agent, was watching the President. Both were operating on three hours of sleep. Lewis was looking at a video of Washington D.C. or what was left of it. He was amazed at the damage. He called McIntyre over and said, "Sit here beside me. I'm not really familiar with Washington and I don't know where anything is. You're more familiar with the area than I am."

"Yes, Mr. President."

Lewis handed him the remote control and a laser pointer. "Pause it when you need to point something out."

"Okay, directly under the camera was where the Washington Monument was located." The video had been shot by a helicopter from five thousand feet. "The Capital was located there as you can see it was completely destroyed."

"Any chance anyone in there could have survived?" asked Lewis.

"I have been told no. If by some miracle the blast didn't kill them the radiation would have. It's been four days now. The radiation dosage would have been far too great for anyone to have survived."

Lewis leaned forward in his chair and looked closely at the video. "Is that water there? It looks like a lake."

"Yes, it is. The crater extended to the tidal basin and when the tide came in…"

"It filled with seawater," injected the President.

"Yes, Mr. President."

"How deep is the crater?"

"We don't know. Right now I think they have more pressing needs they are trying to figure out."

"Do you think it can be rebuilt?"

"Mr. President that is way beyond my expertise."

"If it was the Iranians, and we have been monitoring their nuclear program, how could they accomplish this?"

"Have you ever seen a magician do his act?"

"A few times, mostly on T.V."

"He distracts you with one hand and you take your eye off the other then he performs the trick."

"So we were watching the wrong thing. We took our eye off the ball."

"If it was the Iranians, yes, Mr. President, we took our eye off the ball."

"Let's get back to the damage. Do you know how far out people have died from the blast and from the radiation?"

"Mr. President, we can't even get close enough to determine that. I've been told they are finding bodies from as far as five miles. People standing in the open in direct line of sight were either killed instantly or died within twenty four hours."

"Do you think we will ever find his body?"

"Whose body?"

"President Carson's. He was a good friend. I don't like losing friends."

"No one does," answered the agent, and then added, "I lost maybe a hundred."

"I didn't think about the Treasury department being destroyed."

"Yes, it was. I lost a lot of friends."

"I heard on the news someone is filing suit. They contend since there is no body there is no proof he's dead and I shouldn't have been sworn in."

"We have video evidence to the contrary."

"We do?"

"Yes, Sir. We have high speed cameras that can freeze a frame every twenty five thousands of a second. He's dead, Mr. President."

"You know I certainly didn't ask for this job."

"I have gathered that, Mr. President."

"What would you do, man to man?"

"The Constitution is a very simple document, Mr. President. It is as plain as day, he's dead, by law you're the New President. It's that simple, no court is going to change that. There will be people who are going to try to fight you every step of the way. Do what your heart tells you is right and you will be fine."

"I hope to God you are right."

"I know I'm right, Mr. President."

"You know why I don't resign and hold a special election?" asked the president.

"No, Sir. That's not my concern."

"The Constitution. It lays out how it is to be done. If we don't follow the Constitution this great experiment in democracy will fail and the entire world will suffer. I will stay as the President. Once I have a vice president, someone to follow the rules of succession, I may consider my options." "Again Sir, that is not my concern. I know you will do what you feel is right."

"We have been in this building for five days. Is it possible to step outside for a few minutes?"

"We can do that, Mr. President."

After exiting the building Lewis realized it was nighttime. "I've lost track of time, Ron."

Agent McIntyre was unsure how to answer and the President calling him by his given name puzzled him.

"I think we all have, Mr. President."

"I am not a violent man Ron. I love peace."

Agent McIntyre didn't say anything. He realized the President wasn't finished. "There are two things I need to accomplish while I'm President. I need to find out who did this to us and then I need to kill them."

The two men stood in silence for a few minutes. Lewis pointed to the North and said, "Polaris is shining bright tonight."

"Yes, Sir. It seems very bright tonight."

"People have used it for a guide for thousands of years."

"So I've heard," answered McIntyre.

"My wife and I always enjoyed watching the stars with our children. My wife has always been my guiding light."

McIntyre glanced at the President and saw a small smile on his lips as though remembering a pleasant memory.

"She once told me when she was a little girl she thought the stars were angels shining their light down on her."

Agent McIntyre didn't answer. They went back inside.

JACK IN THE BOX

Jack had been watching the news every chance he had. He couldn't believe the damage inflicted on America, the Great Satan. He could hardly contain himself. The damage had far exceeded his expectations. When he was at work it gave him great satisfaction watching the owner. The man was in obvious pain and grief.

"We'll get them. You mark my words. We'll get them."

Jack had to force himself from laughing at the man.

"Get who?" asked Jack.

"Ever who did this. You mark my words Jack. We'll get them. I bet it was the Iranians. They're crazy, every last one of them."

Jack had to control his temper. He was boiling inside.

"And what do you think America will do?" asked Jack when the owner had his back to him.

The owner turned around and tapped Jack on the chest with his index finger. "Throw open the gates of Hell and unleash the dogs of war."

Jack couldn't answer. The words just wouldn't come.

CHAPTER FORTY FOUR

TICKED OFF

KERNEY, WYOMING

Beverly read the editorial calling for Lewis to resign. She was mad as a wet hen. It had been published two days after Washington and it was already Saturday. She still had not heard from Lewis. She was thankful Josh and Deborah were home. They sat up late each night talking. Both had decided to transfer to colleges in Casper. Josh was still planning on going into the Air Force and Deborah would continue her art studies. Alice had moved in because reporters were hounding her for interviews. Hardly anyone was getting enough sleep. The four of them were bone tired with no end in sight.

"When will this end?" Beverly asked her Mother.

"I don't know," was the only answer she could give.

On the morning news show on Sunday, the announcer said the President and his staff would be moving to Independence, Missouri on Monday. "They will be located in this building here behind me," she said, turning where the cameras could show the new capital.

"As soon as I know, I'm going," said Beverly.

CHAPTER FORTY FIVE

THE CAPITOL

INDEPENDENCE,

MISSOURI

When Lewis walked into the new Capital he was greeted by the people who had made this possible. They were waiting for him in the lobby. Alex Jacobs meet him and shook his hand.

"It looks like I sent the right man to do the job. Well done, Mr. Jacobs."

"Thank you, Mr. President."

Lewis noticed everyone had cards pinned on that said, 'Hello My Name Is' and a name was written under it in bold magic marker. Lewis smiled. Government on a shoestring looks like this. Lewis walked around and shook each person's hand saying, "Well done, I'm proud of you."

When he reached LTC Dexter Jenkins, Lewis placed his hand on the man's shoulder and shook his hand. "I need you, Colonel Jenkins."

"At your service, Mr. President."

Lewis moved on shaking everyone's hand. It didn't go unnoticed that the President paid closer attention to Jenkins than the others. Upstairs on the eighth floor Alex Jacobs held his breath when the President walked into his office. The former conference room was only twelve by sixteen feet. The desk with the 'Office of the President of the United States of America' was there. The desk had come from a secure site near Springfield, Missouri. There was a couch, coffee table and two wing back chairs.

Lewis looked around the room then went to the window and looked out. The window faced west. He looked a little to the right and said, "I wish I could see Wyoming from here, but other than that, it's fine. Mr. Jacobs, thank you."

"Thank you, Mr. President. There is a small kitchen and a room for the bedroom and living room. It's like an efficiency apartment. It was the best we could do."

"It will be fine. I'm sure my wife will like it," answered the President.

KERNEY, WYOMING

THE ROARING MOUSE

After dinner, Deborah washed the dishes and Josh fed and watered the horses. Alice was helping Beverly pack.

"What if they won't let you go?"

"I'm going Momma with or without them. Lewis needs me."

She dressed in blue jeans, sweater, boots and a coat. At the door she put on her cowboy hat. She walked to the vehicle that had the most agents. Beverly figured the ranking agent was inside. She knocked on the door. Agent Compton opened the door. Beverly walked in; she noticed everyone stood when she entered.

"May I speak to the agent in charge please?"

Compton looked to a man on the right side of the vehicle, standing behind a desk.

"Yes, Ma'am, I'm agent Gilmore, Dean Gilmore, how may I help the First Lady?"

"I understand my husband is in Independence, Missouri."

"Yes, that is my understanding, Ma'am."

"My husband needs me, and I am going there with or without the Secret Service."

"Ma'am, I will try to schedule an aircraft to fly you. It will take a few days," said Gilmore.

"I've never flown before," said Beverly.

"If you are worried about safety Ma'am, flying is the safest mode of transportation."

"So is riding a horse if you know what you are doing," answered Beverly.

Dean Gilmore had seen the First Lady ride. He knew she knew what she was doing. He got to thinking she's crazy enough to go by horseback. He had no answer for her on that one.

"Why can't we use the SUVs that are here? They are all over the place. You have sixteen agents here if I've counted right."

"You mean drive?"

"That's what you use a car for isn't it?"

"Well, yes Ma'am."

"Good, we'll leave in half an hour."

Beverly turned and walked toward the door. When she got to agent Compton she said, "I like that outfit. It looks nice on you." Then she was gone.

Agent Gilmore stood there and said, "Everyone thought she was mousy. She weighs a hundred pounds soaking wet. We better pack, half here, half to Missouri." Then he added, "Better be on time or you'll get left behind."

Marsha Jefferson had to smile. She wasn't in a hurry. She was already packed. Marsha looked at the First Lady as she walked towards the corral. She watched as she led her horse to the pasture gate and let it go. The horse trotted off to join the herd. It never looked back. As the First Lady walked past Marsha she said, "It wants to be free."

The First Lady walked to Lookout Point. Marsha followed at a discreet distance and saw the First Lady take a small jar and spoon out of her pocket and scoop dirt into the jar. As she walked past Jefferson she said, "To remind me of this very special place."

Jefferson answered with a question. "It's your favorite place in the world, isn't it?"

"By my husband's side is my most favorite place in the world," she replied then she walked toward the house.

Jefferson wondered if she could ever love someone like that, probably not. Jefferson walked up to the top of Lookout Point and looked around. It was indeed one of the most beautiful places she had ever been to. She had to admit she liked the ranch, but Marsha liked stores, lots of stores. She wanted another pair of shoes like she was wearing. It's hard to find good kicking shoes.

INDEPENDENCE, MISSOURI

Toby Burke was standing in front of the new Capitol Building. It was about the plainest building in the area. He had arrived yesterday after seeing it on TV. It would be in all the papers tomorrow. No wonder newspaper sales were down drastically. He had taken a roll of film of the place. People had been allowed to tour most of the building. Once you've seen a gray metal desk you've seen them all. Reporters, including himself, had been allowed to see the President's office.

Toby Burke was hanging around because he believed there was a story inside. If he could get a glimmer of what it was, he might just be able to write about it. There were lots of people hanging around, mostly locals he judged, nothing like this had ever happened in Independence, Missouri.

He saw three black SUVs pull up to the curb and stop. Men got out of two of them. They were wearing navy blue suits and sunglasses. Three women got out of the SUV in the middle. All of them were wearing navy blue dress suits and sunglasses.

A petite blond woman also got out of the middle SUV. She was wearing blue jeans, a sheepskin coat and boots. She put on sunglasses and a straw cowboy hat that had seen its better days. It was country come to town. She removed two suitcases from the SUV.

Toby Burke knew they were Secret Service. The men moved in front and cleared a path towards the steps. Toby Burke was snapping away with his digital camera. He looked to his left and saw other men that looked like Secret Service agents moving toward the arriving agents. In the middle of these agents was the President. Toby looked back to the woman in the cowboy hat. She had a suitcase in each hand. They met directly in front of Toby Burke.

The lady set the suitcases down, took off the hat and put her arms around the President. She leaned her head on his chest and said, "I'm here, Lewis."

The President kissed her on top of the head and said, "I've missed you." Toby Burke heard all of this as he snapped away with his camera.

The woman picked up one suitcase in her right hand. The President picked up the other in his left. They held hands as they walked into the new Capitol.

"No way am I going to be part of trying to destroy these people," Toby Burke muttered to himself.

He went back to his motel room. Fired up his laptop and typed his resume. He printed ten copies. Then he typed his resignation. The 'WORLD NEWS EXAMINER' was now history to him. He dropped it in the mail and headed to the newspapers and television stations in the area.

He got an interview at his first stop. The editor was interested in what it was like to work for a huge news organization. Toby said,

"You wouldn't want to go there." He got a job as an investigative reporter. The first one the paper had ever hired. He started the next day. His first article appeared four days later. "A Man From a Place No One Has Ever Heard Of." It was about the new President and Kerney, Wyoming. He painted a favorable picture of the new President, his family and his community. Beverly read it the next day. It made her homesick. She wrote a letter to the editor. She included being homesick because the journalist had described it just as it really was. Then she included a P.S. "Even though I love Kerney, I love my husband more and that's why I'm here with him."

When Beverly found out the First Lady of the United States was getting mail, lots of mail, she saw a chance to help Lewis. She asked Alex Jacobs if he could locate a small office to handle the mail. "There is a small room next to my office. It's small but it has a kitchenette and powder room."

"Perfect," said Beverly.

A week later she realized she had bitten off more than she could chew. She selected a former English school teacher to help. She found out the lady had written two children's books that her children had loved.

Beverly and her assistant, Myrtice Thompson, had read and answered hundreds and hundreds of letters. She would write handwritten notes to children all over America. She had received letters from all over the world. She tried to answer those also. She answered letters long after most people had gone to bed.

Lewis worked late every night. He wasn't getting much sleep. When he finally made it to their quarters…Beverly liked the word quarters, because in this situation it was about a quarter the size of their house in Wyoming. She would prepare him something to eat. The two were living like two newlyweds in a cramped apartment. Millions of young people lived like this. She figured they could also. It didn't seem to bother either of them.

CHAPTER FORTY SIX

CRISIS

LTC Dexter Jenkins was seated in the back of the briefing room with the other staffers. Anthony Miller was fielding questions from the press about the day's events. Anthony liked to be called Tony by his friends. The Press wasn't his friend so therefore he was Anthony. President MacDonald had done something no other President before him had done. The daily press conference was broadcast live. Lewis figured if people saw it themselves the news media couldn't use bits and pieces to sway people's judgement. Tony Miller agreed. He knew the news media chose sides. They were either conservative or liberal. Lewis told Tony Miller to just tell the truth. If you do that you don't have to remember what you said.

Tony said, "Just one more question," when a lady LTC Jenkins didn't recognize approached Tony from the room next door. Tony leaned to the right. The woman covered her mouth and his ear with her hand and whispered something. Then she handed him a piece of paper.

Tony said, "Excuse me for a minute" and read the sheet of paper. The press sensed something was going on and leaned forward in their seats. Toby Burke was among them and sensed a story in the making. The First Lady had obtained a press pass for him after his article about Kerney. Tony Miller looked at the press pool and said "I would like to read a brief statement to you. I will not be answering any questions at this time. We have just been informed that the United States Embassy in Cairo, Egypt has been seized. This occurred fifteen minutes ago. We do not, I repeat do not; know if there are any casualties. We will hold a briefing in this room every hour, on the hour starting at noon to keep everyone updated. Thank you." Tony Miller closed the briefing book and left the room. LTC

Jenkins had left as soon as Tony Miller said 'The United States Embassy in Cairo, Egypt had been seized.' He was on the eighth floor before Tony finished.

THE PRESIDENT'S OFFICE

The Secretary told Jenkins to go in. Jenkins was the first to arrive. Minutes later others were flowing into the room. There were ten men including himself and three women. The four Generals in the room were the only ones he could identify. Everyone else was in civilian attire.

Lewis came around his desk and sat on the edge, feet on the floor, arms crossed on his chest. He wasn't wearing a suit jacket, his tie loose and sleeves rolled up. He had been working. This was not a photo op, there was no photographer.

"How did we find out?" asked Lewis.

"One of our people was outside the compound. He had a satellite phone and called Langley." Everyone knew Langley, Virginia was the headquarters for the CIA.

"So the person who called was a CIA officer?" asked the President.

He got no answer and when dealing with the CIA sometimes that's the answer.

"Will he be able to continue giving us intelligence reports by phone?" asked Lewis.

"We believe so, if he isn't caught."

"Okay, I want to make sure when we give our hourly briefing that we don't expose him. Do we know if there are others outside the compound that may be seeking a safe place? In our hourly briefing we need to make sure we don't divulge that information."

Lewis turned to Tony Miller. "Tony we don't say how many are assigned to the Embassy. We certainly don't say if we have anyone outside. Let's say we believe everyone was on the inside. We can say some returned to the States last week. This may misdirect whoever did this as to how many are supposed to be there. Now to the big question, what do we do about it?"

"We have several contingency plans available Mr. President from a show of force to tactical assault and negotiation. This is an act of war Mr. President. Our Embassy is considered sovereign soil. It is the same if you would invade Miami, Florida," said the Marine General.

Lewis nodded his head. "Get the plans and brief me within the hour on all of them."

"Yes, Sir," said the Air Force General.

Lewis looked at the Navy Admiral. "What forces do we have in the region?"

"Mr. President, when Washington was destroyed our carriers in the Mediterranean and the Persian Gulf steamed toward open water in the Atlantic and the Indian Ocean to protect the United States and to have maneuver room in the event of being attacked. It was done automatically without orders. Hopefully that won't hamper this. No one saw this coming."

"I agree, no one saw what happened in Washington coming either, but you have to agree someone took advantage of it. Tony get ready for the next briefing. If nothing changes I still want someone giving the briefing and we don't answer any questions. That will be all."

Lewis nodded at LTC Jenkins. Jenkins nodded his head and stayed in the room.

"This is a test of your will, Mr. President. They sense weakness in America and they are trying to find out how strong we are," said Jenkins after everyone had left the room.

"I agree with you. When they brief me on the contingency plans I want you to give me your opinion. They use terms and initials I don't understand. It's been a long time since I was in the Army. I know some of that stuff but it has changed in the last twenty five years at least I guess it changed."

"We may be lucky about the carriers being in open water, Mr. President, but we need them closer to Egypt in case we need them for some sort of strike."

Lewis picked up his phone and called the Navy Admiral and directed both carrier battle groups closer to Egypt.

At twelve noon, Tony Miller gave his second briefing of the day. There was no change. He answered no questions. He informed them as new developments occurred they would be told. The press was restless, they wanted more information. The network news analysts were having a field day with speculation suggesting weakness on the part of the new President. It was pointed out over and over that as of now, he still didn't have a Congress. The elections were still over a month away and candidates came out of the woodwork. It doesn't take vast sums of money to run a campaign that is less than forty five days. The President insisted on a congress being seated in forty five days. Some states allow the Governor to appoint someone to fill an unexpired term. Governors in those states appointed themselves. However they were not sworn in yet. Some State Legislatures can appoint someone. Lewis looked at it like a pot luck dinner. He knew Representatives have to be elected by the people.

After all the contingency plans were presented Lewis looked at his options. He informed the Generals he wanted to think on it for a few hours. The press briefings were held on time with nothing new to add.

Egypt has a seven hour time difference with the East Coast. The worldwide news coverage had live coverage on the ground. Pictured newscast showed thousands in the streets around the Embassy.

Lewis watched the broadcast to try to get a feel of the situation. He estimated the crowd was forty to fifty thousand. It filled the streets for several blocks. Several men with bullhorns were speaking to the crowd inciting them even more. Groups of men, mostly young, were burning and stomping on American flags. People were throwing bottles and other things over the compound walls, Lewis guessed vegetables, probably already spoiled. Signs were everywhere. Some homemade and some professionally done. Most were in, Lewis guessed, Egyptian but a lot were in English. Most had the same message 'Death to America.' The people were chanting 'Death to America-Death to America.'

Lewis watched in silence. He showed no outward emotion. Inside was a different story. Lewis knew full well this was his crisis and his alone. One news organization had conducted a poll and only twenty five percent had confidence in the new president. It was pointed out that this was the lowest in polling history. Lewis thought about that, polls meant nothing to him. He had started at twelve percent.

Lewis knew he had to address the American people on the Egyptian crisis. That night in the first family's quarters he worked on his speech. Advisors had given him some points that should be covered. Lewis wanted a speech that would cover all the talking points the staff had presented. He noticed several were contradictory to other staff members suggested talking points.

Beverly was answering letters as Lewis worked. She looked at Lewis. She didn't want her husband suffering like this.

"Lewis, let me tell you what Grandpa Thomas would say if something like this happened to him."

CHAPTER FORTY SEVEN

THE SPEECH

EXODUS 4:12

After the next morning staff briefing, LTC Jenkins was alone in the room with the President.

"Mr. President, the American people need to hear from you. They need a strong speech. One to boost their morale and give them confidence."

"I know. I've come up with one."

"You have?"

"Yes, I have, how well can you act?"

"I don't understand, Mr. President."

"Let me explain."

It took an hour to work out all the details.

"This might work," said Jenkins.

"It's dark over there now and the crowds are still out in the street. Let's hope it stays that way. I want that crowd...I need that crowd."

Lewis called Tony Miller and Admiral Douglas. Only four people would be in on the plan. It was important that information wasn't leaked out.

The Admiral said he could get the assets in place. The aircraft carriers would have to leave their task force in order to do it but he didn't see any problems. LTC Jenkins made the first phone call. He was connected immediately. They had been waiting on a call since the Embassy was captured. He had a script to go by and didn't deviate from it at all. He was calling the Egyptian United Nations Ambassador.

At nine p.m., Tony Miller stepped up to the microphone and said, "I'd like to turn this briefing over to the acting Secretary of State, Mr. Dexter Jenkins."

LTC Jenkins walked to the podium. He was wearing a rumpled suit with Ben Franklin glasses pulled down on his nose. He looked like a college professor.

"I have been in contact with the United Nations envoy to Egypt. We are currently negotiating for the release of our Embassy staff in Cairo. The President will address the nation tomorrow night at 9:00 p.m. He will speak for about twenty five minutes. The staff is currently working on his speech. That is all I am ready to say right now. Mr. Miller or someone will continue to give hourly reports. Thank you."

DETROIT MICHIGAN

In Detroit, Michigan, LTC Jenkins' wife, Mildred, was watching the broadcast. She sat forward for a closer look. "What in the world is going on?" she said to her youngest son. The boy was only twelve.

"What do you mean?" asked the boy.

"Your dad. He doesn't wear glasses and his hair is turning gray. Look at that suit. He wouldn't be caught dead wearing something like that."

She tried to call her sister but didn't get an answer.

"What is going on? They said he was acting Secretary of State." Which was true…he was acting.

BRIEFING ROOM

All the network cameras were in place. There was a standing room only crowd. Agent Ronald McIntyre walked up to the news reporter from Wyoming and said "Ma'am, you have to move your camera to over there."

"Why? I won't be able to get a frontal shot of the President from here. Look this is my first assignment covering the President. We're both from Wyoming."

"I'm sorry to hear that, now let me show you where to put your camera."

"And if I don't move?" asked the reporter.

"Then I will escort you out and make sure you lose your press pass."

"I can't believe this. We won't be able to see him well enough from over there."

"Let's move, Ma'am, I'm not going to ask again." He picked the camera up and placed it precisely in front of the double doors where the President would enter and leave the room.

"If I were you I would leave the camera on until he leaves."

At precisely 9:00 p.m. Eastern, 8:00 p.m. Central, Tony Miller entered the press room. He walked to the podium, leaned over and said, "Ladies and Gentlemen, the President of the United States."

Two staffers opened the double doors. A long hallway led to the briefing room. President Lewis C. MacDonald walked down the hallway, turned and walked twenty feet to the podium.

The President opened the briefing book and looked at the cameras. He turned to the first page. Then he shook his head slightly. He took the speech out, folded it in half and put it in his pocket.

Then he looked back at the cameras, with resolve showing on his face. He leaned forward and in a loud, clear voice said, "Let my people go." Then a pause, "Get off our property." Another pause. "You have twenty four hours."

Then he turned and walked back the way he had come. Fifteen feet further down the hallway, three Generals and an Admiral stepped out of an alcove and fell in behind the President. At the end of the hallway, they turned right and out of sight.

The reporter from Wyoming said to her cameraman, "We got the best shot. No one else has this view. I can tell that of everyone here, we got the best shot. Can you believe they made us move here and we're the only ones that had that shot? Where's that agent?" She looked around and didn't see him. "Where did he go?"

Ten minutes later, Lewis looked at Jenkins and said, "Make the call."

"Gladly, Mr. President."

The people in the President's office were quiet as a mouse.

"Mr. Ambassador, Dexter Jenkins. Mr. Ambassador I don't know what happened. Mr. Ambassador I think he's insane. He's lost his mind. No, I can't talk with him. As soon as he got to his office he fired me. He's talking to all those Generals now. He said he's going to level Cairo if anyone's hurt. Listen if you have any family there, I'd have them leave. I'm serious the man has gone crazy. Yes, I know the speech was supposed to last twenty five minutes. I don't know how long it lasted. I didn't even get to hear it. What did he say?"

Ten minutes later after Jenkins hung up, Lewis asked, "Well?"

"He bought it hook, line and sinker."

Lewis smiled, looked at Admiral Douglas and said, "It's your show now."

Lewis had no intention of giving them twenty four hours. He wanted this done at night. The crowd seemed to peak at ten o'clock Cairo time. He wanted that crowd outside the Embassy. He believed the crowd would be bigger tomorrow night. He was right.

CHAPTER FORTY EIGHT

REACTION

NEW YORK NETWORK

NEWS

As soon as the President finished speaking, the network news shows covering the event went back on the air. Some of the seats were empty. Some had run to the restroom thinking they wouldn't be back on the air for at least twenty minutes.

The first one said, "What kind of speech was that? We waited for that? What did it take a total of ten seconds? How many words were there in his speech, if you want to call it that?"

"It sounded more like a threat to me," said one analyst.

"What is he doing or what is he trying to do. Is he going to back it up if it's a threat? This came out of the blue. Last night, Mr. Jenkins said the administration was negotiating for the release of the hostages," said another analyst.

"Ladies and gentlemen, we don't know what to say. We expected a twenty five minute speech and we got this. We are going to replay it in case you sneezed and missed it. I've never seen anything like this before and I have covered a lot of Presidential speeches. This, I have to admit, is something I never saw coming."

Three blocks away in an Irish pub people were watching. Everyone in America was watching. People in the pub stood up and held their glasses up. Someone said, "A toast to the President."

The owner/bartender called out, "Drinks are on the house." Big mistake.

Someone put three quarters in the juke box and pressed two buttons. Ten seconds later, Lee Greenwood could be heard singing 'God Bless the U.S.A.'

The men quieted down and stood a little taller. Their drinks were held at half-staff, a little over their belt. Tears were flowing down some on their cheeks. No one bothered to wipe them away. It wouldn't have been proper. Then slowly but surely all of them joined in. A sense of pride welled up inside of those ordinary working stiffs.

In living rooms all across America, people were smiling and calling their friends and family.

"Hey man, did you see the President? Yeah, he's serious. He said let my people go and he means it. We ain't taking any more of this trash.

"Yeah, he gave them twenty four hours to get off our property or else. Make's you proud to be an American."

CHAPTER FORTY NINE

FLATTOPS

Under the cover of darkness, the USS Abraham Lincoln slipped through the Strait of Gibraltar into the Mediterranean Sea. The USS Harry S. Truman entered the Red Sea from the Gulf of Aden.

Both aircraft carriers went to full speed, fast enough to water ski. Sailors were manning night vision and infra-red devices. The ships were blacked out, no lights what so ever. The radar was turned off. Each carrier was four and a half acres of American power and they were moving with a purpose. A mission in life. There was nothing within a thousand miles that would want to pick a fight with these mighty warships.

When the USS Abraham Lincoln was in range she turned into the wind and launched its aircraft. A radar jamming aircraft was already in the air to jam the Egyptian air defense radar. Sixty five F-18 super hornets were spread out four hundred yards apart. They were on the deck. Ten miles from Cairo they went to afterburner flying 1400 miles per hour. Destination Cairo. They carried only air to air missiles.

The sonic boom reverberated all over Cairo. Windows broke, light bulbs shattered, houses shook and alarms went off everywhere. People literally fell out of their beds from the jarring of the sound.

The crowd in the street at the U.S. Embassy stampeded. Lewis and his staff were watching it live. The news vans were shaking, some losing their signal. The last few seconds that was captured on one of the network stations was of a mass of humanity standing fairly still. It reminded Lewis of a lake when a stone is thrown into the center. A ripple moved out from the center gaining speed and momentum, leaving a void in the center. Bodies were everywhere, some still moving. Some were perfectly still, obviously dead. Panic was everywhere and it was spreading faster than the people in the crowd.

When the Egyptian anti-aircraft opened up the jets were gone. Panic broke out all over Cairo. The planes from the Abraham Lincoln were headed to the Truman who had launched its aircraft for another Sonic boom, and then they would land on the Lincoln.

For the second time in recorded history there was an exodus from Egypt. People thought it was the end of the world. People would claim the United States had dropped an atomic bomb on the city.

In the basement of the US Embassy, the hostages were sitting on the floor when the first sonic boom occurred. Dust fell from the ceiling, light bulbs shattered. The whole building shook.

"My God, what was that?" asked a secretary.

"That was the sound of freedom," answered a Marine.

All of the guards ran out of the room and didn't come back. The Marines quickly barricaded the door with tables, filing cabinets and anything else they could move.

The President made a phone call to the Egyptian counsel to the United Nations in New York.

"You tell your President if a single embassy personnel is hurt I will track him down and kill him. I'm sending a contingent of Marines to secure the Embassy. You fire one shot I will consider it an act of war."

An hour later, a four hundred man Marine assault force landed and started towards the Embassy. A Major was in charge of the Marines. His name was Gerald Reichs. His Marines nicknamed him 'Ace' because he always had an ace up his sleeve.

The streets were deserted, not a soul in sight. Three blocks from the Embassy they started seeing bodies in the street. They had been trampled to death from the stampede. Closer to the Embassy the Marines encountered more and more bodies.

When the Marines reached the Embassy the gates were opened along with the front door of the Embassy itself. Major 'Ace' Reichs didn't want to go inside, he was afraid of what he might find. He took a deep breath and reminded himself he was a Marine and entered the building. They made their way to the basement. One door was blocked from the inside.

'Ace' Reichs pounded on the door and in a commanding voice Marines have perfected for over two hundred years shouted, "United States Marines. Open this door now." He stretched out the words Marine and now. He heard scrapping noises from the inside. Things were being moved out of the way. The door opened and the Marine security officer snapped off a salute. Major Reichs returned the salute and walked inside the room and looked around.

"Did you try to defend our sovereign soil, this Embassy and its staff?"

The Marine looked at the Ambassador and said, "He ordered us not to use our weapons, Sir." The Marine looked at the floor in shame.

'Ace' pulled out a letter from his pocket. He made sure it was the right one. He had two letters in his possession. One letter was relieving the Ambassador. This was the one he presented to the Ambassador. "You will be leaving in two hours."

Then 'Ace' said in his commanding voice, "Listen up people. Clean up this pig sty. We're back in business."

Two hours later, a message was sent to all US Embassies. The United States Marine security detail will never be ordered not to fight in order to protect the US Embassy.

THE DAY AFTER

The speech was replayed over and over again. It simply became known as the speech. Every news outlet had their own opinion; of course, some said it was a quote for the Bible. Moses telling Pharaoh to let my people go, after all it was in Egypt.

It was timed; it lasted exactly seven seconds. There was debate over whether it was twelve words or thirteen. Is twenty four two words or one? They settled on an even dozen. One commentator said, "He said in seven seconds what would have taken another politician twenty minutes." He didn't say if that was good or bad. One full hour was used to discuss the President walking down the hallway with the Generals and the Admiral. That one clip was played almost as much as the speech itself.

One analyst summed it up in a sentence. "This may be the defining moment of his Presidency."

The crisis in Egypt had taken less than seventy two hours. The American people had seen the speech over and over. The scene where the President walked away, to be followed by the Generals was the best. Every news agency had used it, courtesy of the small T.V. station from Wyoming. Polls were taken every hour. The numbers climbed hourly. By lunch time, they were at 55 percent favorable approval rating.

The general consensus from the man on the street was, "Yeah, we got knocked down but we're getting back on our feet." Lewis knew he needed to keep the momentum going. He had awesome decisions to make and he would let his conscience be his guide.

His first step was to appoint a supreme court. He hadn't put very much thought into it since he had no place to put them. Now he did. The United States has twelve district courts. Lewis directed that the senior Judge from each district would sit on the court for a term of one year. The Chief Justice would be from the first district then rotated to the second district then the third and so on.

To change a law would require a vote of 7 to 5. There would be no more 5 to 4 decisions. These Judges had already been approved by Congress in years past. Lewis didn't believe a President should be able to appoint someone forty years old and have them sit on the bench for forty years until they either died or chose to retire. When this plan was put out to the American people, most didn't understand it. Most people didn't know how Justices were placed on the court. A survey was conducted, 45 percent thought Congress did that. Only about 25 percent knew how the system worked. When asked if they thought that it was right to place Justices on the Supreme Court that other Presidents had chosen rather than the sitting President, the vast majority thought that was a good idea. It took the politics out of the system.

Lewis knew Congress could determine how many Justices sat on the Supreme Court. Lewis figured once he had a Congress seated they may want to change it back to the way it was before. This didn't bother Lewis. What he was doing was a stop gap measure. No one could claim he was stacking the Supreme Court to push his agenda. He really didn't have an agenda. He had a war to fight.

CHAPTER FIFTY

LIKE A SWARM OF

LOCUST

After the Egyptian crisis the news media realized the average American was intrigued by this man they had never heard of from a place they had never heard of. They descended like a swarm of locust on the small town of Kerney, Wyoming. This time they had a different reason. They weren't looking for dirt. They had found out earlier there wasn't any to be found. This time they were looking for human interest stories. They found one in particular.

Jo Beth Gordon-Kerney was a member of the Kerney Historical Society. She had married a direct descendent of Doug 'Dug' Kerney. The media wasn't interested in any of that.

She had known Beverly since Beverly was fifteen. She knew how they met at the church dinner. She knew what day Beverly and Lewis fell in love.

When the lady conducting the interview asked her how she knew that exact date Jo Beth had replied, "My brother was killed in Bosnia on May fourteenth 1996. He was shot by a sniper. They were manning a checkpoint. You know checking ID's and stuff like that. The sniper missed Lewis. Lewis escorted my brother's body home. They fell in love during the funeral and the funeral was May 18th."

"They fell in love during the funeral?" asked the surprised correspondent.

"Yep, during the funeral."

"So it was fate that brought them together."

"You could say that. I believe that is so."

Jo Beth also told her about them getting married one day before 9/11 and Beverly rescuing the children because she happened to be near the house when a 911 call came in.

When the article was published the journalist mentioned fate several times. How fate had played such an important role in all their lives.

JACK IN THE BOX

ECCLESIASTES 9:2

The following Thursday Jack was working at the convenience store by himself. The owner always took Thursdays off. The store was closed on Sundays.

Jack hated the owner with a passion. He was always eating ham and cheese sandwiches...the infidel! Jack had already decided when he was able to go back to Iran he was going to kill him and stuff him in the beer cooler. He would be long gone before anyone would discover the body.

He was reading a news magazine. Thumbing through the pages all of a sudden there was a lot of articles about the new President. Jack really wasn't interested in anything about this new President but there was nothing else to do. He hadn't had a customer all day. He hated this job, but it was where he had to be at this time of the plan.

The article was about the MacDonald family and how the President and the First Lady had met. It was like a fairy tale of sorts. The writer had called it fate. Jack believed in fate. He was surprised to find out the man killed by a sniper was also on the same day that Jack was starting his week long journey to Paris. He knew what day he arrived in Paris. It was simple to backtrack the dates. When he read that a sniper had missed the soldier, who now was the President of the United States of America, he knew that the soldier he missed wasn't an insignificant soldier as he had first believed.

Fate had a plan for this man.

Fate had indeed played a role that day when the soldier who was now the President stepped back a foot to let his man open the car door.

Now fate might be like a knife in the back and not only that but then to twist the blade. Fate had allowed the President by some strange twist to be in a position to completely destroy Jack's country of Iran. Did fate step in and save the President's life so he could completely and utterly destroy Jack's country? Jack felt sick.

Fate, what was fate? Was it his fate to die in this God forsaken country called America? This country he knew as the 'Great Satan.' This country of infidels. This country that had no control over their women. A country full of spineless cowards. He believed in prayer. He would pray to Allah not to let him die in this country of people he despised. He believed Allah wouldn't let that happen. Fate, he believed in fate.

CHAPTER FIFTY ONE

PRIMETIME

PSALMS 143:9

Only one current photo of the First Lady had appeared on the news. It had been taken the day she arrived in Independence. She was hugging the President with her head on his chest. It was a very good photo. America wanted to see more of her.

America wanted to meet her, to see her live and to hear her speak. The press secretary, Tony Miller, encouraged her to participate in a live interview on a show called 'The Nation Tonight.' It aired at nine p.m. Beverly had mixed emotions about doing an interview. If there was one person who had less interest in politics than Lewis, it was Beverly.

"Just be yourself," Lewis told her.

"I can do that," replied Beverly.

Beverly was wearing one of her church outfits. A skirt and blouse with a dress jacket. She was wearing her airborne wings and the heart shaped pin. She was wearing a mid-high heel pair of shoes. She never wore high heels. She looked very good, attractive in a wholesome way, like the girl next door.

Kathaleen Dumbar was doing the interview. The questions were easy and it was a very relaxed atmosphere. Beverly was comfortable and smiled a lot as she answered the questions. Not a single political question was asked and after twelve minutes they took a commercial break which lasted four minutes.

When the program resumed, Beverly was smiling into the cameras. Kathaleen said, "Can you tell me where Libya is located?"

The smile disappeared. Beverly blinked and cocked her head slightly and squinted her eyes.

"Kathaleen, are you using me to try to embarrass my husband?"

"No, I would never do that."

"I'm glad you're not trying to embarrass my husband" Beverly smelled a trap.

"Ma'am, back to the question. Do you know where Libya is?"

"Yes, I do."

"Would you please tell us?"

In Wyoming, Deborah was watching the show with a Secret Service agent and said, "Kathaleen is about to get her butt kicked."

"Why?"

"I'll tell you when they go to a commercial."

"Tell you what Kathaleen; we'll play a little game. I will name all the countries that neighbor Libya except one and you name that one. Are you ready?"

"Ma'am, I'm the one asking the questions," said Kathaleen.

"Come on Kathaleen, it'll be a lot of fun. Here goes, Egypt, Sudan, Chad, Niger and Tunisia." Beverly had a small smile on her lips and her eyes sparkled.

Kathaleen didn't answer; she just glared at the First Lady.

"Kathaleen, the answer is Algeria."

Kathaleen's face had a peculiar strain on it as she said, "We're going to take another commercial break. We'll be right back."

With heavy footsteps, she went off stage and found the Director and said, "I want to know who prompted her on my questions. There is no way that woman knows that answer. She made a fool out of me out there."

"No one gave her the questions or answers. You need to get back out there. We need to get back on the air. The break is over now get back out there."

In Wyoming, Deborah explained, "In the wintertime when kids can't get outside much the school had a spelling bees and geography bees. Mom would ask Josh and me questions about things like that."

"Cool!" Secret Service seldom say 'cool.'

Kathaleen warily looked at the First Lady and said, "I understand you raise horses."

"Well, I adopt wild mustangs from the Bureau of Land Management and bring them to the ranch where they stay till they get their health back."

"Isn't the Bureau of Land Management under the Secretary of the Interior?"

Beverly smelled the trap as soon as she said horses. "Yes, it is and when Lewis became Secretary of the Interior we felt it may be a conflict of interest so we stopped."

"I see, and it's my understanding you name these horses after Native American tribes. Is that correct?"

"Yes, I do, as a way of paying respect to those tribes. You see the Indians caught and trained those horses. They were called Indian ponies."

Kathaleen said, "I think that's a little racist."

Beverly said, "Kathaleen, I don't really care what you think. You have the right to your opinion." Beverly smiled and then there was silence.

More silence.

Finally Beverly looked at Kathaleen and said, "Do you need to take another commercial break?"

At the office the following day, the staffers told her she did a fantastic interview and wondered why it was cut short for another segment on something else. Beverly said she had no idea and smiled…everyone smiled.

Other requests came in, but they were respectfully declined. The First Lady's office, which was only Beverly and Myrtice Thompson's office, studied the invitations. They decided she didn't need to do interviews on news shows, especially of the political nature. Beverly told Myrtice First Ladies don't actually have a job. In the past First Ladies would have a project that they were focused in on and energetic about. Beverly had a few ideas of what she would like to support. One was foster care and adoptions. This was an issue that was close to her heart. Another was single moms and balancing a family and work.

When Beverly received an invitation to attend the Gateway Project she had Myrtice research the organization. The organization was semi-local, Kansas City and Independence, Missouri. The organization's mission was to help local women, mostly by encouragement and small business loans to open small businesses. It was a seminar and women could attend free of charge. They would discuss issues such as employee relationships, taxes and the education they may need. Beverly accepted the offer. She wouldn't be making any speeches, just meet the ladies and mingle with those attending.

Three black SUVs pulled to the curb next to a side door. There were three agents in each car with the First Lady in the middle of car. Two agents would remain at the side door to secure the door and the other vehicles. Three agents would go to the front and make sure the local police and a security firm screened everyone as they entered. There was a crowd waiting out front to enter.

Cameramen were setting up their cameras as the first three agents walked in. Toby Burke was also inside. He had just put his video recorder on its tripod when he noticed the second group of agents enter. They moved among the seats and tables on the floor. A female agent, Linda Compton, was to check the ladies room and the dressing room. The two men moved into other areas backstage, then went to the side door and stepped outside, holding the door open.

Toby Burke was filming as much as possible, more out of curiosity than anything. The two agents holding the door open said something into a small microphone attached to their sleeve. Toby could see the First Lady enter heading to his left toward the backstage. The First Lady had a female agent walking one pace behind her and the two agents holding the door fell in behind the female Secret Service agent.

Out of the corner of his eye Toby saw a cameraman reach down into his bag and come up with something in his hand. Toby recognized it immediately and screamed, "Gun."

Marsha Jefferson didn't hesitate. She threw herself into the First Lady who crumpled like a ragdoll under the tackle. Jefferson was drawing her service weapon as the first shot rang out. Marsha Jefferson thought her left shoulder had been hit with a baseball bat. She was still going down with the First Lady when her left hip was hit. Jefferson was down on both knees and her right hand. Her weapon was in her left hand and she felt it slipping from her hand. She heard it hit the floor. The last thing Jefferson remembered was screaming, "Kill him." Then there was the gunshot.

Dean Gilmore, the First Lady's security detail leader drew his weapon. People were running about, turning over chairs and tables trying to get away from the gunfire. Gilmore couldn't tell who or where the shooter was. Another two shots rang out in rapid succession. George Dixon the other Secret Service agent doubled over, he had been hit. His bulletproof vest stopped the rounds, but Dixon was sure he had a cracked rib or two.

Then two shots rang out in rapid succession and the assassin crumpled to the floor.

Gilmore grabbed the First Lady and jerked her to her feet. He grabbed the First Lady's right wrist in his left hand, gun in his right and was running with her. Dixon even though he was bent over was pushing her towards the side exit which was held open by two agents.

Beverly looked over her left shoulder and saw Jefferson crumple to the floor. She screamed, "Noooo" and twisted free. She spun around a surprised Dixon and ran back to Jefferson screaming, "Call an ambulance, call an ambulance." Beverly dropped to her knees and began applying pressure to Jefferson's shoulder wound to try to stop the bleeding. "God, please help her, please help her!" Beverly was screaming.

Police were everywhere now along with the Secret Service. From the time Toby Burke screamed, 'Gun.' until Beverly was kneeling beside Jefferson, six seconds had elapsed. Beverly wouldn't let go of Jefferson. The ambulance driver and EMT medic was inside in less than a minute. Jefferson was on a gurney in another minute and in the ambulance in two minutes. Beverly still wouldn't let go. They could hear her praying. Gilmore jumped in back and Dixon jumped in front with the driver. The ambulance accelerated onto the highway going sixty in thirty seconds.

Ronald McIntyre was in his office when the call came in from Gilmore. He raced to the President's office and knocked. The agent inside looked through the peephole and let him in.

"Mr. President, there has been an assassination attempt on the First Lady. One agent is severely wounded and the First Lady is going to the hospital with her. The First Lady wasn't hurt." Before McIntyre was finished he was talking to the President's back, who was out the door and on his way downstairs.

"Mr. President, the First Lady is alright."

The President kept walking to the elevator and stepped inside. "Let's go."

"We need more agents, Mr. President." Lewis looked at McIntyre and the other agent. "Let's go now," said the President. The two agents got on the elevator.

"We won't draw much attention with three people in one car. Maybe we can beat the reporters." They didn't.

Lewis took off his jacket and holding the collar, had it hanging over his shoulder. The two agents casually walked into the hospital. They weren't wearing their trademark sunglasses. No one even recognized the President.

McIntyre called Gilmore on his cell phone, locating him on the sixth floor with the First Lady. She was secure with the other agents. McIntyre approached Gilmore "Who's at the scene?" Gilmore told him Linda Compton and Dean Morrison.

"Call them and seize all video and audio. Secure the entire scene. How did it happen?"

"Someone had a weapon and fired hitting Jefferson twice, left shoulder and left buttock. Dixon was hit twice. They are bandaging up his ribs now downstairs. Jefferson is in surgery. I doubt if they have started. She was unconscious when we arrived. She's lost a lot of blood."

"Was the assassin apprehended?"

"Compton called and said he's dead."

"Who shot him?" asked McIntyre.

"Well, Boss, that's just it, I don't know. I didn't fire and Dixon said he didn't fire. It had to be Jefferson. There was only the three of us. It had to be Jefferson." Then Gilmore paused.

"What?" asked McIntyre.

"I don't see how she did it, but it had to be Jefferson."

"During the investigation we'll find out."

"Yes, Sir."

McIntyre started to walk away when a thought occurred to him "Why is the First Lady here?"

"She wouldn't get out of the ambulance."

"Why was she in the ambulance?"

"Well, first Jefferson tackled her and we were evacuating her outside and she twisted loose from me and Dixon and ran back to Jefferson. She tried to stop the bleeding using pressure and she wouldn't let go. She climbed on the ambulance, we tried to pull her out but couldn't. So I got in back and Dixon got in front and here we are."

McIntyre was looking dumbfounded. "She got away and went back even though another shooter might have been back there?"

"Yes, Sir, she's pretty tricky. I got to hand her that. One second I'm dragging and Dixon is pushing and the next she's back there with Jefferson."

As soon as Lewis got to the room, he went in. McIntyre had stopped and was talking with another agent. Lewis thought his name was Gilmore, but wasn't sure.

As soon as Lewis walked in Beverly saw him. She had been pacing back and forth. She had removed her bloody jacket. Two agents were in the room with her and moved away from the First Lady. She ran to Lewis and threw her arms around him and started sobbing. "Lewis it was awful. I've never been that scared in my life. One of the agents got shot and another one is in the emergency room now. They say he will be alright, but Marsha Jefferson we don't know about. She was hurt real bad, Lewis."

The two agents glanced at each other. They noticed she knew Jefferson's name. That was a surprise, but not a shock to either agent.

Beverly was wringing her hands and said, "It's all my fault. I should have never come here. I wanted her on my detail. It's all my fault, Lewis."

Lewis put his hand on her shoulders and looked her in the eye. "No, it's not your fault; it's a crazy man's fault. It's not yours and it's not Marsha Jefferson's. Now let's sit down. I feel like it's going to be a long night."

McIntyre came into the room. "Mr. President, we should go."

Beverly looked at Lewis and said, "Lewis, I can't leave her. She saved my life."

"We'll be staying. At least till she is out of surgery and resting well."

"Yes, Mr. President. We can secure the two of you here as well as there."

"Thank you, Ronald."

Agent McIntyre stepped back into the hallway. Agent Gilmore asked, "Are they ready to go?"

"They are staying, at least until she comes out of surgery." Gilmore looked around to make sure they were by themselves. "He's different isn't he?"

"They both are. I've never been on the Presidential detail before and neither have you, but yeah, they're different. The First Lady, she wasn't wearing her bullet proof vest was she?"

"No, Sir, she wasn't. Jefferson tried to talk her into it but she wasn't having it."

"Did she tell Jefferson why?"

"Yes, she did" Gilmore looked around to make sure no one was in earshot. "She said it made her boobs look too big. That's what she said. You know, boss, when the shooting starts everyone runs away from it. You never expect them to run to it. Yep, they're different. I hope it never happens but I'll take a bullet for either one of them."

"Jefferson's vest didn't stop the bullet. She was wearing one right?"

"Yes, Sir, She was wearing one. I went into the armpit."

"I see," said McIntyre.

"She did good, Boss," said Gilmore.

Six hours seemed like an eternity to Beverly. She had her hands clasped together and rocking back and forth, back and forth. She was sitting on the edge of her seat. Lewis had his arm around her shoulder trying to comfort her. It was obvious she was in prayer a lot of the time.

The two agents made note of all this and a sense of admiration went with it. They wondered if in the past a President and First Lady would have stayed under these circumstances. They had no way of knowing, neither had ever served on the Presidential detail before.

Agent McIntyre came into the room. He looked at the two agents and the President, then the First Lady. "I spoke to the doctor. She is out of surgery. They are sure they have stopped all the bleeding in both wounds. They are going to bring her up to this floor. She will be in the room across the hall. They will have everything up here shortly, all of the necessary equipment.

"We're going to have around the clock security up here. We'll try not to make it too obvious, but we're going to protect her."

"I'm staying," said Beverly.

McIntyre nodded his head. "I thought you might. Mr. President, I have a plan to get you out of here if you need to leave."

They discussed the plan for a few minutes. It had its drawback, but what plan doesn't.

Thirty minutes later, the surgeon who operated on Jefferson stepped up to a bank of microphones, cleared his throat and said, "The Secret Service agent who was brought here earlier today is out of surgery. Two bullets were removed from her. She is in critical condition but stable at this time."

McIntyre hoped he would talk long enough for other reporters who were at other exits to come to this location. He spoke for twelve minutes. He steadfastly refused to release the agents name citing patient confidentiality. Then questions were raised about the First Lady. The doctor looked surprised as he should be. No one had said anything to him about the First Lady.

McIntyre stepped forward and identified himself as a Federal Agent and said, "I can assure you the First Lady is not here as a patient. She was not admitted here at any time today. The First Lady is in a secure location while we conduct our investigation. This is the first I have heard anything about the First Lady being injured in any way. It is simply not true. We will be moving our agent shortly where she can be closer to her family. As the doctor said we expect her to make a full recovery. Thank you for your time."

Marsha Jefferson was now on the sixth floor. The President was on his way to the new Capital. The First Lady was in the room with Jefferson holding her hand.

Jefferson was still under and heavily sedated. Agent Gilmore was seated in the room facing the door. McIntyre was in the room across the hall with two other agents. Another agent was pacing the hall pretending to talk on a cell phone.

Jefferson didn't know where she was. She was in a black void. She felt or sensed she was floating up towards a less dark place. It seemed as she got close she would sink back down into the darkness again.

"I'm dead; we're both dead, me and the First Lady." Then she came toward the light again only to sink back down again.

"If I could only go up a little more and get out of this." Then she sank back down again.

"I'm not dead. Dead people don't hurt after they die, do they? I hurt but I can't tell anyone. There is no one here but me."

The light came nearer and she broke the surface. She could feel someone holding her hand and she could hear someone praying. She struggled to open her eyes. She managed to open them slightly and then she saw her. Marsha was barely able to speak.

"Thank God, you're alive."

Beverly answered and said, "And thank God you're alive."

CHAPTER FIFTY TWO

TOBY BURKE RIDES

AGAIN...SORT OF

JEREMIAH 8:8

The doctor said it was an anxiety attack. Toby didn't know if he should get a second opinion, nothing like this had ever happened before.

"I want to keep you overnight for observation. We'll have a heart monitor on you." Then the doctor left the emergency room.

Toby didn't like hospitals. He was actually afraid of them. People came here to die. He never thought about people coming here to get well. His knee was throbbing with pain. The doctor said he would order him some pain medication. Toby laid back and closed his eyes. He could replay it all in his mind.

When he saw the man pull out his pistol he screamed 'Gun' and tried to run. He tripped over his camera tripod and went sprawling on the floor. Chairs were being turned over and Toby scrambled under a table. He saw the Secret Service woman tackle the First Lady and get shot. He heard her scream, and then two more shots were fired. Toby didn't know where they went. He heard someone scream 'Kill him.' It sounded like a woman. Then two more shots. He saw the Secret Service agent grab the First Lady and jerk her to her feet and start running to the exit. Another agent was pushing her.

Then the First Lady twisted away from the agents and ran back to the woman agent on the floor. She was screaming, 'Call an ambulance, call an ambulance! Oh God, please help her.'

Toby felt like an elephant was sitting on his chest. He couldn't breathe. His heart was pounding so loud he could hear it in his eardrums. Then they were gone.

Toby was muttering, 'Call an ambulance, call an ambulance!' He was in an ambulance ten minutes later, siren blaring. He didn't think about where they were taking him. He just wished they would drive faster.

At ten A.M. the next morning, Toby was watching the news in his hospital bed. The announcer said the Secret Service agent would be transferred to another hospital. They couldn't confirm if the First Lady was in the hospital or if it was a rumor.

Toby realized he was in the same hospital. Toby wondered if the First Lady was still here. He would try to find out.

At eleven A.M. Toby was released. He had his discharge papers in hand. He stopped at the admissions office. There was a lady behind the counter. Toby removed a hundred dollar bill from his wallet and walked up in front of the lady.

"Ma'am."

She looked at Toby.

"This is a hundred dollar bill. You can have it but you have to tell me the truth, you understand?"

She nodded her head. She looked both ways and behind her to make sure no one was watching.

"What room is the First Lady in?" Toby felt the bill slip from beneath his fingers. He knew he had her.

"I don't know." She folded the bill and put it in her pocket.

"Why don't you know? For crying out loud, you took a hundred dollar bill from me and you don't know?"

"You said I had to tell the truth, didn't you. That's the truth. You got any more money you want to give away?" Toby pulled out his wallet and counted his money. He checked his pockets for change.

"All I have is forty two dollars and fifty cents."

"I usually charge a hundred but I can answer one more question since that's all the money you have."

"Okay, listen very carefully, is the First Lady a patient in this hospital?"

The woman put the money in her pocket.

"I don't know."

"Can you look? There is a computer right there in front of you. Can you just look?"

"The cleaning crew is not allowed to use the computers. Hospital rules."

"You're the cleaning crew?"

"Yes," she replied and picked up the waste paper basket.

"You didn't tell me that."

"You didn't ask and since you don't have any more money I don't guess you can."

"I want my money back. You took it under false pretenses."

"No, I did not."

"Yes, you did. Now I want it back."

"I'm calling security."

Two minutes later, two security guards escorted Toby out of the hospital and told him not to come back. Toby, being a reporter, had to get the last word in, that's an unspoken rule among reporters. "I've been thrown out of better places than this!" he shouted.

He could see the conference center a few blocks away. His car was still parked there. He headed down the sidewalk in front. The pain medication was doing a good job, too good really, it was slowing his thinking.

A black SUV pulled to the curb thirty feet away and parked. Two men wearing navy blue suits and sun glasses got out in front. Two other men dressed the same also got out of the back seat and looked around then waved a second black SUV forward. Two men in navy blue seats got out of the second vehicle as a third black SUV pulled to the curb. Two men dressed the same got out of this vehicle and waited.

A woman wearing a straw cowboy hat and mirrored sun glasses got out of the middle SUV then a very large man also wearing a cowboy hat got out of the vehicle and started walking very fast toward the hospital entrance with four men in front and four men behind them.

When Toby was three feet away he recognized her. He had seen her photo when he was in Kerney, Wyoming. She's trying to sneak in thought Toby. When she was even with Toby he put his hand around her elbow to stop her and said, "Nice try, Deborah."

He had unintentionally spun her around. The agents started to react. Toby never saw the roundhouse right that hit him between the eyes. Someone turned out the lights.

Toby Burke heard a phone ringing. He slowly opened his eyes. He was on the couch in his apartment. How did I get here he wondered. His head hurt. He felt his forehead. There was a knot there. The phone kept ringing. Toby picked up the phone.

"Hello."

"I am so sorry," said a very quiet voice.

"Deborah?"

A few seconds later. "Yes, this is Deborah. How did you know it was me?"

"Who else would be calling me to tell me they were sorry."

"I just wanted to say sorry."

"How is your Mom?"

"She's fine. She wanted to tell you hello."

"Why is she in the hospital?"

"She isn't," answered Deborah.

"Why is she there?"

"Because Marsha is there. Mom is not going to leave Marsha. She saved her life."

"I know, I saw it happen."

"You did?"

"Yes, I did. She was very brave."

"You won't put it in the paper will you? Neither needs to be bothered right now."

"Deborah, I'm a reporter, what do you think?"

"I think you'll do the right thing."

Toby Burke needed to think on that. In twenty four hours he had seen two heroic acts. Both by women, while he, a man, cowered under a table thinking he was having a heart attack. It didn't make him feel better when he got beat up by a girl. Of course, he wouldn't mention any of that to the First Family's daughter.

"How about you giving me an interview?"

"Okay, I can do that."

"When?"

"Well, I'm going back to Kerney tonight. Have you ever been there?"

"Been there, done that; didn't stay long enough to buy a t-shirt."

"You're funny. We could do it over the phone."

"Let me get some paper and a pen."

His first question was, "How did I get home?"

"The Secret Service found your press pass and your discharge papers. I recognized your name and asked them to take you home."

They talked for two hours. Toby knew no one had really interviewed a member of the First Family. He submitted his article the following week. His article began with a question.

Question: What makes America, America?

Answer: The family.

CHAPTER FIFTY THREE

THE INVESTIGATION

The investigation team from Omaha, Nebraska arrived in Independence. Agent McIntyre met the three men and three women and led them to a small office. They were not here to ruin anyone's career. They wanted to know what happened and to try to prevent something like this from happening again.

Agent McIntyre started out by telling the team that all audio and video records had been seized. All weapons were secured for examination and ballistic tests. He also had interviewed all the agents on the scene with the exception of Marsha Jefferson.

He suggested everyone return to the scene and conducts a walk through and try to reconstruct the events of the previous day. He also had the personal file on all of the agents.

They had a stand in for the First Lady and Jefferson, agents who were not at the scene.

When everyone arrived at the crime scene the agents set up cameras to film the walk through. They intended to compare it to the real event. All of this took the better part of the day. An ambulance was outside for the evacuation.

Late in the afternoon, they started the interviews. They started with agent Gilmore and ended with agent Compton. She was not in the conference center's main auditorium when it happened. They didn't want to leave any stone unturned.

The next morning, they took the personal files of the three agents around the First Lady and studied them. The team wanted to get a better feel for the agent's personality. Then they would view the video.

Agent McIntyre agreed with Gilmore and Dixon that agent Jefferson had somehow heroically shot and killed the assailant even though she was severely wounded. There were several things in Jefferson's file that raised eyebrows 'Too aggressive' was the most obvious, 'Displays anger' was another.

They watched the first video. When the team reached the point where the First Lady entered they noticed Jefferson. Other than being African-American she was taller than most women by at least two inches. They noticed her looking around, surveying her surroundings. What jumped out at them was that she moved with the grace of a cat. They could tell there was speed and strength built into her frame. They heard 'Gun' and Jefferson became a blur on the video. They stopped and reversed it and played it again. They did this over and over.

"She's fast, no doubt about it," said one of the investigators. McIntyre felt pride well up inside of him. They were praising one of his agents and that meant a job well done. He had picked her for the go team.

They watched Jefferson tackle the First Lady and tried to cover her body with her own. A football player would have been proud. They played this over and over. Then they saw her drawing her weapon. It was a fluid motion that only comes from hours and hours of practice, practice and more practice.

When the bullet struck her in the shoulder they slowed the video down. Muscles could be seen rippling along her arm, shoulder and side. They stopped the video.

"The bullet went into her armpit," said McIntyre. Several were nodding their head in agreement.

Then the second shot into the hip. The muscles rippling even more. They saw the weapon slipping from her grasp and falling to the floor. The First Lady was obscured at this point with Jefferson above her on her knees and one hand on the floor. This video didn't show anymore because the camera didn't cover the floor area. Neither the gun nor the First Lady was visible. They looked at other videos from different angles but nothing revealing. The videos didn't show Jefferson managing to pick her weapon up and somehow firing.

The last tape was more revealing than the others. It belonged to Toby Burke, the man who screamed, 'Gun.' Somehow his tripod was knocked over and was at floor level. The agents had to tilt their heads all the way over to watch the video.

The video started right side up and showed the tackle. The camera was on its side about the time the weapon hit the floor. The First Lady's head also could be seen hitting the floor. Someone said, "That had to hurt."

They could see a hand grab the weapon, lift it, point and fire two shots in the blink of an eye. The hand was in the shadow of Jefferson's body. At first everyone assumed it to be Jefferson, but this hand had a man's watch with a wide leather band, the kind bikers wore years ago. The shots came almost as one. At normal speed it looked as one shot, but slowed down two muzzle blasts could be seen.

McIntyre said, "Stop the video."

The video was put on pause. McIntyre rubbed his face with both hands and let out a deep breath. Everyone was looking at him.

"The First Lady."

The other agents didn't grasp what he was saying or implying.

"That's who shot the assailant."

"Who?" asked the team leader.

"The First Lady shot him. Back the tape up and you can see her watchband."

They backed the video up and could see clearly the watchband. They had played the videos with the volume off after the first video. There was too much noise because of people screaming and chairs being turned over when people were trying to run away.

Now they played the video with the volume on. When the pistol hit the floor they heard Jefferson scream, "Kill him."

She was looking directly into the First Lady's eyes. It was obvious she had directed this to the First Lady. The First Lady grabbed the weapon in a classic two hand hold, pointed, and fired two shots, literally in the blink of an eye.

Everyone sat in stunned silence. No one wanted to ask the obvious question. McIntyre finally broke the silence and asked the dreaded question. "What do we do now?"

"We don't know," was the response. They put another video in and watched the rest of it. When the First Lady twisted away and ran back to Jefferson everyone leaned forward in their chair and watched. No one said a word. It was just like the walk through the previous day. They turned the video off and sat back in their chairs.

The team leader finally spoke up. "The evacuation didn't go as it should have. We need to put more of that into training. The protected may go somewhere you don't want them to go. The video where the First Lady shot the assassin should not, I repeat, should not ever see the light of day. Does anyone disagree? If you do say it now or forever hold your peace." There were no objections.

McIntyre said, "Somehow Jefferson managed to kill the assassin. Is that what we are saying here?"

The team leader looked at the other investigators. All nodded their heads in agreement.

"I believe we are all in agreement."

"The reporters are already asking for the video footage. What do we tell them?"

The team leader let out a breath of air before saying "Tell them we will return them…eventually."

McIntyre looked at the group of investigators and asked, "Do we talk to her about it?"

"Let's think about it. We'll meet again tomorrow and will let you know. If we do it will be off the record. Is everybody in agreement on that?"

Everyone nodded their heads in agreement.

"Is she still at the hospital with Jefferson?"

"Yes, she is. She hasn't left."

The following day a decision had been reached. One agent would speak to the First Lady. If she was forthcoming fine, if she wasn't, that was fine also. Agent Ronald McIntyre would be the agent. She was more familiar with him.

McIntyre went to the hospital and waited until the doctor was with Jefferson. Beverly would leave Jefferson's side before the doctor came in and return when the doctor left. The doctor didn't know that the First Lady was in the building.

Agent McIntyre chatted with her for a few minutes. He asked how she was feeling.

"I'm okay under the circumstances. Marsha seems to be getting stronger."

"Can you tell me what happened?"

"Well, everything happened so fast, and it seems like such a long time ago now." McIntyre nodded his head like he understood.

"We're fortunate that no one else was hurt."

The First Lady nodded in agreement.

McIntyre continued, "Agent Jefferson is a very dedicated agent. I'm thankful agent Gilmore was able to shoot the assailant." Beverly's head came up. She had been looking at the floor. She looked at McIntyre and said, "Agent Gilmore?"

"Well, it had to be Gilmore, right? Dixon was hurt, Jefferson was hurt. It had to be Gilmore, right?" The First Lady didn't answer.

"Ma'am do you know otherwise?"

"No, I don't know. It all happened so fast."

"Well, if you can think of anything else please let me know."

Beverly nodded her head and went to the door and pulled it open a few inches. She stood there for a few seconds then closed the door. She leaned her forehead against the door and looked at the floor.

"You know the truth don't you?"

She started crying. McIntyre went near her and put his hand on her shoulder and said, "Why don't we talk about it. Maybe you will feel better."

They talked for twenty minutes. McIntyre took no notes. Beverly ended it by saying "I just wanted it to stop. It was the only way to keep anyone else from getting hurt."

"I understand, Ma'am. Have you ever fired a pistol before?" He knew to fire two accurate shots under duress was difficult.

Beverly nodded her head and said, "I learned how to shoot when I was six years old. My grandfather and my daddy taught me how. I have a colt .45."

"Well, the model 1911 semi auto is a fine pistol," said McIntyre.

"Mine is a model 1873 single action army revolver."

"The colt peacemaker"

"Yes, it belonged to my great, great, great grandfather. I might have put one too many greats in there. I get confused on all that."

"The horse thief?"

"Yes, I see word gets around." Then she smiled for the first time.

"Ma'am, one thing the Secret Service does well is keep secrets."

"I just don't believe the American people should find out I killed someone, don't you agree."

"And they won't, Ma'am. It is obvious to me Agent Jefferson somehow managed to kill the assassin."

Agent McIntyre rejoined the police investigation team. They met at the morgue. The FBI would be the lead investigation service. The Kansas City Police Force had a representative present.

The assailant was on a table and had already been autopsied. He had been fingerprinted after the shooting. The medical examiner said, "Male victim, 68 inches tall, weight one hundred and fifty seven pounds. Appears to have been in fair condition at the time of death. I would estimate his age to be fifty five to sixty years of age. No dental work of any significance.

"Cause of death, two gunshot wounds. One center mass of the chest hitting the heart and one in the forehead. The wound in the chest would have been fatal but not instant. Wound in forehead would have been instantaneous. No indication which wound was first.

"There is no distinguishing marks, tattoos or birthmarks visible. X-rays showed no previous broken bones. The deceased had no identification on his person at time of death. All internal organs appear to be normal. Blood test revealed no illegal substances in the blood stream or stomach. That concludes the autopsy. Any questions?"

There were none.

Everyone met outside to discuss the investigation. The FBI agent who had identified himself as Lee Martin said, "We ran his fingerprints and didn't get a match. We have sent photos to local police departments. We haven't received anything back yet."

"Excuse me," said Agent McIntyre.

"Yes, you have a point to make?"

"Why aren't we sending it nationwide, why just local?" asked McIntyre.

"We believe it was someone local. We put it nationwide and we'll get a million tips and they'll all be wrong."

Then the FBI agent continued, "His clothing was pretty much off the rack at any clothing store. The same with the shoes and belt. He had no watch, no change, and no keys to a vehicle or home.

"We have checked all exterior videos in stores in the area. All vehicles within a mile radius have been checked for ownership. We have a body and that's it."

Agent McIntyre said, "It's the same inside. We have come up with nothing. We can't rule out the suspect somehow picked the lock and defeated the alarm system but that would take a lot of training. Not everyone can do something like that. We are interrogating the personnel of the private security company and have run background checks and have ended up without a clue. He had no press pass on his person. Each signed in when entering. We also checked when they left. One had to be medically evacuated with a possible heart attack. We are missing one name. We checked the news organization assigned that press pass. He was thirty years old. This man was obviously not him. We checked his residence. His vehicle is in the carport. This leads me to believe the assailant somehow obtained his press pass and entered. What he did with the press pass is still a mystery."

The Kansas City police investigator spoke in clipped sentences.

"Checked bus line, no men departed. Local taxi, no results. Motel and hotel, no results. Probably walked. Someone may have driven him. Can't rule out either."

The FBI agent said, "We need to keep working this. Ballistic test show four shots from the assailant's weapon. Two shots from the Secret Service weapon. You need to tell your agent that was impressive shooting.”

McIntyre nodded his head in agreement. “I’ll make sure I pass that along.”

The FBI agent continued, “Right now we have nothing but a John Doe in the morgue.”

Some things remain a mystery regardless of how much you search. How the weapon was sneaked into the building was number one on the list. What happened to the press pass was also a concern.

The missing photo Journalist was solved three days later. His body was found behind a vacant building. He had been stabbed to death. The Kansas City Police took over that investigation. Everyone concerned was sure the murderer was also the assassin. They still looked for clues.

Seven days after Marsha Jefferson was shot, she was wheeled out of the hospital. She was going to Birmingham, Alabama for rehab. There would be no hero’s welcome for her. Secret Service agents liked to remain secret.

Beverly said, “Goodbye and see you soon,” and hugged her neck and then said, “Thank you, for saving my life.”

Marsha said, “Thank you, for saving my life. I will be back.”

CHAPTER FIFTY FOUR

BAD NEWS

President MacDonald was seated behind his desk on the eighth floor of the U.S. Capitol; extra chairs had been brought in from the cafeteria to seat everyone.

"I'm afraid I have some bad news for everyone. Our allies and NATO have respectfully informed me that their nation will not offer assistance if and when we go to war, except one."

"Mr. President, did they say why? We came to their assistance when they needed us in World War II. I don't understand them doing this when we need them the most." Alex Jacobs had asked the question.

"Well, it's quite simple. They are afraid that whoever did this may use a nuclear weapon on them. They didn't exactly come out and say that but the implication was clear," said the President.

"What are we going to do about this, Mr. President? Are we going to have to go it alone?" asked General Stewart of the U.S. Army.

"General Stewart, I'm afraid the answer to that is yes. We are going to have to go it alone. This is our fight. No one is offering help. This is our war and ours alone and I can assure you we will prevail. I don't know how yet, but we will prevail. America is virtually standing alone."

"Mr. President." Director Rosenburg of the Central Intelligence Agency had his hand raised.

"Yes, Mr. Rosenburg."

"Did I understand you to say all of our allies have declined support and then you added, except one?"

"That is correct."

"Can you tell us who is offering their support?"

"Israel."

Every day started with the Central Intelligence agency's daily briefing. The world's situation was presented to the President. This was region by region with the Mideast always first, followed by Europe, then China. Enemy troop movements or suspected weapons displacement. It appeared the military in all of the nations of the world had moved back to their normal posture. It had taken five weeks for Russia to move away from their neighbors borders.

Five weeks without a day off was taking its toll on the new President. The next briefing was always the hardest for him. This was the casualty and damage briefing. The numbers continued to climb. Americans were dying every day from radiation sickness. Bodies were still being found in the rubble. The count was over two hundred thousand. More people lived in Washington D.C. than in the entire state of Wyoming. The number of buildings destroyed or severely damaged was overwhelming. There was no way to put a monetary value on the damage.

It was reported to the President that no accurate count of the number of dead could ever be established. Untold numbers were simple vaporized.

The next briefing was more concrete. The stock market had opened a month ago after one week closure. The numbers had plummeted. This was expected and everyone hoped the downward spiral would slow and finally stop. It did last week but trillions had been lost. It had actually made a few gains, but almost every stock was at levels not seen in over two decades.

The banks fared better. There was no run on the banks that had been anticipated. The cost of gold had quadrupled and silver had tripled, and those costs were on the way down.

His last briefing concerned the violence in the large cities. The National Guard had performed miracles. The State Governors in over thirty states had sent the Guard home. There were a few hotspots mainly Baltimore, Chicago, New Orleans, Los Angeles and Cleveland. Lewis noticed those cities had the toughest gun laws and wondered how law abiding citizens were coping.

CHAPTER FIFTY FIVE

CONGRESS

The new congress was scheduled to be seated in ten days. Lewis was eagerly looking forward to the day he would have a seated congress. He needed help, help to shoulder the load. He hoped and prayed he would get it in the new congress.

When the election results came in political analyst were somewhat surprised. Twenty six Independents won senate seats. Democrats took thirty three and Republicans garnered thirty six seats. What surprised most was socialist won five seats. The American people were getting fed up with the Democratic and Republican parties.

The Independents won one hundred and thirty representatives. The Republicans won one hundred and fifty three seats; the Democrats won one hundred and thirty seven seats. Fifteen seats went to socialist and green party seats.

The President wondered if the Independents knew how much power they wielded if they voted as a block, they could be the deciding factor in any law passed.

There were several court filings on recounts but Lewis saw no radical change in the numbers.

The Senate was sworn in first using the Supreme Courtroom. The house was sworn in groups of four, a hundred and eight at a time. One Representative was in the court for a recount. The winner would be sworn in later. It took over four hours to swear everyone in.

After being sworn in each member of congress was given a number. There would be a drawing of numbers. There would be twelve numbers selected from the House and twelve from the Senate.

Four Republican, four Democrat and four Independents were drawn in each House of Congress. After the House drawings, Lewis spoke to the twelve who had been selected. "I want the twelve of you to come up with a name for a Vice President. You will select five candidates. Those five will then be approved by the twelve from the Senate. If someone passes both selection committees that name will go before the entire Senate for approval. In other words I will not be selecting the Vice President, you will, so choose carefully."

It took three weeks for the Representatives to select five candidates. The Senate only took one week. They forwarded only one name for approval. Everyone hoped it worked because they would start over if it didn't.

The news media covered the hearing in its entirety. This had never been done this way before. This was a unique situation to American politics. In the past the President had always picked a friend or political ally. This President had nothing to do with it except put it into motion. The candidate was approved in one day.

CHAPTER FIFTY SIX

THE VICE PRESIDENT

The new Vice President was named Juanita Hernandez. Political analysts pointed out all three parties were trying to please the growing Hispanic population and the women voters. She fit the bill for all three parties in both categories.

She was the former Governor of New Mexico. She had served in the House and the Senate. She was fifty eight years old, had three children and was a widow. Her husband died on September the eleventh. It was reported she didn't bring a knife to a gunfight. Her family had lived in New Mexico since the early seventeen hundreds. It was also reported she was a workaholic. The new President intended to find out.

Lewis met with her within minutes of being sworn in. He asked her to take care of two things right away. The Supreme Court Lewis had selected needed to be approved by the Senate. The next would be the hardest. Get America back on its feet. Get America back to work. Unemployment was at an all-time high since Washington had been destroyed. He asked her to come up with recommendations that could be implemented immediately.

She already had two. Increase the border patrol and establish an anti-gang task force that could go city to city. She knew the elderly were being preyed on by the gangs. The local police were overwhelmed by large gangs. The Federal government could fight this problem along with the local police cooperation.

The new Vice President said, "When I was Governor, I asked for more border patrol, but was turned down. I think the National Guard did a great job after Washington with the rioting and looting. But I think these gangs are just licking their wounds. I can guarantee you they will be back. The drugs coming across the border is supplying these gangs. The border patrol can help stop that. I remember when I was a young woman I would see people from Mexico working in the fields and packing houses. I actually admired them. They did back breaking work for a lot less than minimum wages. They would live ten and twelve people to a one room apartment. They only kept enough for their basic needs. Now it's the drug cartels that are using them to transport drugs. It is human trafficking. They are now coming for federal and state benefits, and a large number are drug cartel members and criminals. We have to stop it. We have to close our borders. Who knows, the Washington bomb could have been smuggled in to the United States from Mexico or Canada."

They decided that twenty thousand Border Patrol and two thousand anti-gang agents would be a start in National Security and Crime Prevention. It would put twenty two thousand people to work.

He asked her to present other proposals to get the country back on its feet. She promised to have other suggestions within the week. He asked her to sit in with him for the briefing from the director of the FBI.

The FBI director, Hiram Wilcox, arrived a few minutes later.

"Mr. President, we have been able to confirm where the bomb was placed. We looked at thousands of hours of video and found five at businesses approximately five to ten miles away from the blast. We were able to triangulate those images and where those lines converged was the location.

"Let me show you on a map. It was on the rooftop of a five story building in a direct line of sight with the capital, one mile away. We believe since the area was cordoned off for a distance of three miles on Monday it had to be already in place the night of the State of the Union Address."

"We had already assumed that, correct?"

"Yes, Sir," said the director.

"But your investigation doesn't answer the crucial question, who did it? Are we any closer on that?"

"No, Mr. President, I'm afraid we're not any closer on that."

SEARCHING FOR THE TRUTH

A week later Director Hiram Wilcox of the FBI briefed the President. The Vice President also sat in on the meeting.

"Mr. President, we have some new information on the nuclear weapon. Not evidence mind you but information. I want you to keep in mind the crime scene was vaporized. It may not lead us anywhere, but it is information."

"I understand about the crime scene being gone along with a lot of other buildings in the area," said the President.

The FBI Director nodded his head in agreement.

"We believe someone let them do this or was tricked into allowing it to happen."

"So you're saying it could be either is that correct."

"Yes, Mr. President."

"Please continue."

"We have located a few people who worked in the building. We asked them if they noticed anything suspicious or unusual in the weeks leading up to the event."

"And?"

"We found a guard that worked there."

"You are working on the assumption someone allowed it to happen or actively participated, am I correct?"

"Yes, Mr. President."

"And what did this guard tell you?"

"The guard said the only thing he noticed was an air conditioning unit was replaced."

"When?"

"It was delivered on a Friday. Two Friday's before the State of the Union Address."

"So, it could have been in place how many days? If that was it."

"Twelve days. It was delivered on January 27th."

"So, it would have been in place before the area was secured, is that right?"

"Yes, Sir, that started on the third of February. A Friday after most go home."

"What do you think? Do you think that was it?" asked the President.

"Well, I don't really know to be honest with you. No one else noticed anything strange or unusual leading up to President Carson's address."

"So we're going on the assumption that was it?"

"Mr. President, we have nothing else to go on. The Security Guard said the maintenance supervisor told him the air conditioner was being replaced and to let them use the freight elevator. These units are very large and there are several units on the roof. The unit is almost five feet high and six or seven feet long."

"Let me interrupt you again. Will a nuclear weapon fit in something that size?"

"Mr. President, I have been informed it is possible."

"Please continue."

"On the following Friday, the third, the men left and said they would return on Monday. Only two of the men returned, not all of them. The guard doesn't remember if there were five or six delivering it and putting it in place. We're assuming they have to remove the old unit. The actual connecting may be only one or two people. We called several heat and air companies and they tell us they pretty much do the same thing."

"So the security guard doesn't know if the old unit was removed?"

"He said he didn't believe so, but he's not sure. The maintenance supervisor would probably have a key to the building. You know, where they could work after hours. They could have moved it over the weekend. He just doesn't know. This is a private security company. The guard is in his sixties and he works four days on and four days off."

"I see," said the President.

The guard thinks the maintenance supervisors name was Bob but he's not sure. He's only been there for three weeks. We talked to other employees and they gave us a name, not a full name, and it wasn't Bob."

"So the witness isn't reliable, right?"

"Who knows? You know how witnesses are. Maybe the guy told him his name was Bob. We'll never know."

"Is there any other possibilities?"

"Only one I can think of," said the director.

"And that would be?" asked the President.

"It may have been in the basement and at six o'clock put it in the freight elevator and send it to the top floor and disable the elevator where no one could use it."

"So the air conditioner could be just that an air conditioning unit?"

"That is correct, Mr. President."

"In either scenario you presented, wouldn't the maintenance supervisor be the prime suspect?"

"Yes, Mr. President, he would."

"Would there be some sort of paperwork or authorization form for work like that?"

"The paperwork would probably be in the building that doesn't exist anymore."

"Did the guard see the maintenance supervisor on Monday or Tuesday?"

The FBI Director let out a breath of air before answering "He doesn't believe so, but he's not sure. The guard was in the lobby and the maintenance office was in the basement. The guard let them use the freight elevator. The keys are left for the next shift."

"You're saying he might have left after work Friday. He could have been on the other side of the world when it happened."

"That's correct, Mr. President."

No one said anything for at least a minute. Then the FBI Director continued "Look at how long it took to find out which building was used."

"Don't blame yourself or the FBI. You have worked around the clock. You did the best you could."

"Thank you, Mr. President."

"Did the guard get a description of the van or the men who delivered the air conditioning unit?"

"The guard said it was a moving van. He doesn't remember any markings. He said the men looked like brothers or relatives."

"Brothers, what did he mean by that?"

"All of them resembled each other."

"I see, like a family run business."

"Yes, Sir, he said all of them were about the same size and weight. All had black hair. There is one other thing."

"What's that?" asked the President.

"The guard said, "they spoke English but as they were getting in the van, the one that moved the crate in said that one of them said something in another language that he didn't recognize."

"Excuse me, Mr. Director" interrupted the Vice President.

"Yes, Ma'am."

"Would the guard have recognized Spanish?"

"We asked him that and he said he would. He's married to a Hispanic and he said and I quote, 'When she gets mad she cuts loose in Spanish.' His words not mine, Ma'am. He said it definitely was not Spanish."

"I understand. I do the same thing."

"We are on the lookout for the maintenance man even as we speak."

"You have to find him. This may be the only link to who did this," said the President.

"We will do whatever is possible to find him. We will have no boundaries. If he is found in another country we will bring him back. I can assure you of that, Mr. President. No country on the face of the earth will be able to protect him if he's still alive."

"Do you think he's alive?"

"I think someone paid him a large sum of money and then disposed of him. They wouldn't want any loose ends, if it was him."

"We really don't know that do we?" asked the Vice President.

"No, Ma'am, not for sure."

"Question," said the President. "Have you ruled the guard out?"

"We haven't ruled anyone out, Mr. President."

"Question," said the Vice President. "If the weapon was in the air conditioning unit do you think the two men on Monday and we don't know if they were there on Tuesday, were setting the timer?"

"I think they were guarding it. That's why I think that's where it was," said the director.

"So they hid it in plain sight?" asked the President.

"Sometimes that is the best place to hide something."

After the FBI Director left, Lewis thought, 'They hid it in plain sight, sometimes that's the best place to hide something.' He would have to remember that.

That afternoon one of California's two new Senators was shown into Lewis's office. The two warmly shook hands and Lewis asked him to have a seat.

"Mr. President, I want to discuss the new anti-tank weapon the military has in the works."

"Senator, that program has been cancelled."

"It would mean thousands of jobs in California," said the Senator.

"And the loss of thousands in Alabama and South Carolina."

"I see you have been somewhat appraised of this," said the Senator.

"Yes, I have. It cost three times more than the existing system. It has an accuracy problem and a high failure rate. Also it is a different launcher size. All the launchers that are already in place would have to be replaced. It would cost billions to bring this system on board. I'm not going to do it. That's all there is to it, Senator."

The Senator pounded the arm of his chair and said, "I demand you reinstate the program."

Lewis stood up and leaned on his desk and looked the Senator in the eye. At six feet, four inches Lewis was an imposing figure.

"You demand…you demand. Listen Mister, where I come from if you demand something you better be willing to back it up. Are you willing to try?"

The Senator said nothing as he squirmed in his chair.

"That's what I thought."

He turned to the Secret Service agent in the office and said, "Show this…this gentleman out, please."

"Yes, Mr. President."

"I'll go see the Vice President. Everyone knows she runs the country, not you," said the Senator.

"Her answer will be 'No way Jose,'" said Lewis.

When the Secret Service agent returned after escorting the Senator out of the building, he cleared his throat to get the President's attention. Lewis looked up at the agent.

"Should we warn the Vice President?"

"That won't be necessary. Someone should warn the Senator."

The agent smiled. "I started too, but then I thought, live and let learn."

When Lewis finally made it to the President's quarters which were only fifteen feet, Beverly met him at the door.

"Another long day?"

"Yeah, another long day, but I had a little fun earlier today," and then he told her about the Senator from California.

"I talked with Josh this afternoon. He's graduating six months early," said Beverly. She tried to speak with each of them every day.

"Really!" replied Lewis.

"Well, since he's not playing football now he's doubled up on his courses. I understand the Secret Service not wanting him to play football. I think he is doing it to get into the Air Force. He wants to be a pilot so bad. It scares me Lewis."

"Beverly it scares me, too. I remember his sixth birthday party when he got the book on planes. It has been his dream since then. He'll be fine."

"Lewis, we are at war aren't we."

"Yes, but we don't know who we are at war with."

CHAPTER FIFTY SEVEN

JUANITA HERNANDEZ

PROVERBS 5:10

The President's first request was a breeze. Congress went along with the ranking Judge from each district They were more comfortable with the known verses the unknown. If they didn't approve these Judges who would this new president send up for confirmation? Not only that, the district courts had each section of the country represented. They weren't bothered by twelve Judges. Both parties had lost a lot of cases 5 to 4. This stuck in the craw of a lot of people, both citizens and politicians alike. Now it had to be 7 to 5 or it was sent back down to a lower court of appeals.

The second, getting the economy back on its feet was a daunting task. She was going to have to think out of the box on this one. She was good at that. When you have a tough challenge you simply had to get tougher.

She decided she would not present any moral issues to the President. Those would be left up to Congress and the States. Her own personal opinion on abortion, gay and lesbian rights and immigration would be set aside for now. Her mission was getting the country back on its feet.

The Vice President knew when the Federal Government and she hated the term, 'Created jobs' you had to pay for it later and the cost was unbelievable. She believed the best way was for the Federal Government to simply stay out of the way. It makes no sense to borrow more money to pay for it. Just because the Federal Government had done it in the past didn't mean you had to do it that way now. In the past it always failed and never accomplished its stated goal. The Federal Government already owed twenty trillion dollars and it was climbing at a rate unprecedented in world history. No country had ever owed this much money and survived. Manufacturing jobs were leaving and going to other countries. The primary reason was lower taxes and cheaper labor. High paying jobs were leaving and minimum wage jobs were taking their place or no jobs at all. Only people with high paying jobs were actually paying taxes. A large number of people were getting more in refunds that they paid in. Most got all they paid in back in refunds. This had to stop. Everyone should have some skin in the game.

She personally knew people perfectly able to work but chose not to. They had rather live off the other people who chose to work. It was nothing more than a game of numbers, eventually you ran out of money and not one got anything.

The Vice President knew the nation was at war and had the smallest military since World War II.

She would recommend a larger military to cope with the storm that was gathering on the horizon. Not knowing what enemy force the United States would be fighting was beyond her scope of knowledge. The new Vice President called and made an appointment with the President.

THE CARDS ARE ON THE TABLE

When the Vice President arrived she was quickly ushered into the President's office. He stood and walked around his desk and shook her hand.

"Mr. President, thank you for seeing me."

"Please, call me Lewis. Do you mind if I call you Juanita?"

"No, please do," answered the Vice President.

"Before we start I want to tell you we will be moving you out of this complex. I don't want to run the risk of losing both of us at the same time."

"Oh and where will I be moving to?"

"Kansas City, it's actually not that far. Thanks to the Drug Enforcement Agency. They seized an office building last year from a drug cartel. It was supposed to be auctioned off. Lucky for us Alex Jacobs found out about it. Furniture, paintings and everything. From what I understand it is quite plush. We are establishing secure phone lines even as we speak. It will be far easier to secure than here. It sits by itself on twenty acres. It will be a few weeks before you will be able to move in."

"That sounds nice. It is quite cramped here, not that I am complaining."

"Now, please tell me what you have come up with."

"Before we start there is something I would like to point out, actually a few things."

"Okay, let's hear them," said the President.

"I want you to think about two words."

"Two words. I don't understand?"

"Provide and promote."

"Okay, provide and promote."

"They have different meanings, would you agree?"

"Yes, the meanings are different."

"In the preamble of the Constitution it says provide for the common defense. Promote the general welfare, yet it seems that has changed, the meaning, to provide the general welfare. The Federal Government was never intended to provide the general welfare. It was supposed to promote the general welfare.

"The second thing I want to point out is the Constitution gives certain powers to the Federal Government. All power not given to the Federal Government by the Constitution is left to the individual states or the people. That is the tenth amendment in the Bill of Rights. The Federal Government has been grabbing enormous power that should be left to the States. They have done it for so many years that everyone thinks it's supposed to be that way. The United States isn't a nation of three hundred and twenty million people. We are a nation of fifty states."

"I see I need to read the Constitution more," said the President.

"Everyone needs to read it more," answered the Vice President, and then she continued. "The Federal Government has been extorting the States for as long as I can remember. The Federal Government passes a law, a law they shouldn't have passed in the first place, and if the States object the Federal Government politely tells them if you don't do what we say we will withhold funds."

"I can think of a few times I have heard that," injected the President.

"A few times? You must live in the middle of nowhere," said the Vice President.

"Actually, I do. I live in the middle of nowhere," said the President.

"I forget about that," said the Vice President and she blushed.

The President smiled.

"Another thing, the Supreme Court and Court of Appeals, who are supposed to make sure the other two branches of government don't overstep their bounds. The court can't legislate, or at least they're not supposed to."

"You know what I think," said the President interrupting her.

"What do you think, Mr. President?"

"The three branches of government are trying to grab power. Power that belongs to some other branch of government. It reminds me of what would happen if you took three, three year olds and put them in a room with one toy. Each one tries to take it away from the other. Yes, I agree that the Federal Government is trying to control every aspect of American lives. They act like people can't manage their own lives."

"That's right and that brings me to the last item I want to point out before we get started. Do you know what the first three words in the Constitution are?"

"We the People," answered the President.

"Very good," she said with a smile. "Would you believe most people don't know that? Did you realize the constitutional amendments are only twenty to forty words long?"

"I have to admit I didn't know that one," said the President.

"Yet Congress passes bills and regulations that are sometimes twenty thousand pages long and then add more when they realize they left something out."

"How can you leave something out of twenty thousand pages?"

"Good question. Maybe the first twenty thousand pages were nothing more than a smoke screen to hide things they don't want the American people to know."

WE THE PEOPLE

"Can we get started?" asked the President.

"You may not want to hear it, but I will tell you it is all facts. I haven't written it all down so please bear with me and please forgive me if I ramble."

"I know it is going to be bad but let's get it out into the open," said the President.

"Do you know what the unemployment numbers are?" She eyed the President when she said it.

"I saw those numbers yesterday and if I remember correctly it was twelve percent."

"Those are the correct numbers but they are incorrect."

"How can that be?" asked the President.

"After your unemployment runs out you are no longer counted."

"Why?"

"Because it will make politicians look bad if the real numbers were published."

"I think everyone should count. I would hate to think that the government wouldn't count me. That needs to change. I mean the truth is the truth. How are you going to do something about it when you don't even know the truth?"

"I agree."

"What are the real numbers?"

"I don't know. I would guess it's close to thirty percent."

"Thirty percent! You got to be kidding."

"No, almost fifty percent of the American people are receiving something from the government."

"How can we change that?"

"Okay, for starters we have to lure businesses back to the United States. This will increase jobs and jobs increase revenue," said the Vice President.

"Okay, that's a given; now how do we do it?"

"Corporate income tax here is thirty eight percent. Second highest in the world. Some say it is the highest. Businesses leave because of high tax rates. We have to lower it drastically. If we lower it, businesses in foreign countries will move here providing more jobs. More jobs mean more tax payers."

"What rate are you proposing?"

"Twenty five percent. This is lower than most countries. It would benefit those companies to move here. I had rather have two companies paying twenty five percent than have one company paying thirty nine percent."

The President nodded his head in approval then said, "Please, continue."

"We know we are at war, yet our military is smaller than it has been in seventy years."

Lewis said, "I've been told that technology has taken care of that."

The Vice President let out a breath of air and said, "No, technology exists that replaces a nineteen year old pissed off Marine."

The President raised his eyebrows and leaned back in his chair. She doesn't bring a knife to a gun fight.

"Okay, how do we do that?"

"We reinstitute the draft. If we knew who we would be fighting it might be different. I'm assuming you don't know the nation responsible for what happened in Washington. I know we have the usual suspects but don't know for sure."

"Your assumption is correct."

"For starters I am recommending two hundred thousand. This serves two purposes. Number one is jobs and number two it sends a message to our enemy."

"And what message is that?" asked the President.

"We're going to come and get you." Lewis liked her more and more.

"It appears the senate made a good choice selecting you. Now I need you to sell it to the American people."

"Me, not you?" asked the Vice President.

"As you know I am not a politician. I never kept up with politics before I became President," said Lewis.

"Yes, I know. Before you were sworn in I had never heard of you," said the Vice President.

"Likewise," said Lewis and he smiled. The Vice President also smiled.

"You see Juanita, I didn't ask for this job. I really don't want it. You need to start putting a face to our government."

The President paused and took a sip of coffee. The Vice president had to smile. The coffee mug didn't have the traditional presidential seal on it. It said 'DAD.' Lewis noticed her smiling and said, "My wife's has 'MOM.' A great gift from our children a long time ago."

"That's nice. I have one just like it. My husband's is displayed at home."

"Well then, I see we have a lot in common," he said and smiled. "Please, continue with your ideas."

She said, "It gets more difficult as we go along so please bear with me."

"You're going to save the best for last?"

"No, some becomes more difficult to make work."

"Please go on then. Let's get it all out in the open."

"The first item I want to cover is the Department of Homeland Security. The larger a bureaucracy is, the slower it is. It is enormous. All those agencies thrown together after 9-11-2001. Its purpose was to ensure the sharing of information between different agencies at the federal level and to pass that information to state and local agencies if applicable. Presidents in the past appointed friends and associates who in turn hired friends and associates. Most were not qualified for the positions they were appointed to. Almost every agency is now under the Department of Homeland Security.

Information is gathered and passed up the ladder to a bureaucrat who doesn't know what to do with it and then it may or may not get sent back down to the proper agency.

"Our law enforcement agencies know what they are doing and then we hamper them by adding a lot of layers to slow them down. They blame the agencies for 9-11 not being able to connect the dots. So we added a bunch of bureaucrats who can't walk and chew gum at the same time. It didn't stop the Fort Hood shooter, the Boston Marathon bombing and it didn't stop the Washington attack. Every time we thwarted an attack it was because an agency stopped it. There is no evidence that it was stopped by Homeland Security. The New York Police Department has stopped more terrorist attacks than the Department of Homeland Security. The Federal Emergency Management Agency, their purpose is helping after hurricanes or earthquakes and tornadoes. Yet it is considered Homeland Security. Homeland Security should be threats to our safety, not natural disasters."

"Okay, I see where you are going with this. The bureaucrats at the top are making a lot of money. Money that would be better spent at the law enforcement agencies. Is that right?" asked Lewis.

"Yes, it is. Now let's move on to the next item. The Department of Education is another example. Thousands of employees and billions of dollars. They have never taught one child how to read or write or add and subtract. They're good at keeping statistics and making recommendations. Money would be better spent at the local level. Every state has its own Department of Education. All of these departments had good intentions at the beginning but grew into a monster with an appetite for money, lots of money. You try to cut their budget and they scream you're trying to stop kids from getting an education.

"The reason I'm pointing things like this out is how do we expect the American people to expect less when the government wants more?

"Now, let's get down to the nitty gritty. Things that are harder for the people to accept, things that need to be changed. If we look at the real reason the country is in the shape it is in is because of Congress. Our Founding Fathers never intended for someone to spend thirty or forty years as a Congressman. They assumed someone would serve one term. In the beginning our representatives were merchants, farmers, or business owners. They couldn't afford to leave their farms or stores longer than one term. This needs to stop. We need term limits. Before Washington was destroyed that would have been impossible to do. Now we have a clean slate. We can start over. We can get the American people behind us on this. The American people want it to stop. They just don't know how to stop it. We may have the opportunity to stop it, but first a little background on the subject."

"In 1995, the Supreme Court ruled term limits to be unconstitutional. Neither the Federal Government nor the states can limit the terms of Congress. I have found a way around that, or at least I think I have."

The President leaned forward because he never believed our Founding Father's intended for someone to stay in office for forty or fifty years. He hoped she had a solution.

"Number one no retirement pay. It makes no sense for someone to be a congressman for twelve years and draw retirement pay. It's not done in the private sector and it shouldn't be done here. Number two on Federal ballots the D or R or I should not appear. If you don't know what party they are you shouldn't vote for them, and most important, incumbent should not appear. If you don't know who your Senator or Representative is you shouldn't vote for them. I believe this may be a way to limit terms. Only time will tell."

"That may work. So no law against term limits just natural selection. How about one ballot for all candidates from all parties? If no majority is achieved a run off between the top two. Who could object since two Democrats or two Republicans or two Independents might be the two candidates."

The Vice President nodded her head then said, "The Democrats and Republicans would object. They want a fifty percent chance of winning."

"What about the American people? That is who I'm concerned about. Not the parties," said the President.

"I think they will go along, but that's a gut feeling," said the Vice President.

"You know I think Election Day should be a national holiday. Everything closed except hospitals, fire and police departments. I've never liked early voting. It opens the door to voter fraud. What happens if you vote early and a scandal comes up and you wished you hadn't voted for that person, but you already have? What then?"

"You wasted your vote," said the Vice President.

"Will Congress go along with what we are talking about here?"

"Probably not, but the American people will and I trust the American people more than the politicians that run it."

"The next item is even trickier. All social programs should be turned over to the individual states. We lower Federal taxes and let the states determine how much to tax their citizens in state taxes. That money would stay in the state. This makes the states compete with each other. It's easier to move a business to another state and maybe they won't move overseas. If taxes are too high where you are then you move to a state that doesn't give money away. Someone else's money I might add.

"Now the Federal Government robs Peter to pay Paul and when Peter loses his job we have to borrow money from Mary to pay Peter."

"Tell that to Paul," said the President.

"No, you tell Paul to get a job."

"What tax rate are you proposing?"

"Fifteen percent, everyone fifteen percent, and you get a refund on one third of that. The refund should be in U.S. savings bonds. Maybe people would save them and build up a nest egg for the future." She looked at the President to gauge his reaction.

"So people will be able to save five percent of their income is that correct?"

"Yes, it is, and the income should be tax free," answered the Vice President.

"What about the super-rich?"

"Fifteen percent for everyone. Everyone should be treated equally under any law. Now the super-rich use loopholes and move their money overseas. Maybe they will spend it here and that puts more money into the states sales tax revenue, and most importantly gets the economy moving."

"I think the American people will like that. Why wouldn't they." Then he added, "I've heard most people don't object to the tax rate. What they object to is what the government spends it on."

"Well, that may be true, but it doesn't get the economy back on its feet which is our concern right now. We have to put money back in people's hands where they can spend it."

The Vice President felt like she was on a roll and moved forward. "Every year we hear that social security is going broke. One reason is the unemployed are not putting into the system. By lowering the unemployment rate more people will be paying into the system but I have another idea."

"What would that be because I don't think we can do away with it? I don't want to do away with it."

"We have a national lottery with drawings every week and the proceeds go into the social security trust fund, then we don't let Congress borrow from it and never pay it back."

"I don't know about that. Some states don't allow a state lottery."

"I realize that but the state can't stop the Federal Government from selling lottery tickets on Federal property. It should be where they have lots of winners and guess what? They have to pay taxes on the winnings. If the post office sells tickets they get five percent of sales. This helps them stay afloat. If you go in and have to wait to buy stamps, get a lottery ticket, too.

"I think the numbers should be one through thirty one and you have to pick five that match. Also the big buck number should be one through thirty one. Most people pick birthdays anyway. Maybe we'll have a hundred winners every drawing and guess what they will do with that money?"

"Spend it," said the President.

"That's right, they will spend it and that puts money into the economy and more money for the states to run whatever social programs they want to have."

"Okay, I don't gamble but what's the difference between betting someone five dollars on a football game or buying a lottery ticket."

"Morally there is no difference. Gambling is gambling. I believe it was Thomas Jefferson who said 'a lottery is the fairest tax of all.' You don't have to buy one.

"It was not uncommon for states to have lotteries in the eighteenth and nineteenth centuries. Most states have a lottery now."

"Go on," said the President.

"Next is the Veterans Administration."

The President said, "That's like social security. It's a sacred cow. You poke it and it's like poking a hornet's nest. I'm sorry I interrupted you. Please, go on."

"Thank you, first of all our veterans deserve better. They wrote us a blank check. We cashed it and we don't fulfill our obligation. Veterans normally take three months to get an appointment and then drive hundreds of miles to a V.A. hospital. We can do better than that. We should do better than that."

"I'm sure you know I served in the military. I want to do what is right for our veterans," said the President.

"Yes, I know and thank you for your service. My husband was in the Navy and my son is in the Navy now." Then she paused for a moment as if in deep thought of her husband and her son.

"Why do we make our veterans do this while people on public assistance go to the nearest hospital and get the care they need without paying for it? The tax payer pays for it through indigenous funds. It is criminal if you ask me. If Congress had to use the V.A. they would change it real fast.

"We can screen local hospitals and local doctors. We don't want them fraudulently making money off our veterans. Give our qualifying veterans a card and they can go to these doctors and hospitals and the V.A. pays the bill. I want to give them better care for less money. Small local hospitals are struggling financially. This will help keep them open."

"What about existing V.A. facilities?" asked the President.

"They stay open. The entire system has more patients than the V.A. can possibly handle. You know we are at war. What happens when thousands come back? How is an overburdened system going to take on even more patients? It can't and we can't expect it to."

The president simply nodded his head in agreement.

"Next is oil production. I'm sure you have noticed that every time we seem to be improving our economy the oil producing countries raise the price of oil and the economy tanks again."

"How do we stop that vicious cycle?"

"We drill in the Alaskan wildlife reserve."

"I understand that would take seven years."

"It might, that's what people said seven years ago and we did nothing and guess what, until we start it's going to take seven more years. Now I propose we drill but don't pump any out unless OPEC raises the price over seventy dollars a barrel."

"What is it now?" asked the President.

"Yesterday it was one forty two. Oil skyrocketed after the Washington event."

"So why not pump if we drill?"

"We use theirs first. At seventy dollars a barrel we can have growth. Over that and the growth slows down."

"Another thing the world needs the United States more than we need other countries and that brings me to the trade deficit."

"That was a subject President Carson really wanted to focus on before he died," said the President.

"Yes, I know. Countries out there dump their products here and won't let us sell our products there. They place restrictions and high import taxes on American companies. Some such as China use slave labor. How can the American worker compete? From now on if they sell us ten billion we have to sell them ten billion."

"People say the consumer saves money like that. How is it going to fly with the American people?"

"How are they saving money if they buy foreign products? Yes they save that day but pay more in taxes for welfare and food stamps and throw in unemployment. We have to make the American people aware of their actions. Unemployment, welfare and food stamps are costing more than the trade deficit. For every person drawing unemployment that's one less tax payer. We have to educate the American people, buy American and you give an American a job. I know right now we don't make all the products Americans want to buy, but bring back jobs and the products will follow. This is not a quick fix but we have to start somewhere. This has to be done if this country is going to prosper."

"What about the Chinese? We have borrowed and owe them three trillion dollars. What if they suddenly wanted their money?" asked the President.

"The Chinese think they have us over a barrel but we actually have them over a barrel," answered the Vice President.

"How do you figure that? I would like to hear this," said the President.

"If the Chinese think they can cripple us by asking for the money and they might do that, but if we refused or couldn't pay them their entire economy would collapse in hours after the announcement. No they would be fools to do that."

"Are you sure about that because that has been hanging over my head ever since I took the oath of office."

"I'm sure and if they do there is one other thing we can do."

"What's that?" asked the President.

"Print up three trillion dollars in two dollar bills and tell them they have to send ships here to pick it up at a designated port, say Virginia. They have to count it and sign for it. You see they don't have enough ships to transport it back to China. Do you know how many ships that would take in two dollar bills?"

"I have no idea, how many?"

"I don't know and I'm not going to waste my time finding out."

"Well, I'm not either. You know you have a devious mind, Juanita."

"Thank you. I will take that as a compliment," she said and smiled.

"What's next?" asked the President.

"Medicare and Medicaid fraud. We should not coddle these people. You put a few in a real prison for fraud and see how fast it stops. No more country club prisons either. I know you have heard the term 'Don't do the crime if you can't do the time.' Make that hard time with no possibility of parole and see how fast it stops.

"In the past, Judges have made life easier on our prison inmates than the way our military has to live. It is obscene. I don't know how to stop it but it has to stop. Endless appeals are costing the taxpayers a fortune. The lawyers are making a fortune off of the government because inmates get free legal advice.

"The next item is the cold hard facts. I believe you can judge a nation by how charitable it is. There are millions out there that need more help than we can give. People with special needs children, the truly disabled and the list goes on and on. We don't have the money. The reason we don't have the money is we are giving away billions to people perfectly able to work who choose not to. They had rather let the government provide everything. Food, housing, electric bill even cell phones, not to mention free healthcare. Some have never worked a day in their lives. We need to limit that to two years.

"Another thing is food stamps. We're killing our children. The parents buy items that are not healthy. They are overweight and have high blood pressure. They will likely develop diabetes and healthcare cost will skyrocket when they become adults. You think the healthcare cost from cigarettes was costly just wait till all of this comes home to roost. If the government wants to regulate every aspect of our lives, which I'm against by the way. Make them buy fruits and vegetables. Things that are healthy, not items high in salt, sugar and fat.

"In some states food stamps are on an EBT card. You can use them almost anywhere. You can buy liquor, beer, cigarettes and even lottery tickets. If we give money for food it should be spent on food and only food.

"Another word I want you to think about is entitlement. I believe the only things you are entitled to are what you pay into. Social security, Medicare, unemployment and veteran's benefits because you put in something, time.

"Those other programs I mentioned can go broke. Welfare can't regardless of what it cost. Right now for every taxpayer there is someone getting something from the government. We can't afford it anymore. It will be painful but we have to stop it. There is no incentive to work. People are getting tired. They look at their neighbor; they have the same kind of house, drive a better car and spend more on groceries with food stamps. They rationalize things by saying they don't work and look how they are living so why should I work?

"Another item. Foreign aid. We need to completely stop it. We can't afford it any longer. We can't give away borrowed money or money we simply print up. A lot of the countries we give money to, are better off financially than we are. We should have never given foreign aid to countries that don't share in our moral values such as the right to vote, women's rights and religious freedom. Most of the countries we give financial aid to don't even like us. You can't buy respect, you have to earn it. We think they will like us and stand by us if we give them billions.

"We have to stop sleeping with special interest groups and lowering one segment of the population's taxes and raising another. Everyone should be treated equally under the law, everyone."

"Let's move on," said the President shaking his head in disbelief. He had no idea things were this bad and it was overwhelming.

"Tort reform; we will never keep healthcare cost down without tort reform. Let me give you an example. The average doctor pays almost half his income in malpractice insurance. Two people suffer the same problem. One lawyer represents both plaintiffs, but two different juries. One jury awards two hundred thousand and the other awards twenty million. How can that be explained, it can't. That is one reason doctors are getting out and recommending our medical students not to become doctors."

The President looked at the Vice President and asked, "Is there any good news for me?"

"I'm afraid not. That's all I have for now. Give me another week and I will have more."

"Tell you what; let's go with what you have so far. Right now you are preaching to the choir because I agree with everything you have said. Let's see if we can get the American people behind us on this and let them force Congress to act.

"I want you out there pushing this. Right now I have a war to fight. From now on when I get a briefing I also want you to get the same briefing. I want you in the loop on everything."

The Vice President looked at the President and said, "For the last few years there has been a movement all over the country called a convention of states."

"What's that?" asked the President.

"It is article five of the Constitution, if two thirds of the state's legislature's call for a constitutional convention and three fourths of the states meet and agree it becomes an amendment. The difference between an amendment and a law passed by Congress is simple. Congress can pass a law and then change it or the next Congress can abolish it. A constitutional amendment has to be changed by the people of all the states. It bypasses Congress. Most people believe only Congress can initiate any constitutional amendment."

"I didn't know that," said the President.

"It is article five. Read the Constitution."

She picked up her purse and pulled a small pamphlet out. It was only four inches by six inches. She handed it to the President. He looked at the cover. On it in bold letters was written.

THE CONSTITUTION OF THE UNITED STATES

"Your own personal copy. I suggest you read it and the tenth amendment. Pay close attention to the tenth amendment."

"I promise I will do that."

"The states want what is rightfully theirs. Things the Federal Government has taken away for decades. We the government should be helping people succeed not putting up obstacles all over the place and punish them with higher taxes if they are successful."

As the Vice President reached the door she turned and said, "Another thing, Congress shouldn't be allowed to pass a law they themselves are exempt from. That is outrageous. That is one reason the last Congress had an approval rating of eleven percent."

"I started at twelve," said the President and then he smiled. "But you are right about that. Maybe they thought no one would find out."

"We will expose them for what they are."

As the Vice President opened the door she heard the President call her name. She turned and answered, "Yes."

"This tenth amendment you keep referring to, how did the American people ever let it get this way?"

"They are too busy with their everyday lives to notice."

"Do you think it will ever come about, you know the states and the people getting what is rightfully theirs?"

"Are you asking me if the American people will storm the castle with pitchforks and torches anytime soon?"

"Yeah, I guess so."

"I only hope it doesn't happen during our administration. It would be embarrassing."

"Why?"

"Because I would be leading the charge."

Then she left.

She started the next day. If the American people wanted to find out what the administration was doing all they had to do was watch the news. She was on every day. She was a powerful persuader on the agenda. She actually did something most politicians couldn't seem to do, she answered questions without side stepping or dancing around the issues. She was attractive, articulate and had a passion for being honest.

Lewis MacDonald had been in office for eighty days. He had not taken a day off. He had nothing on his calendar and decided to sleep in late. Beverly was afraid he had come down with something.

Lewis couldn't believe how efficient the Vice president was. She was everywhere, giving speeches, doing interviews and calling members of Congress. Lewis hoped she would help shoulder the load but instead she picked it up and ran with it. He was so proud of her yet he had to admit to Beverly he would have never picked her. When Beverly asked him why, Lewis said, "I'd never heard of her."

The Vice President never said, "I". She always said, "We" or "This administration." Yet every idea was hers and she passed the credit to the new President.

CHAPTER FIFTY EIGHT

TOBY BURKE STANDS ON HIS SOAP BOX... TO CLIMB ON HIS HIGH HORSE

JOHN 8:32

Toby Burke was furious. He always read the major newspapers to see what the competition was writing about. He knew the news media had become nothing more than a political arm of the Democrat and Republican parties. In the last ten years, the media had become the attack dogs of the parties.

President MacDonald was an Independent President and both sides were attacking. Some were finding fault with the Egyptian crisis. One side saying he endangered the hostages and not letting diplomacy work. The other side saying it was nothing more than a fluke that the hostages were freed. The draft was attacked by both parties, too large or too small. Both parties said he showed no leadership in letting Congress pick his Vice president.

Toby Burke was going to try to change all that. He knew in all likelihood he would be a lone voice crying in the wilderness. He submitted his article for approval by the editor. He figured the editor would either reject it or approve it, probably with some major changes. He was surprised when the editor called him into his office. When Toby entered his office the editor was reading his article.

"Toby, I want to talk to you about your article for tomorrow."

"Yes, Sir."

"Can you tell me what prompted you to write this? This is more along the lines of something on the editorial page and I write those."

"Sir, I realize that, but you have to admit the article is correct."

"I can see that. How long have you been writing articles, Toby?"

"Not counting the school paper." He noticed the editor was smiling. "Since I graduated from journalism school."

"You still didn't tell me why this article. Remember, Missouri is the show me state." Another smile.

Toby didn't know what to make of the smiles. Was this a kind gesture before turning him down or firing him? Toby took in a deep breath before answering.

"I started reading newspapers when I was twelve years old. My dad would read it first and then let me. I was fascinated by them. My dad would tell me everything in those papers were true. They printed just the facts, no speculation. They let the reader make up their own mind about something."

"Yet you didn't mention any of that did you?" asked the editor.

"No, Sir. I didn't feel it was that important given the space allotted to me in my column."

"What if I gave you more space?"

"That would be great, Sir."

"Can you write a series on this, say ten weeks, once a week and I want specifics?"

"I can do that. That would be easy."

"I want it done right. I want to try to syndicate your articles with other papers. Someone else may want to print them also."

"Yes, Sir, that sounds good to me." Toby knew he would get a portion of any syndication fee.

"I want you to title this series 'THE TRUTH WILL SET YOU FREE.'"

"Sounds like a winner to me, Sir."

CHAPTER FIFTY NINE

JACK IN THE BOX

One of the agents was missing. He should have been on a flight out of New York before the weapon was used in Washington. He never arrived. The Iranian couldn't figure it out. All six of his agents had participated in the nuclear attack and now one was missing. He had a passport and round trip ticket even though he wouldn't be returning. His controller in Iran wanted answers and wanted them fast. The Iranian had driven to the agent's house near Seattle, Washington. He drove by without stopping. No car in the carport. He would have to come back later. The next week he came back. Still no car. Could he have been in an accident? Could he have been in the hospital? Was he dead, or could he have been apprehended? All of these were possibilities. He had to find out. He wasn't sure if he had been arrested and the police were waiting on him. If he was caught, everything would fall apart. He was the only one who knew the location and the identities of all six agents. He had to be careful, very careful.

He decided he had to take a chance. He watched the house all day from a distance. When he was satisfied no one was inside or near the house he drove to the house and parked in the driveway and rang the doorbell. No one answered. He had come up with a cover story. He was looking for a lost dog. He knew Americans loved dogs. He even had a photo of a mixed breed dog. After no one answered he drove away. He would come back tonight.

He parked the car a half a mile from the house and walked. Even though it was dark picking the lock was a piece of cake. He was thankful for the training he had received in Iran. He went to the mailbox and brought the mail in and went through it. Nothing there of any importance, he would take it with him. He went through the closets looking for anything that would give him a clue as to what was going on. He found nothing.

The next week he returned. He went through the mail again. One letter caught his attention and he opened it. It was a notice from the police impound lot in St. Louis, Missouri. What is he doing, he's supposed to be in Iran? He took the mail with him. The Iranian came back the next week. He brought the mail in, no need to look through it, he didn't have time. He had a lot of time consuming work to do.

He started setting the explosives. He had to come up with a plan to retrieve the car in St. Louis, Missouri. He couldn't retrieve the car himself. He needed to mail identities to two of his sleeper cells and let them retrieve the car.

When he left the house he knew there wouldn't be anything left to investigate. He headed back to his job at the convenience store. When he arrived he was exhausted and twenty minutes late. The owner gave him that look that he always gave him when he did something wrong. Jack tried to ignore him which was almost impossible. The owner, the Infidel, was eating a ham and cheese sandwich. His day was coming.

Midway through his shift he started thinking. A dark thought entered his head. The missing agent was supposed to take care of someone, the man who let them plant the bomb was supposed to disappear. Did the agent disappear or the intended victim? Did the intended victim kill his agent and drive his car to St. Louis, Missouri? The list of possibilities was endless. Jack felt sick. He would pass this information to the other sleeper agents tonight.

When he made it home that night it was almost two a.m. He checked the mail. There was a small padded envelope in his mailbox. Inside he looked at the postmark. Laredo, Texas was stamped over the stamps. He had received small packages such as this from Laredo, Texas over the years. He knew the contents had come from Iran to France to Spain then Mexico and drove over the U.S. border. He went into his bedroom locking the bedroom door as an extra precaution. He opened the package and removed a compact disc and a note. The note was in English and was obviously a woman's handwriting. 'You left this in my car last week, sorry. Love, Linda.'

The agent knew there was no Linda. He looked at the disc and its plastic protective container. The disc was older and well used or appeared to be. It was either what Americans called rap or hip hop. He didn't know one from the other. He had a compact disc player, putting on earphones he listened. He opened his nightstand drawer and removed paper and pen. There was a series of what sounded like scratches. To the casual listener it sounded like a defective disc. He wasn't a casual listener, it was a coded message. He wrote it down scratch for scratch. Instead of dots and dashes it was short and long scratches. It was like Morse code. Then he had to decode the message.

Before he finished the coded message his hand was shaking so much he could hardly write. He double checked everything and said, "They are insane. Why do they want us to do this? The risk far outweighs the benefit." Deep inside he knew he would have to carry out the mission from Tehran.

He had been instructed to have his five remaining agents place bombs in churches and schools. These bombs could take place in small isolated churches. The churches had to be over one hundred miles from the agent's base. The churches had to be fifty miles from each other. The worst part was they were to be in different states. Ten states would be bombed. The only justification the agent could see was to stretch the Federal Bureau of Investigation resources thin.

This would be a huge undertaking for his agents. Finding suitable churches in isolated areas could take days. Then they had to make the bombs. One demand by Tehran was the bombs needed to be the same day and Tehran had given him a date. It was only two weeks away. He thought about the date. He knew most of the important dates in Persian and Iran history, he had been taught those in school. The date didn't ring a bell. Maybe that's good. No one could point a finger at Iran.

He removed his world atlas from the closet and started studying. Four hours later, he believed he had a solution. It would require six bombs in the Central Time Zone exploding at twelve o'clock when people were leaving the church. Two could go off in the Mountain Time Zone at the same time when church was beginning. The only real problem he saw was the Pacific Time Zone. Maybe his agent could find a church that had two services on Sunday morning. He remembered one in Seattle but that wasn't in an isolated area. It was in a very large city.

He was also instructed to place ten bombs in schools. Most schools aren't in isolated areas. He had no idea how his agents could accomplish that. The school bombs were to be on Monday after the churches.

He had his work cut out for him and his agents would be doing more than he was. All he did was pass along information. "They are insane," he told himself, again.

"Twenty bombs for five men. Patience, how can I be patient and how can they be careful?"

He didn't have an answer for that and the car, what to do about the car in St. Louis. He would have to delay that for the time being. He needed more planning time for it anyway.

The last twelve days had been nerve wracking for his agents and for him. He needed to find out if the bombs had been placed in the churches and schools. He realized how important tomorrow and Monday could be. If one, just one, made a mistake it could ruin everything and now he had to worry about a stupid car. What if the car was a trap? He had mailed the driver's license this morning. He would use two agents to retrieve the car. The first agent would pick up the car and drive halfway to Los Angeles. A second agent would meet him and finish the journey. He would use the agent in Denver, Colorado for the last leg. The first agent then could get a good night's sleep and go to Los Angeles. He wanted around the clock surveillance on the car. He had a bad feeling about the car. He would fly an agent in from Chicago leaving only one agent, the one in Atlanta.

He thought about the missing agent. They didn't really need him. He was supposed to be already gone now anyway. If he was dead, he was dead. He didn't know how to track down the man who was supposed to be killed. Maybe his agent had taken care of the man already. He still didn't understand why the car was in St. Louis, Missouri.

His agents would retrieve the car in a few weeks. Maybe some answers were in the car. Patience and to be careful. Be very careful.

CHAPTER SIXTY

THE EVIL THAT MEN DO

JEREMIAH 17:9

On Sunday afternoon, Lewis was in his office on the eighth floor of the United States Capitol. Lewis hated working on Sunday but there weren't enough hours in the day. Beverly was in the quarters writing letters.

Lewis's phone rang. He answered on the second ring. It was the Director of the Federal Bureau of Investigation. He asked the President to turn on the TV. The Director was on his way up the stairs. Beverly came in and saw Lewis in front of the TV.

"I came to tell you to turn it on," said Beverly.

"The FBI Director is on the way up."

"Lewis what has happened to the world? Why would someone bomb a church?"

"Beverly, sometimes I think the world has been turned upside down."

"It's more than one church, it's several," said Beverly.

"Yeah, I know, the Director said several."

There was a knock on the door and two Secret Service Agents escorted the Director into Lewis's office.

Beverly went back to the living quarters fifteen feet away.

The Director of the FBI, Hiram Wilcox, nodded at Lewis.

"Mr. President, I'm sorry to inform you, but, and this could change, six churches have been bombed. There may be more, we don't know. When I left my office three minutes ago it was four."

The Director's cell phone rang. He looked at the floor and shook his head then looked at the ceiling. When he hung up he looked at the President and said, "Ten."

Lewis sat on the edge of his desk. "Ten?"

"Yes, Mr. President, ten so far."

"You mean there might be more?"

"Mr. President, we don't know."

"I see," said Lewis.

"We don't have a casualty count at this time. It will take a few hours."

"Where were they located?"

"Mr. President, I can't answer that right now. I can tell you this the first four were in places I've never heard of, small towns and it appears right now to be in ten different states.'

"Ten states? Are you serious?"

"Yes, Sir, Mr. President. The first two were in Alabama and Tennessee and were about seventy five miles apart."

"How large of a group would it take to bomb ten states?"

"I don't know the answer to that but one man could have done the first two, they were only a little over an hour's drive?"

"Has anyone claimed responsibility?"

"Just the usual wackos, Mr. President."

"So you don't take them seriously?"

"We will still investigate, of course, but these groups claim responsibility for everything."

"I see."

"I have a feeling the group who did this, won't take responsibility for it. Churches aren't the same as power stations or trying to derail a train or take down an airliner."

"Do you know what denomination the churches were?"

"Sir, I don't know that at this time."

The Director's phone rang again. He pulled a pen out of his shirt pocket and opened a folder. He started writing. After five minutes he snapped his phone shut.

"Alabama and Tennessee, Arkansas, Louisiana, Illinois and Indiana again fifty or sixty miles apart. Colorado and Utah only forty miles apart on that one. California and Nevada, those were a hundred and ten miles apart, and a little good news. The one in Nevada didn't explode."

"It didn't?"

"You are not going to believe this. The Preacher saw what was happening on the news. He noticed the access to the crawl space was ajar when he went to church so he went in and according to the local sheriff ripped all the wires loose. He's lucky he wasn't killed."

"Someone was watching over him, wouldn't you agree?" said Lewis.

The Director nodded his head and said, "They say God looks after dumb animals and crazy people."

"How long will it be before we start getting casualty numbers?"

"The dead shortly, some may be added later."

"I understand. You said there may be more churches?"

"Yes, Sir, It appears these churches were in isolated areas outside of small towns."

"Anyway we can check all the churches."

"We can't, Mr. President. There are just too many. There are places in this country you can't throw a rock without breaking a church window."

"Can the FBI and the ATF do anything to help the local authorities?"

"Well, of course, we will try to do that. We don't have enough agents to do much, not nationwide. Most police departments have the know-how, but they will be overwhelmed themselves."

"These churches were in isolated areas, right?" asked Lewis, thinking of the church his family attended. The nearest house was two miles away.

"Yes, Mr. President."

"What can the Federal Government do?"

"Mr. President, I don't even want to ask you this, but I think we need to do it."

"What's that?"

"I think you need to address the American people and ask them to stay home tonight. Give the police time to check these churches for other bombs."

"You're right I don't want to do that, but I will."

Thirty minutes later, Lewis C. MacDonald, President of the United States, did something for the first time in American history. He asked, or rather pleaded, that Americans stay home that night and not go to church.

Of course, that message was ignored by hundreds of churches across America. One news channel interviewed a Pastor in Missouri. "We have a constitutional right to be here and no one is going to stop us!" said the Pastor.

"Are you blaming the President? Do you think he's trying to prevent you from practicing your religion?"

"Of course not. What kind of an idiot are you? He's trying to protect us. This is in defiance of whoever placed those bombs. We are not afraid of you. You can bomb all you want. We'll be here next week too, and the week after that."

Several of the churches held their services outside and a few members of the church had weapons and were facing out to protect the congregation.

A sheriff's deputy was on patrol and noticed a black SUV leave the parking lot of the elementary school in Gadsden, Alabama. This wasn't all that unusual. There was an outside basketball court behind the building and kids would play on the weekend. Most of those kids weren't old enough to drive. Maybe it was teenagers drinking beer. He decided he would check the building. He picked up his flashlight off the seat and walked behind the building. He was looking for broken windows or doors that had been forced open. He saw nothing suspicious and headed back to his car. As he approached the front door he noticed a child's backpack leaning against the shrubbery. Some kid probably left it Friday. When he was in his car he started thinking. He sat there a few minutes. He really just wanted to go home. He put the cruiser in gear and backed up where his headlights were on the backpack. He called it in. Thirty minutes later his lieutenant pulled up. He got out of the car and went to the Deputy's vehicle. The Deputy rolled his window down.

"What makes you think it might be a bomb?"

"It rained last night and it is not soiled or anything. No mud splashed up on it."

"Did you get near it?"

"Maybe twenty five feet of it."

"If this turns out to be nothing you owe me a cup of coffee and a doughnut."

The Deputy didn't have to buy him anything. It was a bomb.

The bomb squad was the first to arrive followed by the ATF. They were nearby handling the church bombing that had happened that morning. The FBI arrived an hour later; they had been in Tennessee at a church bombing. The Director of the FBI called the President and informed him within the hour.

"Close all schools starting tomorrow morning. Better yet, close them for the entire week. This is mandatory. I'm not going to put our children at risk."

"How can we secure every church and school in the country? We don't have the resources to do that," said the Director.

Lewis didn't hesitate with an answer. "I'm calling out the National Guard. They can secure the school grounds. I don't want anyone except bomb technicians and search crews going inside. I will issue the order now."

"That would be a blessing, Mr. President."

"Have we gotten the casualty figures from this morning?"

"Yes, Mr. President. 176 confirmed dead. 65 in critical condition. Some of those probably won't make it. I'm sorry, Mr. President."

"So am I. Is there any other targets these people could try to bomb?"

"Mr. President, in America there is a potential target every mile."

"You're right. Please, keep me informed."

"I definitely will, Mr. President."

"Just out of curiosity were any mosques or synagogues bombed?"

"No, Mr. President."

"What do you make of that?"

"Well, nothing really. They have had so many threats and actual attempts in the last twenty years they keep a very close eye on security."

At 10:00 a.m. Monday morning, the day after the church bombings, the Director of the FBI informed Lewis that ten bombs had been placed in schools.

"Seven exploded before we could disarm them."

"Please tell me no one was hurt or killed," said Lewis.

"There were no injuries, Mr. President."

"Thank God," said Lewis.

"The National Guard did a fantastic job. All of the bombs were set to go off at about 7:45 when school buses are unloading children."

"How evil have you got to be to want to kill children. We were very fortunate weren't we?"

"Yes, we were Mr. President. If that policeman hadn't discovered the one in Alabama, I don't know how many children we would have lost."

"Where were they located?"

"The same ten states. These devices were very simple, nothing fancy."

"How did you find them so fast?" asked the President.

"Well, it was really simple. Remember I said one person could have set two off. The one in Alabama and Tennessee."

"Yes, I remember you saying that."

"We concentrated in those areas with additional resources and found the others. We had actually located the ones that exploded before they went off. We pulled everyone back. We figured they would go off between 7:30 and 8:00 a.m."

"Good call, Mr. Director."

"Thank you, Mr. President. We also got some prints off of the church in Nevada and off the one in California. They matched. We ran them through but we didn't get a match in our data base."

"So this leaves us where?"

"I personally think five people did all twenty. Four apiece."

"The dead has risen to 196, Mr. President," Director Wilcox informed the President by phone the next day.

"Any claims of responsibility?"

"No, Mr. President. We are checking all claims but nothing I can hang my hat on."

"Any gut feelings?"

"The labs are working around the clock on this. The bombs in Alabama and Tennessee, two in churches and two in schools appear to have been made by the same person or persons.

"The one in Nevada that didn't explode may tell us a lot, but that will take a while. We are going over that one closer than the others. Maybe we will get lucky but I'm not counting on it."

"I can't believe someone can be this depraved and evil," said the President.

"There is a lot of evil in this world Mr. President. We are seeing more and more as time goes on."

"And the evil that men do can't be understood by everyone else," said Lewis.

CHAPTER SIXTY ONE

WAR FOOTING

The new President had been in office one hundred days when the draft started. There would be no deferments, even medical.

He called the Chiefs of Staff together for a meeting. He was going to change a few things.

He began by saying, "When I went into the Army I went through basic training just like everyone else. You know what I remember most of all?"

The Generals and Admiral didn't answer. They didn't know how to answer a question like that. None of them had gone through basic training. All of them went to the Military, Navel or Air Force Academy.

"I'll tell you what I remember the most about basic training. We spent more time learning to do left face and right face and how to march than we did on how to fight. We spent very little time on how to kill the enemy. I'll give you an example. We had an hour class of the pistol. Fired ten rounds in practice and then fired for qualification. We spent a couple of days on the rifle range.

"Now, what I want is for you to take these new recruits and you teach them every trick in the book. I really don't care if they look good on a parade field or not. I want them to know how to survive on the battlefield, how to kill the enemy and move on to the next enemy and kill them. Do I make myself clear?"

The Marine answered, "Yes, Mr. President. The one question I have is where do we put this many people at one time? I mean, house them in barracks?"

The President answered, "I'm afraid they will be living outdoors in pup tents. The British did it in North Africa in World War II. At this point I don't know who or where we will be fighting. I want them divided into four groups. One in the desert, one in the mountains, one in the jungle and one in a built up area. After thirty days they rotate. They do this for four months so each person has each type of training."

The Air Force General spoke up. "They used a nuclear weapon on us. Why aren't we using a nuclear weapon on them?"

"I don't want them to die in an instant. I want them to suffer."

This answer got a raised eyebrow from the Generals. The Admiral just smiled. That was the answer he was hoping for.

The Admiral said, "Am I to understand you do not want to show mercy on them?"

"That is correct," said the President.

"Mr. President, may I make a recommendation?"

"Yes, by all means."

"I think we should have a few Navy Seals, Rangers and Army Special Forces teach these new recruits. You used the term 'Every trick in the book.' Who better to teach them than those who have been trained."

"I think that is a good idea, Admiral."

"Mr. President, are you authorizing us to pull equipment out of mothball and storage to equip and train these men?" asked the Army General.

"Yes, I am; whatever it takes. Gentlemen we are at war. I want a military that is ready to fight on day one. I want a military that makes the rest of the world think long and hard before they mess with us."

The first group that arrived at each of the training bases was sworn in and paperwork filled out. Nineteen and twenty year olds were making out their last will and testament. This was to let them know that this was serious business.

Then they were marched to the firing range. Each was issued an M-16 rifle for target practice. At the end of the firing range they were fed a M.R.E. (meal ready to eat) an hour later was a class on hand to hand combat followed by bayonet training. They marched from one site to another. If someone fell out from exhaustion, a command was given out. "Pick him up and carry him. We don't leave a man behind."

After ten days, they could march ten miles. They looked like a gaggle, but who cared as long as they got there. In the past soldiers had never been pushed this hard this fast. No one went AWOL. There was no place to go. There was moaning and grumbling, but they kept going. At the end of thirty days they got a change of scenery, from desert to mountain to jungle.

The jungle training was in the huge Okefenokee Swamp in South Georgia. The other three bases were closer together. These were in New Mexico and Colorado for desert, mountain and built up areas. A former Army base closed years ago was the combat in cities site. The draftees were becoming hardened; a twenty mile hike was no problem for them.

At the end of four months, they woke up at revile and were told to go back to sleep. Only in the military would they wake you and tell you to go back to sleep. Somethings never change.

CHAPTER SIXTY TWO

THE INVESTIGATION

Three things happened on one day. Josh MacDonald was sworn in as a Second Lieutenant in the Air Force. The two hundred thousand finished their training and slept the rest of the day, and a man opened a door.

The man opening the door was the break everyone had given up on. His name was Sidney Spivey and he owned a rental house thirty miles from Seattle, Washington. He had rented a house out fifteen months ago. The renter had paid a full years rent up front. He claimed he was a screen play writer and was working on a new TV. series. He told Spivey he may rent it longer than a year. Spivey had given him three extra months. He had called and left messages and gotten no response. Then the phone was disconnected. He had gone by the house twice and left notes on the door and still got no response. The notes were still there.

He used his key. As he was pulling the key out, he dropped it. This saved his life. He bent down to pick up the key and opened the door at the same time. There was an explosion. The top half of the door was blown into thousands of wood splinters. Miraculously Spivey wasn't killed. He was knocked unconscious by the blast. When he came to he called 911 on his cell phone and told the dispatcher what had happened. It took fifteen minutes for a sheriff's deputy to arrive at the isolated house.

The ambulance arrived thirty minutes later, loaded Mr. Spivey and transported him to the hospital. The deputy entered the house and stopped when he saw the other explosives. They were everywhere. He went back outside and called the sheriff's department and requested the bomb squad. The bomb squad arrived, saw all the explosives and called the ATF, the Alcohol Tobacco and Firearms, for assistance. It was determined all the explosives should have detonated at one time. A rat had chewed one of the wires on the bomb by the door. The bomb technicians went to work systematically disarming the bombs. None were very large and each had an incendiary device attached.

Someone wanted this house destroyed in its entirety, but why? Trash was everywhere. It appeared that no one had disposed of trash in at least a year.

One bomb disposal officer would find the most important piece of evidence in his police career. It was beside the commode. Someone had used the bathroom and his passport had fallen out of his pocket. It was a French passport. The police dusted it for fingerprints and entered the prints into the nationwide database. They should have an answer soon if they were in the file. Computers did the work and could do it quickly. While they waited for an answer they had no way of knowing that someone was tasked with watching for that one particular fingerprint. No one wanted it to slip through the cracks. When the match was made she picked up the phone and dialed the FBI in Seattle, Washington. Two hours later the FBI agents arrived.

The first agent out of the car came into the house and said, "I am Special Agent in charge Frank Griffin with the Federal Bureau of Investigation. I want this entire area searched. I want a total lockdown on the news media and I want everyone on site here right now. This is a Federal Bureau of Investigation case."

"Why?" asked the ATF and Seattle Bomb Squad leader at the same time.

"The owner of this passport shot a Secret Service agent and tried to kill the First Lady. No one is getting cut out of the investigation. I want every piece of paper dusted for fingerprints. I want phone records. Is the phone still on?"

"No, Sir, it had been disconnected; probably for non-payment." The ATF had already checked the phone.

"I still want the records. Who owns the house?"

"He's in the hospital. He was injured when he opened the door. He's lucky to be alive. We ruled him out as a suspect because of that."

"I still want him questioned. I want to know if the owner of the passport is who rented the house. We can't question the owner of the passport because he's dead. We are not going to stop working until we get some answers. This passport changes everything."

An ATF agent said, "There is a lot of stuff in the basement we can't figure out."

"Show me."

In the basement were packing cases from different countries. Bolivia, Thailand, Argentina and Germany, there was nothing from France.

"Run a search. I feel like the companies that sent this stuff don't exist. What's all that stuff?" Agent Griffin asked as he was pointing to a pile of metal items in the corner.

"It looks like it came out of a commercial air conditioner. There is another air conditioner over there that has parts missing out of it. This won't fit in there, it's too big."

"Find an agent that knows about air conditioners and get him here right away."

"We found some documents on that table we can't read. It's a foreign language."

The FBI agent looked at the documents. "We have someone here who might be able to read it. Let me get him."

Five minutes later, he asked him, "Can you read this?"

"No, I can't. It's Farsi. But I think there is an agent in Spokane that can."

"Get him here ASAP."

Two hours later, an agent, whose father owned an air conditioning and heating company, arrived.

"I'm going to have to call my father on some of this. He can look it up for me. I can tell you right now this came out of a large commercial unit."

"How large?"

"Well, I guess twice as large as that one over there. It looks like someone pulled this out and replaced it with what came out of that one."

"Why would they do that?" He already knew the answer, but wanted it confirmed.

"Maybe to put something else in there with it and the unit would still work. It just wouldn't do what it was supposed to do, cool a large building."

"But, if there were other units there on the building they might get away with it if it was in the fall or winter, right?"

"Yes, they could get away with it until late spring or summer."

The agent arrived from Spokane. They showed him the documents and he quickly read through them.

"We need everyone outside and get a radiation team in here. We need to check everyone for radiation. These are instructions for assembling a nuclear weapon."

"How long will that take?"

"I don't know. There is a Nuclear Response Team in Ft. Lewis. They can be here pretty fast."

"Alright, everyone drop what you're doing and move outside."

The government moves slow. It always has. The Nuclear Response Team in an exception. When the team arrived everyone was searching the surrounding area for evidence. They found nothing noteworthy. An hour later the all clear was given.

The agent who could read Farsi sat down with the Nuclear Response Team and translated the documents. The Nuclear Response Team was experts on nuclear weapons and nuclear power plants. In the end the Nuclear Response Team leader explained the situation to the agents.

"There are instructions on how to remove those parts over there." He pointed to the air conditioner parts in a pile in one corner. "How to assemble the weapon; place it in the other unit, then how to install the parts out of that unit over there. The instructions are very detailed but easy to follow. Anyone could do it. It wouldn't take someone that is an expert on nuclear weapons to do that. Now the question is, was this the one used on Washington or is there another one somewhere else we don't know about."

"We need to explore both possibilities, don't you think?"

"Yes, we do but if there is more than one we are very lucky."

"How so?" asked the FBI agent.

"These instructions show how to set the timer and the timer was for 9:30 p.m. February 7. That was when the one in Washington went off if I remember correctly."

"That is correct," said Agent Griffin.

"We can't rule out that there is one that didn't go off, can we?"

"But we only have parts for one air conditioner right?"

"You have to ask your air conditioner guy but it appears you are right about that."

Another agent spoke up. "What if there are other places like this? Places we don't know about?"

"We can't rule that out can we?"

At ten p.m., two FBI agents returned to the house. One had interviewed the owner at the hospital. He had identified the renter by the passport photo. He was ninety percent sure they were one and the same. The other agent had the phone records.

"That was fast," said Agent Griffin.

"There wasn't much there. Here let me show you. The phone was turned on fifteen months ago. The day it was turned on over forty calls were made. Care to guess how many since? By the way the phone company turned it off for non-payment a month ago."

"I'm too tired to guess," said the agent.

"Not a single one. That is unbelievable, why have a phone and never use it?"

"Maybe he had a cell phone. One of those disposable ones. If that's the case we'll never find out if we can't find the actual phone."

"Maybe it's in someone else's name. Drug dealers do that a lot."

"What numbers did he call the first day? You said there were forty," said another agent.

"Local stores. Nothing in particular. Several people and it seems they were randomly picked out. We're checking those numbers now. There was one number to a pay phone on the Canadian border. That's not going to lead us anywhere. Who's going to remember something from fifteen months ago? And get this; each call lasted for less than a minute. You know, like it was a wrong number."

"The pay phone bothers me. I didn't know there was any still around. One number out of forty. How long did he talk on that one? Most people don't answer a pay phone, anyway. They just walk on by, I know I would."

"The pay phone was fifty seconds."

"This is a wild hunch. Let's put that pay phone under surveillance."

"Will do."

"When is the last time anyone saw a pay phone?" asked Griffin.

"There is one at the bus station. I saw it last week," answered an agent.

"Was there any incoming calls?"

"Yes, Sir, and as near as we can tell it was telemarketers."

"Over a hundred and all lasted less than a minute. Just long enough to tell them you weren't interested."

"Any duplicates?"

"Yes, Sir, quite a few."

"I'm going to assume that some of those numbers was someone contacting the house."

Another agent came into the room and approached the lead FBI agent.

"Sir, we have a clue."

"Let's hear it."

"We found a pizza box with a phone number on it. When they take the order, this pizza place won't deliver without a phone number."

"Was the address for this house?"

"Yes, Sir, it was."

"We know the phone here wasn't used to order pizza."

"It's not this number, Sir."

"It's a local, the number you just found?"

"Don't know. I believe it's a cell phone. It's not this area code."

"Can we find out whose name it is in?"

"Yes, Sir, with a warrant."

"Get one. I want it tonight. The way things are going there hasn't been a number called from here in fifteen months."

"It's an active number. The phone company verified that without a warrant. They won't give us a name or the numbers called."

"Let's get as many people on that as soon as possible. We need cross checks and listen, see if any went to that pay phone on the Canadian border."

"Yes, Sir."

"Finally!" said agent Griffin.

"Did the owner of the passport have a vehicle?"

"Not in that name, at least not in Washington State."

"Can they check and see if one was registered to this address?"

"Yes, Sir, but that may take days."

"Then we better start now hadn't we?"

"Yes, Sir. I'll get on it right away."

At nine a.m. the following morning, fifteen agents were analyzing the records of the home phone and the cell phone number found on the pizza box. When the two records were first obtained it was obvious something was wrong. The home phone, the cell phone and the renter of the house didn't match the passport name. Four different names had been used.

The FBI made the logical assumption that all four names were fictitious. This didn't slow their investigation. The cell phone was of a type everyone called disposable. A home address or identification was not required to purchase and buy air time. Two years had been purchased when the phone was bought from a department store in Seattle.

Agents were busy entering the calls into computers and using reverse directories to get names and addresses. What jumped out at the agents was the cell phone had made over 1200 calls, each lasting fifty seconds. The agents quickly realized the cell phone user was calling and hanging up. One of the agents remarked to another agent, "He was trying to hide a needle in a haystack. Some of these numbers are important, but which ones. He called almost everything you can think of…probably asking them what time they opened or closed. How are we going to figure this out? The incoming calls were also fifty seconds and a lot of them were telemarketers."

A lot of the calls were to the pay phone on the Canadian border. One call in particular was interesting. It was the last call made on the cell phone in St. Louis, Missouri.

"We have to find this phone. Maybe he made a mistake and put important numbers on his speed dial. We need to find this phone. We'll never figure all this out without that phone."

Special Agent Griffin said, "No calls from it were placed in four months. This phone may have belonged to the man that shot at the First Lady. I'm willing to bet the phone is still in St. Louis."

"You think he left it there?"

"Yes, I do."

"What makes you think that?"

"He didn't have a cell phone on him when he was killed so where would it be?"

No one answered. They had all followed their gut instinct at one time or another. They were usually right. "If this is the man that shot at the First Lady, how did he get from St. Louis to Kansas City? Did someone drive him and drop him off? Someone may have dropped him off and then drove to St. Louis and made that call. It's almost three hundred miles. Check the bus lines and the air lines. I don't think we will find out anything useful but we can't leave any stone unturned."

An agent said, "When I'm on the road I charge my phone using the cigarette lighter. Maybe he did also. We can activate that number and call it. We may be able to triangulate the cell tower and get a general idea."

"Maybe it's still in service. I don't see where it was ever disconnected. Someone go to the phone company and see if they can do that now. Maybe we can get a general area even though we don't know what kind of car we're looking for."

Two hours later, the lead agent was informed that they had it narrowed down to a half mile radius.

"We don't know what kind of vehicle it is. Records don't show a rental car and I don't know when the address search on the vehicle registered to this address will be finished."

The Post Office delivered the information they were seeking that afternoon. The car had been impounded by the St. Louis Police Department. The car was in an impound lot in St. Louis, Missouri. It had been abandoned on a side street and had been towed. The letter was to inform the owner of the towing expense and the daily fee. This was the second notice.

Five agents were on the scene in thirty minutes along with a bomb sniffing dog and a bomb technician.

The phone was in the car. Finger prints were taken of the inside. It had been outside so long it would have been impossible to get fingerprints. The fingerprints were run immediately and a match was made. The fingerprints matched the shooter.

They found a wallet, roadmaps and a box of pistol ammo with eight rounds missing. The wallet contained driver's license and three hundred dollars. They also found an airline ticket, round trip to Paris, France from New York. The ticket was for three days before Washington, D.C. was destroyed. The FBI speculated he missed his flight because he misplaced his passport.

The President was informed about the situation in Seattle and St. Louis the next morning. Agent McIntyre asked to send two agents to Seattle. Threats against the First Family were the Secret Service's responsibility. He was upset that he hadn't been informed earlier. Agents Gilmore and Compton were on a flight in an hour.

When they arrived they noticed there were no vehicles at the search site. When they got out of the rental car, FBI agent Griffin stepped out of the house. "We're not parking here. Go about a mile down the road to a dirt lane on the left. Go to the end of it and park. Someone will bring you back."

"They must think someone might show up," Compton said to Gilmore when they were in the car.

"That would be my guess."

After arriving back at the house Gilmore said, "We would like to see what you have."

"That's no problem; everything is pretty much where we found it. We're fingerprinting everything and I mean everything. There is trash everywhere, food wrappers, cereal boxes and cans."

"How are you eliminating people in fast food places and grocery stores?"

"We're not, at least not right now."

"Will you be able to later?" asked Compton.

Griffin answered, "What we are looking for is duplicates. Odds are a person working in a burger joint isn't going to have his or her fingerprint on a can from a grocery store or a pizza box or a box of cereal. We're playing the odds here."

"Makes sense to me," Gilmore piped in.

Compton started looking around then asked, "Is this all the mail?"

"That's all," answered Griffin.

"Electric bill and phone bill. He must have a water well on the property."

"He does. It's out back in that small pump house," answered Griffin.

"The bills only go back two months?"

"He must have disposed of the previous months because we didn't find any," answered Griffin.

"Why would he do that? I mean look around. Look at all the trash. Why would he dispose of the bills and keep everything else? Does that make any sense to you because it sure doesn't to me?"

"We have noticed that ourselves. The guy didn't know what a trashcan was for," said Griffin.

"How did the bills get in the house?" asked Compton.

"Pardon me?"

"The shooter has been dead longer than a month. How did the bills from a month ago get in the house? Someone has been in here since he was killed."

Griffin said, "That's why we wanted you to park elsewhere."

"I see, and you think they will come back?"

"That's correct," answered Griffin.

Compton looked at the envelope from the St. Louis Police impound lot. She studied it closely. She wanted to be sure. "Where is the car this notice is about?"

"It will be towed to the lab in St. Louis for further analysis," answered Griffin.

"Don't move that car," said Compton.

"Pardon me!"

"Don't move that car. This is the second notice. Who has the first one? Someone may try to retrieve it."

Griffin pulled out his cell phone and punched in numbers. "Don't move the car. Put it under surveillance and put a tracking device on it."

"That was a good call, Ma'am. We have been here a long time. A fresh set of eyes and mind are a good thing right now," said Griffin.

Five days later, a man came into the impound lot. He went into the office and presented the notice and showed his identification. Then paid the impound fee and towing expenses. He had the same features as the passport. The agents were sure his driver's license was the same as the notification. He seemed to look around for cameras. He was being filmed but there was no way he could have spotted the cameras.

He went to the car, pulled an instrument out of his pocket and checked the car for tracking devices. The agents watching him from a distance knew they were dealing with a trained agent. The man started the car and drove away. He stopped a block away and put the cell phone in the back of a parked pick-up that had junk in the back. The agents were lucky. They were able to see this from their vantage point. Had the driver went another block they would have never known it. One of the tracking devices was in the phone. The other was in the car radio. This device only put out a signal every thirty minutes and lasted for two seconds. They made no attempt to follow him. "You know if he was smart he'd dump the car at the airport in the long term lot."

"He may do that when he gets close to where he's going."

"Let's hope you're wrong about that."

The man stopped and spent the night in Albuquerque, New Mexico. The next morning he got on the road at five a.m. and drove to Los Angeles, California. He pulled into a space on the upper deck of an office complex parking deck. He locked the door and went into the building. The two agents who had literally followed him halfway across the country lost him. One agent went inside while the other agent drove around the block. An hour later, they linked back up.

"You call it in?"

"Yep, I called it in. They are not happy about it at all, and I mean at all."

"What do they want us to do about it?"

"They want us to watch the car."

"Did they say why? What's so important about the car?"

"Don't know. Why go two thousand miles to pick it up, drive it two thousand miles here and walk away."

"Beats me. Are they going to send us any help?"

"Yeah, they are flying in agents from other field offices to help."

"You ask me it's just a waste of time."

"You might be right. You know the pick-up truck he threw the phone in?"

"What about it?"

"Round the clock surveillance on it."

"You're kidding me. What did this guy do?"

"I don't know but it must be important."

The two agents watching the car had not been informed of any of the unfolding events in Seattle, Washington. They were simply told to keep the car under surveillance. They moved a block away and watched a beep on a screen for two seconds every thirty minutes.

"What kind of office building is it? The one he went into."

"You name it, doctors, lawyers, travel agents, consultants, real estate and even a few restaurants. Just your typical office building. He could have went into any of them or left before we could follow him. He may be at the airport by now."

At ten o'clock that night, the driver said, "It looks like the building is closed for the night. What are we going to do? We have been in this car since six o'clock this morning. Even the parking deck is closed now."

"We need to wait until we get help to watch."

When the passenger's cell phone rang he nearly jumped out of his skin. He had halfway dozed off.

"Yes."

He finished listening for a minute before saying, "Let me put you on speaker phone where we can both listen."

"I said we have someone else watching him now. Get a hotel room and call in tomorrow at eight a.m."

"Are we staying here in Los Angeles?"

"Yes, we are."

"What's so important about this car?"

No answer. Then a dial tone.

"I've been on lots of stakeouts before and I always knew why. What aren't they telling us?"

"I don't know. Let's get something to eat and a place to spend the night. Maybe we'll find out tomorrow."

At eight a.m., they checked in and were told to go to an office building three blocks from the surveillance site. They went to the sixth floor of an office building and knocked on the door. The door opened and they entered.

The man who opened the door was in his late forties. He was eating a sandwich. His shirttail was out. He looked like he had flown all night. He needed a shave and a shower. His trousers were wrinkled. He didn't look like an FBI agent; he was at least forty pounds overweight.

"Are you with the FBI?" asked one of the agents from St. Louis.

The man burped and hit his chest with a closed fist.   "Shore am, they've been waiting for ya'll."

The agent asked, "Who's here?"

"Don't rightly know. There are a whole slew of them in there now. Ya'll go on in. We's wasting daylight."

"Where are you from, if I might ask, what field office?"

"Behavioral Science at Quantico. But I was born and raised in Lana, Georgia."

"You mean Atlanta, right?"

"That's what I said, Lana, Georgia."

"Did you go to college in Georgia?"

"Yep, Georgia Southern."

"I'm not familiar with that? Where is it?"

"Statesboro, Georgia."

"Did anyone ever tell you that you talk funny?"

"Now that you made mention of it, several of the fellers asked me the same thing."

"Mind if I ask what your degree is in?"

"Logic and I also have one in psychology. Now ya'll better get on in there. Everybody's waiting on ya'll."

"Can you tell us what this man did to have us stay in Los Angeles? I understand other agents are watching the car."

The agent from Quantico looked around to make sure no one else was listening and said, "I shouldn't tell ya'll this but what the man done was drove a car two thousand miles."

"That's it!"

"That's it for right now."

The two agents from St. Louis looked at each other and shook their heads in disbelief. The two agents knew Behavioral Science was profilers. They had heard they were in the basement at Quantico, Virginia. It was rumored that they never really saw the light of day.

"How often are profilers right about suspects?"

"Oh, I'd say maybe ten percent of the time that we are really right. See we play the odds."

The adjacent room was a conference room. There were no windows and two tables were set end to end to hold sixteen chairs. A podium and power point screen was on the far end. A man in a tailored suit was impatiently looking at his watch.

"Please set down where we can get started." The two agents sat in the nearest chair.

"This briefing is top secret. It does not leave this room. This is who we are trying to locate. This is the surveillance tape from the police impound lot in St. Louis, Missouri. The car in this photo is the one we are watching. It is parked on the upper deck of the parking garage three hundred yards away. We have a tracking device on the car at the present time. Our subject picked it up four days ago in St. Louis and drove here and parked late yesterday afternoon. He went into the adjacent office building where we lost him. We don't know if he has an office there or just went through the building. There is the chance he just wanted it out of St. Louis. I can tell you this is important enough to have twenty agents watching."

"What did this guy do?" asked one of the agents from St. Louis.

"I'm afraid I can't divulge that at this time because I don't know."

"Ya know what I think?" Everyone looked to the back of the room. The agent from Behavioral Science was standing there. He had his hands in his pockets. His shirttail was still out.

"Yes, Mr. Jackson. I'd like to know what you think," said the man giving the briefing.

"I think the car is a decoy."

"Would you care to explain?"

"Shore, I think the rascal wants to find out if ya'll are looking fer it."

"But why drive it two thousand miles?" asked one of the agents.

"Well, it's like this. If'in he picked it up in St. Louie and went to the airport and parked in one of them long term parking lots you'da found it right quick like. You'da looked there first. So he had to get back here anyhow and if'in he picked up the car and left it in St. Louie, you'da checked the airline when ya found it. Too many cameras at the airport. If'in you'da checked the airlines and a knowed he took a flight and where he's agoing. So he took it cross country. No he's watching ya'll and if'in onea ya'll go near it he'll know it's not safe to do what he's gonna do next. Ya gotta lure him out. Mak'em come to ya'll."

"And just how do we do that?"

"Let me think on it a spell. I'll come up with sumpin."

"Please, let us know when you do."

"I'll do it. I don't know if the agents that followed him noticed he coulda parked anywhar over dar. Seems to me if'in he was trying to hide it he'da parked on one of tha other levels. He would'na been able to see it himself, so he parks it whar he could see it. That's why I's thinkin he's actin mighty strange. No siree he's watchin fer us. Ya'll can count on that."

The next morning, the car was still on the top deck of the parking garage when the two agents from St. Louis arrived. The agent from the Behavioral Science Unit was the only one in the front room. The senior agent from St. Louis said, "We weren't introduced yesterday. I'm Jonathan Peterson. Everyone calls me John and this is agent James Gray. Everyone calls him Jimmy." The two agents extended their hands to shake.

"I'm Robert Lee Jackson, everyone calls me Bubba." He shook the two agent's hands.

"They call you Bubba?"

"Yep, it'sa lot quicker than saying a whole mouth full of names."

"Then it's Bubba," said Agent Gray.

"Did you work last night, Bubba?"

"Shore did, and I'ma wore slap out. Wore slap out means I'ma real tired."

"What did you do? The car hasn't moved?"

"Ah, did a lotta figurin."

"What kind of figuring?" asked Gray.

"Come on inside the other room and I'll show ya."

In the other room was a young lady maybe thirty years old. She was about five foot seven. Her red hair was in a ponytail. She had a lot of freckles and wore black rimmed glasses. Her dark blue dress and jacket met the FBI's dress code for agents.

"I'll be through in a minute professor."

"Thank you, Michelle." A few minutes later Bubba introduced Michelle to Agents Gray and Peterson.

"Pleased to meet you," said Michelle.

"Likewise," said Gray.

"You just arrived?" asked Peterson.

"I flew in last night from Quantico, Virginia."

"Okay boys, this is what we'a doing. We looking at the angles from all the buildins aroun here an since our man coulda parked anywhere, we kinda figured he parked where he coulda see it all the time. You all following me on that?"

Both agents nodded their heads.

"Now Michelle has computed all that into our computer and this is what we come up with."

"The office building he went into is ten stories. The parking deck is five stories with a concrete barrier to keep someone from driving off the edge. That means the only offices that can see the front and both sides of the car is the seventh through the tenth floors on the corner to our right." She pointed to a large scale photo of the building.

"If he was in another office he would have parked in an adjacent space. Those are the only offices that meet the parameters the professor gave me."

"Have you come up with a plan to draw him out?" asked Gray.

"Yep," answered Bubba.

"Can you share it with us?" asked Gray.

Michelle stood in front of the two agents and said, "It's simple. I'm going to wreck his car."

"That's it. You are going to wreck his car?" said Peterson.

"Oh, there will be more to it than that, but that's the way to draw him out."

"Okay, when are we going to do it?" Peterson asked.

"Today is Thursday. We're giving him a week of watching the car."

"Why don't we do it now?" asked Gray.

"We believe they, and we are guessing here, it may just be one person, but we believe others may be involved."

"You know more about this than we do don't you?" asked Peterson.

"Yes I do and I can not elaborate on that right now."

"When can we find out?" inquired Gray.

"With a whole lot of luck you'll never find out," said Michelle looking as serious as possible. Then she added, "Now we have some questions we'd like to ask you."

"What questions?" asked Peterson.

"You followed him almost two thousand miles, is that correct?"

"Give or take."

"Did the two of you get tired? I'm assuming you took turns driving. Is that a fair guess?"

"We changed every four hours."

"Did you get tired?"

"Yes, we did," both agents answered.

"Yet he drove two thousand miles by himself in three days is that correct?"

"That is correct," said Gray.

"How do you know that?"

"Well, he had to," Gray answered.

"What if I told you the car he picked up wasn't his. We are sure it wasn't his."

"But the driver's license and the notification letter checked out," said Peterson.

"But the fingerprints didn't. Of course you had no way of knowing that."

"Is this one of those things that you know and we don't?" asked Peterson.

Michelle nodded her head for her answer.

"You didn't keep the car under constant surveillance did you? Oh, by the way, you weren't expected to. The tracking device told you where he was, correct?"

"Yes, the tracking device. We couldn't get close without giving the tail away."

"I understand. The man who picked up the car passed the identification test. Remember his license was left in the car."

"But he had the correct driver's license when he picked up the car."

"Both the license he presented and the license in the car was forgeries. We are certain of that."

"Wait a minute," said Gray. Are you implying somewhere between St. Louis and Los Angeles they switched drivers?"

"We believe so. We have no proof of that but yes we believe so."

Both agents were looking at the floor. If what she was saying was true they had been snookered. FBI agents don't like to be snookered.

"We don't know for sure, both men, the real owner and the phony looked so much alike. Black hair, thick black mustache. Almost the same height and weight.

"You remember the first gulf war. You remember how Saddam's body guards looked a lot like Saddam. When the shooting starts, how do you tell the real one from all the others in all the confusion."

"So, we are watching a car and don't know if the guy we followed or someone else shows up…a look alike." Michelle could tell he was agitated.

"We believe they all could look alike or close enough to cause confusion. No one can drive a car two thousand miles and watch it twenty four seven for over a week. We're counting on that. We are hoping he brings in reinforcements just like we did."

"But we don't know where he is," said Gray.

"We evaluated all the offices in the office complex and we believe we know which one it is. We have to prove it first. The car will prove it."

"Which office? There are all kinds of professions over there."

"Yes there is. There are four we are concerned about. Seven through ten. We believe it's the travel agency. We are almost certain."

"How can you know that?" asked Peterson.

"When we searched the car we found an airline ticket. It was copied and replaced along with everything else. We didn't want to raise any suspicions. Care to guess where it was purchased?"

"The travel agency?" said Gray.

"That is correct. It took us a while to piece that part together, but that isn't proof. So he sold a ticket, big deal. He doesn't know why the man left his car."

"So, if you wreck his car and he goes to it that's enough for probable cause?"

"We believe so. I'm willing to bet the car has been wiped down. We are checking gas stations now where he may have stopped along the way. We're assuming you gave him plenty of distance."

"That's right. We hardly ever had visual contact with him," said Gray.

"If we can get him on video with the car, getting in or out and pumping gas, we got him."

"This guy must have done something pretty big to go through all of that," said Peterson.

Neither Bubba of Michelle answered.

CHAPTER SIXTY THREE

SECOND FLIGHT

EGLIN AIR FORCE BASE

Second Lieutenant Joshua A MacDonald had spent two days filling out induction paperwork and taking physicals. He had passed the flight physical with no problem. He had to take the eye exam three times. It seemed as though he had better eyesight than normal, much better than normal. He could see things at twenty feet the normal person could see at fifteen.

He had three days of classroom instruction and tomorrow would go on his first flight with his instructor pilot. With a war on the horizon, flight school was being accelerated.

Josh didn't know anything about his instructor pilot (I.P.). The I.P. knew everything about Second Lieutenant Joshua A. MacDonald. The I.P. was Major Carlton Hunter from Boaz, Alabama. Known by his call sign "MOON PIE."

He had been in the Air Force sixteen years and an Instructor Pilot for three years. When the commanding officer called him into his office and informed Major Hunter that his student was the President's son, Major Hunter said, "I assume I am to baby him and give him passing grades."

The Commanding Officer said, "Just take care of him and don't let him kill himself, alright. You just need to know that he could pick up the phone and call his old man and then what?"

"Can't you let someone else do this? Why me?"

"You're the best instructor I have. If something happens it wouldn't look good if he didn't have the best pilot with him, now would it?"

"Well, I don't like it. I don't like it one bit. If he passes, he passes, if he fails, he fails, that's all there is to it. You can't force me to give him a higher evaluation than he deserves." Hunter was fuming. He had never played favorites before and he didn't intend to start now.

"Just take care of him, alright and remember who he is. He's the President's son."

Major Hunter was waiting on the flight line for his student. He consoled himself he was making a lot of money as a Major in the Air Force. His sixteen year old daughter only made six bucks an hour baby sitting and they were doing the same thing.

Major Hunter saw his student coming. His first thought was maybe he was too big to fit in the cockpit then his problem would be solved.

Josh walked up, saluted and introduced himself as Lieutenant MacDonald.

Major Hunter returned the salute and said, "I want you to perform the pre-flight inspection. I will be grading you is that understood?"

"Yes, Sir," answered Josh.

Josh went through the pre-flight inspection flawlessly. When he was finished he turned to Major Hunter and said, "Sir, this panel appears to be slightly loose and the port wheel strut on the landing gear appears to have a slight leak."

Major Hunter didn't appear fazed, even though he was. He had the mechanics loosen the panel and put fluid on the landing gear strut two hours ago.

"Let's get the mechanic over to straighten this out," said Hunter.

Thirty minutes later Major Hunter lined the aircraft up for takeoff. When he had clearance he roared down the runway. At one hundred and fifty knots he lifted off and began a steep climb. If this kid throws up maybe they will let him fly a desk somewhere.

He put the plane through its paces. He was throwing the plane in some tight maneuvers. He knew the kid hadn't lost his lunch yet. He did barrel rolls and put the plane in some tight G's that even made him queasy.

"You alright up there, Lieutenant?"

"Yes, Sir, having the time of my life."

Major Hunter took the plane in a near vertical dive and pulled up at two thousand feet. The G force was tremendous.

"You okay up there, Lieutenant?"

"Yes, Sir, I'm fine. Can we do that again? That was great!"

Major Hunter climbed to twenty thousand feet, leveled off and said, "I want you to take the controls. Keep it at 350 knots at this altitude and the heading of 240 degrees, you understand all that?"

"Yes, Sir, 350 knots, twenty thousand, 240 degrees," answered Josh.

Major Hunter knew he wouldn't be able to do that. He had never had a student on his first flight able to do that. Most were all over the sky. The Major watched all the instruments, none wavered at all. Up front Josh felt like he was the luckiest man alive.

After twenty minutes, the Major said, "I want you to take it to thirty thousand feet and take up a heading of twenty degrees and increase the speed to four hundred knots, you got all that?"

Josh repeated the instructions and followed them to the letter. Major Hunter was expecting him to miss the mark and start over correcting on all three. He could have waited for the cows to come home before that happened. He was especially impressed on the direction change.

"Okay, you have the controls; if I say I have it you release the controls. Do you understand?"

"Yes, Sir," answered Josh.

"Put the aircraft through any maneuver you want to try."

"Yes, Sir!" answered Josh.

Josh duplicated all the maneuvers Major Hunter had performed earlier. Major Hunter knew it took a lot of concentration to perform the maneuvers and yet he could hear the kid singing a gospel song over the intercom. For some reason Major Hunter joined in as they did the barrel rolls at thirty thousand feet singing 'I'll Fly Away.'

Major Hunter was duly impressed by his flying skills even though he made no comment.

"Let's return to base and land this bird." Major Hunter had never let a student land on his first flight.

"Yes, Sir," answered Josh.

Josh called for and got the landing instructions from the tower. On approach he settled into a nice glide path and made a near perfect landing. After moving the plane to the correct parking pad, both got out of the plane.

"You did pretty good, not great, but pretty good," said the Major.

"Thank you, Sir."

"How long have you been flying?" Major Hunter knew the answer already. He had been told the story of Josh landing in the desert.

"This is my second flight, Sir."

"Lot of simulator time, huh?"

"A few hours at Oklahoma. We didn't have one in Wyoming."

"Go ahead and get ready for your next class."

"Yes, Sir." Josh saluted and started to walk away.

"Major."

"What is it, Lieutenant?"

"Sir, if I become an Air Force pilot I want it because I can fly well enough, not because of who my father is."

"Fair enough. Are you sure you don't have a lot of flying time?"

"Sir, I've been flying in my dreams since I was six years old."

Josh saluted again and said, "Thank you. Major, for letting a dream come true" and walked away.

As Major Hunter watched Josh walk away another instructor pilot walked up and slapped Hunter on the shoulder and said, "How did the babysitting gig go?" Laughing as he said it.

"He can fly as well as you can."

"What!"

"The kid can fly and I do mean the kid can fly. He is a natural."

Major Hunter reported in to the Commanding officer. "I see you didn't let him kill himself out there."

"Sir, I have a question for you."

"What?"

"Could you have landed that plane in the desert under those circumstances?"

The Commanding officer thought about it and said, "Of course I could but then again I lie a lot." He smiled. "Seriously, I'd like to think I could have landed that plane, but I really don't know. That was the first time he had ever been in a plane and from what I understand there were rocks and boulders all over the place. I can't even believe he controlled the plane to get to a landing spot. I don't know if I could have done what he did or not. How about you?"

"I don't know and I hope I don't have the opportunity to find out."

"Did he do alright up there? Did you let him fly?"

"Sir, he made that plane do everything it could do. I had been flying years before I tried some of the stuff he did today. I even let him land the plane."

"You let him land? That's against policy."

"I know, but as I said, he's a natural. He's the first one I have ever seen. He's a natural born flying machine and a pretty good singer."

CHAPTER SIXTY FOUR

TOBY GOES BACK TO

COLLEGE

JOHN 8:32

After his ten articles titled 'The Truth Will Set You Free' was published in over one hundred small town newspapers, Toby was asked to speak to the Journalism Class in Kansas City, Missouri. This was his first speaking engagement.

After being introduced by the professor Toby stood behind the podium. He looked out at the small group of fifty students. He cleared his throat and looked at the expectant faces and smiled. It helped him to remember he sat in a classroom very similar to this one twenty five years ago.

"I want you to write this down. The most important thing I will say today is the truth will set you free."

Toby noticed all the students were writing in their notebooks. Toby felt good.

"If you become a journalist you have a moral obligation to set aside your personal feelings, beliefs and political inclinations. You will notice I said moral. That is a very powerful word, moral. If you don't do that you will just become someone's lapdog. Your reader will see through you and guess what; they will stop reading your articles. A journalist has to be a guard dog. A guard dog, not a lapdog or an attack dog. We have to guard that the government, any government don't abuse the citizens of this country. It doesn't necessarily have to be the government. It can be banks, labor unions, school boards, hospitals or insurance companies. I have investigated all of them as a journalist and guess what, sometimes I find no wrongdoings.

"I'm older than any of you. I'm old enough to remember that if you read the paper or watched the TV. news, what they said was the truth. That's why it was called newspapers. It was the news. Now you can actually call it the opinion paper. All of this has changed in my lifetime and I'm not that old even though most of you probably think I am ancient." Several students nodded their heads and laughed.

"I'm actually what you may consider old school. You see, our job shouldn't try to persuade the reader. The reader is smart enough to make up their own minds. I don't believe a newspaper should endorse a candidate because if they do the reader will think you're biased and they will question your motivation and when they do that you have lost their trust.

"I'm old enough to remember when you could trust the government. I'm old enough to remember when you could trust the news. I'm old enough to say I don't recognize what either has become. It is never too late to make it right. Reporting the truth and only the truth will make it right.

"I want to tell you about my experience in college. I think they are probably a lot like many of yours. I came from a poor family. I was the youngest of six children. For some reason I can't explain my entire family decided I would be the first to go to college.

"My dad was a mechanic and worked in my uncle's garage. My mother worked at the local hospital. No, she wasn't a doctor, nurse or lab technician or anything like that. She was in housekeeping; mopped floors, cleaned restrooms, made beds and yes, she emptied bed pans.

"My dad drove a cab while I was in college. He would leave the garage, go home, shower and drive for six hours at the local taxi company. My mother would leave work and then clean other people's houses. They did this for four years. When the two of them retired on social security five years ago I bought them a house and a new car. You know what? I still owe them. I can never repay what they did for me.

"I worked two and three jobs after school and still had no money. I lived off of ramen noodles, saltine crackers and the occasional can of Vienna sausage. A pack of ramen noodles cost twelve cents back then. Yesterday a pack cost a quarter. If I saw something I wanted or needed I didn't look at it as dollars and cents. If it was three dollars I thought that's twenty four packs of ramen noodles." The students laughed. "I had to wear my clothes two and three days at a time. I couldn't afford to wash and dry my clothes. I had one pair of shoes, one pair and they lasted for four years. When I got to my room I would take them off and not put them back on until it was time for school or work.

"I spent most of my money on paper and pens. I was always writing things to stay in practice. I would write down list of things. Then I would write a paragraph on why I needed to do that particular thing. Yes, I sometimes would have that dreaded problem, the ole mental block. I cured that by keeping a notepad by my bed. If I thought of something at three o'clock in the morning I would write it down. I would write short stories. If I saw something on the news I would write a story about that event. I was constantly writing.

"How many of you realize that the spoken word, once it leave's someone's mouth is gone forever, but the written word last for hundreds of years, perhaps even thousands. Now I know all of you won't become journalist but the skills you learn here will benefit you in the future.

"If you can't get a job at a magazine or newspaper, write a book, but just keep writing. The world has always wanted to read and study what is put on paper.

"It's a tough four years, believe me I know, but the first time you see an article and your name is attached to it you will realize it was all worth it.

"Now some of you want to be an investigative reporter. You have to piece together pieces of a story. Let me ask you this. What did I buy with my first paycheck?"

Several hands went up. Toby called on a young lady.

"A suit."

"No, Ma'am, it wasn't a suit."

"A car," said someone.

"No, not a car. You don't need a car in New York."

"A new pair of shoes!" was shouted from the back of the room.

Toby smiled; sometimes you had to shout from the back of the room. He had done it himself many times.

"That's right, a new pair of shoes. I still have the shoes I wore for those four years. I put them away as a constant reminder of how I struggled and how I had to persevere. Don't judge a man by his shoes. Judge him by how far he has walked in those shoes.

"Next question. Do I still eat ramen noodles?"

No one raised their hand.

"At least once a week. Remember I said they were a quarter yesterday. See what I mean, you have to put the pieces together. You have to listen carefully."

"Can I write about ramen noodles? I know a lot about ramen noodles?" asked a young man in the front row.

"Yes, you may, as a matter of fact that would be a good writing assignment. Thank you and good luck. Remember keep writing and the truth will set you free."

CHAPTER SIXTY FIVE

APPREHENSION

LOS ANGELES, CALIFORNIA

PSALMS 21:8

Michelle O'Conner briefed the FBI agents about the upcoming operation. "Our agent who will wreck the targeted vehicle will be taking off shortly. She will fly from Destin, Florida to Atlanta, change airlines and fly to Dallas, Texas. There is a two hour layover, then to Los Angeles. She will rent a car and drive to the Marriott and rent an executive suite and eat at an exclusive restaurant. She will pay for all of this on her personal credit card. She will be leaving a paper trail of credit card purchases. She will go to bed. After breakfast she will come here. She will park thirty feet away and go into the building. When she leaves she will back up and hit the targeted car. She will call the police and wait for an officer to arrive and give her an accident report. She will put a copy of the accident report on the windshield and drive away. The police officer is not a participant in the operation. He is an actual on duty police officer. She will eat lunch and drive to the airport, turn the car in and return home the same route as she came here. Then she will go into the office, turn in some paperwork and go on a three week vacation. Any questions?"

"Why all the credit card sales? Do you think these guys are going to look at all of that? All of this seems to be pretty elaborate to me. Any of us could have wrecked the car," said agent Gray.

"We don't know if they will look or not. We don't want to take a chance. There is way too much information out there in the computer world. They could run a background check or a credit report, any number of things and discover all sorts of stuff on anyone."

"She's using her real name?" asked Gray.

"Yes, she is, and when they check, if they do, they will find out everything about her. Where she works, where she lives, even her Facebook page. It's all out there for them to find."

"What happens if they find out she works for the FBI? I mean we all have things in our background that we're FBI or government employees. It seems like we are putting an agent at risk," Peterson pointed out.

"Our agent has never, not once, put on a piece of paper or told a friend or family member that she works for the FBI. In other words, she is a deep cover operative and has been since 9/11. No, they won't find anything there and this operation is a mouse trap. If they do check, and we're hoping that they do, we will know and that is more information we will have against them. One other thing I want to point out, we have placed listening devices in the offices above and below them."

"How did you do that? Aren't you worried about those people may be involved and tell the suspects?" Gray was getting a bad vibe out of this operation.

"No, we're not worried. Those offices have the same cleaning crew. An agent slipped in and planted them."

"You won't be able to use it in court. Any judge will throw it out. You're wasting your time there," said Gray.

"We are gathering information, not evidence with the listening devices. We seriously doubt if this portion of the investigation will ever go to court," answered O'Conner.

There was a stunned silence in the room. No one said anything. They were all wondering the same thing, what did these people do?

At ten thirty the next morning a dark blue BMW pulled in and parked one aisle away and two spaces to the right of the targeted car. A dark headed woman dressed in business attire got out. She reached into the car and retrieved a briefcase, glanced at her watch and walked hurriedly toward the parking deck elevators. She never glanced at the targeted car.

An hour later, she came out with her briefcase in one hand and a stack of folders in her other arm. When she reached her car she put the briefcase on the roof of the car. She opened it and removed her keys and opened the door. She put the folders on the passenger seat, got in the car, leaving the briefcase on the roof. As she backed up and turned the briefcase slid off the roof of the car. A second later she impacted the other car. The woman jumped out of the car and surveyed the damage. She was visibly upset. She picked up her briefcase, found her cell phone and called 9-1-1 to report the accident. She started collecting loose papers off the parking deck.

Twenty minutes later, the police arrived. Checked her driver's license and asked questions. The officer gave her a report which she signed and placed a copy under the windshield wiper of the other car. She also wrote a note saying how terribly sorry she was. Then she threw her briefcase in the car and drove away.

Michelle O'Conner looked at Bubba Jackson and said, "She did well!"

Agents Peterson and Gray said, "You think they will buy it?"

"What have we lost if they don't?"

Bubba Jackson said, "Now we wait." And they waited, and they waited some more.

At eight p.m. the following evening, a car pulled into the parking garage. The driver parked in the same parking space where the agents BMW had parked earlier. He got out and went into the office complex. The car was there long after the office complex and parking deck were closed. At three a.m., a man got out of the trunk of the car and retrieved the accident report and returned to the trunk of the car.

Bubba Jackson said, "A regular ole Trojan hoss if I ever saw one."

Twenty minutes later, he got out of the trunk and replaced the accident report under the wiper and returned to the trunk.

"What do we do now?" asked Gray.

"We follow him when the car leaves. He's not going to stay in that trunk forever."

JACK IN THE BOX

At three thirty in the morning, Jack's cell phone started ringing. He glanced at his alarm clock. He sighed before answering it and rubbed his eyes. He knew it was an emergency. He didn't recognize the number, but he knew in his gut it was an emergency.

"Hello."

"We have a problem."

Jack recognized the voice. The man from Los Angeles.

"What is it?"

"The car; I'm afraid something is wrong."

"What can be wrong with the car?"

"A crazy American woman backed into it."

"Tell me what happened."

Five minutes later, Jack said, "You have her address?" He wrote it down.

"I have four people out there now."

"We need to check this woman out. I had a bad feeling about this when we parked the car last week. Someone jumped out of a car and ran in the building and then went back out. He didn't go into any of the other offices, but I think we were followed," said the man in Los Angeles.

"Why didn't you bring this to my attention then? Why did you wait a week?"

"I have no excuse, Sir; can you check the woman out?"

"I can't, but I will have someone check on her."

"Thank you, Allah."

"Yeah, right, are you calling from a disposable phone?"

"Yes."

"Is it safe to use that phone? When did you purchase it?"

"Seven months ago from a drug store. I haven't used it before."

"Good. You will destroy that phone as soon as you hang up. Do you understand?"

"Yes, Sir, destroy the phone."

"And listen, no more calls. You understand?"

"Yes, Sir."

"We're too close to be taking any chances. No more calls!"

He hung up the phone and made a call to Atlanta, Georgia.

"Our friend out west is worried about the car. He just happened to remember he may have been followed last week. I need you to drive to Destin, Florida. It's on the coast of the Gulf of Mexico. Find out what you can. Be careful, be very careful. I don't want any more phone calls, none. It is too dangerous. I'm telling everyone no more calls. If this is a trap we are all caught. Again, be very careful." He gave the man the woman's name, address and phone number and then he hung up. There was no way he could go back to sleep. The idiot waits a week before telling me he may have been followed, what an idiot. This car, this stupid car is using up all my agents. One agent is missing; four agents are on the west coast. One agent is going to the Gulf of Mexico. Everything is at risk because of this car. Why, is the car important?

"Because I made it important," said Jack.

Jack hoped the missing agent was dead. That car can ruin everyone and Jack realized it was all his fault. He was the one who wanted the car retrieved. He was the one that had sent three agents to Los Angeles to watch the car because he had a bad feeling about it. Jack had a sick feeling that things weren't going to end well, all because of a stupid car. A woman driver, a stupid woman driver. Leave it up to a stupid woman driver to wreck everything. No wonder America is the Great Satan, they let women drive. Women aren't allowed to drive in Muslim countries. The only way it should be. They can't vote and they must be submissive to their husband. Women in America have too many rights, the infidels. Yes, America is the Great Satan because of the women.

LOS ANGELES

At 8:00 a.m., the driver returned to the car, got in and drove away.

"Who is following him?" asked Gray.

"An unmanned aerial vehicle, actually two of them from twenty thousand feet. We believe that is better than taking a chance with a vehicle. They might spot a car. Two cars will be five minutes behind and two cars ten minutes behind those."

"We'll see where they go and then make a decision?" asked Gray.

The car drove around for twenty minutes before pulling in a Walmart parking lot. It pulled to the side of the building. The trunk opened and the man inside got out, stretched, then walked into the parking lot and got into another vehicle and drove away.

"Split the drones and get the license plate of the new car. Inform the surveillance cars to move closer to our targets," O'Conner said.

"Let's get more cars on the road," said agent Gray.

"Good ideah," said Bubba Jackson.

"What about the car on the parking deck we've been watching?" asked Peterson.

"We keep watching it. I think they're suspicious. Let's see if we can catch them in our mouse trap. They haven't had time to check on our agent yet. That will take a few hours," said O'Conner.

"You were right, Mr. Jackson, the car was decoy," said Peterson.

Bubba Jackson being a southern gentleman said, "Thank ya, Suh."

At three p.m. that afternoon, a call was made to the agents business in Destin, Florida. A man asked to speak to the lady that backed into his car. He was told she was on vacation. The man insisted on speaking to her. The secretary insisted that she didn't know how to help the man. He asked for her home phone number.

The secretary said, "I'm sorry Sir; I can't give out that information."

"I'll sue her if I can't talk to her today. She wrecked my car and I want her to fix it and not with this rinky dink insurance company the rental agreement provides," said the man angrily.

"Give me your number and if I can reach her I'll have her call you. Will that work for you?"

"You make sure she calls me today," the man said loudly.

Michelle O'Conner said, "All that information was on the accident report which is still on the windshield right now including her home address. Want to bet someone visits. Maybe a little breaking and entering. We'll be waiting if he does."

"How many are involved in this? Unless one of the two we're following is going to Destin, Florida," said Gray.

"Don't rightly know right off hand," answered Bubba Jackson.

At three a.m., a car drove around the block twice of the apartment building in Destin, Florida. The address he was looking for was on the fourth floor. He had called the woman's number several times already, starting at eight p.m. Each time he had gotten an answering machine. He never left a message.

He parked a block away and walked to the building. He looked around to make sure no one was watching. The street looked deserted. He entered the building and took an elevator to the fourth floor. He picked the lock of the apartment door and cracked it open and went to the stairwell and made sure the door would open. He didn't want to take a chance of not being able to use it as an escape route if he needed to. He went down to each floor and checked each door. Satisfied he went back to the apartment and slipped inside. Had there been an alarm it would have already activated. He turned on his pen light and saw the curtains were closed. He turned on a table lamp and looked around. There was mail on the coffee table. He checked the name and it matched. He was in the right apartment. He went to the bedroom and did the same, then the bath. Then he searched the apartment. He was on video the whole time. He looked everywhere for something to tell him that she was a federal agent. He found nothing.

As he was backing out of the apartment, he heard someone yell, "Hey! What are you doing?"

The man turned around, he didn't have a weapon. He didn't need one. He was highly trained in martial arts. He was facing a young college kid wearing a Florida Gators sweatshirt, shorts and sandals with no socks. The kid looked drunk.

The burglar put his finger in front of his lips and said, "Shhh, you'll wake her up."

"Oh, okay, sorry I bothered you I just haven't ever seen you before."

"That's alright, I'm new in town. You have a good evening, or should I say morning," as he winked his eye at the kid.

"You want a beer? I got a six pack," said the kid holding up the beer.

"No thank you," said the man as he walked away. He glanced back at the kid who was walking the other way down the hall.

The man said softly to himself, "Infidel," then added, "That was close." He walked to the elevator. The kid went into an apartment and closed the door. He punched a number on his speed dial and said, "Gator here, that's him."

A block away, the man got in his car and drove away. He never suspected a tracking device was on his car and that he was being followed.

He headed toward Atlanta, Georgia. When he crossed the state line he called and said, "I didn't find anything. She's clean. Yes, I am sure, there is nothing there. I'm headed home now."

He arrived in the Atlanta area and drove through. Thirty miles north of Atlanta he pulled into his driveway. He looked around, didn't see anything out of place. He had spent over twelve hours on the road and two hours in the woman's apartment. A wild goose chase, but better safe than sorry I guess.

He spent an hour dozing on the couch. At nine o'clock, he went to bed. He would sleep as late as he wanted. There were no sounds to keep him awake. His nearest neighbor was a mile away. He like the isolation. It allowed him to do what he needed to do.

At 4:15 in the morning, he thought he heard a sound. The sound wasn't that loud. He knew a house could make noise when the temperature changed. Maybe that was it. He yawned and turned over in the bed and opened his eyes. He tried to scream but a hand was clasped over his mouth. He felt something prick his leg, a needle. He tried to fight for about ten seconds. He could tell there were about five of them. Then he drifted off. His last thought was maybe it's a dream. It wasn't, it was the beginning of a nightmare.

The man who had hid in the trunk of the car didn't fare any better. He had driven to Denver, Colorado.

The third man also had his sleep interrupted that night. He was fifty miles from Houston, Texas.

NEAR ATLANTA, GEORGIA

The search warrant for the house thirty miles north of Atlanta, Georgia was simple. The suspect had burglarized an apartment in Destin, Florida. The suspect had crossed the state line, a federal offense in the commission of a crime.

The agents started searching the house. What they didn't find was a clue in itself. No computer, no list of friend's numbers, no TV or stereo. There was an answering machine, but no tape inside. There was a cell phone.

Quite often when police conduct a search warrant they don't find what they are looking for, but find something far more sinister. You may have a warrant for drugs and find bodies in the basement.

When one agent went into the basement he didn't really expect to find anything. What he found sent chills down his spine. He turned and ran up the stairs. Halfway up he stopped and went back just to make sure he was seeing what he thought he saw. He didn't want to be the laughing stock of the search team if he was wrong. He went back down the stairs and got a closer look. He walked around the table in the middle of the floor. Satisfied that he was right, he ran upstairs.

The agent found the search team leader and grabbed him by the arm and dragged him downstairs. In the basement he couldn't even say anything; all he could do was point at the table.

"What is it?" asked the team leader.

"You are looking at a nuclear weapon."

"Are you serious? You're kidding right? Please tell me you are kidding."

"No, Sir, I'm not kidding. You remember after Washington we had that briefing on what one might look like?"

"Yes, I remember now. Oh Jesus, sweet Mother of God. I'm calling the director. Get everyone outside. I want road blocks set up for at least a mile, no make that two."

Thirty minutes later, a Nuclear Response Team from Dobbins Air Force Base arrived.

"That's what it is, no doubt about it," said the Nuclear Response Team.

The FBI went into full alert. Every FBI agent in the United States received a phone call. Priority urgent, top secret, not a single word would be leaked out.

A device was found in Denver. Another was found fifty miles from Houston Texas.

What had started out as a roundup of suspects had turned into something no one could comprehend. It raised one question though. Are there more out there? The FBI was scared of the answer. They knew the answer was probably.

LOS ANGELES

When the agents in Los Angeles received word about the nuclear weapons being found in the suspects' houses, they changed direction.

"This is a real game changer, if you know what I mean," said Michelle.

No one disagreed.

"Three are in the bag. Two are in the travel agency and they don't have a clue as to what is going on. Is it safe to assume that this is all of them?"

No one answered.

"I say let's bring them in. I don't think we should wait. If word leaks out, and you know that's a big possibility, anything can happen. We have ways to get information out of them. I say let's go ahead and bring those two in," said Gray.

Michelle looked at Jackson. "Professor, what do you think?"

Bubba Jackson slowly nodded his head, "Let's do it."

The takedown didn't go as planned, they seldom do. One man put up more of a fight than anticipated, allowing the other to make it to a window and crash through.

"Oh my God, he jumped!" screamed Michelle.

"Reckon why he went and done that?" said Jackson.

Three agents rushed to the spot he should have landed. He wasn't there. One looked up and saw the man dangling in a tree. He had broken numerous branches at the top. The larger ones at the bottom had stopped him.

A bucket truck was brought to the scene. An agent went to retrieve the body. He yelled down, "He's still alive."

An ambulance was summoned and he was placed aboard. He wasn't taken to the nearest hospital. He was taken to the Naval Base in San Diego, California.

Bubba Jackson and three other men were waiting for the doctor in the waiting room. When the doctor came out he approached the men "I'm sorry, but your friend has a spinal cord injury. I'm afraid he will be paralyzed for life."

"He ain't our friend," they said as they flashed their badges to the doctor.

"What's going on here?" asked the doctor.

"Afraid we can't tell you, Doc. National Security, you know what I mean. Is he gonna make it?"

"He'll live if that's what you're asking," answered the doctor.

"It's important I talk to him right now," said Bubba Jackson.

"He is heavily sedated."

"Tell me what drugs you have given him. All of them. Write them down fer me."

The doctor looked at his clipboard, went to a chair, sat down and began to write down what medications had been administered. He gave the list to Jackson, who gave it to one of the other agents who studied it for a moment, shook his head and put the list in a satchel. The Navy doctor noticed a stethoscope in the satchel. "Are you a doctor?" asked the Navy doctor.

The agent didn't answer.

"Doctor, this is of the utmost importance. You will tell no one about this patient. Do you understand?"

The Navy doctor looked at the four men. "How did he get injured?"

"He took a flying leap."

"He took a flying leap?"

"Yep, a flying leap. I understand you have an isolation chamber here on this base?"

"Of course, we have one for radiation exposure or biological weapons exposure."

"Move him there."

"Now?" asked the doctor.

"Yep, right now," answered Bubba.

"I don't like it. I don't know what's going on here," said the doctor.

"Doc, how many years you been in the Navy?"

"Sixteen. Why you asking?"

"You want to retire from the Navy, right?"

"Of course," answered the doctor.

"What is the best duty in the Navy to spend his last four years?" asked Bubba.

The doctor had noticed the other three men had not spoken a word.

"Pearl Harbor," answered the doctor.

"And the worst?" Bubba was eyeing the doctor to see if he had received the implied threat.

"Probably a weather station at the North Pole," answered the doctor looking from one agent to another before looking at Bubba again.

"I can have you in Pearl Harbor in forty eight hours."

"Is this that serious that you would threaten me?"

Bubba didn't answer.

The next twenty four hours was the longest of Bubba and Michelle's life. They both wondered if they had done the right thing or had they acted prematurely. When they got word that two other devices were found there was jubilation in the office.

Michelle summed it up. "All of us came here to watch a car and try to arrest a few suspects. No one had any idea there were five nuclear weapons out there and we would stumble on them."

Jackson wondered what the five would be tried for. He didn't think they would be tried for the five bombs, probably tried for the attack on Washington and anything else they could think of. America didn't need to know what was going on in Independence.

INDEPENDENCE

In Independence, Missouri, the director of the FBI informed the President about the nuclear weapons being discovered and secured. The President didn't show any outward emotion. He stood and walked to the window facing west and stood there for a few minutes. The director waited until the President returned to his chair.

"I have some very good news on the church and school bombings, Mr. President."

"That's great; those two things have been hanging over our heads for a long time."

"Fingerprint matches have been made. It appears as though the same people with the nuclear weapons did that also."

The President leaned back in his chair, thought for a minute before saying, "Let's not release any information on any of this."

"Are you sure, Mr. President? The news media are criticizing you about the church and the school bombings and the FBI as well."

"I know, but let me ask you this. Has everyone been apprehended?"

The FBI Director shook his head and answered, "We don't know that at this time. We are assuming those five men had a controller."

"A controller, what's that?" asked the President.

"Someone above them that passed along the orders. I wouldn't think any country would allow five men to do what they wanted to do when they wanted to do it. I would think someone is coordinating all this."

"I see," said the President.

"We were fortunate Mr. President; each agent had a cell phone. We are going over all those records now. We were very fortunate."

"I know," answered the President. He then added, "If we release any information the nation who did this will assume we have the weapons. I don't want them to know that. I want them to believe they still have them and can use them when they want to. I think we should say the church and the school bombings weren't even related. Teenage prank of something like that. I don't want our enemy to know they no longer have the upper hand."

"When will we inform the American people, Mr. President?"

"When it's over."

"You mean the war?"

"Yes, the war. Mr. Director, the FBI had done a fantastic job investigating this, but I'd rather our enemy, whoever it may be, think that we are stumbling around in the dark. I had rather they think they have the advantage when they don't."

"I understand, Mr. President."

"What can we charge these five men with that the news media wouldn't even bother to cover it?" asked Lewis.

"Each had weapons that had the serial numbers removed. That's a Federal offense."

"Will the media cover a story like that?" asked Lewis.

"I doubt it. Cases like that happen all the time. We can slip it in while a bigger case is being tried."

"Make it happen."

"Yes, Sir, Mr. President."

PART FOUR

CHAPTER SIXTY SIX

JEFFERSON

PSALMS 21:11

Marsha Jefferson was the first one in the office. Six hours earlier, she left her Mother's house in Birmingham, Alabama, caught a flight to Atlanta then Kansas City and then a taxi to Independence.

The duty officer looked up when she walked in.

"Welcome back, Marsha."

"It's good to be back," said Jefferson smiling.

"Are you on light duty or what? No one told me you were coming back. Have you been cleared by the doctor?"

"Yep, I was cleared. But you know what? I forgot to bring the paperwork. It's in Birmingham."

"Don't worry about it," said the duty officer.

"Gilmore in?"

"Not yet. They worked late last night."

"Worked on what?"

"They wouldn't say. Compton was here also."

Marsha went to her cubicle and started reading threat files on the First Lady.

Dean Gilmore, Jefferson's supervisor, walked past her cubicle, stopped and glanced at her, then cleared his throat to get her attention.

Jefferson looked up. "Hello, Gilly."

Gilmore hated being called Gilly.

"Good morning, Agent Jefferson."

"Good to be back," said Jefferson.

"Can you step into my office?"

"Sure." She picked up a notepad and pen.

"You won't need those," said Gilmore.

Jefferson followed Gilmore into his office closing the door behind her.

"Have you been medically cleared?"

"No, I haven't, but my mother is driving me crazy. I have got to get back to work. There has to be something I can do around here. The duty officer told me you and Compton was working on something. Maybe I can help."

"You don't like doing paperwork, remember," said Gilmore.

"That was then. This is now."

"You never were a very good liar."

"Is it that obvious?" asked Jefferson.

"Yes, it is." Then he studied Marsha for a minute.

"Look, I've got a stack of cell phone and telemarketer records you can go through."

"What am I supposed to be looking for?" asked Jefferson.

"There is a pay phone near the Canadian border we're trying to figure out."

"A pay phone? I didn't know there was any of those still around."

"A few are. Actually I think we just don't notice them anymore. Everyone has cell phones now, but there are a lot of places still with no towers. I guess this is one of those places. The FBI has had it staked out for almost two weeks but no one has answered."

"What's unusual about that? I wouldn't answer one if it was ringing."

"Someone use to answer and now they don't."

Five minutes later, Gilmore placed two stacks on her desk. He pointed to the small stack and said, "Cell phones, there are six of them." Then he pointed to a stack almost ten inches tall. "Telemarketers." Gilmore glanced at his watch and said, "I have to go downstairs. The First Lady is meeting with ten Girl Scout groups. I won't be back until late this afternoon."

"Is Compton coming in today?"

"She will be with the First Lady."

After Gilmore left, it dawned on Marsha that Gilmore hadn't mentioned why she was going through all these phone records. Why was this so important? She had worked lots of cases where she was given a task and not told what the ultimate objective was. That way you were impartial in reaching a decision.

Jefferson jumped in with both feet. She worked through lunch, grabbing a pack of crackers and a cup of coffee at 3:00 p.m. She looked up to see Gilmore standing in her cubicle door.

"You going to work all night?"

"I'm going to give it a few more hours," answered Jefferson.

"Finding anything?"

"No, but that doesn't mean it is not here. You know I'm beginning to think it may be a red herring."

"That's exactly what I think it is, too. To throw us off track or get us bogged down. You know it may be an early warning system to let them know we're looking at them," said Gilmore.

"If it's an early warning system they would have to have someone watching, right?"

"You'd think so," said Gilmore before adding, "But then again if the pay phone is that involved the FBI may go in the store and ask if someone is using it a lot and that would let them know."

"I see what you mean. The FBI didn't do that did they?"

"No, at least not that I am aware of."

"The FBI has an opinion?" asked Marsha.

"They think the owner or clerk at the store may be involved, maybe both, who knows, it may just be coincidence. We have nothing to show any wrong doing on the pay phone."

"They may be right," said Jefferson.

"I hate to tell you this but there is another stack we haven't had time to even look at. We got it late last night. It's going to make it almost impossible to cross check. It's the records on the pay phone. What you have there is the telemarketers and the six cell phones."

"So, no one has checked the pay phone records to the cell phones and telemarketers?" said Jefferson.

"That's right. We have looked through what you have there. The FBI is running all this through their computers, but no one knows what we're really looking for. I guess something that jumps out at us, a hunch so to speak or a pattern. We haven't figured anything out yet. There may be nothing to figure out. They may have just picked a phone number and called it a lot. Who knows, but all six phones called it a lot and someone answered, now they don't," said Gilmore.

"Where did we get all these records from? Did we tip someone off when we got a court order? That may have been their early warning system," said Jefferson.

"We didn't go through the courts to get them. The National Security Agency provided the records."

"Did the NSA record the conversations?"

"They said they didn't but you know how those spooks are."

"They would give them to us if they had them right?"

"Sometimes agencies like to hold their cards close to the vest if you know what I mean."

"Like we do," said Jefferson.

"Yeah, like we do."

"So, we are looking for a needle in a haystack that may not have a needle in it, is that what you are saying?" asked Jefferson.

"Look, you know how things are. We look and look and then look some more. Sometimes we find something, sometimes we don't. We want to touch all the bases."

"I know. You know where I always find what I am looking for?"

"Where?"

"The last place I look."

"Goodnight, Marsha, oh, and welcome back."

"Where are the pay phone records?"

"In the filing cabinet, top drawer."

"What about the key to the filing cabinet?"

"Pick the lock. That's what you always did before."

Jefferson smiled. "I didn't want to bother you at the time."

"Yeah, right. Goodnight, Marsha."

Jefferson was alone in the office. She started talking to herself. It helped to get it out. "This is a needle in a haystack. Who in their right mind would call a telemarketer from a pay phone?"

Then she thought, if you had a rare penny you wouldn't hide it by itself you would put it with a lot of change. So much change no one would bother to look there. That's the haystack, now find the needle. "That's odd; this store must be in the middle of nowhere." She brought the location up on the GPS. "It is in the middle of nowhere."

There had only been about three hundred calls made from there in a year and a half. She checked and saw that the convenience store had a phone inside so they wouldn't need to use the pay phone. She noted that the store was almost on the Canadian border, probably less than a hundred feet.

"You want to have a store where you will have traffic." This obviously didn't have traffic. The nearest small town was twenty miles in each direction. She pulled up how long the owner had been the owner. Seventeen months. She looked to see when the pay phone was installed. Fifteen months. She checked the cell phone records to see when they were activated. Marsha leaned back in her chair, she couldn't believe it. She didn't know what to make of this. The pay phone was installed the same day the cell phones were activated. This can't be a coincidence. This information gave Marsha a little wind in her sails. She continued to work. She knew the computer could figure it out, but Marsha wanted to figure it out. Not some mindless machine.

"There has to be a better way to do this." She knew the telemarketers probably had some type of machine that would dial a number and then go to the next number in order. She wrote the number of the pay phone down on an index card. She made the numbers large enough to see when she placed it against her phone. She could glance at it when comparing it to the cell phones and telemarketers. She decided she would compare it to the cell phones first. An hour later, she sat back in her chair. This is impossible. The pay phone called the six cell phones ten times. All six cell phones received ten calls from a pay phone. The pay phone has to be involved. It has to be. This is out of the realm of possibility.

Like most law enforcement officers, she didn't believe in coincidences. She then went down the list of telemarketers the pay phone had called. She found one number the pay phone had called only one time. Why all the other calls on other lines and only one on this particular line? "What am I missing here?" She looked at the date and time. This was the first call made from the pay phone. The very first one. Who would call a telemarketer from a pay phone? She knew the answer, no one. She made a note to herself and placed it on her desk for tomorrow. 'Find out owner of pay phone.' She looked at her watch. She was amazed it was midnight. "I'll give it another hour. Wait a minute, time, how long did they talk?" She looked at the pay phone record. She knew the calls to the cell phones lasted less than a minute, just long enough to tell someone you weren't interested. This first call had lasted over two hours. Who would talk to a telemarketer for two hours from a pay phone? The answer was nobody.

"It's always the last place I look." She was on the way out of the office when she remembered a case that happened while she was with the Birmingham Police Department. She wasn't involved with the case but had gotten the information after the investigation. A sexual predator was stalking his neighbor. He had run a phone line from her phone junction box on her house to his. It was nothing more than an extension. He could listen in on her phone conversations and determine her boyfriends and what her plans were. It was discovered after his arrest when a new occupant moved in. Could someone be doing the same thing on the pay phone? "Maybe no one is actually using the pay phone but is somewhere else."

She decided she would sleep on it. She picked up an agency car and drove to her apartment. She set her alarm for seven.

She woke up at five, took a shower and headed back to the office. She grabbed a doughnut on the way. She had no food at her apartment. She hadn't been there since she was shot in the assassination attempt.

Something rattling around in her head had woke her up. Her Granny use to say 'Something was tickling her noggin.' She was at her desk before Linda Compton came in at seven.

"Welcome back, Marsha. I've missed you."

"It's good to be back," answered Marsha without looking up.

Linda Compton sat down in front of Jefferson's desk and asked, "Phone records?"

"Yeah, phone records."

"Gilmore and I looked through those so many times I wanted to throw my cell phone away."

"Yeah, I know what you mean." Marsha stopped what she was doing. "You know I have a cell phone. I hardly ever get telemarketer calls. That's one thing I like about a cell phone. Do you get many calls?"

"Now that you mention it, I don't. I get maybe one a month is all."

"How does all that work?" asked Jefferson.

"From what I understand these companies get a whole bunch of lines, maybe even a hundred from a hundred different companies. They buy bulk airtime, maybe fifty thousand hours. They rent a building and the employee's call number after number and give their sales pitch."

"But sometimes it's a recorded message, right?" asked Jefferson.

"Yep, and they have automated dialers. No answer and it goes to the next number," said Compton.

"Where are these places located?"

"All over the place. Some may be from overseas, cheap labor you know."

"But all these numbers are U.S. area codes, right? How do they do that?"

"They have some sort of routing system. The call comes in then goes out as a different area code, sometimes the same as yours. They are really sophisticated."

"Sum it up for me. These numbers I have been looking at to these cell phones and pay phone may have come from anywhere, right? And every one of them may have been in the same building?"

"That is correct," said Compton.

"But why are we looking at these six cell phones and one pay phone? What's so important about them?"

Marsha didn't know it but when she was in rehab she was out of the loop. She didn't know about the FBI investigation. Those arrests had never made the news. All she was doing was looking through phone records without knowing why. The operation was on a need to know basis. Marsha didn't need to know.

Compton didn't answer.

"Linda, what aren't you telling me?"

Compton looked away and said, "I've got to get back to threat assessments." She stood, turned and walked away.

Before she reached her cubicle Jefferson said, "I found it Linda. I found what you and Gilly have been looking for."

Compton stopped and turned around. "Where?"

"The last place I looked Linda."

"Show me," said Compton.

"Tell me," said Jefferson.

"I can't."

"Who can?" asked Jefferson. "Can Gilly tell me?"

"I doubt it."

"Are the two of you going to play show and tell all day?"

Compton and Jefferson turned to look at Gilmore. Neither had heard him come in.

"Well, are you?" asked Gilmore.

Neither woman answered.

"You tell her and you show her." He pointed at each of them in turn.

After Gilmore went into his office both women sat there looking at each other. Both were waiting on the other to speak first.

"I guess you're wondering why Gilly didn't tell you why these numbers are so important."

"Yeah, I wondered about that. I guess he wanted an objective opinion."

"No, there is another reason."

"What?"

"Your temper," answered Compton. Compton knew Jefferson had a temper that would surface from time to time. Gilmore was also aware of her temper.

"I don't have a temper."

"Really, then why do you sometimes kick things?"

"To stay in practice," answered Jefferson.

"To stay in practice for what?"

"In case I ever really need to kick something."

"You broke the drink machine."

"Hey! That machine cheated me out of a quarter," said Jefferson.

"No, it didn't. The price went up a year before you exacted your revenge on it."

"Well, it's not my fault they don't make them like they used to."

"Well, don't go kicking things, alright."

"I won't."

"Promise," said Compton.

"Well, let me think about it for a while."

"Okay, the six cell phones that you are looking at, one of them are dead, and the other five have been apprehended."

"Well, if they have been arrested why is it so important now to do all of this? We can take our time instead of working late into the night."

Compton was seated across from Jefferson. She didn't know how to broach the subject. She didn't know how Jefferson would react.

"Marsha, there is more that I have to tell you."

"Okay, tell me."

"One of the cell phones belonged to the man who shot you." Compton saw Jefferson stiffen and her nostrils flared from the air she took in. Silenced followed for a long time.

"So, he was part of this mystery I have been looking at."

"Yes, he was," answered Compton.

"I actually thought I was working on identity theft or counterfeiting, not the assassination attempt," answered Jefferson.

"Marsha we believe the person who shot you did so because he lost or misplaced his passport and couldn't leave the country. He thought he would do more damage while he was here."

"There is more to this isn't there?" asked Marsha.

"Yes, it started on February 7th."

"What happened February 7th?"

"Washington."

This took Marsha's breath away. She sat in silence for a long time, and then she ran her fingers through her hair. "Start at the beginning Linda. Tell me everything you know and don't leave anything out."

Compton told her everything.

"Okay, now tell me what you found in all of those phone records," said Compton.

"Did you notice all the calls to the pay phone, all of them, during the day were on a Sunday and Wednesday? Any other day was after eleven p.m., none before."

"No, I didn't pick up on that," answered Compton.

"Maybe someone was working except on Sunday and Wednesday and off after eleven p.m. on the other days."

"That could be anyone," said Compton.

"Maybe that convenience store is closed on Sunday. It's out in the middle of nowhere and maybe one of the two employees is off on Wednesday. Maybe it closes before eleven p.m."

"But look at the number of calls. I can't imagine someone standing out in the cold doing all that. That would raise suspicions wouldn't you think?"

"Maybe they were someplace else."

"What are you talking about?"

Jefferson told her about the case in Birmingham.

"But this many calls you would need a switchboard or something. You can make one of those from things you can buy at any electronics store."

"There is something else I was able to figure out. These six telemarketers lines I highlighted called the cell phones in order with no other numbers in between, see what I mean? You have 1714, 1853, 2149, 3282, 4376 and 5055. These are the last four digits on the cell phones. The area code and the first three numbers are the same. Yet, they were called in numerical order with no numbers in between.

The calls always, always lasted fifty seconds, exactly fifty seconds. Each of the telemarketers I highlighted did it the same way. I think it was a recording to pass along instructions. None of the other 94 telemarketer's lines called in order and lasted fifty seconds. They did have a few calls to the cell phones but not this many and there were other numbers in between.

"The very first pay phone call lasted over two hours and this is what I couldn't believe, the six cell phones were activated the very same day. I think that two hour call was the instructions and then it was broken down into fifty second segments, and then passed along at the appropriate time.

"These calls also came in once a week and went out in less than ten minutes, to each of the six cell phones. I think the other ninety four lines are legitimate companies and somehow someone else took advantage of it. All of them may be legitimate and an operator sneaks them in."

"You may very well be right," said Compton

"Linda, I have a favor to ask of you."

"What?"

"Well, we both know that you are a lot better than I am on computer searches."

Linda smiled. This was the first time Marsha had admitted someone was better than she was on anything. "Marsha, what do you need me to do?"

"I need you to track down who installed the pay phone. Do they have other phones elsewhere? I don't know the last time I saw a pay phone. Cell phones have pretty much replaced them. How can someone make money off of something no one uses? What has my curiosity up about this is, the pay phone was installed the same day the six cell phones were activated. Maybe whoever installed the pay phone is involved as much as who answers it."

"It will take a while but I believe I can do that."

"This may be more important than either of us thinks."

"I'll start right now," said Linda as she went to her cubicle and sat down at the computer.

Marsha went back to work doing what law enforcement officers do all the time, sifting through information. Everyone else would call it 'looking.'

Three hours later, Linda was back at Marsha's desk.

"Find anything?" inquired Marsha.

"Yes, I did and I know that this is important, it has to be. The pay phone is owned by a private company, not the phone company."

"I had already assumed that."

"The company is called Far East Oriental Enterprise. They only have fifteen pay phones in the United States. I guess just enough to call themselves a company. The company itself is located in Minneapolis, Minnesota.

"The owner has a Spanish passport and a Spanish name. He left the country the week after 9/11, 2001. The Spanish government said they have no record of the passport. This is where it gets interesting. The Spanish government said they have hundreds of passports in that name but the passport was stolen or a forgery was made. It is a common Spanish name. I connected with Interpol, Scotland Yard and guess what?"

"What?"

"A known Iranian agent uses that as an alias, along with about ten others. He is on the Terror Watch list. He is also on ours with the Department of Homeland Security."

"How was he able to leave if he is on the Terror Watch list?"

"That took months remember. He left the week after 9/11. There was no Terror Watch list and besides there are thousands of people here with that name. I'm quite sure he is safely back home in Iran now and has been for a long time.

"These fifteen pay phones put together couldn't have generated enough income to pay for one phone. In other words they were set up to do what they did without thinking about the cost and profits. They certainly were not trying to make money."

"I kind of suspected something like that," said Marsha.

"I don't know where this will lead us but this company also owned several other businesses. Lots of other businesses."

"Like what?"

"A dry cleaner, a printing company, a used car lot, a check cashing company and a small truck line. It doesn't look like any of them were established to make money."

"But it allowed him to stay in the country, right?"

"Yes."

"How does he do it if he's no longer in the country?"

"These days once you're here you can do that by computer. The phones he had were paid out by a company in France that handles what we call shell companies. You put the money in and they pay the monthly bills."

"Are any still open?"

"Yes, and they have legitimate employees as far as we can tell."

"So, none have gone out of business lately?"

"He had a trucking company that delivered furniture from Canada to the States. They suddenly went out of business."

"Did they sell the trucks?"

"We don't know about that. I guess we could eventually find out, but that could take months."

"Then we better start looking hadn't we, Linda."

"I'll see what I can do."

"How were the nuclear weapons brought into the country?"

"The people the FBI captured didn't know. They went to Seattle, Washington and picked it up in a truck and drove the truck home. It may have been a truck driver who didn't know what the cargo was or maybe another agent. It may have been the man you killed in the assassination attempt on the First Lady. He's dead so we can't ask him."

Marsha canted her head to the left and said, "I didn't kill anyone in the assassination attempt."

"Sure you did. Don't you remember?"

"Linda, I remember. I didn't kill that man."

"The investigation determined you shot him. Maybe you blacked out or something. They have video."

"Linda, can you keep a secret?"

"Marsha, of course I can. I'm a Secret Service Agent remember, or have you forgot that, too?"

"I didn't do it."

"Then who did?"

"The First Lady. I thought you knew."

Linda Compton didn't say anything for a long time. She was thinking maybe Marsha wasn't quite ready to return to work. "Marsha, I read the finale report. They concluded that you shot him."

"They are wrong. The First Lady shot him."

Linda finally said, "That little squirt. I can't believe it."

"Let's get back to this trucking company," said Marsha.

"Would you trust a completely innocent person to deliver a nuclear weapon across the border?"

"No I wouldn't, but these had to be assembled. If you saw a few parts you wouldn't know what you were looking at."

"Does anyone else know about the pay phone and this trucking company having the same owner?"

"I don't know the answer to that, Marsha, and if I try to find out I will have to give a reason."

"Tell you what; let's let that stay between us for a few days okay?" Compton started back to her cubicle and then asked, "What tipped you off on all of this?"

"Last night, I woke up and thought about time. I had analyzed the length of the calls but something else was bothering me. I couldn't put my finger on it at the time. You see, Linda, they made a mistake."

"What was the mistake?" asked Compton.

"Telemarketers aren't allowed to call after 9:00 P.M. local, but they did several times."

"I didn't know that."

"There are thousands of laws and regulations hardly anyone knows about," answered Jefferson.

"You don't have to remind me of that," answered Compton.

"I don't know how lawyers keep up with all the laws on the books."

"I think there is an internet site for all the states that they can refer to. They would have to update law books every day. The average lawyer would have to rent a warehouse to store all of them."

It took over four hours for Compton and Jefferson to cover it in an orderly fashion. Questions were asked and answered by both agents.

"This is a FBI investigation. The only reason we have what you see here is the murder attempt on the First Lady. Actually, everyone is involved but the FBI is the lead agency. They have a task force handling it."

"With all the resources the FBI has why didn't a computer catch what I found?"

"Well we just got the pay phone records and that is what helped you piece it all together. It could be an error of some sort. If just one number is entered wrong it would never find it. Look at all the numbers. Ten in the phone numbers plus the account numbers, time and the length of call. You can bet whoever was entering all this stuff wasn't told what everyone was looking for. Computers are great but to program them for a certain function requires a lot of time. They probably weren't looking for what you found. Why would they?"

"What do we do with this?"

"Turn it over to the task force, that's all we can do," said Compton.

"Why can't we follow the lead? Why can't we investigate it ourselves?"

"You mean run a parallel investigation without telling the FBI?" asked Compton.

"Sure, why not? Our job is to protect the first family. We need to make sure there's not someone else out there trying to harm them."

"I don't know Marsha. The FBI probably wouldn't like us doing that."

"I bet Gilly would let us," said Jefferson.

"You could ask him if you want, but I bet he will say 'No, way.' You know how he is. Professional all the time, strictly by the book."

"Well, it can't hurt to ask. I bet I can talk him into it," said Jefferson.

"Agent Gilmore can I speak with you please," said Jefferson while standing in Gilmore's doorway.

"I see two things wrong already Jefferson," said Gilmore.

"Oh, and what would that be, Sir?"

"Make that three," said Gilmore.

Jefferson said nothing she was waiting on Gilmore to continue.

"You never call me agent Gilmore. You always call me Gilly because you know I don't like it. Secondly, you said please. I didn't even know you had please in your vocabulary. Lastly, you called me, Sir. I almost looked behind me to see if someone else was in the room. Now the answer is no way," said Gilmore.

"But you don't even know what I wanted to talk to you about."

"That's right. I am saving both of us the trouble of hearing it and going ahead and saying no way."

"I want to go to the border and check out that pay phone," said Jefferson.

"Why would you want to do that? That is an FBI investigation."

"I'm the one that got shot, remember."

"Yes, I remember," said Gilmore looking down at the note pad on his desk. He doodled a few lines on his legal pad.

"Wouldn't you want to go if it had been you?"

Gilmore nodded his head slightly but didn't answer. Jefferson knew he would let her go. He stood up and turned facing the window. Looking out as though lost in thought. He nodded his head more, turned and said "Alright, me, you and Compton. Have a plan including travel there and back. You can brief me in say, four hours."

"What about the First Lady?"

"I don't think we should invite her. It might be dangerous," said Gilmore.

"No I meant…"

"She has nothing scheduled for the upcoming week."

Four hours later the plan was presented to agent Gilmore. He listened intently as Jefferson and Compton laid out the plan. His first response was he wanted changes made. Compton asked why. Gilmore answered by pointing out that Jefferson and Compton assumed that everyone had already been apprehended, except for someone on the Canadian border who may have answered a phone, a pay phone at that. He pointed out that there may be others.

What he proposed was in fact quite simple. He didn't want the three of them going to Seattle unprepared.

"This is what we need to do. We don't want to travel as a group. Let's see if we can use different airlines. Let's not rent cars at the same place. We need to make sure we get different colors, make and model. If the three of us arrive on the same flight and rent three cars just alike from the same rental agency it may raise eyebrows. We don't want that. One vehicle needs to be an off road type. Preferably a Jeep.

"Now, Jefferson, since this is your idea I want you to go first. I want a cover story for you and one for the two of us. We don't want to scare anyone by all of us showing up in this area at one time. Another thing to consider is that the FBI will have agents up there. We want to stay away from them. The problem will be that we don't know where they will be or how many. Jefferson, Compton, you have a good plan, but let's fine tune it, okay?"

Back in Jefferson's cubicle, Compton said, "He made some good points or at least I thought they were."

Jefferson had to agree. She wanted to be there too quick. She had not considered all of the finer points.

"We don't want to kick the door down. We want to sneak around without anyone knowing we're there." Compton pointed out that there was a lot they didn't know.

"Have the owner and clerk been fingerprinted?" asked Jefferson.

"Not that I'm aware of," answered Compton.

"That's one thing we need to do. We can at least get a good print from both of them."

"Gilly, I mean Gilmore, can buy a pack of cigarettes from one of them. They would be behind the counter," said Compton.

"I'll buy a map or a magazine, something they have to handle. Gilmore can take them to the Secret Service in Seattle and run them."

"There is a town about twenty miles from the store in both directions. We need to stay in different motels," Compton pointed out.

"We need to dress casual. Have you come up with cover stories yet?" asked Compton.

"Gilly is camping out. I've just broken up with my boyfriend and want to get away as far as possible. I've got you as an insurance appraiser."

"Why can't I be the one that just broke up with her boyfriend?" Jefferson just looked at her.

"I'm joking, Marsha. You need to lighten up."

Jefferson thought about what Compton said. She tried to think of the last time she had just lightened up. She couldn't think of one.

"Do we use credit cards? If we do they may check," said Compton.

"We only use personal cards. We'll have to use one to rent a car. We don't any other time. We don't want anyone to know we work for the government. Don't use any government identification."

Agent Gilmore liked the proposals. He looked at Jefferson. "When you leaving?"

"I'm driving to Topeka, Kansas and will fly to Seattle tonight."

"What about you, Compton?"

"I'm driving to St. Louis and fly out tomorrow morning. I think we should take the cell phone from the car the assassin used. Their agent threw it away so we know he didn't use it. I can leave it with an agent in St. Louis. That's where the last call was from."

"Let me take the phone with me. He won't be able to tell where a cell phone is calling from," said Jefferson.

"Good idea. I don't want anyone else to know about this. It may be a wild goose chase, a complete waste of time. The fewer people involved the better. Where am I flying out of and when?" asked Gilmore.

"Tulsa, Oklahoma at one o'clock and you'll change planes in Denver. This is a ruse. I don't think the bad guys would believe a federal agent would take a connecting flight."

"Good point."

"Can you think of anything else Sir?" asked Compton.

"Just everyone be careful up there. We don't know what all we are dealing with yet."

Both Jefferson and Compton nodded their heads.

Marsha Jefferson would be arriving first. Linda Compton was arriving six hours after Jefferson. Dean Gilmore would be six hours after Compton.

Jefferson rented a dark gray sub-compact car from the airport rental and headed north. She stopped and purchased a GPS at a department store nearby. She entered the airport as her starting point and the motel she would stay in tonight as her destination. She reasoned if she aroused suspicion the GPS would not tell anyone anything of value if it was stolen. She was lucky that her destination took her by the convenience store. Their target site was only one hundred feet from the British Columbia, Canada border.

She slowed down to the twenty miles per hour when she was five miles from the store. She didn't want to miss anything. She planned to stop and purchase a few things and scope the place out.

When she pulled into the parking lot and got out of her car it was hard not to glance at the pay phone. The pay phone was on a pedestal at the edge of the parking lot, maybe fifty feet from the store. She thought it would be mounted on the wall of the store. She wondered about that and made a mental note about it. She would think on it later, not now.

When she entered, a bell sounded to let the employees know someone had come in. A man behind the counter glanced her way and said, "Morning."

Marsha replied, "Good morning."

Two men were behind the counter. There was nothing unusual about either man. One was older, maybe sixty. A little overweight with gray hair and long sideburns. Marsha guessed he was the owner. The other man was about forty to forty five. He appeared to be fit. She sensed he worked out, not a lot, but some.

She went to the cooler in the back of the store and grabbed four diet drinks. She went to the counter and set them down.

"There are a few more things I need to get."

The older man said, "Take your time, Ma'am," then he turned and started putting up cigarettes behind the counter. Marsha thought he's the owner. Marsha noted that he was cordial to her.

The younger man seemed to take more of an interest in her. Marsha often got that attention so it was not that unusual. She went to the aisle that had snacks, grabbed a few candy bars and snack crackers and placed those with the soft drinks.

"Do you have magazines?"

"What kind?" asked the younger man.

Marsha noticed a name tag pinned to his shirt. It had Jack in large lettering; no last name.

"Nothing in particular, just something to read at night," answered Marsha.

The older man turned facing her. Marsha noticed he wasn't wearing a name tag.

"Yes, Ma'am, the magazines are in the corner over there," he said as he pointed to the far corner.

Marsha went in that direction. She could feel the younger man watching. She picked up three magazines. No news stuff, she wanted something that would appear to be just light reading. She picked one on cooking, another on decorating and one on movie stars. She had picked those because each one was priced differently. She wanted the clerk to handle each one. Back at the counter, the older man had moved to the other end and was putting up cigars.

"I guess that will be all."

"You must be having a party?" said the clerk.

"No, no party. At motels you have to use vending machines and everything costs more. Free ice but you pay for it in other things."

"You must be just passing through."

"Actually I might be staying a few days. Hopefully it will just be one though and then I can head back home."

"Where is home?" asked the clerk.

"Birmingham, Alabama."

"That's a long way, isn't it?"

"Yep, and when I left I wanted to get as far away as possible."

"Trouble at home?" asked the clerk.

Before Marsha could answer, she noticed the older man had looked in their direction and knitted his eyebrows and slightly shook his head. "Jack," said the older man.

Jack rang up the items and said, "$21.95."

Marsha gave him thirty dollars. She noticed where his thumbs were on the magazines. She also had the bills he had given her in change for a fingerprint. Marsha knew just because you touch something didn't mean you left a fingerprint that could be lifted.

Jack put the dry items in a paper bag, possibly more fingerprints and the cold drinks in a plastic bag, maybe more fingerprints.

"Thank you," Marsha said as she collected her items.

Jack didn't answer.

Marsha went to the car and put her bags in the front seat, popped open a soft drink and started her car. She could feel him looking at her.

Marsha had purchased a disposable cell phone at the airport. She had already dialed the pay phone before arriving at the store. She pressed the send button as she was pulling away. She could hear the pay phone ringing. After twenty rings she hung up.

Again she drove twenty miles per hour checking both sides of the narrow road. She knew what she was looking for and spotted it easily. A phone junction box was on the same side of the road as the convenience store. She made a note of its location. Then she looked for a place to park. She found one a mile away. She would be able to hide her car off the road and a passing motorist wouldn't be able to see it after dark.

She went straight to the motel and registered. Her room was on the second floor. She parked below the room and was able to observe the car. She wiped down the interior of the car paying particular attention to the GPS. She would leave it in the car. She placed a small piece of thread under the base with a quarter of an inch sticking out. She knew if the GPS was moved she would be able to tell. She locked the car and went inside. She ate a candy bar and finished her drink.

She stayed in her room. She knew nothing would happen until after dark. The TV was on with the volume low. She waited. She had lots of time to wait.

At ten forty five, she turned on the bedside lamp and switched the overhead light off. She moved the chair over into the shadow in the corner. Fifteen minutes later she turned the TV and the bedside lamp off. Then she sat in the dark.

She could see the car through a small gap in the curtains. She drank her diet drink and settled in to wait. She had noticed the store hours displayed on the door. The store closed at 10:00 p.m. If he came right away he could already be here.

She noticed the shadow of a man as he moved past her window. She didn't know if it was another patron or not. She was sure it wasn't the older man from the shape of his shadow. It could be the clerk. She glanced at her watch, eleven P.M.

The parking lot was dimly lit but she could see well enough. She saw him approach the car and take a slender tool out of his pocket. Sliding it between the glass and the door he opened it in seconds. She was right, it was the clerk. She saw him take the GPS and look at the information on the display. Then he went through the glove box and checked the rental agreement. He went through her gym bag which had dirty clothes. He locked the door and quietly closed it. Then he looked in the trunk and walked away.

Ten minutes later Marsha called Compton on her cell phone. Compton answered on the second ring. No names were used. They would talk; actually Compton would talk and Marsha would listen.

"I checked the damage on the house. It looks like it is not too severe. I didn't get a chance to go inside. Do you think I need to?"

"No."

"Okay, I will check in tomorrow. Will you be in your office tomorrow?"

"Yes."

"I'll see you tomorrow," and she hung up.

Marsha was informing Compton she had already been inside the store and had what they needed, the fingerprints. Gilmore would be in tomorrow and purchase a pack of cigarettes and some beer for camping.

They would meet at the predesignated spot one mile from the motel she was in. The fast food place there should be busy and no one would notice. Marsha would pass the items to Gilmore who would drive to Seattle and process the prints.

Next she picked up the phone in her room and said she wanted to place a long distance phone call. She gave the number to the motel operator. It was Gilmores cell phone.

She asked him how he was doing.

"When are you coming home? I don't know how many times I've got to apologize."

"Frank, you say you're sorry all the time and the next day you do it again. I can't believe you would act that way to my mother."

"Marsha, I don't love your mother, I love you. Please just come on back home, please."

"I need more time, Frank."

"Where are you? Are you at your mother's? I'll come get you. All you have to say is you want to come back."

"No, I am not at my mother's house."

"Please come back. We can work this out. I promise I won't do it again."

"Frank, I need to go to sleep."

"At least tell me where you are."

"No, Frank."

Then she disconnected. She had to smile. The three of them had spent an hour preparing the five minute phone call. It was comical to Jefferson to hear Gilmore begging her to come back. The purpose of the call was to reinforce her cover story of a young lady in a relationship that wasn't all too rosy. The three of them knew motel walls have ears.

JACK IN THE BOX

Jack by nature was a suspicious man, he had to be. If he was caught it could be disastrous for him and his country. He knew he had to be cautious at all times. With the deadline approaching he couldn't take any unnecessary chances, but sometimes you have to take a chance.

When the tall African American woman walked into the convenience store he had an uneasy feeling. There weren't many African Americans living up in this area. There weren't many living in the two small towns nearby. Who could she be visiting up in this area? There wasn't much traffic on the highway, mostly hunters and fisherman. She did nothing out of the ordinary. She didn't ask any questions other than about the magazines. Maybe she was just a friendly person, most people in America were. What bothered Jack was she volunteered more information than most attractive women would. She said she would be in this area a few days. She even implied she would be staying in a motel. She indicated that she was having trouble at home. No telling what she would have said if the owner hadn't cut them off. She said she was from Birmingham, Alabama. He had looked Birmingham, Alabama up in a road atlas. That was a long way from here. Jack was thinking she told him an awful lot in a chit chat conversation. He would take a chance and check on her tonight.

He had seen which direction she had taken. There was only one motel in that direction. He had to trust his gut feelings.

Her car was parked in the middle of the parking lot. He didn't know which room she was in but he knew most people park near their room. There were no lights on, on the first floor. He walked past the rooms on the first floor and heard nothing from any room. Then he went up the stairs to the second floor. The room the lights were just turned off was directly in front of the car she was driving. He walked past the room and heard nothing from inside. He could tell the T.V. was off because it wasn't glowing in the dark. He went back down and approached the car. He quickly looked around but saw no one. He used his Slim Jim tool to enter her car. There was a gym bag on the front seat. He quickly looked through it, dirty clothes. He checked the glove box. A rental agreement was inside. He quickly scanned the information on the form. Her license was from Alabama with a Birmingham address. He checked the GPS. It only showed where her trip started from and this motel. He popped the trunk using the lever inside the car. He locked the car then looked in the trunk, empty.

Jack went back to his car in the parking lot next door. He took out a hand set and went to the junction box on the back of the motel. He knew her room number by his walk by. He placed alligator clips on the terminal and waited. He also had a scanner that would pick up cell phone calls.

A few minutes later he heard what sounded like two lovers talking. The man called her Marsha, the same as the driver's license. He knew he had the right room. The man was begging her to come back. She said she needed more time to think. Jack shook his head. In Iran women aren't allowed to think. Americans…their day was coming. Allah would be proud. The great Satan would be brought to its knees.

CHAPTER SIXTY SEVEN

ON THE TRAIL

PSALM 18:37

Marsha left the motel. She placed another string in the door jamb. If it wasn't there when she returned she would know someone had been in her room. She left her suitcase on the bed with the top open. It would have been impossible to look through it without her knowing. She had taken photos on her smart phone to use for comparison. She had brought magazines similar to the ones she had bought at the store. She knew the clerk wouldn't be able to tell. She left those on the night stand.

She went to the fast food diner for her scheduled meeting. It wasn't a meeting in the true sense of the word. Marsha and Gilmore wouldn't even speak to each other. Marsha used the table first. When she saw Gilmore pick up his order, she went to the restroom leaving the magazines and other items in a plastic grocery bag. Gilmore would sit at the same table and leave with the bag.

Gilmore would call Compton with the results of the fingerprints. There was no reason for anyone to suspect Compton. She hadn't been in the store. Gilmore had bought a pack of cigarettes. He only stopped to eat breakfast. Marsha was the only one that had enough contact to raise suspicion. Compton would meet Marsha in the restroom and pass along any information. While Marsha was in the restroom, Compton came in and said, "Gilly got your bag. No one seemed to be watching. No one left when he did. Check in with you later." Then she left.

The next meeting would take place at 6:30 that evening. Marsha returned to the motel. No one had been in her room. Two hours later she left and drove through the small town. She went into several stores to browse around. She picked up a few items, mostly for show. She never had the impression that anyone was watching or following her. She was looking for Jack but Jack wasn't around.

She went back to the motel room. Everything was as she left it. She waited till it was time for the meeting with Compton.

Marsha ordered a hamburger and soft drink and passed on the fries even though the kid asked "Do you want any fries with that?" twice. Marsha thought one day a kid like that will be the president of the United States, it was bound to happen.

She went into the restroom and made sure that no one else was in the room. Compton came in a few seconds later and showed the results of the fingerprint search. Both men had been fingerprinted. The owner was born in the United States and had never been arrested. He had served in the Navy and was also fingerprinted when he applied for his beer and wine license.

The clerk had been arrested and booked for disorderly conduct and solicitation of an undercover vice cop in Minneapolis, Minnesota.

Compton said, "When he was arrested in Minneapolis he used a Muslim name. Mohammed Abdullah Ali-Siad was the name he used. He posted his own bail. When he didn't show for court, Minnesota ran a driver's license check with North Dakota. The driver's license was phony. He also said he worked for the phone company. That makes it a lot more interesting if it's true, but we don't know for sure.

"The other five suspects we've already apprehended were instructed to leave the country if they were arrested or fingerprinted. He didn't leave. That tells me he is higher up on the food chain. He may be the leader of the others."

"There has to be more than that," said Marsha.

"Well Muslims aren't supposed to drink and adultery is frowned upon and can get you killed in Iran. It's obvious he thought he could hide it and has for fifteen years."

"He's been here that long?"

"Honey the others came here during the Iranian Revolution. I think he is a replacement for someone else."

"Well, we know his real name is not Jack."

Marsha returned to wait on her order. Compton came out and ordered a burger to go. Compton was wearing an entirely different style of clothes from lunch time. She had her hair pulled back in a ponytail and was wearing glasses. No one would guess that Marsha was in the ladies room with the same person at lunch time.

Marsha returned to her motel room. Her door and suitcase were still undisturbed. Evidently Jack believed she was just a young lady trying to make up her mind about a relationship. Now Marsha could go to work.

Gilmore had picked up some items from the Seattle Secret Service office. Marsha would meet Compton at a four way stop sign and collect them there.

Jefferson left the motel room at nine p.m. She wanted to be in place when the convenience store closed at ten. She drove to the meeting place. Compton pulled up and handed Marsha a canvas bag.

"I've checked everything. The night vision goggles work fine."

"Thanks Linda. I'm going to park in the woods a mile from the junction box. If it doesn't pan out, I'll call you and meet you here again." Jefferson drove off.

She edged the car into the woods out of sight. She removed the gear Compton had given her and started walking. She was wearing all black including her tactical vest.

She was at the junction box in fifteen minutes. She removed a black plastic tarp and placed it over the junction box then crawled underneath. She turned on her penlight and carefully opened the junction box with a screwdriver. She shined the light inside at the wiring. She knew what she was looking for would be hidden in case the phone company came to do repairs. It was hidden behind the inside panel. She followed it down into the ground. A hole had been drilled for the wire to come out of the back of the box. She replaced the cover, turned off the penlight and folded the tarp placing it aside. She went behind the box, took the screwdriver and pulled the wire up. It was only buried two inches. She knew this line was like an extension for the pay phone. She followed the line by pulling the wire from the ground.

When she entered the woods she put her night vision goggles on. After what she judged to be a hundred feet she knew she was in Canada. She knew she didn't belong here. She kept going. After about four hundred yards she saw the building. It was small, about nine by twelve feet. The cable led directly to the building. There were no windows on this side. She went to the right side of the building, no windows. She went to the other side and saw the door. She did not go close to the building. She stood behind a tree and dialed the pay phone, no answer, and then she waited. She looked at her watch 10:45. Then she saw him. He was walking along a trail she had not seen. At the door he removed a key and opened the door.

Marsha waited. The records indicated that the calls were made after eleven P.M. She would wait until eleven. She wanted to make sure no one else was coming.

She dialed the pay phone with her disposable cell phone. She let it ring six times then hung up. She didn't expect anyone to answer. She dialed the pay phone five minutes later with the cell phone the assassin had in his car.

It was answered on the second ring. Isn't caller ID great.

"Bahram, where have you been?"

Marsha said nothing.

"Bahram, are you there?"

Again Marsha said nothing.

"Bahram, if you can hear me do not go to the rental house. I planted booby traps. Do not go home, Bahram."

Then Marsha said, "This is the Royal Canadian Mounted Police. The building is surrounded. Come out with your hands up."

The phone was hung up. After two minutes the door opened. Marsha turned off her night vision goggles and let them dangle around her neck. She had a high intensity flashlight. She held it to the right of the tree and held her forty caliber service weapon to the left. She turned on the light. Jack put his hand up to block the light from his eyes.

"Jack, you've been a bad boy or should I call you Mo?"

Jack had a bewildered look on his face. "Mo?"

"Short for Mohammed, Jack. That's the name you used fifteen years ago."

Marsha noticed he was wearing a heavy jacket. He wasn't wearing it when he arrived. Marsha moved closer to the tree.

"I want to call my lawyer."

"No, phone calls, Jack."

Jack raised his hand; he was holding a cell phone. He flipped it open. The face lit up. Marsha knew you could trigger a bomb or a suicide vest with a cell phone. She was hugging the tree now.

"Who are you?" asked Jack.

"Marsha Jefferson, remember you broke into my car at the motel."

"You're not Royal Canadian Mounted Police."

"Nope. United States Secret Service."

"You're in Canada. You can't arrest me here."

"I don't intend to arrest you. I'm going to bury you on my uncle's hog farm in Alabama."

Marsha wanted to provoke him into doing something. She did.

"We're going to win. We're going to destroy the Great Satan and then we will crush Israel. You can't stop us."

"I don't think so. We found the bombs Jack. All five of them."

A look of rage came over Jack's face. He screamed, "Praise Allah," and charged Jefferson pressing the send button on the cell phone.

Marsha yelled, "Smith and Wesson," and fired, not once, not twice, but three times. After all, that was her policy.

The forty caliber bullets left the barrel at the speed of sound. The hollow point hydra shock bullet is designed to expand to twice its original size and do major tissue damage. The bullets did all that and more.

The first two bullets hit Jack in the chest. The third shot hit nothing. Jack had blown up. The suicide vest had detonated. He was thirty feet away when the vest exploded.

For the second time in her career Marsha dropped her weapon. She was jumping up and down shaking her hands "Ow, ow, ow, man that hurts." She pulled her gloves off to see if her hands were bleeding and to count her fingers. Her hands felt like they on fire. She shook her hands some more then opened and closed them before picking her pistol up and holstering it. She felt her fingertips.

"Awe man! I broke a nail."

She kicked the tree twice. Now she felt better. Awe, why not, she kicked it again. She tried opening and closing her mouth to make her ears pop. They hurt and were still ringing.

A mile and a half away a FBI agent said, "I heard an explosion on the Canadian side."

His partner said, "That's Canada's problem."

Compton was four miles away. She said to herself "Marsha, what have you done? I take my eyes off of you for two minutes and you go blow something up."

She started her car and headed towards the junction box. She called Gilmore. He answered on the third ring.

"Meet me one mile east of the store."

"Did you hear an explosion?"

"Yeah," answered Compton.

"What do you think it was? It was on the Canadian side."

"I think it was Marsha."

"Oh man, not in Canada."

"Get there Gilly. She's in trouble."

"I'm on my way. On man, she knows where the border is."

He was talking to dead air.

Three minutes later Compton parked her car with the headlights pointing at the junction box. She put on her night vision goggles. She didn't turn them on. She drew her service weapon and got behind the car. Gilmore pulled to a stop and got out "Come on, follow this cable."

After settling down, Jefferson found her spent shell casings. No need to leave evidence lying around. She walked to where Jack had been standing. His legs were still there lying on the ground. His head was a few feet away. His torso was unidentifiable as being a human.

"Jack, you lost your head. Now why would you want to go and do that? A good lawyer could have gotten you off. He could have said, 'Your Honor, my client simply lost his head.'"

Marsha knew the cell phone didn't set the vest off. A cell phone takes about four seconds to go through. She had fired three shots in a second. Knowing this made Marsha feel better. It almost made up for the broken nail.

She couldn't hear Compton and Gilmore coming through the woods. She had put her night vision goggles back on. Her flashlight wasn't working. The lens and the bulb were broken. She put a finger in each ear trying to get her hearing restored. All she could hear was a loud ringing noise that the explosion had left her with. She kept watching the trail Jack had used. She didn't know if the store owner or someone else was involved.

The blast had blown the door inside the small building. Jefferson moved back behind the tree. She noticed that tree bark was missing from several of the trees near her.

Marsha felt lucky to be alive for the second time in her life. Compton got to her first. A few seconds later Gilmore arrived. Compton put her arm around Marsha's shoulders and asked, "Are you alright?"

Marsha nodded her head.

Gilmore turned on his flashlight and looked around and then he looked at the carnage at his feet. "Who's that?" was all he could say.

"What's left of Jack. Suicide vest; he blew himself up. He answered the pay phone from here."

"I want a full report! You understand me. A full report right now."

"Shut up, Gilley. Can't you see what's happened here?" snapped Compton.

"You do realize we are in Canada. Do you know what that means?" responded Gilmore.

"I know what it means. It means we are all in trouble if we get caught. Let's not get caught." Compton was in Gilmore's face now.

Gilmore shook his head in disbelief and walked to the small building door and shined his flashlight inside.

"What's all this stuff?" asked Gilmore.

"I haven't had time to look, I've been a little busy" answered Jefferson.

Gilmore started to enter; Compton grabbed him by the elbow to stop him.

"Watch for booby traps," said Compton.

"I don't see any. What do we do?"

Gilmore realized the three of them were out of their league here. They needed expertise and they certainly didn't have it. They needed crime scene investigators.

Compton said, "I'm going in." She was one of the go team's demolition experts.

"You can't go in there. There is evidence everywhere. We need to get someone here to handle it."

"Gilly, we are in Canada. We're not supposed to be here. You want the Canadian government to do this? We have to get out of here, but we are not leaving this behind, do you understand me?" Compton was jabbing Gilmore in the chest with a finger, "Now move out of the way."

After fifteen minutes, Compton came back out. "It's all clear. You have to see this. You are not going to believe what's in here."

There was barely enough room to move around. Phone equipment was everywhere. Recorders were at different locations. At least a hundred phone lines came into the building from the Canadian side. Only one line was different. It came from the junction box on the American side.

"I'm willing to bet every telemarketer number that called the cell phones was from here. There is a homemade switchboard here, you were right Marsha. There is a box of passports and driver's license complete with credit cards. There's also a box of cash in the corner. These people could change their identities and move all over the world without anyone being the wiser. All they had to do was pick up another wallet and bam they took on a different identity.

"It looks like they could make recordings and call the cell phones. We won't know for sure till all of this is examined and analyzed. This has to be the main place for the entire operation. I had pictured it in my mind as some huge building with lots of people. This is unbelievable."

"What are we going to do with all of this? This is evidence. We sure can't leave it," said Gilmore.

"That is what I was telling you a few minutes ago. Canada won't know what to do with it. They won't know what it means. We know what it means."

"So, what do we do?" asked Gilmore.

"Gilly, get the Jeep. You can make it through the woods on the Jeep. Then we put all this in the cars and get out of Dodge."

"What about the body?" asked Gilmore.

"What about it?" answered Compton.

Gilmore said, "Feed the bears?"

"I don't see any signs saying not to feed the bears," answered Compton.

"We'll take a sample for DNA purposes," said Gilmore.

"And I wish you would stop calling me Gilly."

"Agent Gilmore, please go get the Jeep and take Marsha to get the car."

"Right, I was headed that way."

Compton took Marsha off to the side "You feel like going to get your car?"

Marsha nodded her head and went with Gilmore.

It took six trips in the Jeep to take everything away. As the sun came up they drove past the convenience store and kept going. They had a long drive in front of them. They weren't headed to Seattle. They were going straight to Independence.

CHAPTER SIXTY EIGHT

PROOF

INDEPENDENCE

ROMANS 1:32

The material Gilmore, Compton and Jefferson brought from Canada was analyzed for a month. The FBI, CIA, DIA, NSA and the Secret Service were all part of the investigation. Someone said if it had an initial they were involved. There was no doubt in the intelligence community that the nation of Iran had planned, sanctioned and executed the operation to destroy America. One of the discs recovered was a video disc. The Ayatollah himself had the video made. One of the devices was on the table in front of him. He actually blessed the device. Voice print by the FBI compared the voice to known speeches the Ayatollah had made.

The evidence was irrefutable. What to do about it rested on the shoulders of one man. The President of the United States, Lewis C. MacDonald.

After the investigation a lot of questions were raised. They were the type questions investigators ask themselves after any investigation. Most of the questions began with 'What if' or 'You know.'

"What if they hadn't called the pay phone on their home phone lines?"

"You know if the explosives in the first house had worked we would have lost five cities."

"What if he hadn't lost his passport in the bathroom?"

"You know if they had gotten rid of the air conditioning unit we might not have pieced it together."

"What if they had left the car in St. Louis?"

"You know if they hadn't parked the car in Los Angeles we wouldn't have known about the travel agency."

"You know if the guy in the trunk of the car had gone into the department store we would have lost a quarter of a million people."

"What if they haven't searched our deep cover operative in Destin, Florida? Atlanta would have been hit."

"What if we hadn't found all five bombs?"

"What if NSA hadn't logged all those phone calls? We wouldn't have been able to piece all this together."

"You know if the guy in Canada had set his suicide vest off in the building we wouldn't have this evidence at all."

"You know the maintenance supervisor that allowed them to place the nuclear weapon may be alive somewhere out there."

"You know we were lucky, very lucky."

CHAPTER SIXTY NINE

PLANNING

LUKE 14:31

The President's first action was to have a full briefing to the military, namely the Joint Chiefs of Staff. The Chiefs of Staff had not been a part of the investigation. The Director of the Central Intelligence Agency gave his portion of the briefing first.

"The Federal Bureau of Investigation has located and has control of five nuclear weapons the nation of Iran had infiltrated into the United States. The five cities the devices were to be used on was Los Angeles, Chicago, Dallas, Atlanta and New York.

"We have broken the arming codes. The Iranian agents were instructed to have them in place by December 23rd. Then they were to leave the country. The devices were set to go off on Christmas Eve day.

"These five devices were smaller than the one used on Washington. They are twenty kiloton weapons. The one used on Washington was a fifty kiloton. They were told to park their vehicle on the upper deck of parking garages. This would ensure maximum damage because the devices would be elevated perhaps a hundred feet putting more buildings in a direct line of sight."

"Why do you think they chose Christmas Eve instead of Christmas day? Christmas day is more of a Christian holiday than Christmas Eve" inquired the Air Force General.

"There are millions of people out doing their last minute shopping on Christmas Eve. Most people are off on both days, but a lot more are out and about on Christmas Eve. People outside verses inside raises the number of deaths."

"I see. I hadn't thought of that."

"Mr. President if you remember last week I briefed you on the Iranian-Iraqi border situation," said Director Rosenburg.

"Yes, I remember. You said the Iranians were moving large units to the border area and the Iraqis were also."

"That has escalated in the last few hours."

"How so?" asked the President.

"The Iranians are pouring troops in the border area. These units are out of artillery range now, but someone fired. We don't know who fired first. I suspect the Iranians did. They are moving more and more forces to the border. It appears the Iranians were in a more readiness posture than the Iraqi forces were."

"How large of a force are you talking about?" asked the Army General.

"It appears to be three corps size units. I'm guessing a thousand tanks for each corps size unit and two hundred thousand men per corps."

"Are you sure on those numbers? If I remember correctly they only have a little over four thousand tanks total and my understanding was a standing army of four hundred thousand," said the Marine General.

"You are correct on both of those numbers General. It appears they have activated their reserve forces and they have a hundred thousand volunteers. Volunteer is not the correct word there. Many were grabbed off the street, given a uniform and a rifle and pointed in the right direction. These volunteers have no military training but if you can pull the trigger you can kill someone."

"Where are these forces located?" asked the Marine General.

"One force is between Mosul and Baghdad, one is between Baghdad and Basra and one is directly opposite Basra. Each force is large enough to seize the three major cities. Also the Iranians have started moving their SCUD missile launchers forward to the border."

"Why in the world would they do that?" asked the Marine General.

"You know the answer to that as well as I do," said the Director.

"What are you talking about?" asked the President. He had understood everything up to this point.

"Mr. President, what the General is pointing out is all the major Iraqi cities were already in range of the SCUD missile sites, so why move them."

"They obviously have targets beyond Iraq if they moved them forward," said the Marine General.

"I understand," said the President.

"The question now is what target would the Iranians use them on beyond Iraq?" said the Director of the CIA.

The Army General spoke up. "It could be Kuwait."

"I don't think they would need to use them if it is Kuwait. My best guess would be Saudi Arabia. They could take Kuwait in the operation without very much trouble. They could go from Basra and seize Kuwait like Iraq did in 1990 and then move on to Saudi Arabia at the same time. Can you imagine if the southern force seizes Kuwait and the force near Baghdad heads toward Saudi Arabia and the northern force seizes the oil fields of Iraq? If they had all of the oil of Kuwait, Saudi Arabia and Iraq they could almost singlehandedly cripple the world's economy."

"I don't buy all that. If their ultimate goal was Iraq and the Saudi Arabian peninsula they would have no need to destroy America. We couldn't react fast enough to stop them anyway," said the Marine General.

"I agree with that," said the Army General. Then he continued, "The SCUD missiles, how long before they can reach the border. That has to be at least five hundred miles. I would imagine the roads headed for the border are jammed with tanks, fuel trucks and other supplies. The missiles would have to be behind all of that because they are slower moving. Those missiles can't go cross country like armor or infantry vehicles. They have to pretty much stay on roads through the mountains and rough terrain."

"With this large of a force and with the SCUD missiles being a lot slower, I would say six to eight weeks to launch on Saudi Arabia," said Director Rosenberg.

"If those nuclear weapons were supposed to go off on Christmas Eve and they attack Iraq before that and then head toward their main objective on Christmas Eve before we can get back on our feet they have something bigger in mind. I don't think it is Kuwait and the Arabian Peninsula," said the Marine General.

"General Sandford, what exactly are you implying? You don't think defeating Iraq is their ultimate goal?" asked General Stewart, the Army General.

"No, I don't. If I were the Iranians, I would attack Baghdad with the largest force I could muster. I don't think it would be necessary to attack Mosul and Basra with two hundred thousand men and a thousand tanks. Now I admit they could use one for a frontal attack and they could use the northern and southern force to flank and encircle Baghdad, but that's a long way to go for these two forces to do that. I don't think that is their ultimate goal. I believe Israel is their objective and I believe they think if they attack Israel the surrounding Arab countries will jump on the bandwagon so to speak. The Iranians wouldn't have to include them in their planning. They would just assume the neighboring countries would participate."

The Air Force General spoke up. "Iran knows Israel has enough nuclear weapons to destroy every major city in the Mideast and North Africa. They would use them if necessary."

"I don't think they care," answered the Marine General, and then he continued, "I really don't think the Iranians care if all the major cities were destroyed. We can't even start to understand how much Iran hates Israel. They would think it was worth any cost."

The CIA Director interrupted the Marine General. "Mr. President, I agree with the General on the ultimate objective being Israel. However, I can't leapfrog to that conclusion without more intelligence than we have at this time. I would like to point out that Israel is the only stabilizing nation in the Mideast. You remove Israel from the equation and the Arab countries would turn on each other in a New York minute.

"Look at the map. Every country over there has an enemy on two sides. The Shite hate the Sunnis almost as much as they hate Israel. You've heard the old saying 'My enemy's enemy is my friend.' You remove that enemy, which in this case is Israel and that common enemy is next door and fighting will break out all over the Mideast. All of the Mideast would be involved, but that would only be the start of something bigger, something even more dangerous."

"What?" asked the Army General.

"Civil war. All of the Mideast, Africa, Western Europe, all the way to parts of India, Indonesia and part of Southeast Asia."

"Excuse me, Mr. Rosenberg, did you say Western Europe?" asked the Air Force General.

"Yes, I did," answered Rosenberg.

"Why Western Europe? That's not Muslim."

"Millions of Muslims live in Western Europe. Maybe as many as fifty million. Look at Germany, France, England and the Balkan States. There is a large number of Muslims in just those few countries I mentioned."

"I wasn't aware of that," said the General.

"Most people aren't, and if a civil war breaks out you can see what happens in the Mideast. If you get in the way you get killed. They will go on a killing frenzy.

"We know Iran knows all of this. Their only hope would be the last man standing. Now please I'd like to continue. The main thing I'd like to point out is, if Israel is destroyed and the countries in the Mideast engage in war, the civilian population would probably engage in a civil war the likes of which the world has never seen. Half of Africa, a lot of Western Europe all the way to Southeast Asia. Can you imagine almost a billion people turning on each other and engaged in civil war?

"The Sunni and the Shite against each other. The other Muslims are affiliated with those two. The world would be in a dilemma that we can't begin to comprehend.

"Another possibility we don't know about has Iran managing to somehow sneak a nuclear weapon into Israel. We can't rule that out and they are waiting for the right time to use it."

"Where do you think they would employ it?" asked the Air Force General.

"Well, if I had to guess I would say Tel Aviv. It could be on a ship in the Mediterranean Sea for all we know. They make a dash for the port and set it off. That would be my guess."

"Why would the Iranians be willing to take such a gamble?"

"They have said for over forty years they will destroy Israel. They don't put a price on accomplishing that goal. Iran may believe that in an all-out civil war they can stay out of the conflict. Look at the map, they are sort of out of the way so to speak and they will say they're Persians. The people in Iran are so afraid of the government; a civil war would be crushed before it could get started. I'm sure everyone here knows this is based on conjuncture on our part. The question of the moment is, if Iran and Iraq go to war, what do we do if they don't move on Israel or Kuwait? Then we have to think about

Saudi Arabia and their oil fields. All of this may be an elaborate plan or it may be just a war between two countries that have fought each other before. I don't want to make an estimate on any of this, but we do need to keep a close eye on this and have a plan. Everything can change in the blink of an eye."

Director Rosenberg looked each of the Generals in the eye. He wanted to make sure they understood what he was about to say next. Then he continued. "Mr. President, under no circumstances can we allow Israel to be destroyed. I am saying this as an American, not a Jew." Then he paused for a few seconds. "All of the industrial nations would collapse almost immediately including the United States. No, not under any circumstance can we allow Israel to be destroyed. My best guess is this and you will notice I said best guess. I can't make an estimate on the current situation, I am only guessing. The Iranians want us to believe this is a regional conflict between two countries that have fought each other numerous times throughout history. They may believe we won't get involved in a war like that. If their real objective is the destruction of Israel we will, of course, get involved. If, and this is a mighty big if, Iran launches their attack and we, the United States do nothing and then Iran heads west, they would be halfway there before we could do anything major to stop them. That is just a possible scenario. I believe there will be a war. I hope it is only Iran and Iraq."

The President spoke up for the first time. "Can we stop them if they head west?"

"No, Sir, not without using nuclear weapons. That is way too many targets to hit in a short period of time," answered General Shelton, the Air Force General.

Admiral Douglas said, "We'd have to use every cruise missile we have and we still couldn't stop them."

"What about Israel, could they stop them without using nuclear weapons?" asked the President.

"No, Sir, I don't believe so. Not if Director Rosenberg is right about the other Arab countries also attacking at the same time. I believe like he said earlier, they would all be jumping on the bandwagon," said Admiral Douglas.

The President nodded his head and then asked, "Could the United States and Israel stop them with coordinated attacks?"

The Air Force General answered, "I don't believe so, Mr. President. We currently don't have the assets in place if they attack sooner rather than later."

General Sandford, the Marine General stood up, and looked around the room. "I disagree with those assumptions." Everyone including the President looked at him.

"What are you considering, General?"

"Mr. President, let's let the desert kill them."

"How do we do that?" asked the President.

"They would have to move over a thousand miles. If we let them get halfway there and use our resources to destroy their fuel and water supplies and then use our resources to stop their resupply of fuel and water they will die in the desert. Two things you don't want to run out of in the desert are fuel and water. Then our target list goes from ten thousand to maybe two thousand."

"It is possible, but not guaranteed."

"Mr. President, if we destroy fifty percent of the Iranians fuel and water they won't be able to continue an attack, if it is Israel," said the Marine General.

"Director Rosenberg, do you think Israel if the Iranian's ultimate objective?"

"Mr. President, I don't know. We don't have that much intelligence in the area. If you want me to say its Israel I will say it is. Am I certain it's Israel? A gut feeling, yes. Mr. President I have been with the agency for thirty years. We analyze intelligence and try to make an assumption. Sometimes we can't make that assumption, and when that happens we have to trust our gut instinct. I have trusted my gut instinct on a lot of issues and most of the time I was right.

"Can I connect a bunch of dots? I can if I have some dots to connect. In this instance we don't have any dots to connect. There has been no radio traffic we have intercepted. None what-so-ever. Complete radio silence on the border area and Tehran. We have no intelligence assets in the country of Iran. We have tried that route and they were discovered and executed. The only solid information we have is what we see from satellite photos. A large troop buildup on the border.

"We do know the devices were set to go off on Christmas Eve day. Now, does that mean they launch their attack on Christmas day or do they launch it earlier? I don't know the answer to that. Would anyone like to speculate on that?" He looked around the room. "Well?" The Army General answered the question. "It would take one day to move that large of a force to reach the border. It's only fifteen miles but it's hard to get started then they can move very fast. Now we don't know if Iraqi forces can even slow them down. The Iraqi military is pretty small now after three wars plus they are not trained.

"The Iranians can reach Baghdad in three days if there is only light resistance. That puts it to December 22nd. If they surround and attack Baghdad we'll know Israel isn't the ultimate goal. If it is Israel and this attack against Baghdad is to make us sit back and watch, it would take two days to bypass Baghdad assuming the Iraqi forces don't put up much of a fight. I don't think they, meaning the Iraqis, will be able to slow them down at that point. That puts us to December 20th. This is based on General Sandford's assumption that Israel is the main objective which I am not sure I agree with."

"If they attack Baghdad, Mosul and Basra and that is their only objective, why would the Iranians need to destroy Washington and five other U.S. cities?" asked the Air Force General.

Director Rosenberg spoke up. "Earlier I said my enemy's enemy is my friend. Well, it also goes to say my enemy's friend is my enemy. A quick history lesson, the Babylonians carried the Jews away into captivity to Babylon. The Persians defeated the Babylonians and allowed the Jews to return. Israel now has that land. The Arabs, actually the Muslim world, know Israel couldn't exist without the United States. That is why the Muslims hate the U.S. Israel would have never been allowed to return and exists without the United States. We were the big brother that stood up against the bully. The bully wants to kill the big brother."

"What everyone is saying is if the Iranians limit their attack to Iraq they know we won't get involved. If they attack Kuwait and Saudi Arabia we will get involved. If they head toward Israel they know we will get involved," said the Air Force General.

"We will be at war with Iran. We have been already since the attack on Washington. The question is do we conduct our war with Iran on our terms or do we let this invasion determine that. The timing is what I am referring to now," said the Marine General.

Vice President Hernandez had been listening and thinking of everyone's opinion. It was time to give hers.

"Mr. President."

"Madam Vice President." They referred to each other by their titles if a group was present.

"We have thousands of nuclear weapons, we don't need five more. I think we should give them back to the Iranians."

"We can't give them back. Then they may use…What do you mean, give them back?" asked the President.

"Well, if someone sends me something I don't want nor need I 'Return to sender.' I send it back." A hush fell over the room. You could have heard a pin drop.

"I have just the guys that can do that, Mr. President," said Admiral Douglas.

"We also have some men that can return the weapons," said Army General Stewart.

"I'm going to have to think on that long and hard," said the President. Then he added, "Draw up a plan and present it to me when it is completed."

"Mr. President."

"Yes, Madam, Vice President. You have something else up your sleeve?"

"Yes, I do. This attack on Israel may come at any time or it may never come. I have an idea to start crippling Iran before we are ready to go to war. We can use this massing of troops on the border of Iraq as a legitimate excuse."

"And what is your plan?" asked the President.

"The United States will not buy, sell, trade or conduct any business with the nation of Iran."

"That won't cripple them. We don't do any of that now. How is that going to hinder Iran at all?" said General Shelton, the Air Force General.

"You interrupted me, General. Now if you will be kind enough to let me finish I believe you will agree with what I'm saying. We also will not buy, sell, trade or do business with any country that buys, sells, trades or does any business with the nation of Iran."

"You are saying the world needs America more than we need the world," said Lewis, thinking about his earlier meeting with her a few months ago.

"Yes, Mr. President. We totally isolate them from the entire world."

The Vice President looked around the room. She glanced from General to General and finally the Admiral. She thought it would take an hour to count all the stars on their collars and shoulders.

"How fast can we do that?" asked the CIA Director.

"I think Congress can do that in forty eight hours," answered the Vice President.

"Please, take care of that as soon as possible," directed the President.

"Do any of you gentleman disagree with what has been proposed?"

Juanita Hernandez has never brought a knife to a gunfight. She didn't intend on starting now. All the Generals and the Admiral nodded their heads in agreement.

"How long before Iran will start to feel the effect and how long before they begin to suffer?" asked the President.

"They will feel the effect in maybe a week. They will start to suffer in a month, maybe two. Almost every essential item is imported. Iran can't sustain itself. The Vice President is correct in her analysis. America is one of the few countries that can sustain itself," added the CIA Director.

"Iran imports all of its gas. They have no refineries to make very much fuel. They may seize the fuel from Iraq if and when they attack. Iraq will protect those at all cost including destroying them. We have been talking with the Iraqis about lending support. We need the airbases in Iraq. If the endgame is an attack on Israel and they bypass Baghdad, Basra and Mosul the airbases should be intact or can be repaired quickly."

"Excuse me," said the President. "Will Iraq let us use them if they know the Iranians are going to attack Israel?"

"Mr. President, on any given day the Iraqis hate the Iranians as much as the Jews. They don't see Israel as a threat. The Iranians are their biggest threat. The threat next door," said Director Rosenberg.

The President listened to the Chiefs of Staff. They were the experts. He would order no changes to whatever the plan was. As the meeting came to a close he said, "I want this operation to be called 'Terrible Swift Sword.' I told the American people that retribution would be a terrible swift sword."

"Yes, Mr. President."

Planning sessions began immediately. Three plans would be considered. One if Iran attacked Israel. The second plan if Iran attacked Kuwait and Saudi Arabia. The third plan was the most extensive of the three. The United States attacking Iran.

PROVERBS 20:7

As everyone was leaving the President asked to speak in private with the Air Force General.

"Yes, Mr. President," said General Dennis Shelton after everyone left.

"General, I'm sure you're aware my son is a fighter pilot in the Air Force."

"Yes, Mr. President. I am aware of that. I have already made arrangements to make sure he is in the states if and when we go to war. You don't have to worry about him, Mr. President."

"General Shelton, he has already been assigned to a non-flying post. As a matter of fact, he called me this morning and asked me to do him a favor. He has never in his life asked me to do him a favor. Do you know what the favor was, General?"

"No, Mr. President. I have no idea."

"He asked me not to use my position to keep him out of the war. I didn't know he had been transferred."

"Mr. President, I'm sure you understand that if he is killed or captured that would give our enemy a morale victory and I might add a great moral victory."

"Both of us are aware of that General. You see he asked me a question that I couldn't answer. Do you know what the question was General?"

"No, Mr. President, but I believe I can guess. How can you send someone else's son or daughter and not send you own."

"That was a very good guess. That is precisely what he asked."

"But Mr. President, I admit that is very admirable of your son. I hope you can see my position here."

"Yes, I do and I appreciate your concern. I really do. Let me ask you this, is he a good pilot?"

"From all accounts I have received he is one of the best."

"And we may need every good pilot we can come up with right?"

"Yes, Mr. President," said General Shelton looking at the floor. He had been caught with his hand in the proverbial cookie jar.

"Please, move him back to his squadron and place him back on flight status. I will worry about him like the other parents do when their sons and daughters go into harm's way."

"Yes, Mr. President. I will do so immediately."

Outside of the President's office, LTC Dexter Jenkins was waiting on the elevator with Secret Service agents McIntyre and Gilmore. As they were getting on, Gilmore asked McIntyre, "Have you come up with a code name for the president yet?"

McIntyre answered, "Not yet. He's turned down everything I've proposed."

"What have you tried?" asked Gilmore.

"Well let's see, cowboy, rustler, wrangler, cowpoke, lance, tomahawk and warrior. As soon as he finds out he says try something else. I'm running out of ideas," said McIntyre.

Colonel Jenkins turned to the two men and said, "Use Ghostrider; he won't object to that one."

"Why do you say that?" asked Gilmore.

"He just won't. I'm certain of that."

None of the three men knew. They had no way of knowing the codename Ghostrider was already being used by someone. A Second Lieutenant in the United States Air Force who believed he had actually flown with a ghost was called Ghostrider. His name was Joshua A. MacDonald.

CHAPTER SEVENTY

NAMESAKE

MATTHEW 22:39

As a nation prepares for war, life goes on; not as before, but life does indeed go on. The typical American could tell little difference. That is the way it should be. The nation has to keep producing and selling. Stores would open and close as before. Our most precious possessions, our children must be educated and taught the things needed to succeed in the future. Students would graduate from college and go out and conquer the world, or so they believed.

As Josh MacDonald prepared for war, his best friend was also preparing to help our children prepare for the future. Tommy Parker's lifelong dream had been shattered along with his leg. Like most Americans, when we can't realize our dream we pick a different one.

After Tommy Parker graduated from college, he stopped at a goodwill store and bought a pair of shoes a five year old would wear. He moved in with his mother to help with the bills. When he unpacked he placed the shoes on the fireplace mantel. When his mother asked about the shoes Tommy said, "Just a reminder, a constant reminder." Then he told her the story.

When he finished, Tommy's Mother told him another story. "When your Father died we lost our home. Beverly told me about this house we live in now. It had been empty since Miss May had passed away. It was like she was saving it for something. She gave it to me. I asked her why. She said, 'It's better to give than to receive.' I had always heard that. Then I realized what she meant. You see, she was saying that she was grateful she was able to give. I was receiving because something awful had happened to us. It is better to give than receive and now she is the First Lady. I wouldn't trade places with her."

"And it all began with a pair of shoes," added Tommy.

Tommy would teach history and be an assistant football coach. Coach Sutcliff who was the defensive coach when Tommy played was not the head coach.

"I'm putting you in charge of the defense," said Coach Sutcliff.

"Thank you, Coach. I feel more comfortable there than anywhere else."

"There is another assignment I want you to have. I want to know if there is another Josh MacDonald on the team. Someone I am not getting a hundred percent out of."

"I think I can do that. I know what to look for."

Two weeks later, Tommy had made his decision. The kid wasn't as big or as fast as Josh but then again who was. Tommy called the player over to the sidelines during practice. The boy was big, but not huge and he was smart. He played middle linebacker.

"You wanted to see me, Coach?"

"Yeah, take off that jersey" Tommy started pulling the jersey off.

"Are you kicking me off the team, Coach?"

"Take the jersey off." Tommy could see the hurt in the boy's eyes.

Tommy then picked up a jersey and held it up for the boy to see. The big 94 on the front and back was all that was necessary.

"You know who wore this number?"

"Yes, Sir, Josh MacDonald."

"You got some mighty big shoes to fill son," said Tommy.

"I won't let you down, Coach," he said with bright eyes and a smile. "I saw him play in the championship game. My mom and dad took me to see it. When he scored the touchdown, my dad said, 'Son, that boy's granddad saved your mother's life when she got shot.' I will not let you down." And he didn't. If you expect great things out of someone they usually deliver. The boy's name was Keith Arnold Barber.

CHAPTER SEVENTY ONE

24 HOUR NEWS CYCLE

News organizations had been monitoring every military installation in the country. They were waiting; the nation was waiting, for the opportunity to report large troop movements.

Soldiers were interviewed, even their wives, about when and where they would be deployed. No answers were forthcoming, they didn't know.

The news organizations were assuming the draftees were added to existing units. The media didn't know the two hundred thousand men were still in training at locations out west. They would continue to train. They were America's secret weapon.

They were hid in plain sight. Sometimes the best place to hide something is in plain sight.

K.I.S.S.

LTC Dexter Jenkins had already been told by the Secretary and Secret Service agent in the President's outer office that he could go in. He lightly knocked on the door before he went in.

"Please, have a seat," said the President.

"Thank you, Mr. President," even though the President had told him numerous times he didn't had to address him as Mr. President, LTC Jenkins continued to do so.

"I have a mission for you."

"Yes, Mr. President."

"I don't want this leaked out."

"I understand," said Jenkins.

"Here is a letter of introduction. I want you to talk to the Prime Minister of Israel. We need them to establish an air corridor across Israel. We don't need to lose any aircraft to friendly fire. An executive jet will pick you up and take you to see the Prime Minister and take you back to the airport. I am not writing out our plan. You will have to explain what we are trying to do.

"I need you to leave immediately and return as quickly as possible. The news media are keeping track of everyone in the administration."

"I understand, Mr. President."

LTC Jenkins left in thirty minutes. He had no luggage. He was to quote a term he learned in the Rangers 'travel light, freeze at night.' He would also use a term he had learned in the Rangers. It was called the K.I.S.S. Method, which stood for 'Keep it Simple Stupid.'

He was on the ground for two hours in Tel Aviv. He also did something he learned in ranger school; sleep when you can, stay awake when you can't. Jenkins slept on the flight over and back. He could sleep on a pile of rocks. He had done it many times in the Rangers. No one missed him.

THE FOG OF WAR

The anticipated date of December 20th was fast approaching. The President was meeting with the Joint Chiefs of Staff daily. If someone were to ask, the answer would be yes, they looked older each day. Everyone was under a tremendous amount of stress and it was showing.

U.S. Military Forces around the world were moving. Every attempt was made so that the Iranians or other countries wouldn't know the United States was about to launch an attack against Iran.

The plans to return the five nuclear weapons were finalized. Army Special Forces and Navy Seal teams were being trained to implement the plan. Each weapon was small enough to be placed in a standard automobile trunk or SUV.

Landing sites were selected, routes finalized and target sites picked out. The plan was simple. Land at a remote site, drive undetected to the location and abandon the vehicle and a second vehicle would pick up the soldiers and drive to a pick up site. The military had a high degree of confidence in the plan.

The day before Thanksgiving, all the plans came unraveled. In the Gaza Strip, Palestinians fired three hundred rockets into Israel. The Americans had no way of knowing that the war had started. This action by the Palestinians happened frequently. What happened next caught the Americans completely by surprise.

Egyptian forces moved through the Sinai Peninsula and engaged the Israeli defense force at the border. Syrian forces moved through Lebanon and attacked from the north. Israel was fighting for its life.

There was no movement on the Jordanian border. It was pointed out to the President that while Jordan was mostly Muslim they were moderate and maybe they weren't, to quote the CIA Director, 'invited'.

"Maybe this isn't the start of the attack. Maybe it's a coincidence."

"Let's hope it is," said a wishful President.

"Only time will tell, Mr. President."

Iran launched its attack while the world's attention was on Israel. All three Iranian columns headed toward Baghdad. At the beginning it appeared that Baghdad was the objective.

When Iran crossed the Iraqi border, the Iraqi forces were crushed and had to withdraw. Iraq fought delaying actions, but was no match for the Iranian onslaught. Iranian forces shelled the city for four days.

In the middle of the fifth night, Iran disengaged its forces and headed for Israel. Iran had suffered light casualties in the Baghdad campaign.

The American Generals had not been caught off guard by the attack. The timing was a different story. It had been decided on the ground where the Air Force and Navy would try to stop the attack. With the attack coming four weeks early a lot of assets weren't in place. One thing that helped was someone in the Pentagon had written a staff study years ago. The Army pulled it out of its files a month ago. It had been determined you could put 200 AH64 helicopter gunships spaced three feet apart on an aircraft carrier, leaving enough room on the bow to roll them into place for takeoff.

After the helicopters were gone the Navy could fly the fighters in from the states. The fighters would have to make several mid-air refuels, but it could be done. It had to be done. The aircraft carrier had departed two weeks earlier and was close enough to add its weight to the battle. The AH64 Apache gunships would be used instead of tanks. There was no way to sneak a large number of tanks into the battle area.

The Apaches flew from the aircraft carrier off the coast of Israel. The Apaches flew low level over Jordan into Iraq. Jordan never knew its airspace had been violated. The aircraft carrier then prepared to accept its incoming fighters. CH47 Chinook helicopter came in on an oil tanker. The civilian oil tanker was almost seven hundred feet long and was carrying millions of gallons of fuel for the helicopters.

A Ranger battalion had parachuted into the desert of Iraq in two places. One company was just beyond the Jordanian border to establish an intermediate refueling site for all the helicopters. The other two Ranger companies were deeper into Iraq fifty miles south of the expected Iranian line of march.

The Chinooks were bringing fuel trailers and Humvee vehicles to unload the fuel and to provide scout vehicles. Aircraft after aircraft landed with the much needed fuel and armament for the Apache gunships.

The Apaches were armed with the Hellfire missile. The Hellfire missiles are laser guided and could be used in any weather day or night.

The two hundred Apaches landed in the middle of the night and refueled. They would attack tomorrow morning at sunrise. Right now the pilots were seasick. They needed time to recover.

INDEPENDENCE

A war room had been placed in the basement of the Capitol. Near the end of the hourly briefing for the President the Marine General pointed out to the President that the Iranians would fight to the death.

"I'm willing to let them do that," was the answer the President gave to the Chiefs of Staff. No one offered any objection.

Then the President asked, "How much of their fuel and water trucks have to be destroyed before we commit out light infantry? I want our force to have a high degree of success."

The Army General answered, "Mr. President, in war there are always risk involved. I can't give you a definite answer to that but I'd say forty percent. We are counting on them to abandon their armor and self-propelled artillery."

"So, it would be infantry against infantry is that right?"

"Yes, Mr. President."

CHAPTER SEVENTY TWO

THE IRANIANS

When the Egyptian and Syrian army attacked, a decision was made by the Ayatollah to launch the attack four weeks early. Part of the decision making process was the United States decision not to trade with any country that traded with Iran. Iran had traded oil for gas for decades and the gas had stopped flowing. To postpone the attack would have put the entire attack in jeopardy. It was now or never. In another month the gas shortage would reach crippling levels.

The Commanding General of the Iranian forces pointed out to the Ayatollah that all of his forces weren't in place, namely his air defense and mobile radar systems. The Ayatollah simply said, "You can wait for them when you attack Baghdad."

The Baghdad attack was only scheduled to last one day. After two days, the air defense and radar systems units still hadn't arrived. The Baghdad attack went into the fifth day before he had his forces available. This operation was his plan and adding four days was worrisome to him. He wished the Ayatollah hadn't changed the plans.

"Our Muslim brothers in Egypt and Syria can help us achieve a great victory against Israel," the Ayatollah had said.

"But what about America?" The General asked.

"Don't worry about the Americans. The head has been cut off the snake. America won't be able to help Israel, or to stop us from destroying Israel. America's days are numbered."

The General didn't know what the Ayatollah was referring to. Why was America's days numbered?

The Commanding General wanted to question the decision. He knew he wouldn't. In Iran, you don't question anything.

The Ayatollah went on. "I know in your plan we would attack and the neighboring countries would join us in the attack. This works out better for us. The world won't believe we started the war. It will simply appear as though we are coming to the aid of our Muslim brothers.

"America believed they could cripple us with their sanctions. Now we will cripple them with the destruction of Israel. A chain of unstoppable events will happen that no one will be able to stop."

The Commanding General didn't understand. He was a soldier, now he wished he wasn't. What chain of unstoppable events was the Ayatollah talking about?

"The faith will be cleansed," said the Ayatollah.

What in the world is he talking about thought the General. Islam is already pure.

On the sixth day, the Iranian Commanding General received some disturbing news from Tehran. He was ordered to push his attack at an even greater speed. He was instructed to leave his SCUD missile launchers a few miles west of Ramadi, a scant seventy miles from Baghdad. They were indeed slowing him down and they would be in range of Israel from there. He asked why. The answer was simple, the Israeli defense forces had managed to push the Egyptian and Syrian forces back.

The Iranian General shook his head in amazement. How can a country the size of Israel defeat two much larger countries at the same time even though they were outmanned and out gunned? It reminded him of the Six Day War in 1967. Iran thought if he got there in time Egypt and Syria might renew the attack. The General wondered whose side Allah was on.

The Commanding General of the Iranian force had his Command Vehicle stop for fuel. They were refueling on the go. Each vehicle stopping only long enough to refuel while the rest of the force continued the attack.

While he was refueling he went outside with his prayer rug and faced south in the direction of Mecca, knelt and said his morning prayers. When he was finished he glanced to the east toward the sun and the direction he had come from.

He saw hundreds of tiny specks on the horizon. He thought his eyes were deceiving him. Then he saw the smoke trails of missiles heading towards him, hundreds of them. He knew of only one nation on the face of the Earth that could move that many, that far, that fast. The Americans.

He watched in awe as the first one slammed into a fuel truck and exploded. He shouted, "No, Allah, please not the fuel trucks."

The General dashed into his command vehicle, grabbed the radio and screamed "Disperse the fuel trucks! Disperse the fuel trucks!" He grabbed another handset to order the SCUD missiles to fire. He knew the Ayatollah would execute him if he failed. Then he realized the Ayatollah wouldn't kill him, the Americans would kill him first.

Before he could give the command to launch the SCUD missiles, a Hellfire missile slammed into his vehicle and literally split it apart at the seams when it detonated. For a millisecond he saw what Hell probably looked like.

If he could have seen seventy miles behind him, he would have seen smoke from the SCUD missiles. The missiles had been destroyed ten minutes earlier. Israel had no intentions of letting three hundred missile launchers aimed at them sit there. Sometimes you go to a party even if you haven't been invited.

CHAPTER SEVENTY THREE

OPERATION TERRIBLE

SWIFT SWORD

ECCLESIASTES 3:8

Each Apache helicopter was armed with eight Hellfire missiles plus thirty six 2.75 inch folding fin rockets and a 30 MM chain gun. The Apaches stayed out of range of the Iranian defense weapons, picked their targets and fired until ordnance was depleted. Then flying east before turning south. The Americans wanted the Iranians to think they were behind them instead of south of the main force. The Apaches refueled and rearmed. Two hours later the Apaches were back dealing out death and destruction.

That afternoon, the Navy F18 Super Hornets arrived and started bombing the front of the column. There was no need to use sophisticated smart bombs in this target rich environment. The pilots couldn't miss. To destroy a fuel truck, closeness counted. If a five hundred pound bomb hit close it still destroyed the truck. The Hornets were also armed with Maverick air to ground missiles. The Navy had a field day.

That night, the Air Force F-15 Eagles arrived and started their bombing campaign. Using forward looking infrared radar the pilots could see the heat signature of the Iranian vehicles. Smart bombs were used on vehicles that had clustered together.

The next day was a repeat of the first. The Iranian attack ground to a halt. They had no choice but to stop their advance. The mighty army was in disarray. Someone made the decision to head back to Iran. There was only enough fuel for the trucks and smaller vehicles. Tanks, missile launchers and self-propelled artillery were abandoned. They used too much fuel. The air attacks continued systematically and relentlessly knocking out vehicle after vehicle. Eventually all the fuel and water trucks were destroyed. The Iranian army headed toward Ramadi. They could seize fuel and water there.

The hundred thousand Iranian volunteers; those grabbed off the streets, given equipment and no training, were the first to die. Most had simply dropped their weapons and equipment. The only thing they kept was their canteens. Soldiers dying of thirst were killing the volunteers hoping against hope that there would be water in their canteens, most were empty. The volunteers were simply left behind to die.

The number of Iranian soldiers killed and abandoned was so high neither side could estimate the number. The mighty army was reduced to rubble. The desert started burying them.

The U.S. Navy then turned their attention to the Iranian Navy. The U.S. Navy had been tracking every Iranian Naval vessel for a month. When the order was given, the Iranian Navy was on the bottom in eighteen minutes. Admiral Douglas had told the President and other Chiefs of Staff the U.S. Navy could defeat the Iranian Navy in fifteen minutes. He didn't like being wrong. He was only wrong by three minutes which still counted. He had a five dollar bet with the other Chiefs of Staff. Those three minutes cost him fifteen bucks.

CHAPTER SEVENTY FOUR

DOGFIGHT

BAGHDAD AIRPORT

EPHESIANS 6:10-17

Second Lieutenant Joshua A. MacDonald had arrived yesterday. He was seated in the briefing room awaiting the mission briefing. The 509th fighter wing nicknamed GUNSLINGERS weren't the first ones there.

The last three days the sneaky guys, stealth fighters, F-117 Nighthawks and F-22 Raptors had been carrying the battle to the Iranians. The F-117's were bombers. They only operated at night. The F-117 is almost impossible to pick up on radar.

They bombed airports, bridges, power stations, radar sites and command and control installations.

The F-22 Raptors were the most dominating fighter in the world. They were also impossible to pick up on radar. If Iranian aircraft came up to challenge the Americans they were quickly sent crashing to Earth.

The time had come for the Air Force to use conventional fighters F-15 Eagles and F-16 Falcons. Lt. Joshua A. 'GHOSTRIDER' MacDonald was an F-16 Falcon pilot. The single seat air superiority fighter was just that. It was also a superb bomber using laser guided bombs. It had also taken on the role of close air support to protect ground troops engaged in close combat.

An F-16 pilot never knew what role his next mission would be. Josh liked that.

The Air Force's F-15 Eagles had been targeting the Iranian forces in the western desert of Iraq. Fuel trucks, water trucks and command and control vehicles were high on the priority list. They had been at it constantly for the last two days.

Josh felt like, and rightly so, a Johnny come lately. They had been told Iran had almost one hundred and fifty airports. In Iran it wasn't uncommon to have military and civilians to use the same airports. It was assumed the Iranians had military runways that hadn't been discovered.

The Squadron Commander LTC Stephen 'TEX' Cameron came into the briefing room. The other pilots stood and came to attention when he entered.

"As you were," said 'TEX' Cameron.

The pilots returned to their seats. Cameron was a tall, lanky fifty year old from Wichita Falls, Texas. He was a graduate of the Air Force Academy. He had flown in the first Gulf War during Desert Storm and also after 9/11 over the skies of Afghanistan and Iraq. By all accounts he was a very good pilot.

He was troubled by two things. Being in Baghdad was the smallest of his worries. He had a very young Lieutenant flying under him. He had been discreetly told that if something happened to the young Lieutenant that his head would be on the chopping block. Cameron wondered why he was even over here. Anything could happen. The young flier had been transferred and then transferred back the very next day.

"Listen up gentlemen, our mission is twofold today. We are expecting ground troops to be landing very soon. We will be performing escort duty. We can't afford to lose any aircraft, especially one carrying over two hundred troops. Two aircraft will escort them in. I cannot, repeat, cannot emphasize how important this is to our campaign."

"The other three will conduct bombing raids on bridges, power stations, radio and television stations and last but certainly not least command and control sites. We have to prevent the Iranians from resupplying their army in Western Iraq."

"I will lead the bombing raid. Major Martin and Captain Woods will accompany me. Captain Larkin and Lt. MacDonald will perform the escort duty. We don't have an arrival time so you will just have to be on standby. Good luck and good hunting. That will be all."

Captain Larkin looked at Josh and slightly shook his head in disgust. Josh didn't blame him. Fighter pilots wanted to be where the action was. Josh knew Captain Larkin was blaming him. If I wasn't here he would be on the bombing raid instead of babysitting the President's son. There was nothing Josh could do but just bear it. If it was up to Josh he would be going on the raid, also.

Larkin and Josh watched as the three F-16's took off and headed to their targets in Iran.

"I'm sorry, Sir," said Josh.

Larkin didn't answer. He just walked away.

Two hours later, the operations officer told them the escort duty was cancelled for the day. Bad weather had forced them to postpone it twenty four hours.

"Just great! We get to sit around and twiddle our thumbs," said Larkin.

The two went out on the flight line to tell the maintenance crew. Captain Larkin's crew chief said, "Captain, there are a few things I want to work on. Now would be a good time since you won't be flying today."

"Yeah, go ahead. How long will it take?"

"At least two hours. I can start now."

Josh went to the operations office and had a cup of coffee. There was nothing else to do except wait until tomorrow.

An hour later, the operations officer stopped what he was doing and walked over to the radio.

"What's going on?" There was a lot of chatter coming over the radio.

"Our flight got jumped by ten Iranians."

"Where?"

"About a hundred and thirty miles due east of here, Sir. They are low on fuel, they can't afford to get engaged, Sir."

A minute later the radio operator said, "They are requesting help, Sir. They are out of air to air missiles. They have shot down three of the bad guys. It we can't get anymore there, they are not going to make it back."

The operations officer turned to his standby pilots to get airborne. There was no one standing there. He rushed to the door and saw Lt. MacDonald closing the canopy of his aircraft.

Captain Larkin came in at that time. "What's going on?" he asked.

"Our flight got jumped. Get in the air now."

"Maintenance has my plane. They are working on it. It will take another hour. I was just out there."

They heard an aircraft spool up its engine. They looked out in time to see Josh line up on the runway.

"He doesn't have a wingman! Stop him!"

It was too late.

CHAPTER SEVENTY FIVE

'GHOSTRIDER'

JOSHUA 1:9

The lone F-16 thundered down the runway and lifted off. He didn't climb to altitude. The fighter was streaking across the desert floor one hundred feet off the ground, headed east at six hundred miles an hour.

Twelve minutes later, Josh could see the dogfight from ten miles away. Contrails were everywhere in tight orbits and up and down. He estimated the aerial engagement was between twenty and thirty thousand feet. He was able to see a missile trail followed by an explosion and an ejection seat parachute being deployed. Josh flew on. He could hear the excited chatter on the radio and was able to determine that LTC 'TEX' Cameron was the pilot shot down.

Five miles from the edge of the dogfight, Josh pushed the throttle all the way forward into full afterburner. The mighty engine roared, pushing Josh back into his ejection seat from the thrust.

"I'll fly away oh glory, I'll fly away, when I die hallelujah by and by, I'll fly away."

A thirty foot long jet exhaust looking like a gigantic blow torch was coming from the mighty engine.

'GHOSTRIDER' was supersonic. Pulling back on the stick the nimble fighter went vertical climbing almost straight up. In training flights some pilots called this 'Playing Rocket man.' 'GHOSTRIDER' knew pilots would be swiveling their heads all around and especially up. Their vision blocked by the aircraft they were in, a blind spot. 'GHOSTRIDER' was going to ambush the first one, after that he would be fair game himself.

Climbing through fifteen thousand feet in ten seconds 'GHOSTRIDER' picked his target. A MIG-29 was reengaging an F-16 at thirty thousand feet. At a distance of five hundred yards 'GHOSTRIDER' fired a one second burst from the 20mm Vulcan cannon. At six thousand rounds per minute, the weapon spits out one hundred rounds per second of high explosive incendiary rounds.

'GHOSTRIDER' could see the MIG fly into the stream of traces. Large pieces were coming off the disintegrating aircraft. 'GHOSTRIDER' continued the climb to forty thousand feet before leveling off. 'GHOSTRIDER' was upside down to prevent blackout and to see what was below him without his own plane blocking his vision.

Another MIG was making a turn to engage an F-16 at thirty thousand feet. Snap rolling the fighter and pushing forward on the stick the fighter dove on the MIG.

Selecting an AIM-7 sparrow radar guided missile then centering the MIG on the heads up display. When fired, the air to air missile was tracking the MIG. Turning to the left and pushing forward on the stick even more into a steeper dive. The aircraft was hurdling through the air towards a MIG strafing LTC Cameron. The MIG was making a long turn at a thousand feet.

LTC 'TEX' Cameron was trying to find a place that would offer him cover. This was the third pass the MIG was making. LTC 'TEX' Cameron saw another aircraft pull out at a thousand feet a mile behind the MIG. Then he saw it was an F-16.

He knew his pilots were out of missiles and wouldn't be able to help him. He lay flat on the ground; he saw the MIG open fire. He covered his head with his arms. He saw a missile leave the rail of the F-16. Would it track, better yet would it be in time? He covered his head even more. When he heard the explosion he looked up just in time to see the MIG coming apart. Seconds later the F-16 streaked overhead and started to climb.

"Who is that guy?" 'TEX' said to himself.

'TEX' Cameron stayed where he was. He watched the Iranian pilot float down in his parachute and land fifty feet away. He looked up and saw the Iranian MIG's breaking contact. The Iranians were low on fuel and out of missiles. They also knew there was another dog in the fight and he was loaded for bear.

CHAPTER SEVENTY SIX

THE WITCHATA KID

PSLAMS 25:2

'TEX' stood up and checked his sidearm. He started walking toward the Iranian. 'TEX' Cameron had played cowboys and Indians since he got his first cap pistol when he was five years old. His Daddy had nicknamed him the 'Witchata Kid.' It was time to play cowboy and Iranian.

The Iranian assumed the American was dead and had already forgotten him. He was looking up and watching his countrymen disengaging from the dog fight. There was only four left. Six aircraft had been lost in the aerial engagement with only one enemy shot down.

'TEX' walked to twenty feet away and said, "Draw you yellow bellied dirty rotten scoundrel." The Witchata Kid always said that.

The Iranian turned and saw the American. He understood English as most pilots do, but this was gibberish to him. He reached for his pistol. For some reason folks from Texas are quick on the draw.

'TEX' walked up to the dead Iranian, looked down and said, "You didn't even clear leather. The Witchata Kid is still the fastest draw in the West." Old habits are hard to break.

'TEX' looked up and saw his F-16's returning to base. The other F-16 was flying along with them to make sure they returned safely. It was flying an elongated oval to protect them. It would shepherd the two back to Baghdad. 'TEX' decided he would have a seat and wait, no need to wander off. He knew a rescue chopper would arrive soon.

After his close brush with death, he reflected back on his life. He smiled when he thought about his wedding and the birth of his daughter Madison. He remembered her high school graduation and being able to make it home. Home. He thought a lot about home. Growing up on the Red River Ranch in Texas and Oklahoma was always a good thought. He chuckled when he remembered the kids the ranch hired for the summer. Kids doing simple stuff, fixing fences, putting out hay and filling water troughs. Most of the teenagers could ride a horse but a few had never ridden a horse in their life. They ran around on jeeps and pickup trucks. He wondered whatever happened to those kids. He had no idea that one of those kids was his Commander in Chief.

After the fighters departed, it was unbelievably quiet. There was no sound at all. 'TEX' could hear his own breathing.

Forty minutes later, the sonic boom was deafening. It scared the daylights out of him. He had heard it hundreds of times before, but still.

He saw the plane streaking away before making a turn toward him. 'TEX' was already on his feet. He had jumped up when he heard it. Then the strangest thing happened. The pilot put on an air show for just one person, him. The pilot seemed to know it would make him feel safe and know he would be rescued. It made him proud to be an American.

'TEX' simply watched in awe. "I don't know who he is but he can fly. He can really fly."

The F-16 stayed on station until the rescue helicopter arrived, picked him up and flew to Baghdad.

That night, Lieutenant Josh 'GHOSTRIDER' MacDonald was standing in front of the Squadron Commander's desk. He saluted and said, "Lieutenant MacDonald reporting as ordered, Sir."

LTC Cameron casually returned the salute. "You can fly as my wingman anytime, Lieutenant."

"Yes, Sir," answered Josh.

"That will be all."

Josh saluted and said, "Yes, Sir."

Cameron returned the salute and waved him away.

'TEX' Cameron had viewed the gun cameras on Lt. MacDonald's aircraft. Two kills and one probable. Most pilots would have stayed on the other aircraft to film the missile. They wanted credit for the kill. "Of course, if he had done that I would probably be dead now," 'TEX' Cameron said to himself.

Lieutenant Joshua 'GHOSTRIDER' MacDonald would fly as Cameron's wingman for the duration of the war. It was a good way to keep an eye on him.

CHAPTER SEVENTY SEVEN

THE GROUND WAR

PSALMS 23:4

The AH-64 Apaches departed their base camp and moved to Baghdad. The fighters returned to the airports of Baghdad, Mosel and Basra.

The Iranians caught a few hours of reprieve from the relentless airstrikes. Thinking it was over they bunched up even more. They never even saw the B-52's flying at forty thousand feet. Wave after wave dropped five hundred pound bombs. The Iranian force was pulverized even more. The Apaches and fighters weren't finished. They would return with a vengeance the next morning. The ground war was beginning.

On the eighth day, huge Boeing 747's and Airbus 300's began arriving. American airline companies had leased all available aircraft to the government for thirty days. They were flown into Basra, Mosul, but mostly Baghdad. The huge aircraft had four hundred men each. There was no need for baggage handlers. They were light infantry. They carried all of their equipment on their back. They would travel light and freeze at night. They were spoiling for a fight. Payback.

Transport aircraft were landing every few minutes. Huge C-5A and C-17's were landing, refueling and taking off again to get more troops and equipment. They were landing mostly in Baghdad. C-130's were bringing in ammo, food and water. Vehicles pulling water trailers were disembarked and followed the soldiers. The soldiers were heading west to meet the Iranians who had survived the bombing campaign.

It had been estimated that the Iranian force numbered between fifty and seventy five thousand. Having run out of fuel and water days ago, the number had diminished from six hundred thousand to this small force. They would be met by a force of two hundred thousand light infantry. This light infantry corps had undergone rigorous training for four months. They were hardened but untested. Now would come the time for testing. It was noted that something was missing from this light infantry corps. There was no news media.

The Iranians had only a few vehicles remaining. Over three thousand tanks had been lost or abandoned in the western desert of Iraq. None of the self-propelled artillery had survived. Most were walking and were dying by the hundreds every few miles. The desert wind and sand would bury them.

The three Iranian columns that had started the campaign were now converged into one column. It stretched for fifty miles. Those at the back were near death from dehydration. They would never reach the battle area. Had any of them known what was waiting for them would have lay down and died where they were.

Every hour more and more vehicles ran out of fuel. Trucks designed to carry eighteen soldiers had as many as thirty men aboard. No more supplies, especially fuel and water would reach them. There had been no communications from Iran in five days.

The Americans marched west. Recon drones told the Americans where to block the force moving at a snail's pace to the east.

The Americans had time to dig in and wait. The Americans were ten miles west of Ramadi. Eighty miles from Baghdad. They had marched for four days.

The Iranians with each step, each exhausting step told themselves there is water in Ramadi. Water. This thought kept many of them alive and going, longing for a sip of water in Ramadi. There were also two hundred thousand Americans waiting, just waiting.

To give the Iranians credit they fought bravely when the two forces met. They would fight to the last man. They asked for no quarter and received none. The fire fight lasted for twenty four hours. The Iranians were too exhausted to attack or retreat. Retreat was not an option anyway.

The place where the battle took place was named the Valley of Death by the Americans, even though there wasn't a valley. The American force waited another two days before leaving. The wounded and dead were removed immediately. Casualties were light. The desert itself had killed the majority of the Iranians.

The Ranger Battalion that parachuted into Iraq and established refueling sites was the last to leave. The Rangers were given the mission of destroying the abandoned tanks and artillery pieces the Iranians had left behind. Charges were placed on engines and on the ammo inside. Even the cannon barrels were destroyed. If it could be used for killing it was destroyed. President MacDonald had said, "There are too many tanks in the Mideast." The mission lasted ten days. The world's largest scrap metal site was for sale as scrap metal.

CHAPTER SEVENTY EIGHT

BAD NEIGHBORHOOD

JEREMIAH 12:12

When Iraq realized the bulk of the Iranian army was destroyed they launched an attack. There were old scores to settle. All the neighboring countries of Iran that had been threatened and bullied for what seemed like ages, now wanted a part of the huge oil fields. Turkey attacked from the northwest. Pakistan from the southeast and Afghanistan from the east.

This had not been anticipated by the United States. The plan to return the five nuclear weapons was cancelled by a relieved President.

The Iranian forces couldn't withstand the onslaught from every direction. Tanks and artillery advanced into Tehran and surrounded the Parliament building where the Guardian Council was holding an emergency meeting. The surrounding forces commenced firing and after six hours the building collapsed under its own weight. They continued to fire till it was nothing more than rubble.

Then the bloodbath really began. The civilian population had no way to defend themselves. Personally owned weapons weren't allowed in Iran. They were defenseless. Muslims had been killing each other for over a thousand years, but not like this rampage.

Sixteen days later, the nation of Iran ceased to exist. Not a single nation stepped forward to help or to stop the slaughter. Most felt that Iran was getting what they deserved.

CHAPTER SEVENTY NINE

STATE OF THE UNION

MATTHEW 11:28

President Lewis C. MacDonald looked into the cameras. He was seated behind his desk on the eighth floor of the United States Capitol (temporary). The Vice President, Juanita Hernandez was seated behind him to his right. The Speaker of the House, James Rice, Republican Representative from Minnesota was to his left. President MacDonald had given the two a written copy five minutes earlier. Neither had opened the envelope. Senators and Representatives would receive a copy by Federal Express tomorrow.

The date was February the 1st. The time was 9:00 p.m. Eastern Standard Time. History would later reveal that President MacDonald had not written the speech except for one paragraph.

Each member of his cabinet, which was senior employees in each department having survived the Washington attack, contributed a part.

He read the speech. He did not pause for the crowd to applause, there was no crowd. It laid out facts, good and bad, nothing more, and nothing less. It was grim in some aspects. The National Debt had gone down, but not enough. More people had jobs than last year at this time. Immigration had gone to a trickle. The military was larger and this helped the job numbers. When the American people found out people living on public assistance were making more than the men and women fighting for our country, they wanted an even larger military. The Anti-Gang Task Force had taken over twenty thousand gang members off the streets. Social Security was improving with more people working and paying into the system. The lottery was bringing in millions and over four hundred people had won jackpots which brought even more revenue into the system. Businesses were moving back due to lower taxes. They were hiring which also helped. The trade deficit was evening out because of the 'You buy from us and we'll buy from you' policy. A time limit was placed on welfare recipients, two years. There were jobs to be had now. Many were entry level jobs, but there were jobs. "We can't rob from Peter to pay Paul." He assured the American people that government was back in business, much smaller than before and most social programs would be turned over to the respective states shortly.

Then he surprised the American people by saying, "I'm speaking to our young African Americans now. Get an education. There is no reason you should not at least finish high school. Take responsibility for your actions. If you bring a child into this world, love it, support it and be a good and responsible parent. Be a role model for your children. Many of you are looking in the wrong places and following the wrong people. Your role model should be the father and mother who work hard to provide you with a roof over your head and food on your table. The perfect role model should be the one sitting at the dining room table with you every night. Learn to speak English, not jive. You are not going to get a job or go anywhere in life if people can't understand you. Pull up your pants, tuck your shirttail in and tie your shoes. You can be a part of the American dream if you have respect for yourself and for others. Dr. Martin Luther King, Jr. was about education and peace. One day you may be the President of the United States of America. It has happened before and can happen again."

He praised the military for its great service to this nation. He said, "This nation can never repay you for the sacrifices you have made, but the Veteran's Administration had made leaps and bounds in caring for you. There is no longer two hundred miles of driving or three months of waiting for an appointment. Care is sometimes just a few miles away."

President MacDonald realized all of this was the work of the Vice President. Everything she had proposed had been passed by Congress with the Independents being the deciding swing bloc vote.

Then he read the paragraph that he had written. Only four people on the face of the Earth knew what he was about to say. "In closing, I will now announce I am resigning as your President on February the seventh at 9:30 P.M. Eastern Standard Time to return to my beloved Wyoming. I cannot think of anyone I could leave this country in better care than your Vice President Juanita Hernandez." Then he paused for twenty seconds. When the President said this the camera focused on the Vice President. She was clearly surprised by the resignation. Tears started streaming down her face. She didn't say anything. What do you say, what can you say.

Then he continued, "God bless this great nation of ours and I mean it is ours and it is great! We control our destiny as one nation under God. I believe the American people will keep the dream alive and well. God bless each and every one of you. Good night."

The news stations had all allotted equal time to both the Democrat and Republican parties. The resignation changed all that. The cable news stations had as many as six analysts. They were all talking at the same time. No one could understand what was being said. After ten minutes of insane gibberish, it quieted down somewhat and the anchor was able to restore some order.

Shock and disbelief were the words most often used to describe what had happened a few minutes ago. They finally moved on to the fact the President didn't mention the war in Iran and Iraq. Someone pointed out that that was in the past and "What is done is done." No one had an answer about Iran being carved up by the other nations.

"Maybe that is their concern and not ours," said one of the analysts. "The President didn't mention anything about rebuilding Washington. That's in the future for another Presidency."

Everyone agreed on that.

One analyst brought up the subject of the upcoming Convention of the States. "The article V Convention is scheduled to begin July 4th in Independence Hall in Philadelphia. High on the list is term limits for Congress with twelve years being the maximum anyone can serve in Congress. Another amendment is the Balanced Budget amendment. The Federal Government will have to live within its means. The amendment to set term limits for the Supreme Court is drawing a lot of support from all across the country. What was once a lifetime appointment will be reduced to ten years and each court of appeals district will have to have a representative on the court. The American people will finally have a chance to speak. They're going back to Independence Hall. The place this nation began."

Then there was a lengthy discussion on the new President. The panel never stopped to listen to the Democrat and Republican response. The Democrats and Republicans realized this discussion would last all night and called it an evening. They went home and thought about all that had happened.

In closing the anchor said, "For the second time in a year, America lost a President in the blink of an eye."

Lewis and Beverly stayed for the swearing in ceremony on February seventh and 9:30 Eastern Standard Time. He had been President exactly one year to the minute. He would probably become a trivia question.

They had decided to drive to Kerney. They didn't actually drive. The Secret Service took care of that. Lewis hadn't flown on Air Force One. He spent the year in Independence.

CHAPTER EIGHTY

LOOKOUT POINT

JOHN 12:36

When the five vehicle motorcade reached the MacDonald ranch Lewis and Beverly got out of the middle vehicle. Both seemed to be drawn to Lookout Point. They walked there hand and hand.

Marsha Jefferson glanced toward the house and saw Deborah and Josh coming outside. Josh had a blanket in his hand. They joined Lewis and Beverly on top of their special place. After everyone hugged the blanket was spread out and the four of them sat down.

"It's good to be home."

"Amen to that," said Beverly.

"I remember my first time here," said Lewis.

"That is a day I will never forget," said Beverly.

"I remember my first time here," said Deborah. "I felt safe."

"So did I. It was the first day I ever remember having fun," added Josh.

Beverly said, "I don't really remember my first time here. It seems like it was always here."

They sat in silence for a few minutes just taking in the view and breathing in the fresh air. Wonderful memories going through their minds. It was so peaceful.

"I know you are going to think I am silly but when I was a little girl I believed the stars were angels and they were shining their light down on me."

"I always felt that way," said Deborah.

"So did I," said Josh.

"Maybe there are angels up there shining their light down on us," said Lewis.

Beverly thought for a minute and said. "It's a good thought isn't it. Those angels are shining their light down on us. We do know they are all around us." She looked at her family and her surroundings and said, "We are truly blessed."

EPILOGUE

KERNEY, WYOMING

REVELATION 22:21

I arrived yesterday evening. It took two days to drive here from Independence. This wasn't a two day journey. It was a two year journey. President MacDonald; sorry, he doesn't like to be called that, has been out of office for a year having served only one year before resigning.

I got the book published. It was called 'Quiet Dignity." It was the only one published about the First Lady. Most publishers want to publish books that are controversial. They did not want one about the First Lady that from outward appearances hadn't really done anything.

Well, in my eyes she did a lot if you ask me. She wrote thousands of letters to children and to others needing a healing word. It's true she didn't appear on television a lot or give a lot of speeches. What was most important to me was she left a place she dearly loved to be with her husband, when he needed her. Even though he was busy and didn't have much time for her he was always assured that she was there for support. Not many relationships would have survived what they were thrown into.

Most First Ladies travel a lot on government expense. She made only one flight and that was to Deborah's graduation. She told me later, she couldn't tell if they crashed or landed, so she settled on crash landed.

I'm sure there will be lots of books published on Lewis and I'm sure Beverly will be mentioned. I am sure his presidency will be examined closely, many times.

I just came here to give the family a copy of the book. I was able to get permission from dozens of people who wrote and received answers from Beverly. The little twelve year old girl that Beverly and I held hands and prayed for on my very first day working, a girl I had never met and knew I would never meet. I was actually able to meet and interview her and her Dad. She's fourteen now and she told me how it had changed their life. I told her that it had also changed my life. My book may not sell many copies, but I got it published and feel privileged to have been a part of such a time in history and a wonderful family.

I have also written another book about the MacDonald family. It begins when they first met and ends when he left office. The name of it is 'The State of the Union.' I'm writing it under a different name. I'm a ghost writer. I haven't heard if it will be published. I can only hope. Hope is all I cling to, that and my faith.

It was nice to see the four of them again. I had only met Josh and Deborah once, but Beverly talked about them all the time so I feel like I really know them. We sat up late last night just visiting and after dinner I was able to participate in 'Happy Hour.' Josh was hard to top but Marsha Jefferson gave him a run for his money. I haven't laughed like that in a long time. It felt good. It would be nice if families all across America would get back to eating together and having good fellowship with each other. We have lost so much in this fast paced world.

You know sometimes you meet someone who influences you without really trying. For me that person was Beverly. Their family room is full of their life's history. It is easy to see where their priorities are. Everything that is important to Lewis and Beverly is there. Hey, I got it right.

We had an early breakfast because I have to get back to Independence because I work for the President now. Josh cooked and Deborah washed the dishes where I could visit with Beverly. I love that woman. I sat across from her for a year opening and reading letters, sounds easy, try it sometime.

I even got to write a paragraph that went into the State of the Union address. I'll let you guess which one.

It was still dark when I loaded my car. I hugged the four of them and Marsha Jefferson who is in charge of their security detail. From what I understand Beverly directly asked for her. Marsha said she would come if Beverly taught her how to ride a horse and do the hat trick. Can you imagine a Secret Service detail that rides around on horses instead of a vehicle?

To bring you up to date on everyone; Josh is still in the Air Force. He is an instructor pilot at Mountain Home Air Force Base. He does familiarization flights for ROTC cadets. His first flight was from there. Josh feels like he has come full circle. He flies home in an old piper cub he fixed up. He is also a member of the Civil Air Patrol; after all, he owes them his life.

Deborah, well, she is still Deborah. Still a little bossy, but always in a good way. Once a year she goes to Beal, Iowa and presents the two scholarships in their parent's name. She visits her Grandpa once a month and she has started painting murals in Kerney like she did in South Georgia. From what I understand when people found out it was painted by the President's daughter it has become even more popular. What is most important to me about Deborah is that my daughter wants to be just like her. She will start college soon. I can't believe it! My daughter is going to college.

Lewis, he has become a fulltime rancher again. He does not endorse candidates even though he gets many requests to do so. He respectfully declines. He hasn't made a single speech…good for him. He is doing what he loves.

Beverly bakes a lot of cookies. Josh goes through them quickly. By the way, I am taking two dozen back with me. I got addicted to them back in Independence.

Dawn is approaching as I am driving down the driveway. I stop at the end of the driveway and get out my camera. I have heard so many times about the sunrises on Lookout Point, I wanted to see if for myself. I could see the four of them going to their favorite place in the whole world and spreading out their blanket. As I was getting my camera ready I saw them wave at me. Then the sun popped up and everything turned golden.

All I could do was praise God for such a heavenly sight.

ACKNOWLEDGEMENTS

Kerney, Wyoming and Beal, Iowa do not exist except in my imagination. All other places mentioned do exist. I had to mention my hometown Colquitt, Ga. If you are ever in this neck of the woods drop in and say howdy.

All characters are fictitious and bear no resemblance to anyone living or dead.

I would like to acknowledge my typist Angie Collins Kisfalusi who tweaked here and there. She is truly an angel of mercy.

I would also like to thank Sandra Burch, author of the Seaside Series, for her help in guiding me through the publishing process and Mr. Bill Vincent, publisher, for having patience.

I hope you read the Bible verses as you read the book. They will give you a hint on the upcoming chapter.

I believe there is a story inside everyone. Sit down with pen and paper and let it emerge.

Read the Constitution. You will find it to be an amazing work. That is the only way you can determine if our nation drifts away from its original course.

If you only take one thing away from this book I hope that it is that every family needs a 'Happy Hour.' Find time to gather your family together and enjoy each other.

Hope. Cling to hope and your faith.